Fire

Gunsh...

1969

God's Own Lunatics

outskirts
press

Outskirts Press, Inc.
http://www.outskirtspress.com

Paperback ISBN: 978-1-9772-2987-8
Hardback ISBN: 978-1-9772-4782-7

Outskirts Press and the "OP" logo are trademarks belonging to Outskirts Press, Inc.

PRINTED IN THE UNITED STATES OF AMERICA

DEDICATION

To my wife Mindy, who has opened my eyes and my heart. Without her, this book would have remained a jumble of confused thoughts, drifting in and out of my mind, as it has for the past 48 years.

When I encountered a writer's block, especially when recalling all the people who were killed for no reason I could recall she would with kind and gentle patience help me unpack my memories.

Her help was priceless. I am forever indebted to her, even more than I thought possible.

ACKNOWLEDGMENTS

A very special thank you goes to Alexander Payne Morgan, who edited this book and advised me on many of the aspects of writing a novel. I had the story floating around in my head, but prior to this book, the only thing I had written was a term paper in high school and a master's thesis in therapy school. He guided me every step of the way to turn my memories, notes and drafts into a coherent and readable book. He has been patient, polite, and persistent, working with me to create the book I wanted to write. I could not have done this without you, Alex. Thank you.

A special thanks to my friend Don DeRoeck for his time and invaluable assistance.

Also, a special thanks to my daughter Jennifer and granddaughter Bella for their special computer assistance.

DISCLAIMER

This book is a novel, but it is based on my personal experiences as an Army helicopter pilot with the 71st Assault Helicopter Company during the Vietnam War. Most events are depicted as accurately as I can remember, and most people are described as they were, although I don't use real names. A few characters are composites, as are a few combat missions. However, the descriptions of combat are not in any way exaggerated; I participated or observed each detail as described at some time in my tour of duty. Many other crews performed these same missions as well.

This book honors our pilots, crew chiefs, door gunners, and all the others who kept us in the air. Their contributions and sacrifices must not be overlooked or forgotten.

CONTENTS

I t is 1967. Every young man in America must face the reality of our war in Vietnam, one way or another. Kevin McNally, twenty years old, bored and frustrated with college, decides to see if any of the military services will allow him the excitement of flying jet planes. None will as you must have a 4 year degree; but the army offers him helicopters.

In Vietnam, Kevin – now designated "Mac" – learns the routine but dangerous helicopter chores of insertion of troops and supplies and carrying out the wounded. These helicopters are armed with only two door gunners and are prime targets for the enemy. Mac hates being shot at without being able to shoot back. He volunteers to fly helicopter gunships as soon as he's allowed to; on his 30th day of flying.

The gunships are armed to the teeth, with machine guns, rockets, and canon. Mac can shoot back now, but he is also even more a prime target for the enemy. Flying the gunships is the most dangerous job in the army. Mac is shot down numerous times and wounded twice. Then, he is wounded one more time, and his days in Vietnam are over.

This book pulls no punches in describing the reality of war. The reader experiences the danger, the skill, and the daily spilling of blood. The language is harsh, the humor laced with sick irony, and no apologies are given for doing what needs to be done.

Mac learns to be ruthless in carrying out his duties – saving the lives of American troops – even as he realizes the strategic futility of the whole war. But it's not his job to question his orders. He flies twice into Laos, violating the sovereignty of a neutral country, even as Nixon assures America nothing of the kind is happening.

Mac loses many friends in combat.

Mac hardens more and more as he experiences such losses. He is no longer the bored twenty years old who wants some excitement in his life. He becomes the weary veteran just trying to live through another day.

Vietnam was our first "helicopter war," and this book illustrates the learning curve under fire as our military gained experience through the harsh trial and error of combat.

This is the story of how a naïve kid from Oregon masters the technology of war, takes pride in his skill and expertise, and does what needs to be done to stay alive and protect his comrades. It will be of interest to anyone who wants to know what war is like for the combatants, and especially to anyone who wants to better understand the innovation of "helicopter war."

PROLOGUE

"Big Dog 6. This is Firebird 9-7. Over."

In a whispered voice, I heard, "Firebird 9-7. This is Big Dog 6. Go ahead."

"6, I've got a team of gunships coming your way from the south. What's your sit-rep?"

"We're an eight-man patrol, and we stumbled on a company of NVA. We're on a small hill in some brush. They are 500 meters due west, and there must be at least 200 of those bastards. The area is open between us, but it looks like they are searching a village on the side of a hill. Some are moving towards us, but they have not seen us."

"I'm almost to your location, maybe one minute. When you see me pop a smoke. Throw it behind something so they can't see it."

"Roger, Firebird."

Thirty seconds later, I radioed, "Big Dog 6, I have a green smoke."

"That's me," he replied in that same whisper, "and they are still in the village and the dry paddies."

"6, I'm going to move west of you and come up over those small hills, so they can't hear me coming. If they're in the open, it's no problem. But if any of those NVA moves to the trees, you can direct my rockets after my first shot. Keep hidden but keep your binos on them."

"Roger that."

I keyed the IC (intercom trigger) on my cyclic and asked the crew—copilot, door gunner and crew chief— if they heard all that. The crew chief and door gunner both clicked the switch on the cord that connects their helmets to our communication system. The co-pilot clicked his button on the cyclic. This was a quick way for them to say OK without wasting any time talking. I quickly keyed the transmit button and said, "9-9 (my wingman), did you get that?"

Back came two clicks over the radio. This was all happening in a few seconds, as we were flying 120 knots (138 mph or 222 km/h), just fifty feet above the trees.

The gunship team was very tight, and everyone knew what to do when the action started. Every mission was new and different. If we had a plan, we usually threw it out the window in the first ten to thirty seconds of combat, because when I pull that gunship up and over the hundred-foot hill, a war will begin. And that was a mild description of what was about to happen because we had little knowledge of the W's: what, when, where, who and weapons. We knew why! WAR.

Every NVA on the ground was going to point his AK-47 at us and fire it on full automatic. Two-hundred NVA with twenty-round magazines added up to 4000 rounds coming at us in three to four seconds, and I knew the odds were for someone down there to get lucky. However, one part was lucky for us and the overloaded, slow-flying, ground hugging gunships we were flying: our enemy was poorly trained.

I looked over at my new copilot and said, "Are you ready?" He looked back with very wide eyes and nodded. His job was to shoot the 40 millimeter canon on the nose of the helicopter. The explosive head of a canon shell was equivalent to several hand grenades. I said, "Shoot at muzzle flashes and at people. We're in tiger country, and the only friendlies are those eight guys on the ground a quarter of a mile away."

I pulled back on the cyclic and used my speed to quickly climb up and over the hill. There they were, out in the open more or less. Some were searching the hooches, and others were standing in the village talking to each other and most were in the open.

I dropped the nose, cleared my mind, and looked through the rocket sight at the bad guys. *I wonder if they call us the bad guys.* Glancing at the gauges and with the slightest of hand and foot movements, I got my sight on the targets closest to our guys and punched off four pair of rockets across the paddies and into the center of the village. Then, I picked out hooches. At the same time, my two men in back (crew chief and door gunner) let go with their

M-60 machine guns on targets in the open, including muzzle flashes in the trees. My copilot acquired targets with the nose canon; first, those close by, then in the tree line and in the village. The most difficult thing to learn while shooting any of these weapons was to ignore the tracers coming at you and the popping of bullets passing through the rotor wash. We aimed at the muzzle flashes or where our ground troops guided us. There was some luck involved. After all, bullets were coming through the windshield, which was only a thin Plexiglas.

The targets in the tree line opened up on us with full force. There must have been two companies down there. The NVA in the open were toast, so I switched my attention to the tree line. It looked like a war movie with the tracers whipping past my windshield and a couple coming through but missing me. I punched off three pair of rockets and walked them into the trees at the muzzle flashes, while my crew continued firing into that same tree line. The tracers diminished considerably, and Big Dog 6 said, "Your rockets are right on those sons of bitches. God damn, you got a hell of a lot of them."

I called over the IC, "Ready," which told the guys in back to get inside as we were going to break right. Those two would usually hang outside the ship while we were dropping 500 feet a minute at 120 knots, shooting their machine guns, anchored only by small straps around their waists hooked to the ship, all the while ignoring the tracers streaming by them or hitting the ship. (They had huge cojones.) I called out over the radio, "9-7 breaking right." I liked to break right. Being the gunship commander, I was in the right seat. As I was climbing up, I could look out and see where my wing ship was shooting and where the NVA were hiding when they shot. My wingman then put rockets behind me and under my tail. (Talk about trust!) This served two purposes: First, to hit the enemy, and second, to keep their heads down while my belly was exposed. During his gun run, I was clawing for altitude, so I could be in position to cover him as he made his break. I glanced at my copilot, and his eyes were even bigger now. He looked like he had just seen his grandmother naked. I asked him, "Are you OK?" He just nodded *yes.*

Suddenly, there were several loud noises like a hammer hitting the ship in rapid succession or a woodpecker on a tree—bang,

bang, bang. I felt the ship shutter and start vibrating like a dog shaking after a swim. My engine and rotor blade rpm began dropping. Then, the crew chief yelled, "Mac, we're on fire! There's a 51 down there."

Red master cautions and yellow warning lights on the instrument panel were flashing. *Shit, they had a Chinese Communist 51 caliber machine gun hidden in the trees, a 100 meters from the village.* We called those 51s helicopter killers."

All systems were failing. Instinct and training taught me to call out, "Mayday, mayday, mayday. Firebird 9-7 going down, ten clicks (kilometers) west of LZ Center. On fire, repeat on fire." As I was calling mayday, I was turning the ship away from the bad guys.

A wise senior pilot once told me, "Never crash land in an area you have just blown to hell. The survivors are very angry."

I yelled back to the crew chief that I couldn't jettison the heavy rocket pods because the electrical system was out. So he climbed out into the fire and pulled the cable that released them manually. Then, we were light on his side, so the other side dropped, scary because we were so close to the ground. The Crew Chief yelled to the door gunner to do the same, and he did, reaching right through the flames to pull the other manual release. We leveled out and I flared, and we landed. We would've been a smoking hole in the ground, if they hadn't jettisoned those pods.

Chapter 1.

THE DECISION

I'm so sick of this rain! Every day, all day. How do people do this? I need something different before I get athlete's foot just by walking to class. You can leave your dorm room unlocked and no worries. Umbrellas are a different story. Every day you steal a new one. Of course, they steal yours. You leave them in the hall before entering class and take your choice when you leave.

My name is Kevin McNally, and I'm at a crossroads. I enjoyed my first thirteen years of school. Something changed this sophomore year. I don't know what the problem is.

This is not Medford, Oregon, where I grew up. My life was easy there. I hunted all over the state with my dad and my two younger brothers. I fished on the Rogue River, practically out my back door, and went on camping trips to the high lakes in the Cascades. We had four actual seasons with only twenty inches of rain each year. Eugene has near sixty inches. I really didn't know how good I had it until I left. But isn't that the story for most of us?

I enjoyed high school and had many great friends. I participated in several sports: tennis, cross country and the swim team. Swimming was my best sport. My best stroke was the breast stroke. (Yes, I loved the double entendre, but even so, I did it well.) In class, I couldn't wait for trigonometry, geometry and algebra.

Maybe college calculus was the problem, my first difficult math class. Or maybe math was just harder in college. This weather was also affecting me. Too much change. Now what?

My dad flew in WWII. What little he told me sounded exciting.

He was in Europe for the last 18 months of the war, flying the P-47 Thunderbolt. That was the largest propeller-powered fighter plane ever built. He was shot down twice and received a Purple Heart for being wounded in combat. As with most combat veterans, his war experiences affected him for the rest of his life. He became very stern. He was a disciplinarian with me and my brothers and didn't hesitate to use his belt on us. I respected him very much and wanted to be like him. *Love your abuser. Sounds like the Stockholm syndrome to me now.*

I decided that flying had to be better than this college shit! I had been in college for two years and didn't have a clue what I wanted to do. Studying had become drudgery.

I had met a beautiful woman, who helped distract me from my misery. Just one problem: she wanted to get married. We were only 19 and certainly not ready for that big step. *What the hell was she thinking?* I broke off the relationship. My only skill was working in my dad's pipe yard: loading pipe and plumbing fixtures and then delivering them. My other skill was working in the kitchen in my dorms those past two years. I had eliminated both of those jobs from my future, very quickly.

Thus, began my journey to the various military recruiters in Eugene and Medford. I went to the Air Force first. They said, "You need a college degree to fly. Come back in two years." Next was the Navy. They said the exact same thing. The Marine Corps office was next door, so I walked in. The two recruiters stood up and told me with big smiles, "Sure we need pilots, and no degree is necessary." I said, "Let's talk." They were completely agreeable until I asked if there was any guarantee I would go to flight school after basic training. They said, "Oh, sure." When I requested that on paper, they looked at each other, and everything changed. "Actually," they said, "After Basic, you'll be placed at the need of the Marines." That sounded a lot like I would become a grunt and go straight to advanced infantry training. I had been warned about this tactic by those who knew, prior to my beginning this adventure.

That left the Army. I had nothing against the Army, but I wanted to fly jets. But what choice did I have? I stuck my head in the door, and this sergeant looked up at me. My first thought was, *he is wondering if I am old enough to shave.* I say this because of his chiseled face and enough ribbons on his chest to cover a door. I was beginning to feel intimidated. That was when he smiled, stood up, and extended his right hand. I thought, *Oh shit, this may hurt. I'll never be able to eat with my right hand again.* To my surprise, it was just a firm hand shake. What a relief. I would hate to look like a wimp in front of this guy. He said, "Sit down. What can I do for you?"

I said, "I would like to fly. Do you have anything that doesn't require a four year degree? I just finished my sophomore year of college."

He looked me in the eye and said, "Yes, we've got rotary-wing aviation." He could see my blank stare. So he followed with, "You know, helicopters."

Two weeks later, I took a bus to Portland for a physical and a series of tests to determine my ability to complete flight school. They checked my blood pressure, my shoe size, and my hemorrhoids. It was the first time I ever heard of that last one. Whatever they were, I didn't have any.

After that, the recruiter lined up a half dozen of us naive kids and swore us in to the US Army. We were now GIs, Government Issue. Then, he told us to take out our draft cards, tear them up, and throw the pieces into a small wastebasket he was holding. Well, we all knew this was a trick. We had all seen the long-haired draft dodgers burn and/or tear up their cards on TV. We just stood there. This was the first of many confusing orders I would be given while in the army. He took our draft cards and tore them into many tiny pieces, probably for emphasis, and said, "You don't need them anymore. You are now in the military."

Chapter 2.

THE ARMY

My next step in becoming an army pilot was to be flown to Fort Polk, Louisiana, for nine grueling weeks of basic training. The heat and humidity were unbelievable. Each platoon of fifty guys had two drill sergeants. It was a good cop-bad cop thing. One instructor put fear in you. He looked like a pro football player, and he at least pretended to be a mean son of a bitch. The other one—a skinny guy and six foot four— got his respect by telling us what was expected. That was the method I preferred.

In addition to learning all things military – crawling under barbed wire, marching and running five miles with backpack and rifle, throwing hand grenades, shooting hundreds of rounds at the rifle range, hand-to-hand combat and lots of pushups – I also learned I had signed a blank check to the U S army that included my life.

They occasionally mentioned something about breaking us down and building us up in their image of a soldier, but I was too worn out to make much sense of that. *Hadn't these brain-damaged Neanderthals read my file? I was going to flight school.*

I determined that if they ever give the United States an enema; the tube would be inserted in Fort Polk!

Primary flight school took me to Fort Wolters, Texas, just west of Dallas, for six months. First month, we never saw a helicopter. Just classes: officer training, weather, navigation, weight and balance, mechanical systems, emergencies, along with tons of spit shinning, lots of harassment and pushups. They did vaguely mention something about breaking us down, then building us up. It still didn't make sense to me. One of the students was thrown out for having Mary Jane in his room. We knew women weren't allowed. What an idiot he was.

I kept my mouth closed as per my dad's suggestion. He said, "Listen and you will learn." I was happy with that. I didn't want anyone to know how naïve I was. How could I be anything but naïve coming from a tiny town like Medford? I was shocked when I found out that Maryjane was marijuana.

Finally, we were off to the flight line to begin flying. We met our flight instructor. We still had classes, but only half a day, as the other half was spent learning to fly.

A helicopter has three basic controls. First, the *cyclic*, a rod coming up out of floor between your legs, with a pistol grip for your right hand. This controls right and left and forward when in the air and on the ground. It allows you to move backwards when hovering. Second, in the left hand you have the *collective pitch*. This has two functions: One is a reverse motor-cycle throttle that you rotate, when pulling up the collective, to increase the angle of pitch on your rotor blade. This increases the angle the blade attacks the air. If you do both together, the ship rises farther and goes faster. Third are the two *foot pedals*. You move these as you turn, climb or descend. If not, you will fly like a crab walks: sideways.

We weren't allowed to solo until we spent twelve hours flying under the close scrutiny (and harassment) of the flight instructor. Hell, he would roll up his map and hit me on the head with it. I couldn't feel it because my helmet was fiberglass, but it was humiliating and pissed me off. I found myself flinching like a puppy, where you hold a newspaper over its head as if to hit it for discipline.

While hitting me, he said, "McNally, we can teach a monkey to fly these things. What the hell is wrong with you?" It was difficult enough without this guy distracting me. "If you don't solo by 15 hours," he seemed to enjoy reminding me, "You get washed out." Most of us felt like we WERE a monkey trying to throw a football during the first eight to ten hours of flight training.

Another trainee who hadn't figured out these harassment techniques got in the TAC officer's face (Training, Advising, and Counseling) and was yelling that he was tired of these pushups, and they served no purpose. He was gone in a few hours. My dad warned me about the harassment. It was to see if you could follow orders and not break down. They push you for a reason. You will soon be in combat.

After the first week of flying ended, the TAC officers really increased the harassment. I guess the flying by itself wasn't stressful enough. They kept saying, "Pay attention because you're all going to Vietnam."

After lunch one day—the food, by the way, was great because we had civilian contractors cooking for us—my roommates and I were checking our room before heading out to class. Our TAC officer came down the hall and called out rather loudly, "Everyone fall out in the hall." This meant stand along the wall outside your room at attention with your head and heels against the wall and don't look at him. Just look straight ahead.

He had something derogatory to say about each one of us. When he got to me, he glanced at my name tag on my uniform and acted as if he knew me. He said, "McNally, I've heard about you. Do you know how low you are?"

I replied, while looking through him, "Sir, no sir."

He said, "McNally, you are lower than whale shit."

Someone down the line lost it and gave a small laugh. The TAC officer said, "So you think that's funny? Everyone down and give me 30 (pushups)."

We dropped and started counting. I just hoped I could hold back my laugh until he finished this ordeal and went back to his office. He did manage to belittle each one of us with his wit before leaving.

We went back in our rooms and were almost crying we were laughing so hard. Where did he come up with that gem?

Most of were able to Solo in the twelve to fifteen hour window. We lost a few. Some just quit and were transferred out to who knows where. A few had trouble with the academics.

Our training now consisted of our instructor flying with us to teach us new maneuvers and techniques. We would then practice all the new things for a few hours; then he would fly with us to determine how well we had learned them. If we did okay, he added more. This was the pattern through the next five months.

By the last month of primary training, our total number of hours in the air was nearing 100 hours. The harassment while we were flying had dwindled to nearly nothing. The TAC officer must have been bored. He went into everyone's room and wrote us up for some minor detail or other. When we returned to the barracks, we found a list of various deficiencies, and we were to report to his office.

When my turn came, I marched in and reported as ordered. He looked at me and said, "McNally, I discovered a female in your room today. What do you have to say for yourself?"

"No excuse sir."

He opened his desk and slowly reached in. I'm thinking, *what now?* I knew a female had not been in my room, so I waited to see where this was going to. He pulled out a match box and slid it open. He held it out, and I was looking at a dead fly. "I found this on your window sill. I believe she was trying to sneak in. You are confined to the barracks this Saturday until noon."

I said, "Yes sir."

He said, "Dismissed."

I turned and walked back to my room, shaking my head. He knew how much we looked forward to our weekends. Hell, I wanted to ask him how he knew it was female, but I didn't, as that would have just gotten me more grief. I would have been cleaning toilets and urinals with a tooth brush.

Later that day, I went to the post office on base, and as I approached, there was an odor that almost made me puke. I went in, and they said I had a package. I asked, "What died in here?"

The kid running the post office said, "We don't know. We've looked everywhere. We even had a guy crawl under the building, and he found nothing."

I took my package and couldn't get outside fast enough. As I walked away, I realized that the odor seemed to be following me. I put the small box up to my nose and realized it was making the stink. I stepped off the sidewalk and carefully opened the package. It was a bear's claw with hundreds of maggots crawling all over it. Now I knew why there had been no return address. It was from my two brothers and dad. We hunted bear and ate the meat. They had sent me my share.

I looked around to see if anyone was looking. I didn't want to be blamed for stinking up the post office. I saw a dumpster and tossed the package there. *At least my family is thinking of me. Those sickos.*

"When I returned to the barracks the TAC officer called every one out in the hall and had us stand at attention against the walls and in a loud voice said, "Look here, candidates; you should be taking this a lot more serious. In less than a year, you shit birds will be flying helicopters in Vietnam. You have to be serious, concentrate and develop situational awareness. Hell, some of you might even make it outta here! Some of you may even go home after Nam."

We didn't just pay attention. We had been doing nothing but pay attention. We knew we'd just be hauling in supplies and some troops. No big deal. We were still a bit naïve. I guess it was an army pep talk.

One event really stood out and shook us out of our stupor. Martin Luther King was shot and killed April 4th 1968 while he was standing on a balcony of his motel. There were two black men in our flight class who were very angry, and we didn't know how to console them.

After six months of primary flight school, I graduated and was shipped to Savannah, Georgia, for five months of advanced training and tactics in the Huey (named after Baby Huey in the Sunday comic papers). It's actually the UH-1 Iroquois (all army helicopters are named after Indian tribes, except one, the Cobra). It was hotter and steamier in Savannah than in Louisiana. I heard Vietnam was hotter. *Wow, I can't wait.*

We continued with a half day of classes and a half day of flying. I enjoyed this much more than primary training. However, now they added night flying and instrument training. (That's flying by looking only at the instruments and not outside the cockpit.) This was intense! An hour of this, and you'd sweat through your flight suit twice. At least the harassment was minimal.

Things were going smoothly (and winding up) in flight school when on June 6th 1968 Robert Kennedy was shot and killed after winning the California Democratic presidential primary. We didn't really know what to think or say. We were told to concentrate on flight school and graduate. So we did.

Finally, thirteen months after I raised my right hand and swore an oath to protect America against all enemies, foreign and domestic, I graduated. We had a graduation ceremony in the gym, similar to high school. First, I passed through the line to receive my bars, officially making me an officer and a gentleman. The post commander pinned on the bars. Second, I went through the same line again to receive my coveted wings. I was on a list to have someone else pin my wings on, other than the commanding general. He handed them to me as I saluted him.

My dad flew in from Oregon to pin on my wings. That was a thrill. We went outside for this ceremony. My roommate took pictures while Dad pinned on my wings. Then, we reciprocated for him. Several of us took our parents, girlfriends or wives to the flight line the next day and let them sit in a helicopter. It was over 100 degrees with 100% humidity.

Dad asked me, "How can you sit in this oven?"

"It's easy," I replied. "They order me to."

Dad attended the graduation ball that evening. Mostly, we all hung around the sidelines and talked, as there were no females or booze. Actually, I was too high on life to miss the women.

Later that evening, we returned to his hotel in Savannah and sat at the bar for several hours. I learned more there about him than in my previous nineteen years. He was still very angry because his brother had been killed piloting a B-24 Liberator over Hitler's oil fields in Ploesti, Romania. It was essentially a suicide mission. The planes were flying low, some as low as 30 feet, in broad daylight. Of 177 planes launched, only 89 returned, a casualty rate of 50%. The mission was a "success" because it crippled Hitler's mechanized army. That was August, 1, 1943.

Two of Dad's best friends from flight school were killed while flying in his squadron on combat missions over Europe. He spoke of having a hard time after returning home. He had no patience and argued with Mom a lot. He told me, "You just can't help what you are feeling inside. I'm sorry for yelling at you all the time. Especially for putting you in charge of your brothers while your mom and I played golf." He never spoke about any of this again.

The next morning, we drove all the way to Nebraska, where his mom lived. She wasn't happy about me going to Vietnam. Her husband was in Europe in WWI, and she lost one of her sons in WW II.

After two days of eating fried chicken and mulberry pie and

meeting everyone who knew my dad growing up, we drove to Oregon.

That drive to Oregon was a marathon. I didn't let it bother me. I was thinking, *I'm a proud helicopter pilot. I'm feeling too good to be tired.* I was still elated from my graduation. I was ecstatic.

I stayed at home for ten days. This was both strange and strained as everyone knew where I was going. My dad and mom and my two brothers had been reading about this damn "police action" and watching it on TV for the past year. In that time it had grown from being a small thing to a very big deal. Every night the news would list the dead Americans. It was as if nothing else was happening in the world. I think they dreaded my shipping out more than I did. I hadn't read any newspapers or watched any TV for the past year. My mom surprised me when she asked if I wanted to go to Canada. I was stunned and just looked at her. Then, I remembered. She had waited at home for the last eighteen months of WWII while her husband, my father, flew fighter planes over Europe.

I said, "No mom, I'm not going to run and hide. I believe in what we are doing." I had never seen her cry before and didn't know what to do. Then, she surprised me again by asking if wanted to know anything about the birds and bees. "Mom, I had high school biology and a year of Biology in college. I'm OK with the sex thing." And that was all she needed to know about me at this point of my life.

I told my brothers they could use my new mustang while I was away. They assured me they would take very good care of her.

As a joke, I said, "No sex in the back seat."

They answered with big grins. "Of course, no way."

Shit, I thought, I'll have to burn the seats and buy new ones when I get back.

Chapter 3.

VIETNAM

Those ten days went by in an eye blink. So then, I was off to South Vietnam. It was a fourteen-hour flight: San Francisco, Anchorage, Tokyo and finally Long Binh Post in Bien Hoa, (ben wa) just outside Saigon.

When I stepped out of the plane and started down the stairs, the heat and humidity hit me like a hammer. It was 11 pm. The air smelled like garbage. We walked a short distant and loaded into buses for a fifteen-minute ride to the processing center. I was drenched in sweat. I noticed something strange. There were bars over the windows. It looked like we were in a jail.

My shirt was completely wet, but the bars on the windows distracted me from that discomfort.

The windows were open in a poor attempt to fight the heat and humidity. The ride was pretty quiet. We all felt lots of apprehension as nothing good had been said about this place anywhere in the news back home during my quick ten days. We looked like a busload of students going to school. Everyone looked so young. I'm sure I looked the same. Buzz cuts, some faces with zits, and everyone with eyes wide open.

Finally, someone got up the courage to ask the obvious question, "Why are their bars over the windows?" Without even turning around, the driver yelled out, "It's so the children won't run up to the bus and throw a hand grenade inside." We were immediately silent, more than before. Now everyone was looking outside at every tree, bush, and bend in the road. A grenade in this small area would kill more than one of us.

It really did smell like a garbage dump here. I was going to need some time to get used to this vile odor. I had hauled trash to the dump when I worked for my dad. That odor is unique, and here it was enhanced by humidity and heat. The air actually felt thick, for lack of a better word.

We were checked in and assigned a barracks. They would finish the processing the next day. In fact, it required three days to process my paperwork at Ben Hoa. Over ten years, they moved three million soldiers through that mill and 10,000 women.

Those three days were incredibly boring. The heat and humidity were oppressive. I picked up a Harold Robbins novel. It worked to take my mind off of everything. I couldn't read that stuff at home.

They sent me to Chu Lai (CL), about 60 miles south of Danang and the home of the 71st Assault Helicopter Company. This was part of I Corp (pronounced eye core) located in the northern quarter of South Vietnam. It fell under the command of the Americal Division (created by General Douglas MacArthur in WW II). South Vietnam (VN) was divided into four corps, which defined the areas of responsibility for the military.

After we landed at CL airport—actually, it was a Marine air base full of small jet aircraft—the company clerk arrived in a standard military jeep. He must have been all of 150 pounds, with acne, and with little hair. He looked bleach blond. He had way too much energy for this heat and humidity. We exchanged greetings, and he actually said, "Welcome to Vietnam, sir," and saluted me. I returned the salute and said, "Nice to meet you, Thompson," as I glanced at his name tag. He said, "Stow your gear sir," as he pointed to the back seat of the jeep. I threw my duffel bag there and climbed in. (I had been allowed to bring no more than what fit in that duffel.) We bounced along about a mile south on what someone called a road. The air smelled just as foul as in Bien Hoa. It just stunk everywhere, and now there were columns of black smoke rising up. I could see at least 20. It made for a very smoggy air.

I asked the driver, "What are they burning?"

He didn't look at me. He just said, "Shit," then added, "Sir."

I said, "Shit?"

"Yes sir. That's how we get rid of everything in the outhouses. We are practically at sea level, so we can't dig holes; they just fill up with water. Fifty-five gallon barrels are cut in half and placed under each outhouse hole. When the barrels are full, someone drags them out back of the structure, which varies from a one holer to a four holer, and pours diesel fuel in and lights it. That's what makes the black columns of terrible-smelling smoke. If you smoke, sir, don't throw the burning butt down between your legs; there is always some diesel fuel remaining. We've lost a few outhouses, and some burned GIs had to be sent to the hospital.

I thought, *who gets that job?*

Another surprise came when the driver said, "We're on Highway One, sir, the only north-south road in the entire country."

We passed a few Vietnamese women with large baskets on their heads, black baggy pants and loose fitting tops. The driver said they were headed to the market.

We then turned off "Highway One" and bounced a hundred yards on what must have been a one lane driveway with holes deep enough to qualify as bomb craters. I looked out ahead and to my amazement saw a beautiful ocean of blue-green water and the whitest sand imaginable. *Wow,* I thought, *how bad can this place be?*

Between that poster picture and me were two hundred yards of what my driver called hooches. There were about forty of them, and one would soon be my new residence. At home, we would have called these buildings shacks. As we stopped in front of a small building in an area that looked like the parade grounds, the private said, "This is the CO's office. He' waiting to see you."

I rummaged through my duffel bag to get my orders and went inside. I took off my hat and approached the first sergeant. Now for those of you not familiar with the army, this man ranks just under God and above Jesus. He did not have a name, so to speak. We called him Top or First Sergeant.

I said, "Top, Mr. McNally reporting for duty."

He said, "Just a moment Mr. McNally, I will see if the major is available." He went in, and then came out. "Go in Mr. McNally."

I did and handed over my orders while standing at attention. "Mr. Kevin McNally, reporting as ordered, sir."

In a very relaxed voice and a smile, Major Wilson said, "At ease," which is military parlance for feet apart and hands behind your back, the back of one hand in the palm of the other.

He then surprised me with, "Welcome to the 71st. My clerk is going to give you a tour and show you your living quarters. Then report back here and I will explain your first thirty days."

I replied with, "Yes sir," turned, and walked out of his office to the waiting clerk.

The private said, "Follow me please," and off we went. First, he showed me the motor pool, where they parked and did maintenance on all the vehicles: jeeps, half-ton pickups, one-ton trucks and the big boys, the five-tons. These latter were mostly for transporting everybody to the flight line: mechanics, pilots, crew chiefs and door gunners. They were also used to pick up parts for the helicopters. Civilian contractors lived with us, too, and used these vehicles. They worked on our radio equipment and, as I later discovered, maintained a thing called a computer for operating the gunships' armament (weapons). *I will have to learn about computers.*

Next, we walked to the beach. Thirty yards from the water was a volley-ball net, though I didn't see a ball or anyone playing. Close by was the movie theater, which consisted of several sheets of plywood, nailed to posts driven into the sand. It had been painted white but had seen better times. Someone put a bullet hole right in the center. *All said, not a bad shot.*

Twenty yards away was the officers' club. I really would not call it anything but condemned if I were back in the world. It had two walls. *Shouldn't a building have at least four?* One wall had mail slots, an opening (front door, but without the door), and a long shelf. The clerk explained, "This shelf is for your hat and weapons, prior to entering. Go inside with either, and it's an expensive mistake. You will pay a fine." They fine you for everything I soon discovered.

There was a large bowl on the bar, full of money for various infractions in the club or in the air. You put your fine money in the bowl, which was then available to all. You usually didn't have to pay for a drink. The rule about weapons made sense to me; do not mix guns and alcohol. Hell, we had that rule back home. To finish off this semblance of civility, the officers' club had its very own thatched roof. Warm beer and warm crown royal—there was no ice—both could be purchased for twenty-five cents, if you were not scheduled to fly the next day.

Otherwise, strictly forbidden!

We walked along a sidewalk of pallets lying on the sand and connecting all the hooches. One difference, these pallets were constructed of a metal mesh. I found out the next day that I should purchase some flip flops from the hooch maids. This was important because you couldn't walk to the shower without ripping a toe off if it got caught in the mesh. Imagine trying to run on that diabolical structure during a rocket attack! We threw away our old rubber tires, and the Vietnamese remanufactured them into flip flops and resold them to us. *Wow!*

I noticed there was a four foot wall of sand bags around the Hooches. I asked Thompson, "What are the bags for?"

He said, "We get rocket attacks nearly every night. If the rocket hits outside the hooch, you will be OK. If it hits inside, well then..."

I figured it out.

I was surprised to see some older women walking in and out of the hooches. Some were carrying clothes. Others were sweeping sand out the doors. All were wearing black pajamas and large-brimmed straw hats.

I asked the clerk, "Who are these women?"

"They're hooch maids. They polish boots, change sheets once a week, clean up the place and clean your dirty uniforms. They have been checked out by the MPs and are supposedly not Vietcong (South Vietnamese fighting for the North). You pay them five dollars a month. That totals sixty dollars a month from the twelve guys in the two hooches."

I asked, "Why are their mouths and lips black?"

He told me it was from chewing betel nut, a mild narcotic. He followed with, "I guess in this rotten country, it helps to have a buzz on all day." I thought *Who could kiss those lips?*

We walked along another hundred feet, and he said, "Here is your hooch, home for the next year." It sounded like he had given this tour and speech to other new guys before me. I took the two steps up to the screen door. He had said that all the hooches were built up off the sand for stability. The inside was small with six beds, three to a side, and a five-foot tall locker and a small table next to each bed. The walls were wood for the first four feet up from the floor and the next four feet was screen, our air conditioning. Sheets of plywood hung on hinges on the outside, currently held up by two-by-fours. In the monsoon season, I was told, we would pull out the two-by-fours, and the plywood would drop down over the screen in a so-so attempt to keep out the rain. The hooch had a corrugated aluminum roof which I would learn played a symphony of noise when it rained. But I discovered after a few weeks, it was possible to sleep through anything, including our evening rocket attacks. So, no big deal with the economy roof; it did keep out most of the rain.

I threw my duffel bag on a bed and noticed two of the beds were occupied. I figured I would meet those guys later. I followed the clerk back to the CO's office. I had turned 21 in flight school and would be 22 in four months. Being 21, he told me, made me one of the older pilots in the company. "We have some eighteen-year-old pilots here," he said.

With parental permission, you could take the flight school tests after your junior year in high school. Then get a GED in basic training, do flight school for eleven months, and arrive in VN at 18 ½ years old. *Wow! But, aren't all wars fought by the young?*

I reported to the CO and stood at ease while he explained my orders for my first 30 days.

"You will fly with eight different pilots over 28 days. You will report to the mess hall at 0400, and then choke down some food, but don't complain because we all eat the same mess. At 0430 tomorrow, you will receive a briefing on a combat assault involving all our ships. You will be assigned to the second platoon. A combat helicopter company consists of 200 men. Here, we've got three platoons of helos. The first two are the Rattlers, and you will see the rattle snake painted on their noses. There are ten ships to a platoon. Their job is to haul ass and haul trash, which means people and/or supplies.

"Third platoon are the Firebirds, the gunships. They are the most undisciplined soldiers in this man's army. They are a rowdy bunch of delinquents who don't give a shit. That's because they have the highest mortality rate. Joining that group is purely voluntary."

Actually, enlisting in the army's flight school was purely voluntary. Oh well.

"The guns, as we call them, will escort the Rattlers into the LZ (pronounced ell-zee, for landing zone). They will be between you and the enemy, shooting rockets, Gatling guns, and 40 millimeter cannons, with the door gunners on both sides hanging outside for better movement on their targets. You'll receive the rest of the briefing tomorrow when you meet your pilot. We match up new guys with seasoned pilots. This is how you learn to fly in combat, not like flight school. If you pay attention and practice what they teach you, there is a good chance you might just make it through this war. I usually don't put a new guy in a combat assault their first week, but we are short of pilots.

"OK, here's an alarm clock. For the next thirty days, you are an FNG. My clerk will take you down to the flight line for a check ride and to get your assigned flight gear. See you in the morning McNally. Dismissed."

As I turned to leave, I said, "Sir may I ask you a question?"

He said, "Sure."

"What's an FNG?"

He smiled. "For your first month in country, you are a Fucking New Guy. Then, you are a copilot (also called a peter pilot) until the other pilots think you're ready to be an aircraft commander.

"By the way, write lots of letters home! You have no idea what those close to you are going through back home! This fucking war is all over the TV each night, and the news only shows the worst of it. Here is your blood chit. Keep it on you at all times.

Yes sir. *I wonder what the best of it is. ¿?*

I returned to my new home to unpack my duffel bag and get situated. The two other FNGs were sitting on their bunks, Lance Austin from Kansas City, Kansas, and Dean Perry from Los Angeles, California. Lance was a Bible thumper. (I saw the Bible on his bed.) Dean said he was a surfer. *Hippie* crossed my mind. *This should prove interesting.* California did not have the greatest reputation with my family back in Oregon, and especially with the military. The antiwar crap had started at the University of California in Berkeley. They burned draft cards, American flags and effigies of our leaders. They even pissed on the flag. *Some really fine people.*

Lance enlisted, as it was expected in his family. Their military history could be traced back to the war of 1812. Dean enlisted to beat the draft, so he could choose what he wanted to do.

"Wow," I said, "I enlisted because I didn't like rain in Eugene, Oregon. We all have our reasons."

They both got a laugh out of that. They had arrived the week before. Lance said he had a sister, and Dean was an only child.

"I have two younger brothers," I told them. "One is a senior in high school and the other is in his sophomore year at the University of Oregon. I'm really missing them right now. We used to fight all the time, but we've been getting along better lately." That had hit me when my departure to VN was just a few days away. Why does life work that way? Sibling rivalry really is terrible. *Why does it exist?*

Lance, Dean, and I went to the mess hall together to choke down some mystery chow. I really couldn't call it food. We all agreed it was the worst food we'd ever tried to eat. The tray consisted of gray peas, bland spaghetti, corn bread and some kind of pudding. These were our best guesses. We started trying to gross each other out about what this stuff was. Lance said, "Our hogs in Kansas eat better than this." We were laughing. Dean said, "It's probably left over burnt shit." I said, "This tastes like a long dead animal." We agreed the analysis was correct from all three of us. "Thank goodness for bread and ketchup."

We all got along, and I was relieved by that. It looked like friendships would develop quickly. We wrapped it up early as we all had to be in the mess hall by 0400.

I did not sleep that night. About 0100, a few rockets hit near our company area. The three of us sat up instantly and went to the door, but no one was running to the bunkers scattered among the hooches. Then, I remembered one of the pressing issues we talked about after dinner while I was putting my gear and fatigues in my locker. Someone said, "The rats in the bunkers are two feet long." We had the same chance of survival by staying in the hooch, since it had sand bags four feet high around the outsides.

I was ready at 0300, so I just sat on my bunk, and my roomies on theirs. I think it was ninety degrees. At 0350, I said, "Close enough," and we struck out for the mess hall.

Out of curiosity, I looked up the word "mess" in flight school. Where possibly could that word have come from? Well, it turns out to have originated from an old French word, *mes*, meaning a portion of food. Dinner was a portion of something, but I wouldn't have called it food back home.

Chapter 4.

DON'T TOUCH A FUCKING THING

I grabbed a tray and started down the line: powered eggs, grits, toast and coffee that could hold up a spoon (seriously). I attempted to eat but could manage only toast with ketchup. (I hadn't started coffee yet.)

Then, the door burst open and a tired looking bunch of guys with worn out fatigues—almost white instead of green—came in. They were carrying flight helmets, maps, and chicken boards.

The chicken plate, or board, was a ten pound ceramic plate that we wore in a small poncho over our chests and under the shoulder harnesses. It was bulletproof up to and including a thirty caliber bullet; the AK-47 was 30 caliber. I learned to never leave home without my chicken board.

One of the guys in front stopped and looked around the room and said, "Who's McNally?"

I raised my hand and said in my deepest, most confident voice, "I am."

He came over, dumped his gear on the table, and said, "Don't let anyone steal my shit; I need coffee." He walked over to the five gallon pot and actually put that old sludgy motor oil in a cup. He came back and sat down across the table so we were eye to eye. He looked half dead or at least under slept. Our uniforms were called fatigues. It seemed to me this could also describe his present condition.

He introduced himself as Phil Henry from Florida, and I introduced myself. He seemed not in any mood for small talk, so I just moved my food around on my tray and waited for something to happen.

Then, Major Wilson stood, walked to the front, and said, "Good morning." This was followed by a good morning from the FNGs and some unintelligible mumbling from everyone else. Phil looked at me and said, "Don't be so gung ho."

The major, whom I had met the day before, seemed like a decent guy. He was maybe thirty. He wore a wedding ring and looked very fit. His uniform was clean and seemed brand new; RHIP (rank has its privileges). He gave us the map coordinates for the day's operation, where to pick up the troops and where to insert them. "You will go into the LZ in a formation of threes," he said. "I will hand out a list." He raised his hand and waved some papers. "This has your order in the formation into the LZ. For some of you, it is your first CA (combat assault)." He noted radio frequencies.

"This mission's name is hill 190. That's the name because the LZ is on a hill 190 meters above sea level, or for the Americans, a little more than 600 feet." He was obviously explaining this for us newbies. "Bad news is that you will go in there three additional times. First two insertions will consist of grunts in full battle gear. The next two insertions will be food, ammo and water in and carry out wounded and lastly the dead. We expect it to be hot, so watch the other ships before you pull out of the LZ and check if any of your drinking buddies need a ride out." (He meant if their helo was too shot up to fly.)

"God's own lunatics, or the Firebirds for the new pilots, will prep the area just before we arrive. They will then come out and meet us and escort in the first two groups, and then continue in an oval pattern shooting at anything that moves or shoots back.

"If you are taking fire, call out your number in the group and give the Birds the clock position to shoot into the tree lines, until three groups of three land and dump off the grunts. After that, just shoot at muzzle flashes or origins of tracers. Let's not have any friendly fire casualties. That LZ is going to fill up fast.

"As this assault progresses, our guys are going to be moving toward the tree line and the enemy will be there. If any of our ships go down, you'll have to break formation on short final and find a spot to call your own. After you pull out of the LZ, proceed back to the pickup point in a big hurry. That first group of guys is going to feel very lonely until you bring them help. Any questions?" No hands went up, so he said, "ACs (aircraft commanders) come up and get your info."

Everyone crowded to the door. Half dozen trucks were waiting outside. I sat next to Phil. I asked him about, "God's own lunatics." He said it was from a war correspondent who took a ride with some gunships on a hot mission several years ago. When they landed, he stepped out, puked on his boots, and said, "I now dub you 'God's own lunatics.'" I just sat there in silence and thought, *Wow*.

When we arrived at the flight line a few minutes later, I saw that the crew chiefs and door gunners were already there. They were prepping the ships to fly. I looked down the small taxiway that contained 20 parking slots, or revetments. Each revetment was fenced around in an L shape with a double row of 55 gallon drums filled with sand and another row stacked on top of those. This protected the ships from shrapnel during our nightly rocket attacks. Our 20 ships were called "slicks" because they didn't have any weapons hanging on the outside. They were smooth, or slick, along the outside. Their machine guns were mounted just inside the doors.

Across the taxiway were ten revetments for the Firebirds. There were rarely more than six flying, due to constant exposure to enemy fire, which meant that maintenance was continual. That large diving decal of a Firebird on the side looked to me like it meant business.

We helped the crew finish the preflight. That was when Phil said, "This is your first day flying, isn't it?"

"Yes."

"Don't touch a fucking thing. Just monitor my instruments for any warning lights or master caution lights." (Yellow is a warning and red means *Land now or die*.) "Also be ready to grab the controls if I get shot. I only have two months remaining in this hell hole, and I don't want to die at the hands of an FNG."

Does he think I want to die?

Well, that's twice I have heard the word fuck something, all aimed at me, in less than fifteen hours. Guess I'm nowhere near the top of the pecking order here. Well, not to worry. Everyone new pays the price.

The experienced guys seemed uptight and tense while they were looking over the ships. I wondered what that was all about. I would soon learn.

Chapter 5.

COMBAT ASSAULT

After the preflight, we climbed in and strapped in. As in all aviation, except the gunships, pilots sit in the left seat and copilot in the right. Gunships are the opposite.

Phil yelled, "Clear," as was standard procedure to warn everyone nearby that rotor blades would be turning. The crew chief and door gunner looked out on their respective sides and called back, "Clear left," and then, "Clear right." I looked out my window and yelled, "Clear." Phil cracked open the throttle and pulled the trigger on the bottom side of the collective, and the rotor blades began turning, slow at first, but quickly speeding up to 320 rpm. We called the tower for clearance to take off.

Phil said, "Pulling pitch," as he pulled the collective up. The collective changes the angle of the rotor blades to increase lift. It also contains many switches: landing light, search light (using your thumb), starter ignition trigger, governor, throttle, throttle friction, engine idle, search light movement, and landing light on-off. All of these with the left hand while flying.

The cyclic also has several functions besides flight control: The trigger on front was for communication: depressed halfway for intercom and fully for transmitting on any one of four radios. There was also a cargo release switch for exterior sling loads, a button for armament fire control and one for force trim (holds the cyclic when you let go), and a directional switch. For gunships, the cyclic also has a button on the left side for shooting rockets, and it is also used by the pilot when the copilot was unable to shoot the cannon. All of that while flying with the cyclic in the right hand. All while being on the radio with the ground troops, wing ship, and crew.

We were rattler 2-4.The 2 meant second platoon and the 4 was the number assigned to Phil when he qualified as an aircraft commander, or pilot. Pilots were assigned one number: 0 through 9; 6 was always reserved for the platoon leader. After takeoff, we formed up in our flights of three as per the briefing and proceeded to the pickup coordinates, which happened to be on Highway One.

We landed on the highway, and along the road were several hundred GIs in full battle packs. They looked like shit. Dirty, filthy, unshaven 18 and 19 year old kids who had just completed a mission in the bush (jungle) and were now going to be thrown right back in the fight. They looked exhausted.

I saw two crying.

The ones awake were smoking. (Nearly everyone smoked.) Some had dried caked mud on their fatigues (army talk for a working green uniform).

Their packs were full. They had three and four canteens each and a serious amount of ammunition and grenades strapped to their flak jackets (a sleeveless vest with some metal plates inside to stop shrapnel). They stood as we landed, and many seemed to have trouble getting up. Those packs had to be over fifty pounds. They ground out their cigarettes and slowly walked over to the ships and climbed in. No one was talking.

Their platoon sergeants began barking orders like basic-training drill instructors for the remaining troops to form up in groups of seven for the second insertion and be ready to be picked up in about ten minutes. That second group looked just as nervous as the ones sitting behind me. It was crowded back there. I looked over my shoulder and saw five sitting on the floor, and one on each seat next to the crew chief and door gunner. It had taken them only about a minute to get in. I could see the groups of seven for the second insertion were ready.

A CA worked like this: There was a pre-chosen LZ (landing zone or area). The gunships went in first shooting to soften the area; that is, shooting anything that moved. The gunships would then fly out to meet the incoming slicks carrying the troops and escort them into the LZ. The gunships would engage anyone shooting at those ships. The slicks would then return to the pickup site for the second group of GIs. The gunships remained on station, shooting at the enemy or circling to wait for the second insertion to arrive.

Over the radio, each of the seven flights reported in. There were three helos in each flight, so it sounded something like this: "Flight one, one ready, two ready, three ready." Then, "Flight two, one ready, two ready, three ready." This continued through seven flights and took about ten seconds. Then, the flight leader called out on the assault frequency, "Pulling pitch (taking off)."

About two minutes later, lead said, "Test your guns." Before I realized what he had said, both machine guns let go with a short burst. I would have jumped out of my seat if it hadn't been for my seat belt and shoulder harness. A gun going off just behind your head is painful. Sometimes, hunting back home, we would put ciga-rette filters in our ears. Not here. We had a small amount of sponge rubber built into our helmets with our ear phones. All in all, not much noise was filtered out.

OK, I thought to myself. *This is it: my first combat mission. Thirteen months ago, it all began, building up to this moment.*

We flew about ten minutes. Then a new voice came through those ear phones built into my helmet. "Mission 190 flight lead, this is Command and Control, over." (Flight lead was the lead ship in the first flight. My slick was number two in the group of three in the first flight).

"C & C, this is flight lead, go ahead."

"I'm just behind you and a thousand feet above."

I thought, *That sounds a hell of a lot safer than actually landing in the midst of the enemy.*

C & C had a look-down perspective on the action and could sometimes help redirect forces and/or report on other enemy movements. I was to learn that this didn't always work well.

Then C & C said, "I have Colonel Kim of the South Vietnamese Army with me to observe."

Phil let me know that this was a heads up not to say anything negative or racist about the Vietnamese.

Lead called out, "One minute out. Be alert."

I looked ahead and could see explosions from the gunships' rockets hitting in the tree line around the LZ. I saw tracers trav-eling both ways, from gunships to the enemy and vice versa. Yes, the Intel (intelligence report on the enemy's location) had called it correctly; this was a hot LZ. The gunships turned and flew toward us, then turned alongside us and slightly ahead.

I thought we were moving pretty fast this close to the LZ.

Suddenly, without warning, Phil pulled back on the cyclic until it was in his crotch. He nearly stood the ship on its tail. All I could see was blue sky; actually kind of pretty, no battle smog. I looked at him and thought, *Is he shot?* He looked OK. Actually, it was hard to tell if someone had been shot. We were always sitting up straight because we locked our seat belts and shoulder harnesses when in battle. If we were injured, we couldn't slide out of our seats and interfere with the controls. I checked out Phil's head. It was upright, and very intense, but it didn't look like the head of an injured man. I guessed that crazy maneuver was just to slow us down.

I looked out my side window for orientation and saw tracers, lots of tracers, going by us and hitting the ground, but not us. Every fifth bullet was a tracer. It glowed as it moved because the bullet was hollowed out a few millimeters and packed with phosphorus. This ignited when the powder in the casing exploded and sent the bullet down the barrel. Seeing the glow of the tracers, the machine gunner was able to walk his bullets to the target. (Our tracers were red because we used red phosphorus, and the bad guys used both red and green). The door gunners were firing into the places in the tree line where the enemy's tracers were coming from. I wasn't sure we would get out of this LZ. *Wow, dead on my first day and my first mission.*

More explosions from the gunships' rockets, only this time I could hear them. Many pilots were talking over each other on the radio. To add to the noise and confusion, our machine guns behind me sounded like they were in my head. Smoke and dust were filling the LZ. A strong odor of gunpowder filled the ship. This was all happening so fast.

After what seemed like a minute but was only a few seconds, Phil pushed the stick forward and we leveled out about ten feet above the twelve inch tall elephant grass. I was looking intently at the instrument panel for warning lights when the ship began rocking side to side about six inches each way while we descended. I dared a glance over my shoulder and saw the grunts jumping out the door. We hadn't landed. I wasn't sure what was happening.

Were we on fire? I hoped we weren't because, if we were, there is a good chance of an explosion. Even if we did get out alive, we'd end up grounded. One of our ships would try to pick us up. That was the only comforting thought.

As both lead and our ship pulled pitch to get the hell out of there, I could hear and feel the vibrations as we took hits. When three was lifting off, an RPG (rocket propelled grenade) struck the tail of the ship, where it was attached to the main body. This was where the gas tank just happened to be located. The ship immediately nosed down as the tail boom was blown off, and they lost their center of gravity and hit the ground. Fire spread quickly. The fuel was literally thrown out of the ruptured tank onto the hot engine. It immediately became a large fireball with thick black smoke from the burning metal.

Lead called out in a much higher tone and more rapid speech than usual. "Flight one, ship three is down in the LZ and on fire. Can second flight check for survivors?" Flight two lead asked his number three if their grunts could take a look-see. He said, "Roger." As we were lifting off, trying to get out of there as fast as this ship could at max power, I dared to ask Phil why the grunts were jumping out before we touched down. He looked at me and very calmly spoke, this time in normal tone of voice, saying, "Those grunts are smart. They don't want to sit in this large target with 240 gallons of JP-4 jet fuel when it explodes." I just nodded. *Something not covered in flight school.*

Now the noise on the radio was desperate. I could hear, "Flight three taking fire." Someone else called out they were hit. Someone had lost their tail rotor and was down in the LZ. With all the noise over the radios, Phil spoke loudly over the intercom and asked if everyone on his ship was OK. Fortunately, we were all alive and well. I had learned a few things in those couple of minutes: first, that LZs needed to be larger, and second, about ten to twenty seconds into a combat assault, you could throw the briefing out the window. Gut intuition and experience took over. I also learned that a pilot was in charge of his ship and/or the entire CA and had to keep a clear head and not panic. Everyone in that ship was depending on him.

We were five minutes out of the LZ and five minutes from picking up our second load of grunts, and not a word had been spoken since Phil had asked if everyone was OK. Once again we landed on Highway One. As we were loading up, we heard over the radio that the pilot in our number three ship was dead, the copilot looked like he had some broken bones, and both guys in back had some burns. All three were on their way to the MASH unit (Mobile Army Surgical Hospital) at Baldy. (Baldy was our base northwest of Chu Lai.) They were bringing the pilot out on another ship. This caused another eerie silence among the four of us.

When the grunts were inside, Phil smoothly pulled pitch. We returned to our flight formation and back to the fight. I had about ten minutes to absorb what had just happened in the last fifteen minutes. I felt thankful that I was flying with a seasoned and experienced pilot!

I was knocked out of my reverie and back to war when the lead pilot called over the radio, "One minute out." I looked over my shoulder as I felt and heard shuffling in back. The gunners were checking their machine guns. I then heard "short final" (meaning we were close to landing), and it started again, with machine guns roaring just behind my head and tracers going both ways. The NVA knew we would return. Both sides had been doing this dance for the last four years. The radios were full of confusing crosstalk.

Then, I heard someone yelling over the radio, "Dinks at three o' clock." (Three o'clock is a reference number. Hold a clock in front of you and then place it on the ground, face up, with 12 o' clock straight out in front of you. Then, 3 o'clock would be straight out to your right and 6 o'clock behind you.) We called the enemy "dinks," which just meant little people, dinky. In war, each side has derogatory names for their enemy.

Next thing we heard was a transmission from the C & C ship high overhead, where not only is the colonel safe, and much cooler, he is about to make a significant mistake.

Chapter 6.

THAT WAS CLOSE

The colonel asked over the air waves, "Who said dinks? Say I-D." (In military parlance, that means identify yourself).

Shit, even I, an FNG, knew we were in the middle of a combat assault. We had our own dead and wounded. We didn't have time for stupid interruptions. The next thing I heard on the radio was a pilot keying his transmit button, saying, "I-D." Then another said, "I-D," and on and on. I couldn't help but grin, fighting back a laugh. I looked over at Phil, and he was actually laughing. The C & C ship overhead was silent after that. He got the message! No one was going to admit to insulting our allies and get into pointless stupid trouble after we landed.

Again without warning, Phil pulled back on the cyclic, and we stood on our tail for a few seconds, then leveled out and immediately the grunts were abandoning ship. This insertion was just as hot.

There were more tracers. More noise. More cross talking over the radios. Actually probably not more; I was just more aware.

Suddenly, a bullet passed through my side of the windshield. It passed close to my head, then passed the crew chief, and exited through the sliding door in back. I said out loud, louder than I realized, "Fuck, that was close." At that moment, I couldn't think of anything else to say that would express my thoughts any better or more accurately. Then, another fucking bullet came through. This one hit the outside of my chin bubble (a Plexiglas area on the floor allowing the pilot view the ground) and struck the large instrument panel between Phil and me.

I was dividing my time looking at the instrument panel, looking at Phil, watching where our door gunners were shooting, and noticing how close the Firebirds were putting their rockets and cannon. I must have moved or jerked my head back as several of their explosions hit real close. I saw the bodies of the NVA on the ground, only thirty yards away. Thank god those cannon shots were on target. I reminded myself to buy those guys a drink.

Phil read my mind and said, "They like to work close. That's why we love those crazy bastards. They will do anything to protect us and our troops. They always have our six (cover our backs)."

I heard, "Flight one lead pulling pitch." We were right with him. *Damn*, I thought. (It was just hitting me.) *It's just pure good luck if you survive this shit or bad luck if you don't.* I heard over the radio that another ship just went down. The grunts reported that all four crew members were killed." *Christ, I have twelve more months of this!*

We proceeded back to the troop pickup coordinates, landed and loaded up with hand grenades, mortar rounds, M-16 ammo, machine gun ammo, claymores, smoke grenades and water. While this was going on, I was listening to the radio talk from ship to ship. It sounded like most of the ships were hit. One ship shut down to check for damage and found some critical hits in the fuel pump and hydraulic lines and couldn't continue. Some of the crews were wounded, but only minor wounds so they could keep flying.

As we were returning to the LZ, Phil said, "You got it (which meant I had the controls). Take it all the way to the ground because the guys in back have to throw all this shit out (the supplies we had picked up). Then, they are going to put wounded on board. Be ready. That shit is ugly."

I flew into the LZ ignoring the enemy fire and did fine. I was worried as they loaded the wounded in back. It seemed we were sitting an awful long time in this fucking LZ. Tracers were hitting the ground in front of the ship, right below my feet. They were passing by the windshield with increasing frequency. People were still yelling on the radio, "I'm hit. Ship is down. Taking heavy fire at nine o' clock." It was pure chaos.

The gunships had returned to LZ Baldy, their home base, to refuel and rearm. This had taken them 30 minutes, and now they were back on station and were shooting rockets, mini guns (electric six-barreled Gatling guns), 40 millimeter cannon; the ever effective door gunners worked the tree lines and watched over the grunts.

We were just about loaded and ready, so I glanced back at the wounded and was stunned by the amount of damage that could be done to a human body that still survived. Then, I noticed a medic back there, covered in blood. He obviously had jumped in while they were loading the wounded. (An army medic is essentially a nurse practitioner at first and a surgeon by the end of his 12 month tour.) This one was moving fast, his face focused and serious. Blood was pumping out of two guys like a fountain.

My thought was to get these kids back to medical help ASAP. It seemed to me the ship was not going fast enough until I took another look at the instruments and saw the engine and rotor speeds were both maxed out.

Phil said, "Ease back, Mac (giving me my nickname for the year). We're doing our best. We're only a few minutes out." That would be to Baldy, which had a MASH medical unit. Baldy was the home of the Firebirds and the 196th and 198th light infantry brigades. In fact, that's who we supported on this CA, the 198th, the same as for the rest of my time in VN. Occasionally, we would assist the marines, Aussies, ROKs (republic of Korea), and South Vietnamese.

A combat assault was actually quite involved. We loaded the helicopters with ground troops (grunts, ground pounders, GIs, or dog faces; all the same guys) and took them to the chosen LZ. This was most usually in an area heavily infested with NVA troops. The gunships supported most of these missions by first softening the LZ (shooting and blasting away at the enemy) before the helos full of troops arrived. The gunships then escorted the slicks into the LZ and blew to hell any enemy that shot at them or the slicks. Then, we resupplied the guys on the ground as necessary.

We landed a few minutes later at the MASH unit on Baldy. The wounded were carefully unloaded and placed on stretchers and taken in. The medics had been waiting for us because we had called to let them know we were coming. The doctors and nurses began the triage (arranging wounded in order so the most serious could be treated first).

Phil said, "Let's get out of here. There are trucks waiting with supplies for that miserable LZ."

I thought, *"The word "miserable" is much too kind. It's a fucking death trap."*

It took a couple of minutes to reach the supply trucks. I glanced at the gas gauge and was amazed that we still had half our fuel remaining. This was going to be a very long day. My butt was numb. These seats were not designed for comfort.

The engine was a 1400 horse power jet turbine that was extremely noisy. The grinding of the transmission at the back of the passenger area was worse than fingernails on a chalk board and louder. Also in the same area, the crew chief and door gunner were firing their machine guns, and it felt as if my head was coming off, or at the very least, I was going deaf. The rotor blades were constantly popping and vibrating and producing a wop-wop sound. I guess that's why everyone called it an Italian helicopter. And lastly, and most importantly, some assholes were trying very hard, actually too hard, to kill me! They were constantly shooting at us. Whether it was the helicopter killer, the 51 caliber Chi Com (Chinese Communist), or a Viet Cong shooting at us with his AK-47, all could be lethal to the helos and the guys inside.

There was a very distinct pop when a bullet passed through the disturbed air from rotor blades. That always sent your brain a wake-up call. I was hearing lots of popping. I guess I really didn't know what that was my first two times in this LZ.

We loaded again with more supplies, which included more water, plus one returning army medic. Two hundred guys fighting for their lives in a one-hundred-degree jungle get very thirsty.

Once everything was secure in the LZ, the large Chinooks (large tandem rotor helos) would haul in big tanks of water, which looked like small trailers and held 500 gallons. The Chinooks were too big and too slow to come into an area while it was hot.

Phil said, "We're learning as we go. We've never fought a helicopter war. We lost a few of these Chinooks early on in hot LZs. If a Chinook goes down, it kills 47 GIs and four crew members. They also cost a lot more than a Huey."

Shit, I'm in a Huey. So we have to protect the Chinooks but losing a few Hueys is all in a day's work? Why didn't anyone tell me? I'm going to start a "forgot to tell you in flight school" book for the new pilots that follow me.

The remaining ships checked in, and we pulled pitch and formed up into our flights of three. Ships were moving up to fill the spots of ships shot down.

Phil said, "This CA was fucked. They should have prepped the LZ with artillery and then come in with more than two gunships."

We were missing three ships, and seven dead soldiers, with eight in the hospital. Their parents, wives, or girlfriends were going to receive news of their injuries, or the worst possible news, followed by a visit from an army chaplain or local minister. *Hell, I bet my parents hated going to the mail box.* I quickly discovered that it took mail a week to get home and a week to get back to me. The only good part was no stamps. We just wrote free in the upper right corner of the envelope. What a perk.

Chapter 7.

A SIGHT THAT WILL NEVER LEAVE YOU

Phil casually called out over the intercom, "Mac, take it in, and be prepared for something even worse than your last time. They're going to load us up with dead. If they have enough body bags, you won't see any Americans. If our losses are greater than expected and they run out of bags, you'll see a sight that will never leave you.

"Anyway, you *will* see the enemy dead. They are thrown in back without bags or anything. We are fucked if they load any NVA that have been toasted. We didn't use napalm this time, but our guys on the ground have flame throwers they can use if the little shits are down in spider holes or tunnels. Anyway, if we get toasted enemy, we are fucked when we pull pitch. That burnt skin and muscle swirls around inside here. It gets in under your helmet's faceplate, the back of your neck, worst of all, in your mouth and nose."

"What's that about napalm?" I asked.

"Jets drop jellified gasoline on low level passes. It travels across the ground at the speed of the jet. There is no place to run or hide. It consumes everything. Can't use it when we're close, but it's great for softening up an area."

Phil threw me a mock sympathetic grin. "It's OK if you puke Mac. Most guys do the first time. The sight of those dead never leaves you; neither will the smell."

Something else they didn't tell me in flight school.

"Why do they want the dead enemy back at headquarters?"

He shrugged. "They look at clothes, insignia, weapons, info in wallets, their teeth."

"Teeth?"

Phil explained that different countries have different methods of dental repair work. Especially fillings. Our Intel people use this data to determine what countries are providing troops and giving the North Vietnamese equipment to prosecute this police action.

Phil keyed his intercom switch, and let his crew know that we were one minute out from paradise. Now it hit me why everyone was tense back at the flight line. They've done this before. I came in fast, flared and nearly stood us on our tail. Then leveled out and set us down. It was a pretty good landing. The guys in back immediately began throwing out the cargo.

They were throwing it out as fast as possible. It seemed like an eternity instead of the less than the minute it really took. Then came that moment I will never forget. Three body bags were placed in our ship. This was followed by two of our men covered with only their ponchos. The men loading them made an effort to keep them covered, but the wind from the rotors caused the ponchos to fly off the dead in the ship. To their credit, the crew chief and door gunner were attempting to cover our dead. The guys ran up to the ship and hand delivered extra ponchos.

Then came the enemy. They were stacked in back like a wood pile. Their bodies were torn apart. Many had missing limbs or most of their insides hanging out. The burned ones were last, and the odor was overpowering. I could feel the bile rising up in my throat. I swallowed hard. Then we took off, and it was terrible! The chunks of eschar (burnt tissue) were flying around the inside of the ship. Just like Phil had told me, it was everywhere, and then in my mouth. One of the guys in back puked. He tried sticking his head outside, but it was like trying to take a piss into a wind storm. Now the puke was mixed with the burnt tissue. I was trying to spit before I threw up. The only place to spit was down between my legs. The puke was circulating with the eschar. *One more god damn thing they didn't tell me in flight school.* This was the worst thing I had ever endured. I couldn't have imagined this.

Chapter 8.

THREE CATEGORIES OF SHIT

When we arrived at the Baldy MASH unit with the bodies, we shut down the engine, jumped out and went to a wash basin outside. It was for washing mud and blood off the wounded. As the medics removed the bodies, we took off our shirts and hosed ourselves from head to waist. We wrung out our shirts, but it had little effect on the puke, blood and burnt skin. That smell and taste stayed in my nose and mouth until we hauled bodies on a future CA.

Then, I was introduced to the crew chief and door gunner. They weren't particularly friendly. Everybody is pretty cool at first to the FNGs. You have to prove yourself to gain their respect. The crew chief introduced himself as Bob Smith, said he was from Indiana. He enlisted to go to crew-chief school. The door gunner was Ed Cannon from Alabama. He was drafted a week after graduating from high school. Ed said he volunteered for door-gunner school. He said he thought it would be better than running around the jungle fighting dinks, snakes and mosquitoes. I introduced myself as Kevin McNally from Medford, Oregon. I told them I spent two years at the University of Oregon, got tired of the rain, and enlisted for flight school. When Ed heard I was from Medford, Oregon he said, "No wonder you talk funny." *Me talk funny? His drawl was so slow I wanted to finish his sentences.*

As the four of us walked back to the ship, Phil looked over at me and said, "Today was worse than my first six weeks here, ten months ago. Then, he went into teaching mode. "There are three categories of shit: there's the shit I teach you, so you'll know what to do and what not to do. Then, there's shit you will learn about on your own, usually because the enemy is doing something different from what I tell you or you hear in a briefing. How you react to that determines if you survive. Finally, there's deep shit that happens if you don't learn from categories one and two. This day is only half over, and you can't imagine a year here. But these kinds of days make it go fast."

After that bit of preaching, I noticed the crew chief was rummaging through some equipment in the back and came out with a fire extinguisher. He said, "I'm going to fill it with water and wash the blood off the floor. It smells bad when it dries." When he finished, we all checked for bullet holes and found four. Luckily, only holes in the skin. No internal damage.

We flew over to POL (petroleum, oil, and lubricants; our gas station), gassed up, flew to the turnaround next to the runway, and shut down.

Phil asked if any of us were hungry. *I thought, you have got to be shitting me.* He then clarified. "Never past up a chance to eat, sleep, or take a piss. Even C-rats might be a welcome change to the taste in my mouth."

C-rats or C-rations are food in a can, and no telling how old it is. They have everything: powered scrambled eggs, ham and lima beans, chicken noodles, spaghetti, beef stew, fruit, peanut butter and cheese whiz. We choked it down. Oh yeah, the main course was served cold. After trying to swallow this stuff, I must admit I did have a slightly better taste in my mouth. Then, we sat on the floor in the back of the ship, dangling our legs outside, making small talk. We talked about home, siblings, Mom and Dad, and, most importantly, if anyone had a girlfriend. Everyone admitted there was a female somewhere back at home.

Ed, the door gunner, wanted us to look on the bright side. "This here is better than picking cotton," he pointed out. None of us had any response to that. He said, "Back home, everybody picks that shit, not just the blacks."

Chapter 9.

A SNIFFER MISSION

Phil said, "OK, let's check in and see what they want us to do next." He called HQ, and they told us to report to LZ Center, a rather large fire support base in our AO (area of operation). This took about twenty minutes. When we called Center to report we were inbound, they told us to return to Baldy for a sniffer mission.

This got me thinking about what Phil had said. This was our first helicopter war, so we were learning as we went along. We had just departed Baldy; now, we had been ordered to go back. The higher ups sometimes seemed to be playing with us, like kids with toy soldiers, fooling around, changing their minds. What we thought about it didn't matter. We were just their playthings. I'd heard about war's three rules: First, old people start them. Second, young kids die. And last, there is nothing you can do about rules one and two.

By now, I knew not to ask questions. I'd find out what a "sniffer mission" was soon enough. And I did.

A sniffer was a metal box about two feet wide, three feet tall, with many dials and gauges. This box was mounted to the floor behind the pilots in the cargo section. Four-inch-in-diameter hoses came out of each side of this box, and these were attached to a unit under the ship. Sitting in front of the sniffer was a technician reading the gauges. As the ship flew "nap of the earth," which is right on the tree tops at full speed (120 knots), it detected ammonia from human waste and CO_2 (carbon dioxide) exhaled during breathing. If the sniffer was flying over enemy territory, it could pinpoint where they were.

We were loaded and ready to go. Phil called the Firebirds and asked if they were ready. They said they were spending the army's money on JP-4 gasoline circling near the starting point.

We were looking for the bad guys hiding under a 120 foot canopy of jungle. When the technician saw a spike from the gauges, he called out "hot spot" and the Firebirds behind and above us would put a pair of rockets on that spot. Also, whether we detected a hot spot or not, someone might shoot at us. That would also incur the wrath of the Firebirds.

If either of those two occurred, hot spot or shoot at us, we broke off the sniffer and the gunships took over. Occasionally, a Firebird rocket would evoke a secondary explosion telling us that Intel had their shit together on this mission, and we had hit an ammo supply. If it got nastier, the jets would be called in with napalm. The sniffer would pull far off the route, climb high out of range, and circle until it was determined what to do. We would definitely not fly over the napalmed area; it would be scorched earth. We would pick a new starting point.

Another thing we were not told in flight school. How big will this list grow?

We took a few rounds five minutes into the flight, and the gunships put a pair of rockets on the place those bullets came from. That stopped all the nonsense, so we continued the mission. Actually, it was fun flying at top speed right on the tree tops, because we were flying up and down hills, into valleys, and along ridge tops. Nothing was flat. What a thrill!

This continued for another thirty minutes. I flew, and Phil guided me while reading the map on his lap. We had a few hot spots, and they got the Firebirds' calling cards: rockets, cannons and machine guns. I found out later that some spots had been marked for napalm. Eight months later, sniffer missions were discontinued because there was so much urine under that jungle canopy from animals and VC that all areas were hot spots.

We flew back to Baldy to remove the sniffer gear. While we were refueling, HQ called and told us, "Load up with ammo and return to Center for standard resupply until you are released." We acknowledged, loaded up, and returned to Center. *Wasn't that an old Elvis Presley song? Or something close to that?*

Phil said, "Take us to center. I'll show you the way." He was smiling.

So I'm not the only guy in this ship wondering about the leadership. Seems like they're making it up as they go.

After landing, we hauled a few guys back to the MASH unit at Baldy. They were sick with chills, fever and vomiting. "The most likely reason," Phil said, "is malaria. Guys sometimes purposely don't take their malaria pills (quinine and/or chloroquine) so they'll catch it and get out of combat." They were shaking, pale, weak and appearing to want to vomit. Seeing this convinces me to I take my pills.

We then picked up some new guys assigned to Center. They looked apprehensive and very quiet with very big eyes. They looked like they were maybe fifteen years old.

I had an uneventful landing at Center. The new guys grabbed their duffle bags and jumped out.

Chapter 10.

BURNING SHIT

A pickup-size truck showed up full of C-rations, ammo, water and some medical supplies for a patrol out in the bush. We used a grease pencil to write down the frequencies and call signs and to mark the coordinates on our acetate covered maps. *Pretty clever*, I thought. *We can use these maps forever. A plain-paper map would disintegrate quickly from folding and unfolding.*

We were getting close to the patrol when I called, "Texas 6, this is rattler 2-4 with supplies. Pop a smoke and give me a sit rep."

We promptly heard, "Rattler 2-4, this is Texas 6," in that southern accent. Now I knew why he was *Texas*. "I'm popping smoke. It has been quiet here all day." It was about 1500 (3:00 PM).

"I've got your purple smoke and see the open area near it."

He responded, "I will surround the LZ for your protection and give cover fire if the NVA have a surprise waiting."

I said, "Roger that."

I checked the wind direction from the surrounding trees and began my approach into the wind.

Phil said, "Go in fast and stand it on its tail, just in case."

I keyed my intercom button on the cyclic twice for an OK, and in I went. I stood it on its tail, slowed, lowered the nose and set it down. The guys in back started throwing out the cargo. A few grunts came over to help. We were empty in less than a minute. While they were unloading, I called 6 and asked if he had any cargo for us.

He said, "Thanks, but no. You have to haul ass out of here. I'm sure someone saw you land."

I said the standard, "Roger." The guys in back each yelled, "Clear." They sounded just as anxious to get this big target up in the air.

I pulled pitch and called LZ Center. "Your patrol is resupplied, and we have no cargo." Center told us to land at the smoke. This fire support base was large enough to warrant three landing areas for the helos. I called Center a few minutes later and reported we were inbound. I identified a yellow smoke, and their radio operator said, "Put it down there, and we'll load you up for another of the same. You'll receive frequency and coordinates while they're loading." I gave another customary "roger" and landed. I powered down to flight idle, which is similar to sitting at a red light. They loaded us up to the ceiling, gave us the info, and waved us off.

Phil spoke up. "You're doing great for your first day. Why don't you take a break and let me have a turn." I nodded, looked over at him, and smiled. He nodded back and said, "I've got it."

This continued for another three hours with a fuel and piss stop somewhere in the middle. Damn, my butt had never hurt so much. I tried pushing down on the seat and lifting my butt off that rock under me. I think it helped a little. I peeked at my watch and realized we had been out in the AO for thirteen hours. Strange, I didn't feel tired. I was beginning to believe something I had heard in flight school from an instructor who had been over here. The greatest drug in the world is adrenalin. It will keep you going in Nam, but when it runs out, you pass out. I began wondering, *When will the fatigue hit?*

Another hour of resupply and Center turned us loose. Now it was 7:00 pm, oops, I mean 1900. Our fuel looked OK, so off we flew. It would take about 50 minutes to return to Chu Lai. Another 15 minutes to refuel and park in the revetment, check out the ship and report the eight bullet holes, and help the crew chief and door gunner get the ship ready for tomorrow.

Maintenance wasn't too happy to receive that news. The sheet-metal shop would be up all night patching holes in these Hueys.

On our return, Phil said, "Don't ever fly through that black smoke." I noticed about six of these plumes rising up. "They pull the barrels of shit and piss out from under the outhouses, pour in diesel fuel, and burn that stuff."

"I know," I told him. "The clerk who picked me up at Chi Lai airfield told me they were burning shit."

"Well, you fly through that, and you'll pay a fine to the bar. Any fuckup here results in a fine, payable to the bar in the O club."

Chapter 11.

THE BRASS BELL

After we collected our gear--helmet, chicken board, M-16 rifle and maps--we climbed in a one-ton truck and were returned to where this had all begun at 0400 that morning. I had a feeling I would be seeing very little of the beach and ocean. I still felt a little guilty because of how the grunts lived on the fire support bases, and the guys out in the bush had it even worse.

About twelve of us climbed out of the truck and spread out to find our hooches, when Phil said, "Meet me in front of the officers' club after you shower. Say about twenty minutes."

I replied, "I can't, Phil. I'm flying tomorrow."

"Not to worry. We won't be drinking. I'm flying too. I want to show you something."

I was a little confused but told him OK, and then I looked at my watch. Fast showers were easy. I learned that in basic training and flight school. The showers were in an actual cinderblock building; though small, it served its purpose. Next to it was a platform about eight feet off the ground with a large black rubber bladder lying on top. A truck would bring in water and fill up the bladder. It got hot in the sun which could heat the water to an unbearable level. I was told to test it with my hand and, if it was too hot, to fill one of the available buckets and use the water from that after it cooled.

After I had been there a few weeks, I heard of a few dumb shit pilots who were burned while showering drunk. It really pissed off the CO that they had to be taken off flight status by the flight surgeon.

I finished my three minute bucket shower, returned to my hooch, put on clean fatigues, and walked over to the O club. Phil was in front leaning casually against the wall. When I reached him, he reminded me to put my hat and pistol on the shelf. "The military always wants your head covered when outside and in uniform, but not when inside."

From the noise level, it sounded like one hell of a party. There must have been an entire company in there. Was I ever surprised when we walked inside and saw only six guys. Phil said, "Those are Firebirds that have tomorrow off, after five days of flying into that shit we saw today. When they unwind, it's monumental."

I had seen a few college parties, but this one made those back in the world look like church socials!

Phil said, "See that brass bell over the bar?" I nodded. "Go ring it."

I gave him a quizzical look, and he pointed to the bell. I was new and didn't know much yet, so I walked a few steps to the bar, reached up, and pulled the leather strap. With that loud noise ringing in my ears, the place became instantly silent, and all eyes were on me. I looked at Phil for some guidance. He put both hands in the air, palms toward the audience.

He said, "This is my FNG, Mac."

I thought, *MY?*

The drunks hoisted up their cans and glasses, yelled, "Mac," and took a drink.

Phil raised his hands again and said, "Today, Mac lost his cherry."

Now I knew what a cherry referred to, and I knew nothing anywhere close to cherry losing had happened today. Well, the drunks yelled out, "Cherry." and all took another pull on their drinks. Up went Phil's hands, and he looked my way. He was able to speak in a normal tone of voice as the partiers became quiet again.

"Mac, losing your cherry means you got your first bullet holes in the ship. Now since you're are an FNG, it's your fault there are bullet holes in my ship. Four bullet holes at $5 a hole says you owe the bar $20."

Wow, I thought, *that was supposed to be $40.*

I received another loud toast and repeated yelling, "Cherry, cherry, cherry." Phil pointed to a bowl on the bar and told me that's where I put the money. When I dropped it in, I saw quite a pile already in there. I found out later that money was placed in the bowl for a variety of reasons: losing your cherry, receiving additional hits, promotions, orders for R & R (rest and recuperation somewhere out of VN), orders for going home, and a hat or a weapon in the bar. There were more, and if anything new came along, it was added to the list. Usually, you never had to pay for those warm drinks because the money bowl was never empty.

After I put my money in the bowl, the drunks continued to celebrate having the day off, most likely with memorable headaches.

I waited a moment for Phil to look my way. When he finally did, I mouthed a *thank you*. He nodded, and I departed the club.

I returned to the hooch, and Surfer Guy was looking at a *Playboy* and Bible Thumper was writing letters home to his parents and a girlfriend. They both paused and almost said in unison. "Wow, four bullet holes. What was that like?"

Trying to sound cool, I said, "I could hear them hit us when we were on the ground, and I could hear the pop-pop noise when a bullet went through the rotor wash when we were in the air. We shut down a couple of times at Center and looked for bullet holes. When we found one, we would look in it and see if anything was in the way before it exited the other side of the tail boom. There were eight total, most in the tail boom, and they didn't hit anything vital."

The Huey was very thin skinned and made of light-weight aluminum, so bullets passed through easily if they didn't hit a main structural support or a vital component.

"There were eight holes in our ship," I added, "Phil gave me a break."

After some more small talk about their day, one of them said, "Let's give the mess hall another chance and then check the assignment board."

The food was disgusting. Liver and onions, and it smelled terrible. Hell, I couldn't eat that back home. Thankfully, they had rice. I hoped it wasn't locally grown, as I heard rumors that human waste was used for fertilizer. After that disappointing experience, we looked around for the schedule board and found it by following the chatter. There it was, the cork board on the side of a hooch in the center of the company area. We saw the pilot's name we were assigned to, and the time we were to be in the mess hall.

Looked like we would go through the same routine as this morning; all three of us had the 0400 reporting time to meet another new pilot. I just hoped there wasn't going to be a combat assault.

Suddenly, it hit me, I was dead tired. The adrenalin rush was over. Probably happened earlier, but in all the action, I hadn't noticed. I think I fell asleep in ten seconds.

Chapter 12.

THE NEXT 29 DAYS

In what seemed like a minute, the alarm went off. I couldn't believe it. I asked Surfer Dude if there had been a rocket attack in the night. He just shrugged his shoulders.

How am I going to do this 26 times in the next 28 days? I'm never going to get to know my roommates!

We sat up on the sides of our beds, just looked at each other, and almost started laughing. We were all thinking the same thing. Twenty-seven more times after today.

Those two days off will be welcome.

It was too far to the latrine (army for bathroom), actually a four hole outhouse; we just stepped outside the hooch and peed in the sand.

We gathered our gear and went off to the mess hall. For some strange reason, the powered eggs were palatable, and they were served with ham, real ham I hoped. I was starving, or so it felt. I still required all the condiments: salt, pepper and ketchup.

Suddenly, the door flew open and in strode the old timers, fashionably late. One at a time they called out names: their peter pilot, or heaven forbid, an FNG. We raised our hands when called, and over they came, threw their stuff on the table, and said, "Don't let anyone steal my shit. Guard it with your life."

My pilot returned with his tray and coffee, sat down, and joined the small talk. This guy began the day with a much better attitude than Phil had yesterday.

He was Glen Walton from Texas. "I've been here seven months."

"My name is Kevin McNally from Medford, Oregon, and this is my second day."

I cringed, waiting for a put down. Instead, he said, "Yes, I know. I talked to Phil last night, and he said you did damn good. That's a great review coming from Phil."

I was speechless, so Glen continued talking while we ate. He told me he was rattler 2-9, and he would teach me some more tricks of the trade today to help me survive

At 0430, like clockwork, the CO stood up and said, "Good morning." All he got back was a lot more groaning than yesterday. The FNGs had been told to restrain "the gung ho stuff" yesterday, so we just mumbled.

He began by holding up a three inch square booklet, and what looked like a mini syringe. He said, "These are for you FNGs. The booklet contains all the frequencies for the FSB's (Fire-Support Bases) and surrounding air fields for the month. The small Syrette is in case the bad guys use gas warfare. If you suspect that, remove the cover on the needle and shove it into your thigh, right through your fatigues, then squeeze the pouch. It contains atropine to counteract the gas."

Wow, some more shit they didn't tell me in flight school. This list is growing.

He told us to put the booklet and Syrette in the small pocket on the clothing that contained the chicken board. He added, "You FNGs come up and get a survival knife and tape it to your chicken board. Your AC will explain what it's for and how to tape it."

He then held up a list of the day's assignments. Glen and I were to spend the day resupplying LZ East, coincidently, located ten miles east of LZ Center. *Who thinks of these clever names?* Same thing all day, back and forth from Baldy to East, like a bus route. *Sounds like hours and hours of boredom, maybe intermingled with a few moments of sheer terror.*

Glen grabbed his assignment sheet with the frequencies and coordinates of the LZ. The later was not necessary as LZ East has been in the same location for several years.

Just day two and already everything was looking routine to me. *Is it possible to feel like an old timer on your second day? I do have to admit that I saw a lot of shit yesterday.* We threw our gear into a truck and climbed in and sat on wooden benches on each side. It was a short ride to the flight line. Now we began to sort through the pile of equipment on the floor for our individual helmets, chicken boards and everything else. Since it was dark at this hour, I made a mental note to pick up a flashlight from supply.

The five-minute drive to the flight line seemed bumpier this morning. *Is it possible?*

Here we were: The flight line, with the smell of fuel and the feel of heat and humidity. I was wet and sticky, and it was still dark. The air stank and felt thick; just like yesterday. Were they burning the shit on our runway? Thankfully, it would be much cooler once we were in the air. The 120 mile per hour wind whipping through the Huey will both cool us and dry the sweat.

I met the crew chief and door gunner. I think it was Steve and Todd. I was too tired to remember. I would meet two different guys tomorrow, so why bother? I was told that when I made AC, I would have my own crew, and they would be my friends for life.

Glen shouted, "Mount up." That sounded like Texas horse talk. He looked at me and said, "Let's go to Baldy."

I said, "Clear," over the intercom and both guys in back called, "Clear." I cracked the throttle and pulled the trigger, and those big blades began a slow turn with the jet turbine whining. When I got to full rpm, I called the tower and said, "Chu Lai tower, this is Rattler 2-9 for departure out of the snake pit." I had written Glen's call sign on the corner of my windshield with a red grease pencil. He pointed to my windshield, smiled, and nodded, and gave me a thumb's up.

The tower called and said, "What's your destination 2-9?"

"Tower," I said, "2-9 is headed north to Baldy."

He replied, "You're cleared north over the runway. Depart when you are clear (which meant, when I didn't see any other Huey's position lights)."

I pulled pitch and lifted up and out of the revetment. With my head on a swivel, I turned 90 degrees and moved out in a fast hover to the runway. No taxiways for helicopters. I added some right pedal and was pointing north. I lowered the nose and added power. We started moving into translational lift (helo lingo for taking off).

As we flew north out of the traffic pattern, I asked, "Up Highway One or the beach." He said, "Don't care." I clicked my intercom button twice to acknowledge. After about a minute he said, "Test your guns, and you Mac, climb to 1500 feet. Let's not give them too easy of a target."

I clicked twice again. As I climbed as suggested, Glen told me this was the most common altitude for slicks. "We just have door gunners," he said, "no rockets. We're still going to get shot at up here, but only a lucky one will hit us, and our door gunners are good and will make them pay for the errors of their ways."

I asked Glen "What did the CO mean about the survival knife?"

"There are basically two uses. One is for cutting yourself out of the seatbelt harness if you crash and can't get to the buckle. However, the most important use is to open C-ration cans, if you lose your P-38 (a small can opener device hooked on our dog tag chain)."

I found Baldy and called out in the clear, as it's called, to let any other ships around know I was entering the traffic pattern. Baldy didn't have anyone acting as an air traffic controller. All four of us in the cabin had our heads on a swivel on the lookout for another helo. I called HQ and said, "We're going to refuel and then land at the turnaround." HQ rogered.

I landed at POL to top off the fuel. Everyone got out to pee, except me. When they climbed back in, it was my turn. I guess I will graduate from this bottom-of-the-line for peeing sometime in the future. All shit rolls downhill to an FNG. I flew around the hill to the turnaround and shut down the engine. Then I called Baldy headquarters (HQ) and told them we were checking in. They said, "Roger that. We have two trucks of ammo, food and some new guys to be ferried out to East." I rogered.

Here came the trucks. They pulled up to the open doors in back and began transferring their cargo to us. Our crew helped them stack it in so it wouldn't fall over when we made a banking turn. The two new guys sat next to the crew chief and door gunner. In a few minutes we took off. It was 12 to 15 minutes to LZ East, straight south.

Glen still hadn't touched the controls. I called East and said, "This is rattler 2-9 approaching from your north with food, ammo, and two FNGs."

East replied with, "Looking forward to your arrival here in paradise."

I thought that was kind of cool being able to make jokes,

considering where he spent the night. I replied with, "Yes, just another day in paradise."

I was coming in on short final to their landing pad when suddenly a stream of tracers came out of the jungle canopy no more than a few feet in front of my windshield. Glen yelled, "I've got it," as he grabbed the controls and began evasive maneuvers by banking steeply to the left.

The guys in back immediately leaned outside and opened up on where those tracers had come from. The perimeter defenses on East also opened up with 50-caliber machine guns. Their tracers looked like baseballs.

East called and said, "Come around to our south and approach from there. Damn, we haven't been shot at in a few days."

In the meantime, Glen had climbed back up to 1500 feet. As he was flying south by FSB East, he said over the intercom "Hang on. I'm going to show Mac a high overhead approach." He followed with, "Don't worry, Mac. This is how we get into these hot spots."

I was in the dark. I had never heard the term, high overhead. Another one of those fucking things they didn't tell me in flight school!

He laid the ship over on its side, which is a pretty radical maneuver in a helo. We were falling out of the sky like a bowling ball off a building. I thought, *This is it. We're going to die.* My stomach was in my throat. I did a quick check of the instrument panel, and everything was normal except for the engine rpm. It was down to flight idle.

As we were descending to our deaths, I thought, *well at least we'll die with all the instruments in their proper green zones.* Glen began a turn back to north, pulling the nose up as he rolled on the power. We stopped the dramatic fall and slowed as the nose came up. The ship stood on its tail, like on yesterday's fast approaches. Glen leveled out, and to my amazement, we were over the landing pad. He sat the ship down as gentle as putting a baby to bed.

All I could think to say was "shit." So I kept it to myself.

Glen looked at me and smiled. "Mac, that's a high overhead. Falling fast like that makes us a very difficult target. We'll practice a few of those today."

Now I know why we weren't shown that maneuver in flight

school. Half the guys would have called it quits. OK, maybe a third.

The crew chief and door gunner in back were laughing. One of them said, "Damn, Mr. Walton, those are always so wild and crazy! That was so cool."

I thought, cool? That son of a bitch is crazy.

The two new guys didn't say a thing. They couldn't get out fast enough. I had thought I was going to die. I'll bet they shit their pants.

We unloaded while keeping the ship near full engine rpm just in case mortars started coming in. Then two guys came up to the ship with a sergeant. The sergeant asked us, "Can you take these grunts back to Baldy? The lucky bastards just got their R & R orders."

I said, "Sure thing, Sarg."

The two grunts both smiled and said, "Thanks Sarg. We'll get laid once for you."

He said, "Don't either one of you catch anything, or I'll keep you here an extra six months."

One of them looked at his buddy, and asked, "Can he do that?" The other guy just shrugged his shoulders, and they both climbed in.

Glen rolled up the throttle a little more and said, "Clear."

We all looked outside, up, to the sides and behind, and all called, "Clear." He lifted the ship just a few feet and said to the crew chief, "Coming left."

The crew chief said, "Clear left."

Glen had turned 180 degrees, looked around and said, "Be alert." He added more power, pushed the cyclic forward and pulled up the collective so the blade could grab the air. Over the mike, he said, "We don't want to fly over that machine gun!" Then, he added to me, you got it. I'm tired."

I took us back to Baldy. The trip was uneventful. I called out into the clear, "Rattler 2-9 is entering Baldy's flight pattern from the south." The landing was also uneventful.

Glen said, "Shut it down. I gotta take a leak."

Yeah, me too.

Chapter 13.

HAUL ASS AND HAUL TRASH

A truck drove up to the door, and they began loading. Glen looked over and asked me if I wanted to try a high overhead? *Was this is a trick question?* After his overhead, my sphincter grabbed hold of the seat so tight that I didn't need a seat belt. They nearly had to pry me out of that seat with a crowbar. This was called a high pucker factor.

Of course I said, "Yes." *Was there a choice?*

Off we went, back to East. Just like driving a bus route. We approached from the north like before but farther away from the FSB. Glen said, "I will be on the controls with you, but lightly." Then, he said, "Lay it over on your side." That turned out to be 60 degrees, not the 90 I imagined. Leaning to my side was OK as I had a good look out my window at my target. Then, he said, "Roll back the throttle; watch the rotor rpm. You don't want it to spin off."

I thought, *That's a good safety tip.*

"OK, you are getting close. Be sure to crosscheck out your window. Start your turn and start pulling the nose up. Watch the engine rpm; we don't want an over speed."

I began to feel more confidence, but I didn't want to fool myself; I could feel him on the controls. As we got closer, I made some corrections, or I should say, *we* made some corrections.

The landing was OK, and no one shot at us. All in all, life was good. We unloaded quickly as before.

No cargo for us. When I say cargo, I'm referring to the two main jobs of a slick driver: haul ass and haul trash. People and/or supplies. There were numerous other jobs, as I learned yesterday with the sniffer.

I looked at Glen, and he just nodded. I called, "Clear," and everyone checked their area of responsibility and called back "Clear." I lifted up a few feet and said, "Coming right." The door gunner cleared me. I made a 180-degree pedal turn, so I could take off in the direction I came in.

All went well returning to Baldy. I noticed my butt ached. I tried squirming around and made a poor attempt to lift up off the seat. Glen saw me and took over the controls. Now I could move a little more. He called Baldy and informed them we needed fuel. Then, we'd go to the turnaround.

Between the vibrations from the ship and the 10# chicken board bouncing on my bladder, I understood why Phil had told me never to pass up a chance to pee. We landed on the other side of Baldy at the POL. Glen rolled down the throttle to idle. You had to keep the engine running in case of a mortar attack. You didn't want to be burning around all the fuel or prevent other ships from refueling. Of course, everyone jumped out except me as someone had to hold the controls. *Everything is still rolling downhill to the FNG.*

I finally got my turn. Glen jumped in and grabbed the controls. No words were exchanged or needed. There was one small area on the right side of the Huey, by the gas cap, where the cabin and tail boom were connected. This was the only spot where you could pee and not feel like you were in a shower.

We still had one more trip to East before the trucks were empty. When we got close, I asked, "Can I try another high overhead?"

Glen keyed his intercom and said, "What do you two think about that?"

They both said, "Yes sir, we're getting bored back here."

Glen said, "OK, let's do it."

When we were about three minutes out, I called East and went through the same routine asking to approach from the south. They said the standard, "Roger." I said, "OK." Then, I laid it over on its side and dropped like a roller coaster. All the time, which was only ten to fifteen seconds, I had to keep my eyes on my landing spot and crosscheck my instruments too. (You're supposed to gaze across them every 4-5 seconds.)

Suddenly, I heard pop-pop-pop. The crew chief said, "It's coming from my side," and he immediately returned fire. I slowed the drop and broke hard right away from the enemy. I heard Glen say, "Those sneaky bastards." As I was putting some distance between us and them, the crew chief said, "East is hitting them with 50's and mortars. They sneaked around to the south side."

"Let's try it again from the north," Glen said. I was far enough away, so I climbed as I turned north. I said, "OK" and laid the ship over on my side. I could see Glen was a little tense because it was much more difficult due to limited vision across the cockpit. I was watching everything, and I could tell he was maintaining a very light touch on the controls. Shit, I didn't blame him. He was flying with an FNG. I started my turn and brought the nose up and then leveled out onto the pad (a wood platform made out of the crates that artillery shells were shipped in). We unloaded as usual but in a big hurry. I lifted up and told the door gunner I was coming right. He said, "Clear." I did a 180-degree pedal turn and had my head on a swivel. I took off and returned to Baldy.

I called in the clear as I approached Baldy.

HQ called back and said, "Rattler 2-9, shut it down for about 45 minutes and eat something. We heard you guys were playing dodge the bullets with the bad guys." He continued by asking, "Did you take any hits?"

I said, "I'll call you back with the answer after we eat."

"See if they're still open for business," he said. "Call me back if they're closed, and I'll open it up." I didn't think I was talking to the radioman. It had to be an officer talking, and since I was a lowly W-1, lowest ranking officer in this man's army, I said, "Thank you, sir."

I turned off the radio, climbed out, and took off my helmet and chicken board. I laid them on my seat and shut the door. Then, I went to the front of the ship and opened an access door and disconnected the battery. This was to keep those so inclined from getting in and doing something stupid; something very stupid. As I did my thing, the crew chief and gunner were tying down the main rotor blade and putting a cover on the Pitot (pee toe) tube. We have to keep it clean. Air rushes into it while we are flying, and it tells us how fast we are moving, or how dangerously slow.

The mess hall was up and running, so we grabbed a tray and proceeded down the line. Two guys with big spoons were slinging slop onto the trays. It looked like we were getting a chili burger. I decided I wouldn't have any problem swallowing that, after I loaded it up with all the standard condiments: salt, pepper and the proverbial ketchup.

We ate like starving dogs and drank about a quart of water each. The food tasted good. The warm water was usual. We had canteens in the ship, and they were cooler than this bath water, because they cool off at altitude.

We returned to the ship and did a post flight and found three bullet holes. No major damage, thankfully. Glen turned to me and said, "Didn't Phil tell me you took four rounds yesterday?"

I said, "Yes."

"Shit, you're a fucking bullet magnet."

"Actually, Phil cut me some slack, Glen. I had eight holes, and he surprised me in the club when he said four."

"Mac, Phil told me you guys took eight hits. He asked me to tell you about four hits and see what you'd say. He wanted to find out what kind of a person you are. You are very honest and that impresses us."

Well, back to reality. *Three holes, that's $15. I'll be broke in a week.*

Glen called HQ and said, "I have the answer to your question regarding the hits. It was three."

The radioman said, "Wow, I'll pass that along."

"By the way, the chow line was still moving. We're ready to go when you need us. We emptied your trucks."

"Roger that. Just hang loose until I call."

Hang loose? *Must be one of those California hippy dudes.*

Glen said, "Take a break."

Chapter 14.

WHAT STARTED THIS WAR?

The door gunner walked up to me and said, "Mr. McNally, I heard you went to college for two years."

I stopped and said, "Yes I did."

He said, "Sir, can I ask you a question?"

I said, "Sure, but call me Mac. This is only my second day, and I've got a lot to learn. I'll try to answer your question." I put my hand out to this shy kid. He said his name was Todd, and I said, "I'm Kevin," and we shook hands.

He said he was 18 and drafted three days after he dropped out of high school, halfway through his senior year in the state of West Virginia. He actually said, "I ain't too smart, but I do recognize danger."

I said, "Yes I recognize it too; and very fast."

He asked, "What started this war? I know they call it a police action, but my pa says it's a war when you're drafted and sent somewhere to kill people. And they are trying to kill me. My pa says this is no different than WWII. He was in the infantry. My ma said he came home different and he'd got mean. I couldn't wait to get out of there."

I said, "Todd, I don't really know. I've read a few papers. There was a lot of stuff on TV, while I was home after flight school. It just seems we were looking for a reason to come here. They say a couple of North Vietnamese patrol boats attacked one of our war ships in the South China Sea. I grew up hunting in Oregon, and I'm sure you hunted too. Now a patrol boat against a war ship is like a squirrel going after a bear. We know the squirrel is smarter than that. Our government is afraid of this thing called the domino theory.

If Vietnam goes Communist so will Laos, Cambodia, Burma and finally India, falling one after the other like dominos."

"That sounds like somebody's planning a lot of years of war."

"You're right Todd, and that's a very smart observation. The people who have been here longer than us call the Pentagon 'the Puzzle Palace.' We wait while they guess what the next piece will be and where it fits in.

"We can't do anything about any of this, Todd. We're stuck here, and nobody's asking our opinions. So all we can do is watch out for each other and do our best to stay alive."

He thanked me as a jeep drove up. "You're needed out near Cacti," the driver told us. "A patrol was a few clicks out, returning to Cacti when they received fire. They have two wounded, pretty bad, and no Dust off available."

"Dust off" was the call sign for the helicopter ambulance corp, the medevac Hueys. They were used only to pick up wounded, and believe it or not they were unarmed. The bad guys knew they were unarmed and used the large Red Cross on the side door as a target."

"Here are the frequencies, location and call sign."

Glen said, "Mount up. Cacti is only a few minutes away." He was in another world, so I didn't say anything. He was moving on adrenalin and seven months of war. He handed me the paper with the frequency and call sign. I set the frequency.

Glen called in the clear while pulling the ship to a hover and said he was taking off to the west. He did a petal turn to face nearly west and called, "Clear." We all answered back, "Clear." He rolled on max power and pulled the pitch up to the red line on the torque meter (like the red line for engine rpm in a car). We were off like a dragster. Flying full speed at this altitude is a thrill like no other. After flying fifteen feet above the rice paddies that surrounded Baldy, for maybe, a minute, he pulled the nose slightly up so we could look for Cacti. It is less than nine clicks from Baldy. He called Desert 6 and asked them to pop smoke where they wanted us to land."

We could see a red smoke, and it was close, only a click from Cacti. The wind direction indicated we had to fly around on the south side and then land straight east. The smoke grenade showed us both, where to land and gave wind direction. Glen called and asked, "Are any unfriendly folks around?" Some of the action had become matter-of-fact for him. *How long before I talked so nonchalantly?*

Desert 6 said, "Roger that, we think it's a sniper up in those trees, and a few on the ground, about 75 meters north of the smoke. We are ten feet from the smoke next to an old dry rice paddy and some BFRs. It's large enough for you to land. We are concealed behind some palms. Please hurry; these guys are bleeding badly."

"OK 6, I want you guys to hose down that area on my approach. My door gunners will be doing the same. There will be a lot of bullets flying around, so I want to do this quickly. We are scrambling the Firebirds, but they are out on another mission. I can't wait for them because of the bleeding, so here we come."

"OK, hose down those trees" was all Glen needed to say. All of us had been listening to the radio. But only the crew chief was able to shoot because the bad guys were located on our left. Glen came in fast and low. He said to me, "Get on the controls in case I get hit. And don't let me overtorque this engine."

What are the next eleven months going to be like for me?

I lightly held the cyclic in my right hand and placed my left hand above the collective pitch lever. I was also monitoring the instruments and watching for yellow warning lights and red master caution lights. If Glen managed to pull in too much torque, the engine would tear itself apart, and we would become members of the infantry patrol.

We are coming in fast, like the combat assault yesterday, so just do your job, Kevin, I told myself.

Then, it started. They were shooting at us from several locations in the palm trees. The crew chief was shooting into the palm leaves. I glanced back and could follow his tracers. I looked out to my side and could follow the infantry's tracers from their location, but that was all, as Glen had stood this ship on its tail. He was coming in fast, maybe too fast. I looked at the instrument panel and all was OK. Then, I glanced at Glen, and he looked calm, amazingly calm. Now I felt the collective lever coming up. I saw he was passing through forty-two inches of torque and the red line was forty four, so I stiffened my elbow and kept my palm on the collective. I didn't grip it because that would interfere with his use of the throttle. I slowly pushed down on the collective so he would know he was close to the torque's limit. He gave me a quick glance and had a look of concern on his face. I just shook my head, *no*.

I leaned my head out my window and could see the trees our guys were hiding behind. I knew we were running out of space to land.

That meant we might splatter into those big palm trees. And they were getting bigger. We began to slow. The crew chief was still shooting, and I could see his tracers going into the palm fronds. Miraculously, we slowed. Glen leveled the ship and set it down a little hard. We bounced a few times. I didn't care about the bouncing. I was glad we were still in one piece. Running toward us out of the palms were eight guys, each holding a limb of the two wounded. They slid the hurt guys in and two ponchos to cover them and ran back to the palms in a crouching position. This was the shits. I was thinking, *How in the hell are we going to get out of here.* The only way out was to turn 180 degrees and go out the way we came in. This just happened to be right past the guys who had been shooting at us, except now they were on my side of the cabin.

Suddenly, my door frame and door were blown off and pieces of aluminum were sent into the cabin. Glen said, "What the hell? Mac, are you OK?"

I gave him thumbs up.

Glen keyed his mic and said to the men in back, "Keep shooting, if you're not hurt. We're taking off." In one swift maneuver, we came up five feet off the ground and started across the open area. I could see rounds hitting the ground in front of us and throwing dirt up on our windshield. So much was in my face I couldn't help but flinch. There were so many holes and so much structural damage I thought we were going to fall apart. The ship was shaking violently, and the yellow caution lights were coming on. Then, the shit really hit the fan when a red master caution light came on for low oil pressure. Now it was just a matter of time before we lost the engine. Glen saw the red light. He said to me, "I'm going to point this ship toward Baldy and go as long as the engine holds up."

No tracers were seen from the palm trees. At least that threat had been eliminated. Now, the crew chief was shooting into the surrounding vegetation.

We were running out of takeoff space and getting pretty damn close to the trees, all at 130 knots. Without warning, Glen pulled back on the cyclic, and we shot up in the air (a cyclic climb: use your forward air speed and convert it to altitude) so quick my helmet felt like a 50 pound weight. We must have pulled a G or two. (One G is your body weight.) We had just done an Air-Force maneuver. I hope we didn't break anything on the ship because I'm the FNG. It would be my fault.

As we rose up, Glen leveled out and flew for a minute or two before he spoke. He said, "Everyone OK?" One guy in back said, "OK." The chief said, "It's a good thing these two wounded were asleep. That takeoff was a masterpiece, but it would have scared them to death." He followed with, "Both have a 1 on their forehead."(This tells the MASH unit the total number of shots of morphine they've received. It prevents overdoses.)

"Shit, Mr. Walton, Todd is lying on the floor. I'm going to check on him." He was lying on his side, so the chief rolled him over onto his back and looked through the hole in his chest to the floor of the ship. All he said was, "Todd's dead." He turned his head and tried to puke out the door. It never works. Soon, Glen and I were eating it. A few moments passed, and we heard the Firebirds calling Desert 6, saying they'd arrive in a few minutes and asking for a sit-rep. Desert 6 informed them of the situation. The Firebirds acknowledged.

We changed the frequency to Baldy and told them we would be landing in less than two minutes. Glen told me to take the controls. "Land at the MASH unit, not on the taxiway. We're running out of time for those two in back."

I said, "OK." I called out in the clear and told the world I was landing at the MASH unit with two wounded and one dead. HQ acknowledged. There were six medics with three stretchers and a jeep waiting as we shut down. The jeep had been converted and had a place for two stretchers behind the driver. Todd's body was placed in a body bag and secured to one of those stretchers. The aids put the wounded on their stretchers and took them inside. The Jeep drove around behind the MASH.

Shit, that's it. It's over. No more Todd. I will give those assholes some pay-back.

I flew over the concertina wire (barbed wire) and set down in a cloud of dust.

Glen called headquarters and reported the low oil pressure. "We're grounded until we get another ship and a door gunner."

The oil pressure was near zero; we shut it down. *We were lucky.* We climbed out, stretched and began walking around the ship. We were looking for additional holes. Then it hit us.

Todd was dead!

"Damn this war," I said out loud. Todd was a nice kid, eighteen years old. SHIT. He hadn't even begun to live life.

The crew chief called out, "I've got a hit in the rotor blade."

I stopped my search and walked over to him.

He looked at me and pointed straight up over his head. There it was: a hole. He looked at me and said, "Wait until you see the top side."

I wasn't sure what he was referring to, so I continued my search for bullet holes. Meanwhile, Glen got on the radio and asked HQ if they could send a deuce and a half (two-and-a-half-ton truck) to the taxiway, so we could repair a bullet hole in a rotor blade. HQ knew what he was talking about.

The truck arrived in a few minutes. It had been converted to carry troops, with benches on each side of the bed.

I thought, *This will be interesting. No one taught us how to fix a bullet hole in a blade in flight school. They said the sheet metal shop would repair holes in the ship. Another item to add to the list of things to be learned.*

The crew chief pulled the damaged blade around so it was over the bed of the truck. He grabbed a large roll of silver tape and climbed into the back of the truck and up onto the bench seats along the truck bed. He said, "Climb up here, Mr. McNally, and I'll show you how we fix a blade out in the field. We're grounded, but this is a good time to show you."

He pulled the blade down so we could see the top side. The top-side hole was four or five times larger than the entry hole on the bottom. "The honey comb inside the blade is blown out and creates a larger exit hole. The bullet also mushrooms. It's soft lead. Illegal in the international rules of war. It's supposed to be a full metal jacket so it doesn't mushroom. Only the US and the Aussies obey the rules. The mushrooming causes hydrostatic shock waves and destroys internal organs."

The next few things he did totally astounded me. He pushed the sharp edges of the top side of the aluminum blade down with his knife so that it was flat and covered part of the hole. "The wind peels back the metal. Now, we wrap this hundred mile an hour tape around the blade to keep the metal from peeling open from the wind of the blade. Just make sure the tape is wrapped in the opposite direction of the blade rotation so it doesn't unwrap while we're flying. Don't put more on than four wraps or the weight will cause the blade to be out of balance with the other blade. That would cause an up and down vibration. Practice has taught us how much tape to use to use depending on the size of the bullet hole. This is a small one; AK- 47."

I was just a dumb FNG, so I causally said, "That looks like duct tape."

He smiled and said, "That's correct, Mr. McNally." Then, just to change the subject, he said, "Todd was hit with a 51. The bad guy's gun must have jammed because I didn't hear anything but small arms. One Lucky shot for them, and one bad shot for us."

I'm really pissed

We climbed down off the truck. The crew chief and Glen didn't find any more holes.

Shit, that makes four today, $20. I've got to find a new line of work.

Glen called HQ. "How are the two guys we brought in doing?" He said, "Thanks in a quiet and subdued voice. He looked at us standing outside his opened door and said, "One died and the other is still too critical to fly to Danang (10 minutes by helo)." He added, "Mac, there is a large, very modern hospital in Danang, run by the US."

I just nodded. "Plato is correct." I said, 'Only the dead see the end to war.'"

I've read a lot of history.

Glen just sat there in his seat with his head down. He looked up when HQ called. "They're sending a slick up here from Chu Lai,. They've got a truckload of ammo for us to deliver to Cacti. HQ is concerned about the buildup of enemy troops around Cacti." Glen told us that the Firebird gunships had blown the shit out of those guys we had just dealt with. There were even some secondary explosions, which meant that some of their ammo stores were blown up.

Suddenly, my right calf hurt. I looked down and my pants were torn and bloody. I asked Glen if I should go to the MASH unit. His eyes popped open wide, and he said, "Shit Mac, why didn't you say anything?"

"I just noticed it. By the way Glen, what is a BFR?"

He smiled and said, "A big fucking rock."

I walked across the dirt road and into the mash unit. By now I was limping. The medic saw me and fast walked over and said, "Climb onto that table," as he nodded his head to my left. As I climbed onto the table, I could hear the noise from lots of activity behind a curtain across the room. Must be one of the guys we just brought in.

A doctor walked up to the table and asked the medic, "What have you found?"

He replied, "Looks like metal in there," as he pointed to my calf.

The doc said, "Numb it up and get a quick x-ray. Find out how many pieces."

In a few minutes, the doc returned and said, "Looks like just one piece, McNally," as he glanced at the name tag on my shirt. "Lie back, and I'll get that out."

I felt nothing. He said, "I put in four stitches. We'll give you a shot of antibiotic in your butt and then fly you to Chu Lai."

"Doc, can't we just ignore this little scratch. I have to fly. We have to get supplies out to Cacti before dark."

He gave me an incredulous look.

"I'll check in with you tomorrow," I promised. "I'll be here because we have the flare mission tonight. We know where the bad guys are because we were the Huey that brought in the soldier behind that curtain." I pointed.

"Aren't you supposed to see the flight surgeon?"

I said, "Sir, you're a doctor, please."

"This goes against all my training, but you make a good case and this is a war. Check with me in the morning."

I thanked him and walked out the door before he could change his mind. I thought, *that anesthesia is great, but I'll bet this hurts like a son of a bitch when it wears off.*

I told Glen, "I'm fine, just a scratch, and I can fly."

He nodded and said, "Great."

Chapter 15.

THE ARMY IS TAKING CARE OF YOU

When the slick arrived with a new door gunner, Glen said (to no one in particular), "Load it up. General McArthur said, 'Preparedness is the key to victory.' Cacti wants to be ready for those little shits tonight."

We were loaded and running up the engine, when HQ called. "Rattler 2-9, remember you drew flare duty tonight."

Glen said, "Thanks." Then, "Mac, you've got it."

I clicked the transmit trigger twice on my cyclic to acknowledge. I checked the instruments and began pulling up the collective, but the ship wasn't coming off the ground. I added a little more throttle and was now at maximum. The ship came up six inches.

Glen said, "Put it down. We're way overloaded. We're going to have to do a gunship takeoff."

Oh, some more of that stuff they neglected to mention in flight school.

"We're getting low on fuel," Glen went on, "and so we should be OK to land at Cacti. We are way overloaded. Not having all that fuel weight should make this beast easier to land."

Should?

Glen pulled the ship up to a six inch hover. He called HQ and asked permission to hover to the runway.

Calling this a runway was a stretch. It was a dirt strip about four football fields long and sprayed with oil called Penta Prime. This kept the dust down. It also stuck to your boots if you were unfortunate enough to walk on it. Then, your boots would stick to your foot pedals, which made flying dangerous. It tended to break down, and the small particles would be sucked into the inlet strainers that kept foreign objects out of our jet turbine engines. We had to clean those inlet strainers every time we shut down.

Glen had bounced the ship out to the runway and sat it down. He had already informed everyone on Baldy's frequency what he was doing. He pulled it up to that six inch hover and ever so gently nudged the cyclic forward a millimeter or two. The ship moved forward a few feet and dropped to the ground and bounced while still moving forward.

I didn't know a Huey could do this. We gained both speed and altitude, if only a few feet on each bounce. We were making progress. However, the end of the runway was getting closer. No one said a word. If I had been a betting man, I would have bet against our clearing that eight foot concertina wire, only 100 feet ahead. If our skids caught on the wire, we would fly a short distance and then it would pull us to the ground. This would not be a good thing.

We had about 80 gallons of JP-4 in our tank and were loaded to the ceiling with bullets, mortar rounds, hand grenades, hand flares, and who knew what else. All of that would make a horrific explosion. Pieces of us would be blasted at least a 100 feet in the air. Knowing such things had a way of increasing your pucker factor. I did not want to be part of such a display.

We just barely cleared the wire, dropped a little, and then hit translational lift. It was then I realized I was holding my breath.

We were at Cacti in no time, and Glen called in and asked where they wanted our free delivery service.

The radio operator said, "We're popping a smoke."

Glen said, "I see green." They returned with, "Roger that. Put it there." Glen said, "Be alert. We are too heavy for anything fancy."

As we approached, I noticed we were going slower than usual. We were holding our breaths and hoping like hell the Firebirds had, in fact, blown the shit out of those NVA. Glen flared, and we landed a little hard. Immediately, everyone, including the guys at Cacti, began unloading. Actually, it was more like throwing the crates and boxes to the ground in a speed contest.

Glen called. "Good luck tonight. I'm taking off to the south."

The only response was, "Thank you."

Glen yawned and looked at me. "Take us to Baldy. I want a nap before the shit hits the fan tonight."

It can't be any more exciting than the last two days, can it?

After we landed, we completed the routine. We refueled and did a post flight check while the crew chief was cleaning out the dust intake. The door gunner was cleaning machine guns and hauling ammo belts out to the ship. Everything was moving along at it should. I was helping wherever I could. I was shown the flares. They were cylindrical tubes five feet long and eight inches in diameter that fell by parachute and would light up an area like a mini sun, so the Birds could see where to shoot.

Glen said, "It's early, so take care of business and then write a letter home. The company clerk sends a standardized letter to your home when you get here, but it's better when they hear from you. Let them that all is well, and the army is taking care of you. Don't worry them. Tell them the flying is great, the sand is hot, and the water is warm."

I looked in the "Firebird Hilton," as the sign over the doorway falsely advertised. What a fucking pit! Twelve beds where there should be six. Brown stained mattresses from sweaty bodies. The only item of clothing you took off was your shirt, because you had to move fast when the phone rang.

Chapter 16.

ROUTINE, EXCEPT NO ONE WAS SHOOTING AT ME

At 0200 the red phone rang. The Firebirds jumped up and ran to their ship. I followed with our two gunners.

Glen and the Bird team leader jogged out to the ships. Glen jumped in and said, "Cacti's under a Bonsai attack."

The Birds called Cacti and got the sit-rep. They were being hit on the north and west side. We were to throw out flares behind the enemy, which we did.

The bad guys were caught out in the open, and it was a turkey shoot, as we called it in Oregon when hunting and the game was exposed out in the open.

This went on for about 45 minutes. Finally, the enemy broke off the attack. Dead bodies littered the ground. Cacti fired their cannons at the retreating NVA.

We returned to Baldy for fuel and more flares. We had thrown out eight.

We were called out a second time at 0400 when another attack began, but it was small and quickly dispatched. The good news was that if you went out more than once, you got the next day off.

We returned to Chu Lai (CL) in the afternoon anyway, because no ship was able to resupply Cacti but us. We flew all morning. I checked in with the MASH unit before leaving Baldy. They cleaned my wound and said the stitches would remain for a week. They gave me some ointment, antibiotic pills, and a shot of syrup in the butt. That really hurt. I think I was on adrenalin when I got the first one the previous day. I don't remember it stinging so much.

At CL, I cleaned up, wrote another letter, and headed for the dump, oops, I mean the club. Glen was nowhere to be seen. I took off my hat and pistol, laid them on the shelf and walked inside. You couldn't hear anything. The noise level was the same as flying a Huey with both door gunners going full force at the enemy.

Well, I'll be damned! There was Glen.

He was already half in the bag. He was hanging on to two guys and the bar. He obviously had been there since we jumped off the truck thirty minutes before. He definitely was doing his best to unwind and do it as quickly as possible.

He looked over and saw me. He paused and said with thick tongue and slurred speech, "Riiiiinnnnng thaaaat belllll Mac."

I walked over and rang the bell. I did a good job. It had been only 48 hours since I'd learned how to use this piece of machinery. It was amazing how that bell shut up a bunch of crazy drunks. Glen spoke with that same slurred speech and proceeded to tell everyone how I had fucked up his ship. "Four holes," while he held up four fingers. They gave the same toasts as the day before. The only difference being, I was charged only $5. I just had to pay for the day, and not each individual hole. Sounded good to me. I put in my $5, received another rousing toast, and had a warm Crown Royal. Then, Glen held up his hands again and said that I had broke his ship and had barely got it back to Baldy. He announced that would be an additional $10. I don't know how much I drank, but I finally stumbled to my hooch.

My two roomies were on their bunks. They looked up and said in unison, "Hi man, we heard you took some hits."

I said, "Yeah, I'm still thinking about Todd."

Lance looked at me and asked, "Were you afraid?"

I paused a moment and then said, "No, I really don't think I had time. I did catch myself holding my breath."

Lance looked at me and said, "I'm scared shitless!"

"I don't know what to tell you. Maybe try to concentrate on the instruments and watch the pilot."

No answer, he just looked down at his feet.

Dean, the surfer dude, asked, "Did you worry that you might not go home?"

"Not until now! Like I said, Dean, I didn't have time. Everything's happening so fast. It's like you're on instinct."

We could hear the guys in the O club and wondered how they

had so much energy. No more small talk. We passed out from exhaustion as soon as we were horizontal.

I slept till 1000 the next morning, then wasted the rest of the day.

Day four was routine except no one was shooting at me. It was just a long day driving the bus (flying the Huey back and forth from point A to point B for sixteen hours).

When I returned that evening, I found my bed made, my extra boots polished, the sand swept outside, and my dirty clothes missing. My roomies told me, "We now have a hooch maid. It will cost you five dollars a month. They smell bad, but the word is they're honest."

Lance added, "They'll return your clean clothes in a day or two. They left you some flip flops. Just put five dollars for them on the bed tomorrow."

The flip flops were made of tire tread. We threw old tires away, and they sold them back to us as flip flops. They wasted nothing and were very entrepreneurial.

"By the way, Mac, I've been told they smell so bad so you won't want to fuck 'em, at least not till you've been here six months."

That drew a few laughs.

I asked Dean and Lance, "How'd you guys learn all this shit?"

They said they'd got back earlier than I did and were given the info from two guys in the hooch next door. They were peter pilots. They got off FNG status six weeks ago.

We were told two months later that we were to pay the hooch maids only two dollars a month. With the maids getting five dollars from twelve people, that made sixty per month. A VN doctor made fifty a month. We were causing inflation.

The next day I met my pilot at 0400 in the same mess hall with the same lousy food. We exchanged names. He was Pete Nixon from New York. He had a strange accent. He was missing some letters in his verbal alphabet, especially the letter R.

Chapter 17.

EVERYTHING IS DEAD; I MEAN EVERYTHING

We received our orders for the day. We were to report to Baldy for a defoliation mission.

What's that? Another new one for my list.

We climbed aboard the trucks and went off to the flight line. We arrived in time to help finish the preflight. Pete called the tower, said he was Rattler 2-8 for takeoff clearance. We were to proceed straight north to Baldy.

He said, "Mac, meet Don, the crew chief and Jerry, our fearless gunner. This is the best crew in this fucking country."

I replied over the intercom, "That's quite an introduction; nice to meet you guys."

Pete said, "Mac, you've got it."

So I took over. Pete went on, "I talked to both Phil and Glen and—not to give you a big head—they both said you're a natural.

"Today, we're going to spray Agent Orange on our enemy. It's a potent weed killer that kills everything. It's not orange. It's clear. It comes in an orange barrel, so a grunt doesn't mix it up with hydraulic fluid or Kool aid. We spray it on the jungle. Hell, we spray their rice paddies if we think it's food for the enemy. After we spray, everything is dead in less than a week. I mean everything."

After refueling, I flew to Baldy and landed. I hovered to the large turnaround area next to the runway and set it down.

"This is where the Firebirds live," Pete said. "I stayed at that wonderful hotel two nights ago."

I walked over to the Firebirds' hooch. I looked inside and instantly knew I would die of some dreaded disease if I stepped inside again. It was worse in daylight. As I walked back to our ship, a truck arrived and unloaded the defoliation equipment and began installing it on our ship. They placed a large tank in back. It had a few gauges. They anchored a control unit to the floor and then filled the tank with Agent Orange. Next, long pipes were attached, extending outward on each side of the ship with holes drilled in them at intervals for the spraying. These long spraying booms essentially made us a crop duster. The installers added a pump to the control unit for the operator in back.

A man walked over and handed each of us a large bulky gas mask. "Wear these while spraying." Then, he walked away. I thought *what a personality!* I put mine on. It was near a hundred degrees, so the sweat ran into my eyes and burned like hell. I had no peripheral vision. As I was evaluating these issues, Pete walked over to me and said, "How do you like that mask?"

I explained the problems.

Pete said, "You can add one more problem. The spray gets on the faceplate, and you can't see a damned thing. We drop them on the floor behind our seats. The crew doesn't wear them either. Neither does the spray operator."

That made my mind up real quick.

I bet the man delivering these has never put one on.

A lieutenant (LT) arrived and carried with him his mask and a map. He talked to Pete, and they looked at the area to be sprayed. Later, Pete told me we just spray the hard-to-get-to places. Large areas were sprayed by the air force or army with larger planes.

Pete called in the clear, and we took off towards the area marked on the map. In fifteen minutes we were there. The LT and Pete were discussing where to start and in what direction. After they had a plan, we started. This spraying was dangerous. We were only fifty feet above the jungle and going only sixty or seventy knots. Not much room for error or evasion.

I was surprised to hear the gunships call. "Rattler 2-8, Firebirds are on station; will be up and behind." Now I felt a little more comfortable. We started our back and forth passes over the trees. We flew into narrow canyons. We sprayed over terraced rice paddies. We sprayed over villages.

While cruising along, Pete told me, "One of our slicks flew over this area yesterday and threw out leaflets warning the locals and the bad guys to depart the area as we were going to kill everything with poison the next day. It amounted to telling the enemy where we were going to be. Makes it easier to shoot us down."

Soon after Pete said this, a string of tracers came out of the jungle and passed in front of the windshield. The Firebirds called and said, "We put rockets on that bastard. Are you continuing?"

"Roger that," said 2-8.

And we continued. So did Pete's story. "This area will be dead in a week, brown and crisp. Then we will burn it by shooting tracers or a rocket in there."

Pete was correct when he said the spray would cover the front of the gas mask. It was in my eyes and mouth. It stung my eyes and tasted bad.

Our spray tank was empty in 20 minutes, so we returned and refilled. Pete said, "You do the next round. How is everyone back there?" All three said they were OK.

That was bullshit. My mouth tasted like an army had marched through it in their stocking feet, old sweaty socks at that.

We completed six or seven additional trips before informing HQ that we were getting low on fuel. They told us to grab some chow after gassing up. That sounded great. No objection from any of us.

All the spray equipment was removed while we were eating. Little did I know I would be spraying this shit five additional times as an FNG. I also escorted many spray missions as a gunship pilot. I found out fifteen years later it's carcinogenic. *Wonderful.*

We sat in the cargo bay with our feet dangling outside and ate C-rations. I was lucky and opened the box with spaghetti and meat balls, peanut butter with crackers, and pears; all in cans. I put the two packs of two cigarettes in my cargo pockets. I discovered real quick that cigarettes were worth more than money. Nearly every-one smoked but me. I could trade those smokes for some of the better C-rats. I also pocketed the toilet paper as those malaria pills would tear up your insides.

Sitting on the metal floor of that cargo bay, I leaned back against the fire wall and fell asleep almost instantly. It seemed like only a minute later that a deuce and a half pulled up and roused us from our rest. Two grunts started loading us with numerous large red bags. I spoke before I thought and asked, "What's in the bags?"

They looked at me like I was from another planet. One of them said, "They're mail bags for LZs East, West, Center and Young."

Off on another mission, and this one would include a cast of thousands. The word would get out to those troops before we took off. They'd be waiting like dogs looking at their empty dinner bowls. Anybody who's ever been in the military will tell you that nothing can make you feel better than a letter from home.

Pete said, "Go to Center, West, Young, and finally to East. Don and Jerry are sorting the bags by their destination. Land and then listen for them to say go after they have thrown the bags on the ground. Then, you haul ass out of that LZ and do the same thing at the next three."

I clicked my transmit trigger twice. I called no one in particular and said, "Rattler 2-8 taking off Baldy to the west, then breaking south." We all had our heads on a swivel as I did a fast hover to the runway, then added power, and we were off. I looked at some of the thick green jungle and thought, *It' a shame there's a war here; this place could be another Hawaii.*

I played mailman at the first three LZs without any incidents. Number four was different. East called and said, "We've been receiving sporadic sniper fire all day. You might try coming in on an east to west direction; there's a valley and not as much jungle for cover." (All FSB's created a kill zone around their perimeter out at least 400 meters and removed all vegetation down to the dirt.) "The valley is open, so I hope you can approach without taking too much fire."

I was coming in fast, since this made us a more difficult target. I nearly stood the ship on its tail to slow my forward speed, when those bastards opened up with a machine gun. I was committed and had to land. Both our machine guns in back were firing long bursts. Now came the dilemma; one of them had to stop shooting to throw out the mail bags. The tracers were coming on our right and behind, so Jerry, the door gunner, continued to fire and the crew chief on the left stopped shooting and started throwing out bags when were 10 feet above the ground. Just as I touched down, he yelled, "Go, go Mac." He yelled so loud he didn't need the intercom.

I didn't have to be told again. I pulled pitch while rolling on the throttle and GTFO (in army aviation talk: GOT THE FUCK OUT). *No one mentioned GTFO in flight school.*

As I was returning to Baldy, we received a call from HQ informing us that we had been chosen as tonight's flare ship at Baldy. Pete read my mind, keyed his radio, and said, "This day is getting longer. When you land at Baldy, go to POL and then to the Hilton. Hover near the Firebird revetments and park. Don't block their way into the revetments, if they're not home."

I did as told and shut it down. All four of us crawled out slowly and immediately began looking for bullet holes. What a surprise; we couldn't find any.

Pete said, "Mac, follow me," and he walked over to some large conex containers (metal boxes long enough to hold two cars and eight feet tall) ten yards from the Firebird revetments. The doors were open. I looked in the first one, and it was full of rockets. The second contained about fifty shiny metal tubes, each five feet long and eight inches in diameter.

"These are flares," Pete told me. "We hook their rip cords to a metal ring on the tie down on the floor. They deploy a parachute when we throw them out. These are so the Firebirds can see if it's a dark overcast sky. We fly on the opposite side of the bad guys from the birds. We throw the flares out, and they fall slowly with the parachute and light up the countryside for miles. It doesn't expose our guys as much, because the flares are behind the NVA. Then the Firebirds can blow them to hell.

"The bad news is we have to spend the night in the hooch with the Firebirds, in their 'Hilton.' If we're lucky and our guys are not ambushed or if a FSB isn't attacked, we can sleep. If not, we could be flying for hours tonight. It's crowded in the hooch. There are twelve bunks; eight for the birds and four for us. Now let's load the ship and then grab some chow."

I said, "Pete, I let you keep talking as I always learn, but I was flying flares two nights ago."

"What? That's really shitty luck. It was my turn. They just forgot about my copilot."

He didn't call me an FNG.

This mess hall was better than ours. I don't know what I ate; some kind of mystery meat, and, of course, rice.

We walked back to the Hilton, and I was introduced to the

Firebirds. I hadn't met any of them the other night. They didn't look military. In fact, they looked like bums. They hadn't shaved in five days, probably hadn't slept in six, and smelled like they'd been dead for seven.

Their team leader was Steve Meadows. He said he was from Washington.

"That makes us neighbors," I said. "I'm from Oregon."

"How long have you been in paradise?" he asked me.

"This is day five."

"Shit, I can't remember day five. All I know, this is month ten."

He was the fire team leader. He was also the platoon leader, which made him 9-6. He introduced his crew chief, Ski, and door gunner, Tyler. They were from Boston and Ohio, respectively.

Meadows said, "If Pete didn't tell you, I will. Don't take off anything but your shirt. When that phone rings, everyone runs to the ships and fires them up. I get the call sign, frequency and grid coordinates of where we're going. I will give them to my wingman, Dennis Boyle, who is asleep on that bunk." He pointed to an occupied bunk. "I will also give one to Pete. We will all be on the frequency of the ground troops. If I can't see shit, you will throw out some flares behind the bad guys. Just help Pete watch for the falling parachutes. You don't want to fly into them. They are hell on the control rods."

I thought, good safety tip. It's amazing what I'm expected to pass on to new FNGs!

Pete said, "OK, Rattlers, let's go give our ship a final preflight. When that phone rings, we want those blades turning in sixty seconds. Those guys out in the bush are depending on all of us." He then turned to Meadows and said, "My copilot was here two nights ago."

"What the hell! Don't they like him?"

Pete said, "It was just a fuckup."

After the preflight, I could see that all the crew chiefs and gunners knew each other. Even though we were in different platoons, we all watched out for each other.

I lay down on one of the bunks at the end of the hooch. Steve slept by the red phone. Sort of like a James Bond movie.

Suddenly, the red phone started ringing, and loud. Everyone

jumped up, grabbed their shirts, and ran to the ships. I followed the crowd. We untied the rotor blades, uncovered the Pitot tube, plugged in the battery and strapped in. I was given a small piece of paper with the radio frequency, call sign, and coordinates. We were going to FSB Dragon. I looked on my map for its location. I had been adding locations on my map since day one. Pete yelled, "Clear." Back came the same from Don and Jerry. I looked at my watch. It was 0200 (2 am). Strange, how you don't feel tired when the adrenalin is pumping.

We lifted up and followed the gunships off Baldy's runway, while Firebird 9-6 did the radio work. The Firebirds were low leveling out to the target so they could arrive as quickly as possible. They climbed slowly because they were so overloaded with armament, and that's with only a half a tank of fuel, 120 gallons.

Firebird 9- 6 called, "Dragon base, this is Firebird 9-6, a team of gunships and a flare ship five minutes out. What's the sit rep?"

The radio operator replied, "Must be at least a company coming up the hill from our south and east. Our big guns are useless; we can't tip the barrels down far enough to shoot beehive rounds (similar to a shotgun shell). We're practically shooting our mortars straight up in the air. We are about out of flares, so I hope your flare ship is loaded. Resupply said they were back ordered! Can you believe that shit?"

9-6 said, "Rattler 2-8, throw out your first flare on the north side." 2-8 said, "Roger." Firebird 9-6 then asked Dragon to stop shooting the mortars. He told his wingman that they'd be coming in from the south, punch off rockets, then make a slight pedal turn right, shoot at the east side, then break right.

On the other side of the NVA, we threw out a flare at 2000 feet. It lit up the area for a mile around. I could have read a book by that light.

I could see some tracers going back and forth between the wire and the jungle. Then I heard, "Firebirds rolling in. After my wingman breaks right, give 'em hell with everything you've got for about three seconds."

We caught them in the open. They all began running back to the trees, but the trees were small and few and provided minimal protection. The enemy had nowhere to hide. Another turkey shoot.

I could see the rockets ignite in the pods and burn out as they exited. (A five-foot-long tube of solid fuel ignites and burns out in two tenths of a second. A rocket leaves the pod at 2300 feet per second. Its fins open as it exits and start the rocket spinning like a bullet, at nearly the speed of a bullet exiting one of the machine guns. The spin creates accuracy.)

I could see the rockets explode on those bastards. They were trying to shoot at the Firebirds, but they had no accuracy. The first ship put about eight rockets on the south side of the LZ, both in the open and in the trees. I could see the nose cannon shooting. Both door gunners were shooting. The first ship then moved his nose right, to the east side, and punched off eight more rockets. I could see smaller explosions in the same area from his 40 millimeter nose cannon. Then, I heard, "9-6 breaking right." As he was turning, his wingman put rockets just behind his tail, and the Gatling gun was right on target. His door gunners were also on target.

Pete called and said, "Firebird 9-6, looks like you could use some more light."

"Roger that 2-8."

The flares went out the door, their parachutes deployed, and it was definitely bright below us. This all looked like a maneuver they had done many times before.

The Firebirds made two more runs.

Then, 9-6 called Dragon and said, "It looks pretty quiet down there."

Dragon said, "Roger. Hold your fire. We are sending out two platoons to do some clean up."

9-6 said, "We have enough ammo for one more pass, so I will circle for a while. Need any more light down there?

"This is Devil 6. We are almost to the bodies on the south side. Looks like they didn't haul away their dead. (The NVA would haul away their dead so we wouldn't know how many we killed.) And yes, we could use more light. I want to thank you guys for hanging around."

"Firebirds and flare ship, this is Angel 6 on the east perimeter. Same story to report. These guys were caught with their pants down."

I was thinking, *Devil and Angel. I wonder if those names referred to their personalities, attitudes, or a song I heard?*

2-9 threw out two more flares.

Pete Nixon said, "Take it, Mac, and keep circling over the north side. I'm going to take a nap."

Nap? I figured he was just messing with me. I gave the radio two clicks and took over the controls.

After 15 minutes, both patrols called in to Dragon and said they were returning with some bodies and lots of weapons. "Looks like they have a good supply line. Lots of AK-47's, Russian grenades and RPG's."

We threw out one last flare. As soon as it ignited, 9-6 said, "We're returning to Baldy. Call if these guys want to try act two of this drama." He then said, "2-9, you got that?" I just keyed the mike twice and followed them to Baldy.

Chapter 18.

I WANT TO SHOOT BACK

First, we refueled, and then we went back to the Hilton to re-arm. We did our customary post flight and found nothing of significance. Then, I helped Don and Jerry load a few flares. I went over to the gunships and asked if they needed any help.

The crew chief, Ski, and door gunner, Tyler, looked stunned. Then, they looked at each other and shrugged.

"Sure. Grab some rockets," said Tyler, "and bring them here, and I'll show you how to load these pods."

Ski looked over at Tyler and said, "Why do you get the help?"

"Because I spoke first."

"I'm Mac" I said. They both nodded.

I helped the birds for about an hour. They thanked me, and I returned to the Hilton. That "Hilton" was an oxymoron on the same level as military intelligence, but I guess it was really just wartime irony.

That night I made up my mind. I was going to be a Firebird the minute I got off FNG status. Sitting in those LZs with only a thin piece of Plexiglas in front of me and a thin piece of aluminum for a door was just a crap shoot. Eventually, you're going to get hit, either shot or splattered with shrapnel, worse than my first time. I wanted to shoot back. After all, this police action seemed like a war to me.

Suddenly, I realized I was tired. I took off my shirt and looked at my watch. It said 0430.

That was the last thing I remember.

I opened my eyes, and it was light. My watch said 0600. No one else was awake, so I just closed my eyes.

Damn, it was that red phone again.

Steve jumped up like a cat, grabbed it and said, "Firebird hooch." After a moment of silence, I heard him say, "Yes sir." Steve was a captain, so he wasn't talking to the radio operator. He put the phone down and said, "Get up Rattlers. Those patrols last night at Dragon found some wounded, and intelligence wants to debrief them. So you lucky guys get to bring them here, while we birds go eat breakfast."

I lifted my head up and said, "Breakfast? I think we got a better deal." Surprisingly, at this hour, that statement got several laughs.

Pete looked at Steve and said, "Are you sure you don't want to escort us."

Steve laughed. "No, we killed all of them last night."

"Yeah, good point. Actually, you didn't kill all of them. You left a few alive."

Steve laughed and hit Pete on the shoulder. "I'm just trying to help out our military. Come on guys let's eat. Pete, I'll have them keep the mess open."

Pete nodded, smiled and said, "Thanks, I think."

Sounds like we shouldn't leave anyone alive *in the future. Hell, what does some lowly NVA grunt know anyway? The troops at the bottom of the pecking order don't know anything important. That goes for both sides.*

We did a quick once around the ship for a half-assed preflight. We had checked everything last night. We untied the blades and climbed in. Pete was always trying to be funny, so he told me, "Go find those prisoners. Don't hit any large objects."

Once in the air, the guys in back asked if they could test fire their guns. I said, "Great idea." So, they did.

Ten minutes later I saw Dragon and called for a sit rep and a smoke (so I would know where they wanted me to land). I acknowledged the red smoke.

They said they had four prisoners, two with flesh wounds. They asked if we wanted any help getting them to Baldy. I gave Pete a confused look. He looked at me and mouthed, "I've got it." I nodded back.

He said, "Dragon, as long as they're tied up securely, with bags over their heads, there's no problem. All my crew are armed." It was quiet on the other end; I could hear Don and Jerry laughing on this end.

We landed, and here came four guys with their hands tied securely behind their backs and sand bags over their heads. There was an armed escort, of course. Pete told me, "The sand bags are for intimidation. None of these guys have ever been in an aircraft, especially a noisy one with the air whipping around their heads. They will be terrified by the time we get to Baldy. You never know, we may have to do some evasive maneuvers and jerk this ship around." He said that with a sly smile. The prisoners were helped in and sat on the floor, leaning back against the firewall. Pete said, "If any of those fuckers so much as moves, shoot him."

The reply from the back was, "with pleasure."

I called and said "Rattler 2-9 is departing Dragon for Baldy."

We pulled pitch and Pete said, "I've got it. Let's get this started on the right foot, so they know who's in charge. Hang on." Then, he dove off the side of dragon. Five seconds later, he pulled back the cyclic, and we climbed up so quick my head felt like it was going down between my shoulder blades. He followed that with a sharp bank to the left.

Hell, I thought, *I might get air sick*, but then it hit me. *This is fun.*

Ten minutes later, he called in to Baldy as we entered the traffic pattern and then called HQ. He told them we were delivering "some guests."

The radio operator laughed and said, "A truck is on the way with some MPs (military police)."

After the prisoners were taken away, Pete said, "We'll gas up and be ready to go in ten."

I guess when you draw flare duty you are screwed the next day. I think Pete read my mind.

"Since we only went out once last night, we are good to go today," he said. "Two flare missions, and you get the next day off."

I said, "I got lucky the other night because we went out more than once."

HQ called and said to shut down. "We are going to load you up with canisters of CS. Someone will go out with you and give you the coordinates. The Firebirds will accompany you in case you stir up trouble. Now go eat."

I shut down and asked Pete, "What's CS?"

"It's a type of tear gas, but more potent," he told me. "We

throw the canisters into the jungle, they break apart, and we shoot anything that runs from the gas. We just have to watch where we dump it because we don't want to fly through it."

Another item to put on my list of surprises.

A LT came up to Pete's side of the ship and showed him the area on a map. Pete compared it to his map. I watched and then marked my map. The Firebirds came over to look at the map, too. All three ships took off for Dragon. The only difference today was we were leading.

We flew to Dragon, then five minutes more west of Dragon. I guess someone thought there were more bad guys out there, or the prisoners talked. We started on the marked route. The LT and the crew in back were getting the canisters ready to be pushed out. Pete called, "Coming up on target." Then, he said, "Now," and out it went. We continued on the marked route while pushing those fifty-five gallon drums out the door. This took about ten minutes.

One of the Firebirds said, "I just punched a pair of rockets at some tracers that came up behind your tail. How much more gas do you have to dump?"

Pete said, "Just one."

Firebird 9-6 said, "Save it, and let's go back to that hot spot."

The LT said, "Great idea."

Pete said, "Take it," so I did. I made a climbing turn to the right so I could see what was going on. The Firebirds also turned back and started a climb.

9-6 was talking to his wingman, giving him instructions for the gun run. "Let's punch our rockets a little higher than usual." Meaning he didn't want to go low enough to fly through the gas. It burns your skin wherever your clothes and sweat make contact. If it gets in your eyes, they burn and flood with tears. You can't fly very well in that condition.

Firebird lead said, "Rolling in. Let's stir things up a little." He shot several pairs of rockets and then as lead turned, his wingman put some rockets behind him. *What a team! These guys fly like they've being doing this for years.* More tracers came up out of the jungle. *Those guys are stupid. They instantly gave away their position.*

9-6 said, "2-9, put that last canister on them." I gave him a roger and turned toward the action. The crew pushed out the canister, and then I turned and climbed.

I looked out and saw the Firebirds shooting rockets at the NVA as they ran out of the trees to escape the CS gas. Suddenly, a huge explosion climbed 100 feet in the air. The flames rolled into the sky in billowing clouds and seemed to grow in volume as they rose. It blocked out the sun for 30 seconds.

Nothing was said over the radio. The lead gunship broke steeply to the right. The wing ship fired only one pair of rockets, and then broke right as well.

Pete said, "That was the largest secondary explosion I've ever seen."

Both guys in back agreed. I heard the LT behind me call HQ and ask for some "fast movers with nape" (military talk for jets with napalm).

The Air Force usually had some fast movers circling in the area, waiting for work. HQ called an Air Force spotter plane, carrying rockets like ours, except they were colored smoke for him to mark targets for the jets.

The spotter called us and reported, "Two fast movers are inbound and two minutes out." He followed with, "I see your three ships east of the target. You're OK if you keep flying in the same direction you're headed. The jets will be making one north-south pass, OPHA, (one pass, haul ass)."

However, as we turned to clear the area, we flew through the tear gas. The gunship pilot told me after the mission that the huge explosion probably carried it up into the air.

Shit, it burned like fire everywhere I perspired. It really burned at my collar where it was in contact with my wet skin.

The pilot yelled, "Keep blinking your eyes but don't touch them. Put your head outside and hope for fresh air."

I thought to myself, *I hope he can see better than me.* Then, I felt clean air. No gas.

Pete yelled, "Mac, take the controls if you can see and get us out of here."

I keyed my mic and yelled, "Got it," and moved the cyclic back and forth so he could feel I had control. The guys in back were coughing, and I heard one yell, "Fuck." I could only agree with that profound statement. My eyes were still burning, but at least I could see I was flying in the right direction.

The forward air controller cut in and said, "They'll make their one pass now. I don't need to mark the target as you guys did a good job of that."

9-6 said, "Thanks."

Here they came, and fast. I could see the long canisters drop off the lead's wings. They tumbled into the trees and behind the jets. This allowed the jets time to exit the blast area. Right behind the lead and off to the side came the wing ship. He dropped his ordinance. Their napalm exploded and rolled through the trees for hundreds of yards at nearly the speed of the jets. If you were on the ground, the end came quick.

Pete called up the spotter and fast movers and told them, "Thanks for such a quick and accurate response."

They said, "Call us any time. Always glad to help."

With nothing else to do here, we returned to Baldy. We took on some fuel and were told to shut down and grab some chow.

We checked for holes, found none. We rearmed our door gunner's machine guns. I then helped the birds rearm as the slicks only required some machine gun ammo. With all that completed, we all walked over to the mess hall together. Eight birds and four Slicks. It was cool. *I was walking with the Big Boys.*

We ate and really talked. Not just the small stuff, but the real things: What did you do before VN? Got any brothers or sisters? Your dad military? We were actually getting to know each other. I didn't think these guys were crazy, as I had been told. I thought they were just asked to do crazy things! They flew lower and slower than the slicks. This certainly made them an easier target. There were even rumors that the NVA put a bounty on the Firebirds. I didn't ask about that rumor.

We spent the afternoon resupplying patrols in the bush and some FSB's. I flew five hours, including a fuel stop. My pilot must have thought he had a day off. I completed five high overhead landings and killed no one. Around 1800 we were released.

As I flew back to Chu Lai, Pete asked me, "What is it you remember most about today?"

Without looking over, I said, "My ass is killing me." All three crew members just roared with laughter. Pete said, "So is mine." Don and Jerry both checked in with the same comment. I said to them, "At least you can sort of stand up, even if you are bent over like your grandma." A little levity never hurt, even in combat.

The same routine awaited me. Shower, eat, or least try, write a letter home and make small talk with the roomies. We decided that with all this flying to exhaustion, we wouldn't get to talk until we were off FNG status. One good thing: I would not have to ring that bell tonight.

"Shit," I said out loud. "I haven't checked the schedule board." They both said they hadn't either, threw their pens and paper on the bed, and stood. Off we went. Same schedule with resupply for all three of us. I said, "I guess this is bringing us closer together." They laughed but were too tired to reply. We fell asleep before we could lie down.

Days seven and eight were routine. Resupply, resupply, and resupply. Only shot at twice and no holes. Did the enemy forget about me? However, each day had been different in many ways. Sure, we always fly, but over new landscapes with new cargo, talking to grunts we will never meet again, and learning all sorts of things I'll eventually have to pass on to the new FNGs.

Chapter 19.

TWO COLONELS, FOUR LOST SHIPS, TOILET PAPER

D ay nine was different. It was a CA, and we drew the C & C (command and control) ship. We had the usual briefing, and I got another pilot and crew: Ed Place, rattler 2-2, from Colorado; crew chief, Steve Atchison, from Chicago; and door gunner, Todd Burnett, from Nebraska. (Names can get confusing. Obviously, this was not the Todd from West Virginia who got hit by the 51). I had met those two my second day in the AO. We smiled and shook hands.

Ed said, "You guys know each other?"

Slick crews were moved around a little more than gun crews.

I said, "Yes, we flew together a few times when I was a new FNG. They were the guys that taught me what a rotor blade was." They all laughed.

When the briefing ended, we climbed into the trucks to be driven out to our ships. The old timers were upset about something. They looked at each other and shook their heads as if saying "no" while we were being driven to the flight line. Tension was high. Why? I had no idea, but it made me worry.

The Rattlers formed up into the first flight of three ships; flights two and three consisted of two ships each; seven total. Fifty minutes later, we were at Baldy, and the troops were climbing in. Half were our guys and half were Vietnamese. I had been told no one liked working with the SVNA (South Vietnamese army), as they couldn't be trusted.

Two colonels were in charge of the mission. We exchanged a quick salute and a good morning, and then we all climbed in. This was my first time in the C & C ship.

This will be another learning experience.

We took off and climbed to 2000 feet and aimed for the LZ. We were going 270 degrees on the compass, straight west and 10 clicks from Baldy. This LZ was in a valley two clicks south of LZ Cacti. The two colonels—one American and one South Vietnamese—were in back with the crew chief and gunner. I heard these joint missions were a cluster fuck. Besides not trusting the SVNA, the Americans couldn't understand Vietnamese and didn't know what our "allies" were being told, and vice versa.

The slicks had picked up about 50 men from Baldy. Several of the slick pilots got out and, while grunts were loading, the pilots talked to the Firebirds, who were not coming with us. I didn't know what that was about. The slicks all pulled pitch a few minutes later. We in the C & C would go ahead to scout the area. The others would arrive ten minutes later. We made big slow circles, waiting for the slicks. The colonels in back were looking at the area with binoculars. I wondered if the enemy was curious why we were circling overhead. It was strange listening to the VN colonel talk to his men in a language I didn't understand.

The slicks arrived, already in formation, and the first flight was making an approach.

A moment into the combat assault, the briefing went out the window.

Those first three ships were coming in to land in the LZ when they exploded 10 feet off the ground. They were hit by multiple RPG's. The LZ was a blanket of tracers. Exploding helo parts were flying in the air. I was stunned for a moment trying to absorb what was happening. I snapped out of that when the lead pilot of the second flight told us that the rockets were coming out of the trees all around the LZ, aimed at the three downed burning slicks. *Overkill.*

As the LZ was engulfed with fire, exploding fuel, and ammo, the lead ship in the second group immediately called out, "Abort, Abort, breaking right." Third flight also broke right.

Now I understood why everyone was pissed at the briefing, when told the LZ was NOT hot and we wouldn't need the Firebirds. What genius said no gunships? They knew someone was out there, or why else would we be inserting troops?

Chaos was a mild term for what was happening. Now, the bad guys turned their attention from the burning slicks and aimed at the retreating four slicks. Everyone was talking over each other on the radios.

Everyone was reporting hits. Those hit had to be in the cockpits as you didn't usually feel the hits anywhere else, unless it was a 51 cal or you were on the ground. One slick reported "engine out" and was auto rotating (landing without an engine) near Cacti. Two other ships reported wounded: a copilot was hit in one slick and a crew chief in another. Neither injury was life threatening. Baldy called Cacti about the downed ships. Cacti was sending out a patrol to bring them in.

The door gunners didn't stop shooting until they were far away from the chaos. Tracers from the edges of the LZ had followed the slicks for that same amount of time. The door gunners had been aiming along the LZ's perimeter in an attempt to get those NVA out of the game.

Someone asked, "Can anyone be alive down there?"

An answer came back, "Maybe at first, but not now."

The mastermind of this mess in the C & C ship said, "All ships return to formation and return to Baldy."

There was dead silence on the radio until the second flight lead called Baldy to report he was entering the traffic pattern with three ships.

The radio operator said in a confused voice, "Three?" He had cleared seven to takeoff just fifteen minutes before.

No one answered him.

All landed and hovered to the large turnaround area near the Firebird Hilton and its revetments. The Firebirds were working on their ships and looked at us, probably wondering about the missing four ships.

As everyone shut down and climbed out, including the lucky-to-be-alive grunts, the Firebirds walked over and said, "What happened?"

One slick pilot had tears in his eyes. Someone said, "The LZ was hot. The first three in blew up before they were low enough for anyone to jump out. Twelve dead Rattlers and twenty-one grunts! I could kill that fucking colonel from Intel (intelligence). I knew those three pilots, and so did you." Then, the Firebird put his hands on the slick pilot's shoulders and held on while he sobbed.

When everything had hit the fan a few minutes earlier and the CA was aborted, the American colonel said, "Get back to Baldy as fast as possible." When we landed the C & C ship a few minutes before the other slicks, a jeep was waiting to haul their worthless asses off to safety. I was told the jeep was called on a separate and secure frequency that we didn't monitor.

We lost people and ships all the time, but never three ships in three seconds.

Who planned this mission? Would they face any repercussions? My list of things left out in flight school is quickly becoming a book.

Ten minutes later, a jeep from HQ drove up and a private got out. He said, "HQ wants you to gas up and report to your assignments for the rest of the day. Frequencies, call signs, and coordinates are on these papers." He called out names and handed out the sheets of paper.

Then, he called out, "C & C." Ed raised his hand. The private walked over and handed Ed a map with a route that took us over ten hamlets (small villages). He said a truck would be here in a few minutes to load us with Chieu Hoi, (open arms) to throw out over those hamlets.

Another new bit of info left out in flight school. Pamphlet dropping?

I just stood there until I decided it would be a good idea to help Steve and Todd check the ship. They were both quiet. Finally, Steve looked at me and said, "I drank beers the other night with those guys." I didn't know what to say.

Here came the truck full of what looked like thousands of sheets of three-by-eight inch pieces of paper, bundled together on wooden pallets. Ed pulled one sheet out and handed it to me. One side was in Vietnamese, so I turned it over and saw some pictures. Ed said, "These are pictures of what was written on the other side. It had five pictures: an NVA soldier reading a letter from home. Then the soldier sitting in the jungle and not looking happy. In the next he turns himself in to the SVNA, and then he shows where the booby traps are hidden, and the last one shows everyone in a village is happy and receiving him with open arms."

If it were that easy, why are we here?

We all pitched in and transferred the cargo. Then off we flew toward the first area marked on the map. Ed gave me a mocking look. "You know what we're doing?" I didn't say anything, and he went on. "We're giving them toilet paper." As we approached, I felt movement in back and turned to look. Steve and Todd were cutting the ties around one of the bundles. Ed said, "Thirty seconds."

As we approached what looked like six straw huts, out went the first bundle. This routine continued for nine more drops. I liked the low-level flying. It was a hell of a lot of fun. We were fifty feet off the ground. It beat that bus route I had been flying since I arrived. Otherwise, it was uneventful. I had flown more in my first nine days here, than in the first half of flight school.

The Chieu Hoi mission only took thirty minutes. No one shot at us. I thought that was strange.

I called Baldy to report the mission completed. They said, as nearly always, "There is another mission waiting."

A couple of resupply missions and one bringing the guys in the bush some replacements filled in the afternoon. I knew everyone was thinking about our fellow pilots. Someone took a few shots at us, and I got another hole. Damnit, I'm getting a reputation. We were released early and returned to Chu Lai.

We landed, checked the ship, notified sheet metal in maintenance of the hole, and jumped in a truck for the company area.

Chapter 20.

CARRIER QUALIFICATIONS, FOOTBALL, FACE ANOTHER DAY

As we dismounted the truck, Ed said with a smile, "See you in the bar in thirty minutes. You are buying me my first drink tonight."

"Yes, you and nineteen others." (Drinks were 25 cents each divided into five dollars; you do the math.)

When I got to that club full of drunks, I laid my hat and gun in the pile. I felt pretty safe there, except from my fellow pilots.

I walked in and saw Ed. He had gotten dead drunk in just thirty minutes. They were toasting the dead Rattlers. Not only were they drunk, but angry. It was *fuck this* and *fuck that, fuck the war,* and especially *fuck those goddamned guys in intelligence.*

One pilot said, "That LZ . . . from now on we're going to call it MILLION-DOLLAR HILL." (The average cost of a slick was $330,000.)

I learned several other new phrases because of that morning's fucked up CA: FUBAR (fucked up beyond all recognition), SNAFU (situation normal, all fucked up), FTA (Fuck the army), BOHICA (bend over; here it comes again), and the best was FIGMO (Fuck it, got my orders). That one is saying, "I'm outta here and returning to the world. Going home!"

Damn, I wanted a drink. I hadn't done much drinking in the past, but this seemed like a good time to start. Except I was flying the next day.

I took the liberty of ringing the bell. I was still amazed at how this mad house instantly went silent when that bell talked. I threw five dollars in the bowl and said, "Nine holes in nine days. How can I transfer out of this chicken-shit outfit?" That drew a monumental laugh. I turned and walked out.

No sooner had I sat on my bunk when the door opened, and Ed walked in with two drinks. "Mac, I just talked to the platoon leader, and you get tomorrow off!"

I said, "Are you serious?"

He handed me a glass of warm Crown Royal. He then clicked his to mine and said, "Here's to being in the C & C."

It took me only a second to get the implication of what he had said. *We're alive because we weren't in that first flight.* This reinforced my thoughts about my first CA, nine days before. *It definitely was a crap shoot, whether you survived or not. I don't think I will pass that one on to the new guys.*

I returned to the bar with Ed. It was actually pretty cool because one of the pilots I had flown with said, "You'd be a copilot today, if it weren't for that thirty day rule."

I had to admit I had flown a lot, and learned a lot, and one thing for sure: these guys were amazing.

I noticed other guys I hadn't seen except in the mess hall at 0400. I guess we all had the day off together, which gave us a chance to get to know each other.

The three platoon leaders walked over in front of the bar and announced there would be carrier qualifications tonight. I thought, *What the hell is that? Only the navy takes off from carriers.*

Then, things started to happen. Three guys came in carrying mattresses. Three more had a gallon each of ketchup, mustard and mayonnaise. (Where had they been hiding those last two?) The crowd was getting rowdy now. Almost everybody had a drink in each hand. Most of the pilots I had met since my arrival—both slicks and guns—were screwed up twisted fucks, at least when they had a day off. I supposed I'd be one soon enough.

The mattresses were placed up against a partial wall at the end of the room. Next, the three gallons of condiments were spread with a broom on the floor from the bar to the mattresses across the room. This was one big red, white and yellow mess. I still wasn't sure what was next, but I knew it was going to be messy and not army regulation.

Four pilots grabbed an FNG and put him on the floor on his stomach. They each grabbed a limb and lifted him up a foot and started rocking him forward and backwards. One of the guys said,

"Put your hands out in front of you after we throw you towards the mattresses so you don't break your neck." This was followed by a count of one, two and three. They threw him on the floor, and he slid through the condiments creating a grotesque rainbow of colors going everywhere. The mixture was flying over his head, in his face, and splattering the guys standing too close to the runway. But no one gave a shit. They were yelling, screaming, drinking, and pouring booze on the FNG sliding into the mattresses. He hit those mattresses pretty hard, but he bounced up and was handed a drink. That was a pretty good reward for that messy landing.

Now it started to get serious. Some of the FNGs tried to escape, including me, but the place was surrounded by pilots and copilots. So we all stood there waiting our turn.

One by one, we were thrown down the runway. If too much of the condiments were pushed to the side, the old timers swept the concoction back on the runway to keep it slippery. We all started taking off everything but our pants.

By the time I arrived at the runway, the human catapults were too inebriated to launch us in a coordinated manner. Guys were launched sideways, spinning, and even feet first. They traded off launchers, but to avail.

I was launched almost sideways. What a mess! The ketchup, mayo and mustard were flying up in the air. It was in my face, ears, mouth, eyes, and every place else on my body. Only one small part of all this was good. It was a short ride, just two seconds at most, sliding across the floor. When I hit the mattresses, it was a sponge. Everyone near them was soaked from the spray. I didn't care because someone handed me a drink, or maybe it was two drinks. When I thought about it later that night, I didn't remember much.

Two FNGs were so drunk they volunteered for a second landing. Wow, the power of alcohol.

The platoon leaders tried holding up their hands for quiet. This didn't work so someone yelled, "Shut the fuck up, assholes." This worked, so one announced, "Congratulations, you're now officially helicopter pilots in Vietnam. Not many out there can say that!"

Yeah, I suppose that's true. And of course, there was no mention of this in flight school.

I don't remember if I ran through the shower or the ocean. I don't even remember when or how I returned to my hooch. I did wake up with a headache. I thought, *Thank god I have a day off. I have to remember to drink less before the next day off.*

Before entering the mess hall, I paused to read a notice pinned to the door. TONIGHT WILL BE A FUNERAL SERVICE AT 2000 (pronounced "20 hundred hours"; that is, 8:00 pm) IN THE MESS HALL. THIS WILL BE HONORING THE RATTLERS WE LOST YESTERDAY. NO ALCOHOL ALLOWED INSIDE.

The guy in line behind me said, "That means we get fucked up before the service, so we don't think too much about the possibility of the service being for us."

I slowly continued into the mess hall. I ate something, not sure what was served with those powered eggs, but the potatoes were OK. I just hoped it would stay down. I sat there, alone, and thought about what I had just read. As I returned to my hooch, I noticed piles of puke outside the doors of several hooches. I wasn't the only one feeling like shit. I tried to go back to sleep, but that didn't work.

I heard someone outside yell, "Football game! FNGs and copilots against the EMs." (An EM was an enlisted man; the guys in our crews and maintenance and anyone that wasn't an officer.)

I thought *what the hell. I wouldn't feel any worse playing football on the beach than I do now.*

I put on a pair of shorts and grabbed a T-shirt, choked down some APCs (all-purpose capsules; in other words, aspirin) and ran out the door. The beach was only 30 yards away. I ran onto the beach, so I wouldn't look as bad as I felt. (It's all about appearances.) No one knew me except the crew chiefs and gunners I had been flying with. A crew chief yelled, "Hi Mac, put your shirt on. We're the skins. This is a friendly game of touch. We'll kick off. The goals are marked with 100 mph tape."

Turns out, this was a different version of touch football. It was rugby; football without pads. These guys wanted us to know they were our equals and stronger, even though they were enlisted.

From there, it only got more physical. After a few hard hits, I was ready to kick some ass. Now, we were playing full on tackle football. I think everyone was working off yesterday's frustration and anger. I had only been blocking, so in the huddle I told the quarterback to "throw me a long one. They've only seen me block and won't expect it." He nodded. The ball was hiked, and I took off as fast as I could run in sand. The blocking was good, so the QB was able to give me several seconds to get down field. He cocked his arm and threw it 30 yards. I saw it might be long so I tried running faster. I timed it right and jumped up with my arms stretched out. The ball fell into my hands, and I fell forward into the end zone. Touchdown! 6 to 0 in favor of FNGs.

We kicked off, and they ran it back to midfield. We intercepted their first play, a wobbly short pass. In the huddle, I asked the quarterback to throw me another long one. "I'll act like I'm blocking, and then I'll take off. Block hard guys and give Rosey (the QB) a few seconds. Hold them if you have to. (Illegal, but there're no rules in war.) I will drift out to the wet sand where I can run faster than the guy trying to cover me running in soft dry sand."

The ball was hiked, and I stood up, hit my guy in the chest, and he stopped. I then rolled off of him, did a 360, and took off down the beach. I looked back and here came the ball. Another long one, but this time I was running in the hard wet sand. A fast defender was running diagonally towards me and had an angle at me so he didn't have to run as far. As I jumped up with outstretched arms I caught the ball and tucked it in with both arms as I knew there was going to be a serious collision. I was correct. The guy hit me so hard that we both stayed in the air what seemed like another second or two. I could feel pain as we both tumbled over the 100 mph tape and into the end zone. Half the crowd came running and yelling as the FNGs were now up 12 to 0. The other half were both pissed and hung their heads.

I think my guys were running toward me to see if they were going to need to call a medic if I didn't get up. As I was lying there in the sand, I slowly started moving my arms and, to my surprise, one contained the football. *Shit, I had held on, even with that hit.* Good news, both arms moved. The legs were out of the question because someone was lying on them. He slowly began moving and rolled off. That gave me a chance to move my legs. They moved, like the arms, without pain. It was then I realized he had knocked the wind out of me, and it hurt my right side when I tried to breathe. As I was giving it my best effort to get up without showing any pain—remember, it was all about appearances—the human wave arrived.

I looked down, and the other guy was Ski, the Firebird crew chief. As I was surrounded by well-wishers, I instinctively reached down and offered my left hand to him. My right side hurt like hell. He looked up at me, smiled, and put out his left hand and took mine. (His right side also hurt).

I pulled him up and asked, "Are you OK?"

He said, "OK."

Then everything changed.

We had been at this Neanderthal activity for about 30 minutes, and everyone was talking about those two catches when the CO, Major Wilson, and Top drove up in the CO's jeep. We froze and just stood there. Everyone knew something was about to hit the fan.

The CO climbed out and said, "At ease." We stood motionless, feet apart, hands interlocking behind our backs. I dropped the football. "Men, I know how you feel," the Captain told us. "This is my second tour, and I have lost some friends, some really good friends. One was the best man at my wedding. He was my roommate at the academy. It was a year and a half ago, and I still think of him every day.

"My problem here is injuries. If one of you gets hurt out here, I have to replace you. I know if that replacement is injured or killed, you'll never forgive yourself. You'll have to endure that memory, not just a loss like I have, but loss and guilt for the rest of your life.

"Keep playing, but go back to touch. It doesn't mean you are a bunch of pussies. It just makes more sense. Take out the anger on the enemy. Have a good day men. I will see you at the memorial this evening.

"Nice catch McNally and nice hit Ski," he said, as he was turning back toward his jeep.

Wow, the CO is human, through and through, as well as a good leader.

We continued playing, but it was lackluster. I think we had already released most of our anger.

The game broke up. Most of us jumped in the ocean to cool off, but it was difficult to cool down in a warm bath. Then, I went back to the hooch for a nap and another letter home. Or at least, start one I could finish later after a long day "driving the bus."

There was a knock on our door. We said, "Come in," in unison.

The screen door opened and in came the company clerk. He introduced us to a new FNG, Robert J. Clearwater, another Texan. We all shook hands.

He said. "It's Bob."

We said, "OK," and then we helped him get settled.

I said, "We'll take you to dinner and show you the schedule board in about an hour. You got here on a shitty day. There is a memorial service at 2000."

He looked at us with really big eyes and said, "OK."

While he was moving his gear into that mini closet (locker), we finished our letters. We alternated this with telling Bob a few things to help him fit in. We told him not to send anything home that might scare his mom, girlfriend, or wife. Keep it neutral: Meeting guys from all over the US, swimming in the warm South China Sea, or a movie on the beach; in other words, describe a pretty good life and leave out the blood and guts. "Try to put them at ease," we told him.

He said, "Thanks" and continued his unpacking.

As kind of a joke when I was in college, I would send home a post card that said, "No Mon (pronounced mun), no fun, your son." Dad would send back to me at the bottom of Mom's letter, "Too bad, so sad, your dad." I still added this in my letters, the third year of this now traditional tension distractor.

Finally, we decided it was time to walk to the mess hall. As we entered, I leaned over to Bob and whispered, "Don't get your hopes up." We went through the line and sat down.

We quizzed Bob about his home, which was San Antonio. Next question, "What did you do before the army?"

He said, "I flew corporate jets for my dad's oil company."

I said, "Jets! Why aren't you in the air force?"

He said what I already knew. "You need four years of college. I'm a commercial pilot with a half dozen Jet ratings, so I'm sent to helicopter school. I'm not impressed with the army's use of personal. I guess all those cushy slots are filled with career butt kissers, commissioned officers. Not us lowly warrants." (Historically, warrant officer was a rank in the navy and air force designed to keep long-serving enlisted men with valuable skills in the service, once they had reached the pinnacle of enlisted rank. They receive an officer's pay, an increase for them of a factor of ten or more.)

The army decided if they trained us in officer training and flying at the same time, they could eliminate six months of separate officer training. This saved money and got pilots to VN much faster. I'm now seeing why they wanted more pilots over here. The bad guys were shooting us at a greater rate than anticipated.

We filled Bob in on us. "We've been flying so much, we've hardly had time to get to know each other. Don't take it personally if we only see you when the alarm sounds, or we go to sleep at night."

We told him about the rocket attacks. We almost forgot that one.

Bob had great stories about some of the people he had flown around Texas, the US, and the world. He had been to some very exotic places.

Someone said, "We should call this mess hall 'The Choke and Puke.'"

Bob agreed.

"Let's show Bob the schedule board."

The board was always easy to find, due to the loud discussions there on who was flying with whom. And questions like, "Is he any good? How long has he been an FNG?"

Bob found his name next to an AC I didn't know. He had the standard 0400 wake up and would meet the AC at 0430 in the mess hall.

We had about an hour and a half to kill before the memorial (poor choice of words).

At 2000, we walked into the mess hall. It was fairly dark except for 12 burning candles on a table at one end of the room. There were 12 white flight helmets on the table behind the candles. It was quiet, not a word spoken. Behind the table was a chaplain wearing a white robe. Chaplains were trained to perform all services: Protestant, Catholic and Jewish.

I'm not religious, so I thought this was just opening a wound we had tried to close earlier on the beach. You could hear a few sniffles. Some of these guys had been friends since flight school. The chaplain spoke quietly and reverently of the 12 individuals. What had happened was just sinking in for me. It hurt. You made close friends and then lost them. You had to become cold inside and say, "Fuck it," and keep going. Even so, it was going to take me a long time to rid myself of the picture of those three exploding ships, if ever.

The ordeal in the mess hall finally ended. On the way back to the hooch, Bob asked if we had any booze. We told him, "No, the penalties are pretty stiff."

"So I've heard."

I was thinking to myself, *tomorrow should be OK. I'm assigned to fly with Phil, same guy I flew with on opening day.* As usual, I was asleep as my head was approaching the pillow. The rockets started arriving at their usual time, around 0200. Four rockets total. I opened my eyes and closed them just as quickly and went back to La-La Land. They are not very accurate. I don't know what Bob did.

No matter how long I was in VN, 0400 was too early. Most eighteen and nineteen year olds are still in bed, thinking about their date next weekend or how to get some beer. All we want here is sleep and hope to live another day. Priorities sure vary with the circumstances.

The alarm made its usual announcement, telling us we had to face another day.

I met Phil in the mess hall. He said that Bob (the crew chief, Bob Smith, not the new FNG) and Ed Cannon were down at the flight line. He asked "How are you doing?"

I said, "Great, I'm still here."

"What flight were you in on the cluster fuck two days ago?"

"C & C."

"Shit damn, Mac. I was in the second flight, and I still can't get it out of my mind."

"If it's any consolation, neither can I, and I was 2000 feet above you."

"Well, let's hope we draw a safe one today."

Bob and Ed were waiting when I climbed out of the truck. We greeted each other. They said, "Mac, you don't look so new anymore."

"I don't know if that's good or bad," I replied.

"It's good," they said. "You have that new look all worn away. You are one of us now."

"Thank you, I think. Maybe I look like an old timer because I haven't slept since I flew with you."

"Neither have we," they replied.

Wow! Maybe I really am getting to be an old timer. My uniform looks faded already, my white-toed boots don't look military anymore (supposed to be polished black, but they're not off my feet long enough to polish), and I talk with a potty mouth. I don't have time to do anything but fly, including no time to sleep.

"We drew a good one today," they told me. "We're going to be moving some rocks around the AO."

"Rocks! What? Someone talk to me. We fly, right, not lift heavy things?"

Those three assholes started laughing. I should have kept my mouth shut.

"Well guys, looks like I'm still new, because I don' have a clue what you assholes are talking about."

Still laughing, the three of them climbed in. "I'm going up to HQ," I grumbled, "and see if there's a better crew to fly with."

Now, they were laughing so hard they had tears in their eyes. Bob asked Phil if he could wait just a minute. "I've got to pee before I wet my pants."

Phil said, "I'll join you."

"I'm so happy to make you laugh in a war zone," I said.

They peed, I peed, and then we took off.

Phil said, "I can't fly when I'm laughing this much."

I looked in back and said, "I'll bet those guys can't shoot worth a shit when they're laughing." They both nodded.

I guess it was just a big tension release from that costly CA we were all trying to forget.

Chapter 21.

ROK

I had no idea where we were headed. Finally, Phil said, "Mac, I'm going to tell you what a rock stands for."

"Hey, no problem. I'm going to take a nap. You just keep flying, Phil, and talk to yourself."

I pretended I was disgusted, but actually I liked these guys.

"No Mac, I'm serious. R-O-K stands for Republic of Korea (South Korea). They are some of the most feared and ruthless fighters in this war. The VC and NVA fear them. They ask a prisoner a question only once. If the prisoner falters, the ROKs kill him and move to the next prisoner. They even look mean and nasty; I've never seen one smile. We're going to pick them up at Baldy and take them wherever they want to go.

"They work as patrols looking for the bad guys, forming their own ambushes and taking prisoners for questioning. They fight the war as it ought to be fought. Not this shit we're doing. Fight for an area, win it, then give it back and fight for it again. And each time gets more of us killed.

"By the way, don't stare at them. They think we laugh too much."

We called HQ. "Rattler 2-4 inbound, about 10 minutes out." We asked HQ to inform the ROKs we were going to refuel and then meet them at the turnaround by the Firebird Hilton. Twenty minutes later, we landed at the turnaround. The ROKs were waiting for us. They had full battle packs and no smiles. One of them, an officer with a map, came over to Phil's window and began talking, pointing to a specific spot circled in red on the map.

Phil nodded, and they all climbed in back. Eight total. We can carry more Asians than Americans, because they are smaller. I later

---

saw nine or ten in a slick.

Everyone in back was ready, so we cleared ourselves, and took off. Our destination was 25 miles straight west, past a marine artillery base and across the Song Thu Bon River. We would definitely be in tiger country (enemy territory). The flight was quick at 120 knots, 12 minutes.

We called the marine base to make sure they didn't have any fire missions. They said we were clear to go through their AO. Even an FNG knows better than fly in front of a shooting artillery battery. The marine base was on top of a pinnacle. It was safe because no one could scale that mountain.

Five minutes past the river, we began making false approaches, in case anyone was watching us. We inserted them on the fourth landing out of five total. The LZ was on a line of hills rising out of rice paddies.

They jumped out, gave thumbs up, and disappeared into the jungle. We made our final false approach and then got the hell out of there. We were instructed to fly to the marine artillery base a mile and a half on the other side of the river and land. We then sat and waited for the ROKs to call, so we could extract them with their prisoners. We heard they were fast and efficient. It just depended on how long it took them to make contact.

I locked my shoulder harness to hold me in my seat and promptly fell asleep for at least an hour. When my eyelids lifted, I saw the rest of the crew also asleep.

After we all woke up, the marines approached us and asked if they could take pictures of each other sitting in the pilot's seat and in back in the door gunner's seat. We were happy to accommodate. It was nothing serious; these pictures would be sent home to girlfriends. A little harmless pictorial bragging. I put my helmet on several of them. Todd and Ed showed them how to hold the machine gun downward as if shooting.

At the four-hour mark, the ROKs called and gave us their coordinates. They asked us to hurry as they were evading a company of NVA (200 men). We were off in two minutes, racing to the pickup point. Phil had me take off and never said a word. I saw their green smoke when we were a half mile out.

They moved into a small clearing, and I practically landed on top of them. They climbed in with two prisoners, one an officer. The Huey can handle the weight; it was just crowded back there. As I was adding power to take off, the bad guys caught up with the patrol and started shooting.

Our door gunners immediately returned fire. To their credit, half the ROKs leaned out and returned fire. I then pointed the nose toward Baldy and put some distance between us. As I did this, Bob told us over the IC (intercom) in an excited voice that Ed had been shot in the leg. Both Phil and I looked back so fast that I had to remember to fly. Bob was tying a tourniquet to stop the blood flow. The ROK medic was also helping with a compression bandage. I couldn't tell how bad it was as he was surrounded by all the ROKs in that small space. I wanted to compare it to some of the wounded I had flown to the MASH unit, but I couldn't see his leg. I saw the ROK talking to Bob and then give Ed a shot of morphine. This put Ed to sleep. I called the MASH unit and said we would be landing on their doorstep in about 15 minutes with a wounded crew member.

As I finished that, the ROK's highest ranking person in back spoke to Phil and said there were probably several hundred NVA back there. He requested a napalm strike, and we were happy to oblige.

I called HQ and requested transportation for the ROKs to meet us at the MASH unit instead of the turnaround. They rogered.

In back, I could hear the ROKs yelling at the prisoners. They were hitting the prisoners in the face. They had sand bags over their heads, so they couldn't see the punches coming. Phil was right; they didn't waste time.

Suddenly, they pulled the bag off the officer's head, grabbed the other prisoner and threw him out the door. At least, they threw him out on the correct side. The tail rotor is on the other side.

I keyed my intercom switch and told Phil what they had just done. He looked at me and put his index finger to his lips in the 'be quiet' sign.

Needless to say, the remaining prisoner was speaking as fast as his lips would allow. I wished I could understand what he was saying.

We arrived at Baldy 15 minutes after picking up the ROKs. When we landed at the MASH unit, they took Ed inside immediately. He was unconscious, and it wasn't clear how bad off he was.

The MP's met us with a truck, and all our passengers climbed on board. As they departed, I yelled "thanks" to the ROK medic for helping with Ed. He nodded and surprised me with a smile. That was the last we saw of them.

Phil said, "I told you they are mean and nasty. They don't waste time with pleasantries. Let's go get some fuel for all of us, the ship and the crew."

After eating, we flew to Chu Lai to pick up a new door gunner, Ralph Fredrickson from Iowa. We then spent the rest of the day resupplying FSBs and repeating some of our other previous missions as well. When we landed our last time that day at Baldy, we were informed that Ed Cannon had died. They said the bullet had hit the large femoral artery in his thigh, and he had bled to death. Just stupid dumb fucking bad luck. It reinforced my theory. It was a crap shoot as to whether or not you survived. Sometimes being good is not enough.

It was a quiet ride back to Chu Lai, then another memorial service which I did not attend. Nothing changes here.

I spent the next nine days essentially doing the same type of missions, including a CA with just moderate resistance.

I received a letter from my two brothers telling me that women were burning their bras outside the building where the Miss America pageant was being held. I reread that sentence twice. Wow, I wondered what that was all about. Does this mean women won't wear them anymore? That sounded OK with me. My brothers told me they took my Mustang to the drag races and included a picture with large slicks (racing tires) on the back. Oh well, what the hell? It wasn't very smart buying that car while in flight school because I knew where I was going the minute I graduated. *Enjoy it guys.*

Chapter 22.

NEW MISSIONS WITH THE OLD

had picked up eight additional holes in that span of days. I think I must have become the most welcome guest to the O club. I put money in the bowl but still couldn't drink in the bar. Not counting the carrier qualifications, I'd had only the one drink in the hooch after the Million-Dollar Hill fiasco. I was still waiting for my second day off.

Then, I discovered another type of mission the helos provided. We resupplied troops in a village. I was told that our troops go through the villages looking for contraband and evidence of stored food and ammo for the enemy.

When we landed near the first village, the gunners pointed their machine guns at the children who tried to walk up close to the ship and yelled at them to "go away."

I asked Phil, "What's that all about?"

"The kids have been known to toss a hand grenade in the chin bubble. You have just a few seconds looking at that grenade down below your feet before it blows up and kills you. Our gunners have orders to shoot any of them who come too close. It sounds harsh, but so is dying."

I just nodded. *No one mentioned this in flight school. I will pass that one on to the new guys.*

The next day I flew with Phil again. We returned to Chui Lai early, and for lack of anything to do, we picked on Ralph Fredrickson. We kidded him and asked which country Iowa was in. He ignored us.

We performed all the post flight rituals and returned to the company area. I was surprised when Phil told us, "Go take a nap.

We have a firefly tonight."

I said to myself, *Don't ask. You'll find out before the night ends.*

Then, Phil said, "Mac, after you clean up, come over to my hooch, and I'll explain tonight's mission."

I nodded, and said, "Sure."

I finally remembered to pick up a flashlight at the supply hooch. It's a lot easier to find bullet holes in the dark with a flashlight. However, I soon learned that flashlights are just metal tubes for storing dead batteries.

Twenty minutes later, I knocked on Phil's door. He had already pulled up an extra chair from one of his roomies. He pointed to the chair and then sat in his own.

"The good news first: After a firefly, you get the next day off.

"We take off about two hours after sunset. We'll have installed in back a portable rack with six landing lights mounted in a ring. One guy will run the lights and the other a machine gun. Both will be on your side of the ship, and you will run the mission. You will fly north to Baldy and then position yourself on the left side of the Song Ly (river) 200 yards from the river and at 200 feet altitude. Whoever's in charge of the light will shine it on the river, and we destroy anything they find. The crew can shoot, and also there'll be a Firebird team behind us and a few hundred feet above us. They will be shooting with all their weapons. We trade off. Sometimes, we get the first shot. The birds will also switch off with ships and who gets to shoot first: gunners, crew chiefs, pilots or copilots.

"We do this because no one is supposed to be on the river after dark. If we find any sampans, we consider them to be hauling food, ammunition, or troops to our enemies.

"We will follow the river south on the east side of Baldy for several miles where a tributary dumps into the river. We follow the tributary to its end. Then, go back to the river on the other side of the tributary. Then, we turn south at the river and follow it to Hawk Hill. We turn around, and go north back to Baldy on the other side. Then, we look for any tributaries not on the map and continue the firefly as long as we have fuel and ammo. And then we go home and have some drinks. I'll have a buddy put some booze in my hooch." In a louder voice he added for emphasis, "And then we get to sleep in."

He stood, so I stood, too.

"Now, get some sleep. We'll eat late. We go to the flight line at 2000 (twenty hundred) hours. We meet the birds at Baldy a little after 2130."

We had moonlight that night which made it much easier to find the starting point. As we neared, Phil just sat there, not saying a word.

I called the bird's fire team leader, 9-3, Dennis Boyle, when we were ten minutes out. (He had been promoted from wingman.) I arrived at the starting point when 9-3 called and said, "I am over the river and 300 feet above."

I said back, "I am breaking off to the left bank. When you are set 9-3, let me know and we'll light up this river."

In just a few seconds, he called, "All set."

The light came on, and immediately two boats appeared directly in the beam. In another instant, two rockets struck those boats. Water and debris lifted fifty feet in the air.

Wow, that happened in a heartbeat.

We continued for 15 minutes and destroyed another 17 sampans. Then, a stream of tracers came up from the river's edge and several passed through my windshield. Two holes appeared in the bottom of the Plexiglas between my feet, and two holes at eye level, where they exited. Over the radio came a quick, "Firefly break right."

I broke and heard the explosions behind me. Everybody was aiming at the hooches below where the shots had come from. Both my gunners were shooting (one of them had turned off the light and picked up his machine gun) and the Firebirds were firing rockets. As all of that action was taking place, I put distance between us and the enemy.

Then, 9-3 called and said, "Ready to resume." It was easy to find my continuation point since there was one hell of a serious conflagration from the burning hooches.

The Firebirds switched positions so the wing ship could get some practice. Then, it was door gunners only. When the copilots got their chance, the Gatling guns stitched sampans and the 40 millimeter cannon blew them to hell. One sampan was hit, which caused a tremendous secondary explosion that rose a hundred feet. We saw it, heard it, and then were buffeted by it. Our gunners said the Firebirds broke right around the blast. No one wanted to fly through that debris field and those flames.

An explosion of that magnitude has a life of its own. As it expands upward and outward, it consumes oxygen and grows like rolling boiling water. Impressive, if you're not part of it.

I got back on course, and we continued to eliminate enemy sampans full of contraband.

It was amazing how quickly the gunners walked their tracers into those small boats. It was also amazing how quickly the Vietnamese jumped into the river when the firefly light found their sampan. Some of those bastards shot at us while in the water. That wasn't very smart as our door gunners quickly targeted their four-foot muzzle flashes.

We ended the night with 40 dead sampans, two more secondary's, and four holes in the ship. Those secondary explosions were spectacular at night. Messes up your night vision for a while, but you recover.

I was pissed at the new holes in the ship. *That totals 26 hits in 23 days. I see a pattern here.*

We were all running low on fuel, ammo, and energy when the ACs decided to call it a night. We returned to Chui Lai and the Firebirds to their nest at Baldy. Nest was a much more appropriate term than Hilton to describe that small shack. I was surprised the Hilton family didn't sue someone: the army, the 71st or the Firebirds. It certainly wasn't a positive advertisement for the Hotel. I'd never been in a Hilton, but I knew they had to be way better than this shit hole.

We were shot at twice on our return trip home. No big deal, they missed. The door gunners loved it because they loved shooting. We landed, refueled, completed a post flight and reported the holes to maintenance. The flashlight helped me find the holes. Maintenance worked 24 hours a day in a war zone. They just nodded when I pointed out the holes. Those sheet metal guys asked me how I found those holes. I showed them my flashlight. They nodded. They have large lights mounted on trucks for their night work and don't have to use the small toys like we do.

True to his word, Phil had some beers and crown royal waiting under his bunk. We had a couple of quick ones. We debriefed (talked about the mission), discussed tactics, any changes I should have made. We didn't do anything else; just went to sleep. It would be years before I caught up on my sleep!

I didn't hear the bad news until the next morning when I hauled my fatigued ass into the mess hall. Posted on the door was a notice that Bob Smith, the crew chief from Indiana, who I had flown with several times, had been killed the day before during a resupply mission. A single bullet struck him in the heart as they approached a FSB. A memorial service was scheduled for that evening at 1800 hours in the mess hall. It would be followed by a John Wayne movie shown on the plywood screen out on the beach.

It just occurred to me that Phil's regular crew members were both dead. I wondered what he was thinking? I returned to my hooch and tried to lose myself with my friend, Harold Robbins. I liked Bob. And these memorials were becoming all too frequent.

This shit is getting very real.

Harold Robbins was not working for me right then.

A hooch maid was sweeping out the hooch when I returned from morning mess. I said, "Hi," and she said, "Hi," back in very broken English. She smiled and kept working. I sat on my bed and wrote a long letter home.

I told Mom and Dad all about the volleyball court, the theater, the O club, the beach, and the water. I had pictures of everything. We could get pictures developed in 2-3 days. The company clerk had the film flown to Danang, developed, and returned to us. My parents were probably catching onto my bullshit. How many times can you read about paradise and then get a body count from the news media? After I wrote everything, a lot of lies to convince my parents all was well, I put twenty pictures in that envelope to give my story some credibility.

With all my domestic work completed, I decided to try the beach. I guess everyone else felt the same, and they were setting up their chairs on the sand. With chair in hand, I ventured from the water's edge to the theater, twenty feet inland and pushed the chair legs firmly into the sand with the chair back tilted to the perfect angle for viewing.

My name was on the chair. (There were four crossed out names of pilots before me.) Everyone respected the ownership and did not take your chair.

Then, I went to the bar for two quick shots of Crown Royal. With three beers in hand, I returned to my chair.

The movies were always John Wayne or heroic WWII movies. It was very relaxing to sit there and sip beers as the Crown Royal kicked in.

Naturally, as if scripted, the rockets were early that night. It was funny as hell to watch the new guys running. They didn't want to get in the bunkers with the rats, and they couldn't find their hooches. The movie continued, and they eventually returned.

After the movie, I had trouble standing up. I eventually found my hooch and passed out after setting the alarm for 0700. *Thank you Army.*

The next morning I went to the shelf at the other end of the hooch which was filled with used books and very used playboys. These helped us tolerate the humidity. Included with the books were several issues of "Stars and Stripes." This was a newspaper for troops overseas. It told us how well we were doing. We appeared to be winning. We had very high body counts, enemy KIA's (fighters killed in action).

Today was my twenty-fourth day as an FNG; six days until I was a copilot. I had continued talking to Firebirds every chance I got. They appeared to always have openings. I tried not to dwell on why.

The day was long. It felt like I had been flying Hueys for years. Actually, it had been only 22 days of the past 24. I was told by some old timers, who had gone through flight school after years in the enlisted ranks, "War gives you ten years of experience in twelve months." I could believe it.

I had discovered that becoming complacent with these long days could be dangerous. I had to remain in a constant state of readiness, what's called "situational awareness." Readiness is being able to react. Situational awareness is knowing where you are, what's around you, what could possibly happen next, and what you will do if it happens. Where to go if your engine quits. What to do if you are shot at. What to do if one of the crew is hit.

The 0700 wake-up time was a reward for good flying. I was told this at 0730 in the mess hall. I was glad no one had seen me falling-down drunk trying to find my hooch in the night.

Chapter 23.

DOUGHNUT DOLLIES

Sometimes, we shuttled Doughnut Dollies around to the various FSBs. Of everything I did in VN, I believe that this assignment was the strangest. And the most fun.

Doughnut Dollies were young ladies who worked through the Red Cross. They traveled to various bases and visited the troops, passed out doughnuts, performed skits, and played games (cards, monopoly, and charades). This was very brave of them and a very positive contribution to morale. In the normal routine of war, our young horny troops wouldn't get close to a woman for months.

The Dollies were very nice ladies, especially to us pilots. Someone had told them flying a helicopter in VN was dangerous, and that pumped us up in their opinion. The ladies sure were something to look at, and they smelled better than us, too. It was embarrassing being around them all day, when they looked so nice and we were so dirty and battle worn. I didn't realize how we looked until, seeing them, I noticed the way we looked in our faded and wrinkled fatigues, grimy faces and unwashed hair.

We were given their destinations for the day, beginning with our maintenance crew. WOW, were the guys ever surprised. And delighted. And forget about work while the dollies were there. That took care of an hour and a half. Then, the ladies said goodbye and climbed in the helo.

Glen Walton was our pilot. We started the blades turning and couldn't help noticing the difficulty the girls had holding their pretty baby-blue dresses down as the swirling air was blowing them up. Despite that technical difficulty, they loved flying, and we loved carting them around. I know the crew chief and door gunner had no complaints. They had to help the Dollies with their seat belts. Six seats across the back of the cargo area and a seat on each side of the crew. Those lucky bastards were sitting next to females.

We asked them how long they had been in country. The answers varied from two to eight months

We had some small talk with the Dollies after we landed and again just before we started the engine to travel to their next stop. Not much real communication. Their favorite question to us was, "What state are you from?" It was boring doing taxi service. However, it was exceptionally nice to see some American women. I was happy to tolerate boredom just to see them and smell their perfume.

One of them asked me, "How long have you been here?"

I meekly replied, "Less than a month." I followed with, "You all have me beat."

One of the guys in back just couldn't help himself. "Mr. McNally is an FNG."

A Dolly immediately asked, "What's that?"

Steve Atchison, the crew chief, asked the pilot in a formal manner, "Mr. Walton, should I tell them?"

"Of course you should. You started this. Now you have to finish it."

Steve moved from his seat and faced the seated Dollies in front of him and the other two were twisting their necks to see forward from their seats on the sides. Steve had their attention and was milking it for everything he could get.

"Mr. McNally is an FNG, a Fucking New Guy!"

I thought the Dollies were going to hurt themselves laughing. They were laughing to the point of crying and screaming. This seemed to allow them to let go of some of their own stress, built up by working in a war zone. When the laughter let up, I quickly said, "It's only for four more days." That set off a new round of laughing that was intermingled with the screaming and crying.

Glen said, "Strap them in tight. Mr. McNally is now going to demonstrate low level flying, and the crew will demonstrate the M-60 machine gun."

I asked them if that was OK. The leader in the group conferred and yelled back to me, "Hell yes."

I pulled it up and nosed it over. I couldn't believe I was being paid to do this. The way to the next stop was over a secured area, so we didn't have to worry about being shot at. I was on the deck going around trees, occasionally dragging the skids through the top of the next tree. They loved it. I laid the ship over on the right and then the left. I hoped I wasn't going to get my ass in trouble over any of this.

I then turned and yelled to them, "The machine gun show is about to begin. Don't be startled. Cover your ears if you want to. It's going to be LOUD. OK, Steve, show them how you earn your pay."

Steve fired fifty rounds. Then, he stopped and explained how the gun functioned and why there were tracers.

Glen said, "Give 'em hell Todd."

And so Todd took his turn. He walked his tracers into many trees, and he gave the Dollies a running narrative as he was shooting. He, too, stopped after about fifty rounds.

Steve called on the IC and said he had just gotten a strange request. I turned and looked at him, trying to figure out what he was talking about. He said, "Mr. Walton, the lady sitting next to me has asked if she could shoot my machine gun." I looked over at Glen and waited for his response.

He said, "Ask Mac. He's in charge today."

I said, "Go ahead. Just keep it safe."

I know I was smiling as I watched her shoot.

When she stopped, Todd said he had a request to shoot from another Dolly. All Glen said was, "Go for it."

This Dolly lit up the countryside and was walking tracers into trees. She was a bit slow to get on target, but what the hell? It was her first time, and I was impressed.

When we landed at a FSB five minutes later, I asked them to keep the low leveling and the shooting our secret. After conferring with Glen, I asked the group if another two of them wanted to shoot. "If you do," I told them, "strap in by the machine guns when we load up your equipment." They talked this over for a moment and then walked over to a group of waiting GIs. As the dollies departed, the FSB commander gave me a thumbs up.

At the next stop, we asked the guy in charge of armaments if we could borrow some machine-gun ammo. I promised him it would be returned the next day.

Hell, he was so mesmerized by the Dollies that he didn't even look at me. He just nodded and told another guy, "Get them two cases of seven point six two (the caliber)."

This was fun. The guys in back said, "Thank you," for the ammo and started reloading.

We continued this pattern the rest of the day. I think the Dollies were ready to either wed us or bed us. I felt they needed that break in their routine. I certainly needed it. The girls each had two turns at the guns. One even asked if she could join the 71st. I was in favor but didn't say it. I just laughed with the group.

We landed at Chu Lai, our starting point that morning. We got hugs at the end of the day. Actual physical contact.

One of them gave me a kiss on the cheek and whispered "We are going to figure out how we can meet again, Kevin, in a room with a bed."

I was stunned and murmured, "OK," while she was grinding her pelvis against me. I looked at her name tag and said, "I would love that, Stephanie."

I hoped no one else heard. As she backed away, our eyes met and held. It was just a moment, but something happened in that moment. I felt nervous and had butterflies in my stomach. I couldn't believe it.

We had been crawling all over the ship doing maintenance and double checking everything at each stop, being extra careful due to our cargo. I would have bet that kiss on my cheek had been salty with dirt mixed into my sweat. I'm not sure I could have hugged one of them if they looked or smelled like me. But Stephanie didn't seem to mind.

As they were walking over to the trucks for their ride home (trailer houses three miles up the road at our Division command), the leader of the group said to me, "That was great flying and thank you so much. No one has ever done that for us before. If you're just an FNG, I can't even imagine how GOOD YOU ARE GOING TO BE."

Glen gave a big smile and said, "Imagine how good he'll become under MY tutelage." We all laughed.

Then came another reward. They hugged all four of us again.

Stephanie winked at me and mouthed, "I'll call," as she squeezed my butt.

I really hated to see them go. "I'll call" was the best news I'd received since being assigned to hell.

Chapter 24.

MY LAST DAYS AS AN FNG

We did the post-flight routine and then went home. I grabbed some mail, then off to the showers. *If I make it through this mess, I will never take a shower for granted. I promise.* I got a letter from home. It read like they had nothing to say. *I will ask direct questions in the future.*

I was just thinking about the club when there was a knock at my door. "Come in."

It was Major Wilson's clerk. He said, "The major wants to see you immediately, sir."

"OK." I followed him to headquarters.

I stepped up to Top's desk and said, "Top, Mr. McNally reporting to the CO as ordered."

"Mr. McNally, follow me please. The Major said to bring you in as soon as you arrived."

As we entered, the Major said, "Top, would please close the door and then sit down and listen to the latest escapades of Mac. Apparently, all the Doughnut Dollies are asking to be escorted around our AO by the 71st and even more specifically by a cute guy named McNally."

I felt my face burning and my knees go shaky. I heard Top trying not to laugh. I heard him say *cute* a couple of times. The Major was not doing a very good job of holding back his laugh.

Major Wilson said, "Top, I'm going to have Mr. McNally tell you this in his own words. One of the Dollies was telling an incredible story in the Division's Officers' Club. It seems she doesn't hold her liquor very well. She has only been here two months. I'm sure time will take care of that little problem. Mac, please start at the beginning and don't leave anything out."

Top looked at me, and then the CO, and then his eyes fixed back on me.

What could I do? I told the story. I left nothing out. I didn't defend myself. I occasionally heard a snicker. I saw eyebrows raised more than once. I finished with how good they smelled and how bad I smelled.

Now they were both laughing out loud. The Major asked Top if he knew the penalty for what I did today.

Top spoke up without a moment's pause, "Sir, was that singular penalty or plural?"

"McNally, did you think that through? Speak candidly."

"We were in a friendly area," I replied. "They were strapped in, so I figured, *Why not?* It will give them a story to tell their husbands and kids. To be honest, I almost did a high overhead, but then I remembered my first one, how I almost puked. The machine guns were mounted, and I knew the crew was sitting very close. I watched a couple of them shoot, and you could see their eyes when they realized the power they held. They didn't have that look when they were playing charades."

"I didn't call Mr. Walton in here because he's a seasoned pilot, and he would never do anything like what you did today. I can only surmise that Mr. Walton must have fallen asleep, and then you took over. You can go now, Mac. I have to talk to Top about this."

"Thank you, Sir. Sir, could I ask you a favor. I know it's not a good time."

The CO looked stunned and said, " You are correct about the bad timing. Tell me what you want!"

"When the Dollies were at LZ Ross, I borrowed two cases ammo for our M-60s. I promised the man in charge I would get it back to him as fast as I could. Maybe a little extra as a thank you."

"Go take a shower. I will talk to the pilot taking supplies there and give him your request. I'm sure this will get you a heavy fine in the club. I'm not sure what to call it. I don't want any of these other hot shots trying it."

As I turned to leave, the CO said, "Mac, did you really get a hug from each dolly?"

"Yes sir. We also got a second round of hugs."

"Be candid, Mac, about those hugs. I heard two of them gave you long grinding hugs."

"It surprised me," I admitted, "especially when one stuck her tongue in my ear. I was glad she didn't grab the front of my pants like she grabbed my butt. I was ready."

Now the CO and Top were howling. They mumbled something that sounded like, "Dismissed."

When I got outside, I was relieved to see that the MPs weren't waiting for me.

I had only a few days remaining in the Rattlers. It was all routine stuff. I did several more high overheads. I repeated several prior missions; with some, there was a new twist. I was flying with Pete Nixon when we received a frantic call around 1300 from Center, which we had just departed. We had brought in supplies but had no cargo going out. They wanted us to return ASAP. One of our ships had just crashed while landing at Center. The slick struck the ground very hard, and the blade flexed downward and cut off the tail so the ship began spinning wildly and out of control as there was no tail rotor (anti torque blade). Somehow, a piece of the main rotor blade struck a GI standing close by and cut him into three pieces. The blade struck him at the belt line. That atomized 18 inches of his body, 9 inches above the belt and 9 below.

As we landed close by, we saw the destroyed Huey. There were pieces scattered out 50 yards. Luckily, it did not burn or explode. I could see the GI on the ground moving his head back and forth, while a medic was trying to stop the bleeding. The troops lifted his torso into the back of our ship, using a rain poncho. The medic climbed in with him. Blood was spraying everywhere. The poor guy was still rolling his head. Two guys walked up and placed the remaining pieces of his mutilated legs in back. A very indelible image was set in my brain to remain forever!

He died a moment later. We took the body to Baldy and turned him over to the MASH unit. They said they would haul him to Chu Lai and give him to graves registration. That must be the worst job in this country. *Even worse than burning shit.* We filled the old fire extinguisher with water and washed out the blood.

The pilot from the crash was shipped out the next day. No one ever found out what happened to him.

The next day was unusual because I had not flown this type of mission before, or even heard of it. We hauled HOT food to the troops in the bush. The hot foods were in marmite cans, metal insulated boxes. They were filled with mashed potatoes, gravy, roast beef and cooked carrots. It was tempting to highjack some of those delicacies, but we didn't because we knew those guys had very few moments like this. They had smiles on their faces when we landed. That was a feel-good moment for them and for me.

One of the units we delivered the hot food to was quite unique. The patrol had cut down trees (up to 4-5 inches in diameter) on the side and top of a steep mountain. They were monitoring enemy movements and calling in air strikes, artillery barrages, or grab-and-run missions by the ROKs. My only option was to hover slowly, move sideways into the small opening over a large rock that jutted out over a cliff, and put my skid on it while we unloaded. I had called them and asked if they had removed the cut trees so they wouldn't fly up into my rotor blades. They said, "Yes," and in I went. It was fun holding the ship on that rock. I didn't look inside at the instruments. I just looked out my window and down at the rock. On the other side, it was 2000 feet to the ground.

When I got the all clear from my crew, I yelled to the guys outside, "We were up all night cooking this shit." They were able to laugh in spite of their surroundings. I slowly lifted up two feet and moved away sideways from the patrol.

Their 6 called and said, "Thanks. Hot food, unbelievable! We've been out here five days and just ran out of C-rats. We get picked up tomorrow. Hey, I didn't know a helicopter could do what you just did."

"Neither did I."

The pilot took over the controls and yelled, "That was my copilot. Is he ready for the promotion to pilot?"

Mountain 6 said, "Hell yes, I hope he's the one to pick us up tomorrow."

The mission was going smoothly until I saw Million-Dollar Hill not too far in the distance.

Shit, I will never forget that sight, and how close I came to dying.

We returned to CL after that delivery service, did the usual to the ship, and returned to the company area.

I was informed that evening to report to the CO at 0730 in the morning. I wondered what the hell was happening. *Did I fuck up today?* I thought it went pretty well. *Maybe it was the Doughnut*

Dollies. I don't know. Shit.

I was up at 0600 getting my last clean uniform out of my locker. *Where are the hooch maids with my laundry?* I gave my boots a spit shine like they hadn't seen since flight school. I shined my brass belt buckle and was ready for whatever.

I was on the CO's front porch 10 minutes early, so I walked away from the door and waited. Thirty seconds later, Top came out and walked up to me. He must have seen me come up the steps. I didn't know what to do. I think I was standing at attention.

He said, "Relax **Mr.** McNally and follow me."

I walked in and stood in front of his desk as he sat down. I said, "Top, Mr. McNally reporting as ordered."

He said, "Stand at ease." He turned and walked into the CO's office, then came out and said, "The Major will see you."

I said, "Thank you, Top" and walked in. I stood at attention and said, "Mr. McNally reporting as ordered, sir."

He said, "At ease, McNally." I did. He asked if it would be OK with me if we flew together today.

I said, "Sir, I'm a little confused here."

"Since it's your last day as an FNG, I will be your pilot today."

I said, "That's great sir. If I may say, your flying history is legendary."

"Legendary where? In the club?"

I didn't answer. I'm not very good at sucking up

"Let's get down to the flight line. Those grunts on the side of that mountain are expecting us."

We had Phil's new crew consisting of crew chief Arny Fox (Jim Williams' crew chief) and Ralph, the new door gunner. The ship was ready. The CO introduced himself. Arny cornered me when I was on the other side of the ship and whispered, "What's going on?" I looked at him and turned my palms up as I shrugged my shoulders.

It was 0800 as we took off north. Forty-five minutes later we were nearing the mountain patrol south of Million-Dollar Hill.

Damn, I can't get the thought of that mission out of my head, and now I will be close enough to see it again in less than 24 hours.

So far, the CO had not touched the controls, so I called Mountain 6 when I was three minutes out.

Mountain 6 said, "Hurry if you can. We are tired of pretending to be mountain goats."

I understood and said, "How in the hell did you get up there?"

"We climbed!"

"I'm impressed. Seen any bad guys today?"

He replied, "No."

I could see the small area they had cleared for me the day before. I glanced over at the CO, and he looked a little tense. Probably because he was about to hover alongside a cliff less than half the size of our ship and pick up the grunts we fed the previous day.

He finally spoke. "Is that the rock you balanced the skid on yesterday?"

I replied, "Yes sir. That opening is only large enough for half our rotor blades."

He said with slight hesitation, "I can see that."

As I hovered closer, I could count seven grunts, all with big smiles on their faces and a few carrying the Marmite cans. As I reached the rock, I asked mountain 6, "Are you seven and the cans all the cargo?"

He rogered, so I sat the skid on the rock and said, "All aboard."

The area was so confined they could only climb in one at a time. As soon as number three climbed in, a machine gun located 50 yards down the hill opened up on us. They put three bullets in my windshield. Fortunately, all three passed over my helmet. The remaining grunts immediately returned fire and simultaneously waved me off. "Go, go, get out of here."

My crew chief, sitting behind the CO, opened up with his M-60 machine gun and was doing a good job of keeping the bad guys at bay. (He will be immortalized someday.) The sweat was running into my eyes. I had to tell myself to relax and take my death grip off the cyclic.

I yelled without the radio or intercom, "Everyone climb in. I'm not leaving anyone here to take up residence in the Hanoi Hilton (the NVA prison)."

The door gunner put down his gun and helped the last four grunts into the ship.

Shit, we just may get out of this mess alive.

I called to the Major. "How are my instruments? Keep your hands on the controls in case I get hit. There won't be much time to grab them."

The enemy machine gun was firing intermittently, or maybe it was another one. I yelled at everyone in back, "Shoot at that gun!"

The bad guys were only occasionally getting off an AK shot. A few were hitting the ship. No major damage yet as the warning lights were not flashing. I felt something hit my right forearm. As mountain 6 climbed in, I yelled "Everyone shoot out the right side at those bastards. It's their only way to escape."

As the guys in back shifted around to shoot, my door gunner started shooting. He couldn't before because the grunts were climbing inside in front of his gun barrel. Simultaneously, I was hovering sideways left to make sure I had blade clearance, and then I turned and dove off that mountain. I was crosschecking instruments and hearing that wonderful sound behind me of numerous weapons tearing loose on the bad guys. There were two machine guns, several M-16s, an M-79 grenade launcher, and I think I heard a 45 cal. pistol.

It was so fucking loud my head was pounding. *I can't believe some of the shit that goes on here. I guess it's all new in your first war. Should I put this in my manual?*

As we flew out of range, I pointed the ship toward Baldy, about 85 degrees on the compass, and asked the CO, "Would you like to fly to Baldy, sir."

He looked startled at my request but nodded. "Sure." He grabbed the controls as I let go. I think he was holding his breath.

I lifted up my clear faceplate to wipe off my forehead. The sweat was burning my eyes, and I could hardly see. I turned and yelled to everyone in back, "Nice fuckin' shooting. Those guys were afraid to look out from behind their trees." I got nods and smiles.

With that said, 6 climbed over a few of his guys to get about six inches from my face. He was teary eyed as he grabbed my shoulder and said, "Thank you so much for not leaving me and half my patrol on that fucking mountain."

I didn't know how to respond. Finally, I said, "LT (I saw the 2nd lieutenant bars on his collar), I wouldn't want you to leave me there."

At Baldy, 15 minutes later, the patrol climbed out and into a truck and off to a debriefing. I called Baldy and said we needed some gas. They said to call when we were finished. As we fueled up, the CO got out to pee. When he returned, I did the same. I asked my pilot, the CO, "Would you like to fly around Baldy to the turnaround, sir?"

He said, "No, you take it."

As I was about to shut it down, I received an urgent call from HQ. "We are scrambling the Firebirds. Rattler 2-9 just called mayday. He went down five clicks straight west. He's landed in a dry rice paddy and is waiting behind a dike for help."

I told the CO to take it, and I ran to the Firebirds. "What's the frequency? We're the rescue ship." I noticed the AC was 9-3, Boyle. He smiled and said, "Let's go." I saw Tim Rivers at the controls of the wing ship.

I waived to my door gunner. When he arrived, I grabbed his left shoulder and put my other hand on his back and yelled as I pushed him toward the Conex containers. "Grab an extra case of ammo for your guns." He smiled and nodded.

It was a five-minute flight to rattler 2-9, when it struck me that 2-9 was Glen Walton. I monitored the radio calls between 9-3, his wingman, and me. Rattler 2-9 was off the air. Boyle was telling his wingman and me to come in a little north. We could see their smoke grenade and the crew behind a dry rice paddy dike in a bomb crater. My guys were unloading the extra ammo and making it ready to reload in the pouches mounted to their guns. The NVA had been shooting at the downed Huey, and now it was smoking intensely. It would begin burning any time.

The birds made two passes and not much remained standing. That included trees, brush, and some bad guys crawling along the dike on the other side. As the birds were rolling in on their third pass, I blurted out on the radio for them to keep shooting. "I'm going in to pick these guys up."

I couldn't wait for troops to get there, and the Firebirds would soon be low on ammo and fuel. We didn't know how many NVA were hidden in the area. There were several fires burning from the Bird's rockets, and I thought the smoke would give me some cover. I could see a few NVA crawling along the other side of the dike towards the downed crew, 75 yards away.

Before I got a response, I started in. I asked my crew how much ammo they had remaining. Bob said only about a hundred and fifty, and Ralph said the same. I said, "Shoot at anything that shoots at you. Reload from the extra ammo, and then blow the shit out of those fucks. Just hold the trigger down. If you run low, take the pouch off and feed the ammo into your gun with the other hand like the Firebirds do."

They responded, "Yes sir, and thank you."

On the way in, I remembered the CO. I looked over and said, "Sir, are you OK?" He nodded. I flared and stood the ship on it tail and held it there longer than usual as I had come in too fast, and sat it down between the smoking ship and its crew. Now a few tracers went streaking by our ship. It looked like time was short, so I looked across to the CO and said, "You've got it."

As he grabbed the controls, I unhooked the cable to my helmet, opened my door, jumped out, and ran to the downed crew. I was now the bad guy's target of choice as bullets were hitting the dirt all around me. I wondered how in hell they could miss me with a machine gun, especially with the number of rounds they were shooting at me. I jumped up on top of the two foot dike and slid down the other side. I was now in the bomb crater with its other four occupants. I indicated the mound of dirt above us and said, "Jump down the other side—it's only two feet high—and run like hell, shooting all the way to my ship. There are NVA crawling along the dike on the right. Shoot at them if they're still there. Stay away from your ship; it's starting to burn."

The three of them took off. Glen didn't follow. He was bleeding from his left leg. I pulled a cord out of my chicken board pouch and tied off a quick tourniquet. I asked him how he felt.

He said, "Pissed."

I said, "You're OK. Let's go."

Glen was smaller than me, so I pushed him out of the bomb crater to the top of the dike. I climbed up behind him, and then we both slid down the other side.

The crew was waiting for Glen and me at the top of the dike— what great guys—and were shooting at the enemy along the dike. The Firebirds were keeping them at bay. Without thinking, I threw Glen over my shoulder and told his crew, "Shoot as you run for the ship."

The three of them gave us great covering fire. Glen yelled in my ear, "What the hell are you doing?"

I yelled back, "You walk too fuckin' slow."

I know this sounds strange, but time seemed to slow down. The bullets were spraying dirt up in my face, but I was able to avoid them. I know that's bullshit, but that's how it seemed at the time. I suppose the truth is I was lucky, or they were lousy shots. Probably both!

I could smell Glen's ship burning. I could smell the exploded powder from the crew's shooting. I just kept running, and the NVA kept missing me. Or if I was hit, the adrenalin was masking the pain. It seemed a lot more open out here than when I flew in. *I hope they don't hit Glen.*

I got to the ship and handed Glen to the two guys in back who had been giving cover fire along with the birds. After Glen was in place on the floor, I jumped in, strapped in, and yelled, "TO sir," as I plugged in my helmet. "TO back out the way I flew in."

Then, I called the birds to thank them for the great cover fire. "Those little shits never got a bullet close to me." My crew was firing behind us all the way out.

Suddenly, a bullet came through the door and hit my cyclic just below the pistol grip. The ship jerked left as I glanced at the cyclic to see if it was still attached. It was OK. The bullet had hit the side of the round tube where the grip is attached and not through the center of the tube. The gunners pulled their guns off their mounts and handheld them on near constant fire. *Damn those two would make great Firebirds.* The CO had us ten feet off the ground and was flying around trees and making us a very difficult target.

9-3 said, "Good! Now let's get out of here. We are low on everything (fuel and ammo)."

We pointed our nose toward Baldy and were getting ahead of the birds. We were still no more than ten feet off the ground. I called the birds and said, "Rattler 2-9 has a hole in his leg, so we're going to drop him off at MASH."

I told the CO, "Your flying is incredible."

He smiled and said, "Thanks."

He took us to Baldy. I asked him if he had ever flown into the MASH unit.

He said, "No."

I said, "I'll talk you in, sir."

He seemed to think that was funny. I called in to HQ at Baldy to tell them what we were going to do.

"Hey Arny," I said, "Is everyone OK back there? It's awfully quiet."

He said, "Yes, Mr. McNally. I think we're all in shock."

I said, "OK, but what's this Mr. McNally shit? It's Mac."

He said, "I know, but the CO is with us."

I said "Oops." I turned to the Major. "Sir, for expedience, we use nicknames."

He said, "I know, Mac. Last time in country, I was Will."

We landed at the MASH unit and as they removed Glen on a stretcher, he yelled, "Thank you, Mac and sir."

We left Glen and flew around the FSB to POL to gas up. We looked for other bullet holes at the same time we were pumping. We only found one, near the end of the tail and no damage. Those three in my windshield and the one in the door had my attention.

I climbed in, sat in my seat, and looked straight ahead at those three holes. They were lower on the windshield than I remembered. Maybe six inches lower. *That would place them at eye level. Shit, why am I alive? Maybe I moved my head more to the right to keep my eyes on the rock? Damn.*

We landed near the birds to grab some machine gun ammo. The birds were rearming as well. I went over with the CO to talk to Boyle, 9-3.

Boyle froze. Here he was with no hat or shirt. Actually, neither did the crew.

The CO said, "At ease men. We're in combat. I know the Army regulations say to keep your head covered when outdoors." With a smile, he said, "I don't have any knowledge of this un-military behavior."

Wow, more stuff for my after-flight-school manual.

They asked me about Glen. I said his pride was damaged more than his leg. This drew a laugh.

One of the crew asked me if I had any medical knowledge. I said, "Yes, I dissected a frog and a fetal pig in Biology class. Look guys, all I did was tie a piece of cord around his leg. With a little training from me, I'll bet you could do that."

Now, they really laughed. Strange what's funny in a war. It can be very dark humor. Glen's crew, Steve Atchison and Todd Burnett, were OK, just still in shock. They were realizing how close they had come to dying. Their FNG was my roomie, Bob Clearwater, the commercial pilot. If he was scared, he was doing a good job of hiding it.

I said to no one in particular, "I'm going to the MASH unit and check on Glen."

The CO fell into step with me and started talking as we walked. He asked about my family, and I asked about his. He had a girlfriend from an army family. I told him I had two younger brothers. Now we were at the MASH unit, and we walked in. We saw Glen sitting up in bed, arguing with the nurse and doctor, telling them he was fine. He added that he would like to return to flying.

When he saw me, his eyes lit up and a big smile covered his face. He called me over to his bed and said, "Thank you so much," as tears welled up in his eyes. "I had hoped you would be in the area because you're such a damn good pilot. You were there, and you carried me out of that hell hole." Now he was sobbing.

I didn't know what to say. I still didn't know how to handle a thank you.

About then, he saw the CO and tried to sit up straight in his hospital bed and wipe away his tears.

The CO said, "Relax, Mr. Walton. Nothing leaves this room."

Glen was able to say, "Thank you, sir."

I asked the medic to look at my forearm. He pulled out a piece of metal. It was only an inch long and the diameter of three tooth picks. He put some ointment on and wrapped it as a nurse told me to pull my pants down, then attacked me with a syringe full of syrup. That was more painful than the wound. I can't tell that to the Birds. These medical people are sneakier than the NVA.

I called out to the nurses, "Make sure Glen checks in with the flight surgeon about his mental condition before he is returned to flying." I winked at the nurses, and they nodded, and we walked out. I could hear Glen yelling, "Just wait till I get out of here, Mac, you goddamned FNG." The CO and I just laughed.

I asked the CO if he wanted to fly to Chu Lai. He said, "Yes, I would. I really miss flying, but that's the price you pay if you're a career officer and move up in rank. It's mostly paperwork and very few flying hours. Paper cuts are my biggest worry."

Glen's crew climbed in back, and we cranked it up. Major Wilson and I talked all the way back to Chu Lai. He told me he liked my flying.

He said he would call HQ, and they would determine the fate of the downed Huey. "Either we'll bomb it, if it's not all burned up, or bring in a Chinook and haul it back to Chu Lai. Even if it can't be fixed, we'll place it next to the maintenance building and use it as a hanger queen (use it for spare parts) and then haul whatever remains out to Target Practice Island."

Since we landed early on my thirtieth day, around 1500, I couldn't wait to talk to the Firebirds. I was very tired of those bad guys trying to kill me, when all I could do sit in my seat. *Well, that shit ends today.*

When we entered the company area, I extended some final pleasantries to the CO. Then, I jogged to my hooch, dropped all my gear, and continued jogging to the platoon leaders' hooch, hoping to find Steve Meadows, call sign 9-6.

I knocked on his screen door, and he said, "Come in." Some days you just get lucky. He could have been flying. I walked in and re-introduced myself, and he told me he knew who I was, and that surprised me.

I asked if there were any openings in the Firebirds. He answered, "Yes." He asked me my flight status.

"I finished my FNG status 30 minutes ago."

"You got any free time right now?"

"Yes!"

"Grab your gear and meet me in front of the mess hall in 30 minutes. I've been here for five hours doing paperwork. I need a break!"

I didn't say a word. I just shot out the door and back to my hooch.

I returned in five minutes. Ten minutes later, Steve drove up in a jeep.

"Hop in."

I threw my gear in back and jumped in, trying not to look overly enthusiastic. *Look calm Kevin, this is just another learning phase.*

Chapter 25.

THE FIREBIRDS

W e drove to the flight line. The sun was beating down on the PSP, pierced steel planking, invented in WWII to build instant runways: 10-foot-long pieces of metal plate with holes cut out to make it lighter. The pieces interlocked, and you had a runway. A metal runway, and thus hot. With the humidity, it was oppressive.

The air smelled like burning shit. It was so humid, I was wet from my neck to my boots. *Fuck, how does anyone live here? I can't wait to get in the air.*

We stopped at maintenance and asked if 728 (each ship was identified by the last three numbers on its vertical stabilizer, the tail) was ready to fly.

The sergeant in charge said, "Yes sir. It's been test flown. It's in a revetment waiting for you. I'll send some guys to bore sight you."

We drove down the flight line until we found 728.

All I could think was, *What a beast. This is my choice for a weapon of war.*

We did a preflight with Steve pointing out the differences with a slick. "A slick is a race car, and a gunship is a loaded 18 wheeler going up a steep hill. You can't cowboy this ship or you will die." While he was pointing out the differences to me, I noticed something I couldn't believe. There was a 1 inch gap between the vertical firewall and the floor of the ship. I could look through this gap and see the ground! I wasn't sure what to say, so I pointed and said nonchalantly, "What about this?"

He said, "No problem. It's only an inch."

I thought, *OK, but it looks like this ship is breaking in half.*

Essentially, it was an old B model. The slicks were just now getting the more powerful H model. The army chose the B for guns because it sat and flew in a nose low position. This made it a great platform for shooting rockets, mini guns and the cannon. Slicks sat nose high which meant you would have to dive in a much steeper angle to shoot rockets.

The B model had been modified for the Gunships by adding a larger transmission, engine, and rotor blades. This modification of the B was called a C model. It was not officially on Bell Helicopter's books. Most of the time you had to slide a C model off the ground like an airplane because it never took off less than 1000 to 1500 pounds over-gross. And then with only half a tank of fuel (120 gals). The load you could get away with depended on the age of the ship.

"There are two types of gunships," Steve pointed out. "There's a lead ship and a wing ship. The lead carries 38 rockets (19 per side), 500 rounds of 40 millimeter canon shells, belt-fed like a machine gun.

Like a slick, there are two guys in back, the crew chief and the door gunner, but they hold their 30 calibers freely or with an occasional bungie cord, not mounted like the slicks. These bird gunners have balls bigger than basketballs, and they are truly made of brass. You'll have to see it to believe it. They'll have one foot in the helo, and the other outside on a rocket pod."

Actually, I had seen this, and it was truly amazing. Only a small strap (called a monkey strap) around their waists hooked at the other end to the firewall to keep them in the ship. All the while, the ship would be dropping at 500 to 600 feet per minute with a forward airspeed of over 120 knots. (Try putting your arm out a car window going 60 miles per hour.)

"They can shoot under or behind the ship," Steve said, "not to mention straight forward or out to the side. They can empty those ammo cans in less than 20 minutes, if need be. It's a badge of courage for them to step out on the rocket pod and let the rocket exhaust blow out hot primer fragments and burn holes in their pants legs. The more holes, the bigger your balls.

"The wing ship has smaller rocket pods with seven rockets per side. It also has two electric Gatling guns (also called mini guns) with 15,000 rounds of ammo. You could cut down trees with a stream of those bullets. The wing ship has the same door gunner setup. Wing's job is to protect the lead ship. You'll pick all this up quicker once you're flying."

Steve and I jumped in. Startup procedure was the same as for the slicks. Then, before we could fly, we also had to go through the bore-sighting calibration procedure for the rockets. We hovered out to the taxiway and set it down. Steve pulled down his rocket sight and slid the ship a few inches right and left until his sight was aimed at a shack 800 yards in the distance. The armament crew placed a tube in the center hole where the first rocket would be loaded. It had a sight and was aimed at the same shed and locked in place. The crew then repeated this procedure on the other side.

We hovered back to the Firebird revetments and shut down. Steve said, "Follow me." We walked 50 feet to the rocket storage container. There were hundreds of rockets.

Steve said, "Grab some." I watched him carefully as he cradled four across his arms. The warheads ware 17 pounds and the body was five pounds of solid fuel. That was 88 pounds in his arms. I figured I should take the same amount. I loaded my arms, hoping I wouldn't trip and blow us into tiny pieces. I followed him to the rocket pods. We laid them down and went back for two more each. There were 12 rockets lying on the ground.

Steve said, "Pick one up and follow my lead. The rocket is pushed into the front of the pod, back in first, so the warhead is facing the same direction we'll be flying. We slide it in until you hear and feel a click. Then it's locked in."

After all 12 were snug in the pods (six to a side), we went to the back of the pod and moved the mechanical arms (like a latch type door handle) so they touched the back of each rocket. This area is the size of a dime and is like a primer on a bullet. One and a half volts are sent to the primer from the mechanical arm, and the exploding primer ignites the five-foot-long tube of solid fuel. The fuel burns out in two tenths of a second, and the rocket leaves the pod at 2300 feet per second, nearly the speed of a bullet. We loaded six on each side. The 12 tubes were numbered so we could load them in sequence, one to six. We repeated this on the other side.

Steve said, "Strap in and let's go for a ride and shoot something." He hovered back out to the taxiway and aimed his rocket sight on that same building. "Sit back and look at the building, then draw a two inch circle on your Plexiglas with the red grease pencil. Then put a dot in the middle."

That was easy enough.

We took off and told Chu Lai we were flying south to Target Practice Island. About two miles down the coast and a half mile out to sea was an island that looked like it had been used for target practice for many years. There were lots of holes in the ground and scorched palms without leaves, destroyed trucks, jeeps, and an old Huey.

Steve said, "Do you see the last palm before the ocean?"

"Do you mean that tall burnt pole?"

"Yep, that's the one."

"I'm going to make a rocket run on that tree, but I'm not going to shoot. I want you to look at the circle and dot you drew on your windshield back at the Firebird line. Then you make the second run and shoot. The red button by your thumb on the cyclic shoots rockets. Push gently so you don't move the cyclic. In all the John Wayne movies, he squeezes the radio switch and shakes the stick. That would move a Helo's nose up and down, and you wouldn't hit a damn thing. Make sure you are in trim (foot pedals) and descending at around 500 feet a minute. I've set the rockets to fire one at a time, first one side, then the other.

"OK, here we go. I'm on target. How is your sight picture?"

I said, "Pretty close."

"OK, Mac, break left."

Left was my side of the ship. Pilots sat in the right seat in a gunship and tried to always break right so they could see the locations of anybody shooting at wing. Then, we could identify the targets when we made our next run.

I turned and climbed as I flew away from the tree.

Steve said, "Before you turn to make a run, make sure all your systems are on. When I first got in the birds, I rolled in to punch rockets, and they were turned off. I had to hit switches and knobs while trying to fly with the NVA shooting at me. It was a mess. You want to go hot as soon as you take off in a gunship."

As I started toward the target, I had everything set up. I punched the red button. The rocket was low. I pulled back ever so slightly on the cyclic to raise the nose and punched again. It hit at the base of the tree. Dirt and dust rose up with a large flash.

Steve said, "Shoot again."

I did, and the rocket was 15 yards past the tree.

He said, "Break left, and don't worry about that last shot. These rockets have a large killing radius."

We kept this going for four more runs of three rockets each. I shot from a higher altitude, farther away, and in closer. I learned how steady you had to be on the controls. You can move the cyclic a half inch, and the rocket will miss the target by a considerable distance. I had to relax my grip, rest my arm on my right thigh, put the dot on the target, and gently depress the little red button. In combat, I'd have to do all that while flying, monitoring instruments, talking to the crew, talking to the troops on the ground, and watching where the bad guys' bullets were coming from. *Easy, just make minimal movements with the cyclic.*

"Now, let's try the cannon. We have to school you on all this quicker than previous pilots because the AO is really heating up. Since Johnson stopped the bombing of North Vietnam, they are bringing weapons down through Laos that can shoot down jets. How do feel about flying a helicopter against those weapons?"

"I try very hard," I said, "not to think about the bullets coming at me. And now, I'll be able to shoot back."

Steve talked me through the process of pulling down the sight, holding it snug touching the front of my helmet, with the pistol grip in my right hand. He flew all over the island calling out targets. I started hitting them after about ten misses.

He kept up a steady stream of advice and guidance. He would make a rocket run, and I was to shoot at targets on the periphery. "On a real run, you'll be watching for enemy troops, barrel flashes, tracers, and enemy equipment such as a mounted machine-gun position. That's usually a 51 cal. Again, remember you'll be monitoring the instrument panel and where the gunners are shooting. And where your copilot is shooting. All the while talking to your wingman and the guys on the ground. Don't forget you are flying the gunship. You are the choreographer of the entire dance. And just think, while you're doing all of this, the bad guys are shooting at you."

He looked at his watch. "Take us home. I have a meeting with the CO. I have to tell him I'm going to take one of his promising copilots over to the birds. A warning: some of the Rattlers you've flown with will try to talk you out of your decision. They think we are a little screwed up. They think we unwind too much, and too loud."

Well, no shit, I thought. *Do what Firebirds do all day and half the night, and anyone would become twisted.*

"By the way, you have a great touch on the controls. You're smooth, controlled, and always in trim. You don't cowboy the ship.

"Let's go out about the same time tomorrow and shoot the nose cannon again. That will be one of your primary jobs as a copilot in the lead gunship. We'll do another round with the rockets as well. You'll learn how we run missions, how we cover and protect each other, and—most important—how we drink together.

"You'll see how difficult it is to unwind after a mission. You'll be stationed at Baldy for four to six days, and the stress and fatigue will build. That's where the drinking comes in when you return to Chu Lai.

"This lead ship—the one you're in—is called a hog because it looks fat with the rocket pods on each side and the big bulbous nose in front (the cannon). We almost always fly as a team of two. Number two is the wingman. When you become pilot of the wing ship, you will receive your Firebird number; a 9 followed by 0-5 or 7-9. The 6 is reserved for the platoon leader.

"Both ships have two door gunners. The crew chief is a door gunner when in the air. The door gunner is behind the pilot. They are trained to look for the same things we are. You can re-direct their shooting if you think there is a greater threat elsewhere. And they can also find targets for you.

"You will progress from copilot in the lead ship to copilot in the wing. Then, pilot in the wing, then to pilot or AC, and fire team leader. Then, you are in charge of everything when in the air. Pay attention to all you learn on your way up to fire team lead. There are a ton of responsibilities. Everything will depend on you!

"I'm going to get us a loaded gunship tomorrow and some new crews to check out. You'll learn how to take off with an overloaded ship, 1,000 to 1,500 pounds overweight, and that's with only a half tank of gas, 120 gallons."

All I could think to say was, "OK."

"In two weeks, I'll leave this shithole and return to the world.

I've already begun thinking about my responses to protesters. If I do what I'm thinking right now, I will probably go to jail. Oh well fuck it. Let's go. Nothing could be more fucked up than this." He swung his arm out in front of him to indicate everything we could see out of the windshield.

I called Chu Lai tower. "Entering the pattern from the south for a straight-in approach to the Firebird line."

Tower said, "Roger, cleared to land."

Chapter 26.

WELCOME TO THE BIRDS

After we landed, Steve held out his hand. "Welcome to the birds, Mac," and we shook.

As we were walking over to the jeep, he asked me what I thought of the one-inch separation between the floor and firewall.

"You're flying that ship, so it's probably OK, but I sure as hell don't know how."

He laughed. "When it gets to one-and-a-half inches, then maintenance crawls underneath and welds in L shaped brackets to keep the ship from breaking in half."

"You know Steve, I've learned more here in a month than my first two years of college and flight school."

He said, "Don't ever stop learning; that's when you die."

Wow, that was a pretty heavy-duty statement.

"We're not flying a real mission tomorrow, so I'll see you in the bar after chow and introduce you to some of your new brothers. Technically, you and I have tomorrow off. That makes tonight a drinking night!"

I said, "Thank you," and headed to my hooch. I was looking forward to showering off the war dirt and smell.

The mess hall was as bad as ever. *I really think they could try harder with the food.* After eating the bad food alone, since I guess most people were still flying, I was ready for the bar. I went into a very loud and rowdy scene. This actually looked like fun. I would just have to watch how much I drank, if I was going to remember any names.

I saw Steve and Major Wilson at the bar, along with about six others. It looked like a lot of drinking had already happened. Steve was just as shit faced as his friends. The CO didn't look quite so wasted.

Steve had already let him know that I was transferring to the birds, and Steve told me later that the CO agreed I was ready to fly AC in a wing ship, probably AC in lead. He told Steve I was "extremely calm under fire." I was glad to hear that I had impressed him.

Steve looked at me and yelled, "Ring the bell, three times."

I said, "I only took four hits today, and it's $5 a day." The crowd yelled back, even louder, "Ring the bell."

"No," Steve explained, "you also received two promotions today!" He pointed at the bell, and now all his drunken friends were trying to out yell the guy next him. "Ring the bell, ring the bell." The poor CO was probably trying to figure out how he was going to extricate himself from this certifiable group of future felons.

I rang the bell, and as before, the place was instantly silent. Steve put his hands up and said, "Mac took a hit today, and he is now a copilot."

That drew some cheering and toasting. Then, he followed with, "He has also been promoted to the Firebirds. His new MOS is 100 B." (That is, my military occupational specialty was now gunship pilot).

Well, that brought out as many boos as congratulations. The Rattlers and Firebirds had some animosity toward each other. I think most of it was just a strange comradery. Then Steve said, "That's $5 per promotion, and the hits. Throw $15 in the bowl!"

I did, and here came the drinks. I was handed a beer and a crown royal. I had no choice but to drink. *I will label that as peer pressure in my post flight manual.*

I saw Phil Henry and Glen Walton looking at me and shaking their heads. (Glen was out of the MASH unit. That was good). I had flown with them and their crews several times and learned a lot about flying in combat situations. I immediately felt bad and couldn't maintain eye contact.

Thankfully, I was swallowed up by the birds. Everyone wanted to shake my hand and names were flying at me like bullets.

While everyone was busy, the CO slipped out. No doubt he

figured he'd drunk enough to soothe his nerves, and he didn't want to drink any more than that.

Finally, someone asked me, "Why the birds?"

"I'm tired of being shot at. In a slick, all I can do is sit on the ground and hope I take off before they take my head off. I want to shoot back!"

The birds cheered.

Then for levity, I asked Steve if I would be fined for any other deeds tonight. He said, "No."

"I wouldn't be surprised," I said, "if you bastards started charging me to use the shit house."

That brought more cheering from the birds. One of them said, "Bastards, wow, he's going to make a great bird. Talks like us already."

This party continued, and I could see that the birds really did drink a lot.

Finally, Phil and Glen approached me. "Why, really, why the Birds?"

"You two are the greatest. I really don't like someone shooting at me, when I'm helpless. It's just me guys. It's not about you. It may sound sick to you, but I really enjoyed punching off rockets today. Don't get after Steve. I approached him two weeks ago and told him every chance I got that I wanted to fly with the birds."

Glen spoke to me almost in a whisper. "We had an idea this was coming. We were sitting around one night shooting the breeze and talking about FNGs. We do that occasionally to remind ourselves that we were once FNGs. We also talk about everyone's skill level, so we can identify future copilots and ACs. You grow up so fast here and learn so much in a very short time. We feel and act like old pros after three months. Then we look at the new guys and picture you as babies, which you are not. You are us, a few months back.

"Steve asked about you. Your reputation for being cool under fire has impressed a lot of people. He noted that, and I think he was thankful that you came forward. I'll be honest. It's not an easy job recruiting Firebirds. Those guys ... you guys have a short longevity. Four things happen: you quit and return to the Rattlers, you're wounded, you are killed, or occasionally, you get to go home. If you go home, you are fucked up and have to work hard to assimilate back in the real world. My mom's a nurse and has told me this in several letters. Try to keep your head screwed on."

"Well, good luck Mac," Phil said, "and I hope you are in the air when we need you. I've seen you fly. I know you'll be great."

With that, we shook hands, and I said, "Thank you for everything. You're the two that taught me how to fly!"

Then, they left the bar. The goddamned Firebirds were still at it. *I hope this behavior isn't mandatory.* I slipped out and went to bed. I was four weeks behind in sleep, and I was still under the naïve assumption that I could catch up.

I woke up at 0900! I couldn't believe it. I peed out the door and went back to bed with that nasty Harold Robbins book. I was getting too really like this guy.

The day contained no surprises. The air and the hooch maids still smelled bad. I was sticky and wet immediately. Everywhere were trails of black smoke streaming skyward and killing my appetite. *This 'shit' cannot be good for my lungs.* I still didn't know who got the shit burning details. *It has to be captured enemy. I'm going to ask someone.*

I eventually got dressed in shorts and a T shirt and went to lunch and then back to the hooch. I was killing time before 1500, when Steve and I would fly back to Target Practice Island. I picked up a C model tech manual from supply, and the supply officer said I could pay him later. I didn't want to ask what that meant.

I opened up the manual and began reading. I read for two hours.

Steve picked me up in the jeep and then, with a big grin on his face, drove to the CO's office. To my surprise, out came the CO and TOP. Major Wilson asked us, "What weapons are we firing today?"

Steve said, "The 40 mike-mike (short for millimeter)."

The major said, "Sounds like fun."

Steve quickly tempered their enthusiasm. "Sir, we have to load it first."

TOP and the CO looked at each other, shrugged, and the major said, "Be safe" and walked back inside.

We got going on Highway One. I asked Steve, "What's going on? It sounded like they wanted to come with us."

He said, "They did, until they discovered the cannon required loading. I purposely asked maintenance not to load it so you can learn. It's work. The shells are shipped in crates of ten. Each shell is six inches long and they're heavy. We link them together like machine gun ammo. We'll clip together forty to fifty rounds at a time.

"You climb in back and lift the shells up to the top of a long tall box. The one you saw yesterday. From there, you drop them in and then move the band of shells forward and back as I feed them to you. We will keep adding bands of forty to fifty until we load 450 into the magazine. As it fills, we slide the last band of fifty into a chute at the top of the magazine, down to the gun in front."

After we completed that part, we went to the front of the ship where the cannon was mounted, and Steve guided me through the rest of the process. I took off the top cover and reached into the chute that carried the ammo to the gun. I pulled that belted ammo another foot to the gun and loaded it and then chambered a round.

As we finished, another jeep drove up, hauling two new guys. One was a crew chief and the other a door gunner, both fresh out of their respective schools. They were first trained state side, and then they got some more training down south near Saigon. They had flown on slicks for two months, and then they were assigned to the 71st and the Firebirds.

Steve would be multitasking this afternoon with three of us in training: Me on the frog, as the 40 mm cannon was affectionately referred to, and the rockets and crew chief Joe Gibbs and gunner Paul Walsh on their M-60's.

Steve said to me, "Take me to the island. By the way, Mac, this ship is loaded with 38 rockets, the entire gunner's ammo, a half tank of fuel (our normal amount), and 500 rounds of 40 mm. So today you learn a gunship takeoff. Pull it up carefully and let's hover out to the taxiway."

I added power and pulled up on the collective, and to my surprise we only lifted up one inch off the ground. I sat it back down and looked at Steve. He had a huge shit-eatin' grin on his face.

He said, "Follow through on the controls with me." I just nodded.

He then added, "You guys in back don't worry about this takeoff. It's a normal takeoff for a 1,000+ pounds over grossed gunship. We're going to slide and bounce our way into the air. Does that sound cool or what?"

What's his definition of cool?

He rolled on the power and up we rose, that same one inch. He then moved the stick so slightly I couldn't see the motion, but I felt it as I lightly followed him on the controls. We slowly moved sideways right, out of the revetment, and the ship gently settled back to earth as the rpm dropped (both engine and rotor speed). We only moved three feet.

We sat there for a moment as the rpm climbed back into the green range on the tachometer. He then repeated the same maneuver three additional times. All of this, and we were only out of the revetment, sitting on the ground between the parked gunships and the slicks.

Now, he repeated the same maneuver and moved the cyclic forward a millimeter and we moved forward six or seven feet and back to earth. I'm wondering, *how long will this take?* After a few of these somewhat successful tricks of the trade, we reached the taxiway.

Steve told the guys in back, "Keep your guns cold (unloaded) as I'm going to take off, stay in the pattern and come around and land, and then Mac's going to take this thing off. Then you'll all know one more reason why this ship is called a hog."

Steve called the tower and made his requests. We were cleared for some touch and go's, as they were called. *This is going on my list of things they omitted in flight school. I believe they omitted more than they taught me. Take off like a plane? Right.*

Steve lifted up an inch and pushed the stick forward. We slowly moved forward, but at a downward angle. Same thing he did to get us from the revetment to this takeoff point. However, this time he kept the stick in the forward position and the front of our skids hit the ground and we bounced up off the ground. While going forward we bounced twice more, then the skids remained in contact with the ground. We continued sliding as Steve pushed the stick forward and we were now gaining speed. This was a good thing as I could see the end of the runway ahead.

I dared to take my eyes off the instruments and glanced at Steve to see if he had a worried look on his face. If he had, I would have put one on my face too.

He looked cool and seemed to be enjoying this. So I tried to do the same. Our air speed was approaching take off speed and then we lifted up just like an airplane. *But wait, I'm in a helicopter.* This gunship flies like a loaded bus. We weren't this heavy yesterday. The slicks were sport cars compared to this beast. He did tell me that yesterday.

Steve called the tower and said, "I am flying down the beach for a mile and then turning back to land on the taxiway."

He followed with, "A new pilot in training."

The tower said, "Roger, and welcome to Vietnam."

He said, "Mac, get on the controls with me." We made a long straight-in approach, and he was so smooth. No standing on your tail in a gunship. We leveled out and sat it down. Actually, it sat itself down. He looked over and said, "You've got it," and pointed straight ahead. Then added, gently, "You're cradling a baby, not in the ring with Muhammad Ali."

I slowly pulled up to a hover, and with full power, nosed it over. At the same time, I began forward motion and started dropping toward the ground. I hit, bounced, and repeated this non-flight school maneuver three times. I was gaining airspeed and hoping those skids would come off the ground. I needed altitude with the speed. Both are very important when taking off. *No shit Kevin.*

I did not move the controls until I was at 70 knots, (80 mph), then back ever so slightly came the cyclic, and we started climbing.

I had repeated Steve's maneuver and came in for a landing. Not quite as smooth as Steve's, so he suggested I do a few more. Burning off some fuel made the entire process easier as we continued.

Steve said, "Now, let's go blow up something." As I flew south, he told the guys in the back to go hot. He then explained to me, again, how the cannon sight swung down from the metal bar at the top of my window (co-pilot's side). As I turned east, out to sea, he told them to test fire their guns. They shot some salt water. When we approached the island, he said he would give them some targets and see how quickly they could get their tracers on target.

Both guys clicked their mike buttons to acknowledge. He said to Paul, "In back on the right, two palm trees at 2 o'clock (a little forward of straight out)." Paul didn't hesitate. He was on target by the third tracer. (There are four bullets between each tracer). Then to Joe, "Rock on the hill 9 o'clock (straight out to the left side)." He was also on target in three tracers.

"Great shooting. Now, I'm going to swing around and punch one rocket. Wherever it hits, Mac, I want you to put some 40 mm, fifty yards left and fifty yards right of my rocket. You two in back, shoot around his cannon shots. Pull down your sight, Mac, and hold it to the front of your helmet with both hands like yesterday. Do you see the round ring of light with a dot in the middle? That light is projected onto a glass plate bright in the day light and dim at night."

I said, "Barely."

"With your left hand turn the rheostat (switch) up till you can see the light to your satisfaction. At night, you will turn it down so you can see the target.

"Grab hold of the pistol grip with your right hand and very lightly feel the trigger with your index finger. Center the oblong sight, so the light is directly in front of your face, and the sight is touching your helmet."

I did all three and clicked once. I was glad he was repeating everything.

"The gun shoots single shots or full auto if you hold down the trigger. The gun barrel turns wherever you look."

I clicked again.

"All set?"

He received three clicks in his ear phones. He turned back toward the island and punched a rocket. I was looking through the rocket sight and pulled the trigger. My shots on the left side were long, so I turned the sight downward and shot twice. I then turned the sight right of the rocket and fired three times. A little better, but still long. All the while the gunners were pounding the area with their machine guns. They scored higher than me on that run! Those tracers helped."

He said, "Stop shooting," and made a gradual right turn.

"On this next run, I'm going to punch one rocket and everyone hose down the area around the explosion. Then I'll say, 'Ready,' to warn you that in a second or two I'm going to call, 'Breaking right.' It will be a hard turn so I can get out of the way of my wingman's rockets. You will feel the force of the turn because we will be mushing. That means we are still falling towards the ground due to our weight and speed. That's how it works in combat; except, in combat, I will punch off three to five pairs of rockets. Ready, tells you to get back inside, in case you are hanging out the door shooting. When I'm coming out of the turn, I can look out to see where my wing is shooting and who is shooting at him. All of us should be looking out. Now, if Joe and Paul have a shot, they take it. I'll also be trying to gain altitude, so when wing says, 'Ready,' I can get into position to put rockets behind and under him, as he breaks. That's also what he would have done when I broke, if he were here.

"OK, here we go, two passes, and kill everything around my rocket."

As Steve was descending at 500 feet per minute and 120 knots, or 138 miles per hour, I was splitting my time scanning instruments and looking through my sight waiting for that rocket. Swoosh! The rocket sped by my leg out of the pod at 2300 feet per second. It hit the ground in less than a second. We all started shooting around the explosion. There was a huge dust cloud from the impact of all those bullets and shells. A few seconds later, Steve said, "Ready," followed by, "Breaking right."

We climbed up and out. Paul was still shooting since his side faced the target. Joe then did something extremely crazy in my opinion and my limited experience. He leaned out of the ship, hanging by a small strap and actually fired his machine gun under the ship so he was shooting at Paul's targets. These guys were as crazy as the pilots, or at least they took some very crazy risks. That crazy crew chief was sitting behind me with a loaded machine gun. *That must make me some kind of crazy or very trusting.*

We had the altitude, so we turned for another pass and rolled in on a target. Steve saw an old pickup truck that had been hauled out there by a helo and dropped. It had been shot practically to pieces. He called out on the intercom, "Shoot the truck." All three of us opened up. I actually hit the truck a few times out of 10 shots. Some of my other shots were close. The gunners however, were all over it.

Steve called, "Ready," and paused, and then "Breaking right." He said, "Great job, you guys can fly with me any time. That includes you, too, Mac. Good shooting for the first time."

We continued this training for another hour. I ended up hitting the target pretty regularly.

"Take me home. I'm thirsty," was all Steve said.

As we were about to enter Chu Lai's traffic pattern, he said, "Go cold." This told everyone to shut down the weapons systems and for the gunners to empty the bullets out of the receiver. We landed, did a post flight, and debriefed. He asked questions, made some good suggestions, and asked if we had any questions. There were a few.

Then, he reminded us we needed to rearm the ship.

I had forgotten about re-arming. That won't happen again.

With all of that completed, he said, "Let's go back and check the schedule to see if any of you birds can drink tonight."

We checked the board and saw that all three of us were off the next day until 1500. Then, it was back to the island with Steve for training in the wing ship.

I shot the mini guns (electric Gatling guns made by General Electric, like my mother's refrigerator) one on each side of the ship. They were capable of shooting five times as many rounds per minute than our door gunner's guns. I read that General Custer had three hand cranked Gatling's, but he felt it unnecessary to take them to the Little Big Horn. We can learn by our mistakes, unless they kill us.

It was only 1600, an hour before dinner. A shower and the bar sounded like a great idea. I did both. Three warm crown royals later, in came some Firebirds. I met a few, and we talked. I had had too much to drink to remember names. I made a mental note to write down names. I was told several times that when I made wingman, I would be assigned a number and move into the Firebird hooch. *Sounds cool, but I'll bet they don't sleep too much.*

I also discovered they were short-handed, very short-handed. They had lost a ship and its crew the same day I was out shooting the ground and some dead trees. A wing ship, 717, broke in the wrong direction and flew into a mountain and exploded. Everyone assumed the two pilots had been shot.

I was confused at how they were behaving after losing a ship and crew. Finally, I figured it out. They had booze in the Firebird hooch and had started their Irish wake two hours earlier. I mentioned something about it, and all they said was, "This is what they would want," meaning the dead Firebirds.

I thought about that for a while and came to the same conclusion. I wouldn't want anyone sitting around feeling sorry for me.

The only people that suffer are the live ones. Dead is dead; you just go to sleep. Think about it. You don't know when you go to sleep. You only know when you wake up.

Hell, if I had wanted safety, I would have joined the Navy. For sure, this will go in my book.

There were other reasons the Birds were short-handed. They had a pilot going on R & R. Another had already gone home. A co-pilot had been wounded and sent to Japan for medical treatment, and one guy had said, "Fuck it, I'm going back to the Rattlers." Things can happen fast around here. I guess that's war.

I met Firebird 9-4, Stuart Muse. We talked about the weather. He agreed with me that it was fucking hot here, especially considering he was from Minnesota. I met Jimmy Hanson, Firebird 9-7, from Utah. He had less than one month remaining. *Lucky guy!*

I met Jim Williams, Firebird 9-8, nicknamed, Black Death. He was black and a wingman. There were only about 10 black guys in our entire company. Jim and I hit it off great. He had just made wingman and hadn't moved into the Firebird hooch yet. We talked about the military. He had been enlisted for eight years before he went to flight school. I had all of 15 months in the army.

Jim grew up in Alabama. He got into the Birds late as he enjoyed flying slicks. The Birds kept bugging him until he gave in.

He said he liked me because I wasn't prejudiced.

I said, "Why would I be prejudiced? I know some white assholes. I don't know any black assholes." I thought he was going to fall over from laughing and, of course, the booze. I really liked this guy. He would be great pilot and teacher. He wasn't full of himself.

Time passed. It was late. The Rattlers, and even the Firebirds, were leaving the bar. I left with Jim. It turned out that Jim's hooch was just two away from mine. He said "Good night" and staggered inside. I went on to my place, though I have to admit, a bit unsteadily. I sat on my bunk and took off my boots.

I had a sudden urge to pee, so I walked outside and down the two steps. As I began the process, I looked over and saw flickering lights coming from Jim's Hooch. I thought, *that can be only one thing, fire.* I ran over and up the two steps. There, lying in bed with his mattress on fire was my new acquaintance and fellow Firebird, Jim Williams.

I grabbed him by the shoulders and was yelling for him to wake up as I pulled him out of the fire and onto the floor. I grabbed his mattress and took it outside and threw it down on the sand, flaming side down.

I went back inside, and he was still on the floor, still passed out. He had on only his boxer shorts. I rolled him slowly onto his left side because I could see burnt cloth on his right. He was breathing normally with a slight smile on his face. I made a mental note to ask him what the smile was all about.

He had a six inch burnt circle of skin on his right butt cheek. All that came to mind was one word, "Shit." By now, two of his roommates woke up and said, "What the hell is going on."

"I think Jim fell asleep while he was smoking. He's got a large burn on his ass. I pulled him out of bed and then threw his mattress outside."

I told one of the roomies, "Go to the CO's office and get a vehicle so we can take Jim down the road to the flight surgeon. Also, tell the night clerk to let the CO know what we're doing, then call the flight surgeon." Two minutes later, the CO entered the hooch with the clerk and Jim's roomie. All three were breathing hard. They hadn't wasted any time getting there.

The CO got down on one knee and looked at Jim's burn and told his clerk to get that truck in front of his office. He looked at the roomies and said, "Find some help, get two men here. Then you two carry two mattresses to the front of my office."

He then looked at me and said, "Pull two sheets off these bunks." I put the sheets on the floor, one on top of the other. Two guys from the hooch next door ran in and just stared at the scene. We rolled Jim onto the sheet and the four of us each grabbed a corner and carried him about 30 yards to the truck waiting at the CO's office. Major Wilson said, "Throw those mattresses in back and stack them up."

It was a job getting Jim onto the mattresses, but we managed. We laid him on his stomach so the burn wouldn't get any worse.

The CO told his clerk, "Drive down to the flight surgeon and try to miss some of the bomb craters." *So, I'm not the only one who thinks these roads are fucked.* He told the other guys to go back to bed.

He said, "Mac, jump in back with me and help hold him on the mattresses. You can tell me all about this on our trip down the road."

I told the Major everything in detail. He just nodded. The drive was short, and Jim still had not awakened.

We drove up to the building, and the flight surgeon was waiting. The Doc took a corner of the sheet; the major and I, along with the clerk grabbed the other three. We carried Jim inside and put him on an exam table, face down. The doc checked the burn and gave his body a once over.

I think the pain from the burn was waking him from his drunken stupor. The doc checked his dog tags in case he needed blood. Jim was getting louder, so the doc gave him some morphine. That put him back in la-la land.

He turned and looked at the major. "These are second degree burns, sir. I'll clean the wound and start him on some antibiotics. Then I'll call Dust off, here in Chu Lai, and send him to Danang for additional treatment. Our biggest problem is infection.

"Great job getting him here, sir. You can all return to your company area. I'll let you know how he's doing, sir."

The CO said, "OK, Let's go."

We all three sat in front on the return trip and talked rather casually. When we drove into the company area, we all climbed out of the truck. The CO said, "Mac, come see me at 10 hundred hours tomorrow."

I said, "Yes sir." I went back to my hooch and realized I still hadn't taken that piss. I got up, went to the door and down the two steps, when I realized I had taken off my boots and socks. I was bare footed during that entire episode. I bet that impressed the CO.

I just fell back on the bed and was out. I woke up at 0900, cleaned up and shaved, put on a clean uniform, polished my boots, grabbed a ball cap, army issue, and walked to the CO's office. I was still wondering what I had done wrong.

I walked up the two steps and went inside. I stopped in front of Top's desk and said, "Mr. McNally reporting as ordered, Top."

He said, "Just a moment, Mr. McNally." He went into the CO's office. He came out a moment later and said, "The major will see you." Then under his breath, he said, "Nice work last night. You saved several lives, all while staying cool and calm."

I looked at him, somewhat stunned, and said, "Thank you, TOP."

I reported in to the CO, and he said, "At ease, Mac, that was quite a story you told me last night. That was quick thinking."

He stopped talking, so I said, "Thank you sir."

"You have been here a month and have made quite an impact. I also want to thank you for waking me. I hear you are going to be one of 'God's own lunatics.' From what I've been told, you are a great slick driver. Hate to lose you from the slicks, but the birds will make good use of your talents. The birds have a very dangerous mission here. Be prepared.

"What are you doing the rest of the day?"

"I'm flying to the Target Practice Island with Steve Meadows at 1500," I replied. "I'm going to shoot the mini guns. It will be my third time in a gunship."

"Steve told me a while back that on flare night you helped re-arm the gunships. Were you a boy scout?"

"Yes sir, all the way to life scout. Then, our troop disbanded before I could earn enough merit badges to be an eagle scout."

"I already knew that answer. I just hope the birds don't destroy everything that makes you who you are."

As he dismissed me and I turned to leave, I wondered, *what the hell was that last comment about?"*

"Mac," he said, as I was just stepping out of his office. "Nice shine on those boots." *He was kidding me about my bare feet.*

"Thank you, sir."

Top was laughing as I walked past his desk. The CO had talked to him.

I managed to waste a few hours until my watch said 1450. I grabbed my gear and went to meet Steve. As I showed up, so did yesterday's crew chief and door gunner. We greeted each other in approved military fashion, in case the CO was watching. At the flight line and in the air, the Firebirds were all equal, officers and enlisted men. None of that sir shit. It's just an extra word that takes up time we don't have on a mission.

We arrived at the ship, 641, just in time to help finish the loading of the Gatling guns. They each carried 15,000 rounds (bullets). We went through a preflight, and I was shown the many differences from yesterday's lead ship.

I thought about the stages in my training: First, learning to fly a trainer in primary. Then learning to fly the Huey in advanced training. I followed that with learning to fly a slick in combat. Now, I was going to learn how the lead gunship runs a mission, as well as fly it, and shoot the cannon and rockets. Then, I would learn to fly the wing ship, shoot the Gatling guns, and pilot in the wing ship shooting rockets. Finally, I'd be flying the lead gunship and shooting rockets at the bad guys as a fire team leader, with the copilot on the cannon. All this assuming I remained alive long enough to reach each stage, and the next stage, whatever that may be. *Is there a next stage?*

All gunships fly close to the ground. They are overloaded, slow flying, thin skinned, and unarmored (except for the chicken boards and parts of our seat; the back and the bottom.) This is why gunships and their crews had a high mortality rate. *This also belongs in the forgot book.*

We loaded 14 rockets, and the door gunners had 1500 rounds apiece. The loading was slow, as it was a training session. Finally, we were ready.

I felt like a little kid getting ready for trick-or-treat action. I tried not to look the part.

On the short trip to the target, Steve explained the weapon-system switches, which are all on the panel between the pilots, same as in the lead ship. He showed me how to select rockets or mini guns. He pointed out the master-fuse panel overhead and between us to turn off and on all weapons.

We arrived on station, which is gun talk for at the target.

Steve began rolling in on the island and told the gunners to shoot the truck we killed yesterday. He then told me to do the same. I looked through the sight. It was nearly identical to yesterday's sight, so the familiarity helped.

I aimed and pulled the trigger for a three second burst. I walked them into the target. They chewed up the ground. I did a little better on each run. I learned where to aim, depending on distance and/or altitude. Of course, the guys in back were all over the target, as usual.

After six runs Steve said, "Lean back and put a circle and a dot on the dead truck." I made my drawings, and he said, "OK, swing back around and shoot some rockets at something. Just tell me what you're aiming at so I'll know if you miss." And all of that was with a big smile. He added, "Whatever Mac shoots, I want you two shooting at the same target." They both clicked their mikes. He then switched the rocket button to my cyclic and set it for a single rocket with each press of the red button, alternating sides, like yesterday.

As I began the run, I said, "The three palm trees." I punched three times with about two seconds between shots. All three were close enough to be a hit.

"You don't have to be as accurate as with bullets," Steve said. "These rockets have a 50 meter killing radius."

I then did a slight turn left and said, "The truck." They hit the truck with their tracers. One hit with his first tracer, and the other guy with his second. As I broke right, I was thinking, *How do you put the bullets coming at you out of your mind, so you can remain calm and on target? It will be more intense than in the slicks.*

We continued the fun for three additional runs. I only fired one rocket per run. Everyone was having fun.

Steve said, "I have five rockets. Kill whatever I kill."

I was high on anticipation. Then, he did something unexpected. He fired a rocket at some dead trees as he was turning. He hit the target. I was stunned. Then, I realized I was watching him as he was still turning left, and I didn't have a chance to shoot. As he kept turning, the door gunner on the right had a perfect view and fired a five second burst into to those trees. As he ended the turn, he climbed and dove and fired another rocket.

That rocket was far out in front of us. I thought that was a long shot. As I was getting on target, he was moving the cyclic left and right to make my targeting more difficult. I shot three- three-second bursts. He definitely made it more difficult.

He called out, "Breaking right. OK guys, one last pass. Shoot all around my rockets, and then we are going home. I'm thirsty." The dust in the air was getting thicker, making it more difficult to see the target.

After he punched his rockets, he started moving the cyclic left and right again. This made accuracy difficult, but I understood how to compensate.

He said, "I had to evade some AK-47s. Didn't you guys see those tracers? I had to move a bit to evade those bastards?"

No one said a word. Of course, there had been no one there, but Steve was a great instructor. He had a reason to take evasive action. It was just training, and it was great. He added in an element of intrigue. It pushed our training up a level.

"Why do you think I fired that first rocket while in my turn?"

I said, "The enemy can be anywhere?"

"Good answer. It was to show you that. But it also said, 'always be ready.' The enemy doesn't like gunships. Here's an old cliché. 'Be ready for the unexpected.' There are no rules in war, despite what you've been told."

More info to add to that "What they didn't tell you" list.

We talked about the training session on the return flight. This also included the crew chief and door gunner. "There are two extra set of eyes back there, Mac, and they want to stay alive as much as we do here up front! So listen to what they say."

We landed at Chu Lai and added fuel. We hovered to our revetment and shut it down. As we completed the post flight, I looked at that separation between the floor and the firewall, and immediately was thinking, *Where can I find a tape measure?* Nothing came to mind. When Steve walked by, I stood and walked to 728, stopped, and asked, "Is that an inch and a half?" as I pointed to my concern.

He looked for a moment and said, "An inch and 7/16."

I thought, *Shit, I'll bet it is closer to an inch and ¾.*

We then rearmed the gunship. With the four of us, we finished in 20 minutes.

We climbed in the jeep, and he drove past the road that takes us to Highway One and stopped at the maintenance hangar. He waved his hand to indicate, *follow me*. The three of us jumped out.

He found the maintenance chief and said, "Sarg, 728 is ready for the L brackets. It's over the 1 ½ inch gap."

He said, "Will do, Captain Meadows."

Steve looked over at me and smiled, then said, "Good call."

As we pulled into the company area, Steve said, "No drinking and get some sleep. You three are going to Baldy tomorrow as my crew for the next four to six days. We will be on call 24 hours a day.

Take a tooth brush. You'll live in squalor and smell worse than the burning shit."

I said, "OK" and quickly departed for my hooch before he changed his mind.

He called out to me and said, "Meet me in the mess hall at 0600."

That sounded much better than my usual 0400.

I woke up at 0400, but was easily able to go back to sleep. Probably because the 0200 rocket harassment kept me awake for an hour. They are shitty shots. Everyone works with sleep deprivation here. But, since I'm now an old seasoned pilot, I will get by with whatever I can.

Chapter 27.

THE BALDY HILTON

Breakfast with Steve, Joe, and Paul included small talk. I knew Steve was from the state of Washington. Joe was from Milwaukee, Wisconsin, and Paul came to us from Portland, Maine. Steve had two years of college and had gone to OCS (officer candidate school) and then flight school. He would go home two weeks after this Baldy assignment. Joe and Paul both enlisted after high school. We all came from military families.

The four of us did a "walk around" our ship, 728. It looked ready to fly. I took a quick look for those L brackets. I was pleased to count eight. That made me feel a lot better about flying.

I happened to look down the flight line, past two revetments, and another ship was getting a preflight. After we put our gear on board 728, we walked over for introductions. It was 641, the wing ship I had flown when learning to shoot the Gatling guns. We met Firebird 9-2, Jim Morton, from Chicago and his copilot, Tom Rivers, from San Diego. We shouted, "Hi," to the crew chief and door gunner, although they were busy finishing up.

Steve looked at Morton and said, "Let's put on the music and do some training on our way to Baldy."

Morton said, "Roger that."

Steve said, "We've got four or five days at Baldy to get to know each other. Let's get out of here."

We cranked up the engines, called the tower, and pulled pitch for Baldy. Once in the air, Steve turned inland, flew down to the deck, 30 feet above Highway One. After five minutes of this, he turned off the highway and began flying around trees and between them. He said, "Mac, HF radio has armed forces Vietnam radio beginning at 0600. They rotate the music: an hour each of Rock, classical, country and for some reason, big bands. That's something our parents danced to, I believe. You never know what you'll get when you tune them in."

We were lucky that morning. It was rock. The Doors singing "Light My Fire." This was the perfect song for our training. Jim had the same music on.

"Now," Steve explained, "I'm going to fly around trees, over trees, and any other crazy maneuver that comes to mind. Jim's co-pilot will try and stay in position to cover us if we take any fire (get shot at). I want you, Joe and Paul, to watch them. He is supposed to be in a position to punch a rocket at anyone taking a shot at us. If I turn left, he should turn right and remain behind me and above. If he turns the same way I do, then he will be in front and out of posi-tion. I want you two to grab a smoke grenade and throw it out on whichever side he gets out of position. Tell me the color before you toss it, so I can call, practice taking fire, 9 o'clock, or 3 o'clock, and the color of the smoke. This is fun, but keep your guns ready, as we are low level, and always vulnerable."

Steve then called out, "Lock your shoulder harness Mac, and test those guns back there," he yelled to the gunners. I could still hear the music over the machine guns.

The Doors were smoking hot. Steve told me to take the con-trols. I was really enjoying this. We called it "rat racing."

The spell was broken when Joe in back on the left said, "He turned the wrong way."

Steve gently keyed his mic so as to not interfere with my flying and quickly said, "Practice, 9 o'clock, green smoke, continuing my right turn."

I looked out the back door on the right and saw the wingman out in front of us. He screwed the pooch on that one.

Steve very calmly said, "Jim, your copilot owes everyone a beer." Jim, being a talkative individual, said, "Roger that."

Wow, for a moment I thought of home. *Get back in the game, Kevin.*

"Mac, try to lose him. Let's see if we can get another beer. I hope you're taking notes, because that copilot seat in the ship be-hind us is your next stop."

I was in the left seat, so every time I broke right I was supposed to see him on my left. It looked like he made the same mistake again. I said, "Joe, throw one out." I called out, "Practice taking fire 9 o'clock, red smoke."

Jim in the wing said, "Steve, can we trade copilots? Mine is making me look bad."

Steve told him, "No way."

Steve called Jim and told him to take lead and try to lose us.

Jim said, "Roger that." Then, in his most eloquent speech to date, he said, "Since we are out of position on your right, I will keep on that heading."

"Don't let him lose you," Steve yelled, "or you'll be buying beers. Just turn opposite of him, and stay behind and a little above. Don't lose visual."

I stayed on him for the next 30 minutes with the Beatles, Beach Boys, Danny and the Juniors, Safaris, and the Four Seasons. This had been my best day yet in this Stone Age country.

We landed at Baldy and hovered into the turnaround by the Firebird Hilton. We called the fuel truck. We were too heavy to land at the POL as the TO area was too short for a heavy gunship. (We were heavier because we hadn't spent any ammo.) We certainly didn't have the required runway to slide off to get airborne. One bounce only. We hovered into the revetments and were gassed up.

Steve said, "As copilot, you are responsible for the fuel. DON'T let it go over half a tank!"

After we completed all the routine post-op for our ships and knew they were ready for combat on a moment's notice, we sat down by the ships and talked tactics.

After a few hours of that, Steve and Jim took us back to the gunships to review the weapon systems and other differences with the slicks. We spent time with the sighting systems and how to set them for night use.

The rockets were next. The most commonly used type was HE (high explosive). It had a 50 meter killing radius. Another type was filled with Flechettes. These rockets were the same size as the HE rockets but carried 2000 nails in the warhead. Some were shaped like miniature arrows. A proximity fuse was set to explode 50 feet above trees or the ground, and the nails were dispersed in a pattern like a shotgun. This was a nasty weapon. When a nail struck a human, it began tumbling through the body, leaving a gapping exit wound. It could also pin limbs to bodies or people to people. Last was the WP (Willie Pete, Wilson Picket) rocket. This was white phosphorous which burns at 5000 degrees Fahrenheit. It could kill in many ways. Besides blowing a person apart, it was lethal when inhaled. It could burn through a person. If you put water on the phosphorous, it burned twice as intense. One other use: it produced a thick white smoke. This could be used to create a smoke screen. There were smoke rockets, but we didn't use them. Forward air controllers (FAC) used them to mark targets for the jets.

The radios were the same as in the slicks. FM had a 50 miles effective range and was line of sight. We used that to talk to the grunts. UHF was used for ship to ship, and it was also the frequency for emergencies. VHF was sometimes used in place of UHF. Lastly, HF was basically for music.

"I have a very important safety tip for you guys in back, Steve said. Did they teach you about a cook off in school?"

"It was mentioned," one of them mumbled.

"For you, Mac, a cook off is when a machine gun fires without anybody pulling the trigger. This is caused by the heat of the barrel and/or receiver (where the bullet sits). It can get so hot after being fired many times, it explodes the powder and sends a bullet down the barrel. If the barrel is pointed inside the ship, anything can happen. So keep the barrel pointed outside when you take a break from firing it!"

Another one of those flight school omissions. No one mentioned the Flechettes either.

"Now, it's time to teach you how to build rockets. On real busy days, the troops here on Baldy help us out," Steve said. "Those large pallets of crates are the rockets. The motors, six to a crate, are in the long boxes, and the short boxes contain six warheads each. We open them up and screw the heads to the bodies. When that's completed, we store them in these metal conex containers. We don't use the torque wrench recommended. We just give the two pieces a sharp snap with our wrists when we reach the end of the threads.

"If you drop one, no one dies. The warhead has to travel through a certain number of revolutions before it is armed.

"What I call the motor is a five foot tube filled with solid fuel. It burns in two tenths of a second. The rockets are fast and accurate. We shoot a pair each time the red button on the cyclic is depressed. Once a rocket leaves the pod, four fins open up causing the rocket to spin. This both arms the warhead and provides accuracy, like a bullet. Lead ship has 38 rockets, and wing has 14.

"Lead also has 500 40 mm shells, and wing has 15,000 rounds for the mini guns. Each door gunner has 1500 rounds of standard NATO ammo, 7.62mm or 30 caliber."

I had been told this many times.

"Our biggest challenge from ground fire is the Chi Com 51 (Chinese Communist 51 caliber). If we're facing one of those, I will reach over and turn the selector knob for more rockets. It could be three, four or five pair. I don't have time to look. I punch the button two or three times and out go 12 to 30 rockets, and I call out 'Chi Com 51, breaking right.' Then, Wing will shoot most of his rockets and our copilots will be shooting on full automatic, and the door gunners will not let up on their triggers. That's called shoot and scoot. You must hit the 51 quickly, or you'll be shot down.

"Oh, in case nobody's mentioned it, when we're on the ground, the pilot assists the crew chief, and the copilot will do whatever the door gunner needs with rearming.

"99% of our job is to protect American troops. Don't ever forget that. Mac, you now have a new MOS. That's 100 B, Helicopter gunship pilot. There are not many of us, and we usually don't last too long here. We only fly when there is trouble. And since this is a war zone, we fly often.

"Let's go eat. We've been lucky to have all this time together without any interruptions. After we eat, we'll build rockets."

Wow, that was a fast change of subjects. I'm quickly learning how life is in the guns.

Chapter 28.

FIRST GUNSHIP MISSION

Sure enough, four bites into lunch and one of our grunt helpers came running into the mess hall yelling, "Firebird scramble." We dropped our forks and ran to the ships.

We untied the rotor blades and pulled off the pitot tube cover. We climbed in, strapped in, and yelled, "Clear," all at the same time. The blades were turning while I called HQ, since the mission hadn't come over the red phone. They gave me the call sign, frequencies and coordinates. The bad news followed. One of our slicks had been resupplying troops in the field and was shot down. They had injuries and were in a fire fight along with the patrol they were resupplying.

Everyone in both ships monitored the radio calls. Some slicks were in route to bring out everyone. They needed the Birds to soften the area, as we call it. The patrol and helo crew were outnumbered and about to be overrun.

Steve took my map and gave me a heading. He said, "They are 22 clicks NW at a large horse shoe in the Song Ky Lam River. I got the radio and will call the patrol and the slicks.

"Get us there yesterday," he yelled without using the radio.

The area we were flying into was pure tiger country, so everything was fair game. I could see the tension in Steve's face. A quick glance in back and I saw that same tension on their faces.

As Steve spoke to the slicks, he asked their location. They were flying straight north from the LZ Ross area and would arrive about the same time we would. Slicks were faster, but these were farther away.

Steve got off the radio and said, "Everyone, go hot, and test your guns. This could be a real gunfight. Mac, go ahead and shoot something with that 40 mike-mike. I got the controls."

I aimed out ahead and fired off a round into a clump of small trees. Boom, they were dead. Both gunners blew the dust out of their gun barrels. We were ready.

We were over half way to the troops and our buddies, when Steve called the Air force spotter plane and explained the situation. He requested they nape the area after we picked up everyone. The spotter said, "I'll see what I've got." He was back to us in a minute, and said, "I've got two fast movers almost here. They'll circle and wait. They will see your rockets and use them for markers."

Steve said, "Roger."

I was almost to the LZ. I asked Tiger 6 to pop smoke. He did, and I said, "I've got your purple smoke." *Where were they?* I was gaining some altitude for my own look-see. This would also give Steve a better angle to shoot rockets.

I saw the Huey on its side in a dry rice paddy, 20 yards from our guys. I could now see the enemy troops only 50 yards from ours, and on two sides, with the river behind the patrol. Our guys were behind some large rocks and some palms near the riverbank. Essentially, they were trapped. One thing in our favor was that the enemy had to come out from the cover of the tall trees and cross a dry rice paddy. I was glad; that jungle was thick. *Christ, how do they live in that thick shit? Bugs, mosquitos, snakes and no flat ground to sleep on. All brush and roots.*

Steve called Jim Morton, Firebird 9-2, and asked, "You get all the info?" Back came two clicks on the radio.

Steve said to me, "I've got it."

"It's yours." I pulled down my cannon sight.

Steve called Tiger 6 and said, "We are coming in from the south and will put some rockets on them, then turn west (left) and shoot the second group. I will break east, right over you. My wingman will follow. Have your guys ever had help from gunships?"

Tiger 6 said, "Roger that."

"How many in your patrol?"

"Eight," he said with a nervous tone in his voice.

"OK, then stay behind those rocks and flat on the ground when we shoot. Our rockets throw out lots of shrapnel."

"Thanks," was all he said.

Steve said, "My copilot will be shooting a 40 mike-mike, and the wing will be shooting Gatling guns."

All Tiger 6 said was, "Please do."

Steve was in position and called, "Rolling in." Immediately, we all started shooting. The enemy had some protective cover from our ground guys but not from above. They shot a few rounds at us. A couple of them even switched to automatic fire. Their bullets were streaming by us. I could hear the familiar popping as they passed through our rotor wash.

Steve shot four pair of rockets at the first group, while I followed with the cannon. Both gunners were hanging outside and shooting at targets of opportunity. Steve did a slight turn left and fired another four pair of rockets at the second group. We all followed suit. The rockets expended their fuel about the time they passed by my left leg. I hadn't really noticed the noise a rocket made coming out of the pod, until now. It was a swoosh. I could smell the burnt fuel. The machine guns sounded louder. I could smell the strong odor of gunpowder. I just kept shooting.

My windshield exploded! I was pushed back into my seat. I didn't feel a thing.

Steve asked me if I was "OK."

I nodded.

Steve said, "Ready." This warned everyone he was going to start a steep turn and climb out while flying away from the action, so he could be in position to cover the wingman when he broke.

I hope the wingman will be putting some fire under us because our belly will be exposed.

Then Steve followed with, "Breaking right." I had to stop shooting as I couldn't see anything. The two gunners were firing at a furious pace at both targets. The crew chief shot from the left side, and most of his empty shell casings (called brass) were ejected into the ship. The entire door gunner's brass went out the door. We would have to sweep the crew chief's brass out of the ship when we were flying back to Baldy. We didn't always find it all. It got mixed in with our equipment and barrel bags (the crew's tools and extra parts for their machine guns).

Every so often, some Colonel would come down to the flight

line and tell us to pick up the brass that we didn't dump on the countryside.

Police brass (pick it up) in a war zone? Bullshit!

Joe, the crew chief, was shooting out the door when he swung his gun around to shoot straight out and a very hot brass casing hit me in the back of my helmet. (They were so hot that you couldn't pick them up for 15 seconds after firing.) The casing immediately dropped to my shirt collar and dropped down my back. It was between my skin and my shirt.

I had no idea what was happening. When it touched my neck, I leaned forward instinctively to get away from the burning. When I leaned forward, the casing dropped lower, and that burned. So what did I do? I leaned forward two more times. I still had no idea what was happening, as this casing was making its way to my waist. I thought maybe I was shot or we were on fire. I had to work to concentrate on my job. By the time it reached my belt, it had cooled down. The crew explained what had happened to me after we landed.

By breaking right, Steve could see the bad guys' locations, as they were shooting at 9-2 instead of the downed crew. We would fly over friendlies, but we didn't shoot over friendlies.

Steve *keeps reminding me: don't shoot over friendlies. I just may ask him why he keeps repeating that bit of info.*

The wingman put two pair of rockets behind us on the first target, while his mini guns were roaring. I knew that because there was a four foot flame coming out each barrel. It was bright enough to be seen in the daylight. Their door gunners were just as crazy as ours, as they were standing up and shooting with complete disregard of their own safety. Their guns are not mounted like in the slicks. They stand for better mobility and are able to shoot just about anywhere. Wing then put two pair on the second target and said "Ready," then "Breaking right."

As 9-2 broke right, Steve put rockets under his tail.

We repeated this race track pattern for two additional gun runs. I felt OK, so I stayed in the fight. I was still curious about what had caused that burning.

During this melee, the slicks called and said they were ready to go in and "pull those guys out as soon as we all thought the area had been softened up sufficiently." Steve called the slicks and said, "We just finished the softening." The pilot responding was rattler 2-2. I remembered flying with 2-2, Ed Place.

Steve told the slicks, "I have six rockets remaining, and wing has two. We also have some mini gun and 40 mike-mikes remaining. Door gunners are down to 300 rounds each. So with that in mind, let's do this in one pass. There are eight troops plus the helo crew, that's twelve total, six to each helo." Steve radioed the grunts, "Tiger 6, plan it so when the slicks land on your smoke, six guys jump into each helo."

Tiger 6 rogered. Then he said, "9-6, your helo pilot is dead." Steve and I both said "shit" at the same time, and loud enough to be heard without the I-C. Who was it? I had met and flown with many of them.

Before anyone could respond, Steve said, "Rattler 2-2, are you ready?"

He said, "Yes."

"2-9?"

"2-9 is ready."

Steve said, "Let's do this."

Then 2-9 called Tiger 6 and said, "Keep your heads down. The slicks will be shooting along with the gunships."

Tiger 6 rogered, and in we went. Everyone in my ship was ready. As the slicks flared over the smoke, Steve put two rockets on each target so anyone alive would keep their heads down. They still had someone down there as the NVA shot at us all through our right break and then continued on the wing ship. He put one on each target. As wing called out, "Ready," and then, "Breaking right," Steve was in position.

The slicks said, "Pulling pitch," and they were out of there. Steve called the slicks and asked if everyone was accounted for. Rattler 2-9 responded, "All accounted for. That includes one body bag." The second ship, 2-2, said he had all his cargo as well. Steve was putting rockets on the muzzle blasts as he spoke.

Steve called the spotter plane and told him to "burn that place back to hell."

The spotter said, "Roger. And I'm sorry about your pilot."

Steve answered back, "Thank you. He was also a good friend."

"I just called the F-4's, and they are rolling in."

"That should take care of those fuckers," Steve said, almost in tears. "Even if anyone is still alive down there, the napalm will burn them in their spider holes and tunnels."

He said, "Mac, I'm afraid to ask who the pilot was. Call them for me."

"Rattler 2-9," I said, "this is 9-6's copilot. Who is the pilot?"

There was a pause and then he said, "It's Phil Henry, 2-4."

"Thank you," was all I could get out of my mouth. I had flown at least four times with Phil. I called back and asked about Bob, the crew chief, and Ralph, the door gunner. The other slick answered and said, "Just some superficial scratches. Just enough for a Purple Heart."

It was a quiet flight back to Baldy. Not a word was spoken until Steve called out that a flight of four Hueys was entering the pattern from the west.

Steve followed with, "The slicks will land at the turnaround and discharge their cargo, and the guns will be refueling, before we return to the turnaround. Have two trucks meet the slicks and pick up your patrol and a body bag."

Rattler 2-9 and 2-2 reported that their fuel was OK and they would land at the turnaround.

Phil was in a body bag, so the slick crew didn't see him. The other three had a few bumps, bruises and a little blood. They carefully put Phil's body in one truck, and the other three climbed in an adjacent truck. I saw Bob Jones, the FNG, climb into the truck. He looked the healthiest of the three. They drove up to the mash unit. The patrol remained. They thanked the remaining crews. All eight of them thanked each one of the slick crews individually, and then climbed into the other truck. The slicks waved as the patrol departed for HQ.

HQ called and said, "Guns go ahead and rearm, and slicks you can return to your resupply missions down south in the LZ Ross area, after you grab some ammo for your crew."

Those slick drivers had just lost one of their own, but it seemed to me that we weren't being given any time to think about what had just happened.

Chapter 29.

WARRANT OFFICERS ARE OK

As we landed at the turnaround, Steve told me to hold the controls. He climbed out and walked over to the lead ship. It had already landed and shut down. He found the pilot, and they talked a few minutes. Steve walked back and said, "Shit! Phil only had a few weeks remaining, like me. Let's get this hog re-armed. Shut it down, Kevin."

I heard a truck driving down the hill. It stopped next to our ships and out jumped the eight-man patrol whose lives we had just saved. They literally pulled us out of our seats the moment the blades stopped. They couldn't stop thanking us. Two grunts had tears in their eyes. They wanted our names, our unit, and they were all talking at once. They were trying to shake our hands. One guy wanted to name his first child after me. We were quiet. It was hard for me to get the thought of Phil out of my head. I'm sure all our guys were having the same thoughts.

The grunts had already thanked the slicks. They had come back from their debriefing just to thank us, even more so than the slicks.

"We were just doing our job," was all Steve could think to say.

Their 6 said, "We have to go back and finish the debrief."

We were relieved. I actually felt a little embarrassed. I don't know why. It did help me realize how much we could help our guys. We carried lots of fire power.

It was very quiet rearming the ships. I helped the gunner rearm, and Steve helped the crew chief. I thought this place smelled even worse today. *This filthy, hot, humid, foul smelling third-world country is a mess. What the hell are they burning besides shit? Half the people here are Viet Cong by night and simple farmers by day. We don't know who is friend and who is enemy.*

I found out after we finished with our ships that Steve and Phil Henry had been in flight school together and were FNGs together. Steve looked like he was going to cry. I was too new to know what to say, so I didn't say anything.

I was still trying to grab hold of the fact that Phil was dead.

I remembered my windshield. It looked like several bullets went through. Probably a machine gun blast. The top one third was gone. Shit, I almost joined Phil! Both my shoulders hurt. *Now what's wrong?*

One of the crew chiefs came over and said, "Come on, let's go build rockets. You look at that windshield too long, and it will fuck you up."

I nodded and walked with him over to the conex containers and joined in. This took some time and helped distract us. You had tin snips to cut the metal bands holding the wood crates together, then a crowbar to pry off the nailed-on tops. Lying in the short cases were six warheads in wood cradles. There were six motors in the longer crates. You just screwed them together and put them in the conex containers. We did this for an hour.

We then returned to the gunships for the second time, rechecking the ships for holes, leaks, and loose control rods. (Control rods transfer our cyclic and collective motions to the main rotor blades.) Since we couldn't find anything wrong, I sat down in the shade with the wing crew chief and door gunner and started talking.

They said they liked me because I wasn't so military and didn't throw my weight around like some of the officers. They said that warrant officers were friendlier.

I said, "Hell yes, you are sitting behind me with a loaded machine gun. Do you really think I'm going to ask you if your sister is easy?"

They laughed, and Scott Mayo looked at me and said, "Mac, I have a sister."

I said, "Oops."

Dick said, "I have three brothers."

Scott said, "I'm not worried about you, Mac. You are stuck here in paradise with me, right where I can keep a close watch on you."

Now, I laughed.

Scott told us he had one year of college without a major. He said he had always been interested in flying. He liked working on cars as a hobby. It just seemed natural to work on a helicopter and do both.

Dick, the door gunner, grew up hunting all over the Pacific Northwest. He had been working in the forest, logging since he started high school. He said, "I thought shooting from a helicopter couldn't be any more dangerous than logging. However, now I think I was wrong. Nothing is as dangerous as this."

I said, "I think you're right. No wait, I know you're right."

Scott was 19 and Dick 18. I was 21 and would be 22 in three months.

Wow, at our ages, we should be doing something age appropriate, like chasing women. Anything would be better than my first five weeks here. Good thing I like flying with the Birds.

After two hours of this, we decided to go to bed, even though it was only 20 hundred hours.

I took my shirt off and asked Joe, Steve's crew chief, if he would look at my back.

He said, "You have four blisters from your neck to your belt."

This got some attention, and Scott, the crew chief in the wing ship, came over and looked. "Mac, those are burns from a hot piece of brass. You should go over to the MASH unit and have the medics put something on those before they get infected."

"I'll do it in the morning. I'm too tired now."

Chapter 30.

RED PHONE

A t 2300, the red phone woke us up. (It was more effective than your parents when they tried to wake you up for high school.) We were untying the blades when I jumped in and yelled, "Clear." Both Scott and Dick said, "Clear," and the blades were turning. Steve came running to the ships and gave all the info to the wing and flare ships.

He jumped in and gave me the same info. I dialed it in and marked my map. We were heading west about 14 clicks (8.4 miles) to a marine outpost, call sign: Mountain 6. We called their 6. He said, "A company of NVA is moving up the hill. It's very steep and their progress is slow."

Damn, that wind coming in from the gaping hole in my windshield is distracting. I hope I can hold my gunsight steady.

Steve added, "It's the artillery base we flew by earlier today."

We cleared Baldy's perimeter and headed west, 20 feet above ground for two minutes. Then, we gradually climbed 100 feet as we were approaching some hills. Steve was shaking. I said, "You OK."

He said, "Sure, you take it and make the calls." I nodded and took over.

I called mountain 6 and said, "This is Firebird 9-6. What's your current situation?"

"Same, except they are a little closer. We are dropping mortars on them and have artillery flares in the air. We only have 40 men here. I can't see what they could possibly hope to gain. Our artillery can only reach to LZ Cacti, and nothing is closer. We support marine patrols that come into our area."

"Be there in one minute, pop smoke and tell me where they are."

"We only see them on the north and west sides. There is some cover, but not much. No cover on the other two sides of the compass."

I said, "Save your flares. We have a flare ship with us. We will come in from the north and shoot that group, then swing to the west side and take care of those guys. Both gunships will break over your position. Then you can resume dropping mortars on them if we are in the clear. Our ships are close together as we cover each other. Let me know if anything changes."

Back came, "OK."

I could hear the mortar rounds exploding in the background. I asked 9-2, "You got all that?" He clicked twice.

I asked the flare ship to throw out flares on the west and north sides, and then asked if he could keep an eye on those parachutes. He rogered. The parachute cords can damage the control rods.

I really like this minimal conversation. Things are happening in seconds up here, and there is no time for idle talk.

I said, "Is everyone ready?" I got back two clicks.

I glanced at Steve, and he looked frozen, just staring at his boots. I didn't want to alarm the crew, so I casually said, "OK Steve, it's yours." No response. I reached over and hit his arm. He jumped and looked at me. "We're in position to start the run," I told him.

He looked at me and said, "I heard you." He grabbed the controls, but said nothing. I pulled my sight down and was ready to shoot. The guys in back were ready.

The NVA was immediately shooting at us before we fired off a round. Tracers were flashing by us. I heard that dreadful hammering on the nose. I hoped my cannon was still functioning. Those rounds hit us and struck some hard metal. I could see sparks flying when I looked down between the spaces left by the radio, it being smaller than the space where it was mounted.

Steve came out of his trance and training took over. He put three pair of rockets on both targets. The cannon was OK. That was a relief. I must have fired 50 rounds. The wing ship rolled in, and his second pair of rockets set off a tremendous secondary explosion. He must have seen something. The rest of us continued picking out targets until we broke. We climbed out until we heard 9-2. Then, he broke right, and we started again. As we were going through all of these motions, an explosion buffeted us to the point I thought we were going to be thrown out of the sky. When it first hit our ship, it rolled us over 60 degrees. That's about all this gunship can take.

I assumed we had hit their supply of Bangalore Torpedoes (long pieces of bamboo filled with explosive charges). The bad guys slide them under the concertina wire (coils of barbed wire) and set them off. This blows a hole in the wire, and their troops can storm through faster than the GIs on the FSB can kill them. That rocket might also have struck their main ammo supply.

Our goal here tonight was to hit them before they get near that wire. That explosion would make a difference. Now they would have to cut the wire manually, after climbing a steep mountain.

I called out to 9-2 and said, "Nice shot." I emphasized the words, nice shot. He clicked back, and then said, "So was yours."

Steve gave me a very strange look. I just smiled and nodded.

The flare ship kept the place well lit, while we made two more runs.

We had two rockets remaining and wing also had two. We received only sporadic return fire, but we quickly extinguished that problem with cannon and mini guns. The marines were grateful. They said they were sending out two small patrols to evaluate the situation.

Steve was still in a different state of mind. I had seen this in drunks in my dorm and in our own O club.

I called the marines. "You guys want us to hang out for a while? In case those NVA want to continue this dance. We have some ordnance remaining. Or we can go home and refuel and rearm? We can be back in 30 to 40 minutes."

Mountain 6 said, "I can't thank you enough. Go home and get ready if these bastards decide to come back."

I said, "Hey, we work for the same boss. Call any time."

He just said, "Thanks."

Steve said, "You take it." I took the controls and said, "I've got it"

I flew back to Baldy, wondering what was happening with Steve. The marines called and said, "There are over 100 dead out here. We even have a few prisoners." I called Baldy. They said the slicks would go out tomorrow and get the live ones for interrogation.

They would also haul back a few dead ones.

I'm glad I don't do that ugly shit anymore.

We flew into Baldy and went straight to refueling. After that, it was around the mountain to the turnaround and the Hilton.

We have to do something about that name. I have never been to a Hilton, but I just know they are better than this.

We parked in the revetments and started the rearming. First, I crawled under the nose with a flashlight and saw two holes. I got up and called the crew chief and showed him. He opened the battery access panel and looked in with a light. The battery was OK, but we had lost a radio. It was the high frequency radio. Now we couldn't listen to any tunes. *Not that we had time.*

I thought I better make myself useful and help with the rearming. I carried 38 rockets to the pods in several trips and then started with the 40 mike-mike. That ordnance was heavy.

I will bust my ass for these guys. Hey, I'm discovering that we all depend on each other. This is closer than a football team. These guys will be my fraternity brothers for my next ten plus months.

The crew chief of the wing ship, Joe Gibbs, called me over and pointed to the armor plate on my side of the ship. This is a metal plate that slides forward after you sit in your seat. It protects the pilots from being shot from the side. The bad news is your head sits above this armor plate. I stood there for a moment realizing that a bullet had hit the plate. The plate had done its job.

Joe said, "Jesus, Mac, you're lucky. That was close."

I reached out and put my finger in the hole. It went halfway through the metal. I said, "Damn, that WAS close."

By now, everyone but Steve was staring at the hole. One guy pointed at the hole and said, "Four more inches and you'd be dead."

I was speechless. I sure didn't need to think about that!

We all went back to the Hilton. I couldn't sleep, and I'll bet no one else could either. I was thinking about Phil. In only a moment, he was gone, forever. I was luckier by four inches.

At 0600 our red phone rang. We jumped off those lumpy mattresses, and the adrenalin was pumping, as we ran to the ships. Before we got there, Steve yelled at us, "False alarm."

We turned and walked back to the Hilton. Steve was standing in the doorway. "We have a combat assault in two hours. Eleven slicks will land here to load up, and we'll lead them in."

Joe interrupted Steve and asked him to call maintenance for a new radio and a windshield for Mac. By using Baldy's switchboard in HQ, we could call our CO, Firebird hooch, flight line and maintenance.

"This next part pisses me off," Steve told us, "and the new guys will see more of this stuff soon. We are going back to Million-Dollar Hill. I don't know why. It's been napalmed and covered with Agent Orange, and both of those kill everything they touch. It looks like Target Practice Island. In WWII, we kept every piece of land we fought on until the war was over. Over here, shit, I have been into some of same LZs four times. It should be just once!"

We headed to the mess hall. What a surprise: hot cakes and ham. We all did the starving dog routine. Eat fast or possibly lose out.

An hour later, our slicks were arriving. There was an extra ship with them. It had a rattler painted on its nose with a stethoscope around its neck and the words, "Snake Doctor."

I asked one of the guys, "Is that one of ours?"

"That's the maintenance ship," he said. "They do repairs in the field. It's probably here to change out the radio and windshield. They carry enough parts to practically rebuild a ship. They can even carry extra rotor blades strapped on the belly."

All 11 ships circled around to the back side of Baldy to refuel. Then, they went back to the runway, lined up in single file along one side, and shut down.

Two pilots and two others climbed out of Snake Doctor. One of our crew told me the other two were mechanics.

Another person climbed out, and I recognized him. It was Firebird 9-3, Dennis Boyle, from Maryland. I wondered what was going on. Dennis introduced me to the chief mechanic officer and test pilot, Martin Robertson. We shook hands, and he asked me, "Where is that radio you destroyed?" I gave him a look, you know, when you look at some one, shrug your shoulders, and put your arms halfway out and turn your palms up.

He smiled and said, "Just kidding." I took him over to 728 and opened the access panel and stepped back. As he looked in, the two mechanics walked up with a new radio.

It took them 15 minutes, as they had to remove the battery and a few other parts. They said they'd have to repair the windshield back in Chi Lai. "We can't repair it the field yet, but we'll be able to soon, as new tools arrive."

Several deuce and a half's (large two-and-a-half ton trucks) drove up and unloaded 70 grunts with full field packs. They had M-16's, three M-60 machine guns, a few shotguns, a grenade launcher (similar to our nose cannon), and numerous belts of machine-gun ammo draped over their shoulders. They broke up into groups of seven and climbed in the slicks. The eleventh ship was a spare, just in case.

While they were loading, I noticed Steve climbing into Snake Doctor. Dennis Boyle climbed into 728 with me. I looked at Dennis, and he leaned across the panel of radios and armament switches and said in a low voice, "I'll explain after this CA." I nodded.

A first lieutenant gave a small card to each slick and gun pilot. He climbed into the lead slick.

It was the usual routine with frequencies, coordinates and the call sign. The LT was Big John 6. OK, he didn't look that big. Maybe it was his hat size. Maybe, what he thought was his hat size or maybe something else?

Dennis asked the crew chief to climb out and signal everyone to crank 'em up. This signal is one arm straight up over your head, swinging in small circles.

At that signal, all the blades began turning. While the engines were getting up to flying rpm, I heard Dennis call out, "This is Firebird 9-3, commo check." This was followed by "Firebird 9-2." The 10 slicks reported by calling out their position in the lineup: Rattler 1, Rattler 2, and so on to 11.

Lead rattler, Glen Walton, rattler 2-9, called out, "Rattlers, after take- off, form up in flights of three, three, four and the last ship circle as briefed when we arrive at the LZ."

We all pulled pitch and took off in a long line. The Rattlers formed up into their flights. We turned straight west to the valley of Million-Dollar Hill. The LZ was close, so the guns pulled ahead to prep the area before the slicks arrived. It was a narrow valley; once in, it would be a hard steep turn right to fly out.

The guns rolled in and punched rockets all around the LZ. We were determined not to let history repeat itself.

As rockets were exploding, everyone else was shooting. It looked like a forest fire had roared through. The earth was black, as were all the leafless trees. They looked like crooked poles sticking up in the air. The only place to land was that same small LZ. I saw three piles of melted metal. There was room for three ships at a time in there, but it would be tight for that last flight of four.

We broke right to meet the slicks. We saw nothing on the ground for a quarter of a mile. We called the slicks and said we took no fire. We then turned to get alongside them and take them in.

Since nothing looked alive down there, we hung back to cover first and second flight together. We circled while all three flights delivered their troops without incident.

We all returned to Baldy. HQ told the birds to stand down after refueling. They told two of the slicks to remain and begin resupply for the troops they had just inserted. The other nine would receive orders after refueling. Everyone could shut down on the turnaround.

We landed the gunships and called for fuel trucks. As we were refueling, the slicks were landing in pairs off the runway on the turnaround. Since we hadn't fired much, rearming was quick.

I turned to Dennis and waited for him to speak. It took a moment, like he was wondering what to say, or how.

He started with, "Mac, Steve said he was sick and needed a replacement." He waited, and I waited. Finally, Dennis said, "Mac, he took me aside, just before he climbed aboard Snake Doctor. He told me he was scared." Dennis turned away, like he didn't want to go on, but in a minute he did. "Steve said, 'I saw what happened to Phil, my best friend since flight school.' Steve has two weeks to go until he returns to the world, and he doesn't want to die." Dennis gave a sigh. I could tell he felt embarrassed and maybe ashamed.

I didn't know what to say, so I just said, "That's OK."

Dennis and I continued our talk about life and death, but nothing more about Phil or Steve. I didn't have much to add. This was still my first war.

Dennis walked around the ship. He climbed in, and then out, for no reason. He must have been thinking about Phil. He turned to me and said, "Finish checking out this bird. I have to call the CO."

Chapter 31.

FIRST PURPLE HEART

Dennis was on the phone a long time. When he finally came out of the Hilton, he waved me over. He said, "Shit," so suddenly I took a step back. I stood there stunned. Dennis seemed OK. But, then again, nothing was normal at the moment. He was staring at me. "What the hell happened to you?"

"What are you talking about?" was all I could think to say.

"You have blood all over your face."

I reached up and ran my hand over my face. It did feel wet. I looked at my hand. I saw red.

Dennis said, "Get over to the MASH unit."

First, I ran to the ship to look at my helmet. I picked it up off the seat and turned it so I could see the front. There were two holes with very jagged and serrated edges. The clear plastic faceplate would go up into the helmet only about one inch. Something had struck the front of my helmet while I was flying the last mission. (We lower the faceplate to protect our eyes.) I looked inside the helmet, and there were two bloody holes. One of the holes contained a jagged piece of metal from the window frame, also bloody. I pulled it out as Dennis and Martin walked up.

"You are one lucky SOB," Martin told me.

I nodded and walked over to the MASH unit trying to understand what had just happened.

I have been called a lucky son of a bitch three times today. Coincidence? No, I don't believe in coincidences.

At the MASH unit, I told them what happened and showed them my helmet. A few shook their heads. One doctor looked at my head, while another said he would find a nurse to give me an antibiotic shot. No stitches were required. I asked that this not be reported because we were short of pilots, and I would be grounded. They agreed, but said I had to come in the next day for another shot, and the day after that, if I was still around. They gave me some pills and said I should take two a day until the bottle was empty.

"Try to keep it clean," they told me.

"Oh yeah," I said, "I just remembered. I have some burns on my back." I took off my shirt and showed them. They put a salve on the burns and gave me the tube so I could continue twice a day. I knew I'd never find anyone else to rub this medicine on me. *No point mentioning that.*

I moved my arm and was quickly reminded of the burning. I asked the doctor if there was anything in my shoulders. They were both bloody. He probed around the bloody areas and found several pieces of Plexiglas in each shoulder. The probing hurt worse than the initial wounding. I asked the doctor not to put this in my file so I can continue flying. He reluctantly agreed.

Then, an evil nurse approached me with a large needle sticking out of a small syringe and said, "Drop your pants and lean over the table."

Shit that stung. It hurt worse than all the previous probing.

I returned from the MASH unit with my helmet in my hand and what looked like a long narrow band-aide on my forehead at the hair line. Dennis was walking out of the Hilton. He saw me and signaled me to come to him.

He filled me in on the personnel issues. "Jim Morton was senior pilot, but he was a warrant officer, and CO needed a commissioned officer to be the birds' platoon leader. Bill Knapley would be the new 9-6. Tice had been promoted to 9-1, but he had been killed the previous day along with his copilot. That copilot had had three weeks in that ship and was ready to be promoted to the wing copilot. Dennis shook his head in disgust. "We're now way behind the curve in our training."

Dennis looked at me and, as if suddenly remembering I'd been to the MASH, he asked, "You OK?"

"It was nothing," I said. "Please don't tell anyone. They'll make me go to the flight surgeon, and I'll miss flying."

"Please don't miss any flying. "

He went on talking about personnel. "We have only two other wing pilots. One is 9-8, your buddy Jim Williams. He's still in the hospital in Danang with his burnt ass. The other wing is Damon Steele, 9-0. Captain Knapley has only a month remaining. He's been flying wing for the past month. He got into the birds late in his tour. The new platoon leader will be Captain Jerry Wilder. Do you have any feelings about that Kevin?"

"I don't know him," I said, "but sure, I'll fly with him. He must be OK if you guys promoted him to wing."

"Are you sure? You don't even have a week in the birds, and already we want to promote you to wing copilot."

"I can do it."

"OK, Wilder will fly up in two days to relieve Morton and bring me a copilot. You fly the wing. I'll fly with Meadow's crew. Morton is ready to fly lead with his wing copilot for now, so you can get some wing time."

"We're set for now," he went on. "You'll fly in wing with me. Then, when Wilder arrives I'll go back to lead and start training Wilder and get him to you as your copilot ASAP."

Wow, these promotions come fast.

Amazingly, nothing happened for the rest of the day. I spent most of it with Joe Gibbs. He was teaching me about repair and maintenance of the helicopters, and this was important because they had to be checked constantly, and we didn't always have time to let the mechanics do the official maintenance checks. The gunships and the slicks were supposed to have a maintenance check after 25 hours in the air. Every hundred hours, the mechanics would tear one down and check everything, then put it back together. These checks could take days, and a ship could get 25 hours in the air after just two days of action. We couldn't afford to give up a machine to maintenance every couple of days. So, most of the time, we did the field checks ourselves.

This is why what Joe was teaching me was so important. He taught me about hydraulics, how to set the tolerances on the push-pull rods for the main rotor, how to repair the cannon, and more. The complete checks we did in the field took a long time because we could work on a ship only a little at a time. If we were scrambled, we had to be able to get it operational quickly. We'd learned none of this in fight school. After all, we were going to be pilots, not mechanics. *My manual will have to be a hardbound book, it will contain so much information.*

We ate at 1800 and passed out. It seemed a little cooler that night.

Chapter 32.

FLYING WING

The red phone came to life at 0100, (oh 100). It was the same routine: Jump up, grab your shirt and put it on as you run. Take a leak on the other side of the revetment barrels. Climb in as the door gunner is untying the main rotor.

We all started checking circuit breakers right after the crew chief connected the battery. I was hitting switches and yelling "Clear" to get the blades moving. All this before the fire team leader (Dennis Boyle) came out of the Hilton.

Lead and Flare got the info, and then Dennis climbed into the wing ship and handed it to me. The moment I put in the frequency, he called for a commo check. Lead and Flare called back, "Lima Charley (loud and clear)."

Dennis looked at me and said, "We're flying to LZ West." That was about 25 clicks south by south west (15 miles).The NVA or Charlie, as the Firebirds called the enemy, was attacking the LZ in mass. ("Charlie" began as "Victor Charlie" for Viet Cong and later shortened to Charlie.)

Morton's "Pulling pitch" came over the radio, and we moved out of the revetment, as he made the radio call to anyone in the area. We most always took off into the wind, to the east, as the wind came in from the South China Sea. All aircraft try to take off and land into the wind, which adds to the lift necessary for both actions.

As soon as we were in the air, I called my crew and said, "Go hot and test your guns." Immediately, the machine guns were warming up.

We were at max power and climbing slowly. It was not safe

flying on the deck (that is, close to the ground) at night, especially over that terrain.

Morton called LZ West and asked for a sit rep. West said, "They are coming up on all sides of this mountain."

It was 600 meters. *Not much of a mountain*, I thought.

They had a 400 meter killing field (everything cut down to the dirt), so this would help as Charlie had to cross that open ground.

"Are they in the open yet?"

"Not yet. We got lucky and two of our patrols spotted them five clicks out. We are pointing our artillery down the mountain and loading them with beehives (similar to a shotgun shells)."

I told him, "We're only five minutes out."

"Can you make it sooner?"

"I'll try. If you start shooting the 50's and beehives before we get there, I'll ask you to stop when we make our gun runs."

Morton said, "We'll come in on your north side and shoot there, and then the west side, and then break west. While we're doing that, I want you to tell us where to shoot next. Our flare ship will have the place lit up. Pick the largest concentration and point us there."

We were almost there, so I gave the ship to Dennis. He said, "I've got it."

He called Firebird 9-2 and said, "This mission will be different, as you have already figured out. I'll try to come back around and give you some cover when you break right. Then we fly west, away from LZ West and turn south and do the same thing on the south and east sides and break right. I don't think we'll have as much trouble on the south and east sides. They're steep."

"That's the only way I see this, unless LZ West points us in a different direction. Do you have any suggestions?"

All that came back was, "Nope."

"OK, 9-2 rolling in," Dennis said. "They are coming out of the trees on the north." He called out to the LZ to not fire on the north and west sides. They gave a "roger that.'"

He was punching rockets as he finished the call. He was shooting along the tree line. Gunners were shooting long bursts. It was like daylight out there. The enemy was returning fire from the trees. It looked like they were shooting blind due to the canopy (hundred foot trees). Dennis fired eight rockets and broke right. He didn't climb out; he just kept turning until he was on the wing's tail. As wing broke right, we all started shooting again. Dennis fired only two pair of rockets and flew on to the west side and fired along that tree line as well.

Chapter 33.

SECOND PURPLE HEART

This was working well until a hundred Charlies started shooting at us on full automatic as we rolled in on the south side. My windshield exploded. Shit, I just did this in the Lead ship. Glad we have thick plastic faceplates that slide down out of our helmets. I felt some of the pieces hit me in the arms and around my mouth. I didn't look long enough to see if there was any blood on my gloves.

Dennis called out, "Is everyone OK?"

I said, "I'm OK."

Gibbs said, "I'm OK, but Paul is bleeding from his arm. I think it's minor, because he's still shooting."

I though, *Good, because so am I, and I know I'm hit again.*

The wind felt like it could lift me out of my seat. I kept concentrating on the muzzle flashes and held the trigger down, sweeping the barrels from the trees out across the open kill zone.

As soon as we broke, Jim and his copilot headed in to do the same. LZ Ross called and said, "Stay on the south. The north and west are OK. We've been shooting beehives in there. I think the ones on the east have moved south."

"Roger and 9-2 is rolling in."

They were still shooting, though much less. We pretty much used the same tactics as the first run. Dennis was punching rockets. I was shooting, but shorter bursts to conserve ammo. The door gunners weren't conserving yet.

9-2 called, "Ready," then "Breaking right."

His rockets were on target. We came around again. Suddenly, we felt and heard something hit our belly on our break on the third run.

Dennis said, "How are the instruments? Any warning lights?"
I said, "OK and no."
Lead called and said, "You are leaking something. It's not much."
"OK, let's make one more run and dump everything we got."
"Roger."
We turned, rolled in, and took down the trees. The open area just had bodies, so we ignored it. I held down my trigger until I was empty. Then, I noticed my shoulders were burning. We broke, but from farther out, because he knew we couldn't cover him. Out of ordinance.

As we were pointing our noses north, Dennis called the flare ship and asked if he was still with us. He rogered. Then, Dennis called LZ West and told them we were returning to Baldy. They already knew this as we were all on the same frequency. East said "Good night and thank you. You guys really hung your ass out for us, and we won't forget it."

Dennis said, "Call if they come back." Then, he called Chu Lai maintenance and reported our problem. "No warning lights, so I'm hoping we can make it to Baldy. 9-2 is following and keeping a close watch on the leak. It's hydraulic fluid, oil or fuel, and no warning lights.

"You might send another wing ship up ASAP. Bring Snake Doctor. He may be able to fix Wing's windshield. I heard they can do that now. Almost took off Mac's head when it was shot out. I know you usually work on windshields at Chu Lai, but maybe, just maybe?"

The night chief said he would get right on it. "Thanks," Dennis replied, "and definitely bring up a wing ship." He turned to me. "Hell Mac, two missions, two windshields, and now I see you're wounded again. You sure you want to fly Guns?"

When we were on short final, we got a master caution light for transmission fluid. We landed in the turnaround and shut it down there. It would be easier to get to for repair there than in the revetment.

As soon as Dennis cut off the fuel for shutdown, the transmission seized. "Shit Mac that transmission could have seized up a minute ago, and we'd be dead." He was shaking his head. "I guess it wasn't our time."

"I just got a master caution red on the hydraulics," I told him.

Steve called CL and reported that we were grounded

We unlocked our harnesses and climbed out. Dennis said, "At least we don't have to rearm this ship. Let's go to bed. I feel drained. That was nasty tonight."

I walked with him to the Hilton but kept on to the MASH Unit and had some more Plexiglas removed from my shoulders. And another one of those fucking shots that looked like syrup in the syringe.

The Docs asked me, "What's going on?"

I just shrugged and said, "There's a war going on." Again, I asked them not to report my injuries because I'd be grounded. One of the medics said, "I'll just leave your chart on a treatment table." I nodded and walked back to the Hilton and fell asleep before I could get my shirt off. I think it was 0330.

At 0600, I woke to the sound of helicopters landing on the turnaround. I got up and staggered to the doorway, which didn't have a door. I saw another wing ship shutting down. Behind it was Snake Doctor coming in to land.

Out jumped Snake Doctor 6, Martin Robertson, our chief mechanic, smiling as always. He walked over to 728 and crawled underneath. He came back out and said, "You guys are lucky. The bullets just creased the tranny, two of them, so the leak was very slow. This ship has to be lifted back to Chu Lai. I'll call HQ and request a shit hook." (Shit Hook is short for Chinook, a large tandem rotor helo that can lift thousands of pounds hanging in a sling under its belly.) The gunship was over 9000 pounds empty, but that would be no problem for the hook.

I walked over to the gunship, 528, and Captain Bill Knapley climbed out. WO Stuart Muse was his copilot, with two months as a bird. WO Chuck Norwood, also a fairly new bird, was sitting in back with the crew.

Knapley, our platoon leader, was a short timer. (He was about to go home.) We were wondering who our CO would choose to be the new platoon leader. I had heard rumors that a Captain Jerry Wilder was next in line. Rumors said he was a good leader. I was curious why the rumors didn't talk about his flying.

I knew his crew: Gibbs the crew chief, and Walsh the door gunner. They had both been in combat nearly a year. They were legendary.

I said, "Hi," and they said the same back. I had met them a few weeks earlier when I was an FNG.

Knapley asked, "What happened?"

I told him what I'd heard. "HQ warned us we'd be facing stiffer opposition here, since President Johnson stopped bombing North Vietnam, Hanoi and Haiphong harbor, specifically. The North is able to bring anything down the Ho Chi Minh trail in Laos, including big weapons and troops."

By now, Dennis was up, and he came out to talk to everyone.

Robertson said, "The shit hook will be here in an hour. We'll get the ship ready for a sling load."

"A slick will pick up everyone except Hanson, who'll go with Allen," Knapley told us. "I'll fly lead for now with Norwood. Dennis and Mac, go home. I'll see you in two days."

I was so tired. I felt like I'd been through a shit storm, and I definitely hadn't gotten enough sleep. I went back in the Hilton.

This staying up all night on adrenalin drains you.

We grabbed our gear out of our downed ship and put it the Hilton, their machine guns with equipment bags (called barrel bags) and our M-16's. Then back out to the ships to get the empty ammo cans, smoke grenades, chicken boards, helmets and flak jackets.

The Snake Doctor crew began tying down the blade, securing the door gunners' doors. We didn't have front doors on the gunships. They would have obstructed our view and thrown shrapnel into the cockpit, if they got hit. Martin moved his ship, and then we all jogged to the Hilton to avoid getting sandblasted by the shit hook. One mechanic remained to attach the cable to the Huey. After that, he stepped back and gave thumbs up to one of the hook's crew, who had been hanging out a side window observing the procedure.

The dust was so thick that, for a short time, we lost sight of the Huey. The Shit hook ended up blowing all the dirt off of our Pena Prime. Just great; now we get to walk on sticky oil.

The hook slowly lifted up to tighten the cable, and then pulled the Huey off the ground, climbing as it flew south to Chu Lai.

When the dust settled, we walked over to the gunships to clean out the dirt, a disadvantage of not having a front door.

Thirty minutes later, a slick landed in the turnaround and shut down. The pilot was Ed Place, rattler 2-2, and crew chief Steve

Atchison, along with the gunner Todd Burnet, and an FNG. I flew with them a few times as an FNG.

Ed said, "Come on. Let's help these grounded birds back to their nest."

That drew a laugh, even from us.

Dennis and the birds helped us load our weapons and our gear into the slick. When that work was finished, everyone started talking, as we all knew each other. We told our whole story. Their eyes were wide when we finished.

It occurred to me: Officers have their own club, as do the enlisted men. We are not allowed to drink together. I understand the military's need to separate us. But come on. We just went through a small part of hell together. Shouldn't we at least be able to have a beer together?

Ed looked at Dennis and asked, "Are you birds up for a free taxi ride home?"

Dennis smiled, and said, "Yes."

"Mount up. We're out of here."

We climbed in and settled back for some cool air.

Ed took off and climbed to 1500 feet. Dennis crawled forward a few feet and told Ed, "The Firebirds get nose bleeds at this altitude."

Ed laughed and said, "Be quiet or you can walk."

The rest of the ride was quiet because all the birds quickly fell asleep.

Ed had called Chu Lai and requested a truck to pick us up. The truck drove down the flight line with the birds on one side, slicks on the other, and stopped 50 feet in front of us while our blades were still turning. We started picking up our gear, and Ed's crew chief and door gunner helped us get it all in the truck. Then, the crew climbed back in the ship. They were putting on their helmets and connecting their radio's, when Dennis went to Ed's side window and asked, "Why aren't you shutting down?"

"I have to go back to work," he said. "Don't drink too much." He smiled and called the tower for takeoff.

These 12 to 18 hour days were not mentioned in flight school. *More reality for my book.*

We rode in the truck to the maintenance hangar to leave some of the gear—machine guns and equipment—in a room until a ship was ready. Helmets, pistols, chicken boards, M-16s, and maps stayed with us for the ride to the 71st Helicopter Company.

I was ready to pass out when I got to my hooch. Dean, the surfer dude, was sitting on his bunk reading. I dropped everything on my bunk and said, "Got a day off?"

"When we tried to crank up this morning," he said, "the oil and engine red master caution lights came on. We shut down and called maintenance. They drove down and swarmed all over our ship, and told us, 'This repair will take a day or more. We might have to pull out the engine.' Amazing, how a ship can die overnight when no one is flying the damn thing.

"The good news is they told us there were no reserve ships. Everything is flying or in the shop. The pilot said we get a day off, and here I am."

I told him, "I'm going to sleep before I shower."

I don't remember anything after that.

Chapter 34.

SHOOTING SHARKS

When I woke at 0700, I seemed to remember a few rockets hitting near us in the night. It could have been a dream. *Oh well, I'm a Firebird, so I don't give a rat's ass.*

I cleaned myself to the point of being presentable. The mess hall seemed pretty good that morning. The bacon was a great addition to those powdered eggs.

After breakfast, I was walking back to my hooch, when the day clerk Thompson came running and calling my name. I saw the look of concern on his face.

"What's up?"

"Get your flight gear and report to the CO immediately."

"You know why?"

He just shrugged, turned, and ran back toward the CO's office.

I grabbed my gear and jogged to the CO's office. As I ran across the parade ground, I saw Major Wilson sitting in a jeep. I stopped jogging and walked the next six feet. I looked at him sitting there with a smile on his face.

Before I could say anything, he said, "Hop in."

I tossed my stuff on the back seat and got in.

"How are you feeling today?"

"Fine sir."

He told me I was getting a slight pass today. "You don't salute—snipers could be anywhere—and you don't have to say sir, once we're in the air."

I just said, "OK, sir."

He smiled.

"Let me see that helmet." He looked at the ragged and jagged cuts. "Damn, Mac. Do you have someone watching over you?"

We stopped at one of the gunships. It was a loaded lead ship just out of maintenance.

"Where's the crew?" I asked him.

"Today, it will be just you and me. Let's check out this bird."

While we were doing the preflight, he said, "We're going on a fun mission. Did you know there is a mini rest area, an R & R area (rest & recuperation) a mile or so north on the beach for soldiers who have been in the bush too long? It's a place where they can have a few days to forget the war."

I just nodded. *An R & R setting in Vietnam?* This was news to me.

The CO paused and gave me a slow look over. I knew something was coming. "Why do you keep flying after being wounded?"

I was shocked. I thought I had asked everyone to keep quiet. "It wasn't that bad," I told him, hoping I sounded convincing. "The major said it was OK."

"Rules are rules," he retorted. "What if you passed out?"

I fell back on my flight school training. "No excuse sir. It won't happen again."

Then, he leaned toward me and said, "You did a good job protecting our guys. Battalion called me and told me what a fantastic job you all did last night." He paused but went on before I could say anything. "You were put in for an air medal, maybe a V device for valor."

Then, he surprised me again. "Let's go shoot some sharks."

"What?"

It came out of me before I had a chance to think. I'd been pre-occupied with climbing into the gunship, strapping in, and checking circuit breakers. (The circuit breakers are a backup, so weapons aren't fired by mistake.)

He laughed and said, "I like to fly with you because I never know what will happen next." I didn't know what to say, so I didn't say anything. He yelled, "Clear," cracked the throttle and pulled the trigger. The engine was beginning to whine and the main rotor blade began to move, so I looked out my side and yelled, "Clear."

I was checking instruments in the center panel. On the roof ceiling area above us and between us, I checked circuit breakers. Then, I slowed down to breathe.

The CO called the tower and was cleared to take off north. As we climbed he told me to look ahead and find a tall life-guard tower on the beach. "Some sharks were seen swimming in the area," he told me. "The beach was closed, and they called us. Mac, go hot on the armament."

"You're hot."

We climbed up to a thousand feet.

He said, "Coming right." As he was turning, he dipped the nose down and began his rocket run. I could see two sharks a hundred yards off the beach. He punched off a pair of rockets. The water was only four feet deep. The rockets hit the water and a red water spout rose 50 feet into the air. The CO pulled the nose up and over the huge fountain. He said, "Let's just circle the area and wait. You've got it."

I took the controls as I looked out at a massive circle of red water below me, growing larger as we watched. As I looked back inside to scan of my instruments, the CO said, "We just wait, and the blood will bring in more sharks." After just two circles, here they came. Six sharks coming in on a straight line. It was going to be a mammoth feeding frenzy.

The CO told me, "Bring it around and take a shot. That bloody area is getting big fast. You may be able to shoot three times."

I had already drawn my red grease-pencil circle.

"Look down at those guys cheering," he said, pointing to the men on the beach. "Let's give them a show."

I brought the hog around just in front of our cheering section and dropped the nose and punched off a pair on the left border of the red circle. I gently pushed in an ever so slight right pedal and punched off a pair in the middle and then another pair near the right side of the red chaos. I flew over our targets, and there were large pieces of shark in the red zone.

We circled, and here came more sharks, victims of their own instincts.

The CO said, "Slowly drop the nose. I'm going to turn this 40 mike-mike (nose cannon) on the next group. Let's go out and meet them before they're too close. That red mass is heading for the beach."

The CO started shooting. Three shots on the first shark, and he yelled, "Yeah." He fired maybe four times at another one. He continued shooting at other sharks. He wasn't holding back. The last shark was getting close to the beach, so I stepped on the right pedal. The nose moved right, and he fired probably a dozen times. That shark was history. The CO yelled out, "Hot damn. Do see any more, Mac?"

"Not here, but I bet more are coming. Do you want to fly out from the beach and do some more fishing?"

He said, "Yes."

So, out into the South China Sea we flew. We found two more sharks and created another large red spot. Then, he reached over and turned off the weapons.

"Let's buzz 'em." The CO was grinning. "We'll go low over their heads down the beach and then back to the Firebird line."

This was a real thrill. We flew down the beach 20 feet off the ground while the R & R guys were yelling, waving their arms, big smiles on their faces. After I flew over them, I told the CO, "Hang on." I used all my air speed to climb by pulling back on the cyclic and all the speed was converted to climbing. We rose up several hundred feet. The ship began to slow, so I pushed in my right pedal to turn the ship a hundred and eighty degrees while I was asking the CO if another real low pass was OK. He just nodded, so I dropped the nose to face those troops and dove towards them. This was a big surprise as the guys thought the show was over. They went crazy as we flew back towards them again. Some ran, some stood in place, and a few dropped to their stomachs.

I was low enough to see that most of them were grinning, so I figured everyone was having fun, except the sharks.

I pulled up and turned left away from the ocean and climbed to 500 feet. I called Chu Lai tower and asked for a straight in approach from the south. The tower told us everything was clear. We were the only ship in the pattern.

The tower operator asked us about shark hunting. I said, "We got our limit."

He said, "I thank you for all the guys on the mini R & R. I've been on that beach. It's hard to relax man, especially when you're swimming with sharks."

You've been on that beach? I couldn't help thinking. *What the hell's so stressful about your job? Did three helos and a marine jet all want to land at the same time?*

I gave the CO the controls and leaned back in my seat and

paused as I recalled the past hours at Baldy and now here. No one mentioned shooting sharks in flight school. *I helped American soldiers by killing sharks. Who would ever believe that story?*

We landed and hovered to a revetment. We shut it down and as we climbed out I said, "Sir, I can do the rearming." He smiled and nodded. He climbed into his jeep and drove off towards the company area.

Shit, me and my big mouth. I'll be here for hours rearming this bad boy.

I started with the rockets since they were the easiest. Loading the cannon is physical and time consuming. Just more info that was not included in flight school.

Five minutes into rearming, a truck drove up and stopped five feet from me. I looked up and saw four big smiles from two Firebird crews. I recognized Ski and Tyler. Ski asked me if I needed any help.

I wasn't sure what was going on, so I said, "No, I've got it."

Ski put his hands on his hips. "Look," he said, "we can watch or we can help. Really Mac, the CO sent us down here to help."

After he said that, I understood. "Thank you," I said. "I'd appreciate your giving me a hand."

As they were climbing out, Ski started assigning each man a job. One checked the rocket pods. Ski climbed up on top of the Huey to check the engine and the dust filter, while the other two checked the ammo level of the magazine for the cannon. It was a choreographed routine. These guys were impressive.

I said, "What can I do?"

One said, "You can get in the way."

Another said, "Watch and learn."

A third guy couldn't resist, "Bring us four cold beers."

While everyone was getting a good laugh, including me, Ski said, "Mac. Help them with the 40 mike-mike. That shit is heavy. Tyler will get the rockets."

They were still laughing as I walked behind the revetment to the conex storing the 40 mm shells. I walked in and said, "Load me up." They were laughing, but much less. I held out my arms, and they were draped with 40 rounds of cannon shells. *Damn, these are heavy.* As I started back towards the ship, the two guys who loaded my arms, Arny and Pat, walked past me with only 30 rounds apiece.

When Tyler and Ski saw this, it started another round of laughing.

Tyler said, "Either Mac is stronger or Arny and Pat are pussies."

Now the laughing was getting pretty loud. Ski spoke up and said, "Tyler, you are correct on both counts. Those two wear night-gowns to bed."

Arny, the crew chief, laughingly said, "Fuck you, Ski."

Arny and Pat lay their ammo down on the deck of the ship and pointed to the pile for me to do the same.

After I dumped my load, they said, "Just messing with you Mac. Welcome to the birds" and held out their hands to shake.

Pleasantries were exchanged all around. Arny and Pat were neighbors, I discovered. Arny was from Arizona and Pat, of all places, that crazy state of California. I told Pat I was from Oregon. He made a sly remark that only steers and queers were from Oregon, and he didn't see any horns on me.

That drew another laugh.

"What were you and the CO doing in a gunship with no crew chief or door gunner?" Ski asked.

I said, "You wouldn't believe me if I told you."

Ski said, "That weird?"

I came clean and told him. "We went fishing with Nobel spinners." He gave me a very strange look and asked, "What in the heck is a Nobel spinner?"

"Well Ski, Mr. Nobel invented dynamite," I told him. "We went up the beach and killed a dozen sharks or more. What a kick."

"Now you're shittin' me."

"Believe me," I said. "The place is an in-country R & R. That's what the CO told me. The beach had about 50 guys with haircuts like ours. I know this because we buzzed them twice after our life saving mission was completed."

One the guys mumbled, "Lifesaving, yeah right."

By now, we were done with the rearming.

Ski said, "Let's get out of here. I'm thirsty."

Everyone piled in the trucks. We drove to maintenance and re-ported that 515 would be mission ready after it got some gas. The sergeant thanked us, and we were out of there.

This road is getting worse, or I'm not awake in the morning. Shit, this is like a ride at an amusement park.

We made small talk as we concentrated on holding on.

Finally, we were home. We drove into the parade grounds in front of the CO's office. While I was picking up my flight gear, I looked at those four crewmen and said, "Thanks a lot, you guys." Being with them and seeing how they worked together, I realized there wasn't anything they wouldn't do for each other. A comradery I had never seen before and that includes my participation in sports.

The four just gave me a slight nod and turned toward their hooch.

I then walked up the steps to the CO's office and knocked on the screen door with two moderate knuckle taps.

Top said, "Come in."

"Top, may I ask you a question?"

He smiled (which you didn't see often) and said, "Certainly, Mr. McNally."

"Top, is it customary to thank the CO for something?"

"Well, that depends. What did he do?"

"After we shot the shit, oops, I mean shot the sharks, we returned and he parked the ship. As we were climbing out, I said I could rearm the ship. He smiled, nodded, and got in his jeep and drove off the flight line."

Top said, "Did you just say shit in my office?"

"Yes sir, I mean Top, it won't happen again." I continued. "The CO realized that what I'd said wasn't so smart. Rearming by myself after being in the birds less than a week wasn't a very bright idea. He sent two crew chiefs and two door gunners to help me."

Top asked, "How did that work out?"

"Great. It looked like they had done this hundreds of times. They took over, and I had to ask them what I could do. They put me to work helping load the cannon."

"So you want to thank Major Wilson for sending you the help?"

"Yes Top, if that's appropriate."

He got up. "Just a minute, Mr. McNally. I will see if the Major is available." He walked into the Major's office and closed the door that was usually open, but I could still hear them.

They were laughing!

The Major said, "Top, I didn't think they made them like that anymore. He is so cool under fire and just with flying in general. I told him to buzz the beach after we blew up the sharks. He did a pedal turn and dove down over them so low some were running for cover and others hit the dirt. It was the third time in two flights that he's scared the shit out of me, but he's fearless in combat, and it saves American lives."

Top asked, "Is he dangerous."

The Major said, "No. We need pilots like him in the company. Damnit, I wish he was a commissioned officer. Send him in."

Top exited the office and said, "The Major will see you."

"Thank you, Top."

When Top and I entered the office, the Major had arranged two chairs so the three formed a circle with his desk in the middle. He said, "Everyone sit down. Let's keep this informal."

We all sat, and I waited for someone to say something.

Finally, the Major spoke. "Mac, you wanted to see me?"

"Yes sir. I want to thank you for recruiting those experienced crewmen for me. They got the job finished in minutes. Without them, I'd still be on the flight line. I learned a lot by watching and listening. Those guys work together like a machine."

"Is there anything else, Mac?"

"No sir."

"Mac, what do you think the most important element of leadership is over here?"

I had to collect my thoughts to answer that. Finally, I said, "I think it's to lead by example. The AC's do that every day when they take the FNGs under their wings to train them to fly in combat. Same goes for the crew chiefs and door gunners. They do their job by giving 110% and never complaining."

"Mac, Top and I thank you for your time and your comments. You are dismissed. Oh, and you're welcome for the help."

This entire day will go in my book, which has grown into a manual.

I returned to my hooch. I saw that the large rubber bladder next to the shower was full so that answered my question of what to do this afternoon. I grabbed my shaving kit and a couple of towels.

Glen Walton was in the shower area shaving.

"Glen, how'd you get here so fast?"

"The Dust off was training a new copilot, so they flew me to the flight surgeon's door. He didn't need much time with me. The company clerk picked me up, and here I am. Four stitches, which means a Purple Heart, and I'm grounded for the next week until the stitches come out. The surgeon said the wound was superficial and to keep it clean or it's off to Danang and the hospital.

"Mac, I can never thank you enough for what you did. It was crazy stupid, but we all got out alive. Why did you do it?"

"It looked like you guys needed help, so I helped. Honestly Glen, I didn't give it much thought. I think a guy *would* go crazy if he over-thought things here. I'm just glad you and your crew are OK.

"Anyway, I owe you a lot, Glen. I flew with you my second day as an FNG. You talked to me like I was a human being. I flew with you another four or five times, and it was incredible training. You taught me how to come in fast and stand the Huey on its tail. This time I just happened to jump out.

"Another thing. I guess you didn't recognize my pilot. It was my last flight as an FNG, and the pilot was Major Wilson."

"Major Wilson, no shit! Why him?"

"I don't know, and I'm not going to ask. I didn't ask him if I could go in and pick you up either. I just did it."

Actually, after I got back and had a chance to think about it, I really thought I'd get into trouble. I decided to change the subject.

"You won't believe," I told Glen, "what the Major and I just did. We flew up the beach two miles to an in-country R & R center and blew the shit out of a dozen sharks so the GIs could get back in the water and enjoy their free time!"

"No way. I think you've been to the club and had a few."

"Tell you what, Glen. When we get finished in here, you can buy me a drink and we'll call it even."

"Deal," then under his breath and shaking his head, "Says he was shooting sharks."

Shit, I wouldn't have believed it either.

After cleaning off layers of foul smelling dirt, and shaving my four-day beard, and putting on clean clothes, I felt human again. I felt so good, I vowed I would try very hard to take nothing for granted again, if I lived through the war. I felt like going to the club and getting really fucked up! I'm not sure why. It just made sense. But I had one thing to do before I could begin drowning my brain in warm booze.

I walked over to the EM's club and stopped at the doorway. Someone just inside who was having difficulty standing asked me if I was lost. I replied, "I would like to make an announcement." He turned around and in a very loud voice yelled, "Everybody shut the fuck up. There is an ossifer, I mean an okofer ... this guy wants to say something."

The drunk stepped aside, and I quickly spoke up while the crowd was semi-quiet. There were a few trying to stifle a laugh at the guy who introduced me.

I said in a loud voice, "Would Ski, Tyler, Arny and Pat come here. I have something for them."

The four of them made their way through the crowd and stopped in front of me. They had a confused look and just stared at me.

I handed Ski $100 dollars in twenties and said rather loudly, "Thank you for helping me rearm that gunship. Make sure you each get a couple of drinks for yourselves and do whatever you want with the rest."

Ski said, "I will throw it in our bowl on the bar."

With that the place exploded in cheers, clapping and a race to the bar.

I smiled at them and mouthed a thank you, turned around and walked to the O club, determined to get in that same state of (un)consciousness. I smiled. *Those kids will at least have a good time tonight.* I knew some of them wouldn't make it back to that club as time went on here.

I walked to the O club. It had fewer occupants but twice the noise, most of that from the Firebirds, just like I would have expected. They saw me, and all started cheering. I walked by the penalty bowl and saw enough money to keep everyone on board until closing.

I got a Crown Royal, turned with my back to the bar and yelled, "We have a bell ringer tonight, and it is not me." That drew laughs, but mostly silence. In an even louder voice, I said, "Glen Walton, ring the bell, and then buy me a drink!"

Glen, who was several drinks ahead of me, asked in a slurred voice. "Why the hell would I buy a drink for a goddamned bird? Hell, I used up a lot of my valuable time training you, and now you're going to waste it killing monkeys and trees with your rockets."

That drew a cheer from the snakes and a boo from the birds.

Glen walked over to me, smiled, and put out his hand. I took it, and it felt good. I had never noticed what could truly be communicated in a handshake. Glen ended the suspense and rang the bell.

I put my hands up over my head with the palms towards the crowd, asking for silence. When those fucking guys finally got some control, I said, "Glen, that's $5 for holes, also $10 for getting your ass shot down, $5 for endangering your crew, $10 for letting those bastards shoot you. Also, Glen, $5 for the holes in the Major's ship."

That got everyone's attention. Finally, a drunk said, "Bullshit."

Some in the crowd were laughing at that last remark, and the rest were just confused.

To all our amazement, the Major stepped forward and said, "It's true. I was the pilot in command. You owe $5 for putting your CO in harms way while sitting on the ground taking hits. You also owe $5 for the Purple Heart. I add that up to $45 so far. Mac, anything else?"

I said, "Yes sir, $5 more to make it an even $50. The last five is because you let the enemy shoot at our CO. By the way Glen, do you have $50 on you? If you don't have it, the Major could probably make adjustments to your fines."

Glen said, "Yes Mac, I have $50."

"Hey everyone," I said, "That's 200 drinks. Let's make that last $5 for a record amount put in the bowl. One person for all those fuckups within an hour." More cheering!

Glen pulled me aside and asked, "Did you really shoot sharks with the CO?"

Before I could answer, the CO came up on Glen's other side and said, "Yes, we did, and we followed that with the lowest buzzing I have ever done. Actually Mac was flying. It was worth it to see the guys on the beach go crazy."

Glen was stunned and just nodded.

The CO said, "Excuse me, I am going to go sit in that far corner and meet with the three platoon leaders. Normally, we meet in my hooch, but we'll stick around for a while."

We both said, "Yes sir."

The CO walked over to the table where the three platoon leaders waited and sat down.

Glen and I finished our drinks and were angling toward the bar when in walked Bob Clearwater. He was Glen's copilot the other day when they got their ass blown out of the sky.

Bob said, "I am new here, but I know you always buy the guy a drink that saved your life."

Glen said, "Put your money away."

"Glen," Bob insisted, "I owe you one, too. You got us on the ground in one piece. That autorotation saved my ass. If I had been in one of my dad's jets, we would be dead. As we were falling toward the ground, I realized you don't need a runway in a Huey."

Glen and I were talking about Bob's flying skills when he returned with our rewards. I had recently noticed that booze tastes much better when consumed with friends. Booze also made the heat, humidity and the foul smells more tolerable. It also was making the quiet guys loud and the loud guys quiet (in what could have been misinterpreted as thinking).

The inevitable occurred when a rattler and a Firebird started bad-mouthing each other. The two were getting loud enough to start drawing attention to themselves.

Chapter 35.

TROUBLE IN THE CLUB

Now, to all our surprise, a new captain was pushing his way through the mob that had formed a circle around our arguing pilots.

In his loudest voice the captain—his name tag said Jennings— yelled, "Knock it off! What's going on here?" Before either man could answer, Jennings noticed officer bars on the rattler's shirt and the warrant-officer bars on the Firebird. He then made a serious mistake. He told the warrant to shut up because he was only going to listen to "the real officer."

I stepped into the ring and asked the new guy why he would accuse the warrant of lying. Captain Jennings told me to shut up and join "my lowly warrant buddy."

I replied in a very calm voice, "You don't seem to be acting like an officer. No, wait, you don't seem to be acting like a COMMISSIONED officer. By the way, Captain, the word 'officer' appears in both our titles.

"After you have been here a while, you'll notice that these battles of words are just that, words. A lot of stress is placed on everyone in this room when we are flying around our AO prosecuting this war. We're actually friends. There isn't a man in this room that wouldn't put his life on the line for the guy next to him, regardless of rank or job description."

Just as things were seeming to settle down, Glen stepped into the middle of the circle and said to the captain in an inebriated tone, "Why don't you just shut the fuck up!"

Jennings looked like he was about to explode. "You shut the fuck up!"

Glen said, "Are you aware that this lowly warrant Firebird (he nodded his head in my direction) swooped out of the sky and landed his helicopter between the enemy and me and my crew, when I had just been shot down. He then jumped out of the ship and ran to our position and told us where the bad guys were. He then explained how we could shoot our way back to his ship.

"As we were about to climb over the dike, he noticed I had been shot. He put a tourniquet on my leg, threw me over his shoulder, and carried me back to his ship, and we were being shot at the entire time he was running.

"As we began our run, I asked him why he was doing this and he told me I run too slow. I can remember dirt spraying into my face.

"With all your time and experience here, you can't appreciate anything I just said. You probably have heard about these birds and their heathen murderous behavior? Let me tell you something. He's so humble that he hasn't told a soul about the incident I just told you. Have you noticed how quiet it's gotten? That's because these guys are hearing it for the first time.

"Oh, did I mention that he was flying on his last day as an FNG? Everyone, tell this guy what an FNG is."

In unison 30 guys yelled, *"FUCKING NEW GUY."*

Jennings stood there frozen with nothing to say.

"Now sir, before you start crying," Glen said, "I'm going to finish my drinking with these birds, go to bed, and above all, try to forget about you."

That comment pushed the new captain over the edge. He balled up his fist and took a swing at Glen. I saw it coming and reached out and his fist struck the palm of my hand. That brought a rare silence to the club.

He was standing in an awkward position from his first attempted swing, so when he took the next one at me, I leaned backwards a few inches and let go of his hand. The momentum from his air ball took him to the floor. He hit pretty hard. That brought the noise level up to its normal level.

I put my hand out to help him up, but he slapped it away. I said, "Have it your way, but you better change your attitude if you want any friends."

He jumped up and spit in Glen's face. The room became quiet again.

Now, I'd had enough of this shithead's attitude. I stepped in front of him and grabbed his shirt six inches down from the neck. I jerked him towards me, spun him around, and pushed him out of one of the wall-less sides of the club.

He said, "What are you doing?"

I said, "I'm going pound sand up your ass until your change your attitude. No one in flight school told me I would have to deal with an asshole like you. We're supposed to be on the same side."

I don't think he likes it here. Well, who does?

As he stumbled out and fell face first in the sand, I said "You are a perfect example why parents should consider rubbers!" That drew the biggest laugh of the night.

"You are part of the in-crowd here aren't you? After all a Captain."

He puffed out his chest and nodded.

I said, "Yes you are; indecisive, insecure, incapable, incompetent, inefficient and (worst of all) in the dark. I wouldn't follow you to the shithouse."

The entire groups of drunks, which I then joined, were laughing so hard they couldn't drink. *I thought that was impossible.*

The CO and the three platoon leaders in the corner kept their heads down, but it was easy to see their shoulders bouncing as they laughed.

I turned and asked no one in particular, "Was I drinking a beer or the Crown?" Someone handed me one. I didn't care which. I looked up, and Glen was standing there with some snakes (rattlers). They wanted to thank me for saving Glen.

I said, "Bullshit! As I ran up to Glen, he was beating the shit out of the last two bad guys standing. There were bodies all over the ground! When I ran to my ship, I was actually running from Glen. Shit, don't ever piss him off."

The crowd seemed to like that version of the story, so I stopped talking while they were laughing.

Jim Williams walked up to me and said, "Mac, I believe I'm also standing in line to thank you."

Jim turned toward the mob and put up his hands for quiet.

When the noise level dropped appreciably, Jim explained how I had saved him from being burned alive in his bunk. When he finished, the place erupted with cheers … or was it laughter?

One of the birds said, "That story is funny after it happened, definitely not when it was happening."

Someone else said, "Christ Jim, if we had known, we would have flown up to Danang to make fun of you."

More laughter.

No one had noticed the CO until he stood up, walked over to Williams, and began speaking in a normal tone. The room got quiet because everybody wanted to hear him. "I was with Mac the night Mr. Williams was playing with fire." Now that brought on some laughter. The CO continued. He recalled the entire evening, and there was no laughing then. "Mac not only saved Jim, but three other hooch mates. I think I should move Williams to the Firebird hooch so they can watch over him. Those birds never sleep!"

I see that humor is important in our situation. I will remember that.

I put my hands up and said, "$10 for endangering your hooch mates, $10 for damaging government property. Ring the bell Jim, twice."

"What government property did I damage?"

I said, "When you burned your ass, buddy. GI means government issue. Do I have to continue? Your ass belongs to the government."

The CO returned to the table with the three platoon leaders. Soon, the four of them got up, and one of the platoon leaders came over to talk with me. "That was very tactful the way you handled Jennings. I was about ready to jump in and help you kick his ass, but the CO told us to stay seated. I think he was admiring your work."

I said, "I don't know how that bozo got promoted to Captain. I sure wouldn't want him flying with me."

"I agree, and so does the CO. The last thing he said to us was, 'I'm going to find Jennings and discuss his transfer.'"

As the platoon leader departed, Jim stepped into the spot just vacated. He handed me a beer and asked me, "How am I going to explain my white butt? I told my wife I'd stopped smoking." (When the melanin is burned on a black man, the burn turns white.)

"Hey, I know, give her my name," I said. "I'll explain EVERY thing in detail. By the way, do you remember anything? You had a big smile on your face, but you were totally unresponsive."

"I must have been thinking about my wife."

I smiled and nodded.

Jim said, "Mac, thank you for not saying anything to the birds about what a totally drunk fuck-up I was."

"Jesus, Jim. I plan to get so hammered tonight that your episode will look like a tea party. This place would drive any normal person crazy."

Suddenly, Major Wilson reappeared and was standing next to Jim and me. He smiled at Jim. "You look a lot better than the last time I saw you."

Jim looked at the major, and then at me, and then back at the major. "Thank you, sir."

"How would you two like to fly together the day after tomorrow?"

In unison, we said, "Sure." By now we were too far gone to have any semblance of military bearing.

The CO steered us toward a corner table. (One of the few not destroyed by stressed out pilots). He leaned in toward us and spoke quietly. "Keep this to yourselves until I post the announcement tomorrow." He certainly had our attention.

"Damon Steele, Firebird 9-0, (my stomach immediately felt sick) was killed in the last hour. The gun team just returned to Baldy's MASH unit after they completed their last gun run, but the docs couldn't help him. The wound was too massive. That's all I know right now.

"Everyone here is out of commission, so the 120th assault helicopter company will be covering Baldy's AO. You two will fly wing on Boyle and Jerry Wilder. Wilder will be Firebird 9-6 in a few days, so we are pushing Wilder to advance quickly like you Mac. Everyone else comes home early tomorrow since the 120th has us covered. Any questions?"

I asked, "How did Steele end up at Baldy?"

Major Wilson told us the platoon leader had called up and requested a wing pilot, because Hanson had diarrhea so bad he couldn't fly. Steele was taken to Baldy by one of the rattlers. "Hanson's not ready to fly. The guys in the MASH are doing everything short of pounding sand up his ass to plug him up."

I smiled. The CO had borrowed the phrase I'd used on Jennings. "Any more questions?"

In unison again, "No sir."

The CO got up and walked out.

I can't believe how fast we're losing pilots!

Jim and I resumed our conversation about this hell hole. We started talking about prejudice, and he told me about growing up in the south. "The Civil Rights Act in 1964 was supposed to eliminate all segregation, but you can't change 400 years of prejudice overnight. We're still fighting to sit in restaurants, drink at the same water fountain, sit anywhere in a bus but the back, and be treated better than a rabid dog."

"Jim, you're a human being like me and that's how I'll always look at you. In fact, I'm going to the CO tomorrow and have him change your race to part Caucasian due to your white butt."

Jim looked at me and said, "I need a few days to come up with an answer to that fucking statement. I've been called many things but never a Caucasian."

That seemed like a good time to go back to my hooch. "Goodnight Jim."

"Good night, Kevin"

I don't know what time I went to bed, because I couldn't see the hands on my watch.

Chapter 36.

THREE PURPLE HEARTS AND YOU GO HOME

I woke up with no headache; that was my biggest surprise since arriving in this chaos. Even better, I woke up with an idea. Jim was short. He'd be going back to the world soon. He knew things that could keep me alive for the next ten months, but he'd be gone soon, and I'd miss the chance to learn what he knew. Maybe I could sweet talk him into flying a little extra with me now and give me a chance to learn.

I'd have to get Jim on board, and then we'd have to convince Major Williams. But what the hell? It was worth a try.

First, I went to find Jim.

"How're you feeling?" I asked him.

"Not too bad considering everything."

I grinned. "Yeah, I know what you mean." I was excited to tell him my idea. "How about you and I go talk to the CO and see if we can go to Baldy today? You're getting to be a short timer, and you know every trick in the book about surviving here. I need what you know. I spoke to Dennis Boyle the other day at Baldy, and he said you'd be a FTL (flight team leader) if you were here a little longer. You can't leave until you show me all your tricks."

Jim went serious. "Mac, have you noticed how many birds we've lost this week?" He shook his head, almost in disbelief. "I was still in the hospital last week, but I looked at the casualty list when I got back, and it was just as bad that week too."

"I know. It wasn't on my mind last night. That death list has a way of sobering you up."

"And now you want to go back to it before we are absolutely ordered back into combat? Are you crazy?"

I couldn't explain it, but I knew what I needed from Jim. "Listen," I said, "I hate to do this, but you know you owe me. I saved your ass. Literally."

"Well, hell," he said, but he couldn't suppress a grin. "If you put it that way, I can't say 'no.' but if you get me killed, I'll never speak to you again."

"What could happen if I'm there to keep you out of trouble?"

"OK Mac, let's go talk to the CO. Our platoon leader is currently at Baldy with our soon- to-be new platoon leader."

We planned our speech on the walk to the boss's office. Soon, we were in front of Top's desk asking to see the CO. Top asked if he could tell the Major what our concerns were. I said, "Certainly Top," and I explained our idea. He nodded and said, "Just a moment and I will check with the Major."

When Top entered the Major's office, he made a point of closing the door. But we could hear. They were both laughing. We could hear the CO say, "Top can you believe that? They want to go to Baldy after what we've endured these past few weeks."

The CO agreed to our plan without a single question. "Send Hanson and crew home when you get there," he told us. "Williams, take your crew, Fox and Marshall. I think your idea is great considering it came from a couple of birds. Dismissed."

As we turned to go, Top and the CO exchanged a look and shook their heads. Just after we exited his office, we heard him whisper, "Thank god we have these crazy birds."

We were past Top's desk and were about to go out, when Major Wilson called, "Mac, wait a minute."

I turned and went back. "Yes sir?"

"Ski and Tyler are unemployed. Why don't you talk to them and see if they'll fly with you?"

What a great idea! "Yes sir!"

We knocked on Fox and Marshall's door and told them they had a few days off. Then, we went to the Bird House and grabbed our gear.

We jogged to Ski's and Tyler's. They were both inside. I asked them, "Will you guys fly with me when I make wing?"

In unison, I heard, "Hell Yes." Later, I thought, *my god! That easily they agreed to do something that might get them killed. They volunteered like it was nothing. Like I had suggested we pick up a game of football.*

It took them one minute to get their gear together. It was only twenty yards to the parade ground. That's how quick things could happen there.

The company clerk met us with two jeeps and another driver. We bounced along the bomb-cratered road. Top had called maintenance and had them waiting for us in the snake pit with 738 loaded and flight checked.

We gave the ship a cursory look. We mainly checked the weapons.

Jim told me, "Crank it up. Let's get out of here."

I headed out over the ocean, so we could test fire the weapons: door gunners' machine guns and our Gatling guns. The rockets were too valuable to shoot into the water.

I turned inland and continued low level as we all enjoyed the cool air and the scenery of many small farms.

I asked Jim if we could do some training if we could find some music. Apparently, there had been numerous protests from the troops to play more Rock and Roll. The higher ups had finally realized that the average age of our GIs in Vietnam was only 19. For WWII, it was 27, and the music was much different back then.

I flew over some trees and dropped down to 20 feet, when one of those nice farmers pulled out an AK-47 from under his baggy black pajamas (our name for their baggy pants) and gave us a fully automatic twenty-round burst as he emptied his magazine.

Bad move on his part. He was standing out in the open with a 30 yard run to the tall trees.

I yelled out, "Shoot that bastard."

I knew he had hit us, but all the gauges were normal. I was in a turn to the right and could see the door gunner send that guy to hell. I said, "Nice shootin'."

I looked at Jim and said, "Do you think there are any more in the trees?"

He told me, "Put a pair of rockets in there, and we'll see what happens."

I had completed my turn and gained some altitude. I could see the dead guy on the ground, so I aimed the rockets over him and punched once and said, "Breaking right," when the tall green scenery exploded in a tall fireball. I said, "Jim, I guess that answers my question. Someone was storing ammo."

Jim was busy picking out targets running from the conflagration. He was good with that mini gun.

Jim said, "We're going to go 'off the grid' on some of our missions. We'll be shooting at targets of opportunity in places where innocent farmers are not supposed to be. Our job will be to keep them honest. And they should never shoot at a helicopter, especially a gunship."

Jim called Chu Lai tower and told them about the closeness of the bad guys to their perimeter. They rogered and said they would call security.

Jim and I alternated flying every ten minutes until we had Baldy in view. I called out in the clear that we were entering the pattern. I told the guys in back to go cold and with that Jim did the same to the rockets.

The Birds had been notified of our arrival and were loading the wing ship for the flight to Chu Lai. Jim hovered close to the wing ship and sat it down with enough room for them to get out of the revetment.

I was helping the crew rearm our ship as the other ship was ready to go home.

Then I had a fantastic idea. I looked at my crew and the wing ships and said, "Follow me." Everyone looked at me and a few shrugged their shoulders. As I walked around the Hilton toward the non-existing back door so no one could see us, I said, "Let's moon that Bird taking off." I got a big smile from most of the guys. I said, "Let's line up in a straight line and give them eight bare butts." We did exactly that, although we were laughing so hard it was difficult to bend over. A few of us peeked between our legs to see their reaction, and we definitely got the reaction I was hoping for. They were laughing so hard I thought for a moment they might crash trying to take off.

We had just finished rearming when Wilder ran out of the Hilton and handed Jim a piece of paper with the standard info required so we could do our thing. Wilder would be lead.

Jim said, "Mac, get in the right seat."

I said, "That's your seat."

He shook his head *no* and climbed into the left or copilot's seat. Things were happening fast, so I did what he said. Jim entered all the data, and off we went, flying wing with the old and new platoon leaders at the same time. After two minutes, lead called us and said for me to make all the calls as if I were the lead ship.

I said, "Roger," as I shrugged my shoulders and went to work.

A patrol of ten had made contact with a large number of NVA two clicks south of LZ East in some steep and rugged terrain 20 clicks (15 miles) from us. I called the patrol, Nomad 6, and told them, "We'll be there in five or six minutes."

The radio operator said, "Can you make that four?"

I said, "We'll try. Give me your sit rep."

The young scared kid was whispering and said, "They are a hundred yards away moving slowly. Please Hurry."

"Where are they from your location? And pop a smoke if they can't see it."

I was trying to gain some altitude so we could come in shooting.

The radio operator said, "We are on top of a very steep small mountain, and they are moving through a valley east to west."

"I have your purple smoke. We will come in east to west and break north, right over you, and come in again. We are a team of two. Have you ever worked with gunships?"

The kid said, "No."

"The first ship will shoot rockets and a 40 mm cannon. They have two machine guns working the area. The second ship also has rockets and two door gunners with the addition of two electric Gatling guns. I want all of you to crawl back on the other side of the peak and lay low or behind trees or large rocks. Cover your ears. I can see them and the whole valley. I will let you know if any of those sneaky bastards make it to the top."

We were coming into position so I called 9-6 (lead ship) and asked if they were ready.

They said, "Rolling in."

I watched as they decimated those little shits who had trapped themselves in the valley.

Lead called, "Ready," and followed three seconds later with "Breaking right."

I couldn't believe how far Ski and Tyler were hanging out of the ship. Shit, no wonder they're Birds; they're crazy

As soon as lead was out of my sight picture, I punched two rockets on the guys running back down the valley, away from our guys. Then, I punched two on the right side of the valley in the trees, and then the same on the left. The intensity of those Gatling guns spewing out thousands of rounds per minute was electrifying.

Damn, I was born for this. Just me against them on my gun runs.

I said, "Ready," counted to three, and broke right. I asked Jim to spot me on the next run as there was an increase in tracers on the lead ship. I preferred breaking to my right, so I could look out and see where the shots were coming from that were aimed at the lead. I came out of my final turn, so I could cover the lead ship. I saw an increase in the number of tracers now going by my door on the right, as well as lead.

Jim said, "There are machine guns in the trees, one on each side of the valley, and they are all over us."

My crew chief was leaning out of the ship and pinpointed the guns on the left side as lead would be flying through his line of fire if he shot across the valley on the right side. The enemy was hidden on the ground in large groups of trees.

I was coming in and put three pair of rockets on each machine gun. Jim keyed the mike and in a very southern drawl said, "Nice shootin', cowboy."

Lead called out, "Ready," then followed with "Breaking right." Now wing—that is, us— was supposed to put rockets under and behind the turning ship. The first pair landed under him, on target.

As I rolled in, bullets were hitting the windshield and nose of our ship.

Looks like they held back on showing us everything they brought to this gunfight. What in hell could be so important that the NVA would sacrifice 200 troops?

The next instant, I heard the thumping of bullets coming through the instrument panel and circuit breakers along my left thigh, shin and foot. I couldn't look as I had to get my rocket sight on target. As I punched off another pair of rockets, my side of the cockpit filled with sparks and a crackling sound from damaged electrical wires. My left knee was pushed by something into the cyclic. This caused my ship to quickly lean to the right, followed by a quick lean back to the centerline, since I automatically corrected the abnormal position. *Thank god for training!*

I punched a few more rockets as Jim and I checked the instrument panel, gauges, and the ship's flying ability. Jim called Nomad 6 and asked if he had any other targets.

"We've been hugging the ground," Nomad said. "Let me sneak a peek over the top."

This gunship routine is one big iteration.

I called, "Ready," followed by, "Breaking right." I asked Jim to take the controls as we began climbing out. I said, "I have to check something." My knee felt strange, almost numb. I reached down with my left hand and ran it over the left knee. I felt several pieces of something hard protruding out of my knee. I pulled my hand back and a liquid was dripping off my glove. It could be only one thing: blood.

Nomad 6 called back and said, "I crawled to the top and looked over. Nothing is moving, and there must be over 100 bodies out in the open. I don't know how many are dead in the trees."

I forgot about the blood as soon as lead called, "Ready," then, "Breaking right. Dump half of what you have on top of those bastards. We'll save the rest for escorting the slicks in and out with the patrol."

The two slicks arrived, and the four of us went in for the patrol. We received a couple of errant rounds, and I put a pair of rockets on the muzzle flash. Two loud pops went through my rotor wash. The wing door gunners took care of that issue.

I called the lead slick and said, "We'll shoot a few more times then return to Baldy."

While talking, I dumped the remaining rockets, and Jim was emptying the mini's magazine. I broke right and saw the torn up countryside from the mini guns along both tree lines. "Wow! You go Jim, you go!"

"Thanks Firebirds," Nomad 6 radioed. "You just saved ten lives."

"Firebird 9-6, let's go home."

Damnit, I just called Baldy HOME. I think living here changes everything about you.

I reached down to my knee again because I thought my foot was wet. I saw those two pieces of shrapnel protruding an inch or so from my torn pants.

Jim was cool. He said, "Mac, did you find anything interesting?"

I said, "Yes, blood."

All he said was, "Shit. How do you feel?"

"I feel fine, Jim. I don't feel any pain and looks like the blood flow stopped."

"Do you want me to land at the MASH Unit?"

"No, let's rearm these ships in case we get another call."

"If the CO hears that you flew after getting wounded, you are in deep shit."

"Tell that to those kids out in the bush."

Jim called Baldy and cleared us to land at the POL and then the turnaround for rearming. Shit, the NVA were dropping mortars on Baldy. Wow, everything was going to hell!

Remain calm, Mac. This will settle the nerves of everyone else. They will be looking to you for leadership.

I held the controls while everyone climbed out to check for bullet holes, pee and pump in fuel. I reached out and waved my arm to let Ski know we had half a tank, our max amount.

Everyone climbed in, and we took off to circle around Baldy and land to rearm. On this short one-minute flight, two warning lights came on: electrical for the instrument panel. That included my turn-and-bank indicator. (Difficult to fly on a dark and cloudy night without it). It currently showed me in a very steep diving left turn while I was sitting on the ground. The engine oil-pressure gauge was low and slowly dropping. It required electricity to operate the oil valve pressure switches. *Shit, now both ships have leaking oil.*

I felt some pain in the knee when I climbed out. *Shit, I don't have time for this. I won't put this in my manual.*

When we were nearly rearmed, I told Jim "I'm going to the MASH Unit and see what they can do with this fucking knee."

Jim said he would send a runner if we got any calls.

I had a slight limp when I walked in. Everyone was somewhere else, but I set off a buzzer when I opened the door, and here came the help: two nurses, a medic, and a Doc. When they saw my bloody pant leg they insisted on helping me get on a treatment table. They started to cut off my pants when I put my hand out and said, "Stop.

I have to fly tonight, and I don't have any clothes but the ones you see."

I helped pull the pant leg over the shrapnel. They did take off my boot, but I wouldn't let them cut the laces. I told them that I understood the reason for cutting off clothes. You can get to the injury quicker. My wound was not that serious.

They gave me a several shots of Novocain around the knee, and then waited a few minutes to let it do its job. Then, they began removing shrapnel. I was numb and felt nothing as they pulled both pieces out. I was x-rayed to see if anything else was in there. They found nothing, so they cleaned off the blood, and I was given three stitches for each wound. My third wound in less than two months. *Not good.*

The antibiotic shot in the butt stung like fire, and a bottle of pills followed.

I told them, "I haven't finished the last bottle of pills."

They pulled my chart and the doctor said, "You are a regular here. You told me the pill bottle story just the other day. Don't you have to be cleared by the flight surgeon before you return to flying?"

I stretched things out just slightly with my answer. "Sir, normally yes but in actual contact it can be put off until the mission is completed. Sir, please don't report these injuries. Three Purple Hearts and you go home. I'm needed here. There is nothing for a gun pilot to do back in the world but train Vietnamese pilots. I'd be no good with those guys: language barrier, no desire to fly, and that kid was plowing behind a water buffalo a few months before so anything bigger than a screw driver is machinery."

The doctor looked at the nurse. I think they knew I was bullshitting them.

The doctor told the nurse, "Bandage the knee." He then told me to check in at first light.

I said, "Yes sir and thank you."

As I was getting up to go, he doctor looked at the nurse and said, "I've never heard it put that way about those Vietnamese pilots."

When I walked into the Hilton, Jim was sitting on his bunk. I think he was waiting for me. "Mac, how's the knee?"

I said it was fine. "How many holes did you find in our ride?"

"Two in the tail boom, one in the right rear door and four in the nose, seven total. Lead also has seven. I called Snake Doctor, and they will bring parts or a wing ship if one is available and a lead if possible."

"Both ships with seven. Kind of ominous."

I walked over to find Jerry Wilder and asked him, "How are you doing?"

He looked at me and said, "That's the worst shit storm I've been in since I got here."

Ski came in and said, "I topped off the oil and hydraulic sumps."

Jim nodded, and I sat down on his bunk. He looked me in the eye and said, "I am fucking pissed because of all the Birds those little fuckers killed this month! And Knapley got a call while you were hustling nurses at the MASH. He put the phone down and looked at me and yelled 'FIGMO.' I just said, 'Congrats.' I'm going to bed, Mac. I'm so fucking tired."

"Well cheer up Jim. I saw a news clipping in the Firebird hooch. It said, if a guy named Richard Nixon is elected our President, he would bomb North Vietnam into oblivion. I hope he does."

Jim sat up and said, "No shit!"

"About damned time to end this cluster fuck. Good night, Jim."

I started to lie down when Jerry said, "Is that true?"

"I hope so."

Chapter 37.

FLYING WHILE WOUNDED

We were all asleep when that damn red phone started ringing. It was 2050 and still light out. Most of the crews ran to the ships. I stayed with Jim, Knapley, and Jerry to get the complete picture in case HQ left out something.

As we jogged out to our ship, I looked at Jerry and asked, "What do you think is going on near LZ East? We probably killed 150 bad guys two hours ago, and now they are going up that same valley to the same mountain top, and we are going to do the same thing to them. What's so valuable? Shit, this is crazy."

Jim said, "Mac, I heard in the hospital that the NVA ground troops are given drugs to get them so high they don't care about life and death and will do bonsai charges. The doctors discovered this when examining captured enemy and dead bodies."

That still doesn't answer my question. They wouldn't just throw troops away for nothing.

"Mac," Jim went on, "get in the lead and run this mission like the last one. You take Jerry. Knapley can take his last ride in Nam with me. That was our plan, remember? You think your ship is safe to fly? Shit, Mac, if you're flying with that knee, the Black Death can fly with you and cover your white ass."

"OK, Mister Death, no need to fly with me. Just cover my ass from wing."

I climbed in and yelled, "Clear." I called HQ and cleared two gunships and a flare ship to depart south.

They had sent out another patrol, Nomad 6. Now, it was a race to get there before that patrol was overrun. I called them and asked, "What the hell do you have that's so important, Ho

CHI Minh's girlfriend?"

Nomad 6 said, "If it were that simple, I would have returned her yesterday."

I chuckled and said, "I agree with you. What's your sit rep?"

"Same-same, no change from the last time. They are proceeding slowly up the same valley. They are in the bottom of the valley with very steep sides, with 300 yards of open ground to the steep sides."

"We are two minutes out and will come in shooting. If they get close to you, get on the other side and cover your ears. Let me know if you see anything on those steep sides. Last time they had two machine guns hidden there."

"Roger."

"9-8, you copy?"

"Roger."

"Flare ship, throw two out, one each side, but closer to the peak, so we don't fly into the parachutes. Keep this canyon lit up!"

"Flare ship rogers."

"OK, 9-8 is on your six "

With that said I started punching rockets and was greeted with a hail of bullets. I hit the right and then the left side of the steep canyon walls. My copilot covered the valley floor with the 40 mm. I yelled without the intercom, "Nice shooting, Jerry!"

Then, I said, "Ready," followed with "Breaking right."

I thought wing broke as soon as he called ready. All that enemy firepower had gotten to him.

"How are you doing back there?" I yelled, as we rolled in and I put rockets under and behind 9-8.

Ski and Tyler both yelled, "Great, let's do it again."

Shit, those two have been here too long, but I've got to agree. This is a huge rush, and I've never smoked a joint.

I punched rockets wherever I saw a tracer or a muzzle flash on the right side, and then switched to the left. I glanced at the valley floor, and it was total pandemonium. It was covered in bodies from our first time there. Now, we were piling more bodies on top of bodies that were still warm. The NVA were tripping over their own dead as they were running back down the valley. Only a few of them were stopping long enough to shoot at us. No one had removed any bodies. Usually the NVA hauled away their dead, so we wouldn't have any propaganda to print or publish.

They were still shooting at me, but with less volume and more sporadically. As I called "Ready," followed by "Breaking right," I took a longer look at the gauges and warning lights. There were two yellows: lights and hydraulics.

Everything was tolerable. Hydraulics is an oil-like fluid that helps us move the controls. If it failed, you were usually fucked. You would have a few short motions with the cyclic, and then it would lock and couldn't be moved. Yellow meant a very slow leak or breakdown. I now had a yellow oil pressure along with several additional yellows.

As I was climbing out, I heard, "Ready," so I turned to cover the wing ship's six. He must have punched four pair to both sides of the valley. He had about six rockets remaining, and I had six too.

I called Nomad 6 as I punched one pair to each side and asked, "What do you see?"

"I crawled up and looked over the top," he said. "There are hundreds of bodies. No one has even come close to the top. It doesn't make any sense."

I told him to get his head down. "We are going to dump everything we've got left in the next run, and then go home and rearm."

Nomad 6 said, "I called East, and they are planning on bringing some slicks out at light to gather up bodies. East is sending out a company (about 200) to help us keep the neighborhood as the Firebirds left it."

I said, "Dump everything." I put two pair on the left and kept flying for a few more seconds so Jerry could empty the 40 mm. Ski and Tyler were knocking out one muzzle flash after another. Damn, those two were as fearless as they were good with those machine guns. *I'm lucky to fly with them.*

Jim had six rockets remaining, so he would put two pair on the right and one pair on the left, opposite of lead just to make sure both sides received equal treatment. Knapley had been cutting down trees with the mini guns. Probably his last mini gun exercise. I guessed Jim was giving him a mission to remember. He wasn't leaving the NVA many places to hide. I told the guys in back to save fifty rounds each for the ride home. Damn, there are a lot of people protecting this valley. There must have been 400 NVA down there when we started. I can't remember being shot at by the enemy so many times in such a short time.

Suddenly, the sky lit up under my last rockets on the right side of the valley, and the largest explosion I'd ever seen rolled up into the sky. I called out, "Breaking left," as the explosion was over my exit route if I broke right. I felt the buffeting of the explosion. It lifted the tail of the ship up enough that for a moment I thought we were going over. I pulled the cyclic back on instinct, and the ship leveled after what was a scary few seconds.

Ski said, "Nice flying, Mac. I thought we were going over."

Two secondary explosions followed. They were not as dramatic as the first but still impressive.

"This is Firebird 9-6 (Knapley's number). Now I know why they wanted this area."

I said, "Roger that. Do see any movement? I wouldn't have wanted to be within 300 yards of that blast."

Nomad 6 said, "Roger that. I just got a call from East, and they are calling us in. The men they're sending out will look over your work, just in case you missed one. Thank you again."

"You're welcome."

I called 9-8 and said, "We are lit up like a Christmas tree."

"Any of them red?"

I said, "No, but remember, one is hydraulics."

I was amazed that I could still be flying. Then, I looked at Jerry and said, "You did a great job back there. You kept a level head and were spot on with that 40 mike-mike. Take me to Baldy, Captain. You will be a great 9-6. The great leaders in this fucked up mess are those that lead by example."

He said, "Thank you, Mac. Off the record, I was briefed about you by Major Wilson and Knapley. I was told to learn everything I could from you as you were uncanny with your flying, shooting, running a mission, and your leadership."

"Did you just say you were learning leadership from me? I've been told by a few people, to include Top and the Major and, oh yeah, a Captain who is no longer with us, that some of my activities were borderline."

"I was told you were humble to a fault. Then, I was told stories about your antics and heroism for an hour." Jerry grinned. "They told me not to mess with you because you would pound sand up my ass."

I decided it was time to change the subject. "Have you ever landed at POL at Baldy?"

"No."

"It will be like landing at the Rattlers since you are out of ammo and low on fuel, so just make a normal approach. Turn on your landing light; it's overcast and dark out here."

He was making a fairly good approach. "Be careful and glance out to the side," I cautioned him. "That landing light alters your depth perception. Look for the markers and the coiled hoses. Make sure you land on their left since our gas cap is on the right. Just be ready to turn off the landing light and get us out of here if mortars start dropping."

He was concentrating so hard and trying to stay focused that he just nodded. He had plenty of area to land. You could put five Hueys on POL at one time.

We got to POL with no red warning lights. We refueled and checked for holes. It was difficult at night with flashlights full of dead batteries.

I don't remember if I listed dead batteries on my "forgot to tell you manual." I think I have enough to begin Volume Two.

We had marked the previous holes with some of that special hundred-mile-an-hour tape. Now we can see the new holes and wonder why we were still alive.

We began rearming. There were three new holes in my ship and two in the wing. *Damn, how do these ships keep flying?*

"We'll arm the wing, and only half the ammo on lead in case of a severe emergency. I don't think these ships have much more to give."

My knee was beginning to throb. Or maybe I should say that it hurt like hell. When we finished rearming, I hobbled over to MASH and asked them to check my knee. When they removed the bandage, it even *looked* painful. It was red and twice its size. I couldn't straighten it, and it didn't bend too well either. I got another antibiotic shot in the ass, and they cleaned the wounds again as infection is a big concern in Vietnam. *Damn! Those shots in the ass are the shits, figuratively speaking.*

When I got back to the Hilton I slept four hours. Then, Snake Doctor and a gunship team of two ships landed.

I asked Jim if their ship was flyable. He said, "Probably, the two lights were minor. Robertson will check it out. How about you?"

"Not good. One light is hydraulics."

Robertson and his crew checked the wing ship, and his mechanics started to work immediately. He walked over to my ship, and after a few minutes pronounced it terminal and said he was calling a hook.

"Mac, the CO wants to see you. You, Jerry, Ski and Tyler can ride back with me in Snake Doctor."

"Your pant leg looks like shit. What happened?"

"Shrapnel from the radio electronics bay blew into my knee."

"You're not walking very well."

This is the third time I have gotten in the way of enemy fire power. This won't go in the book.

"By the way, that was one hell of a job you did near LZ East. They estimate you blew up ten tons of explosives. Several of our slicks are flying out to East as we speak. They will be looking for anything that will help us be ready for their next surprise. Blowing up that stockpile saved a lot of lives."

"Just a lucky shot," I replied.

Robertson told us to climb in. "We'll fly back to CL," he told us. "Muse and Norwood will fly lead with 765. Your hydraulics bay was nearly empty, Mac. You have someone looking out for you, like, I don't know, a guardian angel?"

Robertson got all that out in one breath. Then added, "Jim, you lead and Snake Doctor will follow, so we can watch for parts falling off your ship."

Even Jim laughed.

When the Chinook arrived, it attached its sling to the dead lead ship and departed for Chu Lai. Jerry, Ski, Tyler and I climbed in back of Snake Doctor for the ride home. It was almost cold.

We landed at Chu Lai, and the company clerk was waiting for us in the CO's jeep. I looked at Jerry and said, "Shit, this looks bad." Jerry and I climbed in.

Jerry said. "I'm going to say I never met you, and I know nothing."

All we got back from the clerk was a quick half smile. We drove to the parade ground in front of the CO's office. The CO was standing at the top of the steps to his office, as we stopped and pulled our gear out of the jeep.

In a loud and commanding voice, he said, "I want both of you up here, now," as he pointed to a spot one foot in front of his feet.

Jerry and I walked up to him and saluted. I think he saw how much difficulty I was having with the steps. He was not smiling. It was quiet. He just stood there making us very nervous. There were several people watching from thirty yards away.

Great, just enough to get the word out I'm in trouble. I'll leave this part out of my manual.

Finally, he spoke. "Mr. McNally, do you know why you're here?"

"No sir." It was the truth.

"Well then, let me remind you. You are required by military regulations to see the flight surgeon after you have been wounded. Did you know that?"

"Yes sir."

"Who made you aware of that regulation?"

"You did, sir."

"And you, Captain Wilder, are a new guy here, but you come with a resume of good judgement and leadership. Until last night! Anything to say for yourself?"

"No sir."

I looked at Jerry and said, "Tell the Major what I told you to say."

Jerry said, "What?" as if I were crazy.

The CO looked at me and said, "What did you tell him?"

"I told Jerry to say he doesn't know me."

The CO stifled a laugh and said, "You know better! Do you have anything to say?"

I started to say *no* when he interrupted me and said in a low voice so the onlookers couldn't hear, "Tell me the truth."

I said, "Those kids were trapped on a small mountaintop with 200 NVA coming towards them. I thought their radioman was going to cry. The NVA were protecting something so important that they sent a second wave up that valley, another 200 NVA. Fortunately, we discovered what it was. I thought the wound was minor, and I thought those ten GIs were more important. I couldn't call and tell them I scratched my knee and was going to the doctor. In defense of Jerry, he said I should see a doctor. I figured the MASH doctor was as good as any. The MASH doctor asked me if I was supposed to see a flight surgeon before I flew again, and I stretched the truth when I said, if I was in contact with the enemy, I could continue with that mission and then see the doctor."

"The MASH unit called me and told me the same story. He was impressed that you went back a second time to protect and save American lives. He also said you looked like shit when you could hardly walk after flying again. That was when you asked them to check the wound again."

"He said I looked like shit?" *I don't look like shit.*

"Watch it, Mac. I want to say to you two that you were very brave and gutsy to return to that valley after you were shot up the first time. When you retuned to Baldy the second time, Nomad 6 called his HQ at East and raved about you so much their CO was ready to personally pin a medal on you. You can't repeat any of this. Go get cleaned up. You two get tomorrow off, and more. I'm personally ordering you, Captain, to keep Mac out of trouble. Can you do that?"

Jerry hesitated and then said, "Yes sir."

"I also want you, Mac, and Jim to move into the Firebird hooch of squalor tomorrow. Jerry, move into the platoon leaders' hooch. I've sent another gun team to Baldy, as you have seen. You all can get some rest and send Knapley back to the world. You two still have perfect records. By the way, there are some rumors about a mooning incident at Baldy? I'll ask about that later."

That was a relief. The CO stepped back and said in a loud and authoritarian voice, "You two get out of here, now!"

We saluted, turned, and Jerry and I walked fast. I hobbled after him with a severe limp. The CO said, "Mac I want you here tomorrow at 0900. You are going to the flight surgeon."

I stopped and turned and said, "Yes sir."

When we were out of sight of HQ, I asked Jerry, "Would a drink before a shower be appropriate?"

His reply was to turn and walk away from our hooches. I followed as best I could. We dropped all our crap in a heap on the hat and gun shelf and walked in. There were already a few guys drinking. We bellied up to the bar as they say and ordered four Crown Royals. They went down fast and easy, then off to the long awaited shower.

I wondered if anyone back in the world could appreciate a shower as much as I did at that moment. After the shower, which would have plugged up any household drain, Jerry and I were shaving and talking when a shower was turned on behind a partition wall. We said, "Hi," and no one answered, so I looked around the corner to see if that dipshit Captain Jennings had returned.

What I saw surprised me. I called Jerry. He walked over and said, "What's up?"

"Two Vietnamese women are washing their hair with their clothes on in our shower."

He took a quick look. "They value that long black hair," he explained. "They don't have much in personal possessions except the hair. They sneak in here, and we're supposed to throw them out because clean water is a premium."

"Do we throw them out?"

"Hell no, Mac. Let them wash. Just be sure to tell them they have pretty hair."

"Roger that."

"You've never seen them in here before?"

"I don't use this shower very often."

He laughed, and we returned to the sinks and finished shaving. Seeing us with shaving cream on our faces and peeking around the corner probably would have scared the shit out of them. *I think I will put this one in Volume Two.*

Chapter 38.

THE FIREBIRD HOOCH

When Jim arrived, we moved into the Firebird hooch (three times larger than the other hooches). The Firebirds had the Seabees enlarge it the previous year without asking the CO.

Jerry had clued us in to a unique feature of the Firebird hooch before he moved on to the Platoon Leaders' hooch. "The Seabees live up the beach a few hundred yards. They will build anything for booze. It's part of the black-market system. The Seabees don't have an easy way to get booze, no club, no PX. We have one of our slicks fly to Danang and fill it with food, booze, stereo units, reel to reel recorders, and anything anyone might want. Gin and Vodka are a dollar a fifth. They get a wine, Mateus, a really bad rosé, but it gets the job done. Going through channels to get anything here? It takes six months if you're lucky. You'll discover that soon. Our supply officer, Malkovich, can trade for anything. He was a supply sergeant E5 before he went to flight school. You'll meet him. He's always looking for something he can trade."

It took Jim and me only thirty minutes to move all our possessions. While throwing everything in a heap on our bunks, we noticed booze on shelves in every room. There were actual rooms, not one large room like in the slicks' hooches. No doors, but partitions for some privacy.

There were several signs on the walls in a large room with an octagonal table called the Firebird party room. One sign said, "When I die, I'm going to Heaven because I have already served my time in Hell: Chu Lai, Vietnam." The other said, "Kill them all. Let God sort them out."

I thought both were appropriate.

I looked at Jim, who would be my next door neighbor, and said, "This hooch looks like a landfill. They don't pick anything up. They're not very neat."

Jim replied. "Really! Ya think."

We checked out the paperbacks on a shelf and discovered the Firebirds were perverts. That was good to know. I looked in another room with the ceiling covered with centerfolds of naked women. There were a couple of mini refrigerators, and I stood there stunned when I realized I was looking at a real refrigerator. I opened the door and was elated to see it packed with beer. Jim walked up behind me and looked over my shoulder. All he said was, "Shit!"

"This makes me thirsty. How about you," I said.

"Let's go."

We started out the door but stopped instantly as a big man was blocking our way. He said, "Hi, I'm Malko, nice to meet you, can I talk to Mac for a minute?" He looked at Jim and said, "And then you can have him back."

I looked at Jim, and he nodded. Malko (as Malkovich was universally known) asked if he could come in. I said, "Follow me." We sat on my bunk, and he opened a folder. There were four sheets of paper. He handed me the last page to sign.

I said, "Wait a minute. What's this?"

"This is a list of everything that was lost when you were shot down the other day."

I said, "Malko, I wasn't shot down. I crashed from an overload of equipment. This is page four and it says: five, thirty foot long tents, a dozen M-16s, twenty pair of boots, two Huey transmissions, four Huey engines, and there's more here. Let me see the other three pages."

He handed them to me. Page two listed two army jeeps on line one. Twenty folding chairs. "Shit Malko, you couldn't put this in three Chinooks. I'm not going to Leavenworth (the army's prison in Kansas)." I got up and walked out.

At the club, there were at least 20 guys around the bar including Jim. A couple of them were birds, and they said, "Hey, come over here."

I was handed a beer, and it was cold! I asked, "How did you do this?"

"We went out the other night and stole a jeep sitting in front battalion HQ. We filed off all the numbers and helped Malkovich paint some military numbers on it. Then, he traded it for two refrigerators and some other stuff he'll use as trading stock."

The birds were grinning. "I think we got the best deal."

We told them we had just moved into the Firebird hooch. We were each handed a Crown Royal. All four of us toasted and drank. The birds chugged theirs. Jim and I looked at each other and chugged the remainder. My eyes watered, and I felt it all the way down into my stomach.

I asked one of the Firebirds, "Do I have to get a tetanus shot just because I moved into the Firebird hooch?" They all started laughing, especially the slick drivers.

An hour later, Jim and I were getting philosophical and having trouble focusing but kept on drinking. I said, "Jim, I realized the other night that gunship pilots are different. The only time we say 'no' is when asked if we've had enough!"

"Damn Mac, that's heavy."

"All we've got is each other. We all keep saying that. I believe that hooch explains some of it. I believe it explains why we do crazy things. It's the unpredictability that gives us an edge. Everyone thinks we're crazy. I know we have to make our own rules. Example: you and I flying up to Baldy when some asshole shot at us. We took them out. If asked why, we tell them the truth. Someone emptied his AK at our ship. If they say that was friendly, then we ask why the shooting? Then, we say, 'Sorry; it was self-defense.' Easier to ask for forgiveness than permission. It'd have taken months to get permission to blast that hooch."

Jim said, "Flying is a drug for the true pilot. You and I are hooked!"

"Hey, there's something else. We'd rather die than look bad. That says something about us. We take some shit from the slicks, but that's just talk. Talk to ease the stress. I tell myself I'm protecting our soldiers. I don't totally ignore the enemy fire. It just helps me target them. I'm not trying to get the crew killed. They understand the danger."

Jim said, "We fight wars because it's our job. Some days are better than others."

"That's right Jim." The alcohol was really warming me up. "We just do it. It affects us more than we realize. We develop attitudes. We may try to act cool, but our attitude plays out when we drink too much. Christ, Jim, I have three attitudes. Some days it's good, some days it's bad, and lately I just don't give a shit. I have seen some good people die. Who knows when it's my turn?

"Jim, I've noticed that every time we take a helicopter in the air here, it depreciates in value 'cause it gets the shit shot out of it. When you and I go up in the air, we appreciate in value. We learn something new on every mission. If a pilot doesn't learn, he's dangerous.

"Working with, and listening to, the experienced pilots is our only way of learning. Flight school didn't prepare us for this!"

Jim just shrugged, like "What did you expect?" But then I thought of something else.

"Jim," I said, now drunk enough to get philosophical, "tell me how this is a limited war? Aren't those contradictory terms?" I held up my hand, when it looked like he was about to say something. "Don't answer. It was a stupid question. We are killing them, and they are killing us. It isn't murder because our leaders, and their leaders gave us orders to kill each other. That's bullshit."

Malko walked in with Captains Wilder and Knapley. They sat at a corner table and waved me over. As I approached them, I said, "Is this about his list?" I pointed to Malko.

"I'm going home tomorrow," Knapley said, "but I have time to clue you in to the military's black-market system. It works ten times better than the legal path. Malko trades some mattresses for shirts and pants or maybe a stolen Jeep goes for two refrigerators and a mini gun. The mini gun is traded for chairs for the hooches. Then, he trades an extra Huey engine for the fans in here and front bubbles for our ships. Hell, Mac, how many bubbles have you lost? The pentagon doesn't look at anything but the items. They make a list to write off as 'lost in battle' and make a new list for the same equipment to ship to us. Malko doesn't make any money on this. He's working for us, and he's good. Help him by signing."

I looked at Wilder and Knapley, and they both nodded. So I signed.

Oh well, what the fuck. I'm probably not going to live though this war.

My next thought was the bar. So I bellied up and ordered two doubles (that's two beers and two Crowns). WOW, I hope all my future meetings are held here. As I was enjoying the libations which definitely lifted my mood, Jim Williams walked over.

"Mac, are you moving with this spinning room or is my drunken ass completely fucked up?"

"This is the most fucked up I have ever seen you," I told him. "Let's go sleep and finish this tomorrow."

We stumbled outside and went hooch hunting. After a few minutes, I remembered we had moved to the Firebird hooch. It was three times larger than my former hooch. Damn, we could hear noise in the party room. The club was closing when we departed, so it was after 2300.

We walked over the party room's large window (glassless) with two fans sitting on the window ledge to circulate the air. Jim and I rested our elbows on the ledge and leaned in.

Before we asked the moronic question—"What are you guys up to?"—one of them said, "Get your asses in here."

Since the window ledge was only four feet off the ground, we would climb in. Or should I say we tried to scale that obstacle? We were so fucked up that the five guys in the room were laughing and commenting on our ability to get in. They asked if we wanted a ladder. Then, they asked if we wanted a rope thrown over the ledge. Finally, somebody came up with a great idea. "Use the fucking door, Mac." They were as drunk as we were, and none of us could find the door.

Some asshole asked, "Can you fly better than you can scale a four foot ledge?"

I answered, "Not in this condition."

"Well shit, Mac, at least you're honest."

With much effort and swearing, they pulled us in and handed us each a drink in an old beer can. They said, "Be careful, we cut the tops off with a survival knife."

I touched the sharp edge, and it felt like a razor.

Stuart Muse said, "Don't drink just yet."

Steve Meadows walked out of the crowd and said, "Mac, I'm giving you your Firebird number. It will follow you the rest of your life. It is 9-7. There were two before you, and there will be a few after you. You can now sit at this table as the number 9-7, next to Jim, 9-8. We will put on a nickname soon."

I saw that our numbers were carved in the wood. "We were ordered by the CO to present you with your new promotion to AC in a wing ship and then to AC in the lead ship, A Fire Team Leader!" Everyone raised their can and said, "9-7."

Wow, I've only been in the birds less than three weeks, and I'm a Fire Team Leader. That could be interpreted differently. Why is there a need? Better not to think about that. Looks like I owe $20 to the pot in the club.

I looked at Jim, but he didn't look at me. I said, "Jim, is this your doing?"

"Me? Why are you looking at me, Mac?"

"Never mind, you don't lie worth a shit. We'll find out how good you can lie when your wife sees your white butt. Just make sure all the lights are out and fuck her like you did on your wedding night." That drew a laugh.

"Sorry guys," I said, "but I need sleep."

They immediately jumped in and said, "We would have gone to bed hours ago, but we waited up for your two sorry asses."

"By the way," I added, "what were we drinking? It was the worst thing I ever swallowed?"

"Mac, what color was it."

"I don't know. I can't focus on anything."

"If it was purple, it was a purple motherfucker. If it was clear, it was a green motherfucker. Actually, it was Fresca. We named it after the color on the can, green. The purple was grape soda. They are mixed with some of that $1 a bottle of gin we get from the PX (Post Exchange – Walmart of the army) in Danang. We're told that's the good stuff!"

I couldn't think of a single thing to say other than, "Good night."

Chapter 39.

INCOMING ROCKET

As soon as I got in bed, there was a huge explosion. It shook our hooch and threw us out of bed. We recovered and jumped up as did everyone else. We stuck our heads out the door and saw several small fires. We ran out with fire extinguishers (which were small buckets to dip into the large 55 gallon barrels). Other people were running to the same area from their hooches. There was nothing remaining of the hooch that had gotten hit but some burning wood thrown out in all directions. And body parts.

The familiar odor of burnt human flesh hit me so hard I thought I would throw up. A crowd was forming, and I could hear several guys puking. I had told myself six weeks before that I never wanted to smell burning human tissue again. *Never say never in a war.*

Corrugated aluminum had been blown off roofs and thrown all over the immediate area. There were holes in the screen material that comprised the top half of the various walls. Some holes were from pieces of the exploding hooch, and some were from body parts which had blown out in all directions. Burning wood and parts of people lay across several roofs.

I wasn't sure what to do next. I was trying to take in what I saw. Down near my feet was a hand attached to a lower arm. I looked around and saw part of a head. The CO was jogging toward us. I yelled, "Major Wilson!" He looked up, and I yelled again. Then, I put my arm out and gave the big "come here" motion.

He hurried through the crowd and said, "Who lived here? Give their names to Thompson." Thompson had several body bags and gloves. Major Wilson said, "Everyone go to your hooch or the bar. I want five volunteers to help Top and me pick up body parts. If any of

---

you discover body parts in your hooch, get a bag from Thompson."

"I'm in Sir," I said.

"OK, with Top and Mac I need three more." Four EMs stepped out and walked over to Thompson to get body bags and gloves. The major, Top, and I did the same.

Major Wilson said, "Spread out and look very carefully. Treat these bodies as if they were alive." The Major indicated we would start in the hooch that took the hit or what remained of it. "If any of you or your roomies are wounded, get to the orderly room and you'll be driven to the flight surgeon."

We found some burnt pieces of tissue on the plywood that made up the first four feet of the walls. This was twenty or thirty feet away as there wasn't anything at ground zero. We heard someone vomiting. I felt like I might start doing that myself. Top was behind me, and he started gagging and then loudly retching, splattering on my bare feet and pants. I jumped out of the way of his next blast of puke. Then, the CO and I went back to work. Next were the hooches that surrounded the blast. I saw intestines hanging off a roof.

"Damnit" I said to no one. Numerous hooches were missing half their roofs. Some were missing their walls (half wood, half screen) because the sand bags had been blown into the hooches. Many men had been cut by various kinds of shrapnel: aluminum, glass, wood.

Every time I picked up a body part, I thought, *I will kill hundreds of the bastards responsible for this. I will give out some payback for you guys.*

After picking up pieces of humans for two hours, I stopped and sat on one of the pallets. I had been dragging my bag in the sand, which was only half full but still heavy. It was my second bag. I was almost too tired to keep this up.

It occurred to me that I hadn't seen Jim since the explosion.

The CO saw me and sat down by me and said, "This is the second one to hit a hooch. Last time, a year and a half ago, there were two guys inside, both copilots."

Then the CO switched gears. To no one in particular, he said, "We're trying to dig in these bags to determine how many were in the hooch."

Thompson came over. "Everyone is accounted for except six. Top has picked up enough metal pieces to determine six beds were in there. We have pieces of five heads. That rocket must have been huge to atomize so much of those guys."

Without a word, I turned and began digging into my bag. I pulled out an arm with a ring and a watch. "Sir what do I do with this" as I lifted up the arm.

"Put it back. Graves's Registration will here be at first light. They'll do another search. I'll give them all my records on the guys assigned to that hooch. They have a morgue at HQ. They take finger prints, dental records, birthmarks, blood types and who knows what else."

"Sir, I have two wallets and some boots with feet in them. I also found a piece of a beer bottle. Some of them must have been sitting on their bunks drinking and probably bullshitting."

The CO said, "One last thing. We will now go through these other hooches and pick up anything burning and/or any body parts we missed earlier."

I actually dozed off while sitting there. Top said, "Wake up you two!" The CO and I were both startled and jerked our heads up. Top said, "I wish I had my camera because you two were leaning on each other, asleep. It looked cute but also weird."

I said, "Sir, I'm sorry."

"Were we really leaning on each other?" the CO asked. Then he began laughing, and Top and I started laughing. We sitting down with bags of body parts and laughing. War really fucks you up. *I will put that part in Volume Two.*

The CO said, "Let's get some sleep. Zip up those body bags tight. Get on one end Mac, and we'll put 'em in the closest hooch." The CO thanked the four EMs and said, "I'm going to send you soldiers up the beach to the in-country R & R center."

"Thank you so much!" They were talking over each.

"Get some sleep, and then see me at 1000. Thompson will drive you up there." They saluted and returned to their hooch.

"Mac, get some rest. You and Williams will spend the next five days at Baldy. You'll not be getting much sleep. Things are heating up. I want you alert. Meet in the mess hall at 0600."

As soon as I entered the hooch, I saw everyone looking at the dried blood on my shirt and pants. I stripped them off and threw them in a corner and made a note to throw them away. I grabbed a towel, soap, and clean underwear, and couldn't get to the shower fast enough.

Chapter 40.

BACK TO BALDY

Next morning, I saw Jim in the mess hall. I got in line behind him. "What happened with you when that hooch blew up?"

"I just couldn't look at another dead person," he told me, not making eye contact. "I puked before I passed out in bed."

I said, "No problem, Jim."

I saw the CO come in, so I went over to his table, reserved for the CO only.

He said, "You and Jim are going to Baldy for five days. The plan is to make you a fire team leader officially. Do you feel like you're ready?"

I said, "Yes, sir. I can do that."

As I was climbing into the truck to go out to the ships, I realized I hadn't gotten any food while I was in the chow line.

I was flying with Jerry Wilder. We gave our ship a cursory once over and climbed in to light the fire. Chu Lai cleared us for a straight out north departure.

I told Jerry to get on the controls, so he could feel a loaded gunship take off.

"It will be a little easier in this cool morning air I told him. It'll be a lot more difficult as the day heats up." I lined the ship up on the center of the taxi lane and said, "OK, here we go."

We had a nice six-inch hover and started bouncing down the runway. I glanced at Jerry when I did the first bounce. It looked like he was going to scream. We got off with room to spare after the second one.

"You've got it, Jerry."

He looked at me with very large eyes and took the controls. "Got it," he said.

"Test your guns."

They did, and if Jerry hadn't been strapped in, he would've jumped out.

He looked at me, embarrassed.

I said, "Jerry, I jumped higher than you did my first time. These guns are not anchored to a post ten feet back. The gunners move them all over. You'll get used to it."

I spent the next 50 minutes explaining the weapons systems, the cannon, and especially how to fly this overloaded slow-moving hog. I talked about covering the other ships. I included the part about *this is not a slick!* "Move the controls smoothly. Move your head around slightly so you don't get target fixation. If you wait too long, you'll mush right into the ground as you are trying to break and you'll be a smoking hole. Mass times acceleration equals force. Newton's second law of motion. Respect the mass of this beast."

I called up 9-8 (where Norwood was) and asked about some training. He thought it was a good idea. I turned on the music. I told Jerry to fly on the course I gave. Ski and Tyler knew the routine. It took only two turns to confuse Norwood. Out went the smoke, and Norwood had just learned a lesson. I hoped he would remember.

I called 9-8 and asked him if his copilot knew we were flying for beers. "He does now."

After 10 minutes of this, we changed positions, and I explained how we cover them. "This will occur every time we call out breaking right or left. Be careful to make sure you are not getting too low or too close." With that said, out came a smoke, and we were caught out of position. I explained that I let it happen so he could see his mistake.

I called 9-8 and said "We are going to fire the cannon."

He replied that they would shoot the mini guns. We shot about 100 rounds from the cannon. The wing was flying slightly out of position so his ricochets wouldn't hit us.

I called Baldy. "Let the Firebirds know we are five minutes out. Have the fuel truck meet us at the turnaround."

Damn, a hot piece of brass went down my neck. Shit, you can't help moving forward to get that hot casing away from your skin, but then it moves down your back each time you move forward. At this stage of the game, who gives a shit?

I really don't think I will make it through this goat rope. The guys in the bar were right when they said this is a fucking joke. We go back into an LZ we just went into two weeks before. When we went in there, we lost three ships with eight dead. I don't remember how many grunts were killed. You have either good luck or bad luck. It's FUBAR.

I asked Jerry to get on the controls and experience how heavy this ship felt when landing. He tried, but his grip was so slight, I couldn't detect any input from him.

As we slowed our descent and forward air speed, I talked Jerry into gripping the controls a little tighter and feel what I was doing. Now, he was working with me. I said, "Don't be afraid of this ship. Just learn your and its limitations. This ship can kill you. Even if it just barely kills you, you're still dead.

"This job has a high turnover of pilots and crews. You can be careful only to a point. This gunship is a big target. You have nothing in front of you but a thin piece of Plexiglas. If you wanted to be safe, you should have joined the Navy. Remember, it's not just about being a target. We provide the enemy catered suicide."

"I like that, Mac."

We set our ships down in the turnaround as the fuel trucks arrived with our half tank of JP-4.

"Let's get these ships rearmed so those tired smelly birds can return to Chu Lai. They're hanging around in case someone needs our services." We finished in fifteen minutes with the help of eight Firebirds and waved goodbye to the fire team, who looked like they were too tired to make it to CL.

"I'm going to look for holes. Give me a minute or two, Ski, and then I'll clean the plenum chamber." (The plenum chamber is a filter to keep particles out of the engine.)

After all the checks were completed, we waited for the phone to ring.

Jim Williams walked up behind me and asked, "How does it feel to be a gun driver?"

"I'll tell you an hour after the next phone call from the Hilton."

He nodded, and the phone rang. We were confused and stared at each other for a few seconds. Then, Jim ran to the ships, and I ran to the phone. I wrote the info on two small pieces of paper and joined Jim.

"We're going eight clicks north to the Song Ba Ren River to help some GIs who got themselves in trouble. We are to contact Wildman 6."

I handed Jim the info and gave the other one to Jerry.

"Jerry, clear us and TO."

He called, "Clear," and hovered and bounced out to the runway, while I called Baldy and said we were going north. After takeoff, I gave Jerry the heading to follow. "Gain some altitude. We are going to be in mountainous territory in another minute. Stay out of those clouds; they have real estate in them."

Jerry looked at me. "I don't understand."

"Mountains."

He nodded.

"Wildman 6," I radioed, "this is Firebird 9-7, a team of gunships approaching from your south. Pop a smoke and give me a heading to the bad guys."

"We have our backs to the river and are on the north side of the hills. We are behind a dike in a dry rice paddy. It looks like 50 NVA, and there are two dry paddies between us. I don't think they've seen us. They're moving west to east and are in the open."

"Roger that 6. I will come in from the south, shoot, and break over your heads. I have your purple smoke."

"That's us. I think they see the smoke, too."

"Get your heads down. We'll be shooting close, and we'll be shooting mini guns, M-60s, and a cannon along with our rockets. Here comes the first pair of rockets."

They exploded right in the middle of the NVA advancement and caught them flat footed out in the open.

There was so much dirt in the air, I couldn't see the ground, so I pushed a little right pedal and put a pair of rockets 75 yards from our guys, then left pedal and punched another pair.

I called, "Ready," and then "Breaking right," and here came Jim's rockets. On target, and I could see the mini guns tearing up the guys trying to run back to the tree line.

"Hey 6, do you see anything in the trees to your south?" I asked.

"No, all I see are bodies. No one is shooting at us; no troops advancing. You nailed their fucking ass. I called HQ, and they are sending out some ships to pick us up."

"When are they coming?"

"They said they were pulling slicks off their missions and weren't sure when they would arrive. Maybe ten minutes."

I asked, "How many are you."

"20 total; 18 are OK, and two on stretchers."

"6, how are the two on stretchers."

"Both are stable. We have a great medic with us."

The smoke and dust were clearing, and I could see the bad guys running straight west, where they came from. As I turned west, I asked, "Is everyone OK?" They all clicked back, so I called, "Rolling in." I punched a pair into a rather large tent I spotted in the trees. A tremendous explosion rose up. I punched another pair into the group running. "Get on those runners" and followed with a quick, "Breaking right." The jungle lit up with tracers coming up and through our rotor wash. I felt so exposed up there. *Why am I thinking about it now? That's supposed to happen after the mission.*

All this time, the door gunners were hanging outside the ship shooting at NVA and the origin points of tracers. They continued shooting as I broke and didn't stop until we heard 9-8 call, "Breaking right." I put a pair of rockets behind them and under the spot where 9-8 broke. I was looking through the rocket sight with my thumb lightly on the red button on my cyclic. The remaining NVA didn't stop shooting.

Jesus, how many of those bastards are down there? Shit, I could smell the familiar cordite. Well, just ignore it, Mac, and concentrate on your targets and those bastards shooting at you.

I continued the mission and ignored the incoming rounds. "Shoot at the ones you see, and the origin of those tracers." After two more runs, we had gone through half our ordinance.

I called Wildman 6 and asked if he needed more ordinance on those bad boys.

He said, "You kicked their fucking ass."

"We'll stick around and escort you and the slicks outa here. 9-8, let's do a little aerial recon before those slicks arrive." I got back two clicks.

I began a large circle around the area we just blew up. Everyone but the copilot was looking down for any movement. It looked like a nuke had gone off. There was a good sized crater where that ammo had been stored. We kept enlarging our circle for a few additional minutes until the lead of four slicks, 2-9 (Glen Walton), called us and Wildman.

Wildman told them to land in the dry rice paddy east of the smoke. "All your ships would fit in there."

I rogered and told slick 2-9 we would escort them in, then turn 180 degrees and fly out. To Wildman, I said, "Have your stretcher bearer's jump in the lead ship with the wounded. Then do a five, five and four in the last three ships."

We went in, ten seconds ahead of the slicks. We received no enemy fire. The slicks followed us in and created a dust storm that obscured everything for a few critical moments. Four guys with the two stretchers ran towards the lead ship and placed them inside and jumped in.

2-9 called and told the last ship in to lead them out. He got back two clicks.

The new lead called and said, "Four is loaded." The other three followed immediately. Lead said, "Pulling pitch" and the Birds came in again with the two ships on the left side of the four slicks. It was so smooth, it looked choreographed.

Slick 2-9 called and said, "Thank you."

I couldn't resist. I recognized that Texas drawl as well as his number 2-9, my buddy, Glen Walton.

I called up and said, "2-9, no one shot at you because they all fell to the ground with seizures when they saw those large diving red Firebirds on the sides of our ships."

"9-8 agrees."

"This is 2-9's copilot and your ex roomie. I had to take over the controls because the AC was laughing so hard he was vomiting and calling bullshit. He said he always gets sick when one of his students screws up."

"Never heard of a 2-9 copilot, but I do recognize your voice, Surfer Dude."

Surfer Dude said, "No! Now everyone will call me that."

"Glad to help."

"Do you want to call in 2-9, since you have the wounded?"

"Roger."

Glen cleared two birds and three slicks for POL and then the turnaround and one slick to MASH. That slick would then do POL and then fly to the turnaround.

HQ said, "Good job you guys. Guns can rearm and then take a break. It has been a quiet day."

Did that guy think the mission we just completed was quiet?

Things really were quiet for the next two days, and then the phone rang. Everyone ran to the ships, and I answered the phone, as per standard operating procedure (SOP). This call was different.

One of our slicks was landing in a fairly secure area to drop off some of South Vietnam's best. The crew chief and door gunner told them to exit the right side when they landed, then run straight out away from the ship. (They wouldn't jump out like the Americans.) One of those numb-nuts jumped out on the left and ran straight back into the tail rotor. He survived, with a headache and a large dent in his helmet. However, the tail rotor was traveling at nearly 2400 rpm and with that sudden stop, destroyed all its gears. The tail rotor is important as its true name is the anti-torque blades. If the main rotor goes around in one direction, the body of the heli-copter will spin in the opposite direction. (Another one of Newton's laws of motion.) The tail rotor counteracts the force of the main rotor blade. Hence, no spinning.

The pilot kept his cool and rolled off the throttle when he felt the ship wanting to move. The crew chief tried to grab the soldier but wasn't expecting him to go the wrong way and watched help-less as he ran into the blade. A quick call from the crew chief to the AC to shut it down saved the ship from tipping over.

I passed all of this along to everyone. We essentially were es-corting a Chinook in to pick up the ship in a sling and return it to Chu Lai.

We got there before the Chinook to see if any unfriendly people were in the area. I knew our slick crew on the ground was very un-comfortable. A slick was on its way to pick them up. The guns flew around the area waiting for any trouble.

The slick made a quick trip in and out. We kept flying around until the Chinook arrived.

Now it got dicey as the Chinook had to discharge two of its crew to prepare the ship and hook up the ship's lines to the Huey. Then it flew to the end of the sling line to land and pick up the two from his crew. It went well. The Chinook lifted the Huey straight up to 3000 feet and made an uneventful flight to Chu Lai.

We didn't receive any enemy resistance. Unusual but not unwelcome.

Chapter 41.

DEATH IN A FIREBALL

Jim and I finished our five days. New crews came up from Chu Lai and relieved all eight of us. We had had several uneventful missions and no bullet holes. We finished out the week in good order and good spirits. We were going home to party.

After landing, we performed all the required checks. The ships looked good. All the pilots and copilots jumped into the truck. The crew chiefs and door gunners said they would stay and do some cleanup and call for refueling.

As we were on Highway One, it began to rain. A few minutes later, I discovered what a monsoon is. It was literally coming down in buckets. To think I left the University of Oregon and its dark misty weather because I didn't like rain.

I found out later that night from Ski that they had stayed to put tarps over the controls and the door-less openings to the pilots' and copilots' seats to keep them dry. An hour later, they showed up soaking wet. They had on their army ponchos with hoods, but it didn't look like these had provided any protection from the elements.

I did my usual routine, and then I finished a letter home. I told my parents I was in the gunship platoon. It's difficult to soft coat that information.

I stuck my head around the plywood wall and asked Jim, "Ready to forget LZ Baldy?"

"Lead and I will follow."

We were ten feet from the club when our new Platoon leader, Jerry Wilder, yelled, "Mac, Jim, hold up. I have some news for you."

We stopped, and he jogged the last few feet. "Let's get away from the club for a minute." Oh shit, he had that look. "Who is it this time?" I asked.

He gave me a strange look and said, "You know already?" I shook my head and told him he had the look.

"An hour ago, rattler 2-2, Ed Place, and copilot, Dean Perry, were practicing autorotation's at Baldy when a blade broke. They went into free fall the last 100 feet. The FTL was standing in the doorway of the Hilton watching. He says he saw the blade break. They hit the runway and created a huge fireball. The crew chief, Steve Atchison, and door gunner, Todd Burnet, were also killed."

I just stood there staring out into space. I asked Jerry, "Is it OK if I tell his roommate, Lance Austin? I roomed with him as an FNG."

Jerry nodded, his face emotionless. I told the guys I'd meet them in the club after I talked to Lance. I walked over to his hooch.

Lance was sitting on his bunk and Bob Clearwater was on his. I stood there for a moment; I had never done this before. There was another guy on his bunk, who I didn't know.

They were looking at me with quizzical looks.

I said, "Your roommate Dean Perry was killed an hour ago at Baldy while practicing an autorotation. A blade broke about a 100 feet up. They went into free fall, hit the runway, and exploded."

Lance went to the floor on his knees, leaning on his bed, and began praying and crying. Bob looked stunned.

I said, "Come over to the club if you don't have to fly tomorrow, any or all of you."

I walked in the club and noticed Jerry and Jim were already in the bag. They hadn't been there more than 10 minutes. I'll bet they had gone to the Birdhouse first and chugged a few beers.

I had no choice but to begin with whatever they handed me. A big man with a Firebird patch on his shirt came up and introduced himself as Big Randy, the new 9-4. We shook, smiled, and toasted. After we chugged that Crown Royal, Big Randy asked if I had heard about the crash on Baldy. I nodded *yes*.

"Are you OK?" he asked me.

"I will be in another half hour, and then I'll think about it tomorrow. I knew everyone on that ship."

The CO walked in and came straight to me.

I said, "Good evening, sir."

"Mac, I'm going to ask you to do a very difficult job tomorrow, pack up the deceased's belongings. That would be Dean Perry. Come by my office at 0900. I'll give you a large box to fill. Now, use your judgement and screen out anything that might offend his girl-friend or mother. Captain Wilder will assist you."

"Sir, can I buy you a drink?"

To my surprise, he said, "Yes. Can you afford a cold beer and a shot of Crown?"

"Sir, we're probably drinking off my money in the pot."

I walked to the bar and said, "Three crowns and throw a beer in the freezer for the Major." The bartender was a young Vietnamese girl who spoke better English than me.

I handed two Crowns to the Major and kept the third.

He gave me a look, so I said, "It saves me a second trip. I only get one as I'm one ahead of you, Sir."

I was already drunk enough to philosophize. "Sir, did you know that we drink because of our feelings? When we feel good, we have a drink; when we feel bad, we need a drink." There you go, all wrapped up in one sentence. "Cheers," and we chugged them down."

"Did you make that up, Mac?"

"I think so, sir."

The night ended strangely. A chief warrant officer walked in and over to a group of Birds. He said, "Quiet down and stop being so obnoxious."

Big Randy stepped forward and said, "Why?"

That brought on a great cheer from the Birds and Rattlers.

I said to Major Wilson, "Excuse me, Sir."

I walked over to this turd and told him to change his tooth paste and mouth wash. "I can smell your breath across the room." I asked him if he ever bothered to listen to the shit he was spewing out.

Before he could say anything, Big Randy told him, "Get out be-fore we throw you out. This club is private, and a member must escort you until you become a member."

"How does a person become a member?"

Big Randy said, "We would consider a membership after four-teen months here. And then someone must sponsor you."

It suddenly reached his brain; a normal tour was twelve months.

He was getting very angry when someone yelled, "The shit house is on fire." (I mentioned earlier they burn the waste with diesel, and guys throw the cigarettes down between their legs when through smoking while sitting on the pot. The problem is left-over diesel.) The fire was really starting to consume that stinking four holer, so I went back in the club and picked up two Crowns and returned to the fire and tossed them both in to keep the fire roaring.

Everyone was throwing their drinks in the fire. There was yelling and jumping around like kids at a high school dance. "Burn baby burn" really stood out in my mind

The Seabees would be there in the morning and build a new one. It wouldn't stink for a while. We all headed back to the bar. I was told that angry W-2 had been a master sergeant before flight school. He was going to be a problem. He was too much army. He might have had a hard time making pilot.

"He's looking at us as children," someone said.

I decided I would skip the memorial service. There had been far too many, and I didn't want to think about the dead while I was fighting to stay alive.

"Jim, I have a question. I'm not religious, but I would like to know whose side is God on."

Jim looked at me for thirty seconds and then shrugged. "We talked about that before and had no answer then."

I told Jim my take on the memorials, and he agreed with me. I said, "Let's go back to the club."

He said "Lead on. You're the fire team leader."

The only place to go around there was the beach or the Bar. I think the bar offered the most relief from stress. The fire outside was nearly out, so everyone had returned to the stress reliever. I think it was easier to handle death with a drink. Most of these kids had never been to a funeral. Seems Jim and I got into serious conversations when alcohol was involved.

We talked about "fight or flight reactions." I had studied that in biology my first year at the Univ. of Oregon, and I lectured Jim on what I remembered. "Chemicals like adrenalin, testosterone, and cortisol are released into the system causing increased heart and respiration rates. Blood is shunted from the digestive system to the muscles for quicker responses, pupils dilate, impulses quicken, perception of pain diminishes, and we become willing to throw everything into a fight. Or into running away. We can't relax, so we become aggressive. We can build up stress hormones and create physical symptoms; anxiety, depression, poor concentration." I did make one original contribution: "Jim, there's fight or flight, and I've heard of a third one: freeze, where you can't do anything."

Jim and I eventually ran out of things to say, but anyway the bar closed, and we were asked to leave. We decided that was bad.

"Thrown out of a bar with no rules and in a third world country," I said. "Wow, rock bottom, Jim. I think it's cool that two people of different races and different backgrounds and everything else different can come together and work together for a common goal. You said I saved your life. Well Jim, you are working hard to keep me alive by teaching me all your experiences you've learned over the past eleven months. And I thank you for that. Your behavior reflects your values."

By the way, Bob and Lance never did make it to the Bar.

Chapter 42.

SHOT DOWN

We woke up with headaches. Not unreasonable. Jim and I were halfway through breakfast when Thompson, the company clerk, ran in. "Get your gear, Sirs. A lead ship crashed taking off the POL at Baldy."

In unison, we both said, "Shit!"

We ran out of the Choke and Puke to the Birdhouse. We grabbed the essentials, and Thompson drove us to the flight line. On the way I asked him if he had any more news. "Was anyone hurt?" He told us the crew chief had a broken arm and the gunner was burned from hot oil. "That's all I have, Sirs."

Damn, you can never relax and let down. I'm continually being wound up tight like a spring. This goes in the book.

"Why is Jim going?"

"The CO wants him to check you out officially for FTL (Flight Team Leader). When he promoted you in the bar or the Birdhouse, it was not per regulations."

I looked at Jim and said, "I should fuck this up and end all my frustrations here. What do you think?"

"Mac, I know you. You will teach me a thing or two."

"Thompson, the CO wanted to see me at 0900 to pack up Dean Perry's stuff."

"Oh yeah, he told me he would get someone else. They need you two now at Baldy."

On the flight there, Jim and I talked continuously. We covered a lot of subjects. I asked him, "Why did you want to fly?"

He said, "It was a step up in my military career. It sounded exciting, or at least not as boring as a lot of army stuff."

"It's probably because you aren't tall enough to play basketball and not big enough to play football."

He said, "My official stance on such a terrible stereotype is to say fuck you."

Then we both started laughing. Then he said to me, "You probably can't jump worth a shit."

What could I say? He was correct. I said, "That's right, but I know where the ladder is."

Halfway to Baldy, we got a call to proceed ten clicks north of Baldy to help some green beanies (Green Berets). "When you are five minutes out, call HQ, and we'll have the wing ship cranked up and ready to go."

"I hope we sober up before the shit hits the fan. Jim, I forgot to ask who's the wing."

"Its Rivers as Wing with copilot Dave Elliott, CE is Joe Gibbs, DG is Paul Walsh."

I called Baldy HQ and told them we were five minutes out and asked for frequencies and coordinates and a call sign. Jim dialed in the frequencies, and I called Green Monster 6. "Can you hear us?"

"Yes, I can hear you. Oh yeah, now I see you. I'm popping smoke. We're a patrol of eight. There are at least fifty NVA. We are behind some small hills and palms, next to the Cau Lau River right where it flows into the Song Thu."

"I see your purple smoke, and I see movement to your west. Have you worked with gun- ships before?"

"Hell yes, and you guys are the angels from above."

"OK. I'm going to come up over the hills south of you and the NVA. After the rockets and cannon fire with both door gunners shooting at any and everything, I will break over your position and my wingman will do the same except he has two electric Gatling guns. Now with all this going on, I want you to stop shooting. We will continue that pattern until nothing is alive. Here we come. Get your heads down."

Since everyone on board was tuned to the same frequencies, I didn't have to repeat a thing. As I rolled in to punch rockets, I could see those little bastards trying to take cover in the palms, but those trees didn't have heavy enough fronds to hide under, and the trunks were too small to hide behind. The door gunners were tearing them up. There were very few tracers coming by my windshield and rounds breaking through my rotor wash.

I didn't have to tell Jim anything about picking out targets with the nose cannon. Ski and Tyler were on their usual A game. We were fucking unstoppable. I broke and Tom Rivers took over. After two more passes, the trees were burning; black earth and smoke were all that remained. I called the GBs and said, "We're returning to Baldy."

They replied with, "Thanks. Now we'll go check on your handiwork."

The wing ship called and told me, "You're leaking what looks like fuel." At the same time, I gazed across my instrument panel and saw my fuel level dropping rapidly.

"Wing, I'm going to turn east and try to make it to Highway One. We own that road. Lots of friendlies down there."

I called Green Mountain 6 and reported my status. He said, "No problem. We are hattin' up and will be checking out those dead NVA."

"9-7, this is wing, your leak is slowing down."

"I'll bet it is. My gas gauge is near zero. The good news is I see Highway One."

At that moment, the engine rpm began winding down. I bottomed the pitch and called out, "Mayday, Mayday, Mayday. Firebird 9-7 going down four clicks North of Baldy on Highway One, and it's covered with our guys. Everyone go cold."

It was an easy autorotation. As the blade stopped turning, I looked over to my copilot Jim and said, "Since you are the copilot, all of this," as I waved my hand and arm out in front of me to indicate all we could see, "is your fault."

Jim started laughing and said, "Is that all you have to say after getting shot down?"

Then the crew said, "Nice landing, sir, "and they all broke out laughing.

I called wing and asked him, "What do you see in the area?"

He said, "Nothing but our guys."

"I've got a hundred troops around me. Why don't you go back, refuel and rearm? Could you also call Baldy and bring them up to date?"

The grunts had the ship surrounded and were asking questions faster than we could answer. I climbed out and raised my hands to silence the crowd. When I had their attention, I introduced Ski and Tyler and told everyone it was their ship. "They might even be willing to take a picture of you at the machine guns." Ski and Tyler smiled. *When on the ground, it is their ship after all.*

By now, I was standing outside the ship with my helmet still plugged in, so I called Chu Lai for a Chinook to come get my ship. I asked for a lead ship also. I said, "A slick can take me, Jim, Ski and Tyler to Chu Lai to pick up another HOG." *Damn war gets complicated.*

I saw a pair of railroad tracks on one grunt's collar (two silver bars look like railroad tracks) which told me he was a Captain. I walked over to him and introduced myself. We shook hands, and then I asked if he could set up a perimeter around the gunship.

He smiled and said, "Already done."

"I see your shoulder patch is the 198th infantry," I told him. "We are in Chu Lai, actually on the beach about two miles south of your HQ. We are the 71st, and my name is Kevin. We live in that hooch on the turnaround with the name Hilton over the door that we don't have."

He said, "Mine's Matt."

"If you get to CL, call the Firebird hooch first because I essentially live at Baldy and not CL. Buying you a couple of beers is the least I can do for someone who has guarded my ship. The SVN would have picked it clean by now.

"Matt," I added, "there will be a Chinook here soon to haul that dead bird back to Chu Lai. As a warning, a Chinook creates Hurricane winds. Keep clear."

Here came a slick, landing a few hundred yards from the dead bird. The pilots waved us over. Ski and Tyler started throwing their shit in. Jim and I helped. After we got to CL, we picked up a lead gunship and flew to Baldy. We got word on the way that the Chinook had arrived and picked up its load.

As soon as we arrived, we flew to POL for a look see. We were greeted with a sight that made us all shudder. Fifty yards off of POL was a lead gunship lying on its side in a rice paddy still smoking from the hot engine. All the gun pilots knew this would happen eventually. It wasn't easy to get a gunship in the air from the small pad at POL. On a cold day, it required one bounce to get in the air. A hot day required two bounces, maybe a third, and there was barely room enough for the second bounce, but only if you were at the far end of POL.

We flew the lead to the Hilton. (We would refuel when the fuel truck arrived.) Big Randy walked out of the Hilton towards us. I stopped what I was doing and walked toward him. I wasn't sure what to say.

He looked like he hadn't slept in days. His flight suit was covered in dried caked mud. He slowly lifted his head. I spoke first. "Hey big guy, what happened?" *Really brilliant Kev.*

His answer startled me more than my dumb question. He looked at me and said, "I fucked up, Mac. I tried to get off the ground with only one bounce. After that it was disaster in slow motion. I just settled down into the paddy, and when we hit, the nose dipped and the rotor blade struck the water and mud and the last six feet of the tail boom was cut off by the flexing blade from the hard landing and flipped on our side. Rick Rogers, my door gunner for the past four months was burned on his arms from the hot engine oil. Chico Rodriguez, my crew chief has a broken arm. Copilot is OK. Mac, my self-esteem is destroyed. We have a motto in the Guns: I'd rather die than look bad."

"That's a bunch of shit, Randy. It's a great motto, but so is: In god we trust. These REMFs don't have a clue how difficult it is to take that hog off POL. I'd bet you money that 90% of the slick pilots couldn't get that beast off the ground. Shit happens, Randy. Drop it and move on after the investigation. Jesus Randy, you know you aren't a gun driver until you've been investigated!"

"Thanks, Mac. I've already got the crew writing down the incident."

"Don't forget the expediency. They want you back immediately and that's impossible."

"What's the definition of immediately?"

"That's right, Randy. There is no definite or concrete answer. You pushed it and pushed it for what, nine months? I would say they got their money's worth out of you. That slick out there is waiting to give you a cab ride to Chu Lai. Look big guy, no one died.

Now get your crew to CL."

"Thanks, Mac."

Jim Williams joined our little huddle and said, "Try to shake it off, Randy. We'll be back in Chu Lai in a few days and help you drink that refrigerator dry."

We just stood there quietly watching Randy slowly walk to his ride to the Birdhouse.

I turned to Jim and asked, "What do you want to do now?" Before he could answer, I added, "Thanks for covering for me while I was trying to console Randy."

"I'm glad you talked to him. I wouldn't have known what to say."

"Neither did I, Jim. I asked him what happened? Brilliant huh? He looked at me and said, 'I fucked up.'"

Jim looked at me and started laughing.

"What's so funny?"

"That was all you could think to say."

"Next time, you get to do all the talking, Jim."

Jim started laughing again and said, "Maybe I will flunk your ass, then I can order you to do the talking."

"You flunk me and two things happen: You will stay here longer, and I will personally go to Alabama when I return to the world and tell your wife about your white ass.

"Jim, let's go take a nap."

He nodded.

"We're laughing," I said, "when we should be crying."

Chapter 43.

ONE MORE DEATH

As soon as Jim and I sat down on our bunks, the damn red phone rang.

"Jim that phone is wired into our bunks. As soon as there is pressure on that filthy one-inch-thick mattress, the phone rings."

As I answered, everyone was running to the ships.

HQ said, "A 51 Chi Com has those same green beanies pinned down almost on the same spot you left them."

Everything was the same: frequency, grid cords, and call sign. I handed out the info to my wingman, and then climbed in with Jim.

"Jim, I hate those 51's."

He nodded. "Someone should put President Johnson up here with us and show him the effects of stopping the bombing!"

I contacted Green Mountain 6, and they said, "We have determined that there is a 51 cal. hidden 100 yards into the jungle from your last rocket run."

I rolled in and started punching rockets as Green Mountain guided me in to the 51's location. I spread a dozen rockets over the area when Jim's windshield exploded from 51 fire from another 100 yards north of the scorched earth. His windshield was blown apart as I called, "Breaking right."

Ski was laying down constant fire at the new 51's location. As I continued the break, I glanced over at Jim, and he was hanging in his harness and seat belt. I was so stunned I looked a second time and saw blood everywhere. I then looked at Ski behind Jim, and he was covered in blood. I said, "Ski, are you OK?"

He said, "Yes," as he was trying to wipe the blood and other material off his visor. I looked over at Jim, and he had a hole in his chest large enough for me to put my fist in. Jim was wearing a chicken board. It was fractured in many pieces and blown into his chest. The bullet itself continued through Jim and the metal back to his seat and into the firewall behind Ski's head.

Now reality was setting in. My crew was shooting long bursts at targets. My wing was shooting rockets and mini guns, and his door gunners were shooting long bursts. My best friend in this little piece of hell was dead. This piece of hell just got bigger. I wanted to yell, scream, and kill every one of those little bastards! Jim had been talking to me just a moment earlier.

I called Wing and said, "Dump everything on the two 51s and return to Baldy. My copilot is dead." *How could I say that so casual? I learned it from you Jim. Keep calm and everyone else will remain calm and trust you.*

I punched all my remaining rockets at the two 51s, then switched the controls for Jim's cannon and shot it on full automatic at both targets. The wing did the same.

Green Mountain was following our radio calls, and he said, "Return to Baldy. I think you got them all. If they have any more surprises, they are a quarter of a mile into the Jungle. We are headed south to Baldy and have called in Napalm now that we have some distance between us and the NVA." He followed with, "I'm so sorry. I know you gun drivers are tight. You have a shitty job. We all thank you from this end."

I called Baldy and asked for a body bag and truck to meet us at the turnaround, along with the fuel truck. I got back a whisper that I think was a roger. *DAMMIT, I was just talking to him.*

When I landed, the truck was waiting. I carefully helped the medics unharness Jim and place him into the body bag and gently slid the body bag into the truck. When they had him, I just couldn't hold back the tears. I think a piece of me was with him in that bag.

I got back in the ship and called Baldy HQ and asked if he had notified Chu Lai. He said he had, and they were sending up a copilot with Snake Doctor.

I said, "Send a lead ship. This one will take a day to clean up."

I think I was numb. *Goddammit, life is so cheap here.* I walked out to the runway and stood there alone not knowing what to think or do. I was sad, teary, but most of all angry and pissed off. I wanted some revenge. *Someone, anyone to blame, like the REMF who ordered that mission. Or anyone who tries to give me any reason or rational why Jim had to die. That's right, there isn't one. FUCK. I sure as hell won't put this in my after-school manual.*

I called HQ and said, "We're grounded until a ship and copilot arrive."

No one was talking. We were going about our normal routine of rearming the wing ship and checking for holes. Then we began to clean out the blood with the fire extinguisher. We began the cleaning so we would have something to do. That may seem abnormal, but tell me what's normal in a war!

I looked at Ski and Tyler. If I looked like them, we would all be declared deceased. They were at their physical limit. No sleep and constant flying in combat. A human has limits.

Here came more monsoons, buckets of water from the sky. I stood in the rain and undressed down to my underwear. I was rubbing pants and shirt together trying to wash off blood and tissue. Next thing I noticed was Ski and Tyler doing the same. I think Jim would have understood.

Snake Doctor arrived with a lead ship following, as the monsoons departed. The ship had a few holes but nothing serious. The windshield was replaced in thirty minutes. They could fix that front Plexiglas in the field now. Martin said they would help clean the ship, if they didn't have to remove the floor. Otherwise, he would call a Chinook and take it back to CL.

Chapter 44.

LIEUTENANT SHIT BIRD

My new copilot was David Sharp, the Firebird's assistant platoon leader. He was a first lieutenant, and I could tell he was full of himself. I put my hand out and said, "Nice to meet you, David." He stepped back and looked at me with a stern look on his face and said, "That's First LT Sharp."

I said, "That's fine. I'm Firebird 9-7, Fire Team Leader, and Warrant Officer McNally. Now excuse me as I should check on the repair of my ship." I walked into the Hilton and called the 71st platoon leader's hooch and asked for Captain Wilder.

He came to the phone and said, "I'm so sorry about Jim. We thought it might be better to keep you at Baldy for a distraction, Mac."

I said, "Thanks, I'm OK. Where did the 71st find LT Sharp?"

"He is a little stiff. He'll loosen up."

"OK. Call me if you need any flight time." And I hung up. He knew what I meant.

I walked over to talk to Martin Robertson. "Will she fly again?" I had probably already asked that question. I couldn't remember.

He said, "Just give us some time here or in CL, and I will place her back in your capable hands."

I looked at him but couldn't think of anything to say.

Martin said, "Mac, this is my second tour. I was here in '66 as an E-5 crew chief, then to flight school for Warrant Officer and Huey Mechanic. I've lost friends. I still think about them all the time. I can't change anything. I will tell you something about soldiers. We are first, very patriotic. Second, we don't like wars. But it is our duty to fight them. Third, you have minimal decisions to make. Here it is kill or be killed. I know that sounds cold, but it's the bottom line. Be glad it's not you."

I didn't believe everything he said, especially about the decisions, but I thanked him for the quick repair and pep talk. "One question before you leave. Where did they find Sharp?"

"I don't know. Ours is not to reason why, and you know the rest. I will say Mac, that in a very short period of time I have determined that he is an asshole."

I laughed out loud. "I can't wait to fly with him."

Rivers had called the fuel truck as Ski and Tyler were transferring our gear to the new ship. We were now ready to go to work. What you call work in a war.

I gave Shit Bird (my name for Sharp) a tour of the Hilton. He looked like he was going to call his mom. He said, "I'm appalled at this mess."

I asked him if he had had his tetanus shot. He gave me a quizzical look.

I explained about the sleep arrangements. Then, I explained his job as a copilot, and as if on cue, the phone rang, and it was off to the races. Sharp stood there like a mannequin. I waved him off and said, "Go start the Huey." *Not too many hours ago, Jim was running out to the ship.*

This was something new. Apparently several NVA in uniform were waving the Chieu Hoi pamphlets and a white flag. One of our slicks spotted them and called HQ. No one was sure if this was legitimate or a trap. Bottom line: They wanted the birds to check out the area. It was eight clicks due east of Baldy next to the Truong Giang River.

I asked LT Dull (another name for Sharp) to hover the ship out to the runway while I made the calls. He tried pulling the pitch a little too fast, and the ship did not move. He looked at me and said, "Something's wrong."

I said, "Let me try." We came up about six inches and slowly turned 180 degrees and moved towards the runway. We were cleared so I said, "Watch." I nudged the cyclic forward, and we started moving and bounced off the runway two more times. We were slowly gaining speed as we neared the end of the runway. I glanced at LT Dull, and his face was pale.

I know it was a shitty thing to do, but I wanted him to know how much he didn't know.

We cleared the wire by ten feet. I noticed my copilot was breathing again. *That's good, maybe?*

When we got to where the NVA were waving their white flag, I saw the slick flying in a large circle. I called him, and he said he hadn't seen anything in the mile diameter he'd flown in the last twenty minutes.

I said, "Let me fly close to them and see what happens. My wingman has them in his sights. I got back two clicks from Wing. Is everyone ready in back? Two clicks. I told LT Dull to pull down his sight, check the reticle, and be ready to shoot like they showed you on Target Practice Island. I checked my control panel for rockets and called, "Rolling in." All four on the ground ran in four different directions as I closed the space.

As they ran, one pulled an AK-47 out of his baggy black pajamas. He certainly had a death wish or was high on drugs. As he raised the gun up, I told Tyler, "Kill that bastard." He killed him in very few shots. I'll be damned; the other three tried the same routine. I told Ski to shoot the one at 9 o'clock, and Dull to shoot the one at 12 o'clock. Ski got his, Dull fired twenty times and never got close. I called Wing and said, "The rest are yours. I'm breaking right."

Those two were history before I finished my break. I called. "Nice shootin' cowboy." I asked Dull how many times he had shot the cannon at the Island."

He said he had fired it 100 times over two days. I know that's a quick instructional period, but he learned nothing.

I called HQ and explained the mission we had just finished. Then, I requested to delay our trip back to Baldy for a training session. They OKed it.

I called wing and said, "Go for it." I got back two clicks.

"Alright LT pull your sight down."

Instead of doing what I said, he asked, "Why are we doing this?"

I said loudly, "Because you are the worst person to shoot that cannon since I've been in this hell hole. You hear me, shit bird? One more unrequested comment and you are no longer a Firebird. You're too fucking stupid to notice we are in a war here. People are trying to kill us. Now, pull down that cannon sight and look through it. Do you see that small group of palms directly in front of us?" He just sat there. Now I yelled, "What the fuck is wrong? Can't you hear me?"

"Ski and Tyler, are you following this?" They said, "Yes Sir" in unison. I could tell by that response that they were listening to everything.

"Pull the trigger you moron! We in this ship are not going to fly with someone who is afraid to fight."

Finally, I said, "Don't touch the controls. Baldy, this is Firebird 9-7, a team of two gunships to your east and request to land with a straight in approach."

"Firebird 9-7, the tower is occupied today. How about that?"

"Wow, did you just return from a three month R & R?

"No sir, this is my third day in country."

"Welcome to Vietnam. Come over and see us on the turn-around. You will see a sign saying Hilton over the door of our hooch. By the way, can we land?"

"Oh yes, yes, cleared to land."

"Baldy, can you have the fuel truck meet us at the turnaround?" I looked at shit bird and said, "We'll be too heavy to take off from POL. We bounce off POL with only half a tank of fuel and no ammo." I looked closer and saw he had wet his pants. *Shit, this is not going to end well.*

We landed and began rearming. Shit bird went straight to the Hilton. What I didn't know until the next day was that he had called Chu Lai to report me for not showing him the courtesy of his rank.

That night was horrible. Several times, I sat up like a gun had gone off in my ear. I was drenched in sweat, and it was a cool night for a change. I could see Jim's face looking accusingly at me. I started crying, and it lasted off and on all night. I got up and walked outside the hooch. I was so fucking pissed and angry that I couldn't even think about sleeping. I can't remember the last time I cried.

Well, surprise-surprise, a gunship team woke us up at 0700. I walked over to the lead ship to talk to 9-3, Dennis.

He said he had no idea what was going on. All he heard was that the CO wanted to see me. I told Rivers to send a runner to HQ if anything happened. "I'm going to talk to the RTO (radio telephone operator) and see if anyone followed our transmissions."

I walked into HQ and introduced myself and asked if the radio operator from yesterday was available to talk to me. They said "yes" and led me into the radio room. There sat a kid who looked pre-teen. Now I knew I had been there too long.

I introduced myself and told him, "Call me Mac." His name was Montgomery Ellison. He said, "Call me Monty."

"Great, Monty. You wouldn't happen to have recordings from yesterday's missions?"

"Yes sir. Actually, Mac, I've been here ten months and have seen and heard some really weird shit. I anticipated your arrival and made a recording for you." He handed me a tape.

I was stunned. "I owe you big time. I'll be back in a few days. Have you ever shot an M-60 (our door gunners' machine guns) from a gunship?"

He sat up, his eyes looked larger, and he said, "No."

I nodded, and we shook hands, and I headed for our ships.

I had a pretty good Idea why I was called back to home base. Most likely Captain Dull, Shit Bird, Moron or Sharp had a large part in the CO's decision.

I rat raced through the trees, over the trees, and around the trees very close to the ground, as a training session and to scare the livin' shit out of this asshole sitting next to me. I traded off with the wing ship. The door gunners shot a few water buffalo just to be safe. Sometimes, the NVA would strap cases of ammunition on the sides of the buffalo and then throw the hide of a dead buffalo over all of that and disguise it as a fat buffalo. It doubled as a truck.

Fifty minutes later, I landed at the Firebird line. Immediately, Sharp walked away and toward the operation hooch. As he was walking away, I said, "Don't forget about your part in getting this ship mission ready. Anything less is dereliction of duty and will be reported to the CO and Brigade." No answer. *The rest of this day will be wonderful.*

I worked slowly with Ski and Tyler. They knew we were giving shit bird time to hang himself.

After an hour, we finished and climbed into a truck to the company area. On the short ride to the Major's office, I told Ski and Tyler to tell Top and the CO exactly what happened. They nodded.

As the truck came to a stop, the company clerk Thompson was

waiting. He walked over and said, "Get cleaned up and then all three of you have been requested to report back here in twenty minutes."

We all said, "Thanks, Thompson," and we were gone. As we walked away, I said, "Let's meet at the Birdhouse in seventeen minutes." We all checked our watches.

In eighteen minutes, we walked to the COs office. I kept it formal. I knocked twice and Top said, "Enter." I walked in with the two most able and capable crew in this jerk water country. We lined up three abreast in front of Top's desk. I said, "Mac, Ski and Tyler reporting as ordered."

Top stood slowly like he was put out with all this. He went in the CO's office, then returned and said, "Go on in, Mac. Ski, have a seat, and he indicated a chair in front of his desk. Tyler, go outside and wait for me to call you."

I immediately thought, *divide and conquer*. I walked into the CO's office and stood at attention.

He said, "Sit down and tell me what happened."

I proceeded slowly so as not to leave out anything. When I finished, I added, "He even wet his pants."

"Mac, I know you, and you are the finest pilot, quick to change a plan and develop a new one as needed, fair, an incredible teacher, and a great military mind. I'm sorry this is happening."

I was stunned. I knew the CO and I were friends to the point the military allows Field Grade Officers to co-mingle with lowly Warrants. I said, "Thank you, sir."

"As you can imagine, I was told an entirely different story by LT Sharp."

I just nodded.

"Top is getting the stories from your crew. I know you Mac, and you probably told them to just tell what happened. Is that correct?"

"Yes sir."

"Do you have anything to add?"

"Yes sir, I do. As you know, HQ records all missions. HQ records missions of the grunts and the pilots as we are all on the same frequencies."

"Yes, I'm well aware."

"Just before departing Baldy an hour and a half ago, I went to

HQ and picked up a copy of the tape of yesterday's mission." As I spoke, I pulled the small tape out of my pocket and handed it to the CO.

He raised his eyebrows as he took it. He asked me if I had listened to it.

I said, "No sir."

He pulled out a small recorder and placed the tape inside. He turned it on, but with very low volume, and he asked me to slide up to his desk so I could hear. He just kept shaking his head as if he couldn't believe what he was hearing.

"Mac, you and I have always spoken truthfully. Brigade flew a copy of this tape to me this morning, and the Brigade Commander personally handed it to me." He emphasized his statement to me by pulling out the copy he had received a few hours earlier. "I haven't listened to my copy yet.

"Top should be finished with your crew. I'm going to call everyone in and please don't speak unless we ask a direct question." He picked up his phone and made his request. The three walked in, and the CO said, "Grab a chair." He then said, "Did all the stories check out, Top?"

Top said, "To the letter, sir."

"Top and I would like to tell you what the Brigade Commander told us this morning. He said he is well aware of your exploits and bravery. He added that on a couple of occasions he has observed you all working together after a mission, and he was in awe of the routine and teamwork. When Monty, the radio operator, brought this to his attention, he knew there was going to be a problem. A first lieutenant versus a warrant.

"Top and I knew you guys made no mistakes. The army has its protocols, and you followed them to the letter. Sharp is a spoiled, immature individual. His father is a general in the Pentagon. Sharp never should have been in the service. During a war, the standards are lowered. He still should have been washed out in flight school. Daddy just kept backing him up instead of admitting that his kid had something wrong in his brain. I was told that he soloed after 20 hours. And that was a gift. He should have washed out at fifteen hours.

"I'm going to bring him in and let him tell his story again and see how it matches. By the way, Ski and Tyler, don't spread this around, but HQ records all of the missions so they have every word from yesterday. They use most of them for training purposes in the states.

"This will seem like a strange encounter, but everyone gets to meet their accuser."

Sharp was summoned. He came in and sat down and was asked to tell his story. He was very nervous and jumped all around in the chair.

He asked why "we three" were in the room. That was explained to him. He started with a statement that I had no respect for his rank. He added that I wouldn't let him shoot the cannon or fly. He claimed that I had set the controls and done something tricky with the throttle, so that he couldn't hover to the runway. He rambled on for another twenty minutes when the CO interrupted and asked if he wanted to change anything."

He said. "No sir."

The CO reached in his desk and pulled out the recorder, sat it on his desk and turned it on. The room was silent except for the recorder. Sharp's face turned red. He grabbed a waste basket and puked in it. That didn't help with the hot stinking air in the office.

The tape ended with our landing at Baldy. The room remained quiet. The CO said, "You left out the fact that you walked away from the ship and crew after landing here. I'm not going through all the regulations you broke or your behavior in combat or you lying directly to your CO.

"You are going to immediately retire from the army and relinquish your rank of LT. If you wish to fight this, it's your right. I must remind you that a Court Marshall will greatly affect your father from getting any more stars. This is not blackmail. I'm giving you the facts."

I looked at Sharp, then reached over and tapped Top on the leg and pointed at Sharp's pants. Top's eyes almost popped out. Sharp had wet his pants again.

The CO dismissed Sharp and told him, to "start packing." He had some difficulty taking his eyes off Sharp's wet pants.

After Top closed the door, the CO said, "I'm glad that nonsense is over. We have something important to talk about. We need two gunships and crews for a top secret mission into Laos."

Chapter 45.

TOP SECRET

"Since we are not officially in Laos," Major Wilson reminded us, "you cannot tell anyone about this. You will fly without ID. Your tail numbers will be painted over, and the mission is voluntary. It will begin immediately and last for three weeks. You will be inserting LRRPs (Long Range Reconnaissance Patrols, pronounced Lurps) into Laos, and they will call in air strikes on the Ho Chi Minh trail, or should I say, highway. You will insert them on the east side of the Chaine Annamite, and they will hike to the top and look down, west and into Laos, and call in B-52 air strikes known as Arc Lights (the area bombed looked like the glow on hot metal from a welders torch).

"I have picked you three and Captain Wilder would be lead. Wing will be Rivers and Elliott. Ski and Tyler, who are the best two people you would want to work with on this mission?"

Without hesitation, they said, "9-8's crew: crew chief Arny Fox and gunner Pat Marshall."

The CO said, "That's what I thought you'd say, so I got top secret clearances for them as well. The clearances are good until 1980.

"Do you three want this assignment? I've already got Wilder's OK. I also ran this by Arny Fox and Marshall. They're OK as well. I'll talk to Rivers and Elliott.

"I'm sure you'll eat better. We'll get mail to you. You'll be on call 24/7 for three weeks. Insertions are easy. Pulling men out at midnight with the NVA chasing them will be a different story. You'll fly out from Quang Tri near the DMZ or out of a small inland recon base, LZ Rock Pile (RP). You'll fly around Khe Sanh. If you'll recall, after Christmas back in '67, the NVA surrounded Khe Sanh for

77 days and tried to overrun it; 205 Marines were killed and 1600 wounded. Then, we abandoned it."

I said, "Forget all that, Sir. Did you say better food? We're in!"

Surprising all of us, Top said, "Do you need a Top along with you Mac, to keep your crew under control?"

I said, "Yes, of course. I was going to ask." Now everyone was smiling as the tension left the room.

The CO said, "Do you need a CO to keep Top in line?" More laughter.

"Just pack one extra uniform as they have daily laundry. Take your oldest shirts as they will tear off all identification. All right, go pack and keep it low key. Remember, this is top secret. Dismissed."

Everyone began leaving. I looked at the CO and mouthed to him, "Can I stay for a minute."

He nodded, and I remained behind. As Top left, he closed the door. I looked at the CO, and my eyes were getting wet. I said, "Sir, in some fairness to Sharp, I think I took some of my grief about Jim and dumped it on him."

"Yes, you probably did. It was good. You got rid of some grief, and it's about time someone spoke up and stood their ground against that little shit. Don't worry about any of this. Brigade has already talked to his father. Mac, not many people would confess that they had laid their grief on someone. You are a strong person.

"Take out the rest of your grief on the NVA in Laos. They aren't supposed to be there either. Three days from now, you'll be in the air for a two-hour flight to the DMZ. One stop in Hue for fuel. Fly to Quang Tri airport and check in. You'll be briefed.

"Call me, Mac, and keep me in the loop. I go back to the world in 30 days. We might not see each other again. I'll regret that. You've made me feel like I did some good on this tour. I will fill in Major Ron Matthews about our relationship and what you have done here. I know Matthews. You'll enjoy working with him."

"One last request sir," I said, "Actually two. Would it be possible to take Top up in a gunship? He has been very fair with the Birds. He sees how they work twice as hard as anyone else. And I may push him out the door for puking on my bare feet."

"And your second?"

"Can I take the flight surgeon to the Island? I owe him as he has not reported any of my Mickey Mouse injuries. Otherwise, I'd be outta here and training Vietnamese pilots in the states. I can take Top out today and the doc tomorrow."

The CO said, "Let me call the flight line and see what up and running." In two minutes, he returned to the porch where I was waiting and said, "Top is available. I asked him to go to the flight line because I'm going to buck protocol and appoint you ammo officer of the 71st. You tell him when you get there."

"Can you ask him to bring his camera?"

"I'll talk to the flight Surgeon after you leave and have him bring his camera as well."

"Thank you, sir."

Top came out and asked if I was ready to go. He drove to the Conex container at the center of the Firebird line. "Top, did the CO mention that he was putting a warrant in charge of the ammo dump here?"

"Yes, he did, Mac." Top shook his head in disgust. "I don't know what's happening to this fucking army."

I asked him if he could move the jeep off the taxiway. He gave me a strange look. I said, "Here's the CO's helmet. Does it fit?"

He put it on, and I thought it was close enough for government work. I said, "Get in, Top. We're going to Target Practice. You sit in my seat on the right."

He looked stunned.

"I cleared it with all your platoon sergeants." I almost laughed. Top was always in control and had his finger on everything. "Just kidding, Top. But I did clear it with the major. It's OK. We're not going rogue."

"Is all this really on the up and up?"

"The Major said you could call him."

"OK, Mac. Let's go before someone catches us."

I don't think he believes me. I won't put this in my manual.

I cleared us to take off south for a training session.

The tower said, "Another nubee (new person)?"

I said, "Yes and keep your head down. I don't always know where he will put those rockets."

"Shit, are you serious?"

"Absolutely."

I got us in the air.

"OK, Top. Put your right hand on the cyclic like me and rest your arm on your right leg. Start a slow turn to the right. Be gentle. Good, now to the left. You're a natural. Just keep going south. I'm going to take a nap."

I think that got his attention and increased his pucker factor.

"You can see the Island at your 11 o'clock. Now grab a hold of the pitch. Have you ever ridden a motorcycle?"

He said, "Yes."

"This is a reverse motorcycle throttle. I've got it, Top. Pull down your rocket sight. Look through it. See that dot in the middle of your circle of light? Try a slow left turn and push the cyclic forward and the pitch down and roll off some throttle." I was helping. "Look at my right thumb." I gently touched the red button that launched the rockets. I had selected single shots. "OK, Top. Look through the sight and gently push the red button." He did and out came the rocket. It was generally in the ball park, as they say. "OK, Top. Turn right 180 degrees. We'll go out and around, so we can do it again. Pull up on the pitch and add power."

Oops, my bad. I gave him too much information. I had to jump in and recover the ship before we fell out of the sky.

"Top, do you have your camera?"

He nodded.

"Hand it to me, and I'll get some pics so you can show your wife, girlfriends, or kids what an awesome person and pilot you are. They can call me, and I'll back you up. Or as we say in the air, I've got your six."

I got pics of him shooting rockets and with his hands on the controls. (I put friction on the cyclic to keep it in place.) A big left turn with his head leaning a little left and face towards me and the camera. Top's head leaning was poor technique but in fairness I hadn't taught him that. Still, I was happy with how things were turning out. *I should be a Photographer. I'm getting some great shots.*

"Top, you're going to have to show me these pics."

We were shooting at the dead palms, the truck, and some big rocks. He rolled in six or seven times and punched from one to three rockets each run.

He was really enjoying this. I now set the selectors for him to shoot the 40 mm through his rocket sight. He looked like a little kid at Christmas. He shot 200 rounds out of the cannon, and I caught a lot of it on film. He fired single shots at the same targets. That was followed by strafing runs along a beach. He then surprised me and asked me for a rocket and pulled the nose up and punched a rocket.

"Top, did you see a Communist boat?"

"No, I just wanted to see how far a rocket could go."

"Hell Top, I don't even know that." He looked at me and smiled. I grinned back. He got me on that one.

Finally, I said, "Let's go home. I'm thirsty. Put your feet on the pedals. Push the right one and now the left. Easy-easy. True story Top, you're a better pilot than Sharp."

He had a death grip on the controls. I kept saying, "Gently." I called the tower to land, and he asked me, "How did it go?"

"Wait, I have to total these numbers. Let's see. He got twelve trees, six gophers, one naval ship off shore, a monkey, and an erection."

The tower guy started laughing, and so did Top. We landed and called for fuel as we put it in the revetment. As we sat there waiting for the blades to stop turning, Top looked over at me and said, "Why did you do this?"

"Why? Because you're a good person. And a really great person to the birds. It's not favoritism. You know how hard they work and treat them accordingly. You are firm, but fair. I can't tell you how many times I've heard the Firebirds say they wished you were their platoon sergeant. Hell Top, we just look like a bunch of fucked up kids from your point of view. And you're not too far from right.

"Top, you get the jeep and drive back to the office. Ski and Tyler are going to come down here and help me rearm."

He smiled and reached out to shake my hand. With my other hand, I handed him the helmet he'd used and asked him to return it to the CO. Then, he was gone. He looked like he was going to kiss me, so I was relieved when he drove off.

We finished rearming with a lot of joking and kidding. It took about thirty minutes. We drove back to the company area ready for some serious drinking. As we pulled in, Thompson ran out.

"The CO would like to talk to you."

"That sounds like he is asking for my permission."

"I know, Mac. He wanted me to soften my approach, so people wouldn't think they were in trouble when the CO wanted to see them."

I walked in and stopped in front of Top's desk.

He just jerked his thumb towards the CO's door, which was open. I knocked and he said, "Come in, Mac."

I walked in, and the CO said, "I'm pissed, Mac. My top sergeant, the best in the US Army, has informed me that he is quitting and going to flight school."

"Major, I'm not surprised, Sir. He is a much better pilot than Dull, I mean Sharp. He has a killer instinct. However, I can't imagine a Warrant with two years in the army trying to teach him. To be fair, he was very nice to me, and I don't have eighteen months. I didn't even have to threaten him with a push out the door for puking on my feet. Sir, he was grateful and glad to see what his troops went through."

"Mac, that was a good call," the Major said. "I talked to the flight surgeon and how does ten hundred sound? He will meet you here tomorrow."

"Sir, what's his name?"

"Dr. Ralph Weldon, from your country, the Pacific Northwest. He's on a four-month tour here as flight surgeon, and then he will rotate back to the hospital here in Chu Lai or a MASH unit, or FSB. He was ecstatic at the offer. He said he didn't send in the injury reports because he agreed with you that they were picky little things. He told me he also asked around and found out how valuable you are."

I went to the Birdhouse and grabbed everything I needed to scrub off the stench of this country. I returned and grabbed a bottle of Crown and six cold beers. I walked over to Ski and Tyler's hooch and said, "This round's on me."

It took me less than five seconds to empty the first beer. A little longer on the second. Then, we started taking swigs. After the bottle went around twice, I was starting to feel it. Out of nowhere, I said, "I miss Jim, and I'm pissed he's dead. I wasn't even here when they packed his things. SHIT, SHIT, SHIT!" I could feel my eyes getting wet.

I didn't want them to see me crying. To change the subject, I asked, "How's Big Randy's investigation coming along?"

No answer.

We began a drunken philosophical discussion on our thoughts about death. We drew no conclusions. What did we know? We weren't dead yet.

"Would you two like to fly to the Island tomorrow?" I asked them. "I'm going to take the flight surgeon. I'm paying off a debt. He didn't report my wounds, so I got to stay here. You can fly and shoot rockets and the cannon, while the doc shoots the M-60. We'll switch it around so you'll all get a chance at everything."

They both nodded *yes*.

"Be in the Parade grounds before 1000 (ten hundred)," I said. "I'll clear it with Top and the CO."

They liked the plan. They liked it so much, they toasted "Tomorrow." Then, we realized we were getting hungry. Off to the mess hall. I must have been really hungry. Those hamburgers tasted good.

I asked Ski and Tyler if they could eat burgers five days in a row. It took them a moment to swallow before they said yes."

Eating fast is a Firebird habit. I'll put that in the book. It's no different from basic training and flight school.

It seemed we were kept in a constant state of malnourishment and sleep deprivation. I wouldn't think that was a plus for our side. The NVA had only rice and a few veggies, so I guess it balanced out. *I shouldn't bitch so much*, I thought, *even if it's only to myself.*

After two burgers apiece, plus one wrapped in a napkin and stuffed in the thigh pouch of our pants, we left and parted.

I went to the O club, grabbed a bottle of Crown, and found some sympathetic listeners. "I'm going to drink till I puke," I said, "and then continue drinking until I forget about Jim just enough to sleep through *one* night. I'm so pissed at those fuckers who shot him that I'm going to do like the sign says in the Bird's party room. I'm going to kill them all and let God, or someone, sort them out. Shit guys, he died on my watch, my fault. I have to live with that till I die."

With that proclamation, I took two swigs of the Crown. One of the guys said, "Shit Mac, give me that bottle. We lost some good friends when Tice flew into that mountain."

Later, I went to the Birdhouse and grabbed three beers. I really don't know why. I could barely walk. *Damn, life is strange. Standing upright is now high on my to-do list. I'll put this in my manual, so the FNGs will have something to look forward to.*

The night was terrible. I sat up in bed several times in a drenching sweat, even though the night air was cool. I could see Jim's face. That stare on his face looking accusingly at me. I started crying again. I was too angry and fucking pissed off to even think about sleep or the mission into Laos. I got up and took a walk. The crying continued off and on until daylight.

The morning was OK. I was surprised I didn't feel sick. The most difficult part of the day was coming up with a call sign for the doc. Top's was Top Dog, the meanest dog in the whole damn country. I decided Doc's call sign could be: Doc R W, Doc Rough & Wild.

The three of them—Doc, Ski, and Tyler—had a great time. We took lots of pics. Ski and Tyler loved flying the beast. They each had a good touch on the controls. Shooting rockets was almost too much for them. They were intense, especially when they hit their target. Of the thirty-eight rockets, they each shot ten. They were really intent on destroying what remained of the truck. I thought the Doc was going to have an orgasm with the M-60, not that he didn't enjoy everything else. The three of them each shot 150 rounds out of the cannon. They made strafing runs down the beach. *I wonder what that mission cost Uncle Sam? Oh well, who gives a shit? I don't.*

When we returned to the parade grounds, Thompson ran to us and said, "CO," and pointed his finger to the company HQ. Everyone said goodbye, and the doc said, "I hope I never see any of you again professionally." He jumped into his jeep for the one mile trip back to his office.

I reported to the CO, and he said, "Your gunship team leaves tomorrow at 0800."

I said, "We're ready."

"Slight change. They want to begin briefing you in Danang. Here's the call sign and frequency." He handed me a sheet of paper. "But first call Danang Tower to enter their air space. Check out with me in the morning. How about 0630 in the Mess Hall?"

"Everyone?"

"No Mac, just you."

"Sir, I have a request?"

"What? Have you figured out how to stop the war?"

"I'm going to have flight jackets made up for Top and Doc. When they're ready, I wonder if you'd be willing to give them to the honorary pilots."

He loved the idea and said, "Sure. I know Top will really appreciate it."

"I don't know the flight surgeon," I said, "but he tried very hard to fit in. I think I scared him at first. He said, 'You fly differently than the slicks and Dust off.' I had to fight to hold back a laugh."

"You scared me the first time I flew with you."

"Oh, I'm sorry, sir."

"I'm not complaining. I just need to fly more."

After the meeting with the CO, I took Top's and the doc's call signs to Thompson and asked him to have them sewn on two flight jackets. "Sew in a set of wings over the names and the call signs," I told him. "On the right breast, put the nickname underneath a Firebird patch. Put an American division patch on whichever shoulder is appropriate. When they come back, give them to the CO."

Thompson knew people in Danang who could do this. He said, "I'll put it in on the film run tomorrow."

"Perfect."

I walked over to the club/bar, and it was full of its usual and outrageous behavior. I asked Big Randy if he was finished with the investigation.

He said, "Yes. Not my fault. A very short runway for the gunships, and it should be lengthened."

"Good to get that over with," I said. "I'll buy you a drink, or two. I'm leaving tomorrow for some mission in Danang. I'll be gone three weeks. Keep an eye on my shit."

"No problem, Mac."

Someone stuck his head in the bar and said, "There was a service in the mess hall for Jim Williams."

I felt like I had been kicked in the stomach. The bar was silent. I turned and slowly walked out. I didn't see the trail of guys behind me. I walked into the mess hall and went to the front of the room. The guys behind me went to the back of the room.

It remained silent. I stopped at the center of the table where a white helmet sat with a candle burning in front. I was tearing up. I had never felt so bad. I wanted to cry, puke, hit something, and most of all kill someone. I picked up the helmet and held it up level with my face. I swear I could see Jim's face. I picked up the candle and blew it out. I sat both back on the table in their original spots.

Now, I was shaking. Tears rolled down my face. I turned and walked toward the crowd, then another turn and out the door. Damn, my insides, no, hell, my whole being was so mad and pissed off at the world. I went into the bar and ordered two Crowns. I chugged the first and sipped the second, then went to bed.

I couldn't keep my eyes closed. I was sweating as if I were in the hot sun. If I tried to close my eyes, I could see the windshield explode, and Jim looking at me with that pleading expression. The more I reran the mission with its disastrous results through my head, the more I realized I should've been in that seat. *I know I'm placing blame, but if everyone hadn't been in such a fucking hurry to push me through the short course to Fire Team Leader, we wouldn't be where we are now.*

Tonight was much worse than the previous one. Jim's face was there even when my eyes were open. *How do I stop this? How can I kill hundreds of humans without any compunction, and then cry like a baby from one death? Fuck this war!*

I couldn't sleep at all. *Fuck it!* I got up at 0400 and went to the mess hall. The FNGs were there waiting for the morning report and assignments. The CO stopped talking when I came in. I looked up and apologized for interrupting and moved as far away from everyone as possible.

I just sat and did nothing. When the briefing ended, most of the seasoned pilots walked by me and said, "So sorry for your loss." I said, "Thank you." Most everyone knew Jim and I were close. As close as anyone could get in a war zone. *Damnit, I hope I can keep my head screwed on while up north.*

I sat for a half hour, and then the CO came to sit down beside me.

"I guess we can start early. Are you mentally ready to go into combat? I can pull you for many reasons."

"Getting back in the fight is what I need. I'll keep you informed. I just didn't realize how much I liked that guy."

The CO said he wanted to thank me for my efforts here. "We have more requests for the Firebirds than any time in the past. People are trying to emulate you. You've created a team spirit. We haven't had a fight in the bar since you arrived. Be careful and good luck."

I stood up, put out my hand, and said, "It's been a pleasure serving with you, sir."

"As I said earlier," Major Wilson reminded me, "I had a talk with the new CO about you and everything positive you've done here."

I followed him outside and saluted. I went back in and gathered my shit, as we all called our equipment. I jumped in the truck with the other seven guys that were going with me up north. Nobody talked during the bouncing one-mile ride to the flight line.

Chapter 46.

LAOS

We gave the ship the once over, jumped in, and lit the fire. It was about an hour and twenty minutes to Danang. I let Jerry do all the flying. He was very appreciative. We were cleared into their air space and found our way to the Green Berets. They had a long runway, so I knew we would be able to get out of there in the morning. Jerry was directed to land in a secured section of the runway, right by the GB headquarters.

Captain Booth met us and said, "Throw your gear in the truck and jump in after it."

A few minutes later, we found out how the other half lives. These green beanies had actual bed rooms. Their mess hall was a restaurant. The HQ looked like a hotel lobby. They also had a large building for visitors. White sheets!

The Captain said, "Pick a bunk and throw your gear on it and follow me to the briefing room."

Which we did. A long table with sixteen chairs and several pitchers of water with glasses. I hadn't seen a glass since I'd arrived in hell. What could possibly be next? A screen came down out of the ceiling and a projector was stared. It showed helos flying towards a mountain range. They stayed below the summit, so no one could see them from the road below on the other side. They were going straight west. There were several false insertions before the real one and several more false insertions after that. That kept the enemy guessing.

The Berets trained mercenaries (also called mercs) who were inserted as LRRPs, and did most of the observing. They took no ID, just some radios and lots of weaponry.

Next were pictures of the Ho Chi Minh trail. It was not a trail. It was a six-lane dirt road with hundreds of bomb craters on both sides. I was told "they fill in the craters on the road as soon as the dust clears."

The briefing officer said, "It's vital to destroy the supplies at night, because they don't bring anything of value down the trail during daylight hours."

"Gentlemen, we will depart here tomorrow at 0900. We will fly north to Quang Tri (QT) and secure your sleeping quarters. We will then fly west through a mountain pass to LZ Rock pile, RP, which has a single peak rising up nearly a thousand meters. This is occupied by the U S Marines as a lookout post to monitor NVA troops traveling south across the DMZ. There is a FSB around the base of that mountain along with a long runway.

"The briefing will be more exact tomorrow at Quang Tri. We will be on call from Rock pile 24/7 to insert or extract the mercenaries. Tomorrow we will consist of two gunships, three slicks, three King Bees, (old H-34 developed at the end of the Korean war), and two A-1 Sky Raiders flying high cover. The A-1s can come down low level if needed. They carry bombs, machine guns, rockets and can stay on station three hours. They can carry more weight of munitions than the weight of their planes.

"The slicks and Bees will arrive at 0830. The A-1s will fly out of Danang for all missions. Now, before everyone starts trying to take my head off, I will tell you that the Bees were ordered by Division to participate. No Americans will fly in one of those death traps with those shitty pilots. They are old, outdated, underpowered, and flown with reckless abandon by inept pilots (Vietnamese)."

The briefer then pointed at a LT and said, "LT George will take you to lunch. There are no dress codes. And the afternoon is yours."

We followed the LT to the mess (restaurant), and I ate the best meal since I left Medford, Oregon and Mom's cooking. We had BLTs, salad, Coca Cola, and Ice cream for dessert. That last item was not a dream, but the real thing. *How does one become a GB?*

After lunch, I called over to the naval supply depot at the Port of Danang to see if I could locate a high school and college buddy, Will Warren. I actually found him. He was running a Navy storage warehouse at the Danang harbor as ships were unloading supplies for the troops. We talked and he said, "Come on over."

I asked and received permission to fly a gunship over to the docks and land on an unused section. I drew quite a crowd. Will sent two MPs to guard the ship. I was talking to the MPs when Will drove up in a forklift and told me, "Get that piece of junk off this dock, right now!"

Being the uncouth Firebird that I was, I said, "Come any closer, ass wipe, and I'll shoot your dick off. We both started walking faster toward one another with big smiles. We stopped and shook hands. The crowd now relaxed but kept their eyes on us. They thought there was going to be some serious trouble. I turned to face them and in my loudest voice I said, "High school and college buddies. Roommates our first year." I jumped in the forklift and said, "Show me what you do."

He drove me into a huge air conditioned warehouse. What a surprise!

He showed me his quarters: bunk, desk, drawers, closet, desk lamp that could be twisted to serve as a bed light. "Will," I said, "I live in a garbage dump compared to this."

He said, "You look like shit."

"I'm going to tell my mom."

She called Will her fourth son as he spent more time at our house than his own. He thought that was pretty funny.

Actually, I had to agree with him. I said, "Personal hygiene is not high on the Army's list of necessities."

We talked about everything. We caught each other up on all the people we both knew. I knew four guys from our graduation class that had been killed here. He knew of three others. We talked till 1600, when I had to leave.

I hovered very low out to a length of dock that was 400 yards long. It was smooth asphalt. It could have been a one bounce take off, but I bounced four times just to add to the drama. When I reached the end of the dock, I was doing 120 knots and was fifty feet above the water. I couldn't help myself, so I dropped down to thirty feet above the water. Will and the guys probably thought I had bought the farm. While going through all of this, I called the tower and asked if I could buzz the docks north to south which was perpendicular to the dock.

The tower said, "I have you in sight. You are cleared to buzz. It has been a slow day, and you can give us something to talk about at dinner."

I began to gain some altitude as I turned ninety degrees and was flying north. I looked out at the docks, and the people were all waving and it looked like cheering. I laid the ship over on its right side and pointed the nose at the last 1/3 of the docks and started the dive. Now, some people started running. Some crouched down. Others were frozen in place. I was at 130 knots ten feet above the docks. The ship was shaking as I was a little fast.

The tower called and said, "That was great. Now, do it for ten additional docks and get everyone working."

"Thanks tower. I will be flying another few minutes, and then land at the Green Beanies. Good day."

I called the GBs, and they said to "put it in the same place."

I then walked around like a peeping tom trying to find the guest house, as they called it. After I found it, I asked if any new news had occurred. Nothing new, so we napped until dinner. What a life! Dinner was the high point of the evening. We ate white navy beans with ham, salad, green beans and chocolate pudding for dessert. It might not sound outstanding to anyone back in the world, but here it was the second of the two best meals I'd had since arriving in VN. *I'm going to put the shitty food stories in my manual.*

After dinner, the GBs invited us to their club. Everyone could drink. No attention was paid to rank. We began drinking and telling stories of home. As will happen, the challenges started, along with the war stories.

In the center of the table was a large ash tray full of cigarette and cigar butts, along with a mountain of ashes. One of those GBs poured a beer in the ash tray and said, "Drink it." I wasn't that buzzed, but I picked it up and said, "This is for you, Jim," and I took a drink. It was the worst fucking thing I had ever put in my mouth, worse than a purple MF. The room went silent. When everyone started looking at the LT, he got the message. He picked up the ash tray and took a drink. All the GBs were yelling and cheering. "No BS LT, you made the challenge."

The LT put the tray down quickly and ran to the door. As he pushed it open, he began projectile vomiting. It splashed onto the door and door handle and the side walk. He dropped to his knees and was dry heaving. All his buddies were laughing. He finally stood and propped the door open. He returned with a bucket and scrub brushes and began the task of the loser.

I got up and walked over and picked up a brush and began scrubbing right next to him. The room began to quiet. Ski and Tyler got up and joined the party. Two GBs got up and walked out but returned with two buckets and brushes. The rest of the Firebirds joined the group. The biggest surprise was the Captain coming to help. We finished in ten minutes. I took the LT (Robert MacAddo) and led him to the bar and ordered him a 7 up.

Everyone cheered. What a tight group we'd formed in a couple of hours. Someone said they were tired and that was all it took for everyone to head to the showers and bed.

The morning breakfast was whatever you wanted. Imagine that, in a war country.

All the helos had arrived. We topped off with a full tank. I couldn't remember ever taking off with a full tank and full armament. I figured it was good training. My wingman and I slid down the runway for several hundred yards after three bounces each. I know the crowd was waiting for us to crash. Wing called and said, "I hope all our takeoffs aren't going to like this one." Everyone else took off like a helicopter. We took off north and aimed for Quang Tri.

We landed and were shown our hooches. Then, we were taken to a large cement-block building. We sat at another one of those long tables, and the briefing for tomorrow evening's insertion began. The mercenaries were already seated. The insertion as well as the decoys were marked on our maps with frequencies and call sign as well. The Birds would fly cover in case any insertion points were hot.

This briefer looked like he'd never gotten his hands dirty with anything. I was sure he had never spent a day in the bush in the past three years. A hard core REMF.

I change tactics as problems emerge. We'll see how long it takes before we throw this plan out the window and wing it.

An hour later, we landed at LZ Rock pile and topped off again. I estimated it would take half of this very long runway for us to bounce into the air. It was a pierced-planking runway and very smooth.

I had never taken a gunship off at this weight, as we had added extra machine gun ammo. I was 1600 pounds over gross weight. My heaviest TO up until that time was 1500 pounds over gross a short time earlier in Danang. We added only an extra 100 pounds of ammo for the M-60s. Trying something like this back in the world would cost you your license and probably kill people.

At 1500, we took off for the mountains. Everyone sat in anticipation of us crashing in a fireball. I went first. I knew this ship had never been tested at that weight, heat and humidity. If it had been, I wasn't told. They really don't tell us shit. *If we're captured, we can't tell the enemy anything. Even as pilots we're at the bottom of intelligence briefings except for the next mission.*

After five bounces, I was flying. I made a small circle waiting for my wingman. After he got in the air, he said, "9-7, I hope I don't have to do that every day for three weeks. This one was worse than the last TO." I gave him two clicks.

Two of the Hueys had four men apiece. The third one was empty and would be used as needed. The three King Bees had four SVN troops each and would be used for support, if needed. We flew into a valley with such steep sides that the door gunners could not elevate their machine guns to shoot up the mountain sides without shooting our blades. *Now that was a brilliant idea. I've got to talk to someone back at Rock Pile or QT.*

I was keeping a close watch on fuel consumption. The two Hueys with mercs were starting the false insertions. After four, they dumped off the eight GBs and/or mercs in a small clearing. Two more fakes, and it was back to Rock pile and wait for the LRRPs to call for an extraction. We were nearly out of fuel.

We had a hooch close to the runway. The bunks inside looked very good because sleep deprivation was telling us all to lie down.

At 0200, the phone rang. The mercs were on the run. They had guided in the arc light perfectly. (An arc-light mission used 15 to 30 B-52s. Each B-52 carried an enormous amount of bombs, up to 70,000 pounds each, up to 108 bombs internally and externally per plane. One plane could cover an area one half mile wide and two miles long.)

Merc 6 radioed and said they would be at the southern open area about the same time we arrived. The SVN military never fired a shot and ran back to the northern open area and climbed into their ships and GTFO (got the fuck out), which we learned at the debriefing after the mission. *They ran away?*

I called the first slick, rescue 6, and asked if he could take all eight mercs.

He radioed back with, "Yes, a great idea. I wondered why we used two ships to insert those guys. We can get our guys out, and you can help the Bees. I've worked with them before, and they are not dependable or skilled enough to be out here."

I gave him two clicks.

The slick pilot asked the mercs to "shine two flashlights in the air. One from each end of the LZ."

"Firebird 9-7, I'm going in."

I said, "9-7 is on your right side."

A sudden and hurried call said, "The NVA have almost caught up with us. They are above us and coming down the mountain."

I told the slick to break off, and we'd soften the area. He immediately pulled up and gave me two clicks.

I said, "I've got 'em. Rockets away." I shot 200 yards above the mercs and walked my rockets up the mountain. I called Merc 6 and asked if there were any bad guys closer to them. As I broke, wing who was on the same frequency shot a little closer to them, as per their request.

Merc 6 said, "That second ship hit them hard. A couple of them are just sitting. I don't know if they're dead or stunned."

I said, "6, where do you want my next rockets?"

He said, "Cover the area above us up to the top of the mountain."

I thought, *well, we're taking care of our guys.* My thoughts were interrupted by tracers coming up at us and striking back in the crew chiefs and gunners personal space. I told my copilot to shoot the cannon close to our guys. That got them shooting longer bursts as they could see the muzzle flashes. I punched some rockets in their direction. Wing did the same. I called and said, "Rescue 6, come on in. There is minimal resistance, and our fuel is getting low."

"9-7, I'm coming in."

"Perfect, but be aware our 40 mm cannon will be firing all the way in and out."

"Get those flashlights on."

I went in with the slick, and Jerry was shooting all the way. I punched four rockets at a few muzzle flashes. Wing covered him perfectly, as I swung around to escort Rescue 6 out. I came out shooting at everything and anything that provided cover. The slick got out with the mercs and was off to Rock Pile.

What few were alive on the ground attempted to shoot at us, but our door gunners stopped that nonsense.

"Check out each other as there was shrapnel and bullets flying all over back there."

Ski and Tyler said, "We're OK, but we're both bleeding."

I snapped my head around so fast I felt dizzy. They were bleeding from their arms. It appeared it was from shrapnel flying around back there from bullets striking door posts, the firewall and ceiling. "Get your shirts off and check each other for serious wounds."

I looked over at Jerry and just shook my head. "Everyone keep an eye out for shooters on the sides of these steep slopes. Whatever side shoots as us, I will bank the ship in the opposite direction and push in the opposite pedal (the one on the shooters side) that will get the rotor blades out of the way. I got back two clicks. I will be flying out of trim, but I don't have a choice down in this valley." *Fuck, who planned this stupid mission? A REMF*

"Tyler, Ski, did you find any major damage to your bodies?"

Suddenly Ski said, "Taking fire."

I banked hard right with the left pedal pushed in all the way. I was flying out of trim and putting tremendous pressures on the ship's frame. Ski stopped shooting when we had flown past the NVA. I was straight and level and back in trim when I called wing and asked if he had taken any fire and if he had seen what I'd done to clear the rotor blades.

He said, "That was quick thinking. I did the same maneuver, and Fox stopped that guy shooting at you. We saw him fall off the side of that mountain."

Tyler called out, "Wing is taking more fire, and he's doing your maneuver, Mac. The fire is coming from the other side, on their right. I'm giving them some suppressive fire as we are ahead of them, enough to spare the rotor blades."

I said, "Shit, there is someone out in front of you, Tyler." At the same time I was breaking left with full right pedal and stressing this ship even more. I saw the guy drop his weapon and fall out of the tree he had tied himself to; now he was just hanging from a rope around his waist.

"Shoot that bastard Tyler"

"Wing, this is 9-7. How's your fuel?"

"I'm down to the bottom ¼. I should be getting a yellow light any time."

"Yeah, me too."

"This mission was fucked up since we took off. I'm going to put in my two-cents at the debriefing."

The lead slick was calling RP for landing at the GB center. He also told them he was on fumes. And be ready to clear two slicks, two gunships and three King Bees."

The tower said, "Roger. The King Bees came by forty five minutes ago and said they were returning to DN."

I transmitted, "That shit figures."

Wing said, "9-7, I have a yellow light on the fuel gauge."

"Me too. Rescue two and three, how's your fuel?"

"We've been listening and since we have no cargo, we're OK."

Both of them were cleared to land last.

I thought, *I knew those empty ships would have no problems.* A few minutes later, I looked and blinked and said, "Damn, I see the runway."

Wing said, "Don't slow down. I'm on your 6 and pleading with this ship to keep its blades turning."

"RP tower: two gunships from your west are on fumes and would like a straight in approach to the GBs area."

"Cleared to land," was the reply.

'You meet me in the GB bar at 1800, and you can tell me about the Bees. By the way, I'm Mac. What's yours?"

"Mine is Terry."

"Have you worked with the Bees before?"

"I've been here ten months, and do I have some stories for you."

Chapter 47.

THE COLONEL AND THE BEAUTY

As soon as the blades stopped turning, the fuel truck pulled up. I told Ski and Tyler to check in with the medic, "now." At least, they were able to walk to the medic. Everyone else headed to the big room for debriefing. The LRRPs were there, too.

LRRP 6 stood and went to the hanging map. He showed us where they had done their spotting. "The number of trucks on the road was huge, thirty I could see, but there also had been some secondary doings off in the trees north and south of our position. The B-52's began bombing several miles down the road and continued several miles north of our position." He paused to take a breath. "It was great to watch," he said, "as the planes positioned themselves so they all dropped at once, 108 bombs per plane, 500 & 750 pound bombs on the road and a quarter mile on each side. I'm talking complete and utter destruction. We called after the last bomb exploded, and we departed the area for the pickup LZ.

"After our insertion, we spread out and created false trails away from the LZ. That gave us more time to get to the pickup and avoid combat. We left a few booby traps and claymores with trip wires all over the edges of the LZ. Guns, you did a great job. I want also to include that slick driver when I say great job. I wouldn't have wanted to come into that LZ. You saved our ass.

"FYI everyone. The troops with the Bees never showed up. We sent out a spotter toward their LZ and saw no one. They never fired a shot. It's no wonder they didn't stick around here. My guys would have shot'em. Next?" And he sat down.

I stood up. "Did anyone in the planning of this mission have any experience with flying?" I paused but nobody raised a hand or said anything. "OK, so no one? Whoever had us flying so low in and out didn't account for the gunners' inability to shoot at the snipers because they'd be shooting through the rotor blades. It would have been OK to fly in higher and then drop low before we landed in the LZ. We were not sneaking in there. They obviously knew our ships were coming west as we were flying out in a nice straight line.

"Oh, I almost forgot. Where were the high cover A-1s? They could work below the mountain peaks and not have to worry about the automatic 37 mm artillery.

"Also, I would like to know who figured the amount of fuel needed to get there and back. The only reason we made it back was because we got in and out with one clean pass. If we had needed one more pass to cover these guys, we would be sitting somewhere outside your wire. Next," I said as I sat down.

A colonel stood and said, "I believe we have to include more personnel in our briefings. Let's stop for now and have a late breakfast. Mac, can you eat with me?"

"It would be my honor, Sir."

The colonel crashed the line and sat down. He didn't eat anything. I think he was waiting for me. *Wow, this guy is something. This will be an adventure and definitely a learning experience. Cheese burgers, fries, some type of orange juice and chocolate cake. I've got to check into this Green Beret thing. The burgers were better than at Chu Lai and McDonalds Arches.*

When I got to the colonel's table, I said, "Sir, I'm Mac or McNally, 71st Helicopter Co., Americal Division, I Corp," and I extended my hand. He took it and said, "I'm Colonel Derek Wheaton, Special Forces, and I want to learn more about these spotting stations we set up to slow down the NVA. What do you think?"

"Sir, I think you should bomb them every day for a week and extend it into North VN. They'll have no idea what's going on and may even stop moving weapons south. Then, put in the LRRPs to monitor that Freeway and knock the hell out of them for a twenty mile stretch. While we are waiting for this action, we can put patrols at the end of the trails and call in napalm. Sir, I think we've become too predictable. It's like we say in the Guns, 'We win with tactics of surprise and unpredictability.' They don't have tactics. They can't respond quickly to a change in our tactics. I've found that out and used it to my advantage."

"Mr. McNally, what would you suggest about the fuel issue?"

"Well Sir, how safe is the road straight west? And if it's safe, for how many miles from here?"

"As you saw, that road extends 120 clicks, (72 mi) and then just stops at the base of the mountains. We've never used it. Occasionally, we send a patrol out about 60 clicks (36 miles). We've never found anything; even with the LRRP's trackers, we came up empty handed."

"OK. That's perfect. My idea is to drive a couple fuel trucks out there with some troops—good troops, like your Green Berets—and two A-1 Sky Raiders for high cover. If we have to remain on target for even five minutes, we're in trouble. Being able to land for a shot of fuel would take off the pressure. The road is straight, wide and flat. We would have plenty of distance to bounce into the air even if we had all our munitions."

"I saw you bounce off the runway this morning, and as I watched I thought, 'Shit! They aren't going to make it.' But, to my amazement, you did."

"I must admit that's the heaviest Huey I've ever had to coax into the air. I estimated I was 1600 pounds over gross. Sir, I just noticed your pilot's wings. What have you flown?"

"I've flown everything but the Sky Crane (four long legs and can carry a Chinook or those long heavy metal containers or large trucks)."

"OK, Mac, I'll get you over to QT or Danang when we plan the next few Overlook missions. There's one tomorrow; however, it's to the south. We are sending the LRRPs south 20 miles in hopes of getting more traffic on that road. I would love to obliterate twenty plus miles of supplies."

"I hope you can sell it to whoever looks at those plans," I urged him. "Two fuel trucks sitting next to the road would be a life saver."

"Get some rest, Mac. Your group pulls pitch at 2000. Same mission as the one you just finished."

Ski and Tyler returned and gave me two thumbs up as they got in the chow line. They yelled, "The ships and us are OK."

"Briefing will be at 1630," the colonel continued, "then dinner and check the ships and we are set. No King Bees. There is no such thing as a joint mission with them. They'll lose this war a short time after we leave."

I nodded. *Wow. What would people think back home if they knew that?*

"That's it, Mac. See you at the briefing."

I found the radio room and asked the guy on duty if he could call the tower and ask for Terry. Terry was on the phone in ten seconds. "Terry, this is Mac. Can you be here at 1830 and see how the GBs live and eat. We can also talk about those worthless SVN fighting forces."

"I'll be there, Mac."

As long as I was in the radio room and nothing seemed to be happening, I asked the guy if he could get a hold of the Donut Dollies. I figured I might as well push my luck. I said to ask for Stephanie.

It took a few minutes, but then—I couldn't believe my luck—Stephanie said, "Hello?"

I said, "Stephanie, this is a voice from your past."

"Oregon!" She said. "Oh my god. Oh my god. I've been thinking about you every day since you flew me around the AO. I confided with my boss, Donna, about you. She said, 'He must have made quite an impression!' Well, you have, you did.

"I'm so glad you called. Donna has called twice for the Rattlers to ferry us around the AO with you flying. She was told you transferred to the gunships and were currently on assignment up north. So, we are flying around the AO doing our thing, but the flights are boring. I do wish you could come back, so we could be treated as adults. And I could see the person I dream about every night."

I was stunned. *What could I say to that?* Finally, I found my voice. "I will TO in a few hours," I told her, "and I won't return until late. In three weeks, I'll be back in Chu Lai, our town. Do you think you might like to get together then?"

"Yes, of course," she said, without the slightest hesitation. "I got a chill through my body when I hugged and kissed you."

"So did I ... but are you serious? I was so filthy I couldn't stand myself."

"I'm worried about you," she said, "because I've been reading the after-action reports, and one of the colonels here has been explaining them to a few of us at lunch. The colonel said you've saved hundreds of lives, but you've been in the MASH unit five or six times. I'm really worried. You still have nine months to go."

"I don't want you to worry about me," I told her. "I do what needs to be done, but I really am as careful as I can be. I'm in the GB radio room, and I don't know how long this kid will leave me alone. So I'm going to say goodbye ahead of time, in case we get cut off. Where are you from?"

"Lovely Southern California with all the crazy people and beautiful beaches. I even surf."

"I'm impressed. I never tried that. Up in Oregon, the water temperature is 52 degrees. What did you do after high school?"

"I went to UCLA and graduated with a major in history and law. Then three years at UCLA's law school. Passed the bar and went to work at my dad's law firm for a year. I got bored and wanted to do something for our troops. The Red Cross with the Donut Dollies program was the only job for a woman over here unless you're a nurse. I've got you beat by month. I'm in my forth. And your background?"

"You are an extremely intelligent woman. I'm very impressed."

"Well, thank you Kevin. Everyone here thinks most of us are dumb blonds."

"Are any of them familiar with your background?"

"No, I don't say much about myself. They really don't want to know. I think this war thing has them spooked. Now it's your turn."

"Grew up in Medford, Oregon, went to the University of Oregon for two years and majored in math. Wasn't sure there was a future in calculus. And really, I don't like rain enough to live in Eugene; it gets 60 inches a year. I quit and joined the army to fly. Since flying is voluntary, I can't complain. The Airforce and Navy required four years of college to fly jets. So that left the army, and this thing called rotary winged aviation; helicopters. I've learned they don't fly; they beat the air into submission."

She laughed out loud. "Kevin that was the first time I've really laughed since I've been in this little piece of hell."

"It certainly is hell," I said. "We agree on that. I'm the oldest of three brothers. My dad owns a wholesale plumbing supply company. I've worked there every summer since I was fourteen. At sixteen, I was delivering the tons of pipe to job sites, unloading everything by hand and by myself. Needless to say, I do not plan to work for my dad when I get back in the world.

"I don't have a girlfriend nor am I writing to one," I told her. "I have a difficult time just writing to Mom and Dad. All I do is tell lies. Our company commander orders us to write cheerful letters to offset the media's negative broadcasts about VN. We don't have TV or radio here, so I'm clueless about what's really on the news back in the world."

"Likewise, no boyfriend," she said, "and I never dated anyone seriously. The most I've ever been seriously smitten was with you, shooting the machine guns and the low level flying you called rat racing. God, what a thrill. I can't wait to I see you. I want to learn so much more about you. I know this all sounds crazy." She paused, I guess not wanting to go too far. "I can't wait to see you again."

"Damn, someone's coming in. Goodbye beautiful."

"Bye."

It was going to take me some time to take in everything she had just told me. I decided to try to write it down. I began writing. I had had physical sensations too, but what to think about them? It took me an hour to get everything on paper, or so I thought. I read it and had to add more. A lot was said in those few minutes. Then, I had to put aside thinking about her, when the 1630 briefing horn went off.

The briefing room was filing fast and in walked the colonel I had talked to at lunch. He pulled down some maps and marked the insertion LZ and the false ones as well. He added, "There will be two fuel trucks located on the road we call west. They will be hidden off the road just two miles from its end. There will be troops to set up a perimeter. The Sky Raiders will follow the Hueys back to the gas station and provide cover, if needed. Everyone will be on the same frequency, and the fuel trucks' call sign is Traveler 6.

"Take off is at 2100. There will be two strobe lights. That's where you'll find traveler 6. They can gas up two ships at a time. Refuel hot. The strobes will be on as you fly by on your way to the insertion LZ, so you'll know where they're hiding. Call the trucks when you are five minutes out on your return. You will have some help tonight. There are pathfinders. They will mark both LZs. Their call signs are Loaners 1 and 2. Any Questions?"

"Sir, will there be any Bees in the neighborhood?"

"No Bees. What's planned is only here in the hood. I have not heard anything." He gave a wink as he pointed to his eye, so we would not miss it. Everyone was clapping as he walked to his chair. The last thing he said was, "Go to mess."

We did as told. The food was good but not as good as in Danang. Not complaining, just comparing. It was noisy because everyone was trying to get names straight and meet others. The mercs were pretty tight lipped. Some were from the US and others gave origins from all over the globe. An interesting group. I hope they were paid better than our EMs, who were working practically pro bono.

From the door into the hall someone called out loudly, "Terry here to meet Mac."

I got up and walked over to a guy wearing the standard green fatigues. He looked like an NFL linebacker. I put my hand out, and we shook hands. I said, "I'm Mac."

He followed with, "Terry."

I said, "Everyone this is Terry, the tower operator. He helps large planes with cargo make their go arounds, so we won't run out of fuel and crash in jungle."

He put up his hand, though not very high, as the room began clapping.

I said, "Hungry?"

He said, "Starving."

I put him at the start of the line, so he could go ahead and get some food. I took him to the gunship table, and everyone introduced themselves. Someone asked if he was into sports. *I'm sure he's heard that before.*

Terry said, "I was playing football at Notre Dame when I learned my two best buddies from high school had joined the service and were killed. I wanted some revenge, so I tried to join the army, and they turned me down because nothing would fit me—boots, uniforms, just name it—so they sent me to the Air Force and they put me in the tower. I feel like a jerk up there when all of you here are really doing something."

"That's BS Terry," I said. "If you hadn't been up there the other day, we'd all be in the jungle. We all want you to know that. But don't wait up for us tonight because we have no Idea when we'll return."

I spent an hour telling Terry how worthless the Bees were. He told me about incidents where they wouldn't listen to the tower and would land wherever they wanted.

"A few months back," Terry told us, "I cleared two to land, and the trailing ship pulled up fifty feet above the lead ship while the lead ship was slowing and losing altitude to land. The second ship ignored my calls to drop back. It looked like he was trying to fly over the lead ship. He misjudged the distances and landed on top of lead. You can't imagine the mess. Both pilots and copilots were killed."

He told us a few more stories, and we told a few. Terry had a drink and then had to shove off. That still left a few hours before TO.

That left nothing for me to do after we did a re-check on our ships. Since I didn't have my head in the game, I went back to the radio room to see what magic that RTO specialist could create. I couldn't believe he found Steph so fast. *Man, I owe that kid.*

She said, "Hello Kevin, is that you."

"Yes, it's me, and it's so good to hear your voice. How long has it been?"

She laughed and said, "Less than three hours."

"I knew it had been an eternity."

"Wow it felt longer," she said. "Thank you so much for calling. I don't take our connection for granted. I know you're a special person. You give me hope for the future. You are smart, well-liked by everyone here, and they say you are the most fearless and the best pilot in Vietnam."

"Well, I think that may be a little bit of exaggeration," I said, but I was thrilled just the same. "There are many pilots here doing the same thing. They just don't have the cheerleading section I do."

"I believe the people here," she said, "because they watch everything and review it all. They all come to the same conclusion. That's why I'm so worried about you. Everybody says you take too many chances."

"Look Stephanie, I'm not going to do anything that will mess up my future ... our future. We met over here of all places. I've never seen a woman as beautiful as you. I'm serious; two years of looking at college girls who think they are goddesses. Not."

"Goddesses," she said. I felt a note of seriousness come into her voice. "God-desses. The big G-O-D issue. Kev, whose side is god on?"

I tried to keep up with her change of mood. "There's no point asking about God over here. I've asked this before, and there are no answers. But you're a miracle Stephanie. This is a rotten useless war, but it's brought us together, and I'm not going to question that."

"Kev, I feel the same way. I lie awake at night thinking about you. I'm sure I even *dream* about us together. You know, Kev, I've never talked like this before. I've lost all my defenses."

"My crew just walked by and gave me the miniature TO sign (finger in the air and swing your index finger in circles). I will call as soon as I can. Goodbye."

"Goodbye to you."

I heard her crying as she hung up.

I raced by the RTO sitting in a chair in the waiting area and threw him a quick, "Thank you."

I thought, *What in the world is going on? She seems so real and sincere, and I'm just struggling to communicate. I haven't talked to a woman in eighteen months.*

I caught up with Ski and Tyler just as we exited the building. Ski said, "What's so interesting in the RTO room?"

"You're not going to believe this, but she's a Donut Dolly I met on my last week as an FNG."

"Mac, is it true about low leveling the Dollies while they were shooting the 60s?"

"Just where did you hear that?"

"Mac, before we press you into a corner, your crew chief and gunner from that day talk a lot when they're drinking."

"Shit."

They both started laughing, so I joined them and said, "You two are fearsome investigators."

The wing ship was ready to go, so the four of us did a walk around our lead ship. I handed my mission info to Wilder with radio frequencies and call sign Spy 6. *That's original.* We all lined up with me first, wing second, then four slicks. Two A-1 Sky Raiders were in the air for high cover, and lower when necessary.

The first two slicks had five mercs each and the third was empty. The fourth was the flare ship.

Everyone watched us for that soon-to-be crash. We both made

it look like an airplane TO, which it was.

We began a slow climb once we had 120 knots. The slicks were already at 2000 feet. I gave the controls to Wilder, and then checked in with everyone. The A-1 pilots were at 2500. Their call signs were Angel 1 &2, and I was assigned 9-7. Slicks were S1, S2 and S3. S1 was lead ship. At the end of the line was lighthouse 6, our flare ship, just in case we got into a gunfight.

It was after 2200 and dark. The guns finally hit 2500 feet. I could see the strobe five minutes before we passed by. I saw the two trucks, so I called Traveler 6 and said, "We see your Christmas lights. See you later tonight."

"Roger that, gun 9-7."

The mountains were in front of us which meant turn south. Five minutes later, we were all looking for the pathfinders to mark the two LZs. The jungle canopy was over 100 feet high and so thick we couldn't see the ground through most of it. A blinking strobe caught my eye.

I called S1. "Do you see that strobe on the side of the hill at your 10 o'clock slightly low?"

He said, "I'm going to take a look."

I called Loaner 1. "How does it look tonight?" Loaner 1 said he hadn't seen any signs of life.

I told S1, "Let the guns check it first. Ready 9-5?" I received two clicks.

If this LZ was hot, we couldn't insert the mercs because anyone could hear the rockets explode. I said, "Gunners be ready, and watch for that strobe light." I rolled in, and no one shot at me. The strobe was moving south. I returned to pick up S1. He landed in front of the strobe and pointing south for a quick TO. I couldn't see anyone as I flew over the LZ (which is not a good thing ever to do). Wing came in just behind me. I called Loaner 1 and said, "Was that all your deliveries?" I got back two clicks.

"S2, let's go find your blinking light." It would be three miles south according to the briefing. Now if the pathfinder saw bad guys, he would move on. In this case, he moved north 1 mile and turned on his strobe. We all repeated the first LZ landing without any interference.

We turned south for five minutes, and then turned east for five minutes. Our last turn was north. That way we didn't overfly the first LZ. In a few minutes I saw the road to RP, and I called traveler 6. "We're thirsty. How's S1 doing for fuel?"

He said, "I'm landing with you."

S2 said, "Me too."

S3 and the flare ship were OK.

I saw the strobes and flew toward them. This went well. We landed two at a time. No resistance. The guns took off to RP. We climbed to 2000 feet, and no one shot at us. I liked that. We didn't wait for the slicks as they were faster and could easily catch us.

The gunships took only about a quarter of a tank at travelers, because we would be landing with our entire ordinance. I landed as my yellow light said low fuel. That went well. We all hovered to our assigned spaces. Now, we fueled to the max. The four of us checked our ships for anything and everything. It all looked good.

All these missions required a debriefing. This one was fast. We were in and out on both LZs. No shots fired. Traveler's gas station was perfect. It was clockwork.

The B-52s were already up and nearing the target.

We got word that as soon as the bombs began raining down the NVA had started up the mountain. Good news was they were several miles north, where the pathfinders noted their presence the previous day.

The mercs called and said, "Hurry."

When the NVA got to the top and found nothing, they would split forces and start searching both north and south. It looked to be about thirty troops. They probably wouldn't think there were two groups. We possibly would pick up resistance only at the northern LZ. The mercs had left claymores with trip wires there.

My wingman and I bounced off the RP PSP (pierced steel planking) runway. We struggled to fly. The slicks followed, and we added the flare ship. The A-1s were on station.

It was a quick flight to the first LZ. The strobes were operating correctly. Loaner 1 called and said, "Fifteen NVA about 300 plus yards out. Well armed."

"Which direction are they from your position?"

"030 degrees from our original insertion."

I asked 9-5 if he got that info. I got his two clicks. "Get your heads down. We're coming in shooting." Loaner 6 said, "Roger."

I told the flare ship to light it up. He threw out two, and the bad guys on the ground could have read a book by the light, if they'd ever gone to school.

I climbed to position above them and 500 yards out when I started punching rockets. I walked my rockets up the slope and through the NVA. They were in a tight group and not spread out. I had a good look at them as the jungle thinned toward the LZ. Captain Wilder was doing an excellent job with the cannon. Ski and Tyler were putting on a demonstration of excellence.

A few fired at me in full automatic, and to my shock one round came through the front Plexiglas. I heard a few pops as several bullets went through the rotor wash. As I broke left, wing fired a few rockets and the Gatling guns were on anyone standing.

"9-7, I think we got 'em."

As wing broke, I came around to cover him and saw two NVA waving a white flag.

I thought, *Fuck you and this is for Jim.* I punched a pair of rockets and atomized them. Ski and Tyler were shooting at everything. Apparently, I was speaking out loud as Wilder just nodded. I keyed my mic and said, "Off the grid." This was war, and we knew those white flags were a trap to shoot down any ship that came in. Wilder continued nodding.

I called S2 and said, "The area has been softened. Let's go in and pick up our guys. It went well, no resistance. The mercs and pathfinder jumped in and yelled, go, go, go."

I called Loaner 2 and asked, "Is anyone with bad intentions in the neighborhood?"

"No one in sight."

"OK flare light it up." He was listening to the radio calls and knew where to put his flares.

I told the slick to circle while we went in to see who was waiting. As I began my run, four machine guns opened up on me. I began pointing the nose at the origin of those bullets. I was able to get a pair on three of them. Jerry was also shooting at those guns. I called, "Breaking left." As wing was shooting at number four, one of the guns I had shot at became active again and resumed his bad attitude to me. I was picking out targets and yelling at Jerry to shoot at the one on the left. I keyed my mic and told the gunners in back, "Don't stop." Bullets were ricocheting around the cockpit. Smoke was drifting up from one of the radios that we were not using. Something struck me in the chin. Jerry took a direct hit to his chicken board. He was OK, physically. I'd check the other, mental, when we landed. Now we were taking sporadic fire.

Things were calming down, so I called loaner 2 and said, "Where did those guys come from?"

He said, "I don't know."

That answer did not satisfy me. *Shit, it's as if they were waiting for us.*

"OK S2, are you ready?"

"Let's go."

He was flaring to land, when a damn machine gun opened up and was hitting the ship. He had to land as he was low and slow and committed to land. The gun was off to his left about 100 meters away. I turned and got the ship in trim as quick as possible and punched off four rockets.

Everyone on the ground jumped in.

"S2 pulling pitch."

I said, "Break left S2. I'm going to put a few more rockets down there. 9-5 soften up the left." As I broke, I saw wing tearing up the foliage. I told wing I was going to personally escort S2 out of there. We've got to shoot our way out of this one."

As soon as S2 started climbing, he was shot at from two locations. One in front about 200 yards out and another one of those assholes on the left, also 200 yards away.

I said, "Where are they coming from?" This was getting to be another snafu.

Jerry looked at me and said, "North Vietnam, Mac."

I looked at him and started laughing. I called 9-5 and said, "I asked no one in particular where were they coming from and my copilot said, North Vietnam. I think he is ready to move to your ship." While all that was said, I shot at the left side and told S1 to keep banking left so I could shoot behind him at that bastard in front of him. He banked, and I shot some rockets, and it was over.

"Fuel check everyone." S1, S2, and S3 all needed some fuel, and of course the guns were down to less than a quarter tank. Flare was OK.

I called the A-1s and asked if they could drop some of their napalm, and anything else they wanted to, on those guys.

"Roger that. We've been watching and know right where to put it. Also, I would like to say that you helo drivers and your crazy gunners have balls so large that one of our planes couldn't lift one. I don't know how you do it."

"We are practicing to be future felons." That got the A-1 pilots laughing. I said, "Good night," and got back two clicks. *We all speak the same language.*

I said, "Jerry, take me to the gas station. You do it all."

Jerry got us to the road and called Traveler 6. We landed without any resistance. We took only a quarter tank to make the TO easier. Wilder did his TO with only two bounces. We had half of our ordinance remaining, so we were still a little heavy. Thirty minutes later he called RP and asked for a straight in approach for five Hueys. It was another easy landing, as we were low on fuel and had only half our ammo.

After landing, we were checking out the ships for bullet holes, when Tim Rivers hollered, "Mac, come over here."

I walked over and saw his copilot with a bloody arm. "Jesus Elliott, when did that happen?"

"I think it was our second time in. I felt something hit me. I didn't even look. I saw blood dripping off my fingers while gassing up with traveler. I didn't say anything because we couldn't get back here any sooner."

"Let's get you to their medic. Hell, I'll go with you. Something hit me in the chin." We found the medic, who called for a doc. We were there for an hour, getting stitches and antibiotic shots. *Those fucking shots feel like syrup going into your butt.*

While all of that was going on, I slipped away and called the CO and filled him in on the mission and Elliott's wound. "He's been grounded, sir."

"You can wait until there's some light. We do our thing in the dark. Sir, would you like to talk to the colonel here? I will tell him I called for a copilot."

"Please do, Mac."

I went to the radio room and told him the major from the 71st was on the line.

I went back to the ship and Tyler said, "We have a hole in both blades."

"Damn, I wanted to make a phone call. Do I have to go through this?"

The shit just never ends.

It wasn't easy finding a big deuce and a half at this hour. We needed something to climb high enough on to reach the blades with that 100-mile-an-hour tape. The GB didn't believe me when I said, "duct tape," so I told them to call it "100-mph tape." That drew a laugh.

It was after midnight, and I was tired. Everyone looked beat. The GBs were fascinated with the rotor blade repair.

The colonel returned and told everyone, "Take a break and get some sleep. We're going to insert mercs tonight. TO is 0300. We'll insert one team, so everything will be the same except we insert twenty miles north of LZ1. If there are no questions, dismissed. Mac, can I talk to you?"

"Certainly sir." *What else could I say?*

I walked towards the colonel, and he was talking before I arrived. "Mac, I just got off the phone with Major Wilson, and I ran an idea by him, and he liked it. How would you feel about me flying as your copilot? Wilder will fly copilot in the wing."

Suddenly, the colonel stopped talking, a look of shock on his face.

"Jesus Christ, Mac, you've got blood all over your shirt and pants. You're hit in the face. I see some stitches."

I butted in and said, "I remember something hitting me, and then the fighting got even hotter and I forgot. The doc patched me up and I'm fine. I'd love to have you as my copilot, sir. Captain Wilder is ready to fly wing. But you, sir, have quite a bit of knowledge in your head and would be a great catch should you be captured."

"Thanks for your concern, but you won't let that happen. Am I correct?"

"You're absolutely correct, sir. I won't let you be captured."

"Now, Mac, go see the Medic. It looks like you're bleeding again."

I said, "Yes sir," and turned and walked away. I had to wake the medic. Hell, over here you grab sleep whenever and wherever. He injected me to numb the area and then pulled out another chunk of metal. He said, "Sorry, I missed it earlier." He cleaned the wound and added two stitches. He gave me a bottle of pills and told me to check in on return from tiger country.

I asked him not to report this as it was so minor. "Please don't. It would cancel the mission tonight."

"Yeah, I heard you were going back out tonight. I'll write up some shit. No forget that. This never happened, I don't know you, and I've never seen you."

"Thank you. Now I have to check on my guys and the ship. See you tomorrow for another shot. Damn, my butt aches already from the first one."

I found Ski and Tyler, and they brought me up to date.

They had found five bullet holes total, while I was visiting the medic. "It's amazing, five holes, and we didn't even get a yellow warning light. We did lose a radio. The GBs fixed it in five minutes."

I looked at them and just shook my head. "We're leading charmed lives. I have to say you two are crazy sons of bitches, no reference to your mothers. You were literally hanging out of the ship by just a small strap and pinpointing targets. Shit, we would all be dead if it weren't for you two. You're so quick to get on targets."

I told Rivers about the new seating arrangements. He said, "OK." I told him that Jerry was a good stick (meaning a good pilot).

At 0300, we all pulled pitch. I was the first one to go. I turned to the colonel. "Sir, you have witnessed the guns TO. We are 1600 pounds over gross."

He just said, "Shit."

"Get on the controls with me. You can hold on a little more." I think he was timid because he had never been in an overloaded Hog. He had a very intense look on his face. I think he was worried, but we made it over the concertina wire by twenty feet. I said, "You got it. Climb to 1500 feet."

After that, I took over. "OK, sir, I've got it. I'm going to give you a refresher course on the cannon." First, I called Traveler 6 and told him we would be shooting the cannon, and he would hear the explosions. I called all the others and told them the same. I gave the colonel the same speech I gave other front seaters. Twenty shots are not very many, but we didn't have much time. I pointed out targets, and he shot. He was getting the hang of it. I said, "Walk the rounds into your target if you have to. I just hope things don't get too hot.

"There are the strobes. Take us back up to 1500 feet." We had dropped to only 500 feet; the cannons are for close-in work. In about five minutes, I said, "Now, we turn north, as we were told in the briefing." He started laughing, since he had given the briefing.

"Sir, these missions are like going to church," I told him. "The minister has a strong but short beginning. That's when we surprise them. Next is the sermon. For us, it's a continuation of the surprise, but now they know we're there. Finally, the minister wraps it up. For us, it's to make sure all down there are dead. We kill anything that's moving. The key is to make the part between the beginning and end as short as possible. Make it fast and lethal."

I got on the intercom. "OK all, let's start making those four false inserts." The two slicks started down with gunships slightly behind. This continued three additional times with the real one last. There was no pathfinder because there hadn't been time to get them in place.

So far so good, as they say. I asked the colonel, "Could you please take us to the gas station? Be light on the controls as we've lost only 450 pounds of the original 1600." I got on the controls at the end to let him know he had to pull in pitch and slow our descent or we would fall through. (That is, we would not come to a hover but instead hit the ground hard, and there would be no limit to the amount of damage.) The guns took on very little fuel as they had all their armament.

The colonel took off with three bounces, which was pretty good, and I told him so.

I called 9-5. "How's your new copilot doing?"

"Just a moment; let me wake him up."

Jerry jumped right in and yawned when he answered. He said, "Damn, Mac, I was having a great dream that did not include you smelly Birds."

I said, "Never mind."

The colonel looked over and laughed. He said, "I love it. Just enough to lighten things after the tension."

I said, "Yes sir. I might add that you can always tell a gun driver; you just can't tell him very much."

The colonel started laughing again and said, "Mac, do you mind if I go on the extraction mission?"

I said, "Of course not. You are a good stick, learn quickly, and have thousands of hours more than the new Bird they would send me. In fact, you have thousands of hours more time in the air than your pilot (me). Everything I just said is true, sir. I'm not blowing smoke. You're lucky, sir. One of the copilot's jobs is to help the gunner rearm, while mine is to assist the crew chief. Have you ever armed a gunship? This ship is the crew chief's when it's on the ground. Since they are both listening to us, you might tell them about the new American Division's rule about shooting any unruly crew."

I got back, "Bullshit, sir."

"I won't ask who said that because you won't tell me. But I will point out to the colonel that it did sound a little unruly to me."

The colonel agreed, then added, "But only just a little, because, he did say 'sir.'"

Now we all laughed. I couldn't resist adding, "I do have one little scrap of knowledge about flying: A copilot is never right, and then he becomes a pilot and is never wrong. Of course that does not apply here. You outrank me, sir, and those guys behind me have machine guns, so I will just sit here."

"Ski and Tyler, has he ever been quiet?" The colonel asked. "Please be honest."

Tyler spoke first. "Sir, if they ever gave Mac an enema, they could bury him in a shoe box."

I thought the colonel was going to have a heart attack he was so red-faced from laughing. He said, "I'm going to enjoy working with you rearming this ship."

Time to call and report. "Five minutes out for six Hueys west of you on a straight in approach." The colonel did the call, and the tower came back with, "You may land if I'm talking to the guy who invited me to dinner and the colonel who allowed it."

The colonel jumped right in and said, "Hold a moment. I have to wake up Mac."

Terry said, "Clear to land straight in to the east. Sir, you just ruined my mental picture of Mac." The tower got back two clicks from the colonel.

After landing, we did the refueling and rearming and everything else to get ready for going back in. While we were still in a group, the colonel said, "We'll take all six ships for the extraction. Mac, could you and Captain Wilder remain for a few minutes?"

We waited while the rest walked away.

"A couple of things: First, Major Wilson filled me in on both of you. He had nothing but admiration. I know Wilson. We worked together in VN two years ago, and he wouldn't say those things unless he meant it. Second, I had a patrol at the Cau Lau River a week ago who want to buy you beer for life for pulling them out the mess they were in. All eight of them said they owe their lives to you. They were a little embarrassed to call for help. That pride thing."

"That's OK, sir. Just tell them to send cash."

"No, I won't, because they don't know your sense of humor, and they would send the money."

"And there's a third thing. The officer in charge of that mission was MacAddo, the GB whose puke you helped clean up. I haven't told him that. I think I will the next time we're all in the debrief or bar."

The next day was very low key, starting with the colonel holding the mess open till 0900. We were definitely working banker's hours. I checked their small library and found pretty much the same type of "literature." *Guys will be guys.* I grabbed a paperback that looked like it had potential. I read until I fell asleep. That constituted a nap. *I believe that was my second nap.*

The briefing at 1600 included info on Elliott. He had been shipped to the large Hospital in Danang. That was followed by dinner. *I'm going to miss this mess hall.*

Back to our beds. I haven't called it a bed in nearly 18 months.

At 0200, we were awakened by the loud speaker: "Scramble, mercs in trouble."

My heart was racing after that cruel wake up call. I cranked her up and waited for the colonel to bring coords, new frequency and call sign, just in case anything had been compromised. He then climbed in.

"Six Hueys to TO. Two guns, three slicks, and Flare ship makes six."

Someone had a sense of humor. The new call sign was Lonely 6. I hovered out and then remembered my copilot.

"It's all yours, sir."

He bounced four times and was sliding in between the bounces but kept the ship going forward, and we hit translational lift and were airborne.

"Strobes and then five minutes, sir," I reminded the colonel, "and right turn thirty degrees north to the LZ. Mercs will use strobes when they hear us. At least, that's what we got at briefing"

The colonel gave me that smart ass look.

"Sir, I will log you as PIC (pilot in command)," I said, "to make sure you get credit for these hours." He looked skeptical, so I said, "Sir, you've been in the army as long as I've been alive. My gift to you for everything you've done for the guns. You can't let a W-1 take any of your credit. It took guts to fly out to tiger country when you didn't have to."

I decided to check in with the guys on the ground. "Lonely 6. This is Firebird 9-7. How do you read?"

"I've got you Lima Charlie (loud and clear). NVA close behind us. I think they had people up on this mountain waiting for us."

"Flare," I said, "light 'em up."

"I have your LZ," I radioed Lonely 6, "and it looks like they're planning something, because they're in a group. I'm going to come and thin the herd with rockets and 40mm cannon. My wing is 9-5. When I break over the top of you, wing will come in with rockets and mini guns. Both will have door gunners hanging out and picking targets."

"Sir, I'm going to change the subject," I said to the colonel, "do you see that large rock about a half mile away?"

He said, "Yes."

"Draw a two inch circle and when I say, mark it, you put a dot in the center. That's your rocket sight. The red button is just above your right thumb. When you push it, push gently. Now pull down your cannon sight and shoot those bastards on the top of the mountain, sir."

9-7 was rolling in. I glanced over to the colonel. He had walked his shots up the mountain which was only 30 yards to the top. The door gunners were on target.

My turn, so I punched rockets into their huddle before they began running. Some ran down hill, and others ran to the other side of the mountain ridge. I shot at the ones running down towards the LZ.

"Lonely 6, you have some runners coming right to you."

"No problem," he said. "I have 6 claymore mines on trip wires." (A claymore mine is a flat device three inches thick, 10 inches across the front, and eight inches tall. It is packed with high explosives set to blow outward. Hundreds of ball bearings are blown out with force of a rifle shot. A humorous note: one side of the claymore says, "This side towards the enemy.")

"Ready," followed seconds later with 9-7 breaking right over the LZ. And 9-5 was now picking targets and protecting my belly. As I was climbing out, two machine guns started firing at me. I yelled, "Shoot the cannon," then to Ski, "Top of the mountain."

"Lonely, do you see anyone?"

"Five claymores went off after you started shooting. I sent two men to check it out. There were at least 10 dead. Also, there are six running up hill. There were at least fifty when you started shooting."

"9-5," I said, "do you have the source of those machine guns?"

"Yes, after they shoot, they fall back to the other side of this mountain."

"They will kill that slick," I told him. "I'm going over the top and fire some rockets and then jump back on this side. They have artillery down on the Ho Chi Minh trail that can fire air bursts. 9-5 put four rockets on the top and then use those minis all the way to the LZ. When they retreat, I will strike."

"How are you doing, sir?" I asked the colonel. "That was something, the way you handled yourself and that cannon!"

"I'm OK. Major Wilson told me you scared the shit out of him twice in one day, but he loved it."

"Sir, are you ready?"

He tightened his four-point harness. He pulled his cannon sight tight to his helmet, then nodded. "I'm a little nervous, but I'm with you all the way."

I circled back towards the mountain about 500 yards south of the machine guns. I saw them shoot at 9-5. He punched four rockets, and they retreated.

I had enough altitude to fly over the mountain. I had them in my sights and punched off three pairs of rockets. There were six dead, and the machine guns were no longer usable. The colonel got a secondary with the cannon. I quickly flew back over the ridge line.

Ski said, "There were four air bursts. Those bastards were close." (They were using a very sophisticated, very deadly weapon: radar controlled anti-aircraft cannons.)

9-5 asked, "Do you see any targets?"

"I don't see anything. Let's escort S1 and S2 into the LZ."

S1 responded, "I'm ready."

I said, "I'm on you." We flew into the LZ, and the mercs jumped into the ship.

Out of the trees came two mercs with two wounded NVA. S1 called, "We need S3. These wounded look like they should be lying down."

"Damn, I feel the adrenalin rush Mac," said the colonel. "I started out scared, and then I just put it out of my head and was shooting at muzzle flashes and NVA. It was great."

We escorted S3 in without any resistance. He picked up the remaining guys and was out of there.

"9-7 is going to make two more rocket runs for training purposes. 9-5, would your copilot like to punch a few?"

"Yes I would," said Wilder. "In fact, my pilot and I have done the red pencil routine. Hey Mac," he continued, "Can I order my pilot to let me punch a few since I'm his platoon leader?"

"No, but I'll bet he'll let you if you ask nicely.

"Sir, you've got it. Now we look for a target. Gently put your thumb on the red button. Lineup that circle around that pile of destroyed machine guns, then press the button.

"Do any slicks need the gas station?"

S1 was OK, S2 OK, S3 OK, and flare OK.

I said, "All four of you, go home. We'll try to catch you." *That won't happen.*

"9-7 and 9-5 rolling in." The colonel pressed the button. Two rockets shot out and one second later they exploded. He was a little low so I said, "Raise the nose and try it again." He was a little closer.

I called out, "Breaking right." Wilder's shots were almost on the pile.

"OK, sir," I said as he was climbing out, "Let's do it again." He did and was getting closer. 9-5 was on target. I transmitted, for everyone, "Last run."

I turned to the colonel. "Sir, I've got you on single shot. Let's see you blow something to hell."

He said, "Gladly," and started to roll in when an NVA came out of the trees with thirty yards of open ground to the top of the mountain. (You can tell it's an NVA by the uniform.) He saw us and started running.

"Sir," I prompted the colonel, "Do you want that NVA to get away and tell someone about our tactics?" No answer as he gently turned our nose away from the rubble and towards the runner. The runner waved his arms back and forth out in front of him. The colonel saw that and punched anyway. He was behind the guy because he didn't allow for his target's movement. The blast knocked him down, but he sprang up and continued running. The colonel concentrated and punched off a killing shot, and the NVA was atomized.

"Quick sir," I said, "put one on the rubble, and then break right for the gas station." He almost hit it. I said, "Don't feel bad. Those rockets have a fifty meter killing radius. If they had been there, they'd be dead." I looked back and saw 9-5 lining up on us.

"Those were two great shots back there." The colonel was grinning from ear to ear. "That's the only way I can describe it."

"Off the grid," I said to him. He nodded as he turned toward the gas station.

"Maximum fire power theory," I said. "We shoot more at them than they shoot at us. We have a larger choice of weapons, and our weapons are bigger. So we've got the edge, unless they've got a 51."

The colonel did it all, and we made it back to RP. He offered to help us with rearming and checking for bullet holes. He said, "Ski, what can I do?"

Ski looked at me, and I just shrugged. "Sir," said Ski, "climb up here, and you can do Mac's job."

He actually climbed up and helped Ski clean the chamber. When they were finished, Ski thanked him. He said, "You are the first colonel that's ever worked with me."

The colonel climbed down and said, "What can I do, Tyler?"

Tyler said, "Grab some rockets. You have to replace the ones you shot." For some reason, we all started laughing, while Tyler showed him how to load rockets.

I said, "Sir, you've done plenty. Besides, it's time for the debriefing. We'll finish this later."

As we walked into the room, the wing crew started clapping and someone said, "That was a great shot." Wing's crew explained to the slicks and mercs, and that got them fired up.

As the colonel took the podium, he put his hands out palms down and moved them in that up and down motion to quiet the room. He loved this. He was one of the guys for a few moments. Soon, he'd have to go back to the administrative grind where the only bloodshed might come from a paper cut. The debriefing didn't last long. After all, the colonel had been there.

As we were leaving, the sun was coming up. I asked Ski and Tyler if they were as tired as me. They both nodded. We were walking down the hall to the showers when the colonel said, "Halt, all gun crews get in here." He was sitting there with bottles of Gin, Vodka, Rum, Tequila, and a few other bottles, and a tub of ice. *They live pretty well here, when not in the field.*

He said, "Have a drink. I'm buying."

We just looked at each other. Hell, the sun was just coming up. *Kind of early for drinking.*

The colonel then said, "I heard you guys were pussies."

We walked to the table, and each picked up a bottle and took a long pull. We put the bottles down and wing stepped in and followed suit. I said, "We love a challenge." The colonel smiled and said, "Sit down gentlemen. You have shown so much bravery and heroic flying and shooting last night that I don't really know how to thank you for pulling my guys out when it looked so hopeless. All of you put your lives on the line without hesitation.

"Now, let me pour you a drink. Grab a glass and put some cubes in it. As I walk by you give me your choice of these nectars of the gods, and I will pour."

That went really well. We all did it one more time. The showers were harder to find than last time. *I think I know why. This one goes in the manual.*

When I woke up, I was surprised I was alive. After we showered, I had a note on my bed that the colonel wanted to see me. *Hell, what now?*

I reported, and he said, "Sit down. About last night. You came up with new tactics on the spur of the moment, and I was really impressed." He went on with a change of subject. "What do you think about me shooting that NVA?"

I said, "Great shot, sir."

"I mean, was it ethical?"

"Hell yes, that little shit would've shot you without giving it a second thought. There are very few hard and fast rules in this war. It affects your judgement and values. It's kill or be killed. Some people just need killing". The colonel snickered at that comment. "By the way sir, I logged the flight saying you were shot at with a full AK-47 magazine, and you quickly returned fire. We don't do this very often, but that's also how the crew saw it, too.

"It was an honor to fly with you. By the way, I still don't have a new copilot. I actually would prefer you. I'm very partial to your post debrief sessions, and all the gun crews wanted me to thank you as well."

"Mac, here's the latest on tonight's flying," the colonel told me. "It's supposed to rain four inches tonight. Division does not want you to fly when the raindrops are so large that they will dent the leading edge of the rotor blades. It will ruin the blades, and they'll have to be replaced."

This rain lasted three days. I was getting a little bored. I had tried on numerous occasions to talk to Stephanie. No luck.

I talked to the GBs RTO, and he said, "Division anticipated this storm and flew all the Dollies to Bangkok to go shopping. Can you believe that?"

I told him, "Nothing surprises me anymore."

After dinner that night, the Green Berets invited us to free drinks in the bar. "The special occasion is for you guns," said a GB LT. "You bailed out our guys' asses down south a few weeks ago, and most recently got our mercs and LRRPs out of deep shit last night, to include me! And we really appreciate that effort."

I said, "There's one rule when drinking and telling war stories. If it's a true story, you must begin with 'This ain't no shit.' If you don't say that, then we know its bullshit. And we don't need any more of that in this war zone."

They all laughed, and someone added that LT MacAddo will not be speaking this evening because all he talks is bullshit. That brought about even more laughter. That started me thinking that this was going to be a fun night. The best joke of the evening was about all of us.

I said, "There were two guys and two gun ship crews sitting around a campfire after the war was over. One guy was a GB LT; the other was a GB EM. After a few beers, they started with the stories. The LT said, 'This morning a 2500 pound bull got loose and ran toward me snorting and head down. I stepped aside and grabbed his horns twisted his head and pulled him off his feet.' The EM said, 'A little later this morning, I jumped on that bull and rode him till he dropped from exhaustion.' Well, the two gun crews just sat there listening to these stories and were slowly stirring the hot coals in the fire." I paused for effect. "With their peckers."

Guys all around that bar were spitting out their drinks, from the mouth and from the nose. Two fell off their chairs. One guy was trying to write something on paper so he could remember the joke.

After that joke, there was nowhere else to go except bed.

After mess at 0800, I called the CO in Chu Lai and filled him in on the mission since our last talk. When I finished, he said, "Mac, the colonel called me at 0700 and we talked for an hour. He finished with the best joke I've heard in the past year. He raved about the last extraction. How you immediately outfoxed the NVA on the ridge top. He said shooting the cannon was incredible, and then there was shooting the rockets! He said, "I'll call you back when I can describe that sensation.'

"Then, I told him what you said about Top shooting those weapons and what you told the tower operator when you tallied up his hits: he got monkeys, trees and an erection.

"Mac, you are making many friends. Keep it up. Everyone knows about the 71st. Even the Donut Dollies?"

Damn, that sounded like a question. "Yes, I made friends with a dolly, but I haven't seen her since the low level and machine-gun day. I have only spoken to her twice since then. So anything else is gossip, so far."

The Major laughed. "I wish I were staying, so I could continue to hear more great stories. You'll love Major Mathews. I hope you stay in the army. You can get a direct commission to First LT just by mailing a post card to the pentagon. Oh, and I almost forgot to tell you. The GB colonel said he was going to call the colonel in charge of the Donut Dollies and see what they can arrange for you and Steph to meet."

That sent a thrill through my stomach and groin.

I said, "Thank you so much. I'll leave you with a final observation sir. You can't believe how well these guys eat!!!"

"I've eaten there, and I try not to think about it when I walk into our mess hall."

We both hung up laughing. I looked at a calendar on the wall and determined it was Sunday. I decided to see the RTO and call Chu Lai and the Dollies and just maybe get lucky.

Chapter 48.

GETTING LUCKY

The RTO saw me coming through the door and was calling the Dollies as I reached him.

"Hi, I'm Mac and you are?"

He put out his hand and said, "Roland O'Malley, sir."

I said, "Make that Mac."

"I know who you are, sir. Everyone knows who you are." He turned towards me and mouthed, "I'm on hold."

We stood there quietly for a moment, just waiting for the phone to become active. When the voice on the other end said, "I have a Stephanie on the line for Kevin," Roland replied, "I have him right here."

I swear I could feel my heart beating, and I started sweating in the air conditioned room. *Jesus this is strange. I don't feel like this in combat. In combat, I'm planning, thinking ahead, anticipating the enemy's next move, watching where everyone in my ship is targeting their weapons, watching the same in the wing ship after I break, checking my instruments every few seconds, listening for any new sounds in the ship, talking to my crew, copilot and the same to my wing, talking to the guys in trouble on the ground, checking how much armament I have remaining, and looking for places to land or auto rotate should my ship be taken out of the fight. There are many additional items on that list, and I handle them better than speaking to this one lady.*

I was handed the phone, and Roland left the room.

"Kevin, is that you?"

"Yes," and then blurted out, "What's your last name?"

She laughed and said, "You sound nervous. That's not the Kevin

I know, who is so cool saving lives, flying around low level, and letting the Dollies shoot the shit out of the jungle. Well, for the record, I'm nervous, too"

"Well, the last name, please?"

"Rheem. R-H-E-E-M. It's an old European name. When are you coming back to Chu Lai to visit some ladies in need of more excitement, so we can feel alive?"

"Probably not for two weeks. That sounds like an eternity. This situation is almost unbearable. I'm thinking about you on my way to combat and on the way back. And at night when I'm trying to go to sleep. Don't get me wrong. All this is incredible. I feel like I'm in junior high, a nervous kid."

"Well, thank you for that. I'm thinking about you all the time, too. Every time I fly in a Huey, I daydream about seeing you. And I have to admit, shooting that machine gun is a close second."

"I feel butterflies in my stomach, Stephanie. I fantasize about us together. OH crap, one of my crew just ran by the big window in this room and mouthed the word *briefing*. Looks like I will be flying this evening. Goodbye and I'm falling in love with you. There, the nervous kid managed to say it."

"Well, now I know we both feel the same. Goodbye."

After everyone sat down, the colonel walked up to the lectern. "Let's do this a little different today. Any questions?"

The GB captain, Booth, who had helped clean vomit off the bar door stood up and said, "Sir, may I be openly frank with you?"

Colonel Wheaton had an apprehensive look on his face and said, "Certainly. What do you want to say?"

"Sir, I was talking to WO McNally, and he indicated he had an FNG copilot."

Everyone started shaking from holding back their impulse to laugh.

Booth was laughing slightly and said, "Is that true sir?"

The colonel looked at me. I shook my head back and forth *no*. I also shrugged my shoulders and turned my palms up in the 'I don't know pose' and said, "Maybe I can promote him to peter pilot?"

That did it. Everyone was turning their heads back and forth, looking at the colonel, then me. Now everything was out of control again. I'm sure the GB's didn't know that peter pilot was a (derogatory) way to say copilot. They were just laughing at the word peter and the colonel in the same sentence.

The colonel held his hands high over his head with his palms toward the audience. It was at least 30 seconds for the room to become silent.

When the crowd gathered their wits, the colonel said, "Would LT MacAddo and Mr. McNally please come up here."

We stood on his left (the highest rank is on the right). The colonel said, "I have a story to tell all of you and Private Booth." That brought on more laughing; it was quite a demotion from captain to private.

"A few weeks back you'll remember, LT MacAddo and his team got into a little trouble and called the gunships. The gunships came in shooting, and it was a real gunfight. It was back and forth for 45 minutes. The guns were finally able to escort a slick in and pick up all eight GBs. The guys jumped in, and the lead gunship was shooting as the slick got the hell out of there. The gun made a final pass to finish off the few remaining shooters. The slick was not hit because the lead gunship had flown between it and the bad guys! He took four hits, and he and his crew chief were both wounded. LT MacAddo, I would like you to meet that gun driver, Mr. McNally standing here."

We both looked at each, and you could have heard a mouse tiptoe across the room. I finally stuck out my hand while I looked at him. He was shaking and got teary as he put out his hand. I put out my other hand to stabilize him, and the room exploded.

The colonel said, "Would the other seven in that patrol please come up here."

They all shook my hand. Some became weepy.

"Sir, I asked, "is it OK if all the guns come up here?"

The colonel yelled for all the guns to come up.

All seven of the Firebirds came and introduced themselves to the GB's. This went on for ten minutes, then the colonel said, "Go to dinner."

We slowly moved in the direction of the mess hall. Everyone was so busy talking. Even the GBs who did not participate jumped in and said, "We were the guys you pulled out of the hot LZ two nights ago." After we all got seated and were trying to talk to each other, I stood up.

"If I could have your attention for just a couple of minutes. You all know who flew with me these past few nights. That's right, Colonel Wheaton. He has thousands of hours in all aircraft to include the Huey. With me, he flew most of the time. He handled the cannon like a pro. He showed no fear with bullets coming up at him. He ignored them and was walking those shells right up to within just a few yards from you guys. He fired rockets before and after everyone was off to the gas station. Some NVA appeared over the summit and were trying to gather weapons. With a couple of rockets, he ended their mission. I'm telling you this so you see the warrior side of him. Also, I'm not sucking up. I don't do that."

Everybody jumped up and yelled: *Whooo Rahhhhhh,* and clapping.

"I could say more, but I'm hungry." I turned to the colonel and asked if I could eat.

He said, "Continue eating."

I walked back to my plate and finished the meal. My head was still spinning.

After dinner, another briefing. The gist was six mercs were going in tonight. "One of them is a pathfinder. We will fly through a pass in the mountain about halfway to the gas station. Same pass we've been flying by every day. The mercs will be about fifty miles north of our most northern LZ. It is a very dense jungle. From aerial photos, we've seen a few LZs."

"You get up at 2100 and TO at 2130. Same call signs except the mercs will be Dirty 6." That drew laughs from the mercs.

I immediately went to bed and it felt like I just lay down when a very loud voice said, "Get up, we're going flying tonight."

It felt cooler. *That should make for an easier TO for the guns.* The colonel was going to be my FNG again. I said, "Sir would you like to get this Hog off the ground."

"Glad to Mac and thank you for your confidence."

He hovered-bounced to the runway and with three bounces and some sliding we were in translational lift.

"Nice TO, sir. You have a great touch. Ski and Tyler, test your guns. You, too, sir." That killed a few trees.

It was a beautiful night, no clouds and half a moon. "Sir, the pass is coming up. Everyone be alert. Pathfinders were sent out a few times and no sightings, but you never know.

"Sir, turn right to 030 and wake me in fifteen."

"Can you really sleep?"

"In the past I've always had new pilots who were just off FNG status. So, I had to stay alert. I've never flown with anyone with your experience or hours. You're able to do it all. I've seen you glancing at the instruments and then smoothly return to shooting. We're turning north and will be looking for an LZ in fifteen minutes."

As the colonel flew, I was looking down at the thick jungle and shuttered at the idea of someone having to auto rotate into that canopy. "I haven't seen anything. Keep going, sir."

I called, "Commo check." Everyone responded: 9-5, S1, S2, Flare, Angels 1 and 2. "Thank you much gentleman. Now, I can go back to sleep."

I asked the colonel, "How are you doing? Do you want a break?"

He said, "Sure."

"I got it." I took on the controls as he lifted up his hands. I moved the cyclic a little to get the feel. "Sir, I tell the new pilots that you strap on this ship like putting on your pants, and you both move as one. What's your opinion of that?"

"Mac, that's great. I've said it a little differently, but basically the same."

"I've also told new pilots to never auto rotate into an area where you just killed people. The survivors are pissed. Sir, there are predators and prey. Remember you are the predator or you will become the prey."

"I like that, Mac. How about this? Aviation is unforgiving. It can kill you."

"How about this sir? Hope for the best, plan for the worst. I'm not a negative person, but that's the conclusion I've drawn from my four months here."

"That's so true, Mac."

"I tell them, always be thinking, planning, know where you are if your engine quits. Where is that landing area? Sir, many ships are at the bottom of the ocean, but we've never left a Huey up in the air." He laughed. I added, "I use the AMMO acronym: Attention, Mission, Motivation and Objective."

"I love it, Mac."

"Sir, I see an LZ. This might be the big one they were talking about. Shit, we could put five Hueys in that parking lot. S1 what do you think?"

"Let you know as soon as your wingman is through admiring it."

"S1 this is 9-5, and I think it's real pretty. If you want to land there, I will personally check it for you."

I said, "This is 9-7. Did you copy all of that? Let's go check it out. 9-7 is rolling in. Are you ready sir?"

"Yes."

"Let's give it a good look." I was looking everywhere. Hoping there was one mistake they made. Something for me to see, and there it was. A splotch of white. 9-5 saw it too. I was past, but he put a pair on it a few hundred yards behind me.

Click-click, was my thank you.

I broke left, which I didn't like to do because I was in the right seat. I heard wing calling "Breaking left." Suddenly, there was a huge explosion. That small white tent top was their mistake.

"OK everyone, this is 9-7. Let's move another twenty miles north. Everyone fly south of this LZ, so they can't see how many of us are up here. Nice shootin' 9-5. What did you see as you flew close to those bastards?"

"Not much."

"I'm behind you, and I'm going to swing off to your right so I can look in and then shoot from there before we move north.

Click-click.

I saw a few guys on the ground stumbling around while I was talking, so I centered my targets and punched a pair into their nest. There was another secondary explosion larger than the first. "Fuck, what did those little shits have down there? Breaking left."

Wing put mini guns on them. No return fire.

"Let's go find a more hospitable place to land. Really 9-5 what did you see?"

"I saw that tent, and I guessed there was more."

Ten more minutes got us twenty miles north. Then, we resumed looking for an LZ. As I was doing this, I asked, "Angel 1, would you like to give that first LZ some of America's fire power?"

"Thought you'd never ask. We'll make one or two passes south to north to stay below their radar-controlled antiaircraft artillery."

"Sounds good A-1."

The next open area was small. Room for one slick.

"S1 how does that look?"

"I can get in there."

"9-7 is rolling in. No resistance, and I saw no one. 9-5 did you see anything?"

"I'm the same as you."

"S1 come on in. It looks like the best approach is north to south. I'm behind you and same altitude. I'll pull up and get between you and the NVA If anyone shoots. That jungle is so thick, the only way they could get into this LZ is from the west side."

All went as planned. Six mercs including the pathfinder, who just happened to be a tracker, were inserted. We flew east and circled once just in case they were attacked.

Dirty 6 called me and said, "All is good. Tracker says, 'no one has been here in a long long time,' to quote him."

"OK everyone, let's go home."

The colonel did it all. He flew to the portable gas station, got some juice, and took off. He landed at RP and called for fuel. We started checking the ship and doing some rearming. I said "Sir, we can do this; you have to do the debrief." He smiled and said, "Thank you." The debrief was short. The Sky Raiders had blown up everything at the hot LZ. They called HQ and said they could stick around for 30 minutes at the second LZ. We went to bed without visiting the bar.

We all got up around 0900. I'd had about eight hours sleep. *What's this war coming to? I better not put this in the manual. It would raise a kid's hope.*

Everyone had a rare relaxing day. I wrote a letter home since an announcement had said that mail was coming tomorrow.

I went out to the ship and gave it a good look. While enjoying the quiet, Ski and Tyler showed up. We opened the sliding doors, sat down, and just talked about home and women. We must have been talking louder than we realized because when we got to the women part, here came the entire wing crew. They sat down and leaned back against the revetment barrels.

Some of the birds came from comfortable homes and others,

not so much. One had his second drunk-driving charge and was given the choice of jail or the army. Two guys joined to escape parents who were getting high on booze or drugs every day and threatening to kill each other. Two were from divorced parents. One guy was a foster kid, and he told us horror stories about foster care. He joined at 17 and loved the army. "My first real friends and family that I can trust. Guys you trust with your life. It's a home. People you would die trying to help, and vice versa." This went on until dinner and then off to a nap.

Suddenly, the bull horn erupted. "Briefing room, everyone."

In the briefing, we were told, "We just received a call from the mercs. Nothing on the road last night; but a lot of trucks tonight. They spotted a few single soldiers south, several miles away, on the peaks of the mountain range. The mercs think they are expecting us to return to our southerly LZs."

Afterward, I was walking down the hall at a fast clip when the colonel stepped out of a room, and we nearly collided.

"Hey Mac, looks like I'm still with you. That OK?"

"Sir, of course. This whole mission is yours. You worked too hard to become a colonel to take orders from a warrant, and a W 1 at that."

"Thank you, Mac. I've noticed that you don't give stern orders. You ask quietly with a smile. You remind me of a quarterback; you know everyone's responsibility, and you make sure they do it."

"Looks like the mercs are on the run," I told him, repeating part of what we learned in the briefing. "They're just below the ridge on this side and moving north. From what I saw on the insertion, they'll have to eventually turn east to find any type of opening."

"Mac, between us, I heard some urgency in the mercs' call. The arc light hit ten trucks filled with troops, along with the usual artillery and ammo trucks, probably 300 men. To lose all those men probably pissed them off royally."

"Let's go see what we can do."

"RP tower, six Hueys to depart west," I radioed. (An extra Huey in case we needed to extract the mercs with ropes.)

"Hey 9-7, this is Terry. I've got night shift this week. All six cleared for TO west."

"Thank you, Tower 6."

"Hey, thanks for the promotion."

I could make out the gas station's lights and told them to turn them off. We went north through the mountain pass. I turned on the RMI (radio magnetic indicator). When Dirty 6 talked, we could home in on him. A needle on our instrument panel indicated where he was transmitting from in relationship to our position. He was northwest, and that's where we'd find him.

The mercs were frantic on their next call. They estimated over 100 NVA were getting closer. One of their guys was wounded. I told the flare ship to toss out two over the insertion site.

That lit up the place, and I had a good look at the top of the jungle canopy. That didn't help anything. I called them and asked, "Can you hear us?"

The answer was "Yes. We're shinning some flashlights straight up and waving them."

"OK. How far away are the bad guys?"

"Probably no more than 200 yards. They're moving slow and cautiously."

"I've got the lights. Give me a compass heading to their location."

"9-7, they are behind and above us at 270 degrees."

"Sir I've got it," I said. "OK, here comes a pair of rockets. Let me know how effective they are."

"Shit, that was right on those fuckers. You can shoot the next ones a little closer to us."

I shot closer, and as I broke, wing put them close as well. The mercs were ecstatic with both our results.

"Dirty 6, we are going to drop ropes for you to tie on to. We've got no harnesses or jungle penetrators. There are twenty pounds of weight on each rope. Cut it free and tie the ropes around yourselves. This is going to be tight. Slicks 1 and 2 come in over those lights and drop your ropes."

"9-7 is rolling in with rockets and 40 mm. 6, direct those cannon shots."

"Roger, get them closer to us. We've got claymores all around us. We'll set them off when you pull us up."

"Rockets away." I punched off six pair. Our rockets weren't quite as effective in the jungle canopy. The leaves wouldn't set them off, but if a rocket hit a large limb, it would detonate. Still, they were traveling at 2200 feet per second, so all the force of the explosion and shrapnel would be downward.

"6, how close are they?"

"Some have made it through your last pass and are 75 yards away, and they have a machine gun."

"These next rockets and the cannon fire will be only fifty yards out. Take cover. Get behind trees. Tell us when you are all tied in."

"Sir, shoot as close as you can when they come up that hill."

"OK 6, I'm rolling in." I punched off eight pair. That was 12 and 16 for a total of 28. I had five pair remaining. The General was shooting right on and close to the merc's. "Breaking right." Wilder was cutting down the jungle with the Gatling gun, as 9-5 was shooting close to the mercs.

S1 said, "Ours are tied on." S2 said, "We're ready." Up they came, but slowly, not knowing what they were encountering as they were pulled up through the trees. I could see their claymores exploding and now there were several small openings in the jungle and up came the tracers. Several went through the Plexiglas and splattered the colonel, but he kept shooting. We took a few hits in the radio compartments and got several yellow lights.

"Dirty 6, this is 9-7. One of your guys hanging below S2 doesn't look too good. He's leaning backwards and appears to be unconscious. It looks like he's slowly falling backwards."

"9-7, he was unconscious when we tied him in. He has tourniquets on both legs. That damn machine gun cut him down."

"We have nowhere to put down until we are almost to the gas station."

"I know."

It was agony watching that merc leaning farther back and now his feet were higher than his head. That was all it took. He slid out of his makeshift harness and fell 1500 feet into an impenetrable jungle. I've seen people die in many ways. This was just one more. What if he was alive and was too weak from blood loss to help himself?

"SHIT, SHIT, SHIT," I yelled out. "Angel 1, is there anything that needs taken care of back in that LZ?"

"Yes there is and we are rolling in."

"Dirty 6, how is everyone else?"

"We are all OK, and actually we enjoy this method of travel. Hell, I was the one that tied him in. He was a close friend. We went through LRRP School together. Shit, I will never forget the picture of him falling. He was a brother to me."

"This is 9-7. I have the gas station in sight. Traveler 6, two thirsty gunships coming in from your west and two slicks with cargo hanging below. Their fuel is OK. They want to transfer their cargo to first class and move everyone inside."

Traveler 6 said, "I've never seen that before. Those guys have gotta' be crazy."

Those two slicks had to hover very high, over 100 feet, and then the LRRPs were on the ground and untied. They waited for the Hueys to land and then jumped inside and coiled rope all the way to RP.

As we neared RP, I called and asked for a medic to meet us because my copilot took some shrapnel. I felt something on the outside of my left calf as well.

We landed, and the medical field mobbed the poor colonel and hauled him away on a stretcher with him protesting almost violently. I just wanted him to get that Purple Heart. I noticed earlier when he was in his dress uniform (army's version of a tux) that he did not have one.

I helped Ski and Tyler do everything. I called avionics in QT for some radio help as well as a Plexiglas crew. We had seven holes in the ship. I said, "You two need to shoot more and faster." We all laughed.

Tyler said, "I could hold a 60 in my other hand."

I said, "It may come to that. Let's go to the debrief."

It was longer than the last one. We had to wait for the colonel. Then, we discussed tactics and the fluidity of the situation. "And, as I have said since day one, a few seconds into a briefed mission, you throw everything out the window and wing it as you ad lib." The colonel added that he would like Dirty 6, S1 and 9-7 to stick around to fill out some papers on the LRRPs death. Dismissed."

Most everyone headed to the bar. The three of us filled out the papers, and then we were free to go.

I went to the medic because my leg was throbbing. He pulled some shrapnel out. I said, "I have a request. Please don't report this or I'll be sent home."

"OK, but it looks like four stitches, antibiotic shot, and pills, and I want to look at this tomorrow. You know the drill, sir. I just pulled two pieces of metal out of your leg. You should be in bed with the leg elevated."

I was walking to my bed when I heard my name. I turned and saw the colonel trying to catch me. I stopped and met him halfway. "Mac, they took Plexi out of my left shoulder and metal out of the right one. How are you doing?"

"I'm fine sir. I'm searching for my bed, and if I don't find it soon, I'm going to drop in this hallway."

"I have to tell you Mac, I've never felt so alive. My adrenaline is going wild. I want to get back in the fight."

"Adrenaline is the strongest drug there is," I told him. "You are more alert, feel invincible, feel no pain, and your concentration is totally on your mission. You don't worry about the bullets coming at you. You just use them to find their origin and then blow whoever shot them at you to hell.

"Sir, may I buy you a drink before I pass out? We can talk about any questions you have about tactics."

"Sounds good to me, Mac. Follow me."

"Yes sir." We walked into the bar, and I asked the colonel, "What's your poison?"

"Scotch, neat."

I said, "That's OK for me too. Open the bar, sir, and your money's no good tonight. You flew with me tonight and several missions prior like a seasoned pro. You took Plexi in one shoulder and metal in the other and kept shooting the cannon at the bastards who shot you. You did that while blood was running down both arms, and you took them out. I may be overstepping my boundaries, but your balls are harder than brass and a whole lot heavier. You lead by example. I'd fly with you any time."

We sat down. No one spoke. We sipped that scotch slowly, like it was the last on earth.

"Mac, what makes a gun driver?"

"Good question, sir. In my case, I got tired of people shooting at me while I sat on the ground. I thought I could help our troops better in the guns.

"I like what the GBs do, training the Hmong tribes to report on and attack the NVA, whom they truly hate. You GBs help people in this war. I feel I'm doing more for the grunts by flying guns than slicks. I've had slick pilots tell me the birds are too quick on the trigger. They forget who just bailed them out their most recent shit sandwich. The birds covered me when I was in the slicks my first thirty days.

"Some guys have joined the birds and then quit and returned to the slicks because they don't like the killing. They forget this is a war. Most of them are reasonable, but there are a few twisted fucks who want to kiss the NVA's ass or lips. Sir, do any of your guys express these kinds of opinions? After all, these little fuckers are trying to kill them."

"I think our comradery holds us together," the colonel said.

"Same for us, sir," I agreed. "There isn't a guy in the Birds who wouldn't give his life to save a comrade. People look for us when we are on the ground to thank us for saving their lives. My killing is impersonal. You and your men and the infantry have to look at them face to face. Big difference I think!"

"Mac," the colonel said, "this is difficult to explain to you because you are unique. Keep doing what you're doing and pass it on." He paused for a moment, like he wanted to say more. Then he shrugged. "Our groups of GBs are as tight as your gun crews."

"We go on numerous missions where we know our ships are going to be shot down," I said. "We know our fellow pilots will be looking for us. Firebirds and Rattler slicks. It's comforting to have those guys in the sky watching over us."

The colonel stood up and stretched. "Actually Mac, you can look forward to heading home soon. The NVA seem to have stopped all traffic on the Ho Chi Minh trail for now. See you at breakfast at 0800."

"Good night, sir."

I stumbled through the showers and made it to bed. *Damn, this can't be the most efficient use of American troops. Fuck, I don't care if anyone wants to shoot me. I just want to talk to Stephanie.*

I continued these missions with the GBs for almost another week. That was not my idea of soon.

Almost all were routine, as I've already described. We had just one notable incident: a Huey lost power as he was depositing the LRRPs. S1 gave a quick panic call to let us know he was heading down.

As I was rolling in, I said, "Where are they?"

"Across the LZ, straight west. Right where my nose is pointing."

Then, suddenly a hail storm of bullets came up and put a hole in a blade, holes through the floor between the colonel's feet, and up through the floor in back, splattering shrapnel on Ski and Tyler. I glanced back; they just kept shooting. I gave the ship some left cyclic and pedal and started punching rockets all along the jungle and deeper into the jungle. The colonel was doing the same with the cannon. When I broke right, I watched wing punch his rockets in the same place, then the mini guns covered the area like a blizzard. I rolled in and punched twenty more rockets. Then, I called S1. I could see him standing by his open door. I asked, "How are things down there?"

He said in a quiet voice, "It looks destroyed."

S2 called and said he would circle the area with his six mercs on board.

I called S3, the reserve ship. "Can you carry out the crew and the mercs? That's ten total. We're not leaving the mercs here."

"Let's do it."

"I'll go in ahead of you. Wing will be slightly behind. Go in on the right side of S1 and use his ship as cover."

"OK guys, blow that place to hell." I punched a few rockets, and the crew was doing its job. As I broke and wing came in, S3 set down and the ten from S1 jumped, climbed and pushed the guys ahead of them so they could get in.

Now came the moment of truth. Could S3 get that overloaded ship off the ground? As I was rolling in, I shot a pair of rockets to keep anyone alive from shooting at that Huey. The pilot was an experienced driver, but did he have enough bare ground across that field to get the lift he needed?

Up he came and across that field. I thought, *it doesn't look good.* Thirty yards from the jungle, with 100 foot trees, the nose came up as he was trading off speed for altitude. His skids dragged through the top five feet of those tall trees but apparently there were no large branches. He lost some altitude but had that ship flying. It looked like a flying tree house. He said he could barely see out the front. Wing and S2 turned toward the road to RP. I told him his ship was camouflaged if he ever had to land in the jungle. I added, "S3 that was incredible flying."

I looked at the colonel and asked him, "What do you want to do with S1?"

He looked at me and said, "I've got it."

Shit, no copilot had ever said that to me. I called the two ships and said, "We have to take care of S1." I nodded at the colonel and switched the rockets to his cyclic and single shot. "You've got rockets."

He clicked twice, dropped the nose, and punched off one. It was short twenty yards. Close but not quite. I gently pulled the nose up and then stopped so he couldn't raise it higher. He punched off another, and it was a direct hit. A fireball rose up 100 feet. I helped him make a hard left break. That fireball was close because I had let the colonel get closer to his target than we usually get. I wanted him to hit S1, not join it.

I looked over and said. "Please take me home, Killer, sir. All this activity has made me thirsty."

He looked at me and said, "This is the most amazing experience. No one would have ever given me this chance to fly in battle. You've made this tour, my third here, educational and realistic. You pilots have the most dangerous mission. You fly right down their gun barrels. I don't think there are many people that could do your job. Damn, I'm impressed. I will think of many more factors when I plan missions now. You've really opened my eyes. I don't feel like a REMF (rear echelon motherfucker) any more. I don't know how to thank you. I have never talked to an officer like I talk to you."

'Well sir, you are a very intelligent leader. We all learn every day, and then we apply it. Oh, and by the way, no one has ever called you a REMF"

Fifteen minutes later, we stopped at the moving gas station and took on enough fuel to reach RP. In the air again, two yellow lights appeared. They told us the radios had taken some hits and so had the engine. That second one had me worrying. If a bullet hits those compressor blades, they come apart and throw metal everywhere. This happens because they are moving at 6600 rpm. Even worse, if the engine quits and you have to go into autorotation, then you can only hope there is an area on the ground that's open and available for a landing.

We made it to RP and landed without incident. We had eight bullet holes in our ship. Wing had five. The mercs said, "Thank you for not leaving us out there with a 'dump and run.'"

We just said "fuck it" and went to bed.

Walking to breakfast, we saw a team of mechanics working on our ships. I went out and asked one what that yellow engine light was all about. He said it was for a control panel next to the engine. It monitors fuel flow, fuel pressure, exhaust temperature and such. The round didn't hit the gauges or fuel lines. *I seem to be one lucky bastard. I can't put any of this in my book as it is all top secret.*

When we walked into mess, it smelled very good. Pancakes and bacon. "I'm putting in for a transfer," is all I could think of to say to the other seven birds. Several said they were going with me. After we filled our plates, the colonel waved us over to his table and told us to sit down. "I want to know how you all slept last night." We said, "Great, all five hours."

"I won't say this to anyone else except your CO, but I got up last night and opened the bar for a quick couple of drinks to relax. I was so wound up I couldn't close my eyes. I admire you guys.

"Your new copilot will be here before lunch. You head home as soon as your ships are repaired and rearmed. I tried to sign up to fly with the birds but was turned down."

We all chuckled, and someone said, "Wow, a full bird as a copilot in the birds." That caused more laughing. I looked at the colonel and said, "Sir, you can fly with me any time in either seat." Tom Rivers said, "That goes for me too, sir. I watched you on the cannon. I'll bet you would love to fire those mini guns."

"Yes, I would," the colonel agreed. "It looks like you will maybe get two days rest before your ships are ready."

Tom said, "May we be excused, sir?"

"Yes, go back to bed. I may do that myself."

Everyone got up but me. I just sat there until everyone left the mess. I said, "Sir, please don't fight it, but I put you in for an Air Medal along with the Purple Heart."

He just looked at me as I stood up and took my tray to the kitchen area.

It was early, so I detoured to the radio room and gave the RTO twenty dollars. He smiled and said, "I saw you coming and called Chu Lai." He put his hand up to stop me and said into the phone, "Thank you." He handed it to me and left the room.

I said, "Hello."

She said, "It's about time. I thought you had forgotten about me."

I said, "Never."

She laughed. "I have to see you. I only think about one thing all day: you. I have to pay more attention to my job. I even said, 'thank you, Kevin,' to a young soldier as he picked up a handful of games I dropped. He said, 'My name is Roger.' I feel like I'm going to burst. I wrote my mom about you. I hope you don't mind."

I said, "Of course not. I'm amazed that you could like anything about me that first day. I couldn't stand myself. My hygiene was much better back in the world."

"I learned a month ago what the "world" means. I'm sure you were much cleaner. You probably even shaved."

I laughed.

"I may fly out of RP tomorrow," I told her, "or the next day at the latest. I will be in Chu Lai. I've made a few friends in high places, and I will 'call in' those favors to get me to you. We will only be two or three miles apart."

"That sounds wonderful. I feel like a high school girl with her first crush. Honest, I've never felt this way. Never! I told my mom that this isn't a quick fling or a feeling to make up for the loneliness. She wrote me back, 'Steph, I have known you for twenty-four years. You darling, are in love.'"

I said. "Thank you, because I know I am."

"Now to change the subject," she said. "I've been following your activities out 'you know where' Kevin."

"And how do you have access to that top-secret info?"

"The command gave me top-secret clearance because they know I'm crazy about you. They can't believe what you're doing. 'Every day he does something more incredible than his last heroic action.' They ask me, 'What's he like?' I tell them that you are a compassionate person who feels it's his duty to protect American troops."

There was a significant pause on the line.

"You told me you don't take foolish chances," she went on. "I hope you were telling me the truth. I sure hope you're not crazy."

"I'm the sanest, most careful pilot in the army," I assured her.

"The command couldn't believe you had a full colonel as a co-pilot. He was wounded and put in for an Air Medal and a Purple Heart. I'm sure you did that, Kev."

"He earned them," I assured her. "He is a good pilot and a quick learner. He made me promise him that I would not let him be captured because a person of his rank has a lot of valuable information the enemy could use. I didn't promise he wouldn't be wounded or run into the deep shit we got into. Oops. I'm sorry; it's been so long since I've spoken to a woman."

Steph said, "Don't let it fucking bother you."

I started laughing so hard I pulled the phone away from my mouth and held it at arm's length. I finally got some control. I told her, "You are fucking incredible," and now she was laughing.

"I hurt inside, when I go sleep at night," I told her. "It's not the combat; it's you. I'm getting some feelings back. I'd gone numb before I met you. A new copilot asked me how I do what I do. I said it's easy, I don't have a conscience.

"My best friend—the man who taught me how to fly gunships—was killed sitting next to me. It happened in an instant. We were talking, and then he was dead. I was flying, and there was absolutely nothing I could have done even if he had survived. Over a dozen other guys I got to know quite well as an FNG and a Firebird have died. Pilots, copilots, crew chiefs and door gunners; gone in an instant. I've been here only about five months. It changes you. They never talk of the horrors of war in history classes.

"They don't talk about how war affects the soldiers and their ability to assimilate back to civilian life. It's the world's hobby to just to send its men off to fight and kill. It's gone on for thousands of years. I'm so sorry to be preaching to you. You just happen to be the first person that seems to care."

I took a moment to catch my breath. Then, I took the plunge. "Is it too early to say I'm in love with someone I've seen only once? I think about you all the time. You are an angel, and I'm the luckiest guy in the world."

But I was beyond exhausted. "I hate to say this," I said, "but I've slept only five hours in the last two days. I'll call tomorrow and let you know when I get out of here. I love you."

"Love you more. Bye."

I went to bed and slept twelve hours. I woke up, cleaned up, and went to the bar. I had missed dinner. To no surprise, everyone was there. There were a few majors and a LT colonel who looked like they were letting off some steam. The mercs were drinking hard. I asked a guy at the bar, "What the hell is going on?"

"They say President Nixon is going to increase strikes in North Vietnam."

I said, "I'll drink to that. Give me a double."

I was drinking and thinking of Stephanie when some mercs walked up and said they just found out that I'd been the lead gunship these last few weeks. "We want to buy you a drink. We don't know any other way to say thank you."

I said, "That will work, but you guys are crazy. I should buy you drinks. I can't believe what you snake eaters do."

"Yea, we're crazy, but we got a tree to hide behind. You got nothing."

"I believe in the maximum-fire rule," I told them. "Put more bullets and rockets on them than they can put on me."

They laughed and said, "That works for us."

I asked how they got into their line of work.

They said, "Just young and dumb and full of cum. Patriotic and looking for something exciting to do. Hell, you know that adrenaline rush that hits you. Sometimes, it feels as if the action has slowed down for the enemy. They are moving slower, and you are moving faster. It's crazy sounding, but it just happens too often."

"I get that same feeling every time I go into combat," I agreed. "That first shot at me is like a light switch. I can't explain it either. I guess it's in our nature to fight or flight. The only time I ever did the flight thing was when we heard the police sirens getting closer, and we were drinking beer on the fifty yard line after the game on Friday night. I don't know why they didn't turn off those sirens. It would have been easy to sneak up on some buzzed high school kids."

They all laughed and agreed. Then, one said, "We want to thank you for risking your life to save ours. Shit, if I had a girlfriend, I'd let you fuck her." The other mercs laughed and said he only said that because he was too ugly to have a girlfriend. Now I laughed and said, "Shit, I thought you really liked me."

We were interrupted by my copilot, the colonel. Before he could say anything, I said, "Do you snake eaters remember all those 40 mm rounds exploding around you?"

They all said, "Yes," in unison. "Some were close but so was the enemy."

"I have something to tell all of you. My copilot on all missions after the first one did all the 40mm shooting. Now, this ain't no shit."

Everyone in the bar went quiet, and I said, "This is a true story (as was implied when I said, 'this ain't no shit'). I may get busted back to private because this sounds like ass kissing, but I want all of you to know who this person amongst us is. He is a leader of men and superior under trial by fire.

"I want everyone to hold up their drink, and if you don't have one, the mercs will buy it." That drew laughs. "Has everyone got their drink up? That person is Colonel Wheaton!" Everyone just looked at me. So I said, "To the colonel," and downed my drink. The place went wild; the colonel was well liked.

He stood there red faced and held his hands up to quiet the crowd. "Now that private McNally has spoken, I wish I had gone to bed."

A major walked up and said, "Sir, you are one brave son of a bitch, no reference to your mom, but this is your third tour. These Firebirds do it because they are young and patriotic to the limit. Not saying you aren't patriotic."

"I learned a lot these past few weeks," the colonel said. "In particular, I've been reminded how brave all of you are. Also, I've learned how to better plan missions. I don't feel like a REMF anymore." That brought the house down.

Someone said, "This ain't no shit sir; no one has ever called you that."

He said, "Thank you to all my crew," and he took a drink.

As things were winding down, he said, "I'll miss you, Mac. I've never seen anyone scrap a whole briefing in two seconds and change everyone's job without a moment's hesitation, and you're always right. You are the paragon of a gunship driver! And that ain't no shit."

I said, "Thank you, sir, but I was working with the best men out there." *You know, there is not much info I can put in the book from these last few weeks.*

"It looks like a morning departure, Mac. I won't see you off as I have a mission planning session with the jar heads (marines) at 0800."

I said, "Please reinstate me as a Warrant. Privates can't fly."

"I'll get on that first thing. Good luck with Steph. I looked at her background, and she is near genius on her IQ tests, a brilliant lawyer, and a first class lady. The Red Cross is very lucky to have her."

I walked to the sleeping quarters and sat on my bed and began daydreaming, when in walked the colonel.

"Mac, I've just been informed that your ships will be ready to go by 0900 tomorrow. I have some pull around here, and I know everyone in QT, Danang, and Chu Lai. You are going to see that lady. I promise."

I put my hand out again, looked him straight in the eye, and said, "Thank you, sir."

He turned and walked away. I learned that you lose friends in the military as fast as you make them. If not killed or wounded, they are transferred. *This fact goes in the manual.*

I set an alarm for 0700 so I could call Steph. I didn't trust myself to wake up early. I've had such irregular hours, my body was confused.

That 0700 alarm came early. *I don't think you can catch up on lost sleep. If it's lost, it's gone.*

When I finally got to the radio room the RTO said, "The girls took off at eight. They have a full day in your southern AO."

Well, that didn't elevate my mood. I met all the Birds for breakfast. We had a good discussion about the past weeks. We tried to figure out if we had learned anything new.

I said, "I've been wondering how the NVA were in our LZs."

We talked it over, and the conclusion was that they were probably assigned to all the possible LZs within a short distance of the crest of Annamite.

With that said, in walked my RTO buddy with my new Firebird copilot, Norwood. We all knew him and invited him to get some food and join us.

He said, "It has been pretty active in our AO. We lost two slicks and their crews on a CA. We also lost Don Helmsley, a slick crew chief." "A Firebird was also shot down; but all are OK

None of the names were familiar, so I didn't ask for details.

"We also lost a Firebird copilot, Walt Allen."

Now that should have been the first news he gave us. Shit. He was new and copilot in the lead ship. He had been here only two months.

"Let's go preflight our ships," I suggested.

We walked out and crawled all over those shot-to-hell ships. They looked like flying junk piles.

I asked LT MacAddo if he could call Chu Lai for me. I had completely forgotten. We shook hands, and he said, "Thanks for bailing me out of trouble twice; the puke and when we were trapped by the river."

I said, "Glad to. We all work for the same boss. I know you'd do it for me."

It was cooler that morning. We got off with only two bounces. That included full fuel and weapons. We flew the reverse route to Hue and refueled. I let Norwood try to bounce the hog off the runway. He made a good effort, so I told him to fly us home. I turned on the armed forces radio station, and it was country. I asked Ski and Tyler if that was OK. They said, "Anything is better than beating rotor blades." We flew over Baldy, and the Birds were home, so we just kept flying to CL.

Chapter 49.

DOLLIES IN TROUBLE

Then I received A call from CL HQ, the first call I'd taken from CL since coming back from Laos. "One of our slicks was just shot down four clicks north of Hawk Hill. Rattler 2-8, Nixon.

"He's on an oblong hill 500 meters high with 60 degrees slopes on both east and west sides. The hill runs north-south and those sides are almost too steep to climb. There are at least two companies of NVA on each side. The copilot and crew in back saw the NVA as they auto rotated. There is heavy jungle at the base on both sides, and the NVA are just now coming out of the jungle and starting up the hill."

2-8 was carrying eight Dollies, including Steph.

I said, "I've got it. Everyone test your weapons. This is going to be a gunfight. There are 400 bad guys and eight of us.

"9-5, let's hit whichever side shows the most troops. I will go nearly straight south and pour it on any moving piece of shit. Come in a little laterally from me and shoot from there. Not too far out; we don't want to shoot anything on top. Then, we will climb out and repeat the same on the other side. I see the smoking helo."

I called 2-8 and said, "This is Firebird 9-7 coming at you from the north with a team of two. Get everyone down on the ground. We will be shooting in 60 seconds."

We began with ten rockets on the guys in the open. The cannon shot 100 rounds into the trees and on the edge of the clearing. Wing came in with rockets, and the mini guns shot everything trying to get back into the jungle as the cannon shells rained down. I clawed for some altitude as the other side wouldn't be so easy. *They'll be waiting for us. Surprise only works once.* "After surprise,

---

comes deception (Sun Tzu, *The Art of War*)."

The NVA on the other side were trying to run up the hill, so they'd be spread out. I told Norwood to work from near the top and then walk it down the hill. I turned back to Ski and Tyler and yelled, "Don't let anyone get to the top. Keep them away."

I couldn't estimate the number of rounds coming up at us. I could see tracers and lots of muzzle flashes. I punched twelve rockets while yelling at Norwood to shoot those muzzle flashes. My Plexiglas had at least four holes. Smoke was coming out of the radio compartments between me and Norwood. I heard Ski yell, "Shit." I looked back, and he had blood on his left side above his belt. He looked at me and said, "I don't feel a thing."

As I climbed out, I looked at the first side and saw no movement. What I didn't discover until later was that Nixon had left his radio on and his helmet outside the ship lying on the ground so the Dollies could listen to the action. He crawled to the other side of the hilltop, then back to his ship as I was coming to side two again. He said, "Good choice, Mac. There are lots of those little bastards still coming up."

The second pass was just as bad. A bullet hit my chicken board, and something snapped my head back. I moved my head left and right, and everything else seemed to be working. I saw three yellow warning lights.

"Ski, Tyler, are you OK?"

They said, "Yes."

"Then shoot more, dammit. If it's alive, kill it. If it's stationary, destroy it." Steph told me later that the girls got a kick out of that statement.

Norwood said, "Shit, fuck, goddamn it."

I asked if he was OK.

"Something hit my calf. No pain and the foot works OK. Let's get those fucking bastards. This is personal now."

"All right," was all I had the time to say as bullets came through the open back doors and stuck in the firewall near Ski and Tyler. "OK you guys. We're going to hit side one again. If no one is moving up the hill, shoot into the trees."

As I began picking out targets, a few muzzle flashes appeared, and Norwood shot about ten rounds and got a secondary explosion.

I got another yellow light. I called 9-5 and gave him our status. I added, "Save your ammo, so you can keep anyone from thinking it's OK to come up this hill. I'm going to set down there. Keep that fucking cannon on full auto Norwood.

"Fuck, I just got a red oil light. You guys save your ammo because we're probably going down on that hill.

"Mayday, Mayday, Mayday, Firebird 9-7 is going down on the same hill as 2-8. 9-5 is up and flying cover. My copilot has a leg wound, and the crew chief has an abdominal wound."

I shot the rest of my rockets into the tree line and into the trees. I climbed and turned toward the hill and said again, "Empty that cannon. Hold it down on full auto." He emptied the cannon, and I got a red transmission and hydraulics light. *Shit, we're done. Three red lights. How does this ship stay in the air?*"

Ski said in a hurried voice, "Mac, we're smoking pretty bad."

"Thanks Ski," I said. The engine was surging, which meant it wouldn't last much longer. "OK, we're going in. I'll keep this ship away from the slick. Ours may explode." Suddenly, the engine quit on short final. I did a sloppy auto and hit harder than I wanted.

We grabbed the ammo cans, two M-60's, two M-16's, and the ammo box full of thirty-round magazines for my M-16, and the crew's barrel bags (extra parts for the crew's guns). I told Ski to look on the quiet side, and I would go to the busy side with Tyler. Ski said, "There is nothing moving down there." I said, "Keep watch." I told Tyler, "I'll be back. Keep your eyes on the hill side. Remember Janis Joplin: 'Freedom's just another word for nothing left to lose.' You've got nothing left to lose, if the NVA make it to the top."

I saw Steph stand up, and she looked like a goddess, her face so beautiful and body so perfect even though she was in that light blue uniform skirt.

She walked towards me with a hypnotic grace of motion, and I walked towards her. As we got closer, we walked faster. All the crews from both ships were following us. I was oblivious to everything but her.

We met and just stood there for a moment and then grabbed each other and kissed gently, slowly. Then, we paused. As I looked into her eyes and saw such beauty, I actually thought, *how can there be a war? People are so capable of love, caring and forgiveness.*

All I felt right then was that I wanted to be with her for the rest of my life. Then, the reality of the moment forced itself into my brain: *Damn, we're on top of a hill with who knows how many enemies down there eager to kill us for Uncle Ho.*

Steph told me, "Pete said, 'We're lucky because Mac is here. He's the best there is.' Watching you dive in and shoot those rockets was such a turn on. It was like a fairy tale where the knight saves the maiden. God, I love you. You came in with complete disregard for your own life."

"It's all a calculated risk," I told her. "I don't want to die. I've just met the most incredible woman." We kissed again.

I heard some gun shots and that brought me out of my trance. "Let's walk over to Pete."

He and I shook hands, and I asked, "Did you call Chu Lai and request a couple of slicks? There are sixteen people on this hilltop."

He said he'd called. "Mac, thank you for doing what you just did. That attack was incredible. Your balls wouldn't fit in a wheel barrow. I'm sorry, miss. I'm not used to meeting anyone like you out here."

She smiled and said, "Thank you. You can kill all those bastards as far as I'm concerned."

Pete's eyes opened wide.

Before Pete could respond, we heard the mini guns roar on the second side. I called and asked, "What'd you see?"

"Three guys trying to come up the hill. They have to be on drugs."

I walked over and looked down. Four NVA were coming up the slope in two feet of elephant grass. I yelled to Ski, "Bring your gun."

He walked over to the edge, and I pointed. Ski and Tyler both let loose with a thirty-round burst and all were dead, including a few who had just stepped out of the jungle.

Pete was over on side one. I yelled, "See anything?"

He shook his head, *no*. "Not after 9-5 finished," he said.

9-5s door gunners were tracking us and picking off a few still moving. I thought, *off the grid.*

I said, "Keep looking," and now he shook his head, *yes*.

Then, I asked Ski and Tyler, "Are they as good as you two?" They thought about it.

"Maybe," said Ski.

"But probably not," said Tyler.

Then, I noticed that Steph had been following me the whole time. I smiled, and she smiled back.

"You guys are amazingly matter-of-fact in the face of death," she said. "Keep doing what you're doing. It's fascinating. You and your crew have your helmets on. For you guys, it's all work first."

I walked back to Pete and unplugged his radio wire and plugged in mine. I called Baldy first, and Monty answered. "Is that you, 9-7?"

I said, "Yes, and did anyone call you from Chu Lai about two slicks getting our asses off this hill? It's turned into tiger country."

Monty said, "Yes. Two on their way. They'll call on this frequency any time now. I'm not letting anything happen to you; I want my ride in a gunship."

I rogered and then Rattler 1-8 called. "I see your smoking ship. Is it clear to land? 1-6 is following 30 seconds behind. They pulled us off our resupply missions, and his was farther away."

"You've got the platoon leader, Josh, out here where people shoot at slicks more so than usual?"

There was some snickering from 1-8's crew.

I said, "One of you land *in front of* the two downed ships and pick up the eight ladies. The rest of us will catch a ride on the second ship as he lands *behind* the two downed ships.

"9-5, did you catch all of that?" I received two clicks. "9-5 please escort the ladies on their ride to CL."

Again, two clicks.

As we stood there watching that ship get larger, Steph came closer and pressed her boobs into my back. I turned and was met with a kiss. "It was great seeing you in action. You flew until the ship gave out. Wow, you are my hero."

Monty broke in. "Mac, the brass has ordered you to come in with the ladies."

"It might be quiet enough," I said, "to bring out the shit hooks and recover these two ships."

I walked over to Ski and retrieved my ammo box with ten extra magazines and asked him to round up everyone for the second ship.

"Got it, Mac."

I had all the ladies crouch down in front of the downed slick.

"When he lands, you four—I pointed my finger at them—run up on the left side. Watch out for that tail rotor and climb in. Don't worry about modesty. One of you sits with the crew chief and strap in quickly. You four run up on the right side. One of you will sit with the door gunner. You other three, strap in as fast as possible in your usual seats along the back wall. I'll sit on the floor. We don't want that slick on the ground too long. It is a big target."

As his skids touched, I said, "You four on the left, go. OK, second group, up the right side." I grabbed Steph's hand, and we ran to the ship. I gave the two in front of me a boost to get them in the ship faster. The crew chief and gunner were pulling from the other end. I slid my rifle and spare ammo under the gunner's seat.

Steph whispered in my ear, "Will you push my butt?"

I said, "Love to." I put my hands on both cheeks and gently pushed. The gunner pulled me in, and I helped Steph strap in. 1-8's crew yelled, "Go, go, go," and we were up. The gunner slid my rifle and ammo to me. I looked at Steph, and she was crying. The two ladies on each side of her followed suit. I guess they are just realizing how close they had come to death or capture. I emptied three full magazines on muzzle flashes along with the door gunner while on my knees.

I didn't realize how thick and foul the air had been by the two downed ships until I was up at 1500 feet and smelling the cool odorless air.

I sat down on the floor, and Steph unstrapped herself and sat on the floor next to me. I put my arm over her shoulders. She leaned into me and put a hand on my leg. The flight lasted forty minutes. I never let her go. She turned her head up to look at me, and her hand reached up to my chin. She turned my head, so I was looking at her. We did a quick kiss. I think she was self-conscious because we were in such close company. Even so, my butterflies returned.

I said, "Steph, you are my hero and so brave. Bad guys shooting at you and you ask me to push your butt. Wow."

When we landed, there was a large truck sitting near the revetment, ready to take the Dollies away. I was holding Steph's hand, and it was difficult to let go. As I backed away, the army private said, "Mr. McNally, you are supposed to come too." He stuck out his hand to help me up and in. The door gunner said he would put all my gear in the Birdhouse. I asked the private, "What's going on?" He just shrugged.

I sat down next to the love of my life. I put my arm around her, and she settled her head against my chest and shoulder.

It was three miles to HQ. When the truck pulled up to the building, we could see eight officers standing on the platform to the front door. They all had scrambled eggs on the bills of their caps (field grade officers).

Standing there was Colonel Wheaton with a big smile. Seven of the girls climbed out, then Steph and me. The ladies were all standing in a line.

The colonel gave a short speech to the ladies and dismissed the seven. He looked at me. I saluted. He returned it and said, "Not necessary in the compound. Well, Steph, you have had quite a day." He then looked at me and said, "Her dad was my company commander when I began my first assignment as a second LT. I assisted the legal team as a liaison between them and division commanders on the Post."

That was a shock. I had no idea of that connection.

"I talked to him today," the colonel went on, looking at Steph, "and told him about the very scary situation you were in and how it turned out. Your dad wanted to know who the hell this Mac guy was. I said, 'She's in love with him.' I told your dad I'd bring you both back here so you could be together."

"He knew about the flying adventures with Mac and me as his 'peter pilot.'" The colonel gave me a grin. "Then, Steph's father asked me the 24-dollar question: 'What's he got makes him so wonderful?'"

Steph and I just stood there in amazement.

"I told him good things about you," the colonel said, now looking at me, "with only a little exaggeration. And yes, I told him you made me look good including a Purple Heart, an Air medal, and a lot of stick time while commanding troops. Just so you know," the colonel went on, "I've been put on the general's promotion list, although he insisted he'd earned it by years of duty. Anyway, what do you say? Sometimes it really is a small world."

Of course, we had nothing to say.

"You two go get cleaned up. I sent a driver to get your civvies. Relax and rest up. I want to treat you two to dinner at 1730. Dismissed."

Chapter 50.

A TIME TO REMEMBER

looked at Steph and said, "I'll follow you."

She smiled and took my hand. We walked on a long sidewalk until we came to a trailer house with her name on the door. She pulled out her key and opened it.

I said, "Wait," and picked her up to carry her through. She grabbed me around the neck with both arms, laughing, and said, "I love you."

I kicked the door closed and put her down. For a moment we just looked at each other, and then we were kissing and pulling each other's clothes off. When she was standing there in her bra and panties, my butterflies returned. *This is real Kevin. This is real.* We jumped into her bed and continued from there.

Over the next four hours, we couldn't stop making love. We explored each other's bodies, touching, kissing everywhere. We lay face to face, skin to skin. We finally paused. She walked to the bathroom, and I couldn't take my eyes off of her. She walked back slowly and said, "Your turn."

When I returned, she was standing there naked with two glasses of white wine. It tasted like candy.

She said, "When we finish these, we'll take our first shower together. The shower is tiny; we'll be right up against each other. You'll have to help me reach places there isn't room for me to reach myself, if that's OK with you."

I said, "Oh my god, I haven't showered since this morning. Thank you for the previews. I like the coming attractions."

She laughed and said, "How do you spell coming? By the way you smell just fine."

We both laughed and pulled each other together and began kissing.

The shower *was* small. We washed each other until we couldn't stand it anymore, and then we made love standing up. After we dried off, she walked over to the door and found my clothes outside in a box. She brought it in and said, "a present for you."

She poured more wine as I got dressed. Then, she grabbed my shirt and pulled me into her bedroom, so I could help her choose what to wear. We started with choices from her underwear drawer and ended with a tight-fitting mid-thigh-length dress. It was hot, but still ladylike. She looked really gorgeous.

When we walked into the dining room, it became silent and all eyes were on her. I could have been naked, and no one would have noticed. We spotted the colonel and headed for him. The trip across the room took a long time, because everybody wanted to congratulate me on rescuing the Dollies. One officer told me, "What a fantastic effort you made to save those ladies."

I replied with my usual humble answers. "I was with good troops." I didn't know what else to say.

We finally reached the colonel, and he said, "Please sit down. Mac, I want to thank you for what you did today. I know you had a personal interest here, but I've seen you do the same out in Laos. The entire general staff wants to thank you. I know it sounds crass to put it this way, but you can't imagine the negative publicity if eight ladies with the Red Cross were killed or captured."

I felt myself actually blushing. I decided I could get away with nods and smiles. Nobody expected me to say anything.

We had steaks and baked potatoes! *I can't tell anyone in Chu Lai.* There was good wine, a white and a red! This was the day I started to appreciate wine. *I don't think I'll ever drink that shitty rotgut Mateus again*, I told myself, although with seven months remaining in VN, that was more a hope than a promise.

"Mac, you have tomorrow off," the colonel told me, "and then back to the 71st for a day, then off to Baldy. Major Ron Mathews, your new CO, is anxious to meet you. He's a great person. Very much like Major Wilson."

Then, with a very straight face, he said, "Good night and get a great night's sleep."

Steph and I thanked everybody as we left. Then, we were outside in a clear starry night.

In two days, I'll be back killing people. I had trouble holding that fact in my head when I was in such a peaceful setting with Stephanie. *Enjoy it while you can, Kev.*

We stayed outside for a little while. Then she said, "Let's go to bed." I didn't argue. I took her hand. We made our way to her trailer, having some trouble walking, staying on the sidewalk, and staring into each other's eyes at the same time. *I've never felt like this in my 22 years on earth. This is love,* I thought. It was very clear in my mind. The distinction; I couldn't have explained the difference between love and sex for a 22-year-old guy before today, but it was very clear to me now.

We undressed each other very slowly. Kissing, feeling, touching and looking into each other's eyes. We looked in a mirror to see whose were bluer. She said mine were the bluest she's ever seen.

I said, "I haven't got past your neck." She hit me on the arm.

I said, "Wait! I was only kidding. Your eyes sparkle. They are like a mirror, the bluest blue I've ever seen."

"Nice recovery, Mac."

We climbed into bed, and I said, "Let's not come up for air until tomorrow afternoon."

"I was hoping you'd say that." She gave me the most loving soft kiss.

Suddenly, she stopped. "Kevin, what's that on your back? Hell, there's a second. Roll over. There are four!"

I explained the whole hot brass story. She didn't say a word until I stopped talking.

"You're not safe anywhere, are you?" She sounded amazed.

I had no answer. I just shrugged.

We spent the next three hours making love, snuggling and staring into each other's eyes. I thought, *if I die tomorrow, I can say I've had a good life.*

We finally stopped, and she fell asleep. I was left to my thoughts. But I still held her close, trying to be as close to her as possible.

I was so happy and full of life, but what was it going to feel like, killing people and thinking of her and life? What a dichotomy!

We didn't wake until almost noon. I asked her if they had room service.

"Yes," she said grinning. "Me!"

I matched her grin. "I can eat that."

We spent most of the afternoon talking about our lives in more detail. She already knew about me: burnout and the rain in Eugene. She was in VN because she wanted to help and feel useful to her country.

"I was raised in little Medford, Oregon." I told her about my "Mary Jane" misunderstanding in flight school, and my Tac Officer telling me I was "lower than whale shit."

She was laughing so hard she jumped up and ran to the bathroom, telling me over her shoulder that she was afraid she'd wet the bed from laughing.

Seeing her naked body literally took my breath away. I think I held my breath until she came out.

"Your turn," she said.

As I got up, I said, "How come you're always first?"

She gave me a mock-serious look and said, "That's just one of the many qualities I love about you. You're chivalrous."

We both laughed.

"I have never had these feelings for any woman before and that's the solemn truth," I told her. "You know about my experiences in war, but the most difficult thing I've ever faced, or will have to face, will be leaving your side tomorrow." That brought her to tears.

She looked into my eyes, while I was staring into her beautiful blue eyes. We said nothing for a minute, or it might have been longer. I wasn't counting.

She said, "I'm hungry. How about you."

"Now that you mention it, I'm starving."

We took another one of those tiny close-contact showers, and then we couldn't help ourselves. We ran to her bed, not even stopping to dry off.

We returned to the shower and tried again. We dressed.

She looked gorgeous, like a model. Everything was perfect including her tight blue skirt. I told her it matched her beautiful eyes.

It was not formal tonight, so no dress greens for the brass. When we got to the end of the chow line, she said, "Let's go sit with the girls. I want to show you off."

As we sat down, all eyes were on me. I took in that entire audience of Dollies, and I said, "Yes, I have a job, no felonies, have never been married, no paternity suits waiting for me. Only two years of college, but I will finish when I return."

They were all laughing, and one said, "Hell, you just took all the fun out of making you nervous while under cross examination."

Steph said, "I've been talking too much with these girls. They could barely speak English when I arrived." More laughing, and loud.

We were drawing a few eyes from the rest of the room, so Steph put her finger to her lips in the *Be Quiet* sign.

We heard some great stories from the sexy seven as I called them, and I had no problem letting them do the talking. Steph looked at me and mouthed a *thank you*.

They were from all over the US and from very different backgrounds.

One had run away from home because her father was in prison and her mother was a drug addict. "It was so bad," she said, "I won't even take an APC, (all purpose capsule/aspirin)."

Shannon was from West Virginia. She had left school at sixteen and was declared emancipated and got on a bus to LA. There, she met Stephanie Rheem. "She hired me to be her aide and legal assistant," Shannon told us. "She let me live in her apartment. She taught me law every night. She didn't go out. She said it was more important to get me off the streets. I was no longer homeless and had a new big sister who showed me how to make good decisions."

Everyone was stunned. No one had known any of this. I looked at Steph and said, "Wow, I'm so proud of you." Shannon had tears in her eyes. She got up and walked to the other side of the table and gave Steph a long hug.

A corporal walked in and said to me, "Sir, may I talk to you? It's from HQ." I got up, and we walked a few feet away from the group. He said, "You are to pack your things and return to your company here in CL immediately."

I was stunned. I walked back to the table and said, "You'll have to excuse me, but I have to go right now."

Steph jumped up, the shock clear on her face. We walked

quickly to her trailer. I put on my flight uniform, which had been cleaned. I gathered everything that was mine.

I looked at Steph who was helping me. "I'm so sorry. I don't even know why they want me."

She said, "That's the way things work in the military. Please call and write."

"I will. I promise."

We hugged and kissed. Then, I hurried to the sleeping quarters to grab a few things.

I went to HQ and asked my friend in the radio room, "What's going on?

He shrugged. "I'm out of the loop on this one." He picked up the phone to inform the colonel that I was there.

The colonel stopped me before I could say a word. "You get tomorrow off and then go to Baldy for an indeterminate amount of time. Good luck and we'll be in touch. The jeep is outside."

What could I say? "Thank you, Sir."

I threw my small bag in the back of the jeep. It was a short ride to CL.

I was dropped off in front of the CO's building. I said, "Thanks," and took the short walk to the Birdhouse. I threw my bag on my bunk and started to sit down, when I heard, "Surprise!" Most of the birds were there. They handed me a drink and pushed and pulled me to the party room. They sat me down at the 9-7 number on the table and said, "There is your new nickname."

It said, "Irish Killer." I gave them a big smile and said, "Love it," and took a sip of my drink. *Shit, this is awful.* Then, I took another. I said, "Thank you Birds." Some sat down; some remained standing, but they were just barely able to stand. Two bottles of Mateus appeared. (My "never again" statement didn't last very long.) The party continued. Ten or fifteen minutes later, someone yelled, "Attention, CO in the building."

I said, "Yeah, sure." Then I heard, "No shit, Mac, it's the CO." I turned to look and saw a major's gold leaves on the collar. I didn't know him. I jumped up.

As I started to put my drink down, he said, "Don't bother. Give it to me. What's this Mac?" as he indicated the coke can with the top roughly cut off to form a drinking container.

"May I speak freely, sir?"

"Certainly."

"You are holding a purple motherfucker."

"What?"

"Sir, we can get only lousy gin and grape soda or Fresca. Yours is named after the color. The green motherfucker is named after the color of the can."

He took a drink and then spit it out on the floor. "That's fucking terrible." He handed it back to me.

He put his hand out and said, "I'm Major Ron Mathews, CO."

I said, "Pleasure to meet you, sir."

"I understand that some people call you the old man."

"Yes sir. I'm 22," I said with a smile.

"That makes you older than most around here, but let me set you straight. I'm the Old Man," he said with emphasis, but don't ever let me hear any of you call me that!"

We laughed and said, "Yes sir," in unison.

"I've spoken with Major Wilson, and he said the birds are somewhat messy, drink too much and are, at times, unmilitary. But you do the most dangerous job in VN and do it better than anyone else. He also reminded me to tell you to take down those signs: 'Kill them all...' and something about 'I've spent my time in hell.'"

I said, "Sir, if you are deprived long enough, you become depraved."

He just nodded and said, "Mr. McNally, report to me at 0900 tomorrow."

"Yes Sir."

He shook his head and walked out.

The party continued, and things became more and more blurred. For some reason, I said, "Let's go cut out the boobs on big Randy's ceiling wall paper. The ceiling was covered with naked center folds. We grabbed (stole) a ladder from supply, set it up, and took turns cutting out the boobs. We numbered each boob and the corresponding vacant area on the picture. Then, we put the numbered boobs under his pillow. "Job well done. What's next?"

We decided it was time for bed.

I woke up without a hangover. No one was more surprised than me.

I checked in with Top at 0900. He was wearing his flight jacket. I grinned at him. "You look good in that jacket, Top Dog."

Top jerked his thumb towards the CO's office and said, "Go in. He's expecting you."

I walked in and before I could say a word, he said, "Sit down."

I sat and waited, and finally he spoke. "I've been reading up on you. You've had quite a first four months in the Birds. In fact, your month as an FNG was pretty amazing. I'd like you to take the job of ammo officer here in CL. The place is a mess down at the flight line, and we have an IG inspection in a month."

"I'll do it, sir."

"How was your time off up at Battalion HQ?"

"It was great, sir."

"I read about your mission to save the Red Cross ladies a few days past. I also heard rumors that you taught all of them to be door gunners. I was really surprised when I saw that your copilot was a full bird colonel at Rock pile. He was flying, shooting, and helping with the rearming.

"Before that, you left your commanding officer in a slick while you saved four lives, one of which was wounded so you carried him. You pulled out a patrol on the side of a cliff while a machine gun was firing at you. You saved hooch full of our pilots who could have been burned to death. You spent all night recovering body parts. You made Top a gun pilot. It's all he talks about. Colonel Wheaton of the GB wants to give you a direct commission to Captain. Did I miss anything?"

"Yes sir, I'm carrier qualified."

"This is my second tour here, Mac. I'm also carrier qualified. There's a lot more in your file. I know you don't like to go to doctors. I even heard you bribed one with a gunship ride, so he wouldn't report any wounds you received until you DEROS.

"Top adores you. Says you are a man out here surrounded by kids. I heard you bought the bar for the EMs and why. People are calling for you specifically when they want the Birds. Hell, the lady in charge of the Dollies, Donna, said they would walk to the LZs if you didn't fly them around. I tried to explain to her that you fly guns. She said that answer was not good enough.

"I have a favor to ask of you. Now I could order you, but I won't.

Would you please go to the flight line in thirty minutes and get that lady off my back. Fly the Dollies around and through the trees. Get them recertified as door gunners. Whatever will make them happy. Thompson is finishing the documents; he got their names from HQ in CL, with a special one for Stephanie. Perhaps we can sit around some evening, and you can tell me that story. We have the ship set up with six seats, and the other two sit with the crew in back. Your copilot is Wilder. He, Ski and Tyler are already at the flight line. The girls don't know you're coming. So grab your gear, and Thompson will drive. Dismissed."

Wow. That's a man who does his homework!

I ran to the Birdhouse to get my manual on the C model, so I could start on the ammo job after the flight.

I had those butterflies in my stomach as we stopped at the slick. The girls were packing their equipment in a large three-by-three box anchored to the floor. I saw my goddess standing with her back to me. As I walked to her, I was trying to decide what to do or say. I decided to tap her on the shoulder and say, "Do you want some help, lady?" If I grabbed any other body part, she would yell out, "Don't touch me," and put her fist in my jaw.

I lowered my voice to disguise it when I asked her if she needed any help. She slowly turned, and as she told me later, my disguised voice hadn't worked. She was sure it was me.

She said, "Mac," in a very loud voice and threw her arms around me and pulled me in for a kiss. Anybody who didn't already know about us got the message with that kiss.

"What are you doing here?" I said.

"Donna Reynolds specifically asked for me."

I looked at Donna, and she said, "Thank the major."

Steph and I walked out of the revetment to find a little privacy. We kissed and held each other. I couldn't stop looking at her. I'd never seen anyone as beautiful as Steph.

When we came back, I asked Ski and Tyler, "Have either of you guys ever been with eight women at once?"

The ladies laughed and waited for the answer.

Tyler said, "Yes, in the church choir."

More laughter, then they looked at Ski. He said, "Yes," followed by, "in a house of ill repute in Saigon."

The girls laughed. One even said, "What's the name of that house?" More laughter.

He saw they weren't buying it. "Just kidding," he admitted with a *you got me grin*. "But it could have been in an underwear shop."

I said, "If you have any questions when we're up in the air, ask these two. I know them well. We fly together every day. We're the three musketeers. (I liked the sound of that.) They're the best there is. True story."

"Now which two of you wants to fly first with the machine guns?"

They huddled and then two raised their hands. I looked over at the two musketeers and said, "Thanks for the extra ammo."

"We heard you ran out last time," Ski said, "and had to borrow some from a FSB."

"Ladies, this handsome gentleman is Captain Jerry Wilder, my platoon leader and immediate boss."

One of the Dollies said, "Yes, he is quite good looking."

I said, "Captain Wilder, you're blushing," which he was.

It was a nice cool morning with hardly any humidity. I looked over to Jerry and said, "Let's get out of here."

He said, "Where to Mac?"

"East, Center, West, and Karen," I said. "It's a short day, so we are going to play. Ski, Tyler, are our passengers secure?"

"We double checked each other."

"Yeah, I'll bet you did."

That drew a laugh from the girls.

"Here is a pack of cigarettes I stole from the Birdhouse," I said, offering them to Tyler. "Break off the filters for the girls to use as ear plugs.

"We have clearance to fly straight west to LZ East." It occurred to me how confusing that would sound to our visitors.

"Warn the ladies before you test fire your guns. Then, get them in position and before the gun runs. Jerry, give them some maneuvers to remember the Birds by, even if we are in a slick. Warn the girls to hang on, so they aren't thrown around."

Jerry made a turn to the left and then one a little steeper to the right. "I've got it," I told him. I dove for the ground, then a 60 degree turn around some trees, then 60 the other way. A cyclic climb seemed appropriate. That pushed everyone down in their seats. I dove for the ground and said, "Turn them loose." I flew straight and level while they killed some trees.

"That was impressive," I yelled. I banked right and said to Tyler, "See the geese?" And he had his lady shooting into a flock while they were feeding in a field. "OK, here I come left, Ski. You pick her targets. Notice the look on their faces when they shoot."

This went on for fifteen more minutes. I landed on Highway One for a seat change. There were tanks and soldiers on the road, but we didn't stay too long or (especially) let the Dollies be seen.

Up again, and we continued with the low level and turns. I dragged the skids through a few trees. "OK guys, give your replacements some gun time." I looked back, and they were smiling. The guns were roaring as I flew through a little valley, and the girls tore it up pretty good.

I said to Ski and Tyler, "Go cold you two. I'm going to call East in a few minutes and get some smoke. You hold the guns when we land."

At East, we let the girls out to do their thing at the FSB. They were excited and full of energy. It was great to see, and of course the kids at the FSB loved their enthusiasm. The company commanders on the FSB loved it as well. They called Battalion HQ in Chu Lai and reported that these ladies, as they referred to them, were incredibly helpful for morale. (I learned this from Steph when we talked later.)

I waited with the crew at the ships for their return. I spent time talking about flying the Huey with Wilder. I said, "You are cautious, which is good, but you can be a little more aggressive with this ship. More so than a gunship. This thing has power to burn. It's a sports car. You can give the girls a ride."

He said, "I watched you flying. Something is different."

"I think I know what you're talking about. When I get in a helicopter, I don't strap in. I strap it on, and we fly as one. I know it sounds strange, but try it. Don't lean when turning; just sit upright and go with the ship. When we leave here, we're going to take our time getting to Center. We'll have the girls shooting, and you can put a little more adventure in your flying. Let's see if you can turn them on." I winked and he smiled and said, "Thanks, Mac."

The girls wrapped it up at an hour fifteen. We loaded and refilled the machine-gun bag that feeds the gun. We switched gunners. We started south, and Jerry was pushing the envelope. I held my hands close. He looked and smiled, and I gave him thumbs up. We went around the trees and through them until the girls were screaming with excitement. Jerry was excited. I said, "Fly level through this valley that runs just north of Center." Then, I said, "Go hot." Ski and Tyler pointed out targets for the girls. I said, "I'm going to move the ship a little. Keep them on their targets." I moved a little, and they did well with the crew's help. After fifteen minutes, I called a halt and said, "Everyone look forward and watch this landing." They were squealing with excitement.

I doubled back a few miles and landed on the road from Tam Ky. A regular patrol of US troops was there. I called them and said, "I have to land to change seating for training." I told the ladies to change seats but not to get out as I didn't want those troops to see them.

They nodded and played musical chairs. This was the final group of two for the first time around. Off we went, and Steph was in this last group. I asked Ski, "Do something different. Give them a real taste of what goes on back there." Jerry took off for a round-about way to Center. Jerry was flying better. His turns were sharper and his low leveling was lower. I glanced at Steph, and Ski had her shooting farther out. He showed her how to lead when we turned.

I saw a muzzle flash. "Shit. Someone is shooting at us." I asked Ski if he saw it. He had already put Steph on the target and guided her in by looking at her tracers. She hit the guy and never blinked. She looked at Ski and said, "Anything else? Maybe a little more difficult?"

Ski looked at her and said, "Now I think I know what Mac sees in you, besides the obvious. You love a challenge, and you learn fast. Like Mac."

They saw a water buffalo. He keyed his mike so we knew up front. Wilder began a gentle left turn and watched as Steph put 20 rounds in him. The Buffalo just looked at her, so she shot him another twenty or thirty times, and the thing dropped.

She looked at Ski and said, "I fucking love this. Anything else Ski."

He answered her with his mike keyed so I would hear everything he said to her. "Well, let's look. I see a guy down there plowing rice, and he's not supposed to be there. He's tending that rice for the VC or NVA. Do you want to shoot and kill him?"

She said. "Hell, yes."

I heard that and took the controls to make a slow slight turn, and she opened up. The guy pulled out an AK-47 from his baggy pants and pointed it at her, and she said, "No way, you little shit," and fired. It took her thirty rounds, but she nailed his ass, and he never fired a round. Ski looked at her and said, "Damn, you're awesome."

I continued the flight to Center, and the Dollies went on stage to do their show.

They were high on adrenalin. I couldn't resist standing near the stage to watch them. When Steph was up on the stage, she asked the audience a question, and a young guy there answered incorrectly. She put her hands on her hips and told him, "You better get some fuckin' help." The crowd went wild, and someone gave the correct answer. Steph started clapping and told him to stand and take a bow. "I would go into combat with you," she said, to the delight of the guys in the audience.

Steph was unique. I admired her for her work with these kids, as well as everything else. Ski walked up, so I backed away from the stage and turned to him.

He looked worried. "Mac, I've got something to tell you." He told me about Steph shooting the guy in the rice paddy. He said, "I didn't encourage her. I pointed out the guy with the AK, and she said, 'No problem.' I got a lot of pics of her shooting. I told her about 'off the grid,' and she nodded. You know this would be a very big deal if anybody found out."

I said, "No sweat Ski. She's a big girl. She's a smart girl. She won't talk about it."

I brought Ski to the stage and pointed, "Look at her enthusiasm here in the middle of nowhere. These girls are giving a great show." They were now doing a skit with double-meaning words with Steph playing the dumb blond. Finally, at the end, she said in a petite voice, "Good girls get to go places." Then, in a tough sexy voice said, "Bad girls go everywhere." The two hundred guys went crazy. They gave the Dollies a standing ovation. The girls waved as they walked off the stage in single file. They returned for more acclaim. They called the soldier in charge to come up. A lieutenant colonel walked onto the makeshift stage.

Steph went to the microphone and said, "This is the man who invited us." More clapping and cheers. Two girls gave him a kiss on both cheeks. The place was ready to riot. The colonel went to the mic and said, "Thank you ladies." They walked off, a girl hanging on to each of his arms.

Ski and Tyler had reloaded the magazines for the M-60s. When the Dollies arrived at the ships, they put away their props and materials and looked at me. "Do we get to shoot again?"

I looked at Jerry. "What do you think, Captain?" The girls knew all the ranks. I was giving Jerry his due respect.

He said, "Mount up girls. When Ski and Tyler get you buckled in, and I buckle Mac in, we'll take off." That crack drew some laughs. "First two gunners take your position."

Ski and Tyler double checked everyone "That's a policy when transporting civilians," Ski explained.

"Be careful girls," I said. "These guys are young and horny."

They howled at that. We arrived at West in fifteen minutes, shooting all the way. The girls did their thing on a makeshift stage one more time, and they were better than Bob Hope. One encore and the kids were still clapping and yelling and giving the Hooooo Raaahs as the Dollies climbed into the Huey.

We switched gunners again, and Jerry said, "Mac, are you buckled in?" More laughs.

I said, "Yes sir." Then, I keyed my intercom so Ski and Tyler could hear me tell Jerry to call the FSB and request to buzz those kids, as they were still waving. I added, "Warn the girls."

They were screaming as we made the low pass.

It was fifteen minutes of shooting to LZ Karen. We landed, and the girls got the same enthusiastic reception as at East, Center, and West. Wow! I felt tired watching them put out such energy. We switched to another twosome and flew to West. I asked for permission to land for thirty seconds to change the seating for training."

"No problem, land at the platform."

We landed, and I reminded the girls to keep this private. Group four strapped in. Jerry said, "Ski, are you ready?"

"Yes sir."

"Tyler, are you ready?"

"Yes sir."

Jerry yelled over his shoulder, "Ladies are you ready?"

"Yes sir," they screamed.

"Mac, are you... never mind. Alright everyone, let's go." The girls were howling and screaming when he told me, "Never mind."

Off we went and immediately dove down the side of the mountain north and turned east. I cleared the gunners, and they went to work. I really enjoyed watching Steph shoot as she was in the first group on this second time around. The intensity on her face was a new look I hadn't seen before. Ski was taking pictures.

Ski said, "Mac, four runners at 9 o'clock with AK's."

I said, "Take 'em."

Steph got them all. It took 100 rounds, but she picked them off one by one starting at the slowest runner and going up the line to the leader. I don't think any of the other ladies saw her targets.

I called up Ski, "Remind her not to tell anyone."

"I just did, and she nodded."

We continued, stopping at the same FSBs and changing gunners out of sight of the ground troops. It was incredible watching the Dollies. I was getting a stiff neck trying to turn and look over my shoulder.

Finally, I said, "Take us home, Jerry." He went around some trees, through some others. I turned and said, "Ladies of the Red Cross, please enjoy the ride home. There will be no drinks or treats because we forgot the stewardess. We'll be home in 30. I will call CL and have your transportation ready to whisk you to showers and a few cocktails before dinner. Thank you for choosing the Firebirds and hope you enjoyed your flight."

We landed, and I asked the ladies to be slow getting in the truck. Then, I took Steph's hand, and we walked around the revetment. We kissed, and she whispered in my ear. "I wish you could feel how turned on I am from shooting that machine gun. It's going to be a shame to waste it."

"I'm amazed by you," I said. "Everything you do! I can't stand it, being so close and not holding you in my arms for the rest of the night."

One of the girls yelled, "Steph."

I held her hand all the way to the truck. I helped her up by pushing her butt. She turned and said, "I like that."

I said, "I love you," and she said it back.

Chapter 51.

A "FRIENDLY FIRE" INCIDENT

Back at CL, I found a note on my bed to check with the CO. I walked to his office. Top had on his flight jacket and said, "Go on in."

I said, "Top you look like one mean son of – a-a-a whatever."

Top said, "One mean dog?"

"Yes, but the Top Dog."

"It's OK, Mac. I like one mean son of a bitch or meanest dog in the valley."

I reported in. Major Mathews said, "Sit down, Mac. How'd it go?"

"I think the ladies were satisfied. I let all of them fire the 60 twice for most of a fifteen minute session, each time including your friend, Donna Reynolds. She said to tell you 'Thank you very much,' and they weren't going to walk to the LZs in protest."

Major Mathews said, "Thank *you* very much. You are scheduled to fly up to Baldy at 0800 for five to six days. We have two fire teams in the southern AO. We're shorthanded, so don't get hurt."

"Yes sir. Who's going to tell the NVA?"

He smiled. "You do that. Send them your calling card."

I walked out to the front room and asked Thompson if he could get a Firebird Jacket and put on a GB patch, jump wings, combat infantry, helo wings, and Colonel Wheaton's nickname: Mess with the Best, Die with the Rest.

Thompson said, "No problem Mac. I'll send the order to Danang."

"If anyone needs me, I'll be at our ammo dump. Can you take me?"

The place was appropriately named. It was a dump.

Every item from bullets to rockets was mixed together. I opened the C model Huey Tech Manual and checked all the weapons that the C model could carry. One item of interest: It said, "Store white phosphorus rockets nose down." I got all the rockets in order with a name on the rack holding them. Then, I went to the bullets, smoke grenades, lethal grenades, and cannon shells. This took till 1900. I caught a ride back to the 71st.

The chow hall was open. They worked long hours. I walked in and grabbed a tray. Ten minutes later, as I was slowly eating, in walked the CO. He sat down with me.

"I just came from our ammo dump. My god, did the birds help you?"

I said, "No sir. I did that"

"Tell me about the white phosphorus rockets stored nose down."

"It's in the manual. The WP can ignite spontaneously if it comes in contact with oxygen, though not often. If it does with the nose down in these racks, it will burn itself out and not fly away unguided and hit who knows what?"

"This dinner is not up to GB standards, is it?"

"No sir. It's not."

"I hate to add this to your list of things to do, but can you clean up Baldy's FB ammo dump?"

"I can do that, sir."

"Great."

He got up and said, "Good luck," and walked out.

I stopped by the CO's office. Thompson was still there. I asked him if he could fix up a Firebird jacket with the name Stephanie Rheem. Wings above her name and on other side put Dead Eye and a Firebird patch and a U S Army patch, Americal Patch, and First Aviation Brigade.

He said, "No problem, sir."

I gave him a twenty with my thanks. I went to the bar to see if Norm Griffin, rattler 1-8, was there. There he was, drinking with a group of slick drivers. He had a beer and a crown in front of him, so I bought one of each and delivered them personally.

I said, "Excuse me, but I owe this guy for picking the Dollies and me up from a hot area."

He said, "Thanks Mac, but you got 98 % of the NVA before I got there. They were taking some shots at us on TO, but not many. Anyway, thanks. No one has bought me drinks for that before! By the way Mac I had three bullet holes in my ship."

"All the more reason to buy you a drink." I got a crown to chug and a beer to go.

I was in the mess hall at 0630 when in walks 9-5 Rivers and crew. My crew came in a minute later with Bob Clearwater, my old FNG roomie. He walked over, put his gear on the table, and went to the chow line. He returned and sat down.

I said, "What brings you to the Birds?"

"Same reason as you, Mac. I didn't like getting shot at while I just sat there. I wanted to fight back."

"How long have you been in the Birds?"

"Two weeks. I'm familiar with all the weapon systems. I've been on a dozen missions in that big hog."

"Great." I said. "Do you have your tooth brush?"

He patted his chest pocket and grinned. "I pack light. I'm prepared for the squalor in the Hilton. I've slept there a few nights with the Birds while on flare duty."

"We take off in an hour. Have you done a takeoff in a loaded hog?"

"No, I haven't."

"You'll do lots of flying with me. Maybe one day, you'll let me take off in a private jet to a beach in the Bahamas."

He said, "Deal," and we shook.

"Let's go hunting."

All eight of us tossed our gear in the truck and climbed in. It took less than five minutes to reach the Firebird line.

I said, "Rock and roll," and Bob did a nice three bounce and a short slide TO.

Five minutes after TO, we got a call from HQ to help a convoy. They were headed to LZ Motor Pool. "They're in a firefight just east of Hawk Hill, about 22 clicks from here."

"Tell them just a few minutes," I replied. "When we get close, I'll ask for all the info."

"Long drive convoy 6, this is Firebird 97, a team of two gunships. Sit rep."

Long Drive Convoy 6 said, "They're up on two hills on the west side of the road. I'm worried that more troops will come to help them while we're pinned down."

"I see your line of trucks. I'll drop down and come in from their south. We'll shoot and break right over you. HQ said you've worked with guns before. Rockets and 40mm cannon, then more rockets and Gatling guns with door gunners on both sides."

"Yes, I've worked with guns several times."

"OK, we're coming up over a hill for surprise." I punched off ten rockets on the first hill and ten on the second, and then broke. 9-5 was doing great until a 51 cal opened up on him. I turned with cyclic and pedals, put my selector to four, and punched once. Eight rockets hit that gun, and it was silenced. I called 9-5 and said, "Are you OK?"

He said, "My copilot Elliott is dead. Shit, he just got out of the hospital at Danang from the Laos mission. A 51 came up through the floor and blew his leg off above the knee. Fox and Marshall dropped his seat back and pulled him to where they could get a tourniquet on him. It just wasn't enough. The wound was huge."

"I think I got that bastard. Eight rockets and some small explosions after that. You fly back to CL. I'm going to make one more pass and dump everything on those two hills."

"I'm going in on your tail. Elliott would want some payback."

I clicked back twice and rolled in while talking to 6 on the ground. "Are you taking any fire?"

He answered, "No."

I said, "We're dumping everything on this pass. We will rearm and come back after we get another pilot, if you need us."

9-5 said, "I called CL and gave them the info. They said they'd have a few extra hands to help rearm."

We landed at CL, and trucks with a body bag were waiting, along with another wing ship. Ralph Spencer was also waiting to fly with 9-5. When 9-5 landed, Ralph and the 9-5 crew were taken to another wing ship, so theirs could be cleaned. Elliott's body parts were all over the cockpit.

The fuel trucks came and filled us up to half a tank. Six guys loaded rockets and then started on the 40mm. We were ready in fifteen minutes. I got in the air and called the convoy, and they said they were moving without any hostile fire. They also said a team had gone up those two hills and found fifteen dead and three wounded. "The MP's are coming to get the prisoners."

"If you need us, we're going to Baldy."

"Roger that."

We flew to Baldy, rat racing while listening to The Doors and Neil Diamond. It went well. More training for Ralph Spencer. We had just landed at Baldy when HQ called. "A platoon of SVNA regulars with an Aussie advisor have run into resistance." I got the call sign, freq and coords.

It is just fucking incredible how we keep flying as if nothing has happened. A guy just died. We can put that shit out of our minds for a while, but it comes back, especially at night.

Off we went. As I approached, I saw the SVN in some brush with a rice paddy dike for protection. I told Koala 6 that I would be coming in west to east over the village and break to my right away from him, and my wing would follow.

I came in shooting as did the crew. I shot buildings and guys in the street. They were shooting M-16's, our weapons. I got a call from Koala 6 that I was shooting his troops. I said, "This is bullshit. 9-5 follow me. I'm going to overfly that village." As I approached, I received more fire. I said, "Shoot those bastards and keep the cannon on them." I called Koala 6 and said, "The enemy in the village are wearing SVN uniforms and shooting at me. Do you confirm 9-5?"

"Yes, they're wearing SVN uniforms, and they're shooting at me as well."

I said, "Kill 'em. Those could be stolen uniforms, and anyway they're shooting at us. Fuck, this is war. Those little shits are shooting at us. That's a big fucking mistake. Go off the grid. Keep shooting at those sons of bitches. They're still shooting at us.

"Koala 6, if those are your troops in the village they're in big trouble if we make another gun run on them."

"I believe they are," Koala 6 replied. "They had the troops on each end of our line go into the village and plunder it. We told all the VN to vacate the village yesterday. We said we were going in to look for contraband. I guess our guys knew there were some choice items in there. My number two went in to check on the status of those troops. He just returned and gave me the info I just gave you."

"Hey 6, you told me to shoot those fucking vermin, and I did. When I flew over the village, they shot at me, so my wing and I put rockets on their worthless little asses. And unless you get control of those lying bastards, I'm going to make another run."

I circled the village at 1000 feet and a few hundred yards away. Koala 6 had called in Dust Off and some slicks as the body count was high.

I thought *what a fucking mess. SVN robbing their own people and shooting at their allies.*

I circled with 9-5 for thirty minutes while ships came in to evacuate the wounded and carry out the dead. When this was completed, I told Aussie 6, "I'm going back to CL and wait for the investigation."

I told the crew to write down everything they remembered, because we would all be questioned separately. "So, I'm not going to say anything to you. Those stupid people need something to do so fuck 'em. They can look for me."

We landed. I called Monty and asked him if he got that mission on tape. He said, "Yes sir. As I told you before, I've heard some wild shit."

I said, "Great. Monty, could you have someone fly that down the road to the 71st and hand deliver it to Major Thompson?"

"Will do Mac."

"When the slick gets here, my three crew members will have their statements copied for you to deliver to your legal department. The other copy goes to our CO. I'm going to talk to my CO and then go to Baldy and work on the Bird's ammo dump."

I helped rearm the ship, checked CL's ammo dump and then caught a ride to the company area when a replacement lead was ready to travel to Baldy. I went into the CO's office and said, "Sir, this also involves the EMs in my crew." The Major nodded and Top said, "Thank you, sir."

I spun around and looked at Top, and he just smiled. He'd never said *sir* to me.

I reported all to the Major and Top. The Major recorded my statement. "Sir, now you understand why we didn't work with them in Laos. On our first mission, they landed in a field two clicks away. When the shooting began, they all ran back to their King Bees helos

Kelly McHugh

and returned to RP and then Danang. The bad news is we killed forty of those SVN today. I don't know how many we wounded. I know the regulations sir. I'm grounded until the investigation is completed."

They were amazed at what I reported. I asked if I could return to Baldy and go to work at our little ammo dump. "I almost forgot," I said. "I told Ski and Tyler to give you a carbon copy, Top. I assume the copies will get to the Major."

I then caught a ride to Baldy to work on the Bird's ammo dump. As I finished, a jeep drove in from Baldy HQ, and the driver said I was needed in CL.

"Corporal, how soon did they want me, and how am I supposed to get there?"

He said, "A Huey just finished hauling wounded and will be here soon."

I went up to Baldy's HQ and asked if a copy of the cluster fuck had been sent to my CO.

"I sent the original to your CO, Mac, as you asked."

The Huey from CL arrived, and I jumped in. I didn't say a word. A jeep was waiting for me when we landed at the Firebird's revetments. I went to the ammo dump for a quick look. It still looked in order. I was relieved. I caught a ride from a guy who was waiting for me.

I walked in and asked Top, "Who wants to see me?"

He said, "I don't know, Mac."

I said, "I'm going to the Birdhouse. When those assholes want me, tell them you have no idea."

I went to the Birdhouse. There were two new FB sitting in the party room shootin' the shit. They introduced themselves as Neil Bettencourt (Archy) and Neil (Nelly) Alford from Wyoming and Michigan, respectively. They had just finished the FNG flying routine. "Captain Wilder said he had a couple of openings," they told me.

I grabbed a cold beer and chugged it. I was nursing a second beer when a Captain came in with two LT's and the CO. The Captain asked me my name. I said, "What's your name, and why are you asking me mine?" I could see his name on his uniform, and he could see mine. Two could play his stupid game.

That caught him off guard. He fumbled around for twenty seconds, and then he asked me my name again, and I gave him the same answer.

360

He looked at the CO and said, "He is being disrespectful."

The CO said, "No. He's within his rights."

I said, "You're the most amazing material I've met in this little piece of hell where you want to hang our people. You come in here with the attitude that I'm already guilty. I have to get an attorney before I deal with you and your kind. Why don't you grab both ears and pull your head out of your ass … sir?"

He turned and walked out. I went back to drinking. I was curious what anyone was going to say. This was pretty much cut-and-dried SVN army troop activities.

The next morning, an attorney for me drove in from CL HQ, and I briefed him before I was called in for questioning. I was the last one called in. I told my story, and then the attorney who wanted me hung started asking questions. I asked him where he got his info. He said, "From the commander of the ARVN troops in CL."

"It looks like you have been lied to and are very gullible," I said. "Who exactly are you covering for? Is it the Aussie or the worthless SVN army? Everyone has been telling you lies except me and my crew and the wing."

"Wait, what's a wing?"

I looked at him. "Is this your first encounter with aviation?"

"What difference does that make?"

"From the nature of your questions, sir, you are clueless."

I looked at the CO and said, "Is it time, sir?"

He said, "Yes."

As he was pulling the recorder out of his pocket, I added, "My crew chief took pictures of the SVN troops in the empty buildings and hooches. They'll be developed by tomorrow."

I thought the captain was going to have a heart attack. To make matters worse for him, the tape began playing, and it wasn't anything like what he had said.

He blurted out, "What's that?"

I looked at him and put my index finger up to my lips, indicating he should be quiet.

When the tape ended, my attorney, a major, said, "I want your list of all the people you interviewed. I also want the name of the officer who told you to lie and hang this pilot out to dry. An American by the way, just like you. I want that officer's name now, or I go to a quick court marshal and you will be disbarred. And spend time in Leavenworth (Military prison in Kansas). Do you understand?"

He gave a very quiet, "Yes sir." He gave the name of some colonel in charge of working with the SVN army. It figured. The poor guy was ordered to lie by someone above him to cover this up.

The major turned to me. "Mr. McNally, what would you have us do with this attorney?"

"He is pathetic," I said. "I know he was assigned to prosecute me, but he did no preparation and assumed I was guilty. See if you can have any say in who he defends and have him defend the Americans at the bottom of the ladder. He already knows the shitty things they do at the top of the ladder. Also, any case he loses goes up for immediate appeal. I say this because his IQ is the same number as my shoe size."

"Done Mac," the Major said. "By the way, if you ever want to consider the legal field for work, call me."

I said, "Thank you, sir. What will they do with the commander of the VN platoon?"

"Shit Mac, who knows. This is VN. It depends on his father's position in the Government. There will be no charges on the Aussie as he was in an advisory position."

I looked at the CO and said, "Can I go back to work?"

"Yes, you can Mac. What's next on your list?"

"I was almost finished with the Bird's ammo dump at Baldy, and I still have another five to six days of flying out of Baldy. I have one other item, sir. Someone is changing the storage positon of the Willy Pete. I had them nose down as specified, but they are now all sitting nose up. How do I handle that, Sir?"

"It must be a Bird. I'll talk to Wilder. I have one other item. Your last two ships to go down have been recovered. There is a new hog waiting for you down at the FB line. I've sent Thompson to get your crew and Rivers' crew so you can get back to Baldy ASAP."

"Thank you, sir. Oh, by the way, what was the body count?"

"You really tore them up for just one shortened gun run. Forty-two dead and thirty-five wounded, and some of them might not make it. Two have already died at the hospital"

I just nodded. *Shit, they were on our side.*

Chapter 52.

YOU CALL, WE KILL

When I got to the flight line, Bob Clearwater gave me a thumb's up and pointed at the new ship. Rivers was also ready. I said, "Rock and roll," and he took off. I asked him how he was doing. He gave thumbs up.

We cleared CL air space when I called Rivers. "Hey, good buddy, wanna rat race? Rock and roll is on the Armed Forces VN station."

"Let's do it, Mac."

"OK, we'll start slow as this a first time for my copilot."

I turned to Bob. "This gunship has limitations. It doesn't fly like a slick. I'll start with all types of maneuvers, and wing has to always be in place to shoot at anyone shooting at me. Ski and Tyler will throw out a smoke grenade to where he should've been able to shoot. If I break right, he will break left. If he breaks the same way as me he will be in front of us, and that will cost him some beers. After we've caught him a few times, we'll switch, and you will have to stay on him."

While I was talking, I was making slow gradual turns. "Bob get on the controls with me." I called 9-5 and said, "Let's ramp this up."

Click-click

Now, I was making sharper turns, just barely over the trees, climbs and dives. As I broke right, so did wing. "Throw a smoke Ski. What color?"

"Purple"

"9-7 practice taking fire 9 o'clock; Purple smoke."

I asked 9-5 if his copilot knew about the beers.

"He's just been reminded."

"OK, let's go." I gave total control to Bob. He was really enjoying this. It went on for several minutes when Tyler said, "Red smoke 3 o'clock." I transmitted that info, and we got him. Another beer. "9-5 take the lead."

Click-click.

"Stay back and above and off to the side," I told Bob. "When he breaks right, you break left. Then, you will be in position to shoot behind and that means behind the smoke also. Remember he's going 120 knots. It's just more of the same you did with the Birds down south."

For several minutes, Bob hadn't missed a beat. Finally, he lost concentration and made a mistake.

"We just lost a beer," I told him.

I turned the music up, and we relaxed the rest of the way to Baldy.

After we landed, I checked the ammo dump, and all was well. I walked over to the MASH and checked in for a routine exam of my last wounds. For my reward, I was given another injection of syrup. It burned, and my butt cheek hurt when I sat on anything, especially the Huey's seat.

Back at the Hilton, I told my new copilot, "When we get a briefing, you start forming your plan, which should include, 'Hope for the best, but plan for the worst.'"

The red phone rang, and the choreographed maneuvers to the ships were perfect.

"Apparently, a patrol of ten is pinned down by a 51," I told Bob. "They are six clicks south of LZ Center in some real tiger country (steep terrain and no flat spots). This mission might be a GTFO (get the fuck out) while we do an OPHA (one pass and haul ass). That 51 is a powerful weapon. Our only advantage is surprise and unpredictability."

I turned to business. "Big Sky 6, this FB 9-7, a gunship team of two inbound to your location. Can you hear us coming?"

"Yes, I see you now. Here comes my smoke."

"I've got yellow. Where are they from your location? Is it a hill or in a bunker?"

"They're 230 degrees from us. There are some trees up there, and that's all I can tell."

"OK, that helps. I'll come in from their east, very low and rise up to get their attention and fire rockets if able. My wingman will come in from the west. 9-5, do you have questions or suggestions?"

"None."

"OK. Wing break right and go to FSB Motor Pool, then straight south to the river and you're on their blind side. Big Sky 6, you heard the plan. It will begin in about 1 minute."

I flew south staying in valleys so the NVA wouldn't see or hear me. Actually, there were Hueys flying all over this country, so one more shouldn't have been a big deal.

I called 9-5. "Are you in position?"

"Yes."

I said, "Let's go," and in we went. I saw the 51 shoot an occasional burst to keep the patrol trapped. I came in, and they were trying to turn the gun towards me when I put in a cluster of rockets on that 51. Wing came in shooting and surprised the shit out of them. The mini gun got the runners, which were few. They were running towards the dead 51. I kept flying past the 51 site and saw a cave behind where the runners had emerged. I banked away.

"9-5, I'm going straight in and punch some rockets in there. Don't follow me in. If it explodes, you will be in big trouble."

"Thanks for thinking about us."

"I always do."

I had some distance from the cave, so I broke to my right. I said, "Let's rock and roll. Ski, Tyler, kill anything that moves." I turned my rocket selector switch to five, which meant one tap on the red button and five pairs would come out of the pods.

I had everything lined up and pushed the red button twice (twenty rockets total) and broke hard left to put a hill between me and the cave. Twenty rockets tore into that opening and just a moment later fire blasted 300 yards out of the entrance. Then the top of the mountain exploded like a volcano. I was moving farther away and felt the shock wave. It buffeted our ship like a toy. I said, "Let's go home." I called Big Sky and asked how he was doing.

He said, "Thanks, you saved ten lives. People at Center are going to hear about you crazy bastards. LZ Center is forever in debt to the Firebirds."

"Any time. You call; we kill. Our motto. OK Birds, lets return to the Hilton."

When we landed at Baldy, a mutt came up to our ships as we were shutting down and adopted us. We called him Barko. He was a friendly, silly black-and-white mutt. He wouldn't leave. The wing pilot asked if he could be an NVA spy.

I said, "Ask him."

He was always happy when we returned from a mission. We usually had a couple of grunts watch him when we flew. We didn't want to leave him alone because the Vietnamese consider dog a delicacy.

There was one problem with Barko. He would try to jump in the back of our ship when we hovered into the revetment. We were afraid he would get under a skid. Sometimes, either Ski or Tyler would jump out and pick him up and hold him while I hovered into the revetment.

He would occasionally jump into a slick. But then, one of the guys in back would lean out and drop him about one or two feet, then the pilot could pull up six feet and hover away. Slicks had the power to get away.

We came up with a plan we thought would change Barko's mind about helos. Wing's gunner said he would make Barko a parachute harness. He had been in the 82nd Airborne and liked to jump out of perfectly good aircraft. He said "Mac, there is no such thing as a perfectly safe aircraft." I knew he was correct, but a Firebird was the least safe aircraft in Vietnam. I didn't press him about it. He showed a hooch maid at Baldy how to sew together a harness, and he used a parachute we stole from one of the flare ship's flares. When Barko jumped in a helo, we'd go up and drop him out. He'd be OK coming down with the parachute, but maybe it would scare him enough that he'd stop doing it.

The next time Barko jumped in, we implemented our plan. The ship took off and climbed to 1000 feet. Barko was fitted with the parachute and thrown out. He was coming down right over Baldy when a gust of wind pushed him outside our concertina wire and over a flooded rice paddy. The poor dog was struggling just to keep his head above water. The slick saw what was happening and came down over the water, and someone jumped out and picked him up before he drowned.

We all thought this would convince Barko that he didn't want to jump into any more helos. It did not. Old Barko made four more parachute jumps. He was now qualified to be an airborne Ranger Dog. That was something. We were positive he was the only airborne dog in VN. We sewed a set of jump wings on his harness. He loved us. He would run in circles around us when we rearmed the ships. We always brought him food from the mess hall. He liked it a lot more than we did.

After he made his fifth jump, the MP's came to the Hilton when we were on a mission and shot him. There had been a rabid dog on the FSB who bit two people, so the commander had ordered all dogs shot just to be safe.

Shit, it didn't matter who or what you were, you could die in this hell hole. I wonder what those fucking commanders and MPs would think if I fucking killed their dog.

We missed Barko. Another damn casualty of war.

Eventually, we were relieved by another gun team, so we could get back to CL and clean up, write a letter home, and then drink to put everything in perspective.

We were putting everything in perspective when the CO came and said he had a message from HQ. We were to ration our rockets. A large cargo ship with rockets had broken down in the middle of the ocean. It was being towed by another large ship, also filled with our rockets, traveling at five knots (5.75 mph).

We started processing this info. We never wasted any rockets. I imagined what they would tell the ground troops. "Sorry fellas, but we don't have an alternate plan, and we never plan ahead." *SHIT.*

The CO pulled me into a corner and said, "That was an amazing mission blowing up that cave. Center sent a company of men (200) and found parts of 50 people, some were Chinese and Russian mixed in with the NVA. Parts of twenty 51 cal machine guns, grenades, rockets, land mines, mortars, bullets, clothing, and I should add that there were parts of 20 women. From what clothes they found, the women didn't come to fight. They were Saigon prostitutes. Motivators for the troops. Adding the KIA'S found that made 70 people. We don't know how many you atomized. Most of their fire power exploded. HQ estimates twenty tons of explosive were in that cave." As he was leaving, he said, "You guys get two days off."

I said, "Thank you, sir."

Several birds came up to me and said, "Let's go to the Birdhouse." There, we continued drinking but with better booze. We had come by some scotch and rum to go along with our shitty gin. The rocket shortage was the main topic of conversation. After two scotches, I said, "I have an idea. Let's go steal them." This mostly brought out negative responses.

I said, "No, I'm serious. We get a deuce and a half, put on unmarked shirts. I'll get an order from Thompson, and I'll drive. Who wants to go with me?"

Tom Rivers said, "I'll go."

"Great, get some booze for the return trip. I don't want to smell like a brewery driving in there. Anyone got any after shave? I'm going to brush my teeth. Tom, stop over at Ski's and get two unmarked shirts. Allen, steal a truck and a can of spray paint to cover the numbers on the truck."

That was it. The mission was planned. We were ready to go. I went to company HQ and asked the corporal on duty to wake Thompson. When Thompson came in, I explained the plan. "We're going to take the rockets that normally go to the company on the southern edge of our AO. Their source comes in from Saigon. Ours is Danang. Those guys south of us don't see much action. They won't miss their rockets."

He typed the order as I told him, including the number of rockets I suggested. I scribbled a signature and then I told Thompson to throw the carbon copy away. This meeting did not happen.

He nodded and said, "I hope Leavenworth is a better place than they say."

Tom Rivers and I put on the shirts without any identification and got into the truck. I ground some gears looking for first gear, then second, and no more shifting on our bomb-cratered road out to Highway One.

Highway One was a little better. I looked over to Tom. "Got that booze I requested?"

He smiled. "I hoped you would ask because I don't want to be sober when we drive into that ammo depot."

I laughed. "Neither do I, now that I think about this mission.

That liquid courage can help you do what needs to be done."

He handed me a canteen. "Don't chug it. It is pure Crown."

I took a mouthful and tried to swallow slowly. It was more than I thought. My eyes were watering as I handed the canteen back. He took a pull. "God damn that shit is potent," he said after swallowing his own mouthful.

"I know, but one more drink, and I should be as brave as I was back at the Birdhouse."

This fucking war is making us crazy. I sure won't put any of this in my after-flight-school book.

I said, "Tom, do you think you'll make it through your year?"

"Honestly, Mac, No. You and I are living on borrowed time."

"Tom, if you want to fly with anyone else, it's OK with me. I know I fly into a lot more shit storms than the other pilots."

"No Mac. It's not that. Any one of us can get blown away in just a heartbeat. How many bullets have come through our Plexiglas? Fuck, I quit counting. Mac, I love flying with you. I learn something every time we go up."

I thought about that for a minute, and then I changed the subject. "You have to become a person without a conscience," I told him. "Ask for forgiveness, not permission. It could take a week for the REMF's to authorize shooting at an enemy who's in a safe village. But, why did he shoot at us, if it was a friendly village?" This had been on my mind a lot after the friendly fire mission.

Tom seemed to be listening, so I went on.

"Just keep thinking about the entire mission. Situational awareness. And then you're ready for any surprise, or at least most of the surprises. The 51 is the worst." I knew I was preaching, so I shut up. I had said, without a conscience, but it wasn't really that easy.

"Shit Tom, I'm sobering up. Give me some more of that liquid courage." I had two more mouthfuls and more eye watering. Tom took two big mouthfuls.

The ammo dump was huge. I don't know how many acres, but a lot of them. I stopped at the gate and handed the guard the requisition form. He wrote down the number of pallets of HE rockets and handed the form back. "Drive down this row. When it ends, turn right and drive to the man with the flashlight. I'll call him, and he'll load you up and get you out of here ASAP."

"Thanks, these hours suck."

He said, "I already know that."

I laughed and drove. It took ten minutes to load twelve pallets of rockets. The pallets were double stacked, so they tied them down like professional truckers. The loader handed me a form to give to the guys at the gate. I handed the guard the form which itemized what I had received. It also named the company that received them. Hell, I was so gutsy I even signed the phony name with confidence.

We held our breaths for a quarter of a mile. I looked over to Tom for the canteen, and he was already drinking. I said, "Hurry up! I'm dying of thirst."

He handed me the canteen and said, "Fuckin' A man. I wouldn't have believed it, if you'd told me the story of what we just did. Shit Mac. Now you see why I like flying with you. You don't take 'no rockets' for an answer. If you need rockets, you do what needs to be done."

I took two long pulls. *Shit, my throat burns, but it's a good burn.*

Twenty minutes later, we pulled up to the Firebird line. I got on the phone and called maintenance and said we needed a forklift. A few minutes later, it arrived, and we began unloading. I called the Birdhouse and said, "We need bodies down here to build rockets, and I have booze." Fifteen minutes later, a deuce and a half rolled up with many of the pilots and crews of The Birds. They looked at me, and I said, "Don't ask."

Jerry Wilder, the Bird's platoon leader, walked up to me and said, "What's going on, Mac?"

I said, "Sir, if I tell you, you become involved. If you don't know, you have plausible deniability."

He paused to take this in. Then, he shook his head, maybe in disbelief. "Damn, that's a big pile of rockets." He looked over the crowd of Birds who'd come to help. "I'll ask you next month." But he stayed to help.

We left three pallets next to the conex containers and another three hidden behind them. With a crowd of Birds, we assembled and finished those other six pallets in an hour.

Then, I said to Jerry, "You tired?"

He said, "Mac, I'm so tired, I don't care what kind of felony we committed tonight." He'd taken my hint and hadn't asked me anything more. "Fuck it," he said. "Let's go home and get to bed."

"Before you climb into the truck," I suggested to everybody, "look under the passenger's seat."

While that was happening, I checked the ammo dump and made a few changes, just to put everything in proper order. They looked where I said and found two bottles of Crown Royal under the seat with two cases of beer.

I said, "Who wants to drive?" and the crews said, "You do." I started laughing.

Wilder said, "I'll keep you company up front. Besides I saw you grab two beers."

Rivers handed him one and them jumped in the back.

We climbed in the truck, and I drove very slowly, so we could get rid of the evidence. Someone in back was kind enough to hand a bottle of crown through Wilder's window. A voice said, "I want that back, very close to the level you see on that bottle."

Jerry took a pull and handed it to me. I took two and gave it back. "You are one behind me," I pointed out, so he took a drink and put his arm out the window and loudly said, "What do you want me to do with this bottle?" A hand reached out and took it.

We were almost to the parade grounds. The motor pool was fifty yards from the CO's building and hooch. I pulled into the motor pool and coasted past all the vehicles, so it wouldn't be heard.

After I parked, I said, "Be quiet. Put the empties in the large garbage can and then walk down to the water and then turn left and come back in the company area to find your hooch."

Ski said, "We got it, Mac. Thanks for the booze."

I said, "Any time Ski, and if I don't have it, I'll get some."

The next morning, Thompson stuck his head in the hooch and said, "May I come in?"

Someone said, "Hell yes. Whatcha got from the CO?"

"He wants Mac up there in thirty minutes."

Someone yelled back, "You go wake him. I'm in the middle of a really nasty dream."

Thompson came over. "Sir, wake up. The CO wants to see you in thirty minutes."

"OK, OK. I got it. Any idea what it's about?"

"No sir."

Then, he turned and actually jogged out the door.

"Shit, I can't get any fucking rest even when I'm supposed to be off duty."

I reported in, and the CO said, "Sit down Mac. First of all, the IG inspectors are coming through today, and I want to make sure the ammo dump is ready. And before you answer, I was wondering if the Birds had any involvement at CL's main ammo dump?"

"Sir, if you have no knowledge of anything, then you have plausible deniability and can hold to your oath as an officer. If I tell you differently, you then will become involved." I just stood there and waited.

He said, "Thank you, Mac. I'll check with you later, and you can give me the true story."

"OK sir, then it's off to Baldy for a long stay."

Chapter 53.

BIRD ON FIRE

A few minutes after we returned to Baldy, we received an urgent call from a patrol three clicks north of LZ West.

We're starting the war early today.

On the way to the LZ, I thought about how things were really heating up in our AO. The bad guys were everywhere with larger and more powerful weapons. Our ships remained the same. We didn't have more powerful weapons or more gunships. The only thing we had was more vulnerability.

We received a sit rep and a smoke grenade. I rolled in and punched off eight rockets and made my right break, when I began sliding forward. I wasn't sure what was happening. Adding to my confusion, I was now also sliding to the right and was wedged into the right arm rest.

Shit, I forgot to fasten my seat belt and shoulder harness.

I knew I was tired, but I didn't realize how tired. I looked over at Bob. "You got it. Keep climbing until wing says, 'Ready,' and then lay it over on my side." All the time I was fumbling with the straps to get all four of the ends together, so I could clamp them. I got it done, but my heart was racing.

"Thanks Bob, I got it. Keep shooting into the trees on the left, and I'll take the right and in front of us." We rolled in and were on target. As I broke, I could feel a banging on the bottom of my ship.

Wing called out, "51, 200 yards up the hill on the left. I put six rockets on 'em, and they stopped shooting. Fuck Mac, you're streaming fuel."

Ski said, "Mac, we're on fire."

I started looking for a place to auto rotate, when a small

explosion pushed our tail upward and the nose dropped. The sun was behind me, so I could see, and it looked strange, as I went nose low as if to do a summersault. I pulled the cyclic as far back as I could until I hit the stops. Then, we waited. It would all happen in a few seconds. If we went over onto our back, we would be dead. Slowly the nose came up as the engine quit. I bottomed the collective, and we went into autorotation. I knew there was a second explosion coming, a huge one as the gas in the tank exploded.

The fire was being fanned by the speed of the autorotation. I had no choice since I was free-falling without an engine. I gave the mayday call. Now, the fire was coming inside. I didn't have time to look back. Things got worse. The fire was coming around me, the crew, and the copilot, and that made it difficult to see the ground. The cabin was filling with smoke. I was moving my head around in quick short jerking movements to find the ground and get away from the fire. Then, I remembered to jettison the rocket pods to reduce weight.

I leaned my head over my right shoulder and outside. There it was, next to a trail and a line of trees, a bare spot. I pulled back on the cyclic to slow the forward air speed and then up with the collective to let us down gently. It was actually a little harder landing than I wanted. We still had fuel which made us heavy.

I shouted, "Grab anything you can fight with."

Shit, I couldn't see a fucking thing. My eyes were burning and watering. I'm not sure how I landed.

We got out. Ski and Tyler had each managed to take their M-60s. I yelled, "Bob, grab the other handle on Tyler's ammo box." I grabbed Ski's other handle, and then I gave a rare order: "Run! This ship is going to explode." We were about fifty yards away when it blew up. It threw the 6000 pound transmission and rotor blades 100 feet out to the side from the burning ship. The concussive force knocked all four of us to the ground. I looked back and was surprised to see the fire had blown itself out. As we got up and collected ourselves, I saw wing flying towards us. They punched a pair of rockets into the trees 200 yards away.

Hell that meant the enemy was looking for us. It's not difficult to find a burning helicopter. Lots of thick black smoke was still rising from the hot metal. The flames rose fifty feet before the explosion.

"Help should be here any time now," I said. "Let's keep going until we see them. We got wing flying cover. There are a lot of slicks out here."

Wing made three more passes and shot the rest of their rockets and mini gun rounds. Then, they departed. They were probably running on fumes. I worried because those NVA can move fast. They would catch up to us soon. We headed up the trail.

After thirty minutes, those little fuckers were closing in on us. I said, "Let's set up an ambush. This is a good place. The trees are dense, so they'll have to use the trail, and they'll expose themselves completely when they round that bend. Ski and Tyler will be the gunners. Bob and I will feed you. Shoot at the last guys first, so they can't retreat. Bob, have you ever fed an M-60?"

He said, "No."

"Neither have I. I have, however, watched these two cowboys feed with one hand and shoot with the other. Tyler, explain to Bob what you want. You have four or five minutes. Ski, explain what you want me to do."

"Mac, you already know," Ski said. "Just keep the bullets coming. Keep the rounds parallel to the ground. Don't let the ammo belt twist. That will jam the gun."

"Our wingman departed about forty minutes ago," I told them, "so he should be back soon." Then I thought of something. "Did anyone grab a smoke grenade?"

Tyler pulled his flak jacket open and smiled, "Will a red one do?"

Ski opened his and said, "How about purple?"

I said, "You two are amazing. Are you taking notes, Bob?"

"Damn right, Mac."

"Ski and Tyler, pick out your gun positions."

They chose two thick trees. They set themselves up beside those, tight in for maximum camouflage and cover. We moved the ammo boxes and got set. I could see up the trail for 100 yards or so. *At least, they can't come in behind us.* I was hoping there weren't many remaining after the ordinance 9-5 dumped on them.

A few minutes passed. Everyone looked a little antsy. I said, "If you two don't hit anyone, Bob and I are taking over." Ski and Tyler rolled their eyes at that comment.

Ski said, "Don't make me laugh. I'll give away our position."

Here they came. There were only eight. I hoped that was all there would be. They hadn't split their forces the way the enemy had with the mercs and green berets.

I told the cowboys, "Shoot when ready." I saw them looking at each other. *He thinks he needs to tell us that? Well, I was nervous.*

For some reason, in that tiny moment of pause, an image of Steph popped into my head. She was radiant and smiling at me. I wondered if I would ever see her again.

Ski and Tyler nodded to each other, and they opened fire as Bob and I discovered how fast we had to move to keep those guns working. We weren't even looking at the enemy. Their guns were silent, so I looked up and counted eight bodies. "Shit, you two never cease to amaze me. Did they get off any shots?"

In unison, "No Mac and you owe us a case of beer."

"Done, but Bob buys half."

Bob said, "The hell with that. I'm getting each one of them a case. The way I see it, Mac, they just saved our two worthless asses."

"Let's move out before you two break an arm slapping each other on the back. Seriously though, thank you. That was incredible. Not one of those bastards got away."

We gathered up the ammo cans and still had 1000 rounds remaining in each.

Then, we heard it: a Huey with that beautiful distinctive wop-wop of the rotor blades. "Let's get out of these trees and pop a smoke."

"Which of you two has the best pitching arm?"

Tyler said, "I do."

"Throw it out in that dry paddy. As they get closer, we run with all our crap. We don't want to block their gunners, in case someone comes out from those trees."

The slick flared and landed, as we sprinted as best we could with two M-60's and more than half our ammo remaining. We lifted in the ammo cans, the 60's, and then us. I gave the thumbs up. Ski and Tyler were on the floor with guns pointed outward. We lifted and raced across the paddy five feet off the ground and then a cyclic climb. Not a shot was fired at us.

One of the slick crew said, "There are a bunch of bodies back there."

The slick driver turned and yelled, "Mac did you make that mess of bodies?"

"No, Ski and Tyler did."

He just shook his head. Then yelled again, "Your ship looks like shit Mac. I don't think it's flyable."

I yelled, "Don't fly too high. We get nose bleeds."

"Yeah, I heard that about you guys."

Then, it hit me. I was out of adrenaline. I leaned back against the firewall and tried to blank out the world.

"Could you drop us off at the flight surgeon?"

"OK. I'll call CL and the Doc. What are the injuries?"

"Burns."

The CO, Top, Platoon leaders for enlisted men, and the pilots were standing on the edge of the landing pad. We slowly climbed out, recovered our flight helmets, M-60's, ammo cans, and our wits. We walked up to the entourage, and I saluted. The other three followed suit. Then, the CO signaled the slick driver to shut it down. The Doc stepped forward and looked at my arms, neck, and upper chest. My brand new two-piece Nomex Flight suit was singed. These new suits were fire retardant, thankfully.

Doc said, "Do these burns hurt?"

I said, "Not until just now."

"Adrenaline, Mac. I told you after our excursion that I didn't want to see you again professionally."

"I tried, but those sons of bitches had bigger guns."

"Let's get you sorry excuses for Firebirds inside, each one of you on a separate table. I have four in the main room."

The CO said he and Wilder would talk to the pilots, and Top and Sergeant McDougall would speak to Ski and Tyler."

We all looked at each other as if to say, *What? Did we fuck up*?

The CO saw this and said, "You guys are not in trouble. Exactly the opposite. Some wild stories are coming in from all over the AO. Our troops were taken in by Hueys and counted over 75 dead. They hauled some out for examination. They also found ammo and guns of every type. Enough to arm three or four companies (600 to 800 troops).

"We're really interested in how you all survived the fire, let alone landed and got out with guns and ammo. You outran them for forty-five minutes and then set up a perfect ambush. And not one of you is infantry. I know some ground pounders who are going to hear about today, and I'm going to love it."

"Sir," I pointed out, "I used to deer hunt. We always monitored the trails to ambush the deer, so to speak."

We were inside lying down by now. I looked across the room and saw Top in his flight jacket. I yelled, "Nice jacket, Top."

He looked at me, smiled and nodded.

Getting my shirt off brought out some shits, fucks and damns.

The doc said, "Second degree burns are the most painful. Third have the nerves burnt away. I'm going to put medicine on them, and it's not going to feel good. You may even threaten me." He smiled, "Seriously, it will help."

The CO said, "I got some info from 9-5, your wing. When he shut down to refuel and rearm, his ship wouldn't start. I can't believe he stayed so long to cover you. He landed on fumes with five holes in his ship and an instrument panel lit up with enough yellow and red lights to read a book. Now, tell me about the ambush."

I told the story with emphasis on the other three. I knew the pilots always got the credit, so I thought it was time for the crew to get theirs. "All four of us got the job done. However, I really believe Ski and Tyler could have pulled off that ambush alone. I'm sure it was easier than hanging out of a gunship at 120 knots. Anyway, the NVA screwed up. The leader of that patrol let his troops walk right into our trap."

While doc was finishing bandaging our burns, the four inquisitors went outside and compared stories.

I learned later what the CO told them. He was impressed that I gave credit to the other three, and they gave me credit. Escaping from a burning helo is not easy. People are getting burned. They can't see. The ship is going to explode. The CO gave me credit for the escape, and 9-5 for prevented the NVA from following right away. He called our ambush "textbook," which I took as high praise when word of his comments got to me.

Doc was ready to let us go. He said, "Go home, and I want all of you here at 1000 tomorrow. That could give you some sleep time after the bar tonight, if the CO doesn't have any jobs for you as punishment for losing one of his ships."

I said, "Jesus, Doc, you're supposed to be neutral."

The CO brought down two jeeps. EMs in one, pilots in the other. We looked strange with all the bandages on our necks, arms and chests

Word got out that the wounded birds were home. What a greeting. While I was still in the jeep, I was handed a crown, and I gulped it. It burned all the way down. I asked for another, and it appeared magically, and I gulped it down like the first. *I don't know if it was the alcohol or the medicine, but the pain was less.*

Before I could even get inside the Birdhouse, Malko was there with a long list of equipment that was lost on my ship. I looked at the list and asked him if I went down in a Huey or ten large Air Force cargo planes. He smiled, but I could tell he was in a hurry. Then, I remembered the IG inspection. I said, "Malko, when is that IG inspection?"

"Soon!"

"You'll have to come visit me in Leavenworth prison."

He took the list and walked away. Not a very personable guy. I walked in the Birdhouse and grabbed a fifth of Crown and a cold case of beer and discovered I could only get them to the door, mostly with my feet. The case hurt my hands, and the pain would return if I tried to lift it. I walked over to Ski and Tyler's hooch and explained my dilemma, and they shot out their door in seconds. The burns on their hands were less than mine. I had been a dumb shit that hadn't put his gloves on. They could easily open the bottles of god's nectar as we sat on the steps of their hooch door.

We popped the first beer, and it went down easily. Then a crown. After an hour I departed for the club. It was wild. The rumor mill was working as the stories were being passed from slicks to guns and back to slicks. I don't have a clue when I went to bed. I woke up at eight in the same clothes.

We jumped in the back of a truck at 0950, unhappily anticipating the doctor's torture. This bandage change went quicker as an extra medic had come over from the hospital. Then, we got the syrup shot in the butt. *Shit*, I almost cried. Then, back to the company area.

When I jumped out of the back of the truck, Thompson was there with Steph's Firebird jacket. It looked fantastic. I couldn't wait to see her face. The CO walked out and said, "Mac, I'm pissed. Top has turned in his paperwork to go to flight school."

"Sir, I told him it wouldn't work. Can you imagine a nineteen-year-old WO chewing out Top for an infraction and telling him he's lower than whale shit?"

The CO started laughing and said, "I hadn't thought of that. I'll tear up the request. Where the hell did you hear that whale shit thing?" He was laughing so hard I could barely understand him.

"That was used on me my first week of flight school."

Chapter 54.

YOU ACTUALLY KILLED SOMEONE

I walked over to the Birdhouse, and it smelled worse than an outhouse. I was in no mood for jokes. I walked into the party room, and there it was. A hooch maid was steaming rice and fish heads on our small one element burner. *How can they eat that shit?* They had been warned before not to cook that crap in the hooch. We have an extension cord. They could cook it outside.

I just felt like shit today. The body does not tolerate constant pain. I sat down and fiddle fucked with my boot laces and pulled off my boots and wool socks that had not left my sweaty feet in several days. I carefully placed the socks in the pot and put the lid back on and grabbed a newspaper to read while I waited. In about thirty minutes, I heard a group of Vietnamese women outside all chattering away about who knows what? Probably how much they dislike Americans. I put down the Stars and Stripes and retrieved my socks and immediately threw them in the garbage. I picked up the paper as they stepped inside to retrieve the pot and take it outside.

There were six of them. They sat in a circle on the sand outside our hooch, and our hooch maid served the tainted rice to each one. They carried their own bowls with them. Almost immediately, they were spitting out the rice and hitting our hooch maid and talking rather loudly in an angry tone. We never had that problem again.

I went back to the paper. It had a rather good article on the Doughnut Dollies. I decided to save it for Steph.

With the thought of Steph, I went up to the CO's office and asked Thompson if he could call HQ up the road and patch us through to the Dollies. He did and asked for Steph before I had a chance to tell him who I wanted. He handed me the phone and said, "I'll stand guard outside."

"Steph?"

"Yes Kevin, how are you? The colonel just told me what you did the other day. My god I was in tears. You are drawn to danger. You must have a leprechaun on your shoulder."

I started to protest that being Irish did not automatically give me access to the services of leprechauns, but she went on.

"I'm so happy to hear your voice. I've got some news for you. Heads up! The colonel is going to have you come and give a talk to some new pilots, GB's, and mercs about your experiences, how quickly you sized up several problems and created instant solutions. I've been asked to attend since I have a top secret clearance. Come early and stay late. You can't fly with those burns, so I'm going to put you on your back and then climb on top and do everything. Oh god, I start tingling all over just thinking about seeing you."

"You ought to see the condition I'm in," I replied. "I'm tingling more than you. The thought of you and these burns has my body confused."

She started laughing. It was like music: soft, sexy, self-assured and soothing.

"I was thinking about you when all that stuff was happening," I said. "That put me on my A game because I was desperate to see you. I wasn't ready to end our relationship out there in the bush. Where have you traveled lately?"

"We've had such boring flights. We did a stop at Baldy. I saw the Hilton. How do you live in that shithole?"

"That shithole was like that when I got there. It's difficult to imagine, but I don't think about it. They say to the victor belong the spoils. What in the hell are the spoils here in VN? 80% of the inhabitants are Buddhists. Aren't they supposed to be pacifists? Don't they spend their lives trying to reach Nirvana, finding their inner selves and being one with nature? What the hell are the Communists going to do with that philosophy and a bunch of farmers?

"We fall asleep from exhaustion. We don't take off anything but our shirts. We have the rotor blades turning in one minute. The adrenaline starts pumping, and we just go. Just like your feeling when shooting that M-60. It puts you in another place where you're in your own universe. Nothing else is passing through your head. You put fear aside."

She said, "Yes, yes, that's exactly what happened. My god, I didn't know that level of concentration and power existed until I fired that machine gun at people and killed them."

"The CO just drove up, so I have to go. I love you. How many children do you want?"

"Two and I love you, too."

I was sitting on the porch with Thompson when the CO arrived. We both jumped up, and he said, "At ease. Mac, come in and sit down."

I came in and sat down.

"Mac, the brass at CL HQ wants you to come up and give a talk on some of your experiences. Are you OK with that?"

"Yes sir. I'm going crazy sitting in the Birdhouse watching these burns heal."

"OK, go pack a clean flight suit and your civvies. We'll leave in 30 minutes. Thompson will drive us. I'm sure your quarters will be ready." He winked. I just smiled. "I want to meet the woman that's tamed 9-7!"

We were on the road in fifteen minutes and at HQ in five.

Standing out in front of HQ but off to the side for privacy was my beautiful Stephanie. We hugged, and I was so happy to hold her I had to consciously tell myself not to squeeze her too hard. She was gorgeous and smelled much better than my friends in CL. I was still wondering why she loved me. I knew I had to get over that. She was a woman who made her own choices. She had had the world at her feet, yet she had chosen to come over here and help these kids. And (apparently) she chose me. It wasn't something I could question, not that I wanted to question it.

She stepped back and said, "Let me look at you. The fire didn't get to your face. How about anywhere else that's important?"

"No, all other parts are OK." That got me a smile.

The CO hung back, and then I remembered him and stepped away from Steph and got a startled look from her, as if to say *why?*

I turned and said, "Major Mathews, this is Stephanie Rheem, a very good friend. She is one of our esteemed Donut Dollies, who, by the way, is qualified on the M-60 as a door gunner." She looked at me with eyebrows raised.

The CO said, "Please call me Ron, Stephanie. Don't worry. There are very few secrets in the military. And I understand you have a top secret clearance."

"It was the only way I could keep up with Mac's heroics."

"I wanted to meet the woman who tamed Firebird 9-7."

I looked at the Major and said, "Tamed?"

"Yes, tamed. You are a fierce fighter and an incredible pilot. You are a life saver and crazy brave. You've patriotic and generous. I continue to hear all these things about you in combat, but now I get to see you in love."

He shook his head as if to clear it. "Take off you two. See you at 1300 in the briefing room."

I said, "Thank you sir." Steph and I walked hand in hand to her quarters. As we stepped inside, she attacked me. Fast soft touches and deep long kisses. We began undressing each other. It was much slower with the burns. I stopped when her shirt was off. I reached down to my duffel bag and pulled out the jacket. I held it up so she could see the front. The Firebird, her name, the wings and her nickname, Dead Eye. An Americal patch on one shoulder and a First Aviation Brigade on the other. She began crying. She reached out, and I gently placed her arm in the sleeve. She turned and I helped her get the whole thing on. "Look in the mirror." She had a full length mirror on the wall by the living room door. She was crying a little louder now.

I walked behind her and held her tight. The crying softened. We were both looking in the mirror. "You are so beautiful." I turned her around so we were face to face. I kissed her eyes, her cheeks, the tears, and then the lips.

We slowly moved toward the bedroom. We finished undressing.

She said, "Lie down 9-7." She was naked as she picked up the Jacket and put it on. She climbed on top of me and said, "I'm not getting off until lunch."

She proceeded to keep her promise.

At 1200, she said, "I'm hungry. Can you shower with those bandages?"

She helped me take them off. I was very slow entering the shower, and I wouldn't have done it if I'd been alone. When the water hit the burns, I wanted to yell all the four-letter words I had in my vocabulary. I sucked it up because I'm a Firebird. I told her she looked great without the jacket. She punched my arm. "Men!"

"Hey beautiful, this one is different. He loves you so much that he keeps looking for words to describe those feelings. By the way, did you know that men hate two words: don't and stop, unless they're used together in the same sentence?"

She gave me that wonderful laugh as she shook her head. Punched me in the shoulder and said again, "Men!"

We ate lunch with my past copilot, Colonel Wheaton, and some of the brass. Steph was at home with these guys. She spoke as if they were family. The colonel said to Steph, "I like your Jacket."

She said, "Thanks, now I look just like you."

I really don't know what got into her to say what she said next: "I can't describe the feeling of shooting the M-60. I shouldn't say this, but I killed several VC. They shot at me first, or as Mac says, 'If you start it, WE WILL FINISH IT.'" The rest of the table was silent.

One of the new guys said, "You actually killed someone?"

"You're fuckin' A right I did! Several in fact. This is a war. If Mac had shot them, you'd pat him on the back."

I broke in and said, "My crew chief sat beside her. We'd say he took the shots, since she's technically a noncombatant." Then, I excused myself and walked up to the podium.

"I'm Warrant Officer McNally. I read the blurb that was given to you, and that's enough about me. So, I'm here to speak only about tactics. My first rule is: situational awareness. Know what's around you. Not just where you are going, but what's out to the sides, what's behind you. And my second rule is: you have to be ready to throw out the briefing and instantly create a new one. You won't have much time. Your brain has to be on a swivel. Not just your head. And third: don't forget your mission is the troops you're defending. This applies whether you are in the air or on the ground. Those troops could also be you.

"My best friend in VN—who taught me how to fly a wing gunship and then become a fire team leader—was killed sitting next to me on a mission. Hit in the chest with a 51. I know I shouldn't take responsibility. It's a war. But as the pilot in command, I'm supposed to look after my crew. He's never far from my mind. I loved that guy.

These things are going to happen, but you have to save your grief and thoughts of revenge until the mission is over.

"I've also learned that no matter how bad things look, you can get out if you just don't stop thinking or trying."

I continued for another hour. I talked about being NEAR the Laotian border. I wasn't fooling anyone. My disclaimer even got some laughs.

"You have to trust the people around you," I told them. "I went near Laos with a new copilot. I had never flown with him before, but he was confident. He listened when I explained the cannon sight. He was able to ignore the enemy's incoming rounds so well that he completely destroyed a company of NVA by himself. He also learned to shoot rockets with precision. We went on many missions together in the two weeks I was there. He was so good that I did not list his hours as CP. I listed them as pilot in command. I hated to lose him when I returned to CL." I made a dramatic pause. "Colonel Wheaton is that man!"

The place erupted in cheers and clapping.

"My main point is to encourage you to talk to the guys around you. Everyone has something useful to offer. And don't assume anyone knows how to fight just because they were in AIT (advanced infantry training) or flight school. You learn most of it from being in action with the old timers.

"Everything changes when the enemy is trying to kill you." I went on with specific examples of changing the mission as planned and improvising a new plan. "If you have to fall back, spread out and throw hand grenades from different positions. They will think there are more of you."

I also had to say something about the psychology of being at war. "It can wake you up at night when your brain says, 'We were almost killed today.' That's normal. It can also bother you that you did the killing. Think of something else. This shit will stop bothering you over time, and you won't even have a conscience. No problem then. Right?"

I took questions for an hour. Steph raised her hand and asked, "How can you shoot a woman or child?"

"It's easy. You don't have to lead them as much as a man. They run slower."

The place went wild. Even the brass was laughing. Steph had asked me that earlier when we were back in her room. She had said, "They will love your answer."

I decided to say more. "If a woman shoots at me, then there is no doubt in my mind that she's the enemy. The tough choice comes when she and/or a child are working a rice field that has been put off limits to the village. Then, we must assume she is raising food for the VC. If it's off limits, then it's a free fire zone. I usually let the door gunners shoot those people. If there is a very small child nearby or with the target, we try to let them go. We don't shoot them on purpose. We're not animals. Our job is to protect Americans, and occasionally some troops from other countries. We have a scorched earth policy. Kill and destroy everything and anyone hostile. If you make a place uninhabitable, then the enemy has nothing to return to."

Chapter 55.

TET AGAIN AND STEPH ON THE M60

I was wrapping up my talk, when a young private ran into the room and said, "Tet is officially on." Tet is the beginning of the New Year in VN, February 1ˢᵗ for 1969. (Since it's based on a lunar calendar, the date of Tet changes from year to year.) The previous year, it had marked an all-out assault on American FSB's. We were able to repel the attackers but with a significant loss of lives on both sides. We expected trouble again this year. He continued, "They are trying to get over the wire. We have a loaded gunship with a cannon sitting outside. All the other guns are out on missions."

I said, "I'm a fire team leader." I walked down into the crowd and said privately, "Colonel, do you want to go to this dance again?"

"With you Mac, hell yes."

"Colonel, who would you pick for door gunners?"

"MacAddo is good with a 60. Bob MacAddo, come up here."

He appeared and said, "Yes sir."

"How would like to door gun with Mac."

He said, "Of course, sir."

I reached out to shake hands with Bob, when I saw the Captain's Bars, and said, "Congratulation, sir."

He said, "For you, it's still Bob."

"Great, we need one more. Who would you pick?"

They called up a guy who looked older but was a new GB. MacAddo said, "This guy was a 60 gunner in the infantry."

I nodded and said. "Good to have you aboard. There are no rules tonight."

He gave me a big smile and said, "Just the way I like it, sir."

I put my hand out and said, "Mac."

He returned the handshake and said, "Johnny."

I spoke in a loud voice to the crowd. "We're in luck this afternoon. That copilot I spoke of earlier is here with us and will fly with me. That would be Colonel Wheaton."

The place went crazy. Cheering and giving some Hooo-Rahhhhhs.

"OK, everyone, get set. Grab any gear you want to take. I'll be out in a minute."

I walked over to Steph, who was watching all this, and I said, "Follow me." We walked across the tarmac where the ships were parked. Then, down a hill to a small bunker. "Steph this is a weak point. We don't have enough troops to cover the entire perimeter."

She looked at me and said, "OK." No hesitation.

The M-60 was there with three cans of ammo (4500 rounds). "We need you. I need you. If they get through here, it won't matter what I do."

She looked at me and said, "I'm your girl."

I said, "I know that. Did you say two children when our call was interrupted?"

She gave that million-dollar smile and said, "Yes, two are plenty."

"That's great." Then I returned to the here and now. "I hate to put this kind of responsibility on you, but I trust you more than any of the GB's, except maybe the colonel. You can do this, and I know you'll do great." We kissed, and I left her to do her job.

I walked up the hill and down the taxi lane to the gunship. Everyone looked ready and confident. I turned to the two gunners. "We'll be moving at 130 mph, so you'll need to lead your targets by quite a bit. When we turn, you can shoot straight down on the bastards." I pointed to the safety strap and said, "Put this on. When I say 'ready,' you can move back into the ship and hang on if you need to, as I might be making a hard break. There is no wing ship, so you two will have to shoot during the break to protect our belly. I will shoot rockets if I catch the bad guys in the open. If they're in the wire, it will be up to you two, and the colonel on the cannon."

In unison, they said, "Who?"

I said, "Your boss." *I guess they had already departed to get their gear and m-60s.*

The colonel turned to them and said, "Don't let anyone shoot me. Last time I did this Mac let them wound me."

They nodded, and their facial expressions indicated they weren't sure if he was serious.

I called the tower and told him that we would be flying around the perimeter and that the GB's should stop shooting when we came by. At the wire, we would be shooting cannon and M-60s.

He rogered. I said to the colonel, "Sir, it's all yours. Once in the air, I will take it, since you have the close-in work with the 40mm."

He said, "OK." He lifted off the ground twelve inches and said, "This feels more normal." We started forward, did one bounce, and were flying.

I said, "Rock and roll while we TO." Then, "I got it."

The colonel pulled down his sight, adjusted the brightness and said, "Ready."

"Alright," I told the guys in back, "test those 60's. Remember, everything out of or near the wire is yours. Kill every motherfucker down there. No rules and no surrender."

They each had three cans of ammo, 4500 rounds each. Their guns were in order. I called the tower and asked where anyone had contact. I was only 300 feet above the wire.

Tower called back and said, "Keep going about another quarter mile."

I flew for a few more seconds and saw the tracers going both ways. I said, "Here we go guys. Send those fuckers to hell." I saw some NVA coming out of the trees with long bamboo poles, called Bangalore torpedoes. They were stuffed full of explosives to blow open an area of the concertina wire. That would allow the NVA to enter the FSB. To discourage such attacks, the area outside the concertina wire was stripped to bare earth for 400 meters. This was our killing zone.

I fired three pairs of rockets into the NVA out in the open and then three pairs into the trees. Everyone else was concentrating on the guys getting close to the wire. I over flew the area since I had no choice but to stay on the wire. I said, "Look back. Is anyone coming out of the trees?" They both said, "No."

I asked the tower, "Where to next?"

He said they were picking up some enemy comm, but it was all in Vietnamese. "Keep going."

In another twenty seconds, they were almost to the wire. I said,

"Colonel, do you see them?"

He knew what I meant. "Yes," he said and started shooting. One of the Bangalore's blew up twenty yards from the wire.

Shit, that was close.

The two guys in back were awesome. They definitely knew how to operate an M-60.

I told them, "You're fucking good with those guns."

I put a pair into the trees. Everyone was still shooting. Then, I thought of Steph, alone and no communications. I kept flying along the wire when I saw her bunker. She was shooting at the enemy near the wire. More were coming out of the trees. I put three pair of rockets on them. The crew was chewing up the ones close to the wire. It looked pretty good down there. "OK fellas, hang on. I'm going to turn around and will give them a second helping. What da' ya think?"

I received three *yeses*. I climbed and turned.

The colonel said, "Mac, do you know who that is down there?"

I said, "Yes, I put her there after the assignments were given out because you didn't have enough troops for all the bunkers. I chose that bunker because it fills the largest gap between manned bunkers."

"Goddamn," was all he said.

We started our run. I put three pair at the tree line, and a flurry of tracers came up toward us. I turned slightly and punched two pair at those muzzle flashes. I got a small secondary explosion. I had two rockets left. I said, "Keep shooting at everything. If they're all dead, then hose down those trees."

I looked and saw Steph. She had stopped shooting. She was outside the bunker.

I called the GB HQ. "Have guys standing by with 38 rockets to reload me." I turned and made a final rocket run and fired my last pair. I called the tower. "I'm landing for a quick reload of rockets." After I landed, I asked MacAddo to monitor the loading. "Push the rocket all the way in until you hear and feel a click, then go to the back of the pod and make sure the electrical arm is in place." (He told me later that one reloader was a cook, two were his assistants, and the forth was the radio operator.)

I then ran down the hill to find Steph. She was sitting down and reloading the 60 from a fresh can of ammo.

She looked up and said, "How do you do this, especially at night?"

I said, "Because I'm surrounded by incredible people."

She grabbed me and said, "I'll need a week of sex to come down from tonight."

"Hang in there beautiful. I'll send you the radio operator with a radio, so you can call me if those shits come out of the trees."

"How can you be so calm and tender with me when you go through a living hell all day and half the night?"

"I have a lovely motivator. I'll do anything for her." We kissed. I said, "I'll be back soon."

I ran up the hill and told the RTO to take a radio and another can of ammo down to the bunker.

He said, "Yes sir, Mac."

I said, "What's this 'sir' shit?"

"You are saving lots of lives."

"Make sure she's OK."

He said, "WHAT?"

I climbed in and said, "Are you ready, sir?"

"I have half my cannon shells remaining, and the gunners are still in their first can."

"Please take me to the war, sir.

He laughed and shook his head. "Does anything affect you?" Then he had a very good one-bounce take off.

I said, "Hell yes. A couple of those missions with you last month had my pucker factor so high they had to use a crow bar to pry me out of the seat."

He was laughing pretty hard, and I said, "I got it. OK, here we go again. Does anyone on this frequency have contact with the enemy?"

I received an answer. "Keep coming. I can hear you."

I was climbing and asked if they were close to the wire.

He said, "Oh shit, they're running towards us. Must be a hundred."

"Get your heads down. We're coming in." I punched three pair at the leaders and then three pair at the new leaders. I yelled, "Get the ones close to the wire." As they were all three shooting, I heard Steph say, "They are charging me, and there are over a hundred."

I said, "We're going back to the GB's landing area."

As I was making that steep turn, MacAddo said, "Mac, that was a female voice."

"I know, and I love that women, so don't let anyone get near the wire."

I dropped the nose and let go with three pair, then three more. They kept coming. I fired three more. I saw her tracers, and she was shooting near the wire. I yelled out, "Help her!"

I saw her shoot three guys. Their Bangalore was dropped close to the wire, and that was only thirty yards away from Steph. I called and said, "Shoot that long piece of bamboo. Be careful. It's full of explosives to blow a hole in your wire."

She said, "I'll wait until their reinforcements show up. Then, I'll take them all to hell when I blow it up."

"You're a genius. You'll never stop amazing me. I love you, so keep that lovely head of yours down and out of sight. When they make another one of their drug induced charges, we'll both shoot. You get first shot at the bamboo, and then the colonel will shoot."

She said, "You tell my dad's old boss that my nickname is Dead Eye."

The colonel said, "Be careful, pretty lady. I promised your dad I wouldn't let anything bad happen to you. And I think I already broke that promise when I let you go cavorting with a Firebird, the most dangerous, uncouth, unprincipled, undisciplined soldiers on earth."

She said, "Derek, I don't know anyone like that."

"Steph, I've learned to trust your judgement," the colonel said. "You are the smartest person I've ever known, and the only person that uses my first name other than my wife and an occasional General."

"Oh shit," I said. "Here they come, but only about fifty. I think we've thinned their ranks. There are four guys running very fast toward that bamboo." I dropped the nose, but before I could shoot, a hail of bullets hit the front of the ship. Yellow radio warning lights came on. The colonel put about ten rounds into the origin of that last barrage of bullets. I put my remaining rockets on the NVA emerging from the trees, as I yelled, "Is everyone OK?"

The colonel gave me two clicks, and the guys in back yelled. "OK."

I said, "Keep shooting. I'm empty." They continued. I called the GB's and said, "Here we come. We need 38 rockets, two cans of ammo, 300 40mm shells, and a crow bar for me." The RTO started laughing and said, "I have everything but the crow bar."

I told the colonel, "Take us in for ammo. Do we need the fuel truck?"

"It's OK, over half a tank," he replied. "Tower, this is gunship 6 for landing."

The tower said, "Who?"

The colonel said, "6."

"Yes sir. Cleared to land at the GBs."

I said, "It really pays off to bring you along."

He said, "RHIP (rank has its privileges)."

I thought, *For example, look at the party the RTO gathered up for this rearm.* Eight guys standing there. Three were field grade officers. I jumped out and ran down the hill. There was this lady who was so beautiful she looked very out of place in this hellhole. She was covered in dirt and gun grease, and she smelled like burnt powder. I wished I had a camera.

She said, "I got all four of those little fuckers going for the bamboo. Thanks for the radio and extra ammo."

"You are a Firebird. You talk like one, shoot like one, and don't run from a fight."

"This gun is heavy."

I said, "Rest it on the sand bags. That way you are a very small target. You are too brave, darling."

"Oh god," she said, "I love you. I can't wait to get you to my bed. I hope this adrenaline rush lasts long enough to get you there. I see what you mean; you block out everything and keep going. It must feel like hell the next day without any sleep."

"Yes, it does. I've gotta go. See if we can end this quickly." I ran up the hill, and they were still loading the 40mm. The colonel was checking in with the bunkers and other security.

He said, "How's she doing, Mac."

"Incredible, just like we knew she would sir."

He nodded.

"I could see it in her eyes. She wanted to do something. I would have put her at a door gun if the base were being overrun."

One of the LT colonels stuck his head in the colonel's window and said, "Are you OK?"

"I've never felt better. I could do this all night. We are one hell of a team. Stand by in case we need more ammo. Thanks, you guys."

The colonel hovered out, and I said, "I've got it. Let's get you a rocket sight." He picked up the red grease pencil, while I looked for a target. I picked out a building about five hundred yards away. I said, "Circle that building. Put your dot on the window, sir."

"Got it, Mac."

"You've got it, sir."

As he took off, I said, "Rock and Roll." He then called and asked if anyone had contact. Two bunkers said they had killed a few guys running towards them with satchel charges. The fuses had been smoking, and they had exploded after their guys were dead.

"OK, sir. You've got rockets. One pair with each punch of that little red button."

The colonel nodded and flew over the wire at 500 feet.

"Sir, this looks like an 'off the grid' night."

There were a few NVA trying to haul away their dead. The colonel put a pair of rockets on them, and we kept moving. The gunners were shooting short bursts at NVA darting out from the trees to take a shot as us.

"Colonel, do you see those NVA?"

"I sure do." He dropped the nose and punched twice. Those guys never knew what hit them. Suddenly, a fucking machine gun opened up on us. Several bullets came up through the floor where the gunners were. MacAddo got shrapnel in the arm but didn't tell me and kept on shooting. I saw it when we landed, and I sent him to the medic.

"Sir, let's check on Steph. Oh shit, we have two yellow lights: engine-exhaust temperature and our position lights. Nothing serious."

He increased his air speed, cutting corners where he could. There she was behind some sand bags with her gun on top. There were three dead guys hanging in the wire.

I called her and asked how she was doing.

She said, "If you fly with burns, I should be able to hold this position. Right?"

"Steph, that's the wonderful adrenalin not letting you feel the pain. You are incredible. How did those guys get so close?"

She said, "I was trying to clear a jam in the gun. " (The ammo belt can get twisted and interfere with the bullets feeding into the gun.)

"It looks like you cleared it in time. I'm impressed and very proud of you. You're doing the work of two men."

"I wondered why it was so easy." That got everyone laughing. "Sir, do you see why I love that woman." That was transmitted to everyone.

She said, "Kevin, thank you so much. I was never told that. I was told you are supposed to get straight A's in school. I did and no one said, good job, we're proud of you, Nothing. I love my parents. Not sure why, other than I'm supposed to. However, I love you for many... shit, fuck here come some more."

We heard her M-60 open up. Her radio was still on. Immediately, the colonel turned around. It was all I could do not to grab those controls. We were only ten seconds away and saw a platoon advancing on our hero's positon. She was slowing them down. The colonel put two pair on them and got all but two, and the gunners did the rest. I shot the cannon into the tree line and inward. Fires were burning. Some tracers were coming up from the jungle. The colonel put rockets in there, and I put a few cannon shells in as well. I think we killed most of their troops. Now, we could get the bodies to the pathologists, find out how much and what drugs were in them to make those suicidal bonsai charges.

We turned and made another pass by Steph. She waved. We shot three pair of rockets into the trees about thirty yards in from the tree's edge. No one was moving. "Let's go home. Maybe we can get someone to relieve her."

The colonel said, "Good idea," and he called HQ and told the RTO to get someone down to Steph's bunker and some mechanics to work on our ship. We flew around the perimeter one more time with the colonel shooting at any possible place where troops could regroup. I shot the cannon and watched a few explosions and some fires. They were totally defeated. All in all we had had a great night, and there had been some incredible individual acts of heroism: the three in my crew, Steph, and the guys in a few other bunkers that had repelled attacks.

We landed, and I saw Steph. There she was, sitting against the building. She looked fast asleep. I walked over and sat down beside her. I opened up some C rations, and put the peanut butter under her nose. *Shit, no response.* I held it longer, and she finally moved.

"Thank god," I said.

"Hey, why not," she said? "Is he on our side or the NVA? Is everyone praying to the same god?"

I have no idea, and I'm not going to worry about it. It's a rhetorical question.

"We're in a foreign country," she said, maybe still asleep, "don't speak their language, don't understand their culture, religion or politics."

"Steph, wake up! You just repelled an NVA Tet assault. You were incredible. I don't have words to describe what you did. You saved a lot of GB's lives. You are beyond belief, gorgeous."

She shook herself fully awake. She threw her arms around my neck. "My hero. You came charging in and destroyed those shits. You turned around several times just to make sure I was OK, even though you had lots of people to protect. Just like you did when I was on the hill with the dollies."

I pulled her in to me. "I'd bet there's not another female in the American forces that could have done what you did tonight, or nine tenths of the males. You are one in a million. Make that 250 million, the population of the US. Hell Steph, I couldn't have done what you did tonight."

She looked at me and said, "Really, is that the truth?"

I said, "Yes that's the truth. Now let's get back to you. How do you feel?" Then, I took a look. "Shit Steph, you're bleeding."

"Yeah, I know. Something hit my arm when I was shooting. It didn't hurt, so I kept shooting. I guess what you said about the power of adrenalin is so true. Anyway, it's not bleeding now. I'm tired Kevin. Really-really tired. Thank you so much for coming to my rescue and saving my life, again and again. You are so special. Remind me tomorrow to tell you about my parents. I sent them pictures and told them some stories about you. Dad called Colonel Wheaton ..."

"I know, Steph, but right now you need to rest. Let's go clean up. We look like we've been in a war." She gave me a tiny laugh.

I carried her to her trailer. She slept most of the way. I laid her down in the bathroom with a rolled towel under her head. I turned on the bath water and undressed her. *God she is beautiful.* I took off my boots, picked her up, and stepped into the tub. I let her down slowly and put the towel back under her head. I used one of her several bottles of soap and washed her entire body, even her hair using another bottle that said shampoo. Hell, I did a pretty good job for my first time.

After I put her to bed, I took a very long shower. I put our dirty clothes outside in front of the door including her new flight jacket. I slipped into bed and held her close.

Chapter 56.

THE DAY AFTER

When I woke up, it was 0900. I was impressed with Steph's library. I picked out a world history book, returned to bed, and began reading. It was fascinating. We don't seem to notice that we're always at war with someone or helping someone fight a war. It must be awfully lucrative for those involved.

At 1000, she began to wake up and gently touched my leg. "How did I get to bed and how did I get so clean?"

"I'm guilty. Just one of many talents. I'm going to post a notice about my new service."

"No you won't, or I'll break your arm."

I laughed.

"You actually carried me home, undressed me, bathed me, and put me to bed?"

"Yes, that's exactly what I did."

"Wow, how did I find someone like you? You can do everything. What's your IQ?"

"I don't know, but it was high enough that I got to skip the fourth grade. Hey, do you remember last night?"

"Fourth grade, yeah right you bullshitter," she said. "Yes, I remember, but it seems a little blurry. I just remember trying out several different ways to hold that M-60. It was heavy. I did walk out from the sand bags several times to shoot the ones that were getting close. Kevin, I was never scared."

"You had your mind on your job, and you handled it like a pro. You are amazing. Let's spend the rest of our lives surprising each other."

I added, "Be careful of your arm. I had the Doc come in last night after I put you to bed. He said it was minor, but he did give you three stitches and a shot of antibiotic in your butt."

"My butt hurts but not the arm."

"The doc put a bottle of pain pills next to your bedside, just in case. I almost stopped him when he started to stick the big rusty nail of a needle in your beautiful butt because I know how sore I get after one of those shots."

She said, "OK, now let's fuck each other's brains out. I think that's how that crude statement is stated."

For two hours, we did just that. By lunchtime, no one had any brains remaining.

We walked into the mess hall, and everyone stood up and began clapping and chanting, "Steph - Steph." I let go of her hand and moved away. This was her moment.

Colonel Wheaton stood up and put his hands up to quiet the crowd. "Steph, let's go up on the stage."

She was radiant. And she was blushing, and it looked so cute.

The colonel explained to everybody what she had done in the bunker. "She fired 4500 rounds, and there were bodies all over. She walked around the bunker and shot several of them in the wire."

The GB's were transfixed by what the colonel was saying. "She is getting the Vietnam Cross of Gallantry with a gold palm for exceptional heroism. Also, on the ribbon with the Cross will be Bronze and Silver stars representing heroism equal to the military's Bronze and Silver Stars. And men: a Purple Heart. She was hit in her arm and continued fighting for another two hours. The doc stitched her up last night." Everyone could see the bandage around her arm at mid-bicep.

The crowd went absolutely wild, yelling, cheering, whistling, and shouting, "Steph - Steph."

The colonel turned to me. "Mister McNally, you have to return to Chu Lai ASAP. There are lots of missions in the AO."

I said, "Yes sir, let me get my gear and then I'm ready."

He nodded and said, "We make a damn good team. I really like your 'off the grid' philosophy."

I put my hands up to silence the crowd. "I just spoke to the doc doing autopsies on last night's losers. He said they were full of drugs. He also wanted me to tell all of you not to drink the water."

Then, I turned to walk out with Steph. As we were leaving the mess hall, someone called out, "Mac, why not drink the water?"

With a straight face I told them, "Please don't drink the water because fish fuck in it." Steph and I quickened our pace. I could hear a lot of laughing and that would help get their minds off of last night. Humor always helps.

Steph walked me back to her trailer. She had tears in her eyes from laughing. The closer we got to the trailer, her tears increased, and I knew why. Now she was crying out loud. I put my arms around her and said, "I will be very careful. I have so much to live for."

I was in another world during the short ride. I was driven to the Firebird line. There sat a new Gunship with my name on one side and Ski's on the other. There were huge Firebird decals on the large windows on the sliding doors. We always kept them open or the door gunners couldn't shoot. It was fresh from the factory.

Rivers was there, admiring the new ship with me. He asked, "How was Chu Lai's HQ? I heard that quite a few bad guys tried to get through the wire."

"Not one of those assholes got through."

"The CO told us who you put in a bunker with an M-60. Did she really shoot 4500 rounds?"

"Yes, she did, three full ammo cans. She probably killed at least 150 and who knows how many more crawled off to die. She even walked out of the bunker and shot guys in the wire. She shot guys running with satchel charges. She shot and killed four when they were running to the wire with Bangalore's. She shot those Bangalores when about thirty NVA were near them to pick 'em up to run to the concertina wire. I think we would have been overrun if she hadn't been there."

Just then, a jeep drove up and spoiled the moment. The driver gave me a piece of paper with call signs, cords, and frequency. I showed it to Rivers.

"Alright fellas, let's go."

Chapter 57.

THE OLDEST PILOT

An eight man patrol of Marines were trapped on a cliff with a company of NVA were moving in on them. The cliff was ten minutes away. I was talking to Big Dog 6 as we were approaching. He said, "I read the map wrong and got everyone in trouble."

"Don't beat yourself to death," I told him. "A lot of those maps are crap. They were printed before the French were kicked out of here in the early fifties, and some were just pieced together from old aerial photographs.

"I see you. I'm going to move to your left, shoot, and break over your position. Have you worked with gunships before?"

"Yes, and I'll stop our shooting when you guys shoot and begin again when the second ship turns over me."

I said, "Great. 9-5, you get that?"

Click-click.

"I'm rolling in."

I saw 100 bad guys in the open. They turned to shoot but very few had time. I started closest to the Marines and worked back away from them to the trees. The guys behind the trees were shooting on full auto. I yelled, "Get on those guys." That was for the copilot and Ski, but they were already on them. We were getting close, so I broke right. Wing saw the areas where the NVA were about to bonsai the marines, and he put rockets on 'em. I came back around and pounded the trees. Clearwater was very precise on the cannon and of course no one escaped Tyler and Ski.

9-5 called and said, "9-6 was flying."

Wilder (9-6) had been chosen to be the new platoon leader, but right now he was being copilot to Rivers (9-5) who was training him.

I said, "Great. 9-5 has been worrying me because he's short (short time remaining in VN). He's been shooting his rockets from a mile out." That brought out a few snickers.

Back to the war, I rolled in and punched rockets where I saw a few shots come up.

"9-7, this is Big Dog 6. The marine slicks are coming to pick us up. Should be five minutes."

I said, "Call 'em and give them this frequency."

He did, and they called me and said "Lead ship is 4-5." I called 4-5 and said, "Let me know when you're close, and we'll escort you in."

"Roger that 9-7. We look forward to the protection. I think I'll come in from the cliff side, load up, and dive off the edge."

"Sounds great." (It's OK to let the slicks have a say in what they want to do, or think they want to do, once in a while).

Everyone was in the loop. Here they came about 50 yards apart. I started shooting as soon as they were close. I just kept walking the rockets into the trees and brush. Clearwater was doing the same. I always got a feeling of security when the gunners were shooting. No shots were returned. I broke, and 9-6 put the rockets right on those little shits.

The ships dove off the cliff, and I rolled in and put in a few more rockets.

I decided this was an opportunity for a little training. "Bob draw a circle around that large rock and put a dot in the center. OK, you bring us around and line up on anything that doesn't belong to the USA." I set the selector to one rocket. "Start your fall, 300 to 400 feet per minute, 120 knots and in trim. Steady and a gentle punch. That was good, shoot another one." It was closer. "One more and then break." Rivers was working his copilot, too. The mini guns were roaring.

As we broke, I said, "Notice how we're still falling. That's called mushing. It's due to mass multiplied by speed which equals force. You have to watch the ground, instruments, and especially the torque meter, or you'll crash. Feel how this ship flies when loaded and falling. You've got to claw the air for altitude. Also, if you're too low, you're an easy target. Let's fly out a little farther this time."

Twenty seconds later, I said, "Turn and go."

Bob settled in nicely. He had a great touch. I guess flying those corporate jets helped him.

"OK Mac," he said, "I see a guy running out of the trees. I'm going to get him."

"Wait a moment. Let's see what he's doing. He's turning and running parallel to the trees."

The runner stopped and pulled a green tarp off a machine gun. He turned and looked up at us waving his hands across his body and then pointing at the gun.

Bob looked at me, confused. "Is he trying to surrender?"

I shook my head no. "They pretend to surrender, then start shooting at us. Bob, kill that bastard. A minute ago he wanted to kill us. I call it: 'off the grid.' Or in the old days, it was called, 'no quarter' (take no prisoners, leave no survivors)."

Bob's rocket passed by my leg, and the NVA was dead. Not a direct hit, but thirty yards was as good as a direct hit. I said, "Great shot. Now use your pedals and get a shot at the trees where he ran from." He shot, and I said, "Quick, shoot again." Then, Bob broke. 9-5 saw what was going on and put rockets and mini guns on those trees. There was a good size fire burning there. "One more run 9-5?"

I got two clicks, and then a voice said, "9-6 will make the next run."

I said, "Makes sense to me. A future bird has been doing all of my flying and shooting on these last few runs."

We rolled in, and Bob was having fun shooting those rockets.

"Look out in front of you. One of the wounded just got up and is walking toward the trees." I didn't need to say anything else. The rocket hit five feet in front of him, so there would be nothing remaining to pick up. Bob fired another into the trees, and we were out of there. Wing did the same with rockets into the trees.

Back at Baldy, we refueled our two Birds and rearmed them. I went over some of the systems with Bob. He asked a few pertinent questions. He was sharp.

I said, "Are you tired?

He said, "Hell yes."

"Then, let's take a nap."

We walked into the "pig pen," oops I mean "the Hilton" and were both asleep in 30 seconds. The crew on the wing ship was already asleep

The damn red phone rang. Everyone was up and running. A GB patrol, Green 6, had walked into an NVA trap, and one soldier was seriously wounded. They needed a Dust off to get him to Danang ASAP. Before Bob could hover out of the revetment, the Dust off flew over our heads. I called him and said, "Slow down. You're faster than us. Let us make sure it's safe."

The dumb shit didn't answer. I called HQ and said, "Did you hear?"

The RTO said, "Yes. I called on two different frequencies, and I got back nothing."

"Shit. He's going to kill all three of them: pilot, copilot and medic."

This will go in the manual under stupid.

"Bob, pull that collective up and take the rpm to the red line. Watch the torque; you have 46 on this new model. Take it to 46, no more. 9-6 how is everything? We're falling back, but slowly."

Click-click. I couldn't see the Dust off. The patrol was thirty clicks west, almost to the marine artillery base. I tried calling Dust off again and got no answer. Then, we saw a huge black cloud rise up with flames coming out of that cloud. I called the patrol and asked, "Was that was Dusty?"

Green 6 said in a quiet voice, "Yes, an RPG hit the gas tank as he flared. I don't think they felt anything."

I said, "Gunships are one click out. Tell me where those bastards are hiding. I don't need any smoke; I can see the burning Huey." He gave me a heading from the burning ship. I said, "Got it. We will come in shooting and break over your heads. Resume your shooting after the second bird flies over you. Keep it short as I will be covering the wing ship. We'll do that several times. You can direct my rockets or cannon fire if they're trying to hide."

I got close and did a cyclic climb for altitude, then pointed the nose of the ship at those NVA and fired eight rockets. Bob was making their lives miserable with the cannon. The gunners took out a few as well. "Ready, breaking right." I was watching where the shooters were hiding. "You three all concentrate on those shooters while I look for other targets."

We turned in time to shoot at anyone who wanted to shoot the wing. I also saw tracers coming up at wing and me from an area near the patrol. I leveled the ship and fired four pairs and saw a ball of fire rise up. I was smiling when I pulled around as wing was breaking. I put four rockets under wing, and then turned my attention to yet another machine gun placement fifty yards left of the first one I killed. They got four rockets and stopped shooting.

I called Green 6 and asked, "How's your patient?"

"He's still alive. Keep shooting. You guys are deadly. I sent two men out to the two machine gun placements. There were four dead at each placement, and the guns can't be repaired."

I was following the calls from one of our slicks to the patrol. The voice sounded familiar.

"Firebird 9-7, this is Rattler 2-9. Is it safe to land? I'm the new Dust off."

"Let us make another run and then escort you in."

Click-click

"OK, here we go." I noticed we had some holes in the front window. I looked around, and then noticed a hole in my chicken board. I reached in between my shirt and the board and pulled my hand out and there was NO blood. Shit, I never felt anything. Adrenalin! I fired two pair at two suspicious spots. Everyone else was shooting as if their lives depended on it.

"OK 2-9, are you ready? We'll fly in on your left side high and behind you. The patrol and your door gunner will watch the right."

We flew in and didn't receive any fire. The slick came up fast, landed, loaded the wounded and was off to Danang. We stayed as two Hueys were coming for the patrol. I said, "Later Glen."

Click-click

The lead ship called for 9-7. "This is GB 3-6. What does it look like down there? I followed some of your talk and then had to switch freq."

"We just escorted a slick in to pick up your wounded. Not a shot was fired, and he is halfway to Danang."

"Shit, was that smoke Dusty?" he asked.

"Yes, he was overeager to pick up the soldier and didn't wait for us. Two more minutes and we would have been able to soften the area."

The slicks came in twenty and thirty yards from the patrol. The patrol split into two equal groups, and those guys were jumping on before the Hueys had finished landing. They took off and turned away from the burned and blown up jungle.

"Thanks Firebirds, those are the LZs I like."

"You're welcome and glad to help. Say hi to Colonel Wheaton."

"I'll try. He's all over the place. I heard he flew in a gunship and was wounded and continued the mission. They are telling all kinds of stories that make him sound like Superman."

I said, "He must be one hell of a leader. 9-5 or 6, let's go to Baldy."

After landing, we did the routine prep and waited for our next call. Then, we walked over to the mess hall. I admit I had some apprehensions, but we had no choice. The line was fast because there weren't any other customers. We got what we called sloppy Joes back home.

While we were eating, Wilder, who was sitting next to me, said, "Mac, do you have a conscience?"

"Not anymore," I told him. *I had thought about this, and I didn't need to ponder it now.* "As a FTL, you make split-second decisions. You have to focus on your job. Not much time to worry about morals. War will affect your judgement and values. Wars aren't always the best choice, but history is full of them. I think it's the bigger dick theory. Have you noticed bombs and bullets are shaped like dicks?"

He started laughing. We got up and headed back to the Hilton.

"Sometimes, if you hesitate, you die," I told him. "You need to keep it simple. You job is to kill the enemy. You're not a peace negotiator, and often you've got no choice but 'go off the grid.' Here are some calling cards we throw out to our guys on the ground after a mission." I showed him one. It read: *Firebirds: You call, we kill.* "You'll be doing ten to fifteen things at once up there. You're in charge. You can't hesitate.

"Always remain calm, and your crew will follow suit. Listen to those two super crewmen behind you. That's four extra eyes. Don't worry about anything if you get investigated. They have done many investigations on the Birds, and we always walk away clean.

Forgiveness is easier to get than permission.

"By the way, be nice to your crew but firm with the ground troops. Hell, most of them are 18 or 19. They're kids. They need guidance."

I realized I was giving him an earful, but I wanted to share what I'd learned. It might save his life one day. And he was listening.

"You can get scared sometimes in a battle," I told him, "and so I've just decided not to give a shit. The only thing that holds me together is a dolly at CL HQ, and the responsibility for my crews in both ships. By the way," I repeated, "do something nice for your EM crew from time to time. I know you're an officer, and they are E-4s and E-5s, but you have to let them know you're thinking of them."

That red phone started ringing. Everyone ran as I picked it up.

The clerk said, "A platoon of twenty is trapped at a 180 degree bend in the river. On the other side of the river is a 100 foot sheer cliff. The NVA are 150 feet above our troops in caves. They want to get out before dark."

I said to the guys around me, "OK, let's go. The intermission is over. Bob show me a takeoff in this loaded hog."

He did a good job bouncing out of the revetment. He lifted up six inches and eased the cyclic forward, and then I said, "Rock and roll." We had two bounces and then slid fifty yards and hit translational lift.

I said, "Turn straight west. They are 29 clicks from Baldy, about 18 miles. We should get there in less than 10 minutes, depending on what we have to climb over." I called Wet Bar 6. "This is Firebird 9-7, a team of two gunships, and we're 10 minutes out. From my maps, I will have to come in right over you and shoot after we fly by. After we do that, we'll make some very sharp turns and go back out and repeat."

"9-6, are you ready?"

Click-click.

"Let's do this." As I approached the valley entrance, I said, "Pop smoke. I have green."

"That's us."

"Get your heads down. These rockets throw out a lot of shrapnel." I saw the caves and the enemy. I dropped the nose and punched three pair in at about twenty yards apart. I surprised the ones on watch. I fired three pairs at the same area. Bob had the cannon on automatic and moved all over those caves. The machine gun rounds from Ski and Tyler were ricocheting all across the face of the cliff.

"Wet Bar, can you move back while the wing ship is shooting? There is a trail to your south and a little behind you."

The patrol started crawling out when the NVA started shooting from the same spot I'd just hit. They reinforced that by adding a new location, thirty feet away and ten feet above. They were shooting at both us and the trapped patrol. I put four pair of rockets across the face. I was shooting during the turn. That gave me a little more cover.

"Wet Bar, can you move?"

"If we move, we'll be in the open. They're all across the face of that cliff."

"OK. We're going to make one more pass, and then I'm going to get some white phosphorus grenades and drop them to you. You can create a smoke screen, and then get the hell out." I shot rockets into both places that were firing at us. So did Bob.

"Bob, take me SSE to LZ Dragon. I quickly called Dragon and asked if they had any Wilson Picket grenades. "I'll pay you back tomorrow," I promised. "I'd like a couple of cases if you've got 'em."

The CO got on the phone and said, "Mac, you're famous. I heard you borrowed ammo from LZ Karen or LZ West. We've heard many stories. I heard you had a colonel with you as a copilot. What's your plan?"

"A patrol is trapped about 8 clicks north of the abandoned LZ Mellon. The NVA are in caves 150 feet above with machine guns. I take out a machine gun, and they replace it with another. That keeps happening, and it doesn't help the patrol. We have to get our guys out before dark. They have only one way out, and I'm sure the NVA are already sending out people to close the valley door. We need WP so they can make a smoke screen."

"I just got word that we have five cases."

"I'll take two sir. Sir, may I have your name?"

"Major Webster."

We were low on fuel, and I had shot most of my rockets, so I thought it would be doable to land on the slick pad and be able to take off.

As I was talking, Bob brought us in for a landing, and we received the two crates of Wilson Pickets. "Major Webster, would you happen to know Major Thomson in CL? He's my CO."

"Hell yes. He and I fought together here two years ago."

"Sir, could you please call him, and he will have two replacement cases flown out early by the slick covering resupply." Major Webster said he was happy to call, and I said, "Thank you Sir."

As I lifted the ship up, it felt so easy with most of my rockets gone and half our fuel. I warned everyone that I was going to dive off this mountain top. I dove off, and it wasn't too scary.

The crew told me, "We get a bigger thrill jumping out of this ship when landing."

I called Wet Bar and reviewed the plan. "Throw a few in the river. Water causes them to burn hotter and produces more smoke. Throw a few behind you, and a few out in front of you while you're running down the path. Then run through the smoke. We will lead you out of the canyon." I hit the IC and said, "Ammo report."

Bob said, "150 shells."

Ski said, "1/3 remaining."

Tyler said, "1/3 remaining."

"You two save your rounds," I said to Ski and Tyler. "We will most likely have to shoot our way out of there. Bob, save your ammo, too."

I called wing, and he had six rockets, his mini gun was down to 1/3 and the gunners each had 100 remaining.

"I will shoot one rocket at each location," I said, "and save my last eight to help those soldiers get out of there. As I shoot, I will try to break directly over them, and Tyler, push those two crates out directly on them."

This all worked pretty much as planned, and Tyler was able to get both cases near the trapped troops. Then, it was time for part 2.

"Here we come Wet Bar 6. Start throwing."

They were creating a huge smoke screen as I shot. 9-5 shot his and broke. The troops were moving down the trail. I said to them, "Throw a few out to one side, so they'll think you're over there. I saw some movement out to the right. I called everyone involved by saying, "Rocket," and then I shot. When it exploded, four enemy troops started running. I said, "Ski, Tyler," and they dropped them. I saw below me several dead NVA from my rocket. I looked to the left, and two machine guns were on us. Wing hit one with a rocket, and the mini gun made a mess of the second.

"Shit, I said, "I have three yellows: hydraulics, oil pressure, and electrical." Then my exhaust temperature started rising. Something was leaking into the exhaust. "Shit, I don't know how long I can remain on station."

We turned and flew back to the running patrol. They were near the end of the trail that opened up to a dry rice paddy. That was lucky. It would be much easier for the troops to get to the Hueys on dry ground versus a muddy water-filled rice paddy. There were ten NVA spread apart and moving into three-foot-high elephant grass which made them easy targets.

"All three of you, take 'em out." They were ready for us as they were on full automatic with their AK-47's, which could make for a more formidable density of fire. I was moving the ship right and left, hoping to interfere with their accuracy. Most people don't know that a gun on full auto is not very accurate unless it has tracers to guide the bullets to the target.

Still, it was several hundred bullets coming up at us. I punched two pair in response. I hit most of them. Bob finished the job with the cannon. I broke left to see if anyone was on the other side of our guys and noticed Bob hanging in his shoulder harness/seat belt. His head was down.

I said, "Bob, can you hear me?" He lifted his head and looked at me and moved his mouth, but no words came out. He was extremely pale. "Were you hit?" He nodded and pointed to his right calf. I couldn't see anything as the console blocked my view. "Ski, can you see Bob's leg?"

Ski laid down his gun and looked over Bob's shoulder and said, "Mac, I don't see any blood."

Bob said, "I pass out at the sight of blood. I think there's blood on my leg."

"How the hell did you get through flight school? They drew blood from us every month for the medical units overseas."

"I would look away and act like I fell asleep."

"The slicks are going in. Can you shoot that cannon?"

"Yes, I'm with you. Ski said it's a scratch."

"9-6, this is our last run. We'll follow the slicks in and out."

Click-click.

The slick on the left said he was being shot at from 200 yards at his 9 o'clock. Wing put a rocket on the little shit. I punched two into the edge of the jungle on the right. There were nice explosions. *Blowing up things can be fun.*

We followed the slicks out, and then broke off as they were the new H model with lots of power, and they were rapidly pulling away from us. I called Baldy and asked if they had any fast movers in the area. "I would like to see those caves evaporated."

"I'll see what I can do."

We refueled and rearmed, and I sent Bob to the MASH unit. Then, we just sat in the shade of our ships and shot the shit. Too god-damned tired to do anything else. Besides, the Hilton was an oven. We often pulled our bunks outside and hoped for a little breeze. All we usually got were flares going off all night, and machine guns firing from the bunkers at the slightest noise or movement.

We're all friends because we have the same enemy. I think Lincoln said that.

I went over to the red phone and asked for the ammo dump. "Can you order white phosphorus rockets for our gunships?"

"I don't see why not."

I returned to the bullshit session. One of the guys said, "They give a different perspective of this place back in the world."

"Here perception is your reality and vice versa."

Here came Bob. No limp. I said, "Pull up your pant leg." We all began to laugh. Over the wound was a double size bandage (about two inches by three inches).

Bob said, "The doc told me, 'That's a Purple Heart. It's worth ten points on an exam to work for the post office.'"

The red phone rang. It was Baldy HQ telling us that the fast movers had evaporated the cliff. As soon as I hung up, the damn thing rang again. "Mac, you are wanted in CL. 9-2, Morton is coming up to replace you. I don't think anything is wrong. The IG people want to talk to you."

I thought, *Fuck, a bunch of REMF's are going to act like they know who's on first.*

A slick landed 40 minutes later. Morton jumped out, and I jumped in. I told the pilot, "You fly. I don't know how to fly a slick.

Be careful. There are some bad guys around who want to kill me."

He said, "Shit, they didn't tell me *that* when they told me to come up here. Fuckin' Army."

I said, "Right, FTA (fuck the army)."

When we landed, I was taken to the CO's office. I was filthy, under slept, smelly, starving and in a foul mood.

I reported in to Top, and he said, "Jesus Christ Mac, what have you been doing? Smells like you were on the shit-burning detail."

I didn't say anything.

Top jerked his thumb towards the CO's office. The door was closed, so I knocked twice and heard, "Enter." I walked in and saw four REMF's around the CO's desk. I stopped and started to report in, but the CO said, "Sit down Mac. These four officers would like to ask you some questions."

I said, "Certainly, and I would like to apologize for my appearance."

They all smiled and two actually laughed. A colonel looked to be in charge, as he was the highest ranking officer, so I had my eyes on him.

"Mac," he said, "you have quite the reputation. If we had two more like you, this war would be over. The reason I called you in here was to discuss your setup of your ammo dump. It isn't up to army standards. Can you explain?"

"Yes sir, I can. I don't believe the manuals were written for fast war-time rearming and fast turnaround for the guns. First, the 40 mm were at the far end of the dump. Those linked rounds are the heaviest, so I moved them to the front. On the other side of the 40mm, I put the linked 7.62, as the slicks use only that ammo, and it will decrease their rearm time. Door gunners on the gunships also use that ammo. The wing ship could require ten to fifteen thousand rounds for the mini guns, so it made no sense putting that ammo at the far end."

"As for the rockets, well, they don't have to be up front. But next to the first in front. The copilot helps the door gunner rearm, and the pilot assists the crew chief and then moves to the rockets. You can carry 4 to 6 rockets at a time. I'm sure the Willy Pete's are on the list of questions. The C model manual for all systems says to put them nose down after connection of the warhead to the motor. The WP can spontaneously ignite, and the designers didn't want them to take off by themselves, which they would if the noses were pointed up. It can occur if the warhead had a leak and came onto contact with Oxygen. I put the ammo in order of priorities for the 71st order of battle with the priority on gunships. Everything is at an arm's reach after entering the dump. The smoke grenades are up front as all three platoons use them.

"The 38 ammo is rarely used, so it got bumped to the end. Also sitting back there are the smoke rockets. Gunships have no use for those. Flechettes rockets are rarely used as are the WP's. There are other odd items such as grenades, high explosives, claymores, and CS. There are twelve-gauge double-aught buckshot for shotguns, shells for hand-carried M-79 grenade launchers, and 45 ca. bullets for a Thompson submachine gun. Lots of explosive material, but most of it we won't use unless we become an infantry patrol."

"Well, Mr. McNally, we are impressed with the way you've been able to plan ahead and anticipate the needs of the mission."

"Thank you, sir."

"Mac, I'm going to give you the only perfect score I've ever given on an IG inspection. Your CO told me that you could work out all the bugs in a faulty plan. He was correct."

"Mr. McNally, you are dismissed .Thank you for your explanations." I stood up and walked out.

I went to the Birdhouse and got those filthy clothes off my body. I washed three separate times trying to wash the war off me. How the hell can these people write a manual on something they have never seen? *Fuck I'm working for idiots.*

I wasted time until dinner. Turned out that was a mistake. *Fuck it I'm going to the bar.* I had two crowns when someone said, "Mac, Sergeant McDougall, the EMs Firebird sergeant, is at the door and wishes to speak to you."

I walked over and said, "What's up?"

"Sir, I need someone to help bore sight a gunship."

"I'm your man, Sarg."

"Have you had anything to drink?"

I said, "No." How hard could it be for me to hover out of a revetment and land on the taxiway 100 feet away? I had had only two crown royals.

Sarg and I drove to the flight line and climbed in the ship. I called the tower and told them our plan.

I started lifting the ship up out of the revetment, and it was moving very erratically. I sat it down and called the tower. "Wind please," which means give me the direction and speed.

The tower called back and said, "Firebird 9-7, wind is zero-zero." This means there is no direction or speed. *In other words, a calm night with my shitty flying.*

I thought, *S*hit, maybe two crowns are too much. I don't feel buzzed. Shit, I'll try it again.

I pulled up on the collective and was gentle on the pedals. Up we came, and I put the ship down on the taxiway. Now came the hard part. I had to pull down my rocket sight and put my reticle on a tin shed about 800 yards away. In the past, this had been easy and quick, but now I couldn't get my reticle on the fucking shed. I pulled up a small amount torque, so I was light on my skids and could push my pedals a very short amount right and the sight flew right by my target. I then slid back across my target to the left. *OK Kevin, calm down and breathe. The Sarg is getting scared, and I don't want tonight to end poorly.* I went back and forth again, and then I settled down and lined up on the shed. *This won't go in my manual of things they don't teach you in flight school.*

We finished that, and I went back to the company area to do some serious drinking in the club. Captain Wilder was there. Big Randy was putting down the drinks. I met two new Firebirds: Winters and Newhouse. I didn't try for first names, because I would be lucky to remember last names.

After a while, we moved the party to the Birdhouse. We put on some music. Practically everyone had a reel-to-reel tape machine and very large speakers. Most of the music was recorded from Armed Forces Vietnam Radio.

Dennis came in and said, "Goodbye you Mutha fuckers. I'm going home tomorrow."

We cheered him and gave him a beer. Then someone said, "I have Randy's wife's phone number. Do you want it Denny?" That drew a bigger laugh.

The Birds were a really tight group. And really young. They were 18 and 19 years old. I had turned 22 a few months before, and I was one of the oldest pilots in our company.

"It's midnight guys," I told them. "I've had all I can take."

Chapter 58.

STEPHANIE FOR THE DEFENSE

I slept till seven. When I came out of the mess hall, the new clerk Smitty stopped me and said, "The CO would like to see you."

I walked in and said, "Good morning, Top. Smitty said Major Thomson wants to see me."

"Yes Mac, go on in." I did, and Top followed and closed the door.

The CO said, "Those fuckers at HQ are running out of things to do. The legal people received a complaint saying it was your fault Dusty was killed."

I was stunned. I paused and asked if Baldy had a copy of our radio transmissions.

"Yes, Mac. I've got it," and he held up a tape.

I nodded and asked if they had spoken to the 6 on the ground.

"Not yet. What it sounds like is someone higher ranked than Dusty ordered him to go in without the Birds. It backfired."

"I have one request." The CO and Top looked at each other and nodded *OK*.

"I want Stephanie Rheem to defend me. She's a lawyer. You can confirm that by contacting her lawyer father in LA or talking to Colonel Wheaton with the GBs in Danang. They have a personal connection. I want her to be my lawyer because I know when you put her to a task, she will get it done."

A couple of hour later, Smitty came to get me. "The CO would like to see you."

Don't you assholes know there's a fucking war going on?

I walked in, and Top was standing at his desk. I said, "You don't have to stand when I come in." I was smiling, and he smiled back.

"Go on in."

There was Stephanie and Colonel Wheaton. I was fighting emotions and military etiquette.

Steph started moving towards me, so I thought *what the hell? All they can do is send me to VN.* She jumped into my arms. *God she felt good.* I held her, and it was a long kiss. When we broke for air, I said, "Excuse me, sirs, but I couldn't help it. I love this lady who also happens to be my choice for a lawyer. Sometimes I can be unmilitary"

The CO said, "We've been brought up to date."

I looked over at Colonel Wheaton and saw a star on each epaulet of his uniform. "Damn, a General! Congratulations, sir. I know we don't salute indoors, but here you are with stars." I snapped to attention and saluted. I held it until he returned my salute. I reached out, and we shook hands. Everyone else just looked on in amazement.

The CO said, "The general has told us some amazing stories."

He paused, so I said, "Best copilot I ever had. In fact, I listed him as PIC because of our last two missions into, I whispered . . . Laos."

The general said, "They all have clearances."

I continued, "The general did it all. He even helped rearm the ship. What impressed me most was the general's coolness in taking off from RP. When I told him we were 1600 pounds over gross, he wasn't fazed. His touch on the controls was smooth and gentle, and he knew how to get a Bird into the air. I wish I could fly with him some more. I promised I wouldn't let him get captured. I didn't say anything about wounded."

That got a few laughs.

"Now that he's a General, they probably won't let him fly with me. That's a shame because he's a great pilot. He told me as you climb up the ladder, it is more paper than flying. The only way to another Purple Heart for him from now on will be paper cuts."

More laughs.

The general said, "You guys are a very close and tight group. Very special people to work with. I'm sorry I won't be able to go out with you again."

"Steph has known you Gen. Wheaton since she was a toddler," I said. "I almost fell over when she called you by your first name. But it's a relief to me that you know her so well. You know what a good lawyer she is. So, sir, can you assign her to defend me?"

"Of course I can," the general said. "Those legal turds are going to get blasted out of CL faster than we can say innocent." He paused, and then he added, "Mac, is it OK if I come too?"

"I would be honored, sir."

The CO stood up. "I think that's enough for now. Mac, I want you and Clearwater to fly to Baldy. Stay there for a few days before the senseless hearing begins about Dusty."

So Bob and I flew to Baldy. We were just getting settled in when the red phone rang. It was a supply convoy going SW to FSB Ross. They were going out to beef up some of the outlying FSB's. Looks like the enemy saw the plan as well. There were 51's snipping at them every mile or so.

After TO, I called the convoy, Traveler 6, and he gave me an update. "They are shooting that 51 from a long way off. At least a click away on the western side of the road. Sir, we've got tons of ammo in this convoy."

"OK," I told him, I'll come up behind them from the SW and shoot those assholes in the back. Can you hear us?"

"Yes, they're at least a half mile ahead of you, about half a mile off the road."

"9-5," I said, "let's go way out around and behind them and come in fast, cyclic climb and shoot. Let's try a right break. But we may have to change depending on what's waiting for us. For you copilots, this is going to be totally different from anything you've done to date. I'll give you a three word guide for this mission: Evaluate, Improvise, and Perform. Think about those three words when we start shooting. Gunners, if you see that 51, kill the NVA working it."

All the while as I was talking, I was circling around behind those bastards and climbing to 300 feet. We were flying right up to the red lines on our instrument panel. I called 6 and asked him if the 51 was currently shooting.

"No."

"Good. Let's go."

I pulled back on the cyclic, and we climbed to 500 feet. A half a mile out, directly ahead was the 51 and over 100 NVA scattered around. I punched twice, and the 51 was toast. I could see about 50 bodies. My crew was all over the remaining troops. I said, "Breaking right." As I was turning, some 51 tracers went by my windshield. You always knew it was a big gun when the tracers looked like burning softballs. I said, "fifty yards south of the first one."

A hailstorm of bullets was being fired at us from the NVA around that damn gun. Some rounds came through the floor. Then, we had a hole in the windshield. My guys kept shooting, which was good because it let me know they were still alive. As I was clawing for altitude, I heard, "Firebird 9-5 on fire, going down near the highway. I can see some trucks coming toward me."

"I'll stay above you," I said, "until the trucks arrive." He landed ten yards from the road, and I counted four flyers jump out with their arms full of whatever wasn't tied down.

Now, I had to outthink those assholes with the 51. I kept turning and flying low, so the 51 couldn't get a clear picture of me long enough to shoot. I flew behind the hills we had used for cover on the first run. After two minutes, I turned around and dropped to ten feet off the ground.

I asked, "Everyone OK?" I got three loud yeses. "How's your ammo?" Ski and Tyler both had about 1000 rounds. Bob's intervalometer said 400 rounds for the cannon.

I said, "We're going back in the way we came out. I don't think they will expect that. When we pop up over the hill, I want everyone shooting at that 51. If it goes down, then pick off targets of opportunity. I'm going to punch almost every rocket I have to get that damn gun. If it gets too wild and they have a third 51, we'll fly back towards the road and think of something else."

We crossed the road and were able to hide behind trees until it came time to cyclic climb. The Wing's burning ship also provided some concealment. We attacked. Those dumb bastards were doing exactly what I thought: not expecting us from that direction. I shot two pair at the 51 and had a nice secondary explosion in the form of a fireball. I shot two more pairs on each side of the dead 51. I broke right, and the door gunners were on their A game, as always. I called Traveler 6 and asked if he was taking fire.

He said, "No."

Ski said, "Mac, the NVA were chained to that 51."

"I've heard about that." Then I told Traveler 6, "I'm going to make another pass and then go gas up and reload. When I pass over, you resume driving. Baldy just called and said one of our slicks will pick up those grounded birds."

"Are any of them injured?"

"No," said 6. "Our medic checked them out, and all are well. The copilot, as I understand it, is your platoon leader. He told me, 'This shit sucks.' I had to agree with him."

"Shit Ski, were you serious? Actually chained?"

"Two guys had chains. No shit!"

"Fuck! OK 6, I'm going to fly over you, climb and shoot. They would never believe I would be dumb enough to come from the front again."

As I popped up, what few were alive were all waiting for me to come over the hill. The area was burning, and the fire was climbing up the hill. They probably thought I would use the smoke for cover. Actually, that wouldn't have been a bad idea, but I was committed. We shot at anything and everything. No return fire on this pass. I had two yellow warning lights come on: exhaust temp was climbing and electrical. I called CL and asked if Snake Doctor could make a house call. I gave him a rundown on our hits.

He said, "I'll see what I can do."

I told Baldy, "I could fly another mission if really necessary."

I landed as Baldy called me. "CL is sending a new team with both a lead and wing. And a sling for yours Mac. The slick that picked up your wing crew is coming for you and your crew."

I told my crew that meant a shower, cold beer, and sleep in tomorrow. Everyone's mood improved. Mine really went off the scale when Monty told me I was to meet with my attorney tomorrow at CL HQ at 0900.

I sat in the shade and leaned back against a Conex container full of 40mm shells and dozed off thinking about tomorrow. Two noisy Hueys woke me. One ship had Wing's crew, so me and my crew jumped into the empty one. We all fell asleep for the entire ride.

A truck picked us up and took us to the company area, which happened to be in front of the CO's office. We were slowly climbing out when the CO walked out and said, "Mac, you got a minute?"

For the CO, of course, I had a minute. "Be right there." I pulled my gear out and climbed the four steps and dropped everything.

I said, "Good afternoon, sir."

He said, "Follow me," as he walked straight into his office. He pointed at a chair as he walked around his desk and sat down. "First, I want to thank you for your excellent work on both ammo dumps. You got this company's first two perfect scores on the IG inspection. No one, and I mean no one, ever gets a perfect score. You just moved me higher up the line for lieutenant colonel. I also had a long talk with Gen Wheaton, and he insists you did the same for him to get that star.

"While you were flying, I've been snooping around and discovered that a certain major ordered Dusty to go out there and pick up the wounded in a record time. This was to have his underlings make him look good. He was called on the carpet by his superiors as to why there was no gun support. When this wraps up the day after tomorrow, I wouldn't be surprised if he were court marshalled.

"Baldy called me while you were flying here and played a tape that was mind-blowing. I was trying to figure out your next move, and you had already made it. Oh, and we had a meeting and decided your case would require a full day to prepare."

"Thank you very much, sir."

"Be here at 0850 tomorrow, and we'll drive up to the road to HQ. I heard Top ask you a few days ago if you were on a shit burning detail. That was funny, but for god's sake it's time to take a shower. Dismissed Mac. No drinking and get lots of sleep. You will need all your energy tomorrow."

I turned and looked at his smiling face. Then, I grinned and nodded.

After cleaning the war off my body, I went to the bar. The first person I saw was Tom Rivers. I said. "That was a great flaming autorotation. You kept flying and never quit."

"Thanks, Mac. Did you hear about Muse? He took himself off flight status. He got a Dear John letter from his girlfriend of three years. What a shitty chicken shit thing to do behind his back. We should put her in one of our ships for one day!"

"Tom, how's Jerry doing?"

"He's ready to fly wing and should be ready for lead in the near future."

"I'm going back out soon. Set it up so he's my wing. He's going to have to be great following you. How short are you?"

"Three weeks. DEROS and FIGMO until then."

"Shit, you shouldn't be flying."

"I agree."

"Tell Jerry. Hell! I'll cover for you."

Tom grinned. "Hey, want a drink?"

"I don't want a drink," I said. "I need a drink. How about you, Tom?"

"Yes, another one. I'm a beer and a crown ahead of you."

"I'll catch you."

We laughed.

Jerry and the CO walked in. *Well, what do ya know? That should calm this place down.*

Jerry walked over and asked if he could sit down.

We said, "Of course, you're a Bird, and Birds are always welcome. We were just talking about you. And of course the CO may sit wherever he wishes."

He looked down at us and said, "I know. That's why I came over. To see what you E-10's are planning."

E-10 is a made up rank that people sometimes used for warrant officers. Not a real rank, but below an LT and above an enlisted man. A slight put down.

"Are you going to overthrow your platoon leader," he asked us, "and take over?"

"Jerry, nothing of the kind. We were discussing having you fly wing next time out. You OK with that?"

"Yes," he said in a strong confident voice.

"You'll get your official check ride next time you fly," said the CO.

"Guys, I'm outta here," I said. "I gotta be in CL HQ at 0900. Good night."

Once in bed, I started anticipating the next day with Steph. I immediately felt the butterflies in my stomach. Despite being tired, I had trouble getting to sleep. I was so ready to see Steph. I woke up at 0600 and took a shower. You can't take too many showers in this filthy place. This nasty piece of real estate certainly wasn't worth the number of people that had been killed to keep it.

As Smitty pulled the jeep into HQ, the always beautiful Stephanie was standing there with a very big and sexy smile. She was walking briskly toward the jeep before we even stopped. I jumped out to meet her and for that brief moment we melted into each other's arms, and I had no thoughts of war or death. I thought that was proof enough of how much I loved her.

She leaned toward me and whispered, "Would you like to come into my den of iniquity?"

"Oh, please lead the way," I said. "I'll race you."

"No running," she teased. "Let's save our energy for more important things."

I grabbed my duffel bag from the back of the jeep and told Smitty, "Thanks."

Then, Steph and I walked off hand-in-hand to paradise. Inside the trailer with the door locked, we started the most compassionate kissing to date. I was thinking, *how much better can this be?*

"I love you Steph. I've missed you so much. I wish we could stay in here for a month... with room service, of course. God, you look gorgeous. Remember the old song by the Seekers, 'I'll never find another you'?"

We made slow love, thoughtful love, and way beyond what twenty-somethings do: fast and done. When possible, we would stare into each other's eyes. That gave love and sex a whole new meaning. Looking into her eyes, I could better see and feel how I was giving her pleasure. I hoped she knew I was getting the same from her.

We paused after an hour and grabbed the moment just to look at each other.

She said, "You don't have an ounce of fat on you."

"That's because they starve us. Half the food we're fed is not fit to be consumed by humans."

Then I thought of something. "Let me tell you a story about my first year at the University of Oregon. I was in a dorm, which says something about the food I had to put up with. It was worse than at the 71st.

"Besides being a math major, I was interested in biology, in case I ever met someone like you." For that, I received a punch in the arm. "OK, but I was interested in biology. Our first Lab was the dissection of a fetal pig. Pigs and cats have similar musculature to humans.

"When an animal dies, it turns black in spite of being wrapped in rags soaked in formaldehyde. Same with humans. They are black all the way through. The chemicals slow the rotting process.

"When we were finished with the pigs, we were supposed to put them in a large waste basket to be incinerated. One day, several of us wrapped our pigs up and carried them out of the lab in brief cases or under coats. We stored them in a can behind some washing machines in the basement. That evening, we took one to dinner.

"When you finished eating, you placed your tray on a tall rack on wheels eight rows high at one end of the room. There were usually three or four of these tall racks. We walked through part of the kitchen to get to the racks set up for another dorm. We unwrapped the pig and laid it on a tray and slid it into the rack near the top, so the short lady pulling out the trays couldn't see it until it was right in front of her. With everything set up, we went to a large nearby room with chairs and couches and sat down to wait. We didn't have to wait long.

"There was a blood curdling scream that must have gone on for 20 seconds. People ran to help whoever was being murdered. We followed the crowd to look innocent. Several girls were vomiting. There it was, on the floor next to the dropped tray. The pig, which was only about twelve inches long, was very black and smelled bad. The victim was sitting on the floor when some firemen came into the room and told us to leave.

"We all escaped to our dorm rooms. We couldn't stop laughing. We were a bunch of twisted fucks. What do you think of that story?"

"I agree with the twisted fuck part."

"Don't you think it was just a little bit funny?"

"It would be funny here but not back in the world. That poor girl is probably seeing a psychologist as we speak and could become a serial killer."

"We threw out the other pigs. Trying that stunt twice would be pushing our luck.

"I'm horny Steph."

That got me another punch in the arm.

"You're lucky I love you so much."

"Let's talk about something nice," I said, not wanting to leave things at the twisted fuck level. "You told me you sent your mom pictures and told her about us?"

"I sent her about twenty pics with practically a book written on the back of each one. Then, she called and we talked for two hours. She said, 'Steph I have known you for almost twenty-five years, and you are in love. You remind me of when your dad and I couldn't keep our hands off each other. It's such an amazing story: a random meeting, a gentle person but his job is killing people. I didn't mean that the way it came out. I understand he's able to turn it off and love you.'"

"I told Mom about the night I fired the machine gun, you flying in to protect me and then carrying me when I was out cold after three hours of adrenalin, taking me back to my place and putting me to bed. I told her we were wrapped up in each other's arms and legs when we woke up."

"Maybe you shouldn't tell her everything," I suggested.

"I have to tell someone, and I trust Mom. I warned her not to get too specific with Dad. He might be a little shocked and all."

"He might have me taken out and shot," I said. "You're his innocent little girl, and I'm... well, you know."

"Mom is cool. Besides, dad has already checked into your background."

Why was I surprised? "Of course, he did," I said.

She grinned. "All good, honey. Honor roll, varsity swimmer, well liked, didn't have a drinking problem, didn't drink at all, two years at the Univ. of Oregon majoring in math."

"I guess that drinking part doesn't hold over here, but yeah, I used to be pretty straight."

"She told me the FBI went to Medford for your top secret clearance. They questioned your teachers, neighbors and the local police and found nothing suspicious. Their number one question was: is he trustworthy?"

"So, you knew all that? I thought those security reports were confidential."

Steph let this pass. I guess her father and the general could find out whatever they wanted.

"I told Mom I felt like a lucky prospector who had discovered gold." Then, Steph changed the subject. "Tell me about the mission when Dusty was killed."

I took thirty minutes, and she listened and did not interrupt once. She even took notes.

"Tell me, Kevin, is there anything else? I don't think this should have gotten this far. Someone is trying to cover up something."

"My CO told me he did a little snooping around and discovered a major, the CO of Dust off, wanted to show everyone that their work didn't require guns. I think he has a grudge against the guns. Maybe on a previous tour in this lovely part of the world?"

"Inter;esting. You have awakened my lawyer genes. I have contacts through Dad's firm. I'll check on the major's first tour."

"There's something else. Baldy records all the transmissions during a mission. My CO has a copy. I'll ask him to send the tape here via courier."

"Let's keep the chain of evidence intact. I'll send a courier to Baldy for the original and a copy to your CO. It's always nice to have the original to compare to copies. Go shower while I make a few calls. After lunch, we'll put this bullshit in order and bury the chicken-shit bastard that dumped his problem on you."

"Thanks, pal," I said, "but I believe I'm too tired to get out of bed."

She got up and looked so incredible as she walked to her phone, I decided I could manage a shower.

I was just finishing, when she stepped in and said, "Where are you going? I need my back washed."

"It will be my pleasure."

One thing led to another. It was for both our pleasures.

After a very good lunch, we listened to both tapes, and she was pleased. She interviewed the patrol's leader, 6. He told the same story, as we were all on the same frequency. She called the 71st and spoke to Tyler and Ski. Last was a call to my copilot, Bob Clearwater.

She said, "This is a no brainer. It would be laughed out of court back home. I intend to have some fun here. I believe what your CO said. There will be a court martial after our investigation."

The room for the hearing had several visitors: Gen Wheaton, Capt. MacAddo, and their RTO. Also in attendance were my CO, Maj Thompson, Top, Sergeant McDougall (Ski and Tyler's Platoon leader), several Firebirds, Capt. Wilder, Smitty, and a few slick drivers I had pulled out of a fire. Then, the colonel presiding over the investigation walked in with two field officers to make up the investigating court. Next were the Major who was CO of the Dust off platoon and his attorney, followed by Major Webster of FSB Dragon and the three slick pilots that were involved with the mission in question.

We made a dramatic entrance: A gorgeous woman followed by me, my crew, and the four in the wing ship

The opposing attorney immediately called an objection to this person in civilian clothes and a woman. Oops, he had just screwed the pooch.

Steph faced the judge and said, "Your honor, May I answer this?"

He said, "Go right ahead. The counselor is not aware of UCMJ (uniform code of military justice) protocol."

"I'm Stephanie Rheem, graduate of UCLA law school, first in my class and a member of the Order of the Coif. I passed the bar on the first test and immediately began practicing at the Rheem Law firm, the largest in LA. I won every case that I was given to research before one of our attorneys went to court. Then, my patriot genes kicked in, and I became a Donut Dolly for the Red Cross. I also have a General from the GB's here to validate that I understand what's going on in this war. In other words, I have received daily briefings, and I have a Top Secret Clearance.

"Also Captain, the UCMJ states that the accused may choose their defending counsel if they so desire. Warrant Officer McNally, whom did you choose?"

"I choose you, Miss Rheem."

The presiding judge said, "This is going to be the most interesting investigation of my eight months in VN."

Steph turned to the opposing attorney. "Since you called into question my qualifications, it seems fair to note that you required three attempts to pass the bar."

The poor captain just stood there like a statue without a word to say.

The president of the court said, "Everyone testifying must leave the room and will be called in one at a time to give their statements."

The fun began for Steph. She first called up all the birds except me that were involved in the mission. Then, she called Gen

Wheaton as a character witness along with MacAddo. Next were my CO, Top, Wilder, and some Rattler pilots including Glen Walton. They each told their stories in detail. Steph was brilliant in guiding the witnesses to keep them on track testifying to my efficiency, professionalism and attention to detail.

The judge called a break for lunch.

I was sitting in a corner talking to my beautiful attorney when the general walked over and sat down. Steph looked at him and said, "I let them dig a hole, and the burial is after lunch. Here's another wound that will help kill the major. He was kicked out of a gun-team platoon two years ago. The CO went a little soft in his OER (Officer Efficiency Report) because the major is a ring knocker (an academy graduate who knocks on the table with his ring when sitting at a promotion interview to remind the panel he went to the academy). He was a terrible pilot and a poor leader. He is not military material."

"Wow Steph," I said. "You got all that while I was in the shower?"

"No problem Firebird," she said. "You're seeing only a little of me at the base of the mountain. As the elevation rises, you will see more." She paused and looked thoughtful. "Actually, Kev, I didn't mean that like it sounded. I say things like that for the assholes who think blonds are dumber than women in general."

"Are you hungry?"

"No. I'm too caught up in the case. However, it would be my pleasure to keep you company if you'd like to eat."

"I promise, Steph, that I will someday take you to a much more elegant establishment for an evening of very fine dining."

"If it includes dessert, I would be honored."

I said, "Of course. You may begin and end the meal with dessert."

She laughed and said, "I still don't feel hungry, and we're talking about dessert! My lawyer training is in high gear."

As everyone was returning from lunch, the three pilots involved in the mission were talking to Steph. She said, "Be precise. Don't embellish. Answer only the question asked, and ask me to repeat it if necessary. Only one of you at a time will be in the room. Same as in the morning session."

Steph began with the pilots. They didn't hear the initial communications as they were on other missions, but they did hear all exchanges after Dusty went down. They spoke of the ground and gunship exchanges when they were told to report to the gunships at the given coordinates. They told of the expertise of Firebird 9-7 on ensuring the area was safe so we could land and get those guys out of there.

After those three finished, she called up the accuser. He told a completely different story. He omitted the part about Dusty not returning calls after he spoke to the tower. "We're pretty sure his radios were in working order, especially since he spoke to the 6 on the ground before attempting to land for the wounded G I."

"Major, have you ever been involved with a gunship platoon?"

"No, I have not."

"Are you aware that Baldy records all transmissions of the troops on the ground, helos in the air, and anything else in their AO?"

"No."

"President of the court, I would like to play the original tape recording of the mission in question." As it played, the Major went pale.

Everything went as was stated in the testimonies. We could hear clearly the numerous attempts to get Dusty to slow down. Also, the calls from 9-7 to the 6 on the ground to tell Dusty not to land until we got there to take care of the NVA. "We are only two or three minutes behind you." Dusty told 6 to pop smoke as he was coming in without the gunships.

Steph asked Ed, the major, if he was correct in stating that he had never been involved with gunships or in a gunship platoon."

"That's correct."

Steph walked to her desk and retrieved some papers. She handed a set to each of the three Board Members and kept one for herself. She turned and faced the Board and said, "These papers are part of the Major's military file. They were sent here by secured fax and have been maintained by Legal as to their authenticity and a tight chain of evidence.

"You will find the major was a platoon leader of the gunships for three weeks two years ago in II corp. He was relieved of those duties due to poor piloting and poor leadership. He spent the rest of his time in VN working in supply for the same company."

Steph paused for effect and to let the Board read the file. Then, she said, "You have heard his evidence as to the inop radios and then his prevarication as to involvement with a gunship platoon. With that information, we have strike one and two. Now for the third strike. The major was inebriated before, during, and after the mission. I will step back and use the word 'drunk' for the Firebirds in attendance. And 'prevarication' means 'lie.'" Everyone in the room laughed out loud. They were all aware of the Bird's crude reputation.

"I spoke to the major's RTO and his platoon sergeant to obtain this info. They report this has occurred numerous times in the past."

Steph looked to the president and said, "I apologize to the Board, colonel. I couldn't help myself from putting emphasis on the third strike."

"Yes, Miss Rheem, you put a lot of emphasis on the third strike." He seemed to be fighting back more laughter. "Everyone remain seated while the court discusses this investigation."

The three of them got up and walked out. They returned in ten minutes.

"The Board finds this investigation was fabricated to protect the major. It appears that he has done this before. The court apologizes for your inconvenience and an attempt to tarnish the reputation of Mr. McNally. We usually don't apologize, but this is so scandalous we feel we should. We in legal need to check out these complaints in a more thorough manner.

"Mr. McNally, nothing will ever appear on your record here or in Ireland."

"Sir, I'm not worried about here; it's in Ireland. So, thank you very much."

"I'm glad you approve. Would the MP please take the major into custody. (A military police individual is always present in any procedure.) He spoke to the MP. "You've heard enough to file charges. I'll call you later and probably add some more."

The MP just said, "Yes sir," and put on the handcuffs.

"Miss Rheem, do you have anything to add?"

"No sir."

"Before I dismiss the room and the Board, I would like Mr. McNally, Miss Rheem, Gen. Wheaton, Major Thompson, Top, Mr. Walton, Captain McAdoo and Captain Wilder to remain."

All the others filed out. The colonel seated himself on our side of the table and said, "This is an unofficial get together for a bullshit session." That got lots of laughs.

The colonel started off with, "How much of this is true?"

Gen Wheaton said, "Everything you heard and much-much more."

The colonel asked, "Miss Rheem, did you really do everything I read in the after-action report? 4500 rounds? Picking off NVA in the wire, blowing up Bangalores, and for several hours and no relief and wounded?"

"Colonel, I had two guardian angels watching over me. Mac and his copilot flew by my location many times putting rockets, 40 mm, and thousands of door gunner rounds on those bastards. And wait until I tell you who flew with Mac that night: General Wheaton!"

"Mr. McNally, did you teach Sweet Steph to talk like that?"

Before I could answer, she jumped up and gave General Wheaton a hug. "You worked in legal with my dad when he was a second lieutenant. You gave me that nickname."

Gen Wheaton came over and shook hands with the colonel overseeing the investigative board. "I wanted to remain silent so as to not affect your inquiry. I know you are a good friend of Sweet Steph's dad."

Major Thompson said, "I was told some wild stories about Mac from Major Wilson before his DEROS."

I spoke up to answer the colonel's question. "She already knew those words, sir. I've been trying to train her so she'll be able to talk to people when she returns to the world."

"Fuckin' A right, Mac," said Steph.

That brought down the house. Gen Wheaton said, "Get me a bar of soap."

The colonel said, "I'm calling your dad."

"You should've seen my reaction when she called the Gen 'Derek,'" I put in. "I hadn't been in the army long, but I knew that wasn't cool."

Everyone laughed, the general the most.

"Steph, is there anyone you don't know?"

"Yes. That asshole we just kicked out of the army." More laughter.

"General sir," the colonel said, "I know you don't run a dry unit of GBs here."

"No Colonel, I don't and thank you for reminding me. That kind of a reputation could ruin a career." He looked at Captain McAdoo and nodded.

McAdoo said, "I will be back very soon sir."

The colonel said to me, "Did you really carry that pilot through enemy fire?"

"He wanted to walk," I said, "but he was slow and the bad guys were using real bullets. The worst part was I jumped out of the ship and left the CO, Major Wilson, sitting in harm's way. It was my last day as an FNG. When I climbed back into the ship, I looked at him thinking, *How far down the ranks will he bust me (reduce my rank)?*"

The Captain returned with beer, gin, vodka, rum and a bucket of ice. We all thanked him and poured the water out of our glasses.

"Steph, the colonel asked, did you learn to shoot the 60 while he (indicating me) was flying the Dollies to FSBs?"

"Guilty as charged," Steph admitted. "Did you notice how well that training helped at the GB unit?"

"Yes Steph, very impressive. You actually saved the whole base. They could have run 2000 troops through that opening in ten minutes, and it would have been hand to hand combat."

Then, the colonel looked at Mac and asked, "Did you reload the slick with ammo from FSBs?"

"Yes sir," I said. 'They were paid back the next morning."

"For the record," I added, "I know what inebriation is, but I have to admit, prevarication was a new one to me." More laughter.

The drinking continued until 1700 when the general said, "Let's go to dinner." Afterwards, we continued talking until midnight.

As we were breaking up, Jerry said, "Mac, we get the day off tomorrow. There is a large CA the day after: 200 men, 30 Hueys and two gun teams. You and Randy lead. Your wing is me, and the other wing is Norwood. We TO at sunrise."

Someone has been reading too many comic books, I thought. *We are going in with the sun at our backs. I wonder how many more know about the mission?*

"You're in charge Mac," Jerry said. "There will be a C & C at 2000 feet above ground level (AGL)."

Steph and I retired to her place. After we got inside, I said to her, "Let's get naked and play nasty."

"I was wondering when you were going to get around to me," she said in mock indignation. "All those accolades! Will your head fit through my bedroom door?"

"Steph, I'm not a glory seeker. I'm just doing my very best to protect Americans, with an occasional SVNA, ROK and Aussie thrown in. I'm going to change the subject. I'm very impressed with your courtroom presentation. My god, you were smooth and straight to the point. I love you for so many reasons. Steph, you ready for bed?"

"Are YOU ready for bed, Kev?"

"Yes."

"Steph, I have to tell you that I always thought the truth was equal distance between the extremes, but you proved that wrong today. The truth was at the extreme end of guilt."

The next day was wonderful. We didn't go anywhere exotic or romantic (because that didn't exist in Vietnam with that damn war), but we walked on the beach hand in hand, and I had never felt so wonderful and warm inside. I sure felt I could do my job quicker and more efficiently than those guys chained to their machine guns.

Chapter 59.

HALF HIS HEAD WAS BLOWN OFF

Late afternoon, I returned to the 71st and immediately got on the phone with Steph.

"You said two kids, right Steph? I was raised with two younger brothers. I don't know anything about little girls. What happens if we have a girl?"

"I'll teach you! We are very sensitive and must be handled with care."

"Hey beautiful, here comes the CO. Wait just a moment."

In 60 seconds, I got back to her. "The CO put me on flight status, then said, 'Go to Baldy,' all in one sentence. I'm thinking you and I will be out of touch for close to a week. Dammit, this is wrong."

"What did you say to him?"

"I said, 'Yes sir,' the only answer you give to a commanding officer. It will go by quickly. I met my new copilot, Ron Devine, my new wing, 9-6 Wilder, with his new copilot Vic Newhouse. I'm going to miss Tom Rivers, 9-5, as he is FIGMO and headed home in a few days. Fox and Pat are their gunners, and Ski and Tyler are with me (the three musketeers)."

We ended our call with the usual endearments.

The next day, I got back to my job. After Wilder and I checked everything on the two ships and we all had strapped in, I asked Ron, "Have you ever taken off in an overloaded over-grossed hog?"

He said, "No."

"Get on the controls with me. The air has cooled these last few days. That should make this TO easier. Pick it up, Ron."

He had a twelve inch hover. "Move that cyclic forward a millimeter." We began moving, then dropped and bounced. We bounced a second time and were airborne.

I called 9-6 and said, "Let's rat race for beers." I got an *OK*, and 9-6 said he would tell the rules to Newhouse.

I followed with, "I'll do the same here."

I got back two clicks. I explained to Ron that this was an exercise to teach the wing how to always be in position to cover.

"If he makes a mistake," I said, "he buys us beer. Get on the controls with me, Ron, and you'll see that this over-grossed, (over-loaded) ship has limitations. Learn them or die. Let's start fifty feet AGL and race around the trees and even drag the skids through the top of a few trees until you look like a flying forest. OK 9-6, let's go guys."

It only took thirty seconds before Ski called over the IC. "Practice green at 9 o'clock." I quickly repeated that for the wing. The poor guy was caught again a minute later turning the wrong way. Then I said to 9-6, "Let's switch leads." He clicked twice as we slowed slightly, and 9-6 took the lead and the race was on. Ron didn't err for two minutes. He went five minutes before he made a second mistake.

I told him, "That's why we have the copilots give a thumbs up. So we know they have both hands on the controls and don't have a thumb up their ass."

He laughed and said, "I can't wait to use that on my copilot"

I called Baldy for fuel trucks as we landed. While we refueled, HQ called and said, "We have a firefly tonight."

I told my crew and 9-6. "Let's pull out every other rocket and replace it with WP. That should raise some hell in the river." I explained the plan. "We'll start ten clicks east of Baldy, and then turn straight north and follow it to the ocean. Then we'll follow a smaller river that also flows into the Hoi An. We go upstream until we're either out of ammo or the river becomes too small for anything to float on it.

"Let's get some sleep after we eat. We TO an hourxd after sunset. It's a long route tonight. We'll take turns being lead. The copilots will get a turn as will the crew chiefs and door gunners. The slick with the big bright light will be here at sundown."

The eight of us walked into the mess hall, and it smelled good. That got our curiosity working. Honest to god it was sloppy Joes and baked potatoes. *Someone cares.*

We returned to the Hilton and went to sleep. Our alarm went off at sunset. We gave the ships another look see. I told the gunners to throw in another case of ammo for each of them. "You're going to shoot the guys that jump in the water when the light hits their boat."

The slick was just coming in from POL. The slick pilot was Norm Griffin, 1-8. He had pulled me and Steph off the hill when I was shot down a few weeks ago. We reviewed the flight plan.

It was dark enough for government work. It only took a minute to fly to our starting point. The big light came on, and there were four boats. I dropped the nose a few degrees and punched off a pair of rockets. The explosions completely destroyed them. The river was covered with burning debris and floating bodies. My gunners got the few who jumped when the light came on. There were fires burning on both sides of the river. Some hooches, as well as the gardens next to them, were burning. The fires were spreading and gaining momentum. Those WP rockets can really do some damage. I saw all that in just a few seconds as the slick continued down-stream, and I had to be ready to shoot.

The light hit two boats, and I dispatched them immediately. I had to turn right to see because the smoke was billowing up and hid the boats. As I came around the smoke, I saw total carnage again: fires, debris, and bodies floating in our direction. We kept flying. In 30 seconds, a line of six boats appeared. I told Ron, "Sink those boats." He started shooting, and his shots were short. I didn't say anything because I wanted him to figure it out. After ten shots, I said, "Ski, Tyler, help him." The boats had stayed in a nearly straight line, so the three of them quickly destroyed everything.

I called 9-6 and said, "Take the lead in this turkey shoot." I got back his two clicks. "OK," I said, "I'm coming around on your left." As soon as he was beside me, the light found two boats. 9-6 dropped his nose and fired a pair and missed, but the Willie Pete got 'em. Fires were started on the east side of the river. We were leaving a trail of devastation, and it was all drifting to the ocean. I wondered if a larger boat was loading those sampans.

My thoughts were interrupted by the sound of the door gunners shooting. Tracers were being fired toward the big light. 1-8 said, "Lights out," and all outside lights and the firefly went out. Breaking a steep left, I put four rockets on the machine gun, when a second one opened up on me from the other side of the river. I yelled at Ron to shoot on full auto (40 mm). I had to break. I was too close to shoot rockets. I hoped wing was on that guy. Shit, at least four rounds came into the cockpit. Something struck my right knee and calf. I asked how things were in back.

Tyler said, "Something hit my back." Ski said, "I'm bleeding from the back of my right arm." Neither reported any pain. "Ron, are you OK?" All he said was, "FUCK." I was climbing out and up for my next run through all this talk.

"That fucker stitched us pretty good," Tyler said. He took a quick look at Ski's arm and said, "Mac I've cut myself worse shaving." Now it was Ski's turn and, after he looked at Tyler's back, he said, "Whatever it was, it popped one of his zits."

I heard, "Breaking left," then I started punching rockets at the muzzle flashes. Ron was doing pretty good. "Just ignore what's coming up and get on those muzzle flashes," I told him.

The guys in back had burned out the rifling in their barrels with long bursts. Good news was they always carried spares. They changed them in five seconds and dropped the ruined barrels into the river below. They were back on the targets with shorter bursts. We were hitting hard, but there were a lot of assholes down there. They were protecting something valuable. I called the Air Force spotter and asked if he had any workers tonight.

"I just happen to have two fast movers."

I said, "Great, turn, 'em loose. The target is the northern most fires." I called 1-8 and said, "How are you doing?"

"Three holes that we see but no yellow lights. The firefly is OK. Do you want to continue?"

I said, "Why not. The fast movers will take care of those shits and we can use our ammo on the river." I called wing and he was OK. "No holes we can see."

Those fast movers must have wanted to go home. They did a one pass and hauled ass. *Damn, look at that napalm.* Now I know what the sign on the wall in the Birdhouse meant. It said, "Napalm saves."

"9-6, how's your mini working?"

"He's doing pretty good."

"I'm gonna tell him that you're the best mini gun shooter I've ever seen." Of course, I knew his copilot heard as we were all on the same freq. *Nothing like pressure to speed up the learning curve.*

I called 9-6 and said, "Time for copilots to shoot rockets." As soon as I finished the sentence, Firefly lit up five boats. Wing's copilot fired two rockets at the line- up. He had the right idea: fire first at the end boat and at then work your way up the line to the lead boat, a rocket on each boat. Then, let the WP do its thing. We all were on single shots to conserve rockets. Everything below us was burning and sputtering. WP was spraying all over the river and both banks.

We flew around a bend in the river, and a machine gun opened up on us. Two rounds went through the windshield. The ship made an erratic move, and I grabbed the controls. I looked over at Ron. Half his head was blown off.

Fuck, fuck, fuck, another life gone.

I turned the gun switches to five pair (10 rockets) and punched once towards the machine guns and another at a group of muzzle flashes.

I called 1-8 and 9-6. "My copilot's just been killed. Everyone in the ship is wounded. I also have three yellows. We're returning to Baldy. I'll call the MASH and have a truck and body bag waiting, another truck for us. Shoot at any and everything. We're going off the grid."

I called CL and told them the bad news. They told me the CA for tomorrow was cancelled. All gun companies were low on ships.

"1-8, you can return to CL,' I said. 'We're done here. Thanks for hanging in there with us. I saw your door gunners shooting, and they were on target. Are you OK?"

"That last bend in the river was a bitch. My copilot and crew chief are bleeding. It looks like they aren't serious enough for Baldy's MASH. We'll gut it out and go home. Oh, and the little shits hit two of firefly's lights."

"Roger that. See you in the bar."

We landed at Baldy and parked near the revetments and not in them so working on the ships would be easier. Three of us had some difficulty getting out as our pucker factor was max. The medics took Ron's body and carefully placed it in the body bag. I was impressed. They treated him gently, as if he were alive. "I told them so. They just nodded."

We were driven the very short distance to the MASH and then set off the night buzzer, and the doctors and nurses came running. They had us climb onto three of their treatment tables. Tyler's cut was cleaned and a small bandage covered this Purple Heart wound. Ski's required pulling out a piece of metal, followed with lots of cleaning and three stitches. Tyler and Ski got shots and were given pills and were told to report back at 0800 for another shot.

My right calf had been sliced open and my boot had filled with blood. The six inch wound required some stitches inside and I didn't count how many; and fifteen on the outside. They said the internal stitches would dissolve. My knee was next. They x-rayed first to see what was in there and how large it was. Whatever it was, it had torn a very ragged three inch rip on the outside of my knee. They injected the area with Novocain to cut down on the pain. Then the doctors started 'probing the wound' as they called it. This caused more bleeding. The probe found something hard. The doctor pushed in what I would call a pair of needle-nosed pliers. He locked on and began pulling it out. This started a gusher. Someone placed a tourniquet just above the wound. The last thing I heard was "put him out. We're going into surgery." When I woke up, it was still dark, so I knew I hadn't been out very long. Dust off flew me to Danang for antibiotics and to prevent infection.

Shit, I don't have time for this.

Later the same day, some of the Birds showed up including Ski and Tyler. Ski handed me a push-pull rod. These are the rods that translate our movements on the cyclic and collective to the blades. There was a hole in the center of that half- inch-diameter tube. A one-in-a-million AK-47 shot, and a miracle that the rod hadn't severed the tube or weakened it so much that it broke in half from the movements of the controls. If it had broken, I would have lost all control, and we would all be dead. I just stared at that hole, and then handed it back to Ski.

The Birds had brought me some reading material, some of which I would dare read only after lights out. It was nothing but naked ladies. Not too many words. Just typical Firebird literature.

Chapter 60.

STEPHANIE, MY COPILOT

Two days later Steph walked into the ward. She was dressed for a party. She said, "The dress is to cheer you up. It can't be much fun just lying here."

"If I get too bored, I ask for pain meds. They would knock me on my butt if I were standing. Sleep is a good escape."

"The doctor described your wounds to me. They were severe and you still flew for another hour? I'm so sorry about your copilot. I know that as Pilot you feel responsible for everyone."

Then she knelt down over me and gave me the most wonderful kiss. We talked for two hours, mostly about our future back in the real world: marriage, work, kids, where to live. I would owe the army two years after VN, but she said she would follow me wherever I was stationed.

She said, "You could join the army's legal department. I know a few of the lawyers. Even a few colonels and generals."

She said it was time for another kiss. It lasted longer. Then she said, "What in the hell am I going to do with you flyboy? You keep getting hurt. Can't you at least wait until we're married to make me a widow?"

"Would you believe me if I said I wasn't trying to get hurt?"

She said, "I know that. I just worry about you. I found the perfect human being, and I want to keep him alive."

It was getting late, so I asked her where she was staying.

"They have a ward here for visitors."

"Hey, that's great. It's almost like we're sleeping together."

"Kevin, I added a month to my tour, so I can leave with you."

"God, I love you."

We said, "Good night," and she walked out of the ward.

I called Randy, Firebird 9-4, and asked him if he could give Monty a ride around Baldy. "Monty's helped me a lot with the investigations."

Randy said, "For you Mac, I will give him something to remember. Let him take pictures, and we'll take them of him in my seat with a helmet and at the door shooting the gun."

"Damn Randy, that's way more than I would have given him. Thanks pal."

Randy said, "That's bullshit. You are on record with the CO and the Birds for giving the Dollies door-gunner training. I know about Stephanie's heroics. She actually saved the American's CL HQ, so you really saved that place as much as she did. I also know about you on the hill saving the Dollies. I could go on and on, but I won't."

"Thanks Randy, you are a real friend."

As I hung up, I was surprised to hear rockets exploding outside. I asked a nurse, "Is that common here?"

"As of about a month ago, it's become almost every night. But only one or two and never near us."

Steph stayed with me for three days, and we talked about everything. I had never spoken to a woman like this. And then the spell was broken. She had to go back to work.

After a few days, I asked the doctor if I could get out of there. "All I do is fly. I'm never walking or carrying anything. Look around. The bad guys have bigger and better weapons. We need pilots."

An hour later, he returned and said the MASH unit at Baldy could pull out my stitches and keep the wound clean and give me daily shots. I caught a mail flight back to CL and checked in with the CO.

First, I told him about the bullshit I had given the doctor in Danang.

He said, "I know about that."

Second, I got to the important part. "I have a very big favor to ask you, sir. If it's not possible, then I might sneak out and do it anyway."

"I can't wait to hear this one."

"I would like to take Steph for a ride in a gunship as a small reward for saving the CL HQ."

"Request granted. You can set it up with maintenance and Stephanie."

I was stunned and looked at the CO. He smiled and said, "You've both earned this reward together."

"I'm planning to put her in the right seat. Even shoot some of Uncle Sam's ammo. Wow. I really owe you for this one, sir."

"Actually Mac, I'm enjoying this tour more than my previous. What happens around here is unique but always correct.

"Mac, I just got word that Muse flew into a cloud and disappeared. He had turned and was flying along the coast line. His wing didn't follow him as the clouds were dropping fast. They had just been relieved at Baldy."

One more lost bird? I didn't know what to think. I hadn't known Stuart well. "Maybe he'll show up," was all I could manage.

I had Smitty drive me to the flight line. I spoke to the sergeant in charge, and he said a hog would be ready in two days and fully armed.

Then, back at the 71st, I called Donna and told her my plan to fly Steph. "It's completely legal I assured her. I'm not going rogue. The ship will be ready in two days. Have her put on Levis and her flight jacket. It can get cool up there."

Donna said, "I'll get it done at this end. She confides in me and has told me many things, some hard to believe. Is it true about her firing an M-60 for several hours and preventing the base from being overrun? And you taking care of her afterwards?"

"Yes and guilty," I said. "She's the most amazing woman I've ever met. Do you know her background?"

"When we're talking, things will come out. She grew up wealthy but worked hard to become the best at everything. Did you know she finished second in cross country at the NCAA finals her senior year at UCLA? The girl who beat her had been running her whole life and beat Steph by only two seconds. Steph told me she had never been so pissed in her whole life. She couldn't train as intensely because her class load was horrendous. She would run after midnight for an hour."

"She's tough," I agreed. "I would fight with her in any war. I bet I could get her to solo the Huey in five hours. It took me five and that was after five months of primary training.

"OK, so we're on for two days from now. Drive her down the flight line until you see me. I'm excited as a kid before going trick or treating. Thank you Donna, I owe you for this one."

"No you don't," Donna said. "I've got pictures of me shooting a machine gun from a Huey. This may sound gross and crude, but since you're a Firebird, I'll tell you. I was physically turned on when I was shooting. I was wet."

I smiled and said, "Steph told me she soaked through her panties and was glad she was wearing a dress. See you at 0900 in two days."

That next day went by slowly. I went to our ammo dump and ordered more of everything. It was really getting hot in the AO. We were now regularly taking hits from the friendlies (the SVN), so our new policy was that anyone in a free fire zone was enemy, and the Birds had an OK to send them to hell, or wherever.

I went back to our company area and then to the Birdhouse. Several new guys were sitting around our octagonal table in the party room along with some copilots I knew, including Bob Clearwater. I said, "Room for one more?"

One of the new guys said, "Pick your poison, then sit down and tell us a little bit about yourself."

I gave them a rundown of my life up until the army. "Nothing spectacular."

"Shit, Mac, you must have saved it all for here," the other new guy said. "You're a fucking legend, not just here with us, in all the FSB's, HQ in CL and the HQ in Danang and QT. The GB's have you on a pedestal. I've heard your missions included a colonel as a copilot. Then a general! God damn, and I know those missions were so secret that you can't tell us about them. Mac, now don't bullshit us. Did you really have a Dolly shooting an M-60 in a spot in the perimeter the GB didn't have enough men to cover?"

"Here's what happened," I said. "The NVA saw an empty bunker and had their men charge it. It was a choke point and tapered to the wire right in front of her. They had made it to the wire while she was clearing a jam in the machine gun, but she cleared it in time. She probably killed 150, and none got through the wire."

"Shit, let's give Mac a shot of the good stuff."

I said, "What in hell is the good stuff"

Bob said, "My dad shipped me 100-year-old Scotch. Four

bottles, and he said don't just chug it. He said to savor each sip. It's $50 a bottle."

"I've never had scotch," I admitted, "but at $50 a bottle I'll tell you it's good even if I don't like it." I tipped the cup up to my mouth and sipped. *Wow, this is really good.* "Hey where in the hell did these cups come from?"

"We got them from—Who else?—Malko," someone said. "I think they are WWII cups that went with a mess kit."

"I don't know anything about this elegant nectar," I admitted, "but it just spoiled me for anything else drinkable in this hell hole."

That drew laughs, and someone asked Bob if we could do this one more time.

He said, "Of course, but you fucking animals remember to sip."

It was getting late, so we stopped, and for some reason it felt good to be able to walk a straight line. Morning couldn't have come any slower. I woke up a half dozen times. Bad dreams, being on fire and shot and crashing. Nothing nice, like Stephanie, but at least she wasn't in any of the dreams of chaos and death. I was in a river of sweat every time I woke, and it wasn't due to the weather. In fact, it was cool that night. I waited until 0600 to shower, shave and throw some water in my eyes.

I had borrowed someone's flight helmet and chicken board. I asked Smitty if he could drive me to the flight line. I checked out the Hog and all its weaponry. I placed the extra helmet in the right seat and thought about the look she would show me on that beautiful face. At 0845 here came the jeep. Donna stopped, and Steph asked her what was going on. That was my cue, as I was afraid Donna would give it away.

I said, "Good morning, beautiful. I have a surprise for you."

Her face lit up, and she started running toward me. I was afraid she might knock me over. I stood facing her but moved one leg back about three feet, and she met me with considerable force and a kiss to die for. Her legs were wrapped around me. *Does life get any better than this?*

"Steph, you are going to fly a gunship and shoot rockets and the cannon."

For a moment, she looked stunned as she took in what was happening.

She said, "Oh my god, are you serious?"

"Absolutely, but it will cost you a kiss."

"Kiss hell, I'll give you a lot more than that."

With that, Donna said, "Time for me to go back and be trailer trash."

I looked at Donna and winked. She nodded, started the jeep and departed.

"OK, beautiful. Let's do it!" I helped her into the chicken board.

"This is heavy," she said.

I showed her how to relax holding the cyclic, showed her the rocket button. She was five feet ten inches tall. That was taller than some of our pilots.

"There's an outhouse behind the gunners shack if you need it," I said.

"No thanks. I just went."

I climbed in and got settled. I handed her the flight helmet. She put it on and pulled the microphone around so it sat lightly against her lips. I explained the collective pitch and how to start the engine.

I called the tower and asked for a gunship TO north. "We are going to come around and do a few touch and go's. Then, we'll break off and fly south to Target Practice Island."

Tower said, "Cleared for all. You are the only ship in the pattern."

"Roger tower. We are hovering out of the Bird's flight line."

"Steph, follow me on the control in your right hand. You can talk to me by stepping on that button near your left foot or pull back halfway on that red switch by your right index finger. Pull only halfway or you will be transmitting to everyone near this airport. Try it."

She pulled the trigger back and said, "How's this?"

I keyed mine and said, "Perfect. Now step on that floor switch."

"Does it sound any sexier?"

"I'm going to cancel this flight and see what I can do with that sexy voice."

She laughed and said, "No, you're not. Teach me how to fly this noisy beast, fly boy."

"With the index finger on your left hand, pull the trigger on the bottom of the collective just above the throttle and roll the throttle slightly to get some fuel to the turbine."

She did, and the engine began whining and the blades began turning.

She said, "OH MY GOD!" loud enough for me to hear without using the intercom.

"Get on both controls with me. We'll hover out to the runway. Keep your head on a swivel and watch for other aircraft."

I could feel her on the controls. We had twelve inches of clearance above the taxiway. I turned the ship towards the north and sat it down. "OK Steph, feel your left hand. The collective is coming up, and you feel me adding power with the control you're holding with your left hand. Feel it turning. We are at a hover, and this is how a gunship takes off. It's different from the way a slick takes off. Your right hand moves slightly forward, and we start moving. Don't be afraid when we bounce off the runway a few times. This is because we are overloaded. Rock and Roll."

"Steph, where did this fly boy term come from?"

"I really don't know. It just came out."

I saw her tense as we hit the runway and bounced up. "Now we are at 70 mph and rpm looks good." We bounced a second time, and we were flying. I said, "You just hit translational lift; helo talk for beginning to fly."

"Fuck! That was exhilarating and scary at the same time."

"Imagine how it feels at night," I said. "Stay on the controls. Notice how gently I move the controls. We will go straight out and over the trailer trash, then turn 180 degrees and fly down the beach, turn and land. How are you doing?" We buzzed the trailers as I was talking and that got a squeal out of her.

"I don't know yet."

"Off to your right is my company area. The building closest to the water is my club. Now you understand why I love your club."

"That's your club? It has only two walls"

"CL tower, this is 9-7 turning base." I explained flying downwind, base and final.

Tower said, "I see and you are cleared for final and touch and go."

"Roger. Steph, get on the controls a little firmer."

"OK, how's this? I'm shaking a little."

I said, "All the ladies say that to me."

She turned and gave me a smirk, keyed her mic and said, "You better be lying, flyboy!"

"Actually, you are first and only woman I've ever said that to. Honest."

She laughed and said, "Just messing with you, like you do to me."

"Touché. Now push your left hand down. Push your right pedal a little. Good, now pull back your right hand and roll off some power. We are dropping and slowing down. See how the nose turns smoothly?"

Great. She was actually involved in the landing.

We stopped at a 12 inch hover and sat it down. I looked at her and said, "Let's go." As we began forward, I said, "Rock and Roll." We did a double bounce. We didn't need to, but I wanted her to get the full experience. We flew around the traffic pattern at 500 feet above our landing area. I said, "Time your next turn so you are lined up with the runway."

She said, "Roger that, flyboy!"

I lightly helped her with the turn, and we missed lining up on the center but quickly corrected. We went through the same routine again. She was becoming more confident by the minute. I was taking pictures of her by turning my head to the right and snapping the pic with my left hand.

"Let's do something before we fly down the beach and start shooting. Let's buzz the club and company area."

"What's buzz?"

"CL tower, 9-7 requests a low pass over our company area."

"That's what we did over your trailer-trash friends."

"You are cleared. Make it good, I'm watching with my binocs."

"Hang on Steph." We banked hard right. This caused her to let go of the controls, but she quickly recovered. Down we went to about fifty feet over the club and then a cyclic climb three quarters the way over the company area. We re-entered the flight pattern a little low, but she had a firmer grip.

We landed, and she hovered with me. She did a three bouncer on the TO.

She immediately asked me, "Why did we bounce three times?"

I said, "The breeze died down. Aircraft always try to land and TO into the wind." *Damn she's smart. She was keeping track of our TOs.*

"Let's fly down the beach and shoot some rockets and the cannon."

"Roger that. Hey Mac, why do you say Rock and Roll?"

I love this girl. She's quick and smart. "Rock and roll sounds good. I like the music, and it relaxes the new guys, or girl, and it gets you hyped up for some fast action.

"Steph, what's with this 'flyboy' stuff?"

"I think it fits you perfectly. It just came to me several weeks ago as I was lying in bed thinking of you."

"OK Steph, I've got the controls. Pull down the rocket sight. (I had shown her how to do that back at the Firebird line). Now look into the circle of light and see that dot. See if is bright enough to see through it at a target." I dropped the nose and she nodded.

"See that Island that looks like it's been destroyed. Let's add to the ambiance. Put your right thumb on the red button." I pointed the ship at a group of three thirty-foot-tall dead and black palm trees. I think that's what they were before the fronds were blown away. "Push the button when the dot is on the trees."

As the nose came down, she punched. It was a little short but that was my doing. I pulled the nose up and said, "Punch again," and she was right on target. I said, "Again," and she did it again.

She yelled, "Oh god, this is unreal."

"Now we have to break, so we don't become a smoking hole on this little paradise island. We start climbing so we can come around again and kill that truck."

Her shot was close, so I said, "Again," and she was close again. I said, "Steph that was a killing shot. Shrapnel is thrown out in a fifty yard radius."

More pics. Her smile told me all I wanted to know. I said, "You pick a target this time."

I turned on her cannon. "You are now on the cannon," I said. "You can punch like the rockets, or if you hold it down, it fires like your M-60. Let's fly out a little farther. OK, now turn toward the Island and slowly come back on the throttle as you push the left hand down. It's all yours."

She helped lower the nose and gently pressed the red button. Out went the first shot and then a second and a third. I asked,

"Could you feel the thumping on your feet."

"Yes, I wondered what that was."

"That's the recoil from the cannon. It's like the M-60 jumping as you shoot. Rockets don't have recoil because the solid fuel burning out the back isn't pushing against anything except air. We call the cannon the Thumper because of that feeling on your feet.

"You have to tell me what you are shooting at, so I can grade you when I talk to the General."

"I love pressure, Mac. I was born for this shit. Honest, this is the most incredible experience of my whole 25 years of life. Maybe the second most incredible experience."

I said, "Thank you, assuming you were talking about me." I was trying to hold back a laugh.

"You know what I'm referring to. What do you mean assume?"

"I know, I know. Actually, I thought you made a great recovery there, girlfriend."

We turned towards the Island, and she said, "The truck, the damn thing is still standing." She held the button down for two seconds and was short. She did it again and walked the shells up to the truck. She surprised me when she said, "The three dead trees." She shot all around the trees. There was so much dirt and smoke in the air I could only say, "Nice shootin' Dead Eye."

More pics.

We got a call from CL tower. "Are you still in the area?"

I said, "Yes."

"9-7, there is a shark warning at the R & R beach. Could you respond?"

"Yes, I could be there in two minutes."

He said, "Go for it, and I will call them."

I looked at Steph, and she had some sweat rolling down her cheeks. I said, "This is our lucky day. How would you like to kill sharks?"

She nodded and said, "You've got it." Then she wiped her sweaty hands on her pants and looked like she going to start hyperventilating.

I said, "Relax and lean back and take some slow breaths."

She said, "How in the fuck do you do this all day and half the night?"

"Practice."

I turned off the cannon and her rocket switch's while we turned north and flew up the beach. "Now, you are going to shoot for real." We could see the guys on the beach waving arms and towels.

"This is your shot Steph." I turned on her rockets.

As we rolled in, she said, "I see the sharks."

They were 150 yards off shore. She dropped the nose, with a little help and punched once, and there was a bloody geyser. I got it on film. She looked at me, and we were both smiling. I said "OK, let's circle and wait and see if that blood draws any attention."

I slipped my hand down and turned off her rockets. We flew out a half a mile from the beach and as we were coming around she said very calmly, "Here they come, Mac."

I turned on her rockets and said, "They're all yours." I helped her get on target, and she fired once. I added a little right pedal, and she punched again and was dead on. I got it on film. As we were coming around for the third run, I saw several dark shadows coming towards the blood and large pieces of shark meat. The waves were pushing all of this debris towards the beach. I said, "You're on cannon."

She didn't hesitate and started shooting one shot at a time, and as the shots neared the shark meat, she shot on full auto. She walked the shells into the sharks and then moved the barrel back and forth with her pedals.

I said, "Here come some more."

She said, "I'm on 'em."

She used the same tactics as her previous onslaught.

Wow, this girl! I couldn't think of anything else to say, so I said, "Let's circle some more." After two circles and no sharks, I said, "Let's buzz the beach. Are you ready?"

She said, "Yes, I know what buzz means this time. I'm on it." I turned off the rockets, and I noticed her right thumb was on the cyclic grip and not the red button. *Damn, what a fast learner.* We buzzed them and even Steph was cheering.

I said, "Let's make another pass farther out so if any more sharks are swimming in the area towards the blood, you can shoot them before they get close to the beach."

We were out a mile before we spotted one. I said, "Rockets on.

Light 'em up girl." Two punches and they were fish food. More evidence on film. We flew back towards the beach, and she said, "Let's buzz 'em again." She was into this buzzing.

We went back to our larger circle routine for several passes, and nothing. I said, "Let's wave goodbye." As we flew towards the beach, I moved the cyclic to the right and then left several times, and they figured it out and waved back. We made a steep turn left and down the beach. I asked Steph, "How are you doing?"

She said, "Do you mind if I shoot that fucking truck one more time?"

I started laughing, and then said, "You're a Firebird. You shoot like us, and you talk like us. Take us to the Island, beautiful."

As she headed us that way, I could see that she had a firmer grip on the controls. *What have I done here? I've created a monster. She will never be satisfied with the normal Dolly flights. I had better warn the slick drivers.*

The Island was in sight. I said, "Shoot when you're ready." The nose came down, and she was short, on target, and then long with three punches. "Jesus Steph, you've learned this stuff faster than I did. All of those were kill shots." I took more pics.

She said, "If you want it done right the first time, find a woman. Mac, can you take the controls? I want to take this jacket off. I'm sweating."

I said, "Absolutely," and she leaned forward and took it off. I put my hand out for the coat, took it, and stuffed it next to my right thigh.

We made three more passes, and then pointed the nose toward home. We landed at CL and she said, "This is much easier to handle when it's lighter."

I called the tower and requested three more touch and go's for some training with my new copilot. He cleared me.

"You are correct, your honor, about the weight of this ship. You are amazing."

As we lined up on final, I felt her rolling back the throttle and pulling the nose up. As we neared the ground, she began adding power. She was even using some pedal with the power reduction. We touched down. I didn't help her much.

"How are you doing, Steph?"

She looked at me and said, "Hang on."

We did two more. After touching down the third time, I asked, "Are you ready to stop."

"Maybe I'd better. I've sweated through my shirt twice. I look like a wet tee shirt contestant."

I was laughing as we hovered over to the Firebird line. Then I noticed a crowd. "Shit," I said, "Steph, I'm screwed. There's the general, my CO, and my platoon leader."

"Didn't you have permission?"

"I did, but I apparently didn't go far enough up the chain of command. It looks like everyone but the president is standing waiting for us to land."

"I got an idea for an escape." I began using my pedals to turn the nose back and forth as you do when saying *no* by turning your head left and right. Then, I started hovering sideways away from them and towards the landing strip.

Steph said, "Mac, they're laughing and waving their arms to tell us to come back, and since they're all laughing, I guess we're not in trouble."

I stopped and turned around and hovered back and set down into a revetment. I showed Steph how to shut down the turbine. We sat there and took off our helmets and listened to the turbine wind down and the crackling and ticking sound of the exhaust section cooling down.

I said, "Are you ready?"

"Oh hell, nothing could bother me now. I could live another 1000 lifetimes and never feel this way, except when I'm with you."

Nice recovery again, girlfriend.

As we walked closer to the jurors, I started to salute, but the general shook his head for don't.

"Mr. McNally," the general said, "You almost sucked the roof off the shit house, I mean, your club. Sorry Steph. What do you have to say for yourself?"

I looked at the general and then at Stephanie and then back to the general. "Sir, the tower cleared her, so it's all her fault." Steph just stood there and shrugged her shoulders.

They all started laughing, and the general began collecting $5 from everyone. The CO explained. "The general said, I'll bet you all

$5, he will have an answer and we'll all laugh. Mac, we all went up in a ship and watched you two at Target Practice Island. We were amazed at her understanding of the rockets and cannon."

"Sirs, for the record, I did not fire a single shot at any location." I heard a couple of *wows*, an *awesome* and an *amazing*. From General Wheaton came, "I'm so proud of you Steph. Mac, you bring out a side of her I've never seen." Then he added, to her, "Your hair is sopping wet, and you've sweated through your shirt. It's pretty intense activity, isn't it?"

"She also did well flying," I said. "I took my hands off the controls several times. They were still wrapped around the cyclic and collective, but no contact."

Steph said, "You did what?"

"I let you have all the control I could, but I had to shepherd you. I do that with all the new pilots. You wanted to fly and shoot the more powerful weapons. I saw it in your face when I was shot down after you were shot down. You were staring at the gunship with a glint in your eye. I hope I was able to fulfill your dream."

"Oh Kev, I could never ask for any more. I'm still flying higher than a Firebird."

"I like flyboy."

The general broke in, "We followed it all. It was very serendipitous that the sharks showed up for Steph. Mac, you were great. Currently, I know of no other woman on earth flying and shooting from a gunship. I thank you for those moments you gave to my goddaughter."

"YOUR WHAT?" I blurted out. "I mean, sir."

"We decided to keep that quiet. How do you think she was stationed here in CL? I have to watch over her, and now I have you to help me." He turned to his goddaughter beaming with pride, "Steph, you are a firebird."

Chapter 61.

GOD'S OWN LUNATICS

As we were talking, maintenance was rearming the ship, and the fuel man was also there. Then, a speeding jeep screeched to a halt, and Smitty jumped out.

"Mac, there's an all-out assault on LZ East. They estimate two companys at a minimum. The Birds are right behind me." Wilder was first to exit the truck, followed by Ski and Tyler, Newhouse, Fox and Marshal. Then Bob Clearwater, my copilot, jumped out.

I looked at Steph and with a sad look on my face, did a few minimal shakes of my head back and forth, as if to say, *No, this can't be happening.*

I told Steph that I wanted to add something to her flight jacket. "Smitty, could you have a Firebird patched sewn on?" I handed him the jacket as he nodded OK. Steph was crying as I kissed her goodbye. She said, "Mac, other than marrying you, nothing will ever match today's thrill."

I was speechless. I looked at her, mouthed "marriage," and gave her my biggest smile. I told the crowd goodbye, and they stepped back to observe the ballet. I climbed in and strapped on the gunship. Wilder gave me the info, and we were on our way with a rock and roll.

I said, "Go hot and test your guns. You too, Bob," and he shot into a herd of water buffalo. He killed one, and then he looked at me, and we both smiled. I said, "Crank 'em up to max guys, un-ass yourselves and hat up. Its twenty four miles, or for you military types, forty clicks. Ten minutes."

As we were nearing LZ East, I asked for a sit-rep. The RTO replied, "They are coming at the west and east sides where it's not

454

so steep. At least 200, maybe more. We're shooting bee hives and mortars."

"Roger. OK, 9-6, let's fly a little south to the river, then fly north and go where the river turns west. We'll be behind some hills and then we'll surprise 'em. And we won't be shooting at LZ East."

I called LZ East and told them, "Keep your heads down."

As I came over the hill, I'd been gaining some altitude, so I could shoot down at the NVA.

"Son of a bitch," Bob said, "it looks like ants in the kill zone." He meant that because there were so many NVA.

I fired two pair close to the wire and then two pair at 100 meters from the wire and two pair near the trees and two into the trees near the kill zone. All the while, I was getting Bob to shoot close to the wire, and he was doing fair. The tracers coming at us were a massive swarm. I told wing to shoot long, and then come around the LZ with me. After shooting, I only turned slightly away instead of a hard bank right, so I could fly around the LZ.

"9-6, let's fly straight south when shooting, then break right away from them, and go back to the first group and finish with them. Then let's do a slight break right and come back here and finish it."

I had two yellow lights: engine temp and oil pressure. Not to worry. Then, several rounds came through the windshield. One hit the top of my helmet and slammed my head back to the head rest. No blood. I called 9-6, "Is everyone's OK?" I got back two clicks.

I came up over a hill, and it was just like the other side, several machine guns with lots of tracers flying by us. We took a couple of hits as I was walking my rockets from the wire back to and into the trees."

Wing said, "I'm taking hits."

I said, "Bob and gunners. Destroy those damn guns." Bob put 100 cannon shells into them. They were gone. Then, we turned to go hit the first group.

The RTO called, "Perfect, nothing near the wire but bodies. Put some more in the trees."

I said, "Roger," as I turned my selector switch to single rockets and fired into the trees thirty yards from the kill zone. I turned to go around the mountain, and we were hit three times in the tail boom.

9-6 said no one had shot at them.

I said, "I've got six rockets remaining. I'll shoot three here and three back on the other side. Bob you shoot 100 rounds into the trees and empty your cannon on the last pass." We turned to go to the west side. I said, "Bob, remember I said most plans turn to shit after 10 to 30 seconds of action; then, you Evaluate, Improvise and Perform? Well, just like right now. You don't just fly the ship. You can't stop thinking and planning.

"OK guys, last pass, and then we go rearm." I called East and asked if he had any particular spot for my last three rockets. He said, "Just into the trees like the other side." I said, "Roger," as I came up over the hill and fired the rockets 30 yards into the trees, then 60 yards and 90. As I turned south to return to CL, who had been monitoring us, I said, "Returning to rearm."

I had Bob do all the flying. This gave me a chance to ask him about his Bird training to date. He said, "Two weeks of OJT (on the job training)."

"Bob, I have one suggestion. When you're turning, don't lean your head. Just sit up straight and the ship will lean. If you lean over, you can't look through the sights. If anyone sees you leaning your head over in my lap, rumors will start."

I had him call to land at the Bird's revetments. Something urgent must have been happening because there were six grunts waiting for us. We rearmed in fifteen minutes with their help. Then, I called our flight line HQ and said, "We're ready."

He said, "Go to Hawk Hill." A driver pulled up and handed me the freq, coords and call sign. I rogered and said, "Get us out of here Bob. Rock and Roll. Follow the old railroad tracks or Highway One. Both run four clicks east of Hawk Hill which is about 25 miles north."

I called Hawk Hill 29 when we were close and got a sit rep. He said, "We're about to get overrun on the west perimeter. They are also attacking Hill 35 (half a mile from Hawk Hill). Hurry! They're at the wire."

I flew over the wire and had Bob shoot the cannon just on the outside edge. Our troops were on the inside of the wire. He did well and got at least 100 hanging in the wire with cannon shots. I just kept flying along the wire. This was a no brainer. These guys had to be on drugs. It's daylight, and they don't have a chance. They had no overhead protection and were running across dry rice paddies to the wire. It's crazy, but we Birds liked crazy. Surprise was our best tactic. Even if it wasn't needed here.

I called and asked, "How're we doing?" I sometimes asked that because the men on the ground were able to look into the tree line and further, if it wasn't thick jungle. He said, "A few got through the wire before you arrived, but they were no problem. We took them as prisoners."

"We're coming around again with the cannon," I told him, "and I will add rockets on those shits all the way to the river." As I came around, there were only a few out in the open. I took care of them, and then checked the selector switches so I had two rockets, and I said, "Bob, get on that cannon. I don't want a single asshole alive down there."

I saw two NVA look up at us, throw their weapons on the ground, and put their hands behind their heads. I could see Bob hesitate. I said, "Shoot 'em. We're a gunship. We can't take prisoners. There's no room for them, and if we did land, we couldn't take off. Anyway, I don't have a conscience, and you won't either in a month." He fired three shells, and the explosion pretty much disintegrated them both.

He looked at me and yelled, "Yeah."

As everything else was happening, I climbed up about 300 feet and put three pair of rockets into the trees by the northwest corner of FSB 29. I broke, and Wilder came in, but he took some fire.

Tyler said, "I've got 'em," and he gave those shooters a long burst from his machine gun near the southern perimeter of FSB 29. I gave them a pair of rockets as I was turning to cover Wilder's break.

Bob said, "You shot those while you were turning."

I nodded and said, "I want every asshole down there dead."

We were still taking sporadic fire from the west, so I added, "Now, let's hit the west side of 35."

I said to 9-6, "I'm going to give them a few more rockets, and you hose them with the minis." When I was lining up the shot, I noticed about thirty NVA trying to cross the river while at the south end of 29. I shot several rockets at the guys in the open and worked my shots toward the jungle where they were charging out into the open toward 35. Then, I turned my attention to the river. "OK, the three of you are not going to let anyone reach the other side of the river!"

One of them said, "OK."

They walked their tracers into the mob trying to get across the river. I say mob because they were clustered together which certainly made our job easier. Maybe they couldn't swim or maybe they were afraid of being swept away. This time of year the water was moving slow, but during the monsoon season it would become impassable.

The dead guys were falling away from the cluster and slowly drifting downstream. The ones left alive were in a panic when we flew over them. Three of them threw down their AK's and put their arms up. That did not deter my crew. Those three NVA were floating down stream with their buddies in a matter of seconds.

"OK guys, I'm going downstream to see if anyone is faking." We found two and dispatched them. I called 9-6 and said, "Are you ready to finish this mission?" Back came two clicks. The next call went to Hawk Hill.

He said, "They are running out of the jungle across the killing zone. There are lots of bodies. We can hold them off until you finish with 29."

"OK, Hawk 29, where do you want us?" He said, "On our west side. They are coming across dry rice paddies."

I said, "We'll come in with rockets, cannon and a ton of machine gun ammo." I transmitted to everyone and said, "Are we all on board?"

Ski and Tyler yelled, "Yes."

Sometimes, they would yell because they didn't want to stop shooting, which they would have to do to engage the intercom switch located on the wire that went to their helmets.

As soon as I turned north to begin my rocket run, a machine gun opened up on me. Bullets came through the windshield and sprayed Plexiglas on my left arm and on Bob's right arm.

I didn't feel much. I glanced at my arm and saw blood, but not much. I asked Bob how he was doing, all the while dropping the nose and putting a pair of rockets on the machine gun as I began my run. I saw some guys running to the north, so I gave them a pair and some were turning around and running back across the dry rice paddies they had just crossed, so I shot them. As I broke, the guys in back said, "The mini guns are tearing the place apart."

Bob said, "I'm hit but not much blood. I'm OK. You have to teach me that rocket shot in a turn."

I said, "Bob, don't look at your wound again. I want you awake, not passed out. Let's hit the west side of Hill 35." We turned towards the north end of 35 and made a southerly run along their west side, shooting from their wire and across the killing zone and into the jungle. We only heard a couple of rounds go through our rotor wash.

"9-7, this is Hawk 29. I have an update on the west side you just hit. They are bringing in two wounded prisoners. They also counted at least 75 dead and blood trails leading into the jungle."

"Thanks, we are going in on the south one last time. We'll put our remaining ordinance all over that area."

"Breaking right," came from 9-6.

That was my cue to start shooting on this last pass. I put rockets all over the area as it was small. The NVA were trapped between 29 on their north and the river on their south. This was a scorched-earth mission.

When we were done, I said, "That's it, Hawk. We're going back to Baldy to refuel and rearm. If those guys want to try assaulting your home again, call us."

"Thank you. It was great watching you guys work. Man, there wasn't a stone left unturned. You guys are our idols."

"Bob, take me to the Hilton. And by the way, that was some good shooting! This ship will handle like your Slick when you were flying as an FNG now, because we are out of fuel and ammo."

When we landed at POL, everyone jumped out to pee. That chicken board bouncing on your bladder is a killer. As I climbed back in, I said, "OK, I've got it." The poor copilot is always last to pee. As my gauge said the tank was half full, I put my hand out the door with a thumb up.

As we were rearming this beast, Monty drove up in a jeep and jumped out and said "Two things, sir."

I interrupted him and said, "It's Mac."

"OK Mac. First, that big CA is sunup tomorrow. And second, the ride with Big Randy was incredible. He said you told him to do all the maneuvers. I shot the cannon. I was holding the controls while we were flying. I've got pictures of me flying and shooting. I can't begin to thank you."

"You thanked me in advance by recording our missions and giving them to me, twice in fact."

"OK, great. Back to item one, the CA. Mac, you're on one side and Randy's on the other. There will be thirty ships with seven or eight GIs per ship. Drop them off into rice paddies two clicks west of LZ Karen. (LZ Karen was about thirty clicks south and a little west. Five clicks straight west of LZ West). Then, they'll sweep north and around to the east side in very steep surroundings. That's all the info, oh, and here are all the numbers and call signs."

Wilder and I wrote all the data with the red grease pencil on our maps and pre-tuned the radios. Then, we had to help rearm. I had a lot of holes in the windshield and thought I would wait a little longer to call for repairs. We'd probably get more holes tomorrow.

After rearming and cleaning the filters, we checked to make sure the bullet holes were only that; in other words, that nothing was damaged between the entrance and exit holes. They all checked out, so we were good to go.

Bob walked over and said, "Can I ask you some questions?"

I said, "Certainly."

"Mac, why do they call us 'God's own lunatics'?"

"I think it was 1966 or 67. A journalist took a ride on a gunship, and it was a hot mission. When they returned, he jumped out and immediately puked on his boots. Then he said, "I officially dub you 'God's own lunatics.'"

I reached into my helmet and pulled out a typed sheet I'd put there months before. "And here's what TV anchor Harry Reasoner said about us: 'Airplanes are safe and helicopters are not. Airplane pilots are clear eyed, open, buoyant, and extroverts. Helicopter pilots are brooders, introspective, introverts, and anticipators of trouble. They know if something bad has not happened, it's about to.' How about that?"

But Bob had no comment. I think he was still a little stunned from the mission.

"Let's go eat," I suggested.

The food actually wasn't too bad. Some kind of mystery meat with fake mashed potatoes and string beans. For dessert, frosted cupcakes. Now, if we can just get an entire night of slumber.

No such luck. We were all deep into sleep when several loud explosions had us sitting up and confused. If we were under attack, they should have called us. I picked up the phone and asked, "What in the hell is going on?"

The night radioman said Baldy had been given 155 mm and 175 mm Howitzers (large cannons) for troop support. "This is artillery's first night mission. What da' ya think?"

"I think it's pretty fucking loud. We can't sleep with that shit going over our heads."

"Mac, they tell me it's only for ten minutes."

"If it goes one second past ten minutes, I'm going to launch a Firebird assault on those fucking guns. And you can quote me."

They finally stopped, and we went back to sleep. We were not called all night, but we woke to rotor blades, lots of them, landing on the turnaround, and three abreast on our short runway. They were inserting about 250 grunts. Their barracks were up the hill on various flat spots. These guys were geared for combat. They carried every explosive device from bullets, grenades, claymore mines, smokes, grenade launchers, and shotguns for the close-in work.

I asked Big Randy how the briefing went. He said, "Some REMF gave the briefing but wouldn't take any questions. I don't think they know shit. I think the recon was probably done from 2000 feet, and the NVA are waiting for us. I've got a bad feeling about this."

"Hell Randy, I've been out of touch for so long with CL and CL HQ that I don't have a clue. What did they say about the guns?"

"We go in first and see what's there. Then circle back and escort the ships to their landing. Everything out there is hostile."

I told Ski and Tyler, "Grab an extra two cases of machine gun ammo. Don't hesitate to fire long bursts. This doesn't sound like it was planned very well. I'm getting really tired of these FUBAR and SNAFU missions. It's getting like the civil war. Just throw people out there, so the other side uses up their ammo and then attack with who's remaining when their weapons are empty. Jesus fucking Christ, who would makke up a plan like that?"

Bob walked up to me and said, "Are you religious, Mac?"

I said, "Hell no. Tell me right now whose side is god on? Really, I'm serious. Whose side? Do you really think there is some magical plan for you? Is the other side given the same line of bullshit? Have you ever noticed that all bombs and bullets are shaped like your dick? This whole goddamned war is about mine is bigger than yours. You and I are just pawns on this chess board. I'm here, and I volunteered to fly, and then volunteered again to fly gunships. My job, as fucked up as this war has become, is still to protect American troops. That's your job as well.

"Bob, just be very alert this morning. If you see anything, kill it. I don't fucking care if it's a woman. Shoot her. She'll probably have an AK under her baggy pants."

"Hey," Bob said, "I just noticed my arm and shoulder ache. How's your arm?"

"My arm and shoulder started hurting fifteen minutes ago."

"When this cluster fuck is over, let's walk over to the MASH."

Here came the trucks, seven deuce and a half's and two one-ton trucks. *Wow, those 2ⁿᵈ LT's look so young.* I counted six of them. That means they'll form into six groups before advancing into the jungle. New 2ⁿᵈ LTs don't last too long in VN.

The sergeants were loading the troops. It was time for the birds to go do our thing. The C & C ship took off. (I couldn't help thinking, *so they can arrive earlier and give away our attack*.) That C & C had a small load of REMF's who would try to direct troops to the enemy or away from them. Their call sign was Hawk 6.

"Light up the turbine, we're going hunting. You two have those extra ammo cases opened?" I received two clicks.

"Firebird 9-4, are you ready?"

"9-4 is loaded and ready."

"Baldy Tower, Hawk 6 and two Firebirds are taking off." Those slicks could fly faster, so we went earlier. Our job was to soften the target and then circle back to the flight and escort them to the ground. All thirty were going to land at once. "Watch close for hostile muzzle blasts and tracers," I told everybody.

A minute later, the lead slick said, "Pulling pitch."

I transmitted, "Keep pushing, guns. We're headed toward LZ West then 2.5 miles further. Test fire your weapons. Remember, everything out here is hostile. Even a fucking water buffalo." Then I called, "Lead slick 1-8, can you see us? We are a minute out. There is no cover on the west side, so 9-7 will target the right and 9-4 the left. 9-7 rolling in."

I saw nothing on the south side, so I punched three into the jungle on the right of the entire LZ, and 9-4 was doing the same on the other side. No return fire.

I don't know, this could still go either way. The jungle could be empty or 500 NVA could be waiting. We've been doing the same tactical assaults since 1966. That's three years for the NVA to learn. My money is on the NVA with machine guns to greet us on the left and at the northern end of my side. Shit.

"OK guys, let's go find those slicks."

"Firebird 9-7, this is rattler 1-8. I've been monitoring you, and you took no fire?"

"Yes, but don't trust that. It could be a trap. Have your crew keep a close watch on that jungle.

"9-4, let's hang back and come in with the race track pattern, since they'll all land at once."

I said to my crew, "All right, let's do this."

Just prior to touch down, all hell broke loose. Tracers were crossing at our slicks. One of the guns on my side was a 51. *Shit.* I put my sight on it and punched three times at the bastard. Most all the other rounds flying by and into us were near that 51 I hit. A thousand AK rounds just flew toward us. I was talking to the crew, and they had been splattered by shrapnel, but nothing serious. I think I was hit as well. The slicks discharged their troops and were trying to get the hell out and were talking over each other on radios. One was on fire. One was a rolling ball of fire. Some of the disabled ships' crews were running back to the last of the thirty hoping for a ride out of hell. Two ships had wounded on board and were flying to CL hospital.

I called 9-4 and said, "Answer if you can. How are you doing?"

"I'm OK, but my wing is hit and going down where the last ship landed."

"Can you cover him 9-4?"

"Yes."

I called, "If any slicks can return for wounded, I can cover you in and out."

Slick 1-8, Norm Griffin, who I met when the Dollies were shot down, said, "I'm turning back." Then three more called and said they were turning and following 1-8.

"Thank you men. Why don't you form up in a diamond and land where the last of the thirty ships did?" I got back four click-clicks. While talking, I was also flying in on my second run. I was shooting at muzzle flashes. "Bob, are you OK?"

"Yeah Mac, I'm getting better at blocking out the enemy fire."

"Great, keep it up."

"9-7, we're getting close to descending point.

"OK 1-8, I've got your right, and 9-4 is alone on the left. The guys are in the trees on your left, and I saw two on the ground who look wounded. When you four Dust offs load up, turn around and exit the direction you came from." They were taking minimal fire.

We all started down, and immediately machine guns opened up on us. I put two pair on each gun and felt rounds hitting the cannon on the nose. I turned my attention to the muzzle flashes and gave each one a pair of rockets. I called Morning Hawk 6, the commander on the ground, and asked, "Where are you?" As I started my break, the four 71st Dust offs called and said, "Pulling pitch."

I said, "Tyler, how's 9-4 doing?"

"He's taking some fire," Tyler told me, "but the door gunners are handling that problem."

"OK guns," I said, "let's take these Angels of mercy out of here."

When they were about two clicks out, I said, "9-4, I'm calling Morning Hawk again. We're going to do an air force mission: one pass, haul ass. Then, we'll check in at Baldy to refuel and rearm. 71st dust-off flight, I'm breaking and returning to the LZ to check on the ground troops."

These same slicks would be hauling in water the rest of the morning. 250 guys on the ground in 100-degree and 100-percent-humid air would need a lot of water. The grunts we just dropped off carried four canteens of water each, and it wasn't enough.

Bob said, "Mac, that last pass knocked out my cannon."

"Shit. Well, watch the instruments. 9-4 you ready?" I got back his clicks.

I punched a pair into several flashes along the edge of the trees.

The door gunners were shooting long bursts. There were bodies everywhere and burning trees and large open spaces in the jungle from our rockets.

"OK, let's go to the Hilton." Then, there were sparks coming out of the radios (we had four), and something came up through the floor and hit my right calf and the radios. Probably two rounds.

We had a quiet flight back to Baldy. I called for a new windshield and a new canon. We all helped rearm. Then, when that was almost finished, Bob and I went over to the MASH.

We walked in and they said, "Shit Mac what are you, a bullet magnet?"

I said, "No, it's Plexiglas. Both of us." We lay down on the treatment tables and waited. They used magnifying glasses to look for the glass. They pulled out several pieces from both my shoulder and my upper arm. *Shit, whatever they put on the wounds stings like a son of a bitch.* Then, I heard Bob say, "Goddamn that stings." He got his shot and pills and adios for him.

Doctor Weldon walked in and said to me, "I thought it was you, so I put on my flight jacket to show appreciation. What's it this time?"

"Huh?

"Don't bullshit me, Mac. I've been reading your nonexistent file. Christ, you are a glutton for punishment. I suppose you don't want this in your file? Damn Mac, you're bleeding from your right calf. What do you have to say for yourself this time?"

"I guess I'm just lucky, Doc."

"You're impossible, Mac."

"Doctor Pilot, how did you arrive here? Is this an upgrade from your last assignment?" Everyone in the room was laughing.

"We rotate every three months. We can't stay in the flight surgeon status more than that, or we would lose our fucking minds. Dealing with gunship pilots was not something they prepared me for in Med school. It should fall under a psychiatric specialty."

I laughed. "That's what happens to you when you fly a gunship," I said, "You go crazy." With that, they laughed, even the Doc.

He said, "I agree. You have to be certifiable to fly a gunship."

"To answer your question, sir, I would greatly appreciate it if none of this made it into my official file."

Two nurses, a doctor, and a medic came over and said, "Is this the guy you're always talking about? The one that gave you that jacket?"

I told them, "The doc's done some pretty amazing shooting and flying. He's a fast learner. He was on target quickly. If his medical abilities are as good as his performance out in the wild, then I feel very safe here. I'll bet he didn't tell you everything." Everyone looked at me quizzically. "He shot the cannon 150 times and shot 30 rockets. He assisted with takeoffs and landings."

I was interrupted when a nurse walked up and said, "Bend over." She shoved a large rusty nail into my left butt cheek and injected me with a thick burning substance.

I asked her, "Was that pepper in that syrup you injected me with?"

"It was only maple, flyboy."

I was stunned. "Where did you get that nickname?"

She said, "There are not a lot of girls in this hell hole, so we all know each other and talk. Seems you are famous and a very wonderful human being as well." She winked and walked away.

Weldon said, "Lie back. I want to numb this entire area before I go exploring your insides." He noticed the look on my face. "The insides of your arm," he added, "and your leg in thirty seconds." He touched one of the wounds and said, "Can you feel this?" I said, "No," and he followed with, "Let's go."

He probed inside the arm, and he felt something. He stopped and slid those needle-nosed pliers into my arm until he felt the object. He grabbed it and slowly pulled it out. As it came out, a geyser of blood followed.

He said "Put him out."

When I woke, he walked over to my hospital bed and asked, "How do you feel?"

I said, "Tired and my brain are a little fuzzy."

"That's normal. I had to open your shoulder and tie off the bleeders. That ragged piece of glass made a pretty ragged wound inside. The stitches inside will dissolve and the outside stitches can be removed at my old building, OK, now for the leg. You were struck with a rather large piece of shrapnel. Not too much damage, but it was a large opening and took a lot of internal stitches and fifteen stitches to close you on the outside. You should stay off the leg and not use the arm for two weeks." He held his hands up. "Before you start arguing, I will say two days. How's that?"

"That's an excellent prognosis, Dr. Weldon," I agreed.

"Do you want the shrapnel and Plexiglas, Mac?"

"No, thank you. If anyone asks me, I will say I sprained my ankle." The doctor looked at me and shook his head.

I knew a new gun crew was flying up to relieve us, so I said, "Thank you," and returned to my ship.

Everyone was swarming over the ships. Snake Doctor was there and fixed the windshield and radio. A mechanic was under my ship to check on damage from whatever hit by my feet. They had two mechanics installing a new frog (nose cannon).

Martin, the Snake Doctor, Robertson said, "It will be ready in thirty minutes. The hole in your ship didn't damage a thing. The wing also had holes only." I looked at the guy under my ship, and Snake Doctor said, "That's my assistant double checking me. Mac, both ships got the shit shot out of 'em, and they still fly. It still amazes me. Mac, could I ask a big favor of you?"

"Martin, you have helped me so many times, just name it."

"Could I fly a loaded gunship to CL?"

"Absolutely, and you can do it from the right seat." He lit up like a candle. I said, "Excuse me," and I walked over to my copilot and said, "How would you like to fly back as pilot of Snake Doctor?"

"Sure, if you want me to."

I said, "I'm paying back a debt I owe Martin."

Ten minutes later Martin said "We're ready. Now if your replacements would get here."

Fifteen minutes later, the Birds landed, and we said goodbye to all and took off.

I called my wing 9-6 and said, "How about some rat racing?" Click-click.

"OK, Martin, start flying low level around and through trees. We're teaching the wing copilot how to cover the lead ship. 9-6, Snake Doctor would like to do a maintenance check on our weapon systems. Click-click. Martin could you check my weapons?" This was being transmitted just to account for the ammo should anyone ask. *They haven't yet.*

"Yes, Mr. McNally, I have some time right now. Let's go hot with the new cannon on my side."

I switched the firing for the 40mm to his side so he could fire. "You're hot. Why don't you strafe along the right side of the dike in front of you?"

"OK, sounds good to me. Shit Mac, look at those guys in the trees. Those are NVA. Those trees are too thin and sparse to offer any protection." This conversation was only on the intercom, not transmitting

"I just switched you back to rockets. Hit those fuckers." He punched three pair. The first two were long and short respectively; the third pair atomized them and they never fired a shot. Then, 9-6 said, "We're here and rolling in when you break."

I looked at Martin and said, "Break right, and as you're climbing out, notice where any enemy fire is directed at 9-6 or us. Let's keep shootin' till nothing moves. This whole bullshit fight is supposedly to stop the spread of communism. Communism is just capitalism for a few. Keep their people hungry and in poverty, and then they need you. OK, no more politics."

He said, "Roger," and made his break.

"I never thought of that commie shit that way, Mac. I like it. Shit Mac, this thing flies like a loaded dump truck."

"Welcome to my world."

He looked at me and shook his head. "Mac, I see a few shots going up to 9-6. They're coming from farther into the trees. Christ, I can't believe the damage these rockets leave behind. What's their killing radius?"

I said, "Fifty meters; now kill 'em." He rolled in and punched four pair farther into the trees. He was on his own personal high. I shot the cannon at some flashes and movement in the thin cover.

He was a great pilot, so he could get on target faster than most. He just had to learn how a rocket drops or if he's low, it sails long. There are a few more idiosyncrasies, but that's for another lesson. Up came tracers, lots of them at both us and the wing ship.

"Christ Mac, how many are down there?"

I said, "A whole fucking bunch. Everyone keep shooting." And they did until nothing moved, and there was no return fire. "Why don't you make a few strafing runs with the cannon?" He did, and shit, he was so high, I thought he was going to hyperventilate.

"I think they're all dead, Snake. You ready to go home?"

"No, but I'll go anyway. Thanks so much, Mac. I never would have known what you guys really do. I hear all the time how you help our troops. But flying this Hog is an art form. Just flying this out of combat is fucking dangerous."

I turned on the cannon and told Martin to use his rocket sight and strafe anything and everything on the way to CL. He happily nodded and fired 200 rounds at Water Buffalos and geese in the rice paddies. One dumb shit pulled out an A K-47 and took a shot at us. Martin was quick to end the guy's military career.

Martin landed, and I sent him off to maintenance, and the three musketeers rearmed and refueled our baby.

Back at the company area, I called Steph and asked if she could arrange to have me ordered to HQ. We were only three miles apart, but it might as well have been 1000 miles.

"I will Mac," she said, "especially because I just heard a rumor that you were wounded and have been grounded for two days. I can't let that go by. You have to grab life and hold on tight here. It can be gone in a heartbeat."

"You are so right. I'm so sorry you are thinking about the gunships and me. It sounds negative, but in a war it's a fact. Get to work on your godfather and get me out of here, please. You are my sanity, and my future. I love you! Goodbye."

Chapter 62.

BRIEFING THE GREEN BERETS

Within an hour, I had orders to report to CL HQ to brief the GB's on gunship tactics while I was healing. Smitty had just left the Birdhouse, saying he would be ready to go in fifteen minutes.

I asked him if he could make it twenty because I was in great need of a shower. After twenty minutes, I walked to the company area and threw my gear in the jeep. The rough ride was five minutes, and Stephanie was waiting on the steps of the HQ building.

She ran to me, nearly knocked me over with her all-out body assault. I held my ground and was able to remain standing. It wouldn't have looked good if I had been knocked off my feet by a woman (a Firebird thing). Once I got her to bed, she could knock me down, throw me down, and stay on top of me all night.

As we walked to her place (sounds better than trailer house), we both started talking at once. I stopped to be polite and said, "Go ahead."

Then she stopped and said, "No, you go ahead."

We both started talking again laughing like two nervous kids on a first date. I looked into her beautiful blue eyes and felt like I was seeing into her soul.

Once inside her personal residence, we stopped to breathe. I said, "Let's take one of our famous showers. Here's your Flight Jacket with the Firebird Patch."

She said, "I feel so privileged to have that patch. Great idea on the shower. I just took a shower, so now I'll take another one with you just for fun."

"Same here, I just took one twenty minutes ago, but I'll take another one with you."

The tiny shower stall suited us just fine. I loved having her right next to me with no space to move away. I was in a dream state. I lost count of the number of times I gently washed her entire body.

She was looking at me so intently that I looked straight into her eyes and said, as softly as I could, "I accept your proposal."

She paused for a moment while staring into my eyes and then suddenly, almost yelled, "OK, OK, OH god I want that so much. I guess I'm not so much for tradition. You can ask me any time."

"OK Stephanie Rheem, I will.

Then, we were in bed and able to enjoy the sensations we gave each other without a single word for the first hour.

Finally, I was ready for a break. "OK Steph, what did you and your mom talk about since I last visited this piece of heaven?"

"Everything. She is enjoying our activities nearly as much as we are. I think she is reliving her earlier years with my dad. She hangs on my every word. Even asks for details."

"Steph, I'm going to be too embarrassed to face her. You have an amazing relationship. I guess it is a mother-daughter thing."

"Correct. She was really impressed when I told her you bathed me and put me to bed and let me rest. Said she'd never met a young man with that much compassion … or that much restraint. She also said you're one handsome guy.

"She was just a little skeptical about all the stories of me flying that Huey and firing the weapons and saving the day at the GB's base. She told me Derek went so far as to give you the credit for noting the weakness in his defenses and choosing me over his own troops to defend that bunker."

"I've known you for a while Steph," I said, "and we've been through some harrowing encounters together and survived, and yet every time I'm around you I have those same butterflies I had when we looked into each other's eyes the first time. Just saying, this is all new for me."

"I feel the very same way Mac. I love it, and I'm thankful because I've never heard any of my girlfriends talking about feelings the way we do."

"Let's continue to work on developing our appetite for dinner."

"What a coincidence Mac! I was just about to make the same suggestion."

We came up for air in time to shower and go to mess.

When we walked in the mess hall (which term was an insult to this restaurant), I felt everybody's eyes on us, or at least on Steph. She was a celebrity. A gorgeous celebrity. Everyone had heard the stories, or at least rumors, of her heroics. No one had known she was an attorney until now, and I'm sure it enhanced the interest people had in her.

We served ourselves dinner and looked for a place to sit. The general stood and waved us over to his table. As we walked toward him, a strange thing happened. Everyone in the mess hall began standing until all were up.

The general looked surprised. One of his aides, a lieutenant colonel, stood and said, "Excuse us sir, we just thought it would be appropriate to stand when this lady entered the room. Out of respect for you, sir, we wanted it be a surprise to you as well as her. We wanted you to be proud of her knowing how we feel, and I will add, thankful she is here. Hell sir, we're glad she's on our side. Can you imagine if she weren't?" That drew a laugh from the room and eased the tension created from leaving the General out of the loop.

As Steph sat, so did the GBs. The general said, "I did not tell them to do that. They all love you as much as we do," indicating himself and me. Her face was red. She smiled at everyone and raised her hand as a thank you.

"Well Mac, are you ready to give us a talk on gunship tactics?"

"Yes sir, I'm prepared."

"Mac, you just arrived. You haven't had time to prepare."

"I know, sir, but I've planned this talk for the last six months. It's right here." I pointed to my head."

He smiled and said, "I should've known."

After dessert, I was introduced as "Firebird 9-7, Kevin McNally, who has saved the life of nearly every man and woman in this room."

I took the podium and began, "The guns will come to your aid whatever you're dealing with. Our job is to protect you, so you can do your jobs and prosecute this war. Gather all the info you can about your circumstances and give it to us while we're in route.

That way, we can fly in with surprise on our side. Surprise and unpredictability are our edge. We are a big target, so we have to be quicker. We don't want to have to arrive and circle tor five minutes gathering data. That gives the enemy time to set up a defense.

"Get info on the enemy's big weapons, what they are and where they are located. And remember, we don't like to shoot over friendlies in case we have a faulty rocket.

"When we roll in to shoot rockets, get your heads down. The rockets have a fifty meter killing radius.

"We work in teams of two. The first ship in, the lead ship, has rockets and a 40mm cannon that can shoot on full auto, if necessary. There are two door gunners with free M-60's. Wing ship also has rockets. He has two electric Gatling guns and two door gunners.

"We cover each other's six by flying in a race track pattern. When one ship shoots and breaks, the other shoots to protect his belly. You can shoot short bursts if there is any gap between us. Just don't take a chance on ricochets, since your bullets are as lethal as the enemy's.

"Keep all conversations to a minimum. We're doing a multitude of tasks, and the situation is constantly changing. Just give us the facts we ask for.

"If the enemy is in the open, it's no problem. But if they're behind cover, we need your help to know where to shoot. We look for muzzle flashes and tracers in the daylight. It's no problem at night as their AKs throw out a four-foot flame, as you're all aware. At night, we also bring a flare ship that tosses out flares on parachutes behind the enemy. You can read a book by their light."

I continued for another thirty minutes.

"Let's pause. Are there any questions? Don't hesitate guys. The only dumb question is the one you don't ask. It's a fucking fight for survival out there. They are trying to kill you as much as you want to kill them. They may not have much training, but their bullets still kill."

A GB raised his hand. "What's the best tactic to use until the guns arrive?"

"Show no fear. If you have to fall back, move only a short distance for cover. You guys are better trained, better equipped and are smarter. Set up claymores and then move only back enough to draw the enemy in. Have everyone throw a grenade or two at the same time. Let them think there are a lot more of you than they thought.

"Shoot at those bastards the whole time and stop when we get close. The shooting from several locations confuses the hell out of them. Confusion to an untrained mind is terrifying. That's another advantage for us.

"They live in this fucked up world with its high temperature and humidity. We have an expression in the guns: we own the day and they THINK they own the night.

"There is one issue that I wish you GB's could get over. You are not a bunch of weaklings if you call for the guns. If you wait too long, it gives them better odds to wound or kill you. The guns are here to protect American troops. Use us. Look at us as an extra bandolier of ammunition. Remember, we're as crazy as you." That drew laughs.

"We in the guns are volunteers, just like all of you. We all asked for what we got ourselves into over here in this little piece of hell."

I answered more questions and added to my talk for another thirty minutes.

"If there are no more questions this evening, let's go to the movies. The General told me you've got John Wayne and popcorn!"

General Wheaton stood and said, "Thank you, Mac. The movie is here in the mess hall at 2000, (twenty hundred). Dismissed."

When I was walking back toward Steph, I saw the biggest smile on her face. She stared into my eyes and said, "I'm so proud of you."

I said, "Thank you. I believe I'm improving in my ability to accept a compliment. How about a walk before the movie?"

"I'll walk anywhere with you, flyboy."

I smiled and took her hand. "Do you have any idea where you would like to live back in the world?"

"Certainly not LA. What you've told me about Oregon sounds like paradise. I could live with that."

We walked out of the movie at intermission and spent the next few hours talking about the future. We'd already seen the movie.

Chapter 63.

BACK TO LAOS

I was called into the general's office early the next morning. Two colonels were seated there, and they paused their discussion when I came in.

General Wheaton said, "Have a seat Mac." He introduced me to Colonels Bevans and Stuart. "They're newly assigned here from Danang. They're part of a team following the incursion of weapons into SVN from the north.

"We've been talking about using the arc lights further south. Straight west of Danang are some very narrow valleys that all the soldiers, trucks, and weapons coming south from the Ho Chi Minh highway have to squeeze through. It's just a one lane road through the mountain valleys. We would have them bottled up in there, and we could bomb thirty to fifty miles of those convoys in a single attack.

"There's a road west out of Danang to the Laotian border. We can refuel at the border, then fly on to the Bolaven Plateau, land, and wait for the mercs to call. That plateau is a paradise, rivers, waterfalls, lakes, green trees and fields. And no war!"

He looked at me and smiled. "The only real disadvantage of the plateau is its altitude. I know loaded gunships struggle for altitude. Alternatively, you all could wait at the Laotian-Vietnam border.

"The insertion LZs for the mercs to watch the trail have yet to be determined. If you go down out there your E & E (escape and evasion) is west into Thailand. We have lots of people in Thailand, to include the Air Force with fighters and B-52 bombers."

"OK," the general concluded, "let's see if we can tear any holes in this plan."

"Sir," I asked, "how safe is the border refueling?"

"Very safe Mac. We can put enough troops and Air Force to stop any enemy attack. We are prepared to do whatever it takes to catch those bastards in the valley."

"Same tactics as before sir."

"Yes, we've been continuing missions similar to the ones you and I performed. We've spread them north to the DMZ and south halfway from RP to the Bolaven Plateau. By moving this next mission so far south we should surprise the hell out of the NVA. What do you think?"

One of the Colonels said, "Missions where you two did what?"

I said, "Sir, may I answer that question, please?"

General Wheaton nodded.

"We were inserting LRRPs into Laos to call in air strikes on the Ho Chi Minh highway," I said. "We were concentrating on the east side of the Chaine Annamite. The LRRPs would call in the arc lights, and then we would go in for the extractions, like we're talking about doing now. Anyway, my copilot had just gotten wounded and General Wheaton, he was Colonel Wheaton then, immediately volunteered to be my copilot, so we wouldn't have to delay the mission. He did everything a fighting copilot does, and he did it well, and he earned a Purple Heart doing it. This was just a few months ago.

"Sirs, as you know, a field grade officer doesn't generally go into combat. Someone told me when I was an FNG that Colonels and Generals were pencil pushers. So you don't always think of what they did before they attained that rank. I needed a copilot, and the general volunteered without hesitation. And he volunteered for several more missions, until my new copilot arrived. He is incredible. He is a better pilot than me. After the first mission, he was doing TO and landings, shooting the 40 mm cannon and shooting rockets, all while flying. I would fly as his copilot any day, anywhere. My point is, he knows what he's talking about from immediate hands-on experience, and we should listen to him."

General Wheaton looked to see if the colonels had anything else they wanted to ask. They did not.

"I know this new mission is very important," I went on. "I'm seeing a huge increase in 51's every week. Those damn things are helicopter killers. Another positive about this mission is how many miles the NVA will have to spread out their troops. That's a lot of manpower to put up in the mountains looking for us. We will be on the other side of the trail. They will be looking on the original side. We can grab the mercs, fly south then east to get out of Laos. From there, it's our choice: Danang, if we've got the fuel, and if not, we fly to the traveling gas station. When do we start?"

"Report to our HQ in Danang at 0900 three days from now," General Wheaton said. "Oh yeah, pathfinders will go in today and find a safe area on the plateau."

"Yes sir."

"Steph is off today," he noted with a wry smile. "Dismissed."

I walked double time to her trailer. She opened to door for me wearing almost nothing. She was as beautiful and exciting as the first time I saw her. How could all of this be happening to me? We had our usual passionate initial encounter, but after a while we talked about what was happening outside.

"Did General Wheaton tell you about my next assignment?"

"Yes he did. He said it would be safer than your previous excursions to the Laotian border. I looked on a map, and you'll be halfway across that country, very deep in Tiger country. Why did he tell me it would be safe?"

"I think he was trying to put your mind at ease."

"Well Mac, it didn't work."

We did our best to forget the war for two days, and then I returned to CL to prepare for Laos. I still had stitches in me, but nothing hurt. I was told to keep it clean. *Come on. Jesus this is Vietnam.*

Most of the prep for the mission was studying maps and aerial photos of the valleys and the plateau. I could live on that plateau. *It was spectacular.*

I departed CL at 0730 for the hour flight to Danang. My copilot was Vic Newhouse. Wing was Captain Jerry Wilder and copilot Bob Clearwater. Ski and Tyler with me and Arnold Fox, CE and Pat Marshall DG in Wilder's ship.

Something new: Four Rattler slicks were the insertion and extraction ships. This was cozy. Lead slick was Glen Walton, 2-9. The other slicks were 2-2, 2-4, and 1-8. I didn't know a couple of those slick pilots. I would work on that.

We briefed the mission several times, including the two LZs, two alternates and several false insertions. We maxed out on fuel and armament and waited for dark.

It took only 20 minutes to reach the border. We kept flying across the valley and over the mountains and began our false insertions and the true LZs. We put ten men in each LZ. They were ten clicks apart (six miles). It required two ships in each LZ to drop off ten mercs and supplies.

The first two slicks had seven mercs each and the third had six. The fourth was supplies only and would be our reserve ship on extraction for any situation. Number two landed twice and disgorged some of his troops in both LZs. We received no fire.

We stayed low and flew to the Bolaven Plateau and landed in an area chosen by the four pathfinders. It had a two-mile-long straight road, which we could use to take off. We'd burned less than an hour of fuel, which left us with almost two hours of flight time.

As the crews swarmed over the ships, the four slick pilots walked over to the Birds and were introduced by Glen. I then said, "Let's sit down. Glen and I are going to explain the tactics we use to pick up troops if they are alone or being pursued."

We went over the race-track patterns of the guns escorting slicks in and out of an LZ, picking out hot spots for the guns if we aren't shooting at a particular spot. "Be loose and flexible coming out," I told them. "You may have to go out the way you came in, so the lead ship in may not be the lead exiting. Give your door gunners the OK to shoot at anything other than our mercs."

We went over other issues and answered questions. Then, we broke to get some sleep. The mercs were monitoring the pathfinders would wake us when it was time to go in.

The next thing I knew, the sun was rising. Damn, we were able to sleep through. Of course that meant the Ho Chi Minh trail was empty, no traffic last night.

As people were waking, I thought, *Wow, C-rations for breakfast. It just doesn't get any worse.* I got potatoes and gravy, cheese and crackers and pears. All served in little green cans. After that, someone said, "Bring out the cards." Then later, "Where's the football?"

I said, "Remember, no tackling. Hell, I don't even want to see touch tackling. Just throw it around."

After a few hours, we had all switched to books or magazines.

The GB's threw in some *Stars and Stripes* newspapers. Then, it was time for lunch, which meant more green cans. They listed the contents, but what was inside the cans didn't taste anything like what it said on the outside.

This goes in my book. Exceptionally shitty food. Maybe that will put some pressure on the government to improve it. Fat chance.

Lunch was followed by a nap. The weather was cool with minimal humidity. It smelled like the outdoors back in the world. Just clean; no burning shit. Nothing to remind you of a war. I could smell trees. The river running alongside the road was crystal clear. I took off my boots and dangled my feet in the water. What a sensation! It was cool and relaxing.

About then, the pathfinders returned. They'd been out checking the neighborhood to ensure our safety. One walked over and said, "Mac, is there room for a few more tired feet?"

"Absolutely, have a seat. It's amazing how good a simple pleasure can feel when you're in a war."

He looked so young, about my height and not a pound of fat on him. For that matter, I was pretty thin too.

He sat and took off his boots. "I agree Mac," he said. "We just walked 10 miles around this place never knowing what was behind the next tree. So to sit here is a real pleasure. By the way, I'm Randy Allen;pathfinder." He put out his hand, and I took it.

"We know who you are, Mac. We were briefed by the GB's in Danang. We were led to believe you can walk on water."

"Well, Randy, I can't, and I've been wounded, so I know I bleed red. In fact, I'm lucky to be here. Don't ever think I'm better than you or more important than you. OK"

"Thanks Mac. We're not used to being talked to by an officer the way you talk to us. Tell me something. Did you really have General Wheaton fly with you out to the Laotian border and beyond?"

"I did, but he was a lowly full bird colonel then." (Highest rank before general)

Randy started laughing and said, "I haven't had a good laugh in a long while."

"Any word from the mercs?"

"No, still on radio silence."

We talked about everything. He was a Kansas wheat farmer on

the family property. Enlisted after high school, as he didn't want to spend the rest of his life on the farm in the middle of nowhere. Then, he stopped and laughed. "Here I am in the middle of nowhere. However, it's green, and that's an improvement. There's nothing green in Kansas once you're thirty feet from my mom's garden."

Now, I laughed. "I probably never would have seen this beautiful country if it weren't for the military. What do they say, 'Join the army and see the world?' Or was that the navy?"

"I have to check the gunships to include firing up the turbine," I told him. "I might add a nap after lunch, in case we have to fly tonight. I've been in sleep deprivation since I arrived in VN."

I walked over to the ship, and all three of my crew were asleep in the shade under the ship. *Hell, I'm not going to wake 'em. I'll join 'em.* An hour later, I woke up when I heard someone ask if anyone was hungry.

The slick crews, sixteen total, came over, and we had the greatest bullshit session since I'd been in the army. No booze, so it was all straight stuff from very humble people who all depended on each other. It made eating the C-rations palatable.

We ate and then crawled all over the ships to ensure readiness for tonight. Both of the guns and the four slicks looked good and ready to go. It actually got a little boring in the afternoon. We tried reading, then played hearts, and finally dinner in a can.

The pathfinders hiked out of camp to ensure there weren't any unfriendlies lurking about. They returned in thirty minutes to report they'd gotten a call from the mercs. A long convoy was coming down the trail. It was 20 clicks north of the areas we had encountered convoys two months before. It was moving slowly, not more than ten mph. The B-52's will be on station just prior to the convoy's ETA into the valley of death.

Five hours later, we could hear the thunder from hundreds of bombs exploding. I could only imagine the devastation.

The pathfinders' radio operator said, "The mercs called and are OK. The bomb blasts also covered the lower one third of the valley's walls. He's seen no movement there. He doesn't think they have any troops this far south. Nothing is alive, as far as he can see . . . both north and south."

I thought to myself, *they're going to change that route the next time they come south. They could move to the next valley west. If they do, our mercs will still be able to observe them just as easily as tonight.*

The radio operator called me and said, "The general wants to talk to you."

I walked over and took the phone and said, "Good evening, sir."

"How's everything out there in paradise, Mac?"

"All is quiet, sir. It must have been Dante's inferno in that valley. We could hear the explosions here on the plateau."

"The mercs are OK, and I'm wondering what to do next."

"Well sir, I don't think the bad guys will try to use that valley for a while. There is another valley west, as you know. That would be my guess, and the mercs are in position to watch that valley without moving from their current location."

"I saw that, too, Mac. Why don't all of you remain there for two or three more days and see if they're as desperate to get those weapons into South Vietnam as we believe they are."

"We're running out of books and magazines, but no problem staying here. It's beautiful, quiet, and no bomb craters."

"Great Mac. I just got off the horn with the mercs, and they are doing fine. They will run low on food in two days. That's their biggest concern. They are watching both valleys twenty four hours a day. Call if anything unusual shows up. We'll call you after it hits the fan."

We all spent those two days trying to stay alert, but let's face it, we were bored. The food sucked. We ran out of reading material and got tired of the picture magazines. We learned a little more about each other. It was a large group of kids: sixteen in the slicks, eight birds, and four pathfinders. A grand total of twenty eight. We talked for hours. We just went around the circle, and each guy chose his own topic. After five or six rotations, we knew more about each other than our mothers did.

Glen and I had some great conversations about life in general, and we agreed we would make an effort to reconnect back in the world.

The pathfinders were rotating their turns at monitoring the radio while the group continued with the "getting to know you" session.

Suddenly, Randy interrupted us. "Excuse me guys. The GBs just called and said a convoy was spotted up north by some mercs out of RP. The convoy is spread out and in a long trail formation. I called Danang, and they said wait because the convoy will have to close up, when they come through one of the valleys down here."

Someone asked, "Why will they have to close up the convoy?"

Randy said, "It would most likely be because the road narrows down to one lane. They also do it for protection. They lose their overhead air cover a few clicks south of the DMZ leaving North Vietnam."

We knew it would be five to six hours before they entered our valley. We were 99% sure they would use the new valley to the west.

Sure enough, we later got a call from our most northern patrol that they were entering the new valley. Now, they would be history. The B-52's were in the air and would begin their bomb runs when the convoy was optimally positioned.

The southern patrol called an hour later and said the arc light would begin in an hour. The BUFFs (big ugly fat fuckers; B-52s) were nearly in position to bomb the convoy from the southern end of the valley north for 34 clicks (20 miles). The bombers would fly in a long trail formation in groups of four at the southern end of the valley and of six at the northern end where the trail was wider. They'd all drop at once. A formation of six could kill an area of 5/8 mile wide by two miles long. Each B-52 carried 60,000 pounds of bombs, a combination of 500 and 750 pounders that added up to 108 total bombs. The BUFF's dropped them from 30,000 feet altitude.

The hour arrived, and we could hear the thunder and see the eerie glow in the distance.

The mercs called and asked to be picked up. They reported that everything was dead below them in the valley, animal and vegetable, as far as they could see north and south.

"OK, everyone," I said, "mount up for the extraction. It should be cold but be on your toes. We'll pick up the northern group first, then the southern, and sneak out south of the last truck bombed and east to the VN border. Watch your fuel. We should all be able to reach Danang safely. Remember, we have a gas truck, traveler 6, waiting at the border and a short ways north.

"Randy, have your guys climb in Slick 4. We'll have two ships land in the north LZ, and Slick 1 will take on seven, Slick 2 three. In the south LZ, number 2 slick will take on four and 3 will take six; twenty total. Number 4 is available for emergencies, but he will already be carrying four pathfinders. Guns will hang back behind the second ship in at both LZs. We can cover and shoot from there."

Slick 4 circle west of the LZ. We'll form up and fly ten clicks south. Same thing; guns hang back to cover slicks in the LZs. Then we hat up and GTFO."

All went well until we picked up the southern patrol. As we were flying out, two machine guns opened up on us.

Son of a bitch. The NVA had sent some troops down the next valley west, a third valley.

I called all slicks to break east, and the guns to turn west. Ski and Tyler were already shooting as were the wing's gun crew. I rolled in and began punching rockets at the two machine guns. They were thirty calibers and not 51s. That was a relief. All of those thoughts were just a flash. I called Vic Newhouse, my copilot, and said, "How you are doing?" He said, "OK. I'm seeing AK muzzle flashes that make for easy targets."

I called, "Ready," then "Breaking right," and 9-6 (Jerry Wilder) followed with his rockets. Clearwater was hosing down everything with the mini guns. First run was going smoothly until Wilder called out during his break. "I've been hit in the leg, the calf," he said. "It's bleeding but not enough to be an artery." I was already punching rockets, so I added sixteen more where I saw the tracers coming up out of the jungle.

I called 9-6 and said, "Let's go home."

9-6 said, "The crew dropped my seat back and pulled me out to the cargo area and put on a tourniquet. Bob will be flying us home."

Bob put the petal down and was turning east. "Oh shit, we just got two warning lights, oil pressure and hydraulics, both yellow lights. We're going to keep going until we have to put it down."

"OK 9-6, I'm on your six to the right. Bob, how are you holding up?"

"I'm good, Mac. Flying corporate jets was a lot safer than this. I might add it also paid a hell of a lot better."

I don't know how I'm going to word this in my manuals that explain all the shit they didn't teach in flight school. Actually, I'm being cynical as you just can't teach all this shit. It comes by experience only.

We just crossed the border when Bob called and said, "The oil pressure light is red."

At the time, I was talking to General Wheaton about our situation. He said, "We don't have any troops in that area, so if that ship goes down and you are able to pull out the crew, then blow it up."

The slicks were up at 1500 feet for safety. Glen called and said, "9-7, when they put that ship down, number 4 can pick up the crew. All of us are flying the new H-model with lots of power."

"Thanks 2-9. I've got some armament remaining. I can cover 4 when he goes in for the pickup."

"9-7, this is 9-6's copilot. I see a green flat spot at my 12 o'clock."

I replied, "I see it. Let me fly over it before you land."

As I did, two AK-47s let loose on full auto. They shot early, so the four of us were all able to return fire: two pair of rockets from me, 50 rounds from the cannon and 150 rounds apiece from Ski and Tyler. If they had fired when we were overhead, only the door gunners would have been able to shoot.

"Fuck Mac, I've got a red light on the hydraulics."

"Put it down fast, and I'll make another pass on those bastards. Number 4, are you ready?"

"1-8 rogers, and is on his tail. We should both touch down at the same time."

"9-6, how do you feel?"

"I'm getting light headed. I'm going to need help getting to the slick."

"Bob, can the three of you get him to the slick?"

Before Bob could answer, the fourth slick pilot, Dick Champion, called and said, "My crew just volunteered. You are well aware that the guys in back have big heavy brass balls and are crazier than shit."

I said, "Thanks guys. The Birds will be buying you beers for a long time."

"9-6, they both gave me thumbs up to those words."

As the wing ship was about to touch down, everything failed at once. The engine quit and the hydraulics froze. The ship hit hard from about a six foot fall onto the right skid and leaned right far enough for the blade to hit the ground. That blade strike caused the ship to roll onto the right side and the force from the blade stopping so quickly tore the ship apart. As the dust and grass were flying in the air, the slick crew got to the wreck and asked if everyone was OK. The crew chief and door gunner were OK. They were lifting up Wilder who was unconscious either from blood loss or from the crash. The slick crew had climbed on the side along with the pathfinders so they could help lift Wilder up and out.

Suddenly AK-47s opened up on the downed ship, and the two guys who were pulling Wilder out were totally exposed. It's a good thing we had a clear night, since we didn't have a flare ship. On the other hand, the NVA were able to see, too.

1-8 said, "9-7, we're taking fire from the north of us."

I rogered and punched two pair of rockets. They were on Ski's side, so he fired several hundred rounds. Vic put 100 cannon shells on the target. It was a thick jungle and very difficult to see into that foliage.

The slick crew was able to pull Wilder out, and then jumped to the ground so the gun crew could lower him down as the pathfinders provided cover fire. The slick crew carried him to their ship as the gun crew split up. One looked through the copilot's door and the other went back into the ship to see why Clearwater hadn't climbed out. He was unconscious and bleeding from the forehead and his clear visor was shattered. Something broke loose in the crash and obviously struck his forehead.

I rolled in again realizing I only had six rockets remaining.

The slick crew saw that no one followed them, so they ran back and helped the Pathfinders pull Bob out. This was difficult as some sporadic fire came from the south side of the open field.

1-8 said, "9-7, south side," so I put in one pair and told Vic, "Shoot that cannon dry (empty it)."

1-8 called and said he had two yellows, avionics (radios) and his rpm's were surging (engine was increasing speed then slowing down). He said, "It's only a small amount."

Ski and Tyler were still picking out targets as I rolled in.

1-8 said, "Pulling pitch," so I shot one pair on the north side and one pair on the south. As Vic was emptying his cannon, I noted to myself that I had only two rockets remaining.

The slick gunners were shooting a long continuous burst on both sides all the way out. Once he was clear, I turned my rocket selector to single rocket and rolled in on the crashed wing ship. I came in from the north side to target the exposed belly and the fuel tank. I punched and the ship exploded. *Damn, that hurt.* It was fully engulfed in fire in a few seconds.

"The ship is destroyed," I called out, "and I think I can make Danang."

1-8 called. "I'm returning to Danang ASAP as both my gunners have been shot. They didn't realize it until we were flying out. Crew chief is hit in the arm. Looks like a bullet wound. The door gunner looks like he was splattered in both legs from shrapnel."

I said, "Go. We're OK."

It was then I noticed three holes in my windshield and one in Vic's. I had taken a round in the chicken board. I checked all my instruments, and they were OK. It was the fuel gauge that concerned me. Ten minutes later I had a yellow caution light for low fuel. Well, that certainly wasn't a surprise.

I was ten minutes from Danang. *This will be close.* I called the general and gave a quick mini post action report. He didn't say a word until I finished.

"Mac, everyone wounded is in our medical room. No one is in danger. Clearwater and Wilder are awake and on IVs getting blood and antibiotics. The slick gunners are doing fine. They were sewn up and given some of those syrup shots in the butt as you call it. How's your fuel?"

"Sir, I'm on a fart, fumes, and a prayer."

The general started laughing and finally said, "Dammit Mac, I'm serious."

"So am I sir."

"Check in with me when you land. It sounds like it was quite a gunfight."

"Yes sir."

I turned to my copilot. "Vic, how's she flying? Is the fuel still low?"

He looked at me, and then we both laughed.

I could see the runway lights at Danang and started to believe that we might make it. "Take it up slowly, Vic. A little more altitude would be nice if the engine quits."

I called Danang tower and gave them my situation, and he cleared us for a straight in approach.

"Alright everyone, go cold even if you don't have any ammo." The three of them said one after the other, "I'm out."

I said, "Don't worry, fellas. I'll protect us. I have one rocket." That eased some tension, and I looked back and saw the door gunners laughing while sitting there with their machine guns lying across their thighs. I asked them if they were going to use those empty guns as clubs.

Tyler said, "Fuckin' A, Mac."

I looked at Vic, and he said, "I'll point the cannon barrel at 'em and scare the shit out of them."

I said, "Shit," as I shook my head. "You guys are a hell of a group, and I'm lucky to fly with you. You were incredible out there. Your eyesight and accuracy with your weapons saved our asses."

About then we crossed over the threshold (the beginning) of the runway.

I said, "Vic, hover over to the GBs before you run out of gas. If you run dry before that, it will be your fault as you're the copilot."

"Christ Mac, it never changes. I can't wait until I make pilot."

Chapter 64.

REMEMBER YOU'RE IN A WAR ZONE

As soon as we shut down, the general appeared in a T-shirt and slacks. The others weren't in uniform either. I had never seen the general in civvies. He looked tired. As I climbed out, he came up and said, "Good job, you got everyone back alive."

I looked at him and said, "Do I know you?" He looked at me for a moment, and then he got it. I quickly followed with, "Excuse me, General Wheaton. I've never seen you in civvies."

"I'm glad you're back. Come on in and let's go through that mission."

During the debriefing, I told the general about the slick crew that risked everything, twice, to save the wing's crew. I told him about the pathfinders' heroics, the number 4 slick.

"Sir, I did learn something tonight. I relaxed too soon and let my guard down and flew right into their trap."

After the debriefing, I went to their first-aid room and checked on everyone. I talked to the medic as they were all asleep.

He gave a positive report. "They will be evaluated in the morning to see if anyone should be in Danang hospital to keep the wounds clean and prevent infection."

I asked him to look at my leg and shoulder from earlier wounds.

As he pulled off the dirty bandages, he said, "Fuck, this is a mess. Oh crap, sorry sir."

"You described it perfectly. We ran out of pilots for the mission, so I felt I had to go. Can you clean it and not tell anyone?"

He nodded and said, "OK sir, but I can't lie to the general if he asks. I'll leave it open tonight, and you can clean it more in the shower. Come in tomorrow morning, and I'll re-bandage them."

I said, "Deal, and thank you."

I found the shower and then fell asleep as I hit the pillow.

We were awakened at 0800. I found a clean flight suit on a chair by my bed, along with polished boots. *This overnight room service is the only way to go.* I went to the medic and had my wounds cleaned, and then I staggered to breakfast. I was still exhausted. Most everyone was in civvies.

As I sat down with my food, in walked Steph. That woke me up better than any caffeine. My stomach had its usual butterflies. I couldn't take my eyes off her. As she walked up, I was so surprised I couldn't think of anything intelligent to say. "I can't believe you're here." *Brilliant, huh.*

She smiled and sat down beside me. "The general is giving all of you the day off, so I was flown here late last night and slept in one of the guest trailers. I went to the Intel room early this morning and read the after-action report. I don't know what to say, flyboy. It looks like you set up the rescue mission and then made it work."

"I had lots of help, Stephanie. I'm going to say it again. I'm so surprised and so glad to see you. This is still a war zone, and when we're together, I forget that fact. That's how much I'm in love with you."

"Excuse me, Kev. I'm going to get breakfast."

When she returned, the general walked over with a cup of coffee and said, "May I join you?"

"Of course sir. I've never heard a general ask permission from an officer as far down the line of authority as me."

He smiled and said, "I wasn't asking you, Mac. I was asking the beautiful civilian sitting beside you."

I felt my face redden.

"Don't mind him, Kev," she said. "He's just messing with you. He doesn't get many chances to loosen up."

"She's got me there, Mac. She's known me for 24 years."

Steph said, "Yes, I have, and I've loved every minute as far back as I can remember."

"Mac, have you ever known a ten year old who was smarter than you?"

"No sir."

"Well, I have, and it's been a pleasure to know her. You are a lucky man, though I don't believe it's all luck. I've gotten to know you. I'm her father's age, and I've learned much from you."

I didn't know what to say, so I kept quiet.

Steph saw this and said, "Derek, my godfather, you are embarrassing this poor humble human being. The only luck was meeting each other serendipitously as we did. The rest we made ourselves."

"Sir, I'm going back to college just so I can talk to this gorgeous lady."

The general laughed. "I know what you mean, Mac."

"Yes, it would behoove you two to be cognizant of my idiosyncrasies."

The general gave a chuckle. So did I.

I said, "Sir, would you like to go out and toss the ball around? Something that doesn't require a dictionary."

"I would love to, but I have meetings all day."

Steph said, "Alright you two, how about: Hey man, let's go chug some whisky, tell dirty jokes, and look at pictures of naked women."

The general said, "Excuse me. I must leave. You're on your own, Mac. Good luck. See you later, Steph."

"Come on, Steph," I told her, "That's not me. I just look at one naked woman, and I drink wine with her."

She threw her arms around me, and I told her for the thousandth time, "I love you, and I'll never look at pictures of any naked women."

"Come on," she said. "Let's go for a walk. There's a view of the ocean."

"OK."

As we were getting up, the general's aide approached. "A wing gunship with a new team has just departed CL. Maintenance is crawling all over your ship. They found five holes, besides your windshields."

I said, "Thanks."

I leaned over and whispered in Steph's ear, "Let's go to your place," and then I gently blew into her ear. I remembered when she stuck her tongue in my ear months ago, and I almost went AWOL.

She said, "OK," as she shivered. "That's a real turn on." She was pulling on my hand to hurry me along.

We almost tore her door off the hinges before she could get

the key in the lock. We both tried to get through at the same time and started laughing as we both backed off. I said, "After you." She didn't pause, and I followed and locked the door.

Then, we slowed down and savored the anticipation. Undressing was slow. I think it was to calm us down. At least, it was for me. These moments were so special that we wanted to appreciate every sensation. Then she began crying.

That startled me. "Why are you crying?"

"Your body has scars and bandages all over it. How can you be so loving and cheerful?"

"I see you, and I forget all about pain and this crazy war."

She carefully pushed me backwards until my legs touched the bed. She said, "Sit." We stayed in bed till noon with only one bathroom break.

Next was the highly anticipated shower that started everything over again. Not that I was complaining. Then, we went back to bed.

Being in love with Steph was possibly my best way of coping with this terrible place. I could forget the war when I had the woman I loved in my arms. At the same time, it's like Harry Reasoner said about Helicopter pilots: When everything is going well, you know something very bad is about to happen.

Right on schedule, it happened. An aide knocked on our door and then in a loud voice said, "The general wants you ASAP."

I said, "Shit. I'm so sorry."

Steph threw back the covers and said, "Go get 'em flyboy. Don't apologize. Remember you're in a war zone."

"Yeah, you're right," I said in a dejected tone. "Hopefully, I can come back to say goodbye after I find out what's so damned important."

I got dressed in my cleaned flight suit. "I'll bet this gets real dirty before the day is over."

I reported in to the general. He said, "We have a serious situation northwest of Quang Tri. The northern most observation point for the mercs in the Annamite's near the DMZ has been discovered, and they're on the run. They reported having a two-hour lead as the NVA were spotted early on in their hike up to the peak. Our guys, eight total, are moving down the other side as fast as possible, only occasionally stopping to set a claymore with a trip wire.

"We've checked the maps, and it's 200 kilometers in a straight line, then you home in on them with your RMI (radio magnetic indicator). Here are the frequencies and the coordinates of the direction they're moving. Call sign is Animal 6."

I snickered at that one. "Sir, is my wing ship here?"

"Yes, and they've been given all this information. Norwood is 9-1, as you know. His copilot is Larry Marston, gunner is Joe Gibbs, CE, and Paul Walsh is DG. Your ship is armed and fueled to the max. You should get there in an hour or less. Take three slicks. There are only eight mercs, but you know how hot it is out there. The slick crews have been given extra ammo as have the Bird crews. It's a cool morning, so you should be able to make it off the runway. It's 10,000 feet long."

"Did you say we should make it off? Hell, if I can't get that hog off the runway, I know someone who can," and I smiled at him.

The general laughed. "Would you like me to take it off for you?"

I smiled back. "Of course sir. I remember the last time we flew, and you handled that overloaded bus with ease and grace."

"Well, thank you, Mac, I would love to, but men with more stars on their shoulders than me have told me I've flown enough combat."

"OK sir, but I think they're wasting some of your talent. Keep your ear to the radio. I don't anticipate having to refuel at QT."

I ran to Steph's trailer and walked in without knocking. She was sitting on her bed crying. She stood as I walked up. I put my arms around her and held her tight. I finally pulled back and kissed her salty lips and said, "I'll be careful and see you soon."

As I turned towards the door, she said, "You're lying about the first part."

I smiled and walked out and ran to the ships. They were up and running at TO rpm. I jumped in and strapped the beast on and said, "Vic fly a heading of 340 as fast as you can push this baby. Those mercs are going to need us real soon."

Vic got it off with three bounces and a 100 yard slide. I asked the guys in back how much extra ammo they had on board.

"We went back and grabbed an extra case apiece. That was after they had already given us an extra case. Last time we flew with you, we ran out."

I just said, "Good call, I'm glad I met you two. OK everyone test your weapons."

Ski said, "Tyler is he getting mushy?"

Tyler said, "It sure sounded like it. If it gets any worse, I'm going to transfer to another gunship."

I spent the next ten minutes giving the crew the briefing. "Everyone out there but the mercs is enemy, and I want you to kill every fucking one of 'em. I'll do my share."

I decided to check on my wing. "9-1, how're you doing back there?"

I got back two clicks.

After fifty minutes at 120 knots, we were close enough to call and start homing in on the merc's location.

Animal 6 said, "9-7, I'm mighty glad to hear from you. I'm sure we can run faster downhill than they can run uphill, so our distance has increased. At least a two and a half hour lead."

"Sounds good 6."

I began planning the slicks' approach. I could see two fairly flat LZ locations about another half mile down the mountain from the mercs. I called them back and told them both looked like good areas. I told them about the trap the NVA had set up for us the other day and nearly caught us flat footed.

"The guns are going to make a run on the first LZ and shoot the shit out of it just in case anyone is waiting. Slicks hang back a mile and circle."

"Animal 6, do you see the LZ about 400 yards below you?"

"Not yet, but we're moving pretty fast."

"Can you see us?"

"Yes."

"Stop and get behind a tree or a rock. We are rolling in and will circle the LZ with fire. 9-1 let's approach south to north and break right, flying down the slope as we'll be faster if the NVA are waiting."

While explaining this to everyone, I was turning away from the LZ. We flew parallel to the mountain range with peaks several thousand feet above us. This LZ was small. Maybe it could take in two Hueys at a time.

"OK fellas, let's tear this place apart." My first pair of rockets were across the LZ on the north side, then a pair short on the south and then a pair on the east and west side. The crew was laying down heavy fire. I said, "9-1 just shoot a pair on my break and save your rockets unless they open up on me before the break." Ready, and breaking right."

As I broke, all hell let loose. Tracers from a machine gun and muzzle flashes from AK's showed their positions in the area I'd just put my rockets. The guys in back were hanging out and shooting long bursts. *Damn they're brave.* My wing was laying down good rocket fire, six total, and the mini guns and door gunners were going strong; all on target There was 360 degrees of enemy fire around the LZ, and all coming up at us.

I was coaxing all the horse power my ship could give to get in position to cover my wingman. While doing so, I called Animal 6 and said, "Let's try the LZ half mile straight left of the LZ below you. The one in front of you is full of machine guns and people that don't like us. I don't see any NVA on the peaks yet. It looks like they're still climbing up the other side. Now since company was waiting for us here, there's no reason to think it will be any easier at the next LZ."

I broke towards the LZ and fired a pair of rockets into the jungle at all four of the compass points and then broke right and clawed for air. 9-1 said, "Ready," and two seconds later said, "Breaking right." I shot two pair behind him and that cut down half the enemy's firing from the east side he was flying over, and then I broke in behind him and asked, "Are you OK?"

He said, "We got hit a few times, but the crew's fine and no warning lights."

"6 just keep moving. The guns are going ahead see what awaits us. 9-1, let's do the same approach, except I'm going to punch three pair at the eastern side, so we have a little more breathing room for our right break. Shit, I know they're down there, waiting. They heard all the explosions and gunfire from the first LZ."

This LZ was slightly larger. It could handle four slicks at a time. We only needed room for one

I came in again and spread my rockets to the north tree line, the south, and west. I shot three pair to the east side and then I broke right. Here came 9-1's rockets. He switched to single rocket which was smart as he only carried fourteen. No one shot at us, so he only fired once. That left him with seven remaining, and I had fourteen.

"I'll put a pair under you," I said, "and then I'll do another quick break and fall in behind you. 9-1. I'm suspicious. I know they are down there, and I don't want the slick blown to hell while he's landing for the mercs."

I called Animal 6 and asked, "Where are you?"

He was whispering. "100 yards from the south end of the LZ, and I can see a machine gun and about twenty NVA. They are 20 meters back in the trees but have a clear shot to the LZ."

I said, "Hold that position and get behind something big. We are going to come in from the west, shoot those bastards, and break over you. After the second ship breaks over you, start moving cautiously toward the LZ. On the next pass, we'll come in from the east again and then try to get the slick in." As I was coming around for my run, I called 2-9 and asked if he wanted to add anything.

He said in a sarcastic tone, "Yeah, kill some more of those bastards and then escort me in."

I said, "Roger," then followed with, "9-1, you ready?"

Click-click.

I punched two pair on the south side twenty meters into the trees and got another secondary explosion. As I was doing a slight pedal turn to get my nose pointed west for the next shot, Animal 6 called and said, "Shit that was perfect. I only see three guys staggering around. We'll go in and take care of them."

I put a pair on the west side, the north, and south, and then broke right. Wing shot one rocket into the same areas I had. He then broke right and received no fire, but I said, "Vic, hose down the area behind him." As he was shooting, I asked, "How's everyone back there?"

They said, "We're into our second extra case of M-60 ammo, and we've each changed our barrels."

"Now I know why I have a headache. OK 2-9, come on down, and we'll meet you about a quarter mile south of the LZ."

Click-click

"6, how much ammo do you have?"

"We've got everything. We haven't fired a shot in four days: a machine gun with close to 1000 rounds, grenades, six claymores, grenade launcher with fifty rounds, tons of M-16 and six smoke grenades."

I said, "Keep those smokes handy. We're going to need them. When we escort the slick in we'll come in over you. I want you to throw two smokes at the north tree line, two at the south, and the last two out in the middle of the LZ in case anyone is on the other side and wants to shoot across the LZ from their north location. The slick will come in, land, load up and turn 180 degrees and fly out the way he came in. Is that OK 2-9?"

"Yea, cover my ass, and I'll buy you a beer."

"6, here we come." There were some single shots at us but sporadic. All four door gunners were firing long bursts with the cannon and mini guns following suit. The mercs had thrown two grenades each to the three designated areas.

Glen Walton called out, "Just lost my engine."

As he flared and put it down with a bounce, a merc radioed, "It came from the east." That was on our right and down the slope. I had my rocket selector on single shot and fired one. I called the mercs and said, "Set up a perimeter around that ship and don't save any ammo. We'll only get one more chance. We're low on fuel and ammo. Slicks 2-2 and 2-4 get down here. We have twelve friendlies on the ground. You slick gunners shoot all the way in and out. Use that entire extra case of ammo."

"Glen, are you OK?"

"Yea, we're all fine. Just get down here quick. I don't like working in the infantry."

"Slicks, the only place to land is side by side just ahead of the downed ship. Then go out the way you came in." *Shit that had to be a lucky shot into his engine. I'll leave that out of the book, so I don't scare the new guys. You can be a great pilot and still die here.*

In we came again. As I fired one rocket on the right and one on the left, I said, "No one stop shooting." Both ships flared and landed. The men on the ground were shooting as they ran to the ships. Glen's crew had their machine guns and were shooting as they fast walked. Glen was carrying one case and his copilot was carrying one. Both were trying to pause and pull out belted ammo for those machine guns. The mercs were shooting enough ammo to supply a platoon (50 men). They also had two shoulder mounted bazookas they hadn't told me about, but what the hell, they knew when and how to use 'em. They fired into the east and west position with pretty good sized explosions. The smoke grenades were still doing their job. The rotor wash was stirring up the smoke and spreading it out instead of blowing it away. That was fortunate.

Shit, I have two yellow warning lights on, oil and hydraulics. I called 9-1 and asked if he had any lights on.

"Yea, I've got a high exhaust temperature."

I told the crew to keep shooting. "Vic, empty your cannon. Ski and Tyler save fifty rounds each in case we go down." If we did go down, the cannon wouldn't be useful and neither would my last rocket. I said, "9-1, use all your rockets. Save a little door gun ammo." I flew across the LZ with Vic and the door gunners shooting while the slicks loaded. 9-1 followed and did the same after firing his last rocket.

I heard 2-2, "Pulling pitch and turning 180 degrees to GTFO." I received some fire from the north, but the mini guns ended that. 2-4 said, "I'm right behind you 2-2."

I said, "Keep going. I have to call the general and get his decision on the downed slick."

I called the general, and he said, "Kill it."

"Roger that, sir."

I turned back and punched my last rocket. There was an explosion and a fifty foot ball of fire rose into the sky. I said, "Sir, the slick is dead."

Fuel was going to be tight getting to RP. *Damn, I've got to stop this.* Running out of fuel was about the worst disaster for a pilot and very embarrassing.

We arrived at the highway to Danang and were only fifteen miles out.

I called 2-2 and said, "You make the calls. You'll land several minutes before the guns."

2-2 said, "Roger wilco (OK, will comply)."

Three slicks called in and landed. Slick 1-8 had hung back and was following the guns as we had more warning lights. The warning light came on for my artificial horizon (which helps you fly straight and level at night), which added to my stress.

9-1 called and said, "Three of my four radios are out." All he had left was the FM for talking to the ground. (We all monitored that one.)

1-8 called Danang, as he was 1000 feet above me and had a better view. He said, "There are two very thirsty gunships coming in low level."

The tower called 1-8 and said, "I've got 'em. All three of you are cleared for a straight in approach."

We landed and hovered to our parking spots. Maintenance swarmed all over the guns. Their orders were to get us back in the air quickly, if possible.

Chapter 65.

DO YOU HAVE A CONSCIENCE?

A GB colonel walked over to greet us and said, "Follow me to the briefing room." He looked at me and said, "We have the entire mission on tape. Damn, we were sweating just listening to you guys. That was a hell of a gunfight. Everyone out there is a hero."

He took a good look at me and stopped. "Shit Mac, you're bleeding." I looked at my arms, and they were OK. Then I found a large red spot of blood on my right side just above my waist line and running down the outside of my leg to the top of my boot. "Damn, I don't feel a thing sir."

"Let's get you to the medic."

The colonel's aide said, "Follow me, sir."

I could have found it myself, having been there a few months back. We walked in and the medic said, "Shit, do you need help onto the table?"

I said, "No, I don't feel anything yet." I knew I would soon. I took off my pants, underwear, and boot before they got to me. They liked to cut off clothes, and I didn't have any extras. The medic had called the MD and when he arrived he said, "Lie down please. I'm Doctor Conner."

I did as told, and he put on gloves and gently pulled the edges of the opening apart. I felt that and moved slightly. He said, "I'm sorry. It looks deep but I don't think it's deep enough to have hit anything important. I'm going to x-ray you and see what, if anything, is in there."

They wheeled me into the x-ray room and took the picture. I was returned to the medical unit. Glen walked in and said, "How you doin'?"

I said, "Fine. I was hit with something small."

"In that case, you're an asshole. You let me get shot down. That's twice, and I'm getting to be a short timer (close to going home)."

The doctor walked in and said, "You have a bullet in there. It must have hit something hard to slow it down before it struck you. You're lucky, Mr. McNally. It's sitting between two muscle layers. I'm going to numb that area and pull out the bullet, clean the area, and then at least eight stitches."

"Sir, could I ask you a favor? Please don't put this in my records or I'll be sent home."

"I read your medical records from CL, Baldy, Danang and RP, and you have put in that request with each incident. Why?"

"There is nothing for a gun pilot to do in the states except train Vietnamese to fly. I really don't think I could do that for a year. I feel I can do some good here by helping American troops." Then I flinched and jerked away from the doctor.

He said, "I'm sorry again, but I got hold of the bullet and out it came. We'll wash it and you'll have a souvenir."

"Doctor, I will never forget this place, with or without a souvenir."

"Lie down and try to relax. I'm going to numb this wound some more and then stitch you up."

While the doc was sewing my wound closed, he started talking. "I've heard the stories about you and Dr. Weldon. Are those true?"

"I'm not sure what the rumors are, but he flew with me and shot rockets, the cannon, and M-60 machine gun. He said it was his greatest day since he arrived in hell. He said it gave him a much better understanding of the war, especially when you're just hanging your ass out with no protection in front of you."

"OK Mac, you're closed, as we doctors say. Now a shot in the butt of our special syrup, and some pills to take. I'm going to keep you here overnight for observation. Infection is our greatest concern."

"Is the syrup necessary?"

The doc said as he walked away, "I heard you Firebirds were pussies."

I called out, "I want a shot in each cheek." *What else could I say? That shit really does sting, and so did his answer.*

I was given some meds for pain and fell asleep. I woke up, and it was dark. The nurse brought me some dinner, and after I finished a few bites, I lost my appetite and lay back in bed. The nurse reappeared with a tray full of bandages and bottles. I couldn't see the bottles' labels, but I'm sure they were important. She then had me roll over on my left side so she could clean the wound. That procedure was uncomfortable.

She said, "Sorry this is cold. It's betadine and will kill any germs."

"It looks like the iodine that was put on my cuts and bruises when I was a kid," I said.

"It's the same color," she replied, "but it's better at killing germs." She put on new bandages and said, "I'll get your medications."

More pain meds and antibiotics, and I went back to sleep till sunup.

After a few bites of breakfast, I stopped and asked the nurse, "Why have I lost my appetite?"

"Getting shot and then the probing inside you puts you in a mild shock. That entire trauma has an impact on you."

Doctor Conner walked in and said, "Mac, I just got off the phone with your friend, General Wheaton. You have friends in very high places. Is the general the one rumored to have flown copilot in combat with you?"

I said, "Yes doc, but he was just a lowly Full Bird Colonel then. Please keep that to yourself. He is one great man."

"He would like me to Med-Evac you to Danang's Hospital for observation. We will wrap you up and carry you to the helo on a stretcher. I'm sure that's not your choice, but you were shot. It was nice meeting the man behind the legends. The general did say you were humble to a fault."

"Goodbye, Doctor Connor, and thank you for your help." I was lifted onto a stretcher on top of a gurney and taken to the waiting helo.

Five minutes later or so—I lost track of time—we landed at Danang, and I was wheeled into the hospital with the general and Steph waiting in my room. "What a surprise! My two favorite people in this country." Before I was taken off the gurney, Steph was there with a long soft kiss. When she stood up, I could see the general smiling.

The nurse asked everyone to step back. She took my vital signs, asked some questions, and said, "I'll be right back with your medications."

When she returned with a syringe filled with syrup, I felt a sense of dread. She pulled the curtain to give me privacy and proceeded to physically injure me. *She doesn't like people.*

After that ordeal was over, Steph looked at me and said, "Dammit flyboy, I said be careful."

I said, "It was a lucky shot."

The general stepped in before Steph took a swing at me and said, "Great job, Mac. You left no one behind. I've listened to the mission three times and took notes for future briefings. It was just incredible. You don't have to debrief. I've got the tape, and the stories from the pilots and crews. I'll see you later."

"OK sir, look forward to it."

Steph pulled up a chair and leaned forward with her face two inches from mine and said, "Kevin, do you love me more than flying?"

Without pausing, I said, "Absolutely, no contest. I'm just doing my job. Like a married couple, we both go to work each day. Your face flashes before me when I'm flying to and from a mission. That keeps me going."

"OK, I know you can't think of me when you're punching rockets. I'm just worried about you. I've worked every day since you were dragged out of my bed. Two girls with diarrhea, so it was a good chance for me to keep my mind busy, so I wouldn't worry so much.

"Now that you're here and all mine, I'm going to be your recovery nurse. Maybe even see if I can delay your healing and keep you out of this fucking mess."

"I feel very safe, lucky, and special. I'm so in love that I'm your obedient patient. Anything you want me to do."

"Tomorrow, I'm taking you to my place and begin your rehabilitation."

"Is that rehab or sexual physical training?"

She just rolled her eyes.

After I was discharged from the hospital, we were flown to CL HQ. We didn't go straight to her trailer. We walked and talked for two hours. My wound hurt a little, but I didn't mention it. I ended up knowing more about her than I did my two brothers. This relationship was beyond anything I could have ever imagined. She gave me some pictures that Donna had taken of her. I already had quite a few that I'd taken. These were better. In one, she was in a two piece swim suit. Another showed her in a sexy pose in bed, even though she was covered where it mattered. There were some of her flying my gunship and shooting rockets, cannon, and the M-60 door gun. I thought about getting her in bed, but I didn't want to mess up our wonderful feeling of closeness.

She looked at me and said, "Please tell me the truth. This question will not affect our relationship. Do you have a conscience?"

"No Steph, not when I'm in the air. I can't afford to. I can't think about what I'm doing to those kids on the ground from North Vietnam. When they dig foxholes around our FSB, I call them pre-dug graves. I have thought about your question when I'm alone with my thoughts at night. I realize I'll have to redevelop one. War does things to you. It affects your senses, both physical and mental. I had a conscience prior to arriving here, so I know I can find it when I leave."

Steph listened until I was done. "I believe everything you say," she said. "I'm so happy you can be so honest. When I'm with you, I feel your compassion and I feel a conscience. I don't think you've lost it. I think you compartmentalize it. You are able to turn it off when it needs to be turned off."

"Come here and lie down beside me," I said. "You're safe and don't have to worry about popping one of my stitches."

"I really don't want to be safe, but I will lie down. I will figure out a way we can make love gently. Very gently."

She was true to her word; it was gentle. *Amazing how women can have multiple orgasms. Must be a reward for putting up with men.*

She climbed off so gentle and said, "Don't move. I'm getting the wine."

As she walked in the kitchen, she asked if I'd ever had Scotch.

"Yes, I have."

"It's quite good when sipped. I have some here. I have the same privileges as the generals."

"I tasted my first Scotch over a week ago. One of our Firebird pilots received four bottles from the states. He said if we tried to chug it, we would never taste another drop of his nectar of the gods."

"OK flyboy, two of my finest glasses and the nectar of the gods. I like that name. It's fitting.

She poured, and we sipped. I said, "This stuff is really great. I knew they were lying when they told me that one-dollar-a-fifth gin was the good stuff."

She laughed at that comment. "I was told you firebirds would drink anything. Don't think I'm criticizing you. I know why you birds drink, and I would too. God, how you can fly, literally, into the jaws of death every day, all day, and half the night, is way beyond my comprehension. Alfred Tennyson wrote a famous poem in the 1800's about the 'Charge of the Light Brigade' and that was only one mission. The British charged into a Russian force and were slaughtered. You dummies keep going back."

"I can put those thoughts out of my mind," I said, "because I think of you. One of the birds told me I have pussy brain."

Steph jerked her head forward, dropped her head, and spit Scotch back into her glass and out of her nose, while choking and trying to laugh, all at the same time. The Scotch that missed the glass splattered in her lap. She looked at me and shook her head with the biggest smile. We were sitting together on the bed, so I turned and slapped her on the back a few times. She put her hand up as if to say, "I'm OK," I stopped and went into the kitchen for a glass of water. I handed it to her and said, "Sip this, like Scotch."

She stopped coughing, thank god. Her face was red and tears were running down her cheeks.

"I can't wait to tell Donna and my mom about your pussy brain. They will die laughing. Mac, I almost wet my pants. In fact, I'll be right back," as she hurried to the bathroom.

I thought it was funny, but I had no idea it was *that* funny. I took two quick sips of scotch, so it really wasn't a chug.

As she walked back in the room, she said, "That was close, but I made it. Dammit Kev, if you ever do that again when my mouth is full, I'll smack you with the first thing I can pick up."

I smiled and said, "Roger that, Steph." She sat down beside me, and I handed her the glass of nectar.

"It's going to be spectacular living with you," she said. "There will never be a dull moment. Wow, I bet we make some spectacular kids. I'm looking forward to that."

"I hate to bring this up in the middle of discussing our future," I said, "but I'm supposed to see the doc tomorrow."

"Will they put you back on flying status with stitches? Shit, do you need a lawyer?"

"They need pilots, Steph."

"Why is it always you?"

"It isn't just me. I fly with a lot of great pilots and crews. Every one of them are heroes in my book. We do our jobs. Most every job in a war is dangerous. This is our first helicopter war, so we're learning as we go."

"Yes," she said, "but at what cost? It's an expensive war. It costs young kids their lives. Can you imagine losing a child you raised for eighteen years? And what do the parents have to show for it? A lousy form letter from the government that destroys their lives. I think I understand WWII, but not Korea and not this one. It's just back and forth. No one keeps any ground they gain. They give it back to the other side and then try to retake it again."

"Aren't young kids always the ones to fight and die? Steph, I tell new pilots that there are three rules of war: First, old people start them. Second, young people die. Lastly, there is nothing you can do about rules one and two."

"Oh my god Kevin, that is so true."

"I know, Steph. I'm going to change the subject. Do you think I have a pussy brain?"

She smacked me on the shoulder and said, "Yes, you do. Hell, by bird standards, I have a dick brain."

Now, I spit scotch into my glass. She gave me her biggest smile. "Doesn't that just burn coming out your nose?"

"Tell me about it. I won't be able to taste food for a week."

The next day we were flown to the CL Hospital. Steph had to go back to work, and I had to check in to ensure my wound was infection free. The doc cleared me with a shake of his head. He said he had talked to Dr. Weldon and was told of my history, which meant don't put anything in my file. He told me he didn't like doing this but knew how much I wanted to fly and how desperate we were for pilots. I was put on flight status but had to check in with the Baldy MASH unit daily. "No lifting!"

I said, "Thank you, doctor."

The next morning, I flew to Baldy with Vic as copilot, and 9-1 Norwood flew with Marston as copilot. We rat raced for training and, of course, for beers. Both copilots did very well with only one error apiece in their fifteen-minute segments.

After we landed, the fuel trucks arrived and filled us to a half tank each. The ships had been rearmed in CL, so we were essentially ready to go. The tired Birds who had been at Baldy for the past five days could happily say, "Enjoy," and left for CL and the club.

Well, here we were back at the Hilton with nothing to do. We settled down with the paperbacks for a few hours when the red phone blasted us out of our reverie and started the adrenalin flowing.

The ballet began. The call was to assist an eight man ROK patrol thirty clicks northeast. They had two prisoners and were being pursued by what they estimated to be a company of NVA regulars, about 200 men. When they reached the Song Thu Gia River where the Quan Dai Lo River branches off, they would be out of the steep jungle and in the open without any cover except rice paddy dikes. Two slicks had been called off resupply missions to rendezvous with the birds and pick up the ROKs after the birds had finished with the NVA. The slicks were 2-6 and 1-4.

I received the call sign, frequency, last known coordinates, and about how fast they were moving.

I ran out to the guns, which were running at full operational rotor speed. I gave my wing the info and then I climbed in and told Vic to "TO and fly NW for twenty clicks." Then I would call Kidnap 6 for their location.

"They should still be in the steep jungle," I said, "and hopefully putting some distance between themselves and the NVA."

After five minutes, I called Kidnap 6 and asked for a sit rep. He said he believed he had gained some distance from the NVA, and now he could see the open rice paddies.

I said, "Throw a smoke out into the open." I waited and saw a red smoke, and he said that was his."

I asked, "How far behind you are the NVA?"

He said, "Less than a click. They made up some distance because we slowed down hoping we wouldn't have to expose ourselves out in those rice paddies."

I said, "No problem. I will fly over you, which I don't like to do but I won't punch a rocket until I've passed you. I would like you to spot my rockets and direct me in after my first four. Move to the edge of the jungle and tell me how far they are behind you, and I'll stop 'em right there."

"Roger that 9-7. Nice to be working with you again. You bailed our asses out of trouble a few months back."

"9-7 rolling in." I punched two pair and said, "6, how were those?" Vic was tearing up the countryside with the canon while I talked to 6.

"Add a 100 yards."

Vic automatically added the 100 yards and put fifty more cannon shells on that platoon.

I punched two more pairs and broke right. I watched 9-1 put his rockets and the mini gun in the same area. All four door gunners never paused.

"6, how were those?"

"Right on top of those bastards. They were totally surprised. They are retreating. Add another 100 yards."

The jungle vegetation in their retreating path was much thinner. Now they were exposed. I could see the well-worn trail.

Slick lead 2-6 called and said he could see us working the area and had been monitoring all radio transmissions.

"2-6, after we make this run," I said, "we'll circle out back and escort you in. Kidnap 6, throw out a smoke for your ride home."

"6, this is 2-6. I have your green smoke. Both ships will come in together. When you see us flaring to slow down, it will look like we are pointing our noses straight up. That's your signal to run like hell. Put five in each ship. After you're in, we'll turn around and go out the way we came in."

"Roger. We'll split up the prisoners. They will have empty sand bags over their heads. If you could make the ride to Baldy a little more interesting, it would encourage these prisoners to talk. I'm sure none of them have ever been in one of those noisy ships, and it will scare the hell out of 'em. Sometimes you guys scare me."

"My pleasure 6; we'll give them a ride they'll never forget."

While the pick-up was planned, I put ten rockets on the NVA as they ran into the nearly open area. Everyone was shooting, and I saw quite a few bodies on the ground. I broke, and 9-1 continued the decimation.

We flew out to meet the slicks, and in we came. I called 6 and said, "We will be shooting while you're climbing in those ships."

The two slicks, true to their word, stood their ships on their tails to slow down and here came the ROKs. As the ships touched the ground, the ROKs and prisoners were scrambling to get in.

As that was proceeding as planned, I started punching rockets on the far side of the open area. There was a little more cover but not enough to hide or avoid my rockets. I punched six pair and broke. Someone down there shot at me a few times. I hadn't received any enemy fire on my first two runs. Wing saw the muzzle flashes and put rockets and mini guns on top of them. As we flew back towards the slicks, I asked, "Is everything OK?"

2-6 said, "I wish all our missions went that smooth. I don't think they fired a shot at us."

"OK, let's go home." I called the Air Force forward observer plane and asked if he had any fast movers in the area with napalm.

He said he'd check. Then he said, "I have two. Where do you want it?"

I gave him the coordinates and told him, "We left the area smoking and burning. The NVA that made it to the heavy jungle were last seen moving NW. Maybe a mile from the fires by now, or should I say about a click and a half."

"OK 9-7, I'll take it from here. I say miles every once in a while myself. I guess we just want to think we're back in the world. We should meet and have a drink sometimes. I feel like I know you."

"Sounds great. I'm in CL every five or six days. You could fly to CL, and we can have someone pick you up. We are only three miles down the road."

"You're on."

After landing at Baldy, we checked the ship and couldn't find a hole. We looked at each other, and I said, "Let's look again." It was so unusual lately that no one spoke. We checked again with the same results. The wing ship was also in pristine condition. We just shrugged.

Chapter 66.

THANK GOD FOR KETCHUP

We rearmed the ships and went to the mess hall. We knew our next mission wouldn't go as well as the one we just finished.

We were correct. Whatever it was, I don't ever want to see it or smell it again. And that was the consensus of everyone.

As we walked back to the Hilton, I said, "Let's build some rockets."

Someone agreed. "That will help pass the time."

It was practically impossible for us to relax. We were so fired up with adrenalin from the mission, it was hard to come down. When we did come down, we were tired and irritable. If we weren't asleep, we felt we were crawling out of our skins. Combat takes its toll.

What are we supposed to do back in the world? How can we assimilate? I've never had friends like these guys. We are so close. What could make you closer than facing hot-metal mutilation or shards of Plexiglas in the face together? These last three sentences will go in my manual of things they don't teach in flight school.

The rocket building helped. Three hours was our limit. Then, we read our paperbacks until dinner. Dinner was a disgusting thought. Might as well open up the C-rats.

Some days this place is just depressing.

After the less than tolerable dinner, the flare ship landed and began loading. I walked out to help and discovered it was none other than my good friend Glen Walton, 2-9 from Texas. We shook hands and talked as we loaded his ship with 25 flares.

He said he'd been flying since 0500 and was exhausted.

I said, "Shit, Glen, we're always tired. I thought the slicks were bad, but the guns fly a lot of night missions. I could fall asleep right here." I pointed to the ground next to his ship.

"Come on Mac; let's take advantage of these few minutes."

I nodded, and we entered the Hilton which was as dangerous as combat. This offered a disease-ridden den, and the other offered bullets. What a choice!

Little was said. All twelve of us lay down and were instantly asleep.

At 0300, the god-damn red phone woke us, and we went into our trained response. I heard a few comments as we ran out the door: shit, fuck, god-damn war. The usual.

This mission was to assist a patrol of eight Americans from LZ Ross, six clicks west, very steep terrain and heavy jungle. We were told, "Contact Explorer 6. They are backed up against the steep terrain, and the bad guys are approaching from the west and are crossing a stream one click east."

After a rock and roll, I called Explorer 6. "The NVA haven't seen us. I count 30 moving slowly towards us."

"I'm only a minute out," I told him. "Get behind some trees and flash a light at me. I have a flare ship, and he'll toss one out after our first gun run. OK, I have your light. You're flashing SOS"

6 said, "Yes, that's all the Morse code I know, and it seems appropriate."

"Roger that. We're coming in from the north and will break away from you. The flare will light up the targets even better on our second pass. Keep me informed of the directions they're running. 9-7 rolling in." I punched four pair right into the single-file line. I walked them up the line to the leader. I broke, and wing finished the job. The flare lit up the countryside.

I called 6 and asked, "Is there anything moving?"

He said, "No."

"Are you headed to Ross?"

"Yes, we are."

"OK, we'll fly cover for you."

6 said, "Thanks," and they emerged from the trees and moved across the rice paddies which made the going slow.

About 300 yards into the paddies, a mortar shell exploded near the patrol.

"Shit, did anyone see where that came from?" I got no answer. "9-1, let's spread some rockets into those trees on the right and left of the patrol's location when we arrived. Shoot fifty yards into the trees."

I shot three pair on the left and four pair on the right. Vic and the door gunners were shooting at the same areas. I broke, and wing fired two singles left and three right. The mini guns and door gunners followed his explosions. We were all guessing where to shoot. Hoping to see a muzzle flash from that damn mortar.

"Flare, can you throw out some flares up the slope behind where the patrol was hiding?'

"Roger, they will be out the door in thirty seconds."

Another mortar round exploded closer to the patrol.

6 said, "9-7, they're just about zeroed in on us. The next shot could be lethal."

I said, "Roger," and turned sharply back towards that damn tree line and started punching rockets a 100 yards into the trees. I told 6 to run to the last mortar explosion. The bad guys would be thinking the patrol would keep running away from them and would not expect this. I thought I saw a flash from that last mortar launch and punched two pair. The crew was following my lead. I called 6 and asked if he was still receiving mortar shots.

"They stopped after those first two. I think you hit those bastards. We're moving down the dikes now. Much faster than in the water. We're more exposed, but it's OK. No one is shooting at us. Thanks 9-7, we got out of there without a scratch. We've covered a mile and have two and a half to go. We'll follow the stream that flows directly west to Ross."

"Roger that 6. We'll fly cover for a while until our fuel gauge sends us back to Baldy."

"Appreciate that. Out."

My wingman's copilot and my copilot flew over the patrol, back and forth for thirty minutes, and then we departed for Baldy.

We landed and my watch said 0430. *Shit we still have to rearm and refuel.* We were dragging, and it took forty minutes to finish that twenty-minute task. The sun would be coming up in a half hour.

Just at sunrise, the red phone rang. At least, it was only for a routine mission and not an emergency. We needed to help insert thirty of our guys to an inaccessible mountain top to prepare it for the Chinooks to bring in some heavy artillery.

We were to depart Baldy at 0800. Well, nothing like a leisurely start. This war might become civilized after all. Since everyone was awake, I suggested we eat.

I think they are making up these missions to see if they're possible. This is our first helicopter war. Let's see what we can do with helicopters and artillery.

A slick pilot, our flare last night or Glen or someone, told me once that you never pass up a chance to eat or pee. *This will go in my book. I'll add sleep to that list.*

Powered eggs just don't cut it. Thank god for toast (soggy) and ketchup, or it wouldn't have been palatable. I think the other morsel they splattered onto the tray was grits. Glen from Texas said, "These are better with butter."

I said, "Hell Glen everything's better with butter." He agreed and added, "It's the secret of Southern cooking."

We were back to the Hilton by 0700, and no one was there: no troops and no Hueys. When we got a chance, we always rechecked our ships, to catch a problem before it happened on a mission: a fluid leak, a loose push-pull rod (that moves the angle of the rotor blades), the stability of the tail rotor, the battery, and so on. We looked for anything and everything. I told the copilots to look at the manuals and ask the old timers questions. "They don't mind, and you WILL LEARN something. There's nothing like experience for learning."

The slicks arrived thirty minutes later. I asked the pilots if they had heard anything important in their briefing the previous night. They said it was essentially an in-and-out mission, and the briefing was done within a few minutes.

I said, "Yeah right. We've heard that bullshit too many times. Let's just be on our toes, and if you even think you see something, call out the position immediately. We don't want any more Million-Dollar Hills or any type of cluster fucks." *I'm sick of these SNAFU missions.*

We were taking in four slicks, eight grunts in each of the first two and seven in the last two ships. It was a small LZ, and we could take in only two ships at a time. The sides of the mountain were nearly straight up, so the main concern was that we might fly over some NVA at the bottom of the mountain 1000 feet below.

I said, "Rock and roll," and we took off right on time. Thankfully, there was no C & C ship up above advising us.

We flew nearly straight west past the Song Tinh Yen River four clicks, and there it was sticking up like a monolith. The first two slicks began their approach, and as they slowed, flaring nose up, a steady stream of machine gun tracers rose straight up at them. I dropped my nose and punched off four pair of rockets right on top of those guns and called out, "Abort, slicks, abort-abort, break sharp right."

As they were turning, the other two slicks also turned. Their gunners were working the area over. My crew concentrated on those machine guns. As I broke, wing and his crew put ordinance all over the area. I told the slicks to circle, and we would soften up the area, as we called it. We made another run and received fire from AKs 150 yards to both sides of our first rocket explosions. We hit them pretty good. I told the slicks, "I'm going to take a look at the other side of the mountain and see if that approach would be any better."

No one shot at me, so I thought I would provoke them. I punched off three pair into some trees fifty yards from the open area at the base of the mountain. No response. Hell, now what? They could be just waiting for the slicks. Should we go back to the original approach on the other side?

Shit, I thought as I called the slicks. "We're going to try again on the first approach. I'll be shooting before you flare. Both of us and all the crew will be putting enough heat on them they shouldn't even want to raise their heads to shoot."

In I went, shooting everything, and then the wing followed. No return fire as the first two slicks landed and discharged their troops and equipment to prepare the locations for the big guns. In came the second pair and did the same. All was smooth and no enemy fire. As they lifted and took off the last slick said, "Shit my engine is surging."

I said, "There are lots of rice paddies down there. Pick one and land now before your engine quits, and number three will be there when you land."

"Shit Mac, it's surging to 7200." We flew at 6600 rpm.

I watched as he descended, and I followed him in case he had a welcoming party. Sure enough, he was taking fire from his left, so I stopped that with a pair. Good thing I saw a tracer as the jungle was fairly thick.

The third slick flared and touched down, and the crew of the fourth jumped in, and they were up and out in ten seconds. I had my crew and wing shoot on both sides as we escorted them out. As they were safely at altitude and on their way to Baldy, we circled back to check on the slick. No one was visible, so we fired into our previous targets, as I called Baldy and asked if they wanted to send out a Chinook and if I could get some napalm in the area.

They said they would order up the Chinook and call for the nape.

"No offenses," I said, "but have the spotter call me."

"Roger."

The spotter, Air Force 02, told me two F-4s are coming in with nape for two passes.

"I see you, Air Force 02, and two passes are perfect," I told him. "Do you see the burning jungle at the base of the steep ridge running slightly NE? That's the first pass. The second is on the north side of the rice paddy with the Huey. Drop the nape two hundred yards short of each target, but not on the Huey, and let it run through the area. We are trying to get a Chinook in here and pull out that Huey. Those two areas were the last ones to shoot at me."

"Thanks 9-7. I'll relay that info to my fast movers. I have your location half a mile south of the second target."

"Roger, I'm sticking around to watch the fireworks. It fascinates me. "

I loved it. The two jets came in at 500 mph. The nape ran through the jungle at nearly the same speed. They pulled up sharply and turned to their left, so they could make a north to south run on the second target.

As they completed that second run, I called Baldy and said, "It looks clear. Maybe put in some troops for a perimeter at the base of this mountain."

"Great Idea 9-7. I'll put in the suggestion."

"9-7, this is Baldy. They are loading up thirty guys here from the 198th. Should be there in fifteen."

"Roger, we have fuel and ordinance remaining, so we'll fly cover."

The Chinook appeared and was at 2500 ft. He circled once to survey the area. He checked in with me as Hook 1. I told him the fires were the enemy's last location.

"I'll come in from the south. Then, I don't have to fly over the fire. I'll drop off the troops and lift back up as they form a perimeter and get the ship ready for pick up. Then, I'll go back in and load up everything."

I said, "Hook 1, the guns will escort you in both times."

"Thank you, I appreciate that."

"Hook 1 is on approach."

"So far it's lookin' good."

He landed and discharged the troops. He also left one of his crew to direct the procedure for tying down the main rotor and the apparatus to hook onto the mast of the Huey. That apparatus would connect to the hook on the Chinooks belly.

All was proceeding nicely, when a machine gun opened up from the base of the mountain only a few hundred yards away. I immediately turned, did a cyclic climb for altitude, and punched off four pair. *That leaves me with ten rockets.* I asked the crew, "How much ammo do you have?" Vic had 350 cannon shells remaining and the gunners had opened up the extra ammo crates. They had about 750 rounds apiece and another 500 each in the crates.

As I broke, wing came in firing. The machine gun stopped shooting after my rocket shots, but we had to make sure the sneaky little bastards weren't waiting for the Chinook.

I made another run, fired only one pair, and let the crew work over the area. I broke and called Hook 1. "Are you ready? The smoke from the new fires will block their vision, but we'll be here."

Hook 1 said, "Descending." He flared and sat the ship down. All the troops but two ran up the lowered tail gate. The two remained with the crew member who had to climb up on the Huey and attach the binding strap to the hook as the Chinook hovered down very close to the mast. He reached up and looped his end—a heavy canvas strap—over the hook. He had to be careful not to touch that metal hook or the static electricity from the spinning blades would throw him off the Huey and knock him unconscious. It could also kill him if he landed on his head. The three then ran to the Chinook.

The Hook rose up and tightened the cable and lifted the ship straight up 2000 ft. Next stop CL. I was impressed with the power of that Chinook.

I said, "Vic take me to the Hilton." 9-1 said, "We'll follow."

We had a welcoming committee waiting. We hovered into the revetments and shut 'em down. We had an artillery colonel, major, and captain standing in line to greet us. They thanked us for continuing the mission to get the artillery crew to the top of the mountain. "Tomorrow morning early, we're going to put four 155 mm cannons on that mountain, and they can shoot fifteen miles in all directions. I would like your crew, Mac, to escort four Chinooks out to place those guns on that mountain top. They will return and load up to capacity with 155 mm rounds, food and other equipment to secure the cannons. They will return with additional loads of the same."

"Yes sir."

The gas trucks showed up, so I said, "Let's check this ship for holes and rearm." I had two holes in mine, one through the floor on my side. I didn't hear or feel anything. I checked my boots and then looked around the cockpit and finally located where it hit. It struck the circuit breaker panel in the ceiling between the green houses (the green glass ceiling over each pilot's head so we can look up above for other ships, and the color is to reduce the heat intensity and glare). It struck the metal plate holding the six modules controlling electrical power. Looks like we were OK. Lucky this time.

The other hole was directly behind my head through an eight inch wide panel separating the cockpit from the cargo area in back. This was where the sliding door in back latched. Shit those two bullets were close.

The wing ship had a hole in the tail boom. The bullet was a through and through: in one side and out the other with no damage in between.

After rearming, it was off to lunch. It was such a boring existence here I actually looked forward to the flying. It was such a dichotomy: kill people or sit and talk about home.

The next morning at 0600, HQ called and said the Chinooks were twenty minutes out. They had picked up the 155s in Danang.

We took off to meet them, rock and roll. They went in one at a time and placed the cannons where the arty crews had marked the spots. All four in and not a single shot at any of us. The Chinooks said, "See you in two hours," as they returned to Danang for the 155 mm shells. Most would be HE, a few others WP, and also flares and bee-hive rounds.

We received a call two hours later. They were twenty minutes out. "This will take longer," they told us, "as we have to unload by hand. They loaded us with a fork lift. Too bad we couldn't bring that out here."

"Roger, OK fellas, rock and roll."

The first two went in one at a time. I called and asked if they could take 3 and 4 in at the same time as our fuel was getting close to being a problem. 3 and 4 said they'd give it a try. "One of us at each end of that small base while the other two are on the landing pads."

It was pretty dramatic watching those big Chinooks lowering their tail gates with the body of the ship hovering over the edge with the ground 1000 feet below. The arty crews were carrying ammo out to the cannons along with the helo crews. It was a long thirty minutes to finish the job. Fortunately, no one shot at us. I knew they knew we were here, so why were they waiting? I also figured we'd find out soon. The copilots loved that they flew the entire time, circling over the base and practicing gun runs. Despite my fears, it ended smoothly.

The Chinooks climbed to 3000 feet (very safe altitude) and returned to CL just south of our company area. We dropped to fifty feet and rat raced back to Baldy to the music of the Beatles, Stones, Iron Butterfly, and my favorite, The Beach Boys.

We landed at Baldy and did everything military to our ships. We were too pumped up to sleep, so it was time for a bullshit session.

Thirty minutes later, we were interrupted when a jeep drove up. The driver, a corporal, climbed out and said, "Who's Firebird 9-7?"

"I am corporal. What's up?"

"You're wanted up at HQ for a briefing, sir. Jump in. I'm your ride."

We stopped in front of the HQ for the 196 Light Infantry Brigade. "Follow me, sir."

I was escorted to a Colonel Roth's office. I reported in, and he said, "Have a seat, Mac."

"Thank you, sir."

"Mac, we have a large CA on for tomorrow morning at sunup. We're putting 200 men into an area just north of the marine artillery base west of here 32 clicks between the Song Thu Bon and the Song Vu Gia rivers. Our scouts have found a large concentration of NVA moving in the foothills of the jungle. They are constantly moving, so we can't just nape 'em. We'll find them and engage.

"The scouts have found indications of large weapons: 51s, mortars, AKs and machine guns. We are going to blow the shit out of the area just before we go in. The marine arty base has been stocking up on arty shells for the last three days. Here's the freqs and co-ords; the call sign is Baldy 1-6. We pull pitch a half hour after light. The artillery will shell the area for thirty minutes prior, beginning at the edge of the LZ and working outward, mostly north and west into the jungle and hills which become very steep very quickly. My second in command will be in the C & C ship, Lt. Col. Everett.

"We'll land nine ships at a time for the first two groups, seven to a ship with full field gear. The third will have ten ships with the last four carrying eight troops each. Resupply will begin immediately with food, water and ammo.

"I would like you to remain on station as long as possible. It's supposed to be cool again tomorrow morning so hopefully you can TO with three quarters of a tank of fuel? Then maybe an hour on station?"

"Yes sir."

"OK Mac, see you early. The slicks will be arriving at 0500."

The corporal drove me back to the Hilton. The gun team and the flare crew headed to the mess hall. As we ate, I briefed the crews. When I finished, the flare ship pilot told me was going to join us on the CA as a rescue ship. He followed with, "I hope we won't fly tonight. We're exhausted."

Chapter 67.

JET GOT HAMMERED BY THE NVA A MOMENT BEFORE THE NAPE INCINERATED HIM

We got lucky. The red phone was silent all night. We were awakened at 0530 by what sounded like half the Hueys in VN landing on both sides of our short runway. A long line of trucks was driving down the small hill loaded with 200 wide-eyed and quiet troops. *I've been here too long. These troops look like junior-high kids.*

As the troops filled the Hueys, I sat in the back of my ship with my feet dangling out the door, thinking about Steph. This war was fucking up the good part of my life.

The lieutenant colonel and two aides arrived with helmets, so they could plug into the Hueys' communication with Baldy 6 on the ground. They also brought a radio of their own, and I couldn't think of a reason why. *Yeah right.* The colonel was C & C 66.

It was 20 miles in civilian talk to the LZ. About twenty minutes figuring time for the Hueys to get in formation. The C & C ship took off, so they could circle the LZ and let the enemy know we were coming.

Next was the plethora of Hueys. As they were setting up their formations for flight and landing in the LZ, we guns hovered out to the very end of the runway.

"9-1, are you ready?"

Back came two clicks from his radio, so I said, "Rock and roll," and began sliding and bouncing. I think I willed my ship into the air because for a moment I didn't think I had enough runway.

I heard 9-1 say, "Shit," as he began the same maneuver. As soon as Ski told me 9-1 was airborne, I said, "Test your weapons." After that was finished, I asked Ski and Tyler, "Did you throw in extra ammo for your guns?"

Ski said, "Yes, it's now routine for us."

I certainly knew why it was routine. It was getting so hot in our AO that we always assumed we would encounter 51s.

The lead Huey, Rattler 1-8, Dick Champion, called me and said they were in formation and at 90 knots (103 mph). I was hanging back, so I could cover the first 18 ships landing and swing back around and come in with the last ten ships. The twenty-ninth was the C & C ship. I could see the smoke and dust around the LZ from the artillery we had put in the other day. Looked like they had really saturated the area. I liked that.

"OK, CA team," I radioed. "The first 18 begin your descent." As they started in, I slowed and moved back, up and above, so I could shoot on both sides. All 18 nearly touched down together. The troops began jumping out before most of the ships touched down. No one reported taking fire, which makes for a good day for everyone on the ground.

1-8 said, "Pulling pitch and making a right turn." All ships lifted and began their turn when all hell broke loose.

At least four 51s were pounding the slicks, and I punched rockets at all four locations.

I called, "Breaking right."

As I turned and began climbing out, I saw 9-1 blow up in a large fireball. *Holy shit*

"I'm breaking back in," I said, as I turned. The crew saw where the new 51s were located and was firing steadily. I put four pair on the 51s, and they stopped firing.

Two ships were shot down. One crashed, and one auto rotated. I called Rattler 2-4, Tom Bell, and said, "We have to get your guys in. We've put in only 60% of the troops." Then I called the C & C ship and said, "Colonel, can you get that arty unit back on target?"

He said, "I'm giving them the coordinates from the tree line and up the hill into the jungle."

"2-4, can you have two of your ships pick up the crews that went down?"

"I'll get on that. OK, last group, begin descent and everyone shoot."

Then Baldy 6 called and asked if they could put some wounded in the ships coming in. 2-4 called his flight and had three ships linger in the LZ for wounded.

As they were coming in to land, I punched rockets at any muzzle flash or tracer. Another fucking 51 opened up on the slicks as they were standing on their tails to slow quickly and then land. I put three pair on the new 51 and saw Vic do the same. Ski and Tyler were shooting long bursts, and pilots were talking over each other to report directions from where they were receiving fire. Someone yelled over the radio, "Ship is down." Another said their pilot was shot, and they were flying to Baldy's MASH.

When 2-4 called, "Pulling pitch and making a right turn," the artillery shells began exploding in the trees.

Damn. It was as if they knew we were coming. They were obviously farther back in the jungle than we anticipated. Maybe it was the setting up of the new arty unit. I had followed the two slicks down as they were picking up survivors and fired the rest of my rockets along the tree line as the two slicks were getting some single sporadic shots.

Two slicks called to report they were picking up the crew from the last ship shot down. The other slick picked up the crew of the ship that had auto rotated, but only one man was alive from the crashed ship.

I just said, "Shit. Thanks guys. That was brave of you to land in the open paddies."

2-4 said, "Form up and return to Baldy."

Now, I had time to think of Norwood, Marston and the two gunners that had been in 9-1's blown up bird.

I called CL and reported what had just happened. They said, "Brigade has called, and 9-6, Wilder, is flying up with William Langley, crew chief Joe Gibbs and gunner Paul Walsh. Walsh's arm is healed from his gunshot wound."

I said, "Yeah, I remember."

"Mac, do you want to come to CL for a break?"

"No thanks. I need to keep my mind on the job."

Now I know why the extra radio. They called Brigade to report on the mission. Shit, one gunship team to cover 28 Hueys. We should've had four minimum.

We landed at the back side of Baldy for fuel, and then flew around to our revetments and the Hilton. I went through all the motions of helping, while I was trying to understand why I didn't feel anything. *Shit, four friends just died in an eye blink. I must be really calloused.*

The wing ship with 9-6 piloting landed. He approached me and "expressed sympathy." He was sorry and etcetera. I nodded and said, "Thank you." I followed with, "I felt worthless out there today. Those slicks were so under protected". *I felt numb. It was a new and strange sensation. I didn't even feel angry. I didn't know why.*

Bell, 2-4, walked up to me and asked if I was OK.

Trying to sound calm, I said, "Yeah, I'm OK."

The red phone seemed extra loud. I picked it up and said, "Firebird 9-7." As I spoke, the crews were running to the ships.

"Mac, it's Smitty, are you guys ready to go?"

"Yes."

"They need help at the LZ you just left. The NVA are storming out of the jungle and are too close to our guys for the arty to help. Same frequency and call sign, Baldy 6."

"OK Smitty, we're outta here."

I wrote down the info for 9-6 and ran out and gave it to him, then jumped in my ship. "Vic, we're going back to the CA LZ. The NVA are attacking and are too close to our guys for the artillery to fire, so it's all on us." I said, "Ski, Tyler, go back and jerk out the first ten rockets and replace them with flechettes." Then to my CP I said, "Get us out there."

As soon we were in the air, I called Baldy 6 and said, "Give me a sit-rep."

"9-7, we're in deep shit. How far away are you?"

"Five minutes. Pop a smoke and give their direction from you."

"They're doing a bonsai charge straight west of our smoke. We were advancing toward the tall trees at the jungle's edge when they came running out. I don't know where the fuck they came from."

"I'll come in shootin' south of you and then break over you, and my wingman will do the same. My first 20 rockets are filled with flechettes, tiny metal arrows an inch and a half long. Watch if you haven't seen them before. Those rockets have proximity fuses so they blow up a hundred feet or so above the ground and each rocket will spray the enemy with nearly a thousand of those arrows."

"God damn hurry. We're just holding our own, but more are streaming out of the fucking jungle."

"OK, I've got your purple smoke. Get your heads down, but I'll be shooting away from you so you can peek over your sandbags."

Before he could answer, I started putting rockets on the NVA 100 meters from our guys and then walked them back towards the jungle, away from our guys. My crew was doing the same but a little slower so as to stop anyone that made it through my rockets. Some NVA dropped down and hid behind the rice paddy dikes but that was not enough to protect them from the little arrows. A few took shots at us, but the gunners took care of them by shooting at their muzzle flashes. We were looking down on them. They had nowhere to hide in those open paddies. The Flechettes pinned their arms to their bodies, their bodies to the man beside them. Back near the trees, they were pinned to the trees. It seemed more gruesome than being blown apart as you don't die as fast.

There were over a hundred NVA down on the ground. A few were squirming uncontrollably. I made another pass and fired only five pair (half of the ten Flechettes I had remaining) into about seventy-five willing to try running across those paddies. I got 'em all and told 9-6 to fire into the trees and jungle mix.

9-6 and I made two more passes, and it looked like their gallant charge had been futile. I told Baldy 6 to pull back, so we could get the arty in those trees. Then the question I hated to ask. "Do you need any wounded to be medevacked?"

He answered, "Yes, six wounded and four dead. The slicks are on their way; we called Baldy while you were doing your thing. If you could hang around, it would be great. They are sending out six ships with resupply of the big three (food, water and ammo)."

"Roger that, we have enough fuel and ammo to cover the slicks."

Rattler 2-4 said, "I've been monitoring your chatter with Baldy 6 and appreciate you staying for the party."

"Roger 2-4, 6 is pulling back so the arty can shoot. You will be a click farther away east from the area I just hit. All six of you can come in at once. Fly in west and then turn 180 degrees to exit."

Click-click.

I was flying over 6's location as the arty was again firing into the jungle. *Another tip for new guys. Never fly into an area that's being shelled by artillery.*

The slicks were on final approach. They flared and landed and received a few errant shots. I fired, and the shooting stopped.

This was pissing me off. I called Air Force Spotter One and asked if he had any fast movers with napalm. "Our guys are now far enough away that you can burn those bastards to hell."

Air Force Spotter One said, "I'll get right back to you."

I was monitoring the radios, and Rattler 2-4 had the wounded and 2-5 had the ugly job of hauling out American dead. I hoped they were in body bags, so the crew in that slick wouldn't see their faces. They were all looking like kids to me. *God, did I ever look that young and naïve? Hell yes, I did, but it seems so long ago.*

The arty was pumping the jungle full of white phosphorus. They were shooting in the jungle two clicks and further up the mountain.

The Air Force spotter called and said, "I have four fast movers inbound with napalm."

I was so surprised. I said, "FOUR, outstanding. NVA are coming down that burning steep mountain after we hit them with our gunships and arty. Maybe you could drop some on the other side of the peak. That's the only place they can come from so quickly."

"Roger that."

"We are flying east and will circle over the ground troops."

"We will make one pass and haul ass. We will come in from the south. The first two F-4s will put their Nape on each side of the peak and the second two will drop theirs below the peak on your side several hundred yards apart and beginning below the first drop. Fast movers are ten seconds out."

What a sight. Coming in at 500 knots with a large red shark mouth painted on the nose with twelve inch white teeth. It looked ferocious. It would scare the shit out of me if I saw those teeth diving down towards me.

The first two dropped their loads, and the second two were only five seconds out. They leveled out so the nape would run along the ground. They dropped their loads and pulled up sharply. As they pulled up, a 51 fired into the belly of the F-4 farthest down the hill.

The gun hammered the jet just before the nape incinerated the 51 and its shooter.

The jet called out, "Phantom 3-6 on fire and jettisoning."

I could see the flames. The canopy flew off and the pilot and navigator shot out of the jet in special seats with rockets mounted underneath (a Martin-Baker seat) to get them away from the aircraft. The seat separated and the parachutes deployed. They were falling north of the new arty base that had been shelling the napped area. They looked to be falling just short of the Song Vu Gia River, and I was sure there were NVA down there.

I called Rattler 2-4 and asked, "Can you send one of the empty slicks back so they can pick up the two Air Force pilots?"

He said, "Roger. Rattler 1-1 just volunteered."

"1-1, this is 9-7. Can you see me flying over the arty base north of the LZ?"

"I've got you in sight, and I'm four clicks east of you, and I see the parachutes."

"We've got to make this quick. There are some hooches along the river, and those pilots would be a big prize for some Vietcong. Fly in northwest at 345 degrees, and we will be ahead of you shooting."

"Shit, I see villagers running towards the pilot with pitch forks and bamboo clubs."

"9-6, we're off the grid," I said.

Click-click.

I don't like shooting over friendlies, but we had no choice. I could see the pilots trying to extricate themselves from the parachute harnesses. He heard my ship coming because he waved and then dove to the ground. I fired four rockets, and the crew continued to shoot. We stopped the farmers' advancement. Wing shot a pair, and then he was out of rockets, but the Gatling guns were deadly. As I was climbing out to cover my wingman, Tyler said, "Mac look straight right."

There must have been fifty NVA running out of the Jungle two clicks from the pilots. They were two clicks northwest of the new arty base. The NVA must have something planned for that arty base. I called the arty base and asked if they could see the NVA running towards the pilots. I broke right and dove towards those bastards as I called my wing and said break left and follow me for a quick shot and then get back to the incoming slick. "Vic, how many rounds do you have?"

"Fifty Mac."

"Shoot thirty."

Arty 6 said, "I've had my guys plotting the coordinates to fire. I just got the signal that they're ready."

I said, "Give 'em hell as soon as my wingman breaks away to his right. We got quite a few already."

Ski and Tyler looked back and said, "Mac, the arty just took care of the last few of those guys that we didn't kill."

I said, "Last few? You two will have to work on that."

"1-1, are you ready?"

"Yes, I'm coming in. The pilots are smart. They're running toward me so the parachutes don't blow into my blades. The villagers are shooting at me."

I saw the muzzle flashes before 1-1 called me. I shot my last pair of rockets and said, "Vic, eliminate the rest of the village." He put his last twenty at the few remaining hooches in the village. I broke right and let the wing's Gatling gun finish the mission.

1-1 called. "I have the pilots and am 180ing out of here. See ya at Baldy."

"9-6, ready to go home?"

"Yes, we have nothing left to give the enemy."

"Yeah, I'm out, too."

Air Force Spotter one called and said, "That was the most incredible rescue. God, I wish I had a camera. You guys have super balls."

"Well, thank you, Air Force. Glad to help. You've always been the ones to help us."

"Hell, I've heard you were humble, but I'm reporting this mission to the higher ups. If those pilot's wives ever hear this story, they may sleep with you."

I laughed and said, "Talk to you later. We've got to get these thirsty and ammo-less birds back to Baldy."

Vic flew to POL and then around the big hill to the Firebird revetments and the Hilton.

We just began rearming when Air Force Spotter One landed and taxied off the runway and over to the Firebirds and shut down his little bird.

He climbed out and said, "Who's 9-7?"

Each person from both our ships raised their hands and said, "I am."

He said, "I heard you Birds were an undisciplined bunch of smart asses."

"In that case, I am. Nice to meet you. I'm Kevin McNally, Firebird 9-7, and a lot of what you've heard is not true. We're just a bunch of crazy bastards because we're asked to do crazy things." I put out my hand.

"I'm Captain Steve Connelly." He put out his hand, and we shook. "I want to thank all of you for hanging your asses out to save some fellow pilots. Where are they?"

"The slick flew them straight to the MASH. It's right across the road." I pointed past the Hilton to a large structure, wood on the bottom half and then screen up to the roof with corrugated aluminum on the top.

He said, "Thanks" and headed in that direction.

We didn't follow him as we had to rearm the birds. You never know when that fucking red phone is going to sound off.

We had completed the rearming when Connelly walked back across the dirt road toward us with two men in dirty sweaty flight suits walking with him. We paused and stood still as we were pretty sure who they were, meaning this could get emotional.

They looked at us but didn't blink. They were probably thinking, you've got to be shittin' me. These derelicts, who probably smell as bad as they look, couldn't have been the ones to pull our asses out of that certain death or capture. One said, "I'm Major Anthony Berkshire and this is my RIO (radar intercept officer), Captain Jeff Pound. We owe you our lives."

Capt. Connelly said, "I've never seen anything so courageous in my life, and this is my second tour flying that little cub."

The two pilots added, "We will never be able to thank you or forget you. I talked to the slick crew on the way here, and now I meet you birds and I am totally blown away. They can't teach those heroics in flight school. I still can't get over how fast you set up that rescue. They played back the radio transmissions for me in the

MASH. You were battling on two fronts while orchestrating a rescue. I've heard rumors about you, but now I know they're true."

"Tony," I said, hoping this wouldn't last too much longer, "I had lots of help. We are an eight man team that all depend on each other. Just so you know, right after that asshole shot your ship, your nape incinerated him, so technically you won the duel.

"By the way, you two—I indicated the F-4 crew—are the first DIRTY Air Force pilots I've ever seen." They started laughing, and the rest of the group joined in.

They were still laughing as they walked to the cub.

We waved as they took off and that was the end of that. Just like everything in this fucking war. You see someone once, and one of you makes a big difference in the other's life, and you will never see each other again. You won't know if they made it home or were killed. Damn, it should be more than that.

Nothing else happened that night. We woke up and wondered if we'd missed a call, we were so used to being called out in the middle of the night. Nothing happened the next day either. I wondered if maybe the NVA were recalculating their tactics, since we'd kicked the shit out of them these last few days

After two days of sitting on our asses, another gunship crew flew up to relieve us, and we were happy to go to CL. I needed a shower, some booze, and a call to Steph. Maybe not in that order. God, everything had been so intense with so much death that I was afraid to be near Steph. Everyone else around me had died. Well, at least a lot of them had died.

The last two nights I hadn't been able to sleep. I kept waking up in a drenching sweat, and I could see the dead Birds faces before we took off. Fuck, why did they have to die? *And people here ask me why I'm not religious!*

We rat raced all the way to CL. It was good training for Langley, a fairly new Bird. All I could think of was Steph.

We landed and refueled. No need to rearm as we hadn't fired a round in the previous two days. I checked in with Major Mathews. He'd been my CO for the last two months, but I'd spoken only a few words to him.

He said, "Sit down Mac. How are you feeling?"

I said, "Fine sir, just dirty, thirsty and under slept."

"Then, I'll see you in the bar after evening mess."

I spent an hour in the shower trying to wash this country off my body. Clean clothes followed. I drank a cold beer while dressing. That was the best experience of my time here. Funny how the best refers to whatever good thing you're doing at the moment. Over here, you just never knew. Everything good was so precious you made sure you enjoyed it.

I went up to the CO's office. He wasn't there, so I asked Smitty if he could call someone for me.

He smiled and said, "Mac I saw you double timing up the steps. Here's the phone, and they are locating Steph."

I said, "Thanks," and took the phone.

He said, "I'll go sit on the porch and stand guard."

I said, "Shoot anyone trying to walk through that door."

He looked at me and said in his best military voice, "Yes sir." Then he walked out.

I hope he knew I was kidding. You just never know. Hell, he wasn't even armed.

I heard, "Kevin is that really you?"

"Yes beautiful. God I hate this war. It's definitely working against us."

"I flew out to the bases eight days in a row to keep my mind busy, so I wouldn't worry as much. I don't think it helped."

"I know exactly what you're saying. I have the next two days off, and I want to see you. I worry about you, too, flying around this country."

We talked of love, possible living locations, kids, future work and some more love, and how much we meant to each other. I hated to hang up the phone, but she had some things to do. She added that she couldn't wait to see me tomorrow because she wanted to tell me something, "but only face to face."

"Now I'm curious."

"Tomorrow," she promised.

I walked into the bar and the place went quiet. Someone raised a glass and said, "Here's to Norwood and his crew." I was handed a glass, so I raised it with everyone else and said, "Norwood and his crew," and chugged the Crown Royal. I'd been away from the booze too long; that drink burned all the way down.

In walked Glen Walton, Rattler 2-9. There was a rattler on each side of him making sure he got there. One on them said, "Glen, ring the bell for getting your ass shot down in Laos." Glen rang the bell, threw in $5.

Then, Glen turned to the crowd and said, "Mac, ring the bell, as you let me get shot down."

For a second I thought I might protest. But all I could hear was *RING THE BELL,* over and over, until I rang the damn thing. I threw in $5 and got a loud cheer. Glen and I smiled at each other, shook hands, and chugged some bourbon.

My fatigue was really kicking in, so I excused myself and went to bed.

Chapter 68.

STEPH

A t 0200 in the morning Smitty came in and woke me. "Mac, they need you up at the hospital in CL. Get dressed, and I'll drive you up there."

"What in the fuck is so important at two in the morning?"

"I don't know. They just said get you up there STAT."

I pulled on my shirt and pants and stuck my feet in my boots. "OK, let's go, Smitty. I'll tie them in the jeep."

It was cool that night. With a breeze off the South China Sea, it didn't smell too bad. That was a nice change.

We pulled in front of the hospital and stopped. Dr. Weldon, the doctor I'd taken to the Target Practice Island, was standing in front of the doors.

"Doc Weldon, how are you?"

"Fine Mac. Follow me."

He turned and walked quickly into the Hospital, took several turns, and stopped in a large four corner intersection. I stopped and wondered what the hell was going on.

Out walked Donna, the Dollies' boss. She stopped in front of me and put her hands on my shoulders. "Kevin, I'm so sorry. Steph is dead."

I looked around and saw General Wheaton with red eyes; Captain MacAddo; Major Mathews, my CO; Jerry Wilder, my platoon leader; Glen Walton, the Rattler I saved twice; Vic, my copilot; and another doctor, who I found out later was a psychiatrist.

I was shaking my head and the hallway was slowly starting to move. I looked at Donna and said, "Wha, wha, what did you say? No way, no fucking way Donna."

"Steph is dead. She was in an empty ward doing paperwork. She had spent the evening here cheering up some Vietnamese kids who were burnt from napalm. A rocket hit the ward, and she was killed instantly. She didn't suffer." Then Donna was crying.

My body began shaking. I discovered I was sobbing, tears running down my cheeks. I said, "How do you know she didn't suffer?"

"The rocket destroyed everything in the ward. Everything was blown into small pieces. Please don't ask me for any more information." Donna was crying so hard I had difficulty understanding her.

I turned to look at everyone behind me, and without exception all had tears running down their cheeks. Now, the hallways were spinning faster, and I felt unsteady. I felt Donna grab my upper arm and guide me to a chair. I collapsed into that chair. I didn't know what to ask. This is a nightmare. It couldn't be true. She was my entire future. I dropped my head into my hands.

The support crew was silent, and Donna waved them away. They turned and walked so slow that it didn't look real.

I just looked at Donna, and she said, "There's one more thing."

I didn't know what to say or do.

"Mac, there is only one other person who knows what I'm about to tell you. He is an MD sworn to secrecy. Steph was excited because she was pregnant. She knew you would be excited too. She said she didn't use any protection because she knew nothing would happen in this hell hole. She was so in love with you she never considered the consequences. She said it was stupid because she should have known better. She wanted to tell you face to face because she wanted to see your face light up."

"She was correct," I said. "My face would have shinned like a search light. There was nothing in the world more important to me than spending my life with her," and with that I broke down and cried like a baby." *Why, Why, Why, did this happen to someone who had so much to give the world?*

"Donna, can I see her?"

She immediately said, "No Kevin. Remember her as you last saw her. Please, don't pursue this. It was a mess in that ward."

I just couldn't take all of this in. Dead, pregnant, and now I couldn't even see her. *Fuck this whole goddamned world. I have nothing to live for now. What the hell am I going to do?*

"Kevin, you can stay here tonight. I'll be in the bed next to you. I will be there when the nightmares come."

"OK," I said, "thank you. I know you two were the greatest of friends. She loved you. I'm so thankful you told me about the pregnancy. I would have never have known."

Donna guided me down the hall and into an empty ward. She helped me with my boots and said, "Lie down and try to sleep."

With that said, the psychiatrist walked into the room with a pill and a glass of water.

I took both and laid back and cried myself to sleep as I thought; *the truth is not always what you believe and I can't believe this has happened.*

Chapter 69.

DOMINOS

I woke that morning feeling as if I'd never gone to sleep.

I lay in bed trying to absorb what I had been told that night. All those ranking officers standing there, it had to be true. She can't be gone. This makes no sense. A pure person with nothing but love in her heart and compassion for all. She was the best in all her classes: high school, college and law school. She had a brilliant future.

I sat up and hung my legs over the side of the bed and saw Donna sleeping in the next bed. She opened her eyes and sat up. She hadn't gotten undressed either.

Donna told me, "You woke five or six times in the night, sitting up, calling for Stephanie. Whenever that happened, I helped settle you back to sleep." She gave me a sad little smile. "It made me cry every time Mac."

I looked at Donna in disbelief. I felt my lips quivering, but I couldn't talk. Finally, I found some words. "How can she be gone? She was pregnant?"

Donna nodded *yes*. "She never even thought about birth control. She was so in love."

"I would definitely have said, 'Incredible, I'm so happy'. I feel sick. Donna you're not safe anywhere in the hell hole. You can be mortared in bed, blown out of the air, or hit with a rocket while sitting in a hospital."

Donna offered to stay with me, but I needed to walk. Alone.

Fuck, what am I supposed to do for the rest of my time here? I think I'll stay and just keep killing these bastards. That might help me feel a little better. I'm going to get some payback.

I was driven over to the GB's HQ. I went into General Wheaton's waiting room and asked Top if I could see the general without an appointment.

He said, "I'll tell the general you're here. He's expecting you." He knocked and entered the office. He immediately came out and said, "Go in Mac."

I walked in. He had very red eyes and looking tired. "Sit down Mac. I just got off the phone with Steph's mom and dad. I was crying with them. It sounded like her mom was going to have a breakdown. I talked to Donna this morning, and she said you didn't have a very good night either. For the first time in my career, I hate the military. That rocket should have hit my sleeping quarters."

We just looked at each other. I couldn't think of anything to say.

"What do you want to do, Mac?"

"Sir, I have two months remaining. I'm going to extend and kill a few for Steph."

"You think about that for at least two weeks before you approach Major Mathews. Don't make any decisions while you're so upset."

"Yes sir."

"Steph's parents asked about you, and I told them it ripped your heart right out of your chest. I told them you are a tough man and will pull yourself together. They told me they were looking at pictures of you two when I called. They saw the admiration in your eyes when you looked at each other. They said looks like that can only be the truest love.

"Steph told me a few weeks ago when you two were out of touch that she would steal a Huey and fly and shoot her way into Laos to find you, if I didn't personally get you back. I told her I'd get right on it, but I knew you wouldn't return until you finished your job."

I hung my head and for the first time since meeting the general I didn't look him in the eyes. When I looked at him, I saw Steph.

"Sir, can I go back to the 71st and drink myself into oblivion?"

"Yes, you can Mac, but please call if your mind won't let you move on enough to do your job. I don't want you to be a danger to yourself or your crew."

"Yes sir and thank you. I've just suffered the greatest loss ever and yours is probably worse. She loved and admired you so much."

"My driver will take you as soon as you and I gather items from Steph's trailer. Let's go see what you and I want and what we'll send her parents."

I followed him to her trailer, and he unlocked the door. We walked in and tears began running down our cheeks. The air smelled like her. There were many new pictures on the wall of us just being ourselves and laughing.

The general said, "You are the first person to bring that side of her to the surface. I'm so glad that she was able to have fun and fall in love. I often think of these young kids that die over here who have never experienced any of those emotions."

I took only two pictures: one of her and one of the two of us together. Any more than that would have been too much.

The general also took a few pictures of her and us. "I'll have my staff inventory and pack everything for shipment home. These last two days have been the worst of my life. I want to throw something and break it. God dammit, I'm pissed."

There was a knock on Steph's door, and I was surprised when I opened it to see a Chaplin. He looked at the name tag on my uniform and said, "Mr. McNally, I've come to speak with you about Miss Rheem."

General Wheaton said, "I'll wait outside Mac."

"Please stay sir. This won't take long. Chaplain or Captain (the rank on his uniform), please leave. I don't want to talk to you and listen to your fantasies about a god and that there is a divine plan for all of us. This is a fucking war which means life can have little value, and it's a crap shoot whether you live or die. By the way, whose side is god on in this dirty little war? Yeah right, I didn't think you would have a snappy answer to that question. Please leave before I become disrespectful of your rank and comment on the lies you probably tell these kids. The general and I have some very sad work to finish here."

He turned and walked away without a word.

When the general and I finished our work, we shook hands. He said, "My driver will be waiting for you at the front door."

It wasn't military, but I just nodded. I hadn't had time to bring anything with me the previous night, so I walked into the ward to thank Donna. I found her as she was gathering the few things she had brought with her to watch over me. I gave her a hug and said, "Thank you for helping me last night." She was crying when I walked out.

The short drive to CL was silent. The driver stopped in front of the COs office.

Major Mathews walked out and said, "Come on in, Mac." He stood by the door and waited for me to walk up the two steps. I stopped and saluted. He returned it and turned and walked to his office. I followed.

"Sit down, Mac. I've talked with the guys who went with me to the hospital last night, and we couldn't think of anything consoling to say. I'm giving you today and tomorrow off. I know that's your limit for time off. Then, you go to Baldy for at least five to six days. Wilder will fly with you. Ski and Tyler too, of course.

"Do you think Wilder is ready for Fire Team Lead?"

"Absolutely sir."

"Take him with you for a few days. We need him to replace Big Randy who is getting his DEROS orders. Call me when you pass him, and I'll send you a copilot, and bring Captain Wilder back here to replace Randy. OK Mac, I'll probably run into you in the club tonight. Dismissed."

I walked to the Birdhouse and straight to a cold beer. Hell, it was 1000 (10 am), but I didn't give a shit. I slept for three hours. Then, a shower and back to my bed and letter writing. I received a sharp letter from my parents asking me why I hadn't told them I'd been wounded, twice.

Shit, the army was not supposed to do that. When I first arrived here, they had us fill out a form to NOT notify loved ones unless you were dead or coming home seriously wounded."

I walked to the COs office and asked Top how I can stop these notifications of wounds? They even sent two missions to the local newspaper."

Top looked at me and said, "The army works in mysterious ways, sir."

I said, "Top, my name is Mac," and I extended my hand. Top returned the shake and said, "I know all about you from your copilot, Top. He told me flying and shooting rockets was better than sex. My name is First SGT Frushella."

"Top, I would argue that part about sex."

"Yeah me too. I told him he'd been here too long, and I might have to call his wife. Look, Mac, I'll send another note to Brigade to stop the press releases."

"Thank you, Top."

After I left, I had to decide if I should write the letter and try to talk my way out of trouble with Mom and Dad or go to the club and kill my liver. The death wish won. I had to stop thinking about Steph. I'd faked it here in the company area so far today. I couldn't keep it up without alcohol.

I walked in and looked in the bowl and saw a lot of money, so I ordered two crowns and chugged them. I got a cold beer and walked out through the back of the club as there was no wall. I stopped at the water's edge, sipped the beer as I looked out over the South China Sea and wondered if this country was really worth saving.

The domino theory was probably shit anyway. Let the VC and the Commies have the country. *Let's see what they can do with it. Why do we care?*

There was only one Steph who had walked this world, and I was extremely lucky to have met her. I looked out over the water. I was feeling heartache, but I wasn't feeling sorry for myself. I was feeling sorry for her, for everybody who knew her.

Chapter 70.

TO BE CONTINUED

"I'll warn you now VC," I told the South China Sea, "don't try to harvest any rice in an area we've declared off limits."

I guess I'll never get the word out to those assholes, but we've been here since 65, so they should know by now.

I went back into the club for a beer. I was trying hard to get Steph out of my mind. I knew I'd never be able to accomplish that in my lifetime, but I wanted to be able to do my job here without fucking up.

I'm sorry Steph, but this is war, and I have to protect Americans. I love you and will always love you. I will somehow get through life, though it won't be easy. You leaving this earth is proof there is no omniscient being watching over us with a plan. What a crock.

I tried to avoid being social. Everyone knew. They'd all heard of Steph's heroics, her notoriety on the FSBs, her serving as my defense attorney, and our love. I wanted to be alone, so I walked back to the water's edge.

Jerry Wilder came up beside me and said, "Hey Mac, I hear you and I are doing a check ride."

"Yeah Jerry, day after tomorrow. How do you feel?"

"I feel ready. I've flown with you and behind you as pilot and wing copilot. I've learned from the best."

"I need another beer."

"Yeah me, too, Mac."

We grabbed our beers and walked out to the ocean and resumed drinking.

"How about you Mac. Are you ready?"

"Don't worry. I'll be ready to fly. I may be a little angry, but I won't take it out on you. You're a great pilot and will become even greater."

"Thanks, Mac. That's quite a complement coming from you."

I looked at him and smiled. "Jerry, I'm going to chug two crowns and then try to sleep. You did a great job on my wing out here on the beach. Good night."

"Good night, Mac."

The alcohol didn't help much. I fell asleep immediately but woke up forty-five minutes later in a dripping sweat. I saw Steph's face. She was just staring at me, just like Jim after he was killed. How do you control your mind? *I can't take this shit into battle.*

The rest of the night was more of the same. I remember seeing the first moments of dawn but woke up later at 1100.

Now, I have to kill this afternoon and evening before I get in the air. I'll write mom and dad another letter and see if I can bullshit my way out of trouble and put them at ease. I know they'll be really pissed when I tell them I'm going to extend for six months.

I minimized my wounds by telling them, "I'm flying and walking and throwing a football on the beach." *Hell that might even work.*

I worked up the courage to try lunch. It was some kind of mystery meat. It looked like baloney, so we had affectionately nicknamed it a horse cock sandwich. I ate two but with all the accoutrements: ketchup, salt, pepper and a new one, mustard. *Where the hell is that mayonnaise that we used for carrier qualifications?*

It was difficult to waste time in a war zone, especially in I Corp, the northern most quarter of south VN. Everything was off limits. I'd been there ten months and had never been in a town, village, or the PX (army general store) in Danang. Our slick pilots would fly up there and land inside the concertina wire and load up with booze, snacks, tape recorders, clothes, paperbacks, and whatever else would fit inside their ships.

My time waster was paperback books. Harold Robbins could really write a fast-moving action packed nasty novel. *Thanks, Harold. No shit. I mean it.*

I finally returned to Baldy.

The red phone interrupted my reverie. There was a big CA planned at 1500 two clicks west and two clicks south of Cacti. Pathfinders had reported a large force of NVA in the area.

I looked at the map, and it seemed like a great place to suck us into an ambush. There were three valleys, like three fingers of a hand. The three valleys narrowed quickly with very steep sides, but the middle finger had an opening at its far end and broke out into lowlands and rice paddies. That's where the LZ should be located. Some REMF is having us going in the front door. There are mountains on both sides. This mission is going to be FUBAR.

9-9 Clearwater was my wingman, and his copilot was Vic. I had promoted Vic to wing ship copilot. He was good, and I hated to lose him, but that was how it worked. I would find another guy who didn't want to fly slicks. (*Another tip for my manual.*) Jerry Wilder would be my copilot. I guess, officially I was checking him out so the CO could make him a Fire Team Lead.

1430 arrived along with 22 slicks. Twenty-one for troops and one extra. They loaded quickly. The LZ was only seven clicks from Baldy (4.2 miles).

The guns would TO first to soften the area. *Double S, Double D; same shit, different day.* The slicks would be close behind so we could circle back and escort them into the LZ. The entrance to the three valleys looked very ominous. I didn't have a good feeling about this. The mission was planned too quickly. Cacti couldn't cover the troops because they would have to shoot the arty over mountains and drop the shells into the canyons or their steep sides. In other words, they'd be shooting blind.

"OK Birds, everything out here is enemy until our troops land. There are hills on both sides of the LZ, so let's shoot before we get there, so we have room to break right or left. We'll see from where they shoot at us."

That was all the orientation I had time to give. We were there in minutes.

"9-7 rolling in." I punched rockets to both sides of the LZ and was shot at by some small arms (AK-47). Wing received the same treatment. "9-9, let's go find those slicks. Rattler 2-7 we're ready but be loose. We received a few small arms rounds. They could be holding back the big stuff." I received click-click.

The LZ was large enough for all 21 ships in groups of three to land at once. As the ships were descending, all hell broke loose. There was a 51 on both sides of the valley.

"All ships break right and stay low and get the hell out of here." I put my rocket selector on 3 and punched once on the right side and once on the left, six rockets on each. Both stopped shooting. The small arms were hellacious. There must have been 100 NVA on those hills with lots of jungle around them. "Everyone form up in your threes."

Shit, if they had waited 20 seconds longer, it would have been a slaughter, even with the guns.

"I have a new plan," I told everybody. "I just called Cacti and asked them to arc their shells over the small mountains to the entire area around the LZ. We'll fly six clicks north and west to the north end of the large valley and land there. Hopefully the NVA will think the area is being prepped for us to try again. There is a large flat spot at the other side and the end of this valley with lots of cover on both sides. We might be able to call some fast movers if anyone is waiting. So, we're going to fly around and land at the other end of these mountains. How does that sound?"

"I'm looking at my map," 2-7 said, "and I think it's a great plan. We'll follow you. We have a few hits, but no warning lights or wounded."

"Alright 2-7, circle your flight," I told them, "and we'll soften it up. The Airforce spotter bird just called, and I asked him to come in on the same path we just did and hit both sides of that valley. There's room for them to drop the nape and pull straight up.

"Firebirds, let's do this. 9-7 rolling in." I shot six rockets on the left and six on the right as I was turning to get out of the valley. No one shot at me. That felt good. I turned and shot under 9-9, and he flew out without taking a round. I called 2-7 and said, Let's go." He clicked twice and turned the formation of twenty-one to fly two clicks north, then turn and land in the dry paddies at the other end of the valley. There was some anxiety. I could hear it in their voices. "2-7, I'm just taking swag." I received click-click.

My copilot, Wilder asked, "What's s swag, Mac?"

"Jerry that's a 'scientific wild ass guess.' By saying 'scientific,' it adds credibility."

He was laughing. "Mac, I completely understand, and I haven't even graduated from college."

"OK fellas, let's go." I started punching rockets as usual. I was looking for any movement or muzzle flash. Here they came, fortunately all small arms. We pretty much ended those guys' military careers.

The slicks landed, the troops jumped out, and all was good so far. Then a 51 was shooting from a click away (.6 of a mile) so not very accurate. I turned and arced in four rockets at those assholes. Two hit almost right on them. I thought, *Shit I should do this more often. It's safer.* They stopped shooting.

Then, things started heating up. The NVA had carried their 51s a click away and now a second one was shooing at our guys in this new LZ. They were still too far away to be accurate, mostly because of the terrain, so I put four more rockets on them. Now, I had four rockets remaining and so did wing.

Cacti's arty was now hitting the first LZ and one click north. I asked if they could add half a click. They said, "Here they come." They were right on target and I said, "Don't go any farther north."

One of our slicks called, "Engine failure, going down at the most northern end of the LZ."

"Can anyone pick him up?" I said.

2-7 said, "I'll get them. Since I was first in, I'll be last out. Then they'll owe me a beer."

I loved the humor and casualness of all this. Each of these men was doing his job as a true professional and risking his life, and the story of this casual professionalism and courage would never get on the nightly news. Even a stupid war has moments to celebrate, events that make us proud.

"2-7, 9-7 is coming in to meet you." I saw him flaring to land to pick up the downed crew when he began to receive heavy small arms fire. I put my rocket selector on single and fired twice on muzzle flashes on the right and the same on the left.

The downed crew jumped into the rescue ship, and they were out of there. The downed ship was smoking quite a lot now, and it was only a matter of time before it started burning.

Baldy called and said they wanted to send another fifteen ships into the same valley to reinforce the troops already there. I told them that if they could get some guys to help us rearm, it would go much quicker. They rogered.

I told Jerry to land at the revetments, so we could save time by not flying to POL. The trucks could fuel us while we were rearming. It went quick. Fifteen Hueys were in a line on the side of the runway. Here came the trucks. Another 120 kids going to war. These kids were loaded down with the most weaponry I'd seen to date. Mortars, M-60s with thousands of rounds, and bazookas.

A jeep drove up and screeched to a halt. A colonel jumped out and said "Who's 9-7?"

"I am sir," standing there with no cap on my head and my shirt off. *Not army regulation dress.*

"That was quick thinking changing the LZ," he told me. "You saved a lot of lives. I just got off the phone with your CO, and he said you've been doing a lot of mission changes with 100% success in the last ten months. He suggested I call General Wheaten at GB HQ for more details. I gave the general a call, and he said to call him tomorrow at 0900 and to mark out at least an hour on my schedule. I can hardly wait, Mac, if I can call you that. You're known by that name in the entire AO clear up north to the DMZ." I nodded my assent. "OK Mac, the slicks' blades are ready to turn. Get out there and keep protecting my men."

"Yes sir," then I turned and yelled at the Birds, "Light the fire (get those turbine engines to start turning the blades), and everyone was moving. I grabbed my shirt and jumped in, strapped on, and called 9-9. "Ready? It's about ten clicks so we should be there in a few minutes. 2-7, how are you doing?"

"I hope I have tomorrow off," 2-7 said. "It's going to take a few tonight in the bar for me to close my eyes."

I just click clicked.

"OK Birds, let's soften up this piece of earth. We have time for one gun run before the slicks arrive."

I contacted Baldy 6 on the ground, and he said, "We've moved almost a click into the valley and have received only a few sporadic rounds. We have scouts out 500 yards on both our flanks. They found signs of troops and shell casings, and it looks like the enemy is moving towards the original LZ."

I rogered and then told him, "I'm going to call Cacti and stop their firing until the NVA reach the area near our original LZ. Then Cacti can pound the shit outa' 'em." I then called the Airforce spotter and asked him to call off the Napalm because the NVA were running towards the area I had just asked him to nape. "If we wait awhile, we can nape them all. I'll call 6 on the ground and tell him to stop moving and hold that position." Then I told him about the plan.

"9-7, I can have them circle for thirty minutes."

"That's perfect," I said. "This day just may turn out OK. Airforce spotter, I'm going back and escort in another fifteen slicks. 2-7, where are you?"

"I'm near the valley entrance. I see you now 9-7."

"I'm going to shoot on each side of the valley as I'm flying towards you. I'll stop when you turn into the valley, and then I'll turn and escort you in. Tell your LT that his troops are about a click into the valley and have the NVA on the run back towards the original LZ. Then we'll have them boxed in for a turkey shoot."

I was shooting as I was talking. I'd never shot toward the slicks, so I had to be careful.

9-9 and I covered the slicks by firing a few random rockets around them to discourage any enemy left behind from shooting.

"9-7. this is Baldy 6. The NVA are approaching the LZ area. Call in the nape. Just remind them we're only a click NW and are pulling back to put a mountain ridge between us and the nape."

The spotter called and said his jets would come east to west and burn what was remaining of the jungle on the north, south and west end of that LZ. "OPHA; One pass, haul ass."

I called out for all Baldy troops to get down and behind something if possible. "Here come the jets." *Nape is devastating.*

The jets swooped and dropped that jellified material on the NVA. That liquid hell would run across the ground at 500 miles per hour and turn everything to an ash.

"Cacti start shooting toward that LZ again. Extend a few of your shots a half click south to hit the other side of the LZ in case the NVA had some scouts out ahead of the main force."

It looked like the world was exploding when the arty rounds landed.

Baldy 6 called me and said, "The second insertion has caught up with me. We're ready to move ahead when the arty stops."

I called Cacti and said, "Cease fire. The troops are ready to move in and search for survivors."

I couldn't believe it when Baldy 6 said. "We've found five survivors. They're in a bad way, mostly burns. We called for two slicks for medivacs. Do you Birds have enough fuel to hang around for five more minutes?"

Damned if it wasn't 2-7 and a second ship. "Hey 2-7, who'd you piss off?"

"I don't know, but I've been getting shot at for the past three hours. I wanna go home."

We escorted the ships in and out without receiving a round. All ships from the second insertion returned to Baldy with the Birds. Several slicks landed at the MASH unit. The Birds landed and immediately got ready for the next mission.

We slept through the night. Wow! The advantages of being dead tired. The relief team flew up the next morning, and we were very happy to return to CL.

When it was time to get back to Baldy, I still had to officially pass Jerry Wilder so he could be FTL. I set that up for the following morning when we'd be flying back.

0730 and here came the Birds, laughing and talking until they saw me and all went silent. I called out, "Good morning, Birds. Ready to go hunting?" Loud enough to let them know this wasn't a funeral.

"Hell yes," came from a number of voices.

"For any of you who don't know, Captain Wilder is in charge. He'll be ready for Fire Team Lead after this check ride."

More loud cheers and congratulations.

"In the air guys, I'm Jerry or Wilder. I'm only a Captain when other officers are present."

The EMs said, "OK Jerry. You ready to rock and roll?"

"Fuckin' A man."

This should go well. I took Jerry aside and said, "How do you feel about some more rat racing for Vic?"

"I remember when you had me do that for the first time. I was a little nervous, but ever since it's been a turn on."

"Explain it to Vic. He's only done it in the lead ship. As you know, the wing flies differently than lead."

"Roger that Mac."

Wilder said, "Rock and roll," and we took off.

I was determined to be just a passenger. "Captain Wilder, you tell me what you want me to do." He nodded and turned inland where there were some trees to give him places to make sharp turns and momentarily be out of Vic's view.

"OK," Wilder said, "Go hot." I pushed in the circuit breakers, and then he said, "Test your guns."

We started the rat race when I suddenly said, "I've got it Jerry," and I took the controls. I called 9-9 and said, "There are workers in two paddies on the other side of the last trees, and no one's supposed to be out here. We're going off the grid a little. We'll shoot them before we report them. They might run and hide before we get clearance. I'm sorry, Jerry. I shouldn't have taken your controls."

He said, "No problem. Old habits are hard to change."

"Do you want to take the shots?" I asked him. Then to 9-9: "Follow us in and shoot if you want to. They could be women."

Jerry put down his rocket sight and said, "I've got it Mac."

So I pulled down the cannon sight as we rolled in on the workers. Two immediately pulled out AK-47s from their big baggy black pants, but Jerry punched his rockets first. Both gunners in back had picked some targets as did I. Jerry punched a pair into the other paddy as they also had weapons. He called, "Breaking right" and in came 9-9 firing rockets, Gatling guns and door gunners. Jerry was looking outside to take in all the information: muzzle flashes, people, and weapons.

We rolled in one more time and picked off the stragglers. There were twenty bodies down there and a lot of red in the paddies. They only got off a few shots as we had surprise on our side. They must have thought we didn't see 'em.

As wing broke, Jerry said, "The rat race is on." Jerry broke left around some trees. The wing ship should have broken right so he would have position and distance to shoot at anyone taking a shot at lead. Well, Jerry fooled wing and turned back right after he was behind the trees. It was a hard sharp bank as he practically laid the ship on its side and came out from behind the tree behind 9-9's copilot. Wing should have climbed up to see beyond the trees. His mistake cost him seven beers, eight if he included himself.

I looked over at Jerry and said, "Where'd you come up with that?"

He said it was a story he'd heard about me sneaking up behind some 51s by flying behind hills, then sticking my nose up, shooting, and then dropping back behind the hill. "The NVA swung their guns around to anticipate where you'd come up again," Jerry said, "as determined by the direction your nose was pointing when you dove behind the hill. Instead, you turned 270 degrees and came back up in the same spot and caught them off guard and blew the shit out of that 51. In fact, it worked on both of those 51s. My move was a take from your flying."

"Wow, we can stop the flight check right now. You put what you learned to good use. Let's go to Baldy and see what the NVA have lined up for you."

We landed at Baldy, and the Birds who had been waiting for our arrival were walking out to their ships for the flight to CL as soon as we hovered onto the turnaround and the Hilton. They waved good-bye and were gone. We hovered into the revetments and called for fuel. Then, it was the perpetual rearming, though not much this time.

About two hours later, the red phone rang, and it was off to war. I ran out to the ship and let Jerry tend to the phone. I hadn't run out to a ship in nine months. I got it going when Jerry came with the info. I set the frequencies and pulled out my map as Jerry said, "Rock and roll."

We were headed south of Hawk Hill. The bases there were re-ceiving a heavy mortar barrage from two areas in the jungle about one click from both bases.

Jerry flew south for just a few minutes and made contact. He said he would come in from the east and shoot at both areas and then break right over the bases, followed by the wingman. Jerry asked if they had any arty that could burn the jungle, and they said they had Willy Pete's and could load them now. Jerry said, "Wait until both gunships shoot and break out of the area on our last run. "I'll tell when it's safe to fire."

Hill 29 was running the show, and he said, "Roger. We didn't shoot much before you got here because we weren't sure of their exact location."

We rolled in and fired at both areas and drew some enemy fire for our efforts, and this gave away their locations.

Jerry said, "Shoot around my rockets."

We put a lot of firepower on those muzzle flashes, and the 5000 degrees of burning white phosphorus was soon to follow.

Jerry said, "Hold your fire, and we'll come in again and look for personnel now that the jungle has been blasted open."

We all shot in and around our last run. There was a breeze, so most of the smoke from our rockets was blown away from the explosions. We could see some NVA running south to escape. Both ships fired at them, and as we broke, we called for Hill 29 to open fire south of our last explosions. They were shooting when Jerry said, "Shoot some long ones ahead of them, and they'll be trapped."

This worked. We stopped the arty and rolled in again; it was total chaos. The few remaining NVA that were outside of the WP now were running out in the open between the two Hills, about a click apart, to escape the fires we had caused, and now the Willy Pete's had come their way. As we departed, Jerry said, "Be ready. They may come back after dark. Maybe to save face as that's important in their culture."

We made it back in time for lunch. After the usual rearm and refuel, we went to the mess hall. The food at Baldy was usually better than at CL.

Then we did the usual re-check with the ships followed by a nap. We slept till 1800 and then dinner.

As we were finishing dinner, a runner came into the mess hall and said the red phone is blasting off the hook. It was just beginning sundown. The NVA were attacking early tonight.

They were making a ground assault on both Hills 29 and 35. This time, they were coming in from the north. The flare ship threw out flares behind the advancing troops. The arty on both hills tilted their barrels down and fired beehive rounds at the bonsai charge. We flew in from the east and caught them in the open.

As we were shooting, a machine gun opened up on us and put several through our windshields and a few more in the chin bubble and into our electrical area: the battery, radios and the wiring to our circuit breakers. We were close, so I fired ten cannon shells at that gun, and it kept shooting as we broke. It had to be in a bunker and shooting through a small six inch tall by three feet long opening. As we broke, 9-9 put a pair of rockets on top of the gun, and it stopped shooting. I keyed the mic and said, "Thank you for that shot."

Click-click.

Hill 29 called. "We are shooting more beehives. Keep those flares coming, guys. We're low on flares down here."

"OK, stop the arty and we'll shoot them off the wire on this pass." Actually, none of them made it to the wire. If they got to the wire, they could blow holes in it with Bangalore torpedoes and then continue their charge onto the FSB. We used all weapons except rockets. The door gunners had a field day. 9-9 said he took a few rounds and had an electrical yellow warning light flashing. Then Wilder shot ten Flechettes into their Bonsai charge. It made an ugly scene.

Jerry told the flare ship, "Throw out four at once, so we can look for survivors and end their military careers." We found a few. It was a mess down there. We called Hill 29 and asked if they needed Dust off. They said the few scratches they had could be handled by their medic. "Thank you Birds and good night. I hope you don't have to come back tonight."

Jerry said, "Do call if you need us. We're light sleepers and wake up many times a night with our nasty dreams. You know, just a bunch of young perverts."

"Roger that Birds. You two are an impressive team. We love working with you."

As we flew back to Baldy I said, "Now for the critique on this mission."

Jerry looked over in surprise. I smiled. "It was perfect, Jerry. It was so good that I'm going to say, 'Excellent job Captain Wilder. I'll fly anywhere with you.'" His smile was so big I thought he was going to cry, so I looked away. I also had depressed my transmitting switch so the wing and flare ship would hear my critique, and Jerry would look good, and he would have the respect he deserved. Word travels fast in the military.

We landed at Baldy. After all the work on the ships was completed, I suggested, "Jerry, call CL and ask Snake Doctor to bring windshields and some electrical parts that Ski and Walsh (wing crew chief) need. They'll give you a list in a few minutes."

After all was completed, everyone went to sleep but me. I could see Steph's face, and I was wide awake, still had the adrenalin pumping. *I have to get a grip on this. At least, I'm not thinking of her during a mission. I just can't accept she's gone.* More tears.

I walked out past the ships, stood next to the runway, and looked up. You don't see this many stars back in the world unless you are miles from civilization, away from the ambient light.

Suddenly, I was startled as Wilder walked up beside me. "Thinking of her?"

I nodded, and we just stood there for five minutes, then Jerry said, "As your platoon leader, I order you to go to bed."

We both thought that was funny, and then I said, "Yes sir," and that had us both laughing.

We walked back to the filthy, gross, bug-infested Hilton and went to bed. I eventually fell asleep. I woke up a few times with the same visions.

We slept through till 0600, when the phone rang and the ballet began. Turns out the call was from Major Mathews, asking about me. Jerry stuck his head out the door and yelled, "False alarm."

After breakfast, as we walked back to the Hilton, Jerry told me he'd told the major I was doing well in combat but still having a little trouble with sleep. The major had mentioned the radio transmission of my critique. Jerry grinned. "Thank you for that."

We heard a Huey approaching, so I didn't answer. Yes, it was Snake Doctor. He hovered over near our ships and sat it down. The big surprise was his copilot, Major Mathews, and the new Bird, Gary Vandercamp.

I said, "Sir, what are you doing out in this dangerous country? People out here don't like us."

He said, "I was giving Snake Doctor Martin here a check ride."

Jerry said, "He was probably checking on me to make sure I wasn't lying about you."

"No way, Jerry," I said. "You and I both know that Major Mathews, your CO, is your backup. If he knows you are always straight, he will back you and cover your six."

Major Mathews said, "I just wanted to get out of the office and check on my crews. I haven't flown in so long I needed help starting Snake Doctor."

We all laughed, and Martin shook his head and said, "The major started the ship because I refused to help." We laughed again as we all knew no one says no to the commanding officer.

Martin and his crew went to work on the ships. Snake Doctor always calls Baldy when they come to make repairs. This is so they can call another gun team if the NVA starts trouble.

"Jerry, I hear you were phenomenal on your check ride."

"Yes sir, I did well, but Mac held me back. Once we left Baldy, he took the controls and unplugged my helmet. I just didn't know what to do, sir."

"You fucking Firebirds never quit," the major said. "I think I just ruined a potentially great officer by asking him to be a platoon leader of a bunch of... I can't really say what you Birds are. But I'm impressed. I think Jerry is the right man to work with you maniacs."

With all that said we all ran out in front of Jerry and bowed. Now the CO really laughed. "This is the most discipline I've ever seen from the Birds."

I said, "Oh mighty one, what is your next command?"

Wilder said, "Someone go brush the Dust off my seat that Snake Doctor blew in there."

I stood and said, "May we be dismissed, sir?"

The Major looked confused and said, "Yes, Mac."

I turned towards the Hilton and said, "Let's go read some nasty novels."

As we walked away, I heard the Major laugh and say, "Well, so much for command authority." Jerry said, "You see what I have to deal with." They were both laughing.

As we walked in the Hilton, the red phone blared. Everyone ran to the ships but me. I yelled to Martin, "Are the ships ready?"

He said, "No."

I yelled out again. "One of you sirs is wanted on the phone."

They took off on a trot, and the Major grabbed the phone out of my hand.

The speaker said, "Sir, this is Smitty. One of our slicks went down South of LZ Ross and that's the last I heard. They called a mayday." The major ran to Martin and relayed the news.

Martin said, "Shit sir," and looked at the ships. "Still need repairs but probably good enough for a short mission."

I asked Martin if he would go with us as the rescue ship.

He gave me his famous big grin and said, "Gladly. I get bored patching up ships from you fucking gun pilots."

I looked at the Major and said, "How would you and Martin like a little action and be able to grade Jerry at the same time as he covers you?"

He gave a big "Yes," without hesitation.

Jerry gave everyone the information.

I looked at Jerry and said, "It's your mission." I looked at Vandercamp and said, "You're not being slighted. Captain Wilder is taking another check ride. When we return, you're my new copilot."

He nodded, and then we started towards the ships. The crew had already started getting them ready.

I said, "Martin, do you have machine guns?"

He looked at me and said, "Are frog's assholes waterproof?"

I was laughing and said, "I would suppose so."

I climbed into the lead ship, set frequencies, and found the coordinates. We'd go 14 clicks to Ross, then turn south and start searching.

The guns were ready, and Snake Doctor 6 said he was, too.

When we got close, I spotted some NVA running north, and they were in a hurry. I just hoped the slick crew had a smoke grenade. I spotted a red smoke and said, "Jerry, I have a red smoke fifty yards ahead of the NVA troops." I transmitted that message so everyone was on board.

Jerry was turning the ship slightly away from the NVA, so he wouldn't have to shoot over our guys. Then he said, "Rolling in," and he began punching rockets. I was shooting close to the slick crew and walking my cannon shots south right into the now disorganized NVA. Some were turning to shoot as they were running in all directions from our guys. Ski and Tyler were tearing them new assholes. We broke, and here came 9-9 doing the same thing. Vic was good with the minis, and their crew was spot on picking out runners. We made one more run, and then Jerry asked Snake Doctor 6, "You ready to give a cab ride?"

He said, "Shit, thought you'd never ask, and my crew wants you to leave a few for them to shoot."

Jerry said, "We'll do our best. Come in north to south. That will put some concealment between you and the NVA. We'll be beside you and will be able to shoot anywhere out in front of you. Turn and fly out the way you came in."

Jesus, Martin was coming in fast. He stood the ship on its tail as we began shooting out ahead of him. Jerry shot every rocket but four, and everything was smoking and burning, with a lot of dust and smoke in the air.

9-9 said, "The Rattlers are running toward Snake Doctor."

Damn, I never thought he would make that landing. I thought he would fly right over everyone. His door gunners weren't just a couple of mechanics. They were shooting during that radical flaring maneuver. *Christ, how were they able to stand during that flare?*

I called Snake and asked, "How is everything?" as I broke, and 9-9 came in firing.

Snake 6 said, "The 71st 6 is taking it out. (It was Mathews, our CO)."

I was watching 6 fly out and said, "9-9 break now. I think everyone has been taken care of down there." I followed with, "Look at 6 fly that ship low level and around trees. He's a rock star. It's a good thing he's flying like he's running from a mother-in-law or we would never catch him until Baldy." He was turning sharp and moving up and down. The NVA would never hit that target.

I looked at Jerry and mouthed, "Call Snake and ask about his passengers."

Jerry nodded and called.

Snake said, "All are fine, but they need a change of underwear."

I said, "I thought our CO was flying."

"He wasn't."

The CO cut in and said, "We've just run out of ammo: M-60 and M-16s. By the way, I don't smell any shit in here. I almost did when Martin made that landing, but luckily I held it, so he let me fly out."

The CO added, "I'm going to drop them off at MASH. They need to see a doc."

A call came in from LZ Ross. They said they would secure that slick for a Chinook pick up.

Jerry said, "This is 9-6, great and thank you."

"Roger."

Five minutes later, we were at Baldy. I almost told Jerry to land at POL, but I held my tongue and he did everything I was going to tell him. *Let go Kevin.*

Gary set it down smoothly. After refueling, we began rearming. Snake Doctor deposited the downed crew at the MASH, then flew over and landed near us. We all walked over as they climbed out.

I said, "That was a hell of a rescue gentleman and sir. I'm sure you're a gentleman, too, Major Mathews. You two would make great Bird pilots."

Mathews said, "No thank you. I'm too old to drink like a bird."

"Sir, it's only every sixth day."

Martin said, "I would love to join the Birds, but Majors Thompson and Mathews said I was too valuable as chief mechanic and test pilot. The army has invested a lot of money in me, and I owe them."

"I know that, but I wanted to let you guys know that I was impressed with your flying. You were great. We have to rearm, so we've got to go, sir."

"Go to it, Mac."

We turned and headed towards the conex containers and the armaments. We were done in twenty minutes. We noticed that Snake Doctor was preparing to leave. I walked over and said, "What, no departing comments?"

Martin said, "No, the CO and I have passed each other on this check ride. Mac, I can't believe you do this shit all the time. See ya in CL."

I looked at the CO and said, "Jerry's a Fire Team Leader, sir."

He nodded and said, "Thank you for all the training you gave him. He told me that you spent a lot of time with details."

I backed away from the Huey as they lifted off and hovered to the runway with Captain Jerry Wilder sitting in back.

I yelled at Ski and Tyler. "Did you guys find any holes?"

They said, "A few minor hits; they can't shoot worth a shit."

Great! But we just got lucky; those AK-47s could throw out a lot of bullets. We walked back to the Hilton after rearming and wasted the next few hours.

At 1500 on the dot, the phone screamed at us, and we went into motion. When I arrived with the info, both ships were at full power. "We're to fly ten clicks west of LZ Center and contact Big Dog 6. The patrol is 500 meters from the bad guys and have not been seen."

When we got close to Big Dog 6's position, I called. "We're a gunship team of two. What's your sit rep?"

6 said, in a whispered voice, "We're an eight-man patrol, and we spotted the NVA in an empty village. It looks like the NVA are searching the village for anything left behind when it was evacuated two days ago. There must be 200 NVA. We're behind some brush 500 meters due east of them."

"6 pop a smoke when you see us. Throw it into a wet rice paddy as soon as I see it."

Thirty seconds later, I said, "I see your green smoke."

"That's me," he said in that same whispered voice.

"OK, Big Dog 6, we'll come in behind the small hills so they can't see or hear us. No problem with the ones in the open. If any are hidden under trees in or around the village direct my shots. Then I'll break towards you and my wingman will do the same. Then we'll repeat the process. Stay hidden."

I keyed my intercom switch on the cyclic and asked the crew—Vandercamp, door gunner and crew chief—if they got all of that. All answered with a click. I quickly keyed my transmit button and asked 9-9, "Did you get that."

Click-click.

Chapter 71.

DOWN IN FLAMES AGAIN

When we rolled in, I pulled the cyclic back to trade some speed for altitude, and 200 NVA fired their AK-47s on full automatic: 4000 rounds every three or four seconds. Several rounds came through the windshield, into the radios, and into the overhead circuit breakers. Yellow warning lights were flashing across the instrument panel. It was not looking good. These big overloaded slow flying ships were a great target.

Still, most of those NVA were in the open, and my crew was firing everything they could fire. I said, "Keep shooting. You're doing great."

Gary looked at me with very wide eyes. I said, "Shoot at muzzle flashes and people. We're in tiger country, and the only friendlies are the eight men in that patrol only a quarter mile away."

The bad guys were bolting out of the hooches, running in all directions, looking for cover. Others were standing in groups in the open area of the village, as if they were conferring about something.

I pointed the nose of the ship at the NVA in the open, looked through the rocket sight at those bastards, and kept punching. *I wonder if they call us the bastards.* Glancing at the gauges and with the slightest of hand and foot movements, I turned my sight to the enemy troops down the hill about twenty yards out of the village and punched off two rockets. According to our best information, these guys were the closest to our patrol. Then, I was shooting at everything in the village center. I picked out several hooches as targets. At the same time, Ski and Tyler had their M-60s all over that village.

The most difficult thing for a new crew member was to focus on shooting and ignore the tracers and the popping of bullets through the rotor blades. Of course, some luck was involved for the bullets to miss you.

Then, the NVA in the tree line opened up on us. There must have been two companies down there, 400 total. The bad guys in the open were toast, so I switched to the tree line where I could see new tracers. It looked like a war movie with the tracers whipping past my windshield and a couple coming through but missing me. I punched off three pair of rockets and walked them into the trees at the muzzle flashes, while my crew was now firing into that same tree line. The tracers diminished considerably, and Big Dog 6 said, "Your rockets are right on those sons of bitches. God damn, you got a hell of a lot of them."

But our ship was getting too close. I called, "Ready," to the guys in back, so they could hang on. I called out over the radio, "9-7 breaking right," and then I broke. Those guys behind me were incredible, hanging out of the ship while we were dropping 500 feet a minute at 120 knots.

My wingman put rockets behind me, and his crew was shooting. I glanced at my new copilot, and his eyes were even wider. He looked like he'd seen his grandmother naked. I asked, "Are you OK?" He nodded *yes*.

Suddenly, there were several loud hammering noises in rapid succession on the ship's belly, like a very big woodpecker pounding on a tree. Bang, bang, bang, and I could feel the ship shutter and vibrate like a dog shaking after a swim. My engine and rotor blade rpm began surging and then dropping.

Ski yelled, "Mac, we're on fire. They've got a 51 down there."

Red master caution and yellow warning lights were flashing like the gumball unit on a police cruiser.

All systems were failing. "Mayday, Mayday, Mayday. Firebird 9-7 going down on fire, ten clicks west of Center. On fire, repeat on fire." I was turning the ship away from the NVA. Never crash into an area you've just blown to hell. The survivors will be very angry.

Therefore, I had no choice but to pass the nice landing areas and stretch my flight time to get across the valley. There were no trees on a small hill which was lucky for us, but there was elephant grass, which can grow ten-twelve feet tall.

My neck was burning as were my arms.

Then the engine quit, and I went into autorotation.

As we were falling, I tried to jettison the rocket pods, but the electrical system was out. Those pods still had half their rockets remaining. The extra weight of the rockets and pods would make an autorotation difficult. I had nearly all my fuel because we had just come on station, which was not just a fire hazard but added even more weight.

I yelled for Ski to manually jettison the pods. He had to climb out into the fire and pull on a cable to release a pod. When he did, the ship leaned sharply over to the right, as Ski's pod was on the other side making that side lighter.

Ski then yelled at Tyler to jettison his pod on the right side. He also had to go into the fire searching for the cable and found it five seconds before I flared to slow our forward airspeed.

I looked to the side to see how tall the grass was. I couldn't see out the front due to smoke. I could feel the fire as it was growing, especially while falling in autorotation, which was fanning the fire. The 51 had ripped our fuel tank apart and the fuel was turning to mist as it exited the tank and rose up into the 1200 degree engine exhaust and ignited. It burned back down to the fuel tank and was coming up around the ship and inside to include flames in front of my face. Once it got to the leaking tank, we would have an explosion.

I had once been told by a seasoned pilot to keep flying until the ship is stopped on the ground. "If you ever give up on the way to the ground, you will, without a doubt, die."

And in a helicopter, you can't have any forward speed when you land on a soft surface because the skids will dig into the ground. You will stand on your nose and be at the mercy of the breaking rotor blades, which could tear through the cockpit.

The flames were all around me, but I kept telling myself to keep flying. I think it was pure adrenalin that kept me on those controls. God damn this fire's the shits. I've seen people with third-degree burns.

Luckily the grass was only a foot tall. I was about a foot off the ground when I pulled the collective to cushion the landing. It was a little hard, but I didn't give a shit as that ship would never fly again.

If those guys hadn't jettisoned the pods, the story would have ended differently. We would've been nothing more than a smoking hole in the ground.

My neck was really burning as I was fumbling for my seat belt release, when I had a vision of Steph. I saw her, beautiful, smiling, happy. *Shit does this mean I'm gonna die?* I found the release. Then, I had to slide back a piece of armor plating protecting me from bullets out to my right. I pulled it back and dove out. My head jerked back before I hit the ground because I hadn't unhooked the communication cable attached to my helmet. It unhooked itself without breaking my neck.

While this was going on, Ski jumped out with his M-60 and fell into a six-foot deep bomb crater. If I had landed there, we would have gone over on our side. Ski climbed out. He hadn't broken any bones, which was damn lucky. Then, he pulled his can of ammo out of the fire, and also grabbed the copilot's M-16.

I reached back in and jerked out the can of M-16 magazines under my seat. I turned and saw Tyler standing there without his M-60, just his ammo can. The fire was roaring now, and we had to get out of there as it would eventually explode. Then, I noticed that pieces of the rotor blades were flying off the ship, as were pieces of the rods up to the blades. Suddenly, I realized those sons of bitches were shooting that 51 across the valley at us. I said, "Everyone get down, they're shooting at us."

I don't know what possessed me to reach back into the flames and feel around on the floor for Tyler's M-60. I found it by brail and jerked it out and threw it on the ground. Then I said, *Fuck it*, and reached back into the middle of the ship and fire where the cannon ammo was loaded and felt for my M-16 hanging on the side of the four-foot-tall cannon magazine. I pulled it out and threw it on the ground.

I looked up as I saw my wingman coming in and jettisoning his rocket pods. Hell, he was coming in to pick us up. Then, pieces of his ship were flying off into the air. There was a second 51 by that village, and it was tearing his ship to pieces. He stopped descending and flew over us straight and level and across the valley.

Shit, now we're fucked and I think they are, too.

I said, "Gary, grab the other end of Tyler's ammo can, and I'll grab Ski's. Let's put some distance between us and that village. Stay in a crouch." I put my ammo in Ski's can.

We began a fast walk away from the NVA and the ship, when it blew up in a spectacular blast. I felt the heat on my back. My neck hurt and under my chin was painful. So were my arms. I always rolled up my sleeves halfway to my elbows. My fire retardant flight suit didn't work very well on my arms with my sleeves rolled up. Shit, what pilot ever thinks he'll go down in flames? If you did think about that, you wouldn't fly. Hell, this was my fourth time down and second in flames.

I lost track of my wingman because we were concentrating on getting the hell off this hill and away from that burning Huey. I knew those NVA assholes would be coming after us. Any aircraft was a real prize for them, especially the pilots.

We were on our own, at least for now. There wasn't anything to do but try to put as much distance between ourselves and the enemy as we could.

We had been moving along the ridge line for about two hours according to my watch when the ridge abruptly ended and sloped sharply down into the jungle. I said, "I think we would do better staying together for now as we have guns and ammo. I know they can move faster than us as they travel light. But remember the last time this happened." I got some rueful nods from Ski and Tyler. Gary just looked scared. "We were down, but we had weapons, and we were able to set up some surprises for them. Let's go into the thickest part of the jungle. They won't expect that, and I remember seeing a small river on the map in that direction." I pointed into the jungle.

The thick jungle was the shits. Even so, we pushed our way through making steady headway. After two hours of this misery, I stopped and climbed a tree to look for the NVA. I was sure they were after us. I didn't see anything so we kept going. We were headed northeast as near as I could discern. That would mean we would miss LZ Center by three or four clicks north.

After another hour grappling our way through this hot, humid, and foul-smelling vegetation, I thought how nice it would be to have a couple of machetes. I climbed another tree and saw the NVA several miles behind us and moving more east towards the LZ south of us. We kept moving for another hour, and I climbed yet another tree and saw them a half mile behind us. They had picked up our track and were closing in.

"Shit guys, they're close. That river should be close, too. We might be able to set up an ambush."

Gary said, "Are you crazy? We should keep moving as fast as we can."

I said, "They're closing in on us. They're following in our footsteps. We need a new plan."

I asked Ski and Tyler if we could ambush them in the middle of the river. They said, "Maybe, let's go look at that river and see if it's more than a stream."

We found it nearby, small but more than a stream, about twenty meters from shore to shore. We managed to ford it. We had to be careful to keep the guns dry because the water was up to our waists, but fortunately it was moving slowly. The bank sloped up sharply on the other side. It was work with the heavy ammo and guns, but at the top we found some large rocks among the trees.

I said, "Let's set up an ambush here. We'll wait until they're past the center of the river and then open up on them. The water will be up to their chests as they are at least a foot shorter than us, and they will be slow and cautious. Most third-world people can't swim, even the ocean fisherman. This river will definitely give us an advantage over last time."

We set the M-60s thirty yards apart and had a mini crossfire since we would be able to shoot from two directions. Ski and Tyler would shoot and feed their own guns. Gary and I would be close enough to pick off guys with single shots from our M-16s.

"We'll wait until we can get as many NVA in the river as possible before we start shooting. Agreed?"

Everyone nodded, and we checked our equipment one last time. I gave Gary a few of my M-16 magazines (15 total) and said, "Shoot single shots only. The gun is more accurate, and you'll conserve ammo."

I walked away from the ambush site and into the jungle to look for an escape route. The jungle wasn't as thick on that side of the stream, and there was a well-used animal trail. We'd be able to move faster, but so would they. Then, I had an off-the-wall idea.

We could set up a couple of trip wires attached to smoke grenades. It might scare them a little, maybe even slow them down. What I wouldn't give for a couple of claymore mines. Maybe after the smoke, they might think something bigger was waiting.

I returned to the ambush site and told Ski and Tyler about my idea. They smiled and said, "It's so bad, it just might work."

We split up and went to our respective positions, me with Ski and Gary with Tyler.

Twenty minutes passed before the bad guys approached the river. Instead of sending a scout across, they entered the water in a mass.

This was a stroke of luck for us. *We hadn't had much luck today. Well, I take that back; we did make it through the fire.*

These guys were not well trained. They were jumping in the water as fast as they could, and I didn't see anyone giving orders. Perfect. A trained unit would have someone on point to check out the territory.

Fifty or sixty guys were in the water when we opened up. They were trapped. The water was up to their chests which made for slow travel. The ones three quarters of the way across tried to continue but that just put them closer to Ski and Tyler. A few tried turning back. Gary and I shot them and then turned our guns on the others. After a minute, all were dead. Not a single shot was fired our way.

I told Tyler and Gary, "Set up two smokes with trip wires. One of you remain with each wire, so Ski and I won't set them off. We'll stay and get the next group trying to cross. Then we'll come running. If they do try a second crossing, they will be spread out up and down the river. That will give us time to put distance between us and them, because they'll have to reorganize the ones who were far enough up and down the river to avoid Ski's gun."

Damned if they didn't try crossing again. Someone was giving orders but was definitely not in the assault. Those poor bastards wouldn't be stupid enough to try crossing that river after witnessing their buddies' deaths unless someone of high rank was encouraging them, or should I say, threatening them? Drugs might also have been involved.

We waited as fifteen NVA entered the water. We wanted more,

but it didn't happen.

Ski and I started shooting in short bursts to conserve ammo. We had no Idea how long this game would continue. A few shot towards us, but to no avail. We had great cover and were in a superior position (above them) and behind large rocks.

Again, some tried to retreat and some tried continuing toward us. All was futile. We then put some rounds into the trees to keep them guessing and grabbed the ammo can after I threw my last five magazines in and we ran like hell. I thought, *Those were for you Steph*

We came to Gary, and he pointed to a piece of parachute cord across the animal trail. He joined our track workout, and we ran another 200 yards and came to Tyler who stepped out of the brush and pointed to his parachute cord. The pilots carried that cord in the pocket on their chicken board and the gunners in their flak jackets; all for various uses. We also used it for tourniquets.

I don't remember getting tired from all the running. We occasionally slowed to a fast walk and stopped once to assess our remaining ammo. Of the gunner's original 1500 rounds, Ski had about 600 and Tyler had 900, as he didn't participate in the second ambush. Gary had two magazines remaining, so I gave him one of mine and told him to "shoot slower." He nodded. I had 120 rounds, and he now had 90.

"Let's go guys. We're not out of this mess yet."

Two more hours and the chasers hadn't caught us. However, we hadn't seen or heard a Huey. *Shit, they had to be looking for us.* That was one of the reasons we had the energy to keep going. We knew our fellow pilots wouldn't give up on us.

Damn, it was getting dark. "We can't stop. They'll catch us. Grit your teeth and think what happens if we're caught."

Nobody said a word. We just kept moving.

The jungle is scary at night; strange sounds and bushes moving without any breeze. I knew we were at the bottom of the food chain tonight. In the air with rockets, we were the top of the food chain. How quickly that changed! I was more worried now than when the NVA were closing in on us. At least we had a full moon which allowed us to occasionally see the ground when the jungle canopy opened.

A couple of times I drifted away from the group to create a false trail, then I walked on fallen trees, rocks and anything else that wouldn't leave foot prints back to the group. What I really wanted was Randy, the pathfinder from the Bolaven Plateau mission in Laos. He could be a ghost.

About midnight, Gary told me he was tired.

I said, "Gary, we can't stop unless you want to live in the Hanoi Hilton (the prisoner of war prison in North Vietnam). I'm guessing we killed 75 guys in the river. How many of those fuckers were after us?"

But we really had no idea.

"This jungle stinks," Gary complained, "and the air's so heavy, I can hardly breathe."

"Yeah," I agreed. "There's no breeze, which tells me those moving leaves and bushes are caused by nonhuman life forms."

We had definitely slowed down the past few hours and were barely able to walk when the sun started peeking through the jungle canopy. I don't want to be in a jungle ever again at night. Shit, I don't want to be in one in the daytime either. We were now dehydrated. We had sweated all night.

Time to climb a tree. I couldn't see anything at first, and then I saw smoke. Maybe they were eating. I guessed they were about a mile away. Fuck, I had to figure out something else. We had only one smoke remaining. Had to save that in case we got lucky enough to have a Huey pass overhead.

I climbed down and reported our situation to the guys, and no one smiled.

I said, "Let's go until we find another ambush site or someone comes up with a brilliant idea."

Damn, we came to a small clear stream. We had no choice but to drink. I just hoped there weren't too many animals upstream.

Thirty minutes later, when we stopped to change arms, so we could use a fresh arm to carry those ammo cans, I felt pain in both hands and looked at them and was surprised to see the palms of my gloves were burned and stuck to my hands.

These are Nomex flight gloves; they're supposed to be fire retardant. On closer inspection, the palms looked like leather. The material was burnt, so I wasn't 100% sure. What fucking son of a bitch sold these to the military and what asshole in the pentagon approved the contract?

The more I looked at my palms, the more they hurt.

Ski said, "Mac, we could climb that steep hill over at our 10 o'clock and set up another ambush."

I looked and said, "Brilliant Ski. We're out of gas, and we can't keep going, so this might be our last stand."

We climbed the hill, but we were so tired it seemed like a mountain. We were all out of breath at the top and just rolled over on our backs for a couple of minutes, hopping to slow our heaving chests.

We finally got to our hands and knees and peered over the top. The animal trail continued.

I said, "Let's spread out as much as we can and work a little crossfire like at the river."

We split up as before and set up the machine guns. There wasn't any cover; no rocks or trees.

I said, "Shoot very short bursts. We may have to run again. Gary, only shoot one magazine, so make every shot count. Keep your heads down as much as you can. We wait until we think we have the most NVA possible in the open."

"We've got to get them all. There's a large open grassy area behind us. Running across that field will put us in the open. It must be 100 meters to the trees on the other side."

Here they came, just like before.

"Jesus Christ, there are 20 of those little shits down there. Did they send all of North Vietnam after us?"

Ski said, "Sure as hell looks like it."

"OK guys, it's open season," and we all started shooting. Some dropped to the ground, and others were running in both directions along the trail. A few tried shooting at us, but they had a very poor angle.

I thought I heard something and turned to look right and left and saw a Huey. I screamed at Ski and Tyler, to be heard over the machine guns. "Throw a smoke." They looked at me, and I pointed to the Huey.

Tyler said, "I lost the smoke grenade. It probably got pulled off my flak jacket last night by a branch in the jungle."

I said, "Most of those NVA down on the trail are dead. Let's get out in that field so we can be seen. This two foot elephant grass hides us while we're lying flat to peek over the edge."

We started running with our guns and what ammo was remaining. We were three quarters the way across the open area when the few remaining NVA crested the hill and began shooting at us. We made it to the trees without getting shot.

The NVA crouched down as the Huey went by.

I don't know what possessed me, but I stood and ran out in the open diagonally, waving my arms. As I neared the trees, the NVA rose up on their knees and began shooting at me. Dirt and grass were flying up in the air all around me. I got to the trees and thought, *fuck it. I really don't care if I live or die. They missed me the first time. Who knows the second time? Here goes.* And I started running back towards my crew. The grass and dirt started flying up in my face. I stopped waiving my arms and stopped running and began shooting at the few remaining NVA. My guys were shooting at them, too.

Then the Huey saw me because the door gunners opened up on those shits. The Huey turned sharply and came down in a high overhead. My crew began running out to the anticipated landing spot.

I resumed my running to that same anticipated spot. Those assholes were still shooting at me. *How the hell can they miss me?*

The ship landed perpendicular to us so his door gunner could continue shooting, and the crew chief was pulling guys inside. Ski and Tyler were on their knees so they could keep shooting their 60s out the side with the door gunners.

I arrived five seconds later and was pulled in as the crew chief yelled, "Go-go-go; everyone's in."

I grabbed two magazines out of my pocket as I ejected the empty, and I put my M-16 on full auto and held it on those guys. I knew it wasn't as accurate, but it might cause them to keep their heads down. Gary and I were on our stomachs on the floor of the ship shooting.

Shit, something hit the back of my leg.

When were far enough from our pickup point to stop shooting, Ski said, "Mac, the back of your left leg is bleeding. Don't move; I'll check it. Mac you have a piece of something sticking out of your skin. I can't really tell what it is as there's blood on it. The bleeding is slow. I'll skip the tourniquet since we're starting our approach to Center."

What I didn't discover until we were back at LZ center was that both pilots in the slick were wounded. Their windshield was shot out. Half their instruments were out, since the electrical system was torn up pretty bad. Hell, we could have all died in a crash if the bullets had moved two inches either way. Both pilots would have been dead along with us.

When we landed, I received another surprise. This was good news. All four members of the wing ship had been rescued alive and well. Their hydraulics had been damaged and their ship flew across the valley and into the jungle at a nose up angle equal to the slope of the mountain. They had just enough hydraulic fluid remaining for them to pull the nose up slightly more and they settled into the trees, cutting them down as they were approaching the ground. The blades flexed down and cut off the nose of the ship, so they could unstrap and step forward out of the cockpit. A Huey was able to extract them ten minutes later. They were surrounded by NVA, but the rescue ship's door gunners offered enough protection that they could get in the ship.

On the way to LZ Center, I asked the slick pilot if he could get the Air Force to nape that hill and our rescue location. He nodded. I climbed out at Center and now my burns were giving me a considerable amount of pain. I asked for the medic.

A medic came over and looked at me and said, "Can you follow me, sir?"

I said, "Gladly," and when I started walking to the first aid bunker, I was limping because my left hamstring was on fire. The medic gave me a shot to numb the area and pulled something out. It looked like a piece of a bullet. It must have been a ricochet. He tried to numb my hands and then cut off the leather gloves. That hurt like a motherfucker. I tried not to flinch, but he could see my pain and stopped. The pain med must not have hit the right area.

"Sir, I'm sending you to CL and the flight surgeon. You may end up in the hospital or sent to Japan for infection prevention. Let me put some salve on your neck, face and arms, then put you on a slick. I'm going to wrap your hands as they're bleeding."

A colonel walked in and said, "Mr. McNally, I just talked to your crew. If half of what they say is true—and not the result of adrenalin overload—you should receive a Medal of Honor. I would like you to tell your story on tape before the ship is here to fly you to CL. I can go with you and finish it at the flight surgeons, if necessary."

"OK, sir." It took me thirty minutes with the colonel writing and recording while I was talking. A slick arrived five minutes before I was done, but he had to wait. You know, RHIP (rank has its privileges).

I climbed into the slick with my crew and saw they had some minor bandaging. At least it was minor. I felt responsible as well as concerned as this was the fourth time Ski, Tyler, and I had been shot down.

I leaned over the pilot's shoulder and said, "Not over 100 feet or we'll get nose bleeds."

He turned towards me and smiled. "Yeah I heard that about you Birds," and chuckled.

He took off and pointed his nose toward CL and climbed to 1500 feet, which is a fairly safe altitude. All four of us Birds were asleep in five minutes in that cool air.

I opened my eyes when we began our descent. 1500 feet! No wonder I felt cold. I sat there and clenched my teeth as my hands were giving me considerable pain. We landed next to the flight surgeon's building. He was standing there with Major Mathews and Jerry Wilder. Then, General Wheaton walked out of the building.

The doc asked, "Does anyone need help getting inside?" We all said *no*, and followed him into his aid station. I was limping as the pain shot in my leg had worn off. A nurse took the crew into a large room with treatment tables along the walls. I followed the doc into another room as my entourage followed.

He said, "Sit on the table, Mac." After I tried to sit, I stood due to the leg pain. The General said, "We stayed back Mac so we wouldn't try to shake your hand. Damn Mac, that looks painful," as he nodded toward my hands.

"It is, sir, but it took me over twelve hours to notice. Thank god for adrenalin."

The doc saw that I couldn't sit, so he said, "Lie down on your stomach, Mac, and I'll clean up the leg first." After he finished that, he turned to my burns. "I'm going to put you out," he said, "so I can cut off this leather. If I don't, you'll probably pass out from the pain. These are deep second degree burns." His eyes were a little ironic. "I know you know from experience how much those exposed nerves can hurt. I'll be right back Mac. I have to get a nurse and some equipment."

While the doc was out, General Wheaton said, "You gave us a scare Mac. We thought we'd lost you. Oh hell, we should've known better."

The doc returned. He then asked everybody to please wait outside. This was going to take over an hour. As they walked out, the nurse put a mask over my face and said, "Count to ten." I don't know how close I got to ten. The next thing I knew, I was waking up.

While I was asleep, the doc had cut the leather off of my palms. Essentially, the leather had been heated to a temperature that caused it to fuse to my skin. The operation took two hours. I had been injected with pain killers before I woke up.

When I opened my eyes, I immediately vomited. The doc said, "The nausea is from the anesthesia. Suck on ice and try 7 up. The leg looks good. The medic did a great job. I x-rayed it, and it was clean."

"Doc, we don't have any 7 up."

"I spoke to the general, and he said he could get some. Just small sips or you'll vomit again."

"I'm going to send you back to your company area he told me, instead of the hospital. I think it will be better for your psyche to be around lots of people, especially friends. Come back tomorrow morning at 1000 hours, and I'll change those bandages."

My hands were bandaged to look like two large boxing gloves. At least they didn't hurt. My neck, chin and forearms didn't feel so good. Burns are the shits.

"My medic will drive you to the 71st. See ya tomorrow. Oh, before you go, my nurse has a shot for you. Drop your pants. Your butt can handle the soreness better than your arm. She also has some salve for your face, neck and arms and pain pills for your hands. Don't drink when you take the pills. The alcohol will enhance the pills effect and make you goofy."

Goofy? Isn't that a Disney character?

When she arrived, I said, "You'll have to pull my pants down."

I showed her my boxing gloves. When she finished with the shot, I said, "What have I ever done to you?"

She smiled. "See ya tomorrow, flyboy, and we'll do it again. Don't be such a pussy tomorrow."

I had an instant vision of Steph standing there saying those exact same words. I thought I was going to throw up. I nodded and quickly walked out. Not for fresh air, as there was none here, but I didn't want to puke on their floor. The feeling passed, thank god.

The medic stopped in front of the CO's office, so I automatically looked up, and Major Thompson was standing at the top of the two steps. That was a signal for me to see what he wanted. I told the driver, "Thank you," and limped up the steps. I gave the Major my best salute with my large white boxing glove.

He snickered and returned my salute. "At ease Mac. Come in my office."

We walked in, and he motioned me to a seat.

"Mac, you've been through 24 hours of hell. There is no one in this company or any company I've been in or commanded that would have made it through the ordeal you just went through. Tell me the truth Mac, how are you?"

"Sir, I would never lie to you. I feel fine. The only thing that ever gets me down is the thought of Steph, and that never happens when I'm in combat. Well, once this morning after our second ambush on the NVA at the river, I told Steph that was for her as I watched them floating.

"Would you like me to give Ski and Tyler some time off? You're not going to be flying for a while."

"Yes, I wouldn't be here if it weren't for them."

"What are you going to do while off flight status?"

"I haven't eaten or slept in 24 hours, and I feel the need for alcohol. Those are first on my list."

"OK, Mac, dismissed."

"Thank you, sir," and I walked to the Birdhouse. I sat on the edge of my bed, and the next thing I knew, two hours had passed. I felt exhausted. Then, I suddenly realized that I had to pee. How the fuck am I going to unzip my pants? I can't wet my pants. Firebirds don't do that.

I had a desperate idea. I went over to Ski's hooch and called his name as I stood outside.

He came out and said, "Wow Mac, you really burnt those hands."

I said, "Your arms don't look so good with all those bandages. We're going to have to stop rolling up our sleeves. How's Tyler?"

"Physically about the same as me. He's over at the club getting hammered, which I will be doing soon."

"Ski, I've got a problem. I've gotta pee so bad I can taste it. Could you unbutton my pants?"

"No Mac, I can't do that. No, no, I can't."

"I just want you to undo that button at the top. You don't have to do anything else. Hell, I don't want you putting your greasy hands on me."

"OK, but don't tell anyone." He unbuttoned me and thank god they weren't the fatigues we wore when I first got here. They had seven buttons. These pants had a zipper.

Ski walked back in his hooch, and I bent over and used my forearms to move the pants down a foot and then I fumbled with my underwear and then pissed on the side of his hooch. *Hell, I'm a guy, the world is my urinal.* I got myself back in the underwear and pulled my pants up with my forearms, which hurt like hell with the burns.

I said, "Ski, could you come out here?"

He walked out and looked in all directions, then buttoned my pants.

I said, "Could you please pull up that zipper?"

"Shit Mac, we're good friends, but this is too much."

"Ski, a Firebird can't walk around with his pants unzipped."

"Goddammit, Mac, this had better be a secret." He then pulled up the zipper.

"Ski, I have one more thing to ask you." He looked at me and said, "Now WHAT," which is the only time I ever heard him raise his voice.

"Could you get your scissors out of your barrel bag and cut off the top of these bandages, so my fingers are free so I can use them to pee."

"Gladly, be right back." He returned and carefully cut off the bandages at the finger tips. I had two joints exposed on each finger and one joint on the thumb. They were burnt, but nothing like the palms.

"If you pull my wallet out of my back pocket, I'll give you and Tyler $20 each so you can get fucked up tonight. In fact, if you follow me to the Birdhouse, I'll give you a fifth of gin in case the beer isn't enough to make you forget about our last mission."

He pulled it out and took two twenty's. Then he looked at me and said, "I suppose I have to put this back," as he held the wallet in front of my face.

"Please." He put it back. I said, "Thanks Ski, I owe you." As we walked to the Birdhouse for the gin, he said, "You don't have enough money to pay me for the button and zipper missions. I'll give you a pass on the wallet."

I couldn't help but laugh. "The gin's here," I said. "Sleep in tomorrow. We all have it off. The CO is going to try to give you and Tyler at least seven days off. Probably until we get a new ship. Probably will be another beat up piece of shit."

I made it to the showers and did my best to keep my hands dry. My neck and arms really hurt when the water made contact. I ended up only washing my bottom half, with running water only. *That's the important part, right?* I tried to use just finger tips but the bandages were soaked. *I hope they dry by morning or the flight surgeon will be pissed.*

I went to the club. As I walked in, the ubiquitous noise stopped. Some asshole yelled, "Ring the bell, you dumb shit. You just got shot down for your fourth time. Uncle Sam can't afford you."

That drew a lot of laughs.

I shrugged, held my hands out, palms up, and said, "If you pull out my wallet and take out five, I'll ring the bell." Then someone said, "Five more dollars, since the ship was a total loss." Whoever pulled out my wallet took out a ten and threw it in the pot. Then he said, "Someone else has to put the wallet back. I can't have my hands in Mac's pants twice. I'm a Firebird and have a reputation to maintain."

I don't know who put it back, but I said, "That feels good." Everyone laughed, and the guy jerked his hand out of my pocket and called me an asshole.

"I've never heard of a fine for a ship that's a total loss."

"We just added it because it's your second burnt up ship."

"Shit, I should have surrendered to the NVA."

The crowd cheered, and then people walked over and asked if it was OK to pat me on the back and tell me they were glad I got out alive. I told them from the middle of my back to the waist was OK.

All the previous talk was what we did to lessen the tension of being in this shithole of a country. I still hadn't seen anything worth keeping. I really couldn't imagine what the commies wanted to do with a few million farmers.

A very smart lady, whom I still love, despite the futility of holding on, told me a quote from Winston Churchill: "Socialism is a philosophy of failure, the creed of ignorance, and the gospel of envy, its inherent virtue is the equal sharing of misery."

I was handed a beer and a crown. I announced, after I took a drink, "This is the best I've ever tasted. When we got thirsty, we drank from tiny streams or trickles of water. I will never take water for granted again. I've said that about food back in the world and a shower. Earlier here, I said that about a cold beer. There are many things I won't ever take for granted and that includes friends. You guys are the greatest friends I've ever had and that ain't no shit (which meant it was true)."

More cheering and swearing.

I spent the next few hours talking to the guys and trying not to think of Steph. *Fuck, I'm going to extend for six more months here. I'll do it tomorrow. There's nothing for me at home but teaching Vietnamese to fly.* Faces were getting blurry. I said, "Where's that pilot who picked me up. I owe him a drink!" *Maybe I should slow down on this booze.* I don't remember if I slowed down or not.

I woke up at 0800. I leisurely walked up to the CO's office and asked Top, "Can I steal Smitty for ride to the flight surgeon at 1000?"

Top said, "Yes Mac, the CO left me a note and said to MAKE SURE you go." He said that with a big grin.

"Thank you, Top. Smitty, I'm going to eat breakfast and we'll leave at 0945."

After breakfast, the colonel who debriefed me at Center called me in the Birdhouse and asked a few questions. One in particular: "Did anyone ever disagree? You were in a very difficult situation, and we've seen moral breakdown with stress."

I said, "No sir. I'm not bragging, but a gunship team is a very tight group, and we all pull for each other. We know what the other guy is going to do and trust him to do his part, so the rest of us can do ours. We all depend on each other every minute we're in the air. It turned out we needed each other just as much on the ground in that miserable fucking jungle. We all asked each other for opinions as none of us have ever been in the infantry."

At the flight surgeon's, I told Smitty, "I will call you after the torture." He nodded and drove away."

I walked in and the doc said, "Wow, you're here on time. Hell, you're here. I actually thought you might not show up. Let's go in the room to your left."

I sat at the table. The doc had a puzzled look on his face when he saw my bandaged hands.

"Mac," he said, as he looked at my hands and saw finger tips, "this doesn't look like my work."

'It isn't doc. It's my crew chief's." He still looked puzzled, so I said, "Doc, I had to go to the bathroom."

He was struck with a moment of clarity. I saw it in his eyes.

"Sorry Mac, I'm so used to turning my work over to the nurses to finish for me, so I can move to the next patient. I won't ask for any details, but it appears you managed. Let's cut these bandages off and redo them so they're practical."

It didn't feel good, but he was trying to move slowly, so I sucked it up. When the doc finished, he called in that evil nurse who enjoyed poking a rusty nail in a guy's butt.

When she pulled that rusty nail out of my butt, she said, "Don't forget to take your pills, flyboy. We're going to do this three more times. I can't wait until tomorrow. But don't worry, Mac, it will be our little secret. I don't want you to look bad."

"I don't know why I'm such a puss when I get those syrup shots. It stings like fire. Maybe that's why."

She said, "Get tough flyboy or I'll call the Firebird hooch." Then she winked and smiled and walked away."

I called Smitty for a ride home. When I sat down in the jeep, he reached back behind my seat and pulled out a can of seven up and said, "From the general."

"Smitty, I don't think I need that. Turns out that alcohol did the job for me last night. The Doc wants me back at 1000 tomorrow. Can you clear that with Top?"

"Sure thing, Mac."

"How many cans do you have?"

"Four Mac."

"Take three cans and give Top and the CO one and you get the third. I'll put something strong in mine, as a pain killer, of course."

That night I put a lot of gin in that can every time I drank the level down enough to allow me to add more. The gin didn't taste so bad after an hour of self-medicating.

I spent the next day writing letters home after I returned from the flight surgeon. Top and the CO thanked me for the 7UP. I made up a few stories in the letters home without any blood or gore.

They probably won't believe it, but I try. Hell they'll notice the shitty writing too. These bandages are a handicap. Taking showers hurts like hell. Mine are just a matter of patting the areas with a soapy wet towel before seeing the flight surgeon.

After five straight days visiting the flight surgeon, the pain was letting up. The rest of the burns were also much better. My butt was sore. I scrubbed my body for ten minutes in the shower and could still smell that jungle. All the black smoke in the air from burning shit just made the jungle on me smell worse. *Shit, they have a large burning pit a hundred yards from the Hilton. That probably isn't healthy for me either.*

I was reduced to two more visits for bandage changes. That would mean I could fly soon.

Captain Wilder came into my hooch and said let's go to the MARS station. I have an appointment.

I said, "Yea sure, I've never been to MARS. It couldn't be any shittier than this fucking country."

"No really, Mac. MARS stands for Military Affiliate Radio Service. Not the planet. They're volunteer Ham radio operators. They bounce their radio signals off the upper atmosphere and down to another Ham operator in the states who contacts a phone operator and calls whomever you signed up to talk to. It's non-secure so we can't say anything secret; as if we know anything secret. Now here's the procedure. After you have spoken, you must say 'over' so both hammys know to turn a switch that allows the other party to speak back to you. If one side or the other forgets to say 'over' there is silence until they remember. You're allowed five minutes. It's strange to yell into the speaker, as you must occasionally do and say something like, 'I love you and want to be in bed with you and your hot body, over.' The person back in the world doesn't know that you're not alone and might say something back like, 'I want to fuck you so bad, over.' The Ham operator turns his head to cut you some slack. You have to sign up for your time months in advance and then tell who you're going to talk to and when. Vietnam is fourteen hours ahead of the west coast and seventeen ahead of the east coast."

After Wilder finished his call, he walked out to the porch and found me waiting. I said, "I thought I'd give you a little privacy."

When we returned to the company area, I got a big surprise when Ski and Tyler came to my hooch and said, "Mac, we have to go to the flight line. Our new ship just arrived, and the best part is it's new. We'll have power. The flight line said it's right out of the box."

We snagged a jeep and covered the one mile in four minutes and still nearly ruptured our kidneys. We pulled up to the new ship and stared in amazement. Usually, replacements for the gunships were rebuilds with a new engine and transmission, which means the ships looked like shit inside and out. *I'm gonna be pissed at anyone who puts a hole in this baby.*

My name was painted on the right side just behind the pilot's door, and Ski's was on the left. Mine said AC and his said CE for Aircraft Commander and Crew Chief /Engineer, respectively. The ship shined. It had been waxed. It looked too pretty to fly in combat. *I'm usually too dirty to sit in something this nice.* They also said Martin had test flown it several hours fully overloaded.

The next day Ski, Tyler, and I went to see Malko in supply and check out new equipment to replace everything we lost the week before: helmets, chicken boards and the vests, flak jackets, atropine syrettes, survival knives, maps of the AO, manual of this month's radio frequencies, and some odds and ends. We had gradually thrown away our helmets and chicken boards during our E & E (escape and evasion).

Malko looked up when we came in and said, "I was wondering when you would be coming to see me. By the way Mac, I've got a form for you to sign." He smiled as he handed me a clip board with six pages. I counted them. The first page made me pause.

"Holy shit, Malko, a jeep—a fucking jeep in a gunship? Three Huey transmissions and four turbine engines. I'm not going to read any more. No wonder we're not winning this war. If the pentagon pencil pushers can't figure this out how can they prosecute this war?"

We win every battle but are not making any gains. We just keep fighting over the same real-estate. I can't put this in my set of manuals.

"Did you steal this equipment you're giving us?"

"Come on, Mac. This is how the system works."

"I know, I know, you've explained it enough times."

"Hell Mac, if it weren't for you, I'd be in a tough situation keeping this company together."

"Thanks for that unique reminder. Is there anything new that we should have?"

"No, not yet. How are you guy's burns? I heard some really wild stories."

"No, they're all bullshit. We landed in a field, picked some flowers, and then caught a ride back to Center."

"Right Mac," and then he looked at Ski and Tyler and said, "He's full of shit."

They looked at him and said in unison, "We know." We walked out trying not to laugh.

"After we put this new shit away, I'll meet you two on your steps, and I'm bringing the whiskey."

One of them said, "Make it quick. I want to drink something besides beer."

When we got together, I had the promised whiskey and some paper cups. "We got out of that shit," I told them, after we each had a filled cup, "because we're a team, a fucking good one. I wouldn't be alive if it weren't for you two."

"Shit Mac," said Tyler, "we wouldn't either, if you hadn't kept flying that flaming son of a bitch."

"We were great at setting up those ambushes, "said Ski. "Those shits didn't stand a chance and learned nothing from their futility."

"Damn Ski," I said. "I didn't know you got out of high school. Futility?"

Tyler said, "Ski's too polite, so I'll say it. Fuck you, Mac."

I said, "Thanks, I deserved that." We laughed. We toasted and chugged. I refilled, and we chugged again. "Do you realize we were infantry for a day?"

"OK, now it's sippin' time to ponder that thought."

So we sipped and talked about the mission, mainly our escape, which was amazing. We reviewed every incident in order of occurrence.

"We really deserve to get shit faced. Anyone ready for number four?"

They both extended their cups, and I poured. I asked, "You two still want to fly with me?"

Ski said, "It would be very boring to fly with someone else."

Tyler said, "We do get shot down a lot, but it's not dull. We are so wrapped up in every mission, these days fly by. I'm beginning to think I might make it outta here."

"I know what you mean. I don't know what else could happen to us short of death."

"Number five coming up," I said. "I can feel this. How about you two?"

They said, "Oh yeah, me, too."

"You ready to fly again? I'm gonna' talk to the flight surgeon tomorrow. I'm going crazy."

Tyler said, "You mean crazier!"

"Yeah, that's what I meant."

"You two talk to your platoon sergeant about flying, and I'll corner my platoon leader after we see the doc tomorrow. We'll tell 'em that we'll go AWOL if we can't fly." They nodded. "I know you two still have stitches in you, so it's your decision."

They immediately said, "You still have stitches in your leg."

We emptied the fifth. "I'm gonna try to find the Birdhouse. See you two at breakfast, or if you don't make it, I'll see you after the doc."

"We have to go with you to the doc, so we'll see ya at breakfast."

Sleep was terrible. Steph was looking at me asking, "Why?" I couldn't answer. I woke up with tears rolling down my cheeks. *Kevin, you've got to stop this. You're in a war zone. There's no room for compassion, and you can't live in the past.*

I ate breakfast with a headache. Ski and Tyler were there, and they looked like I felt. They said they would see their Sarg at 1100.

We went to see the doc at 1000. I told Smitty I would call him in about an hour, sooner if I got released to fly.

"Good morning, doc."

"How do those hands feel?"

"Actually, there's no pain. I can grip objects without discomfort. You can release me, doc. I'm ready. Actually I'm going crazy sitting in the company area all day watching these hands heal. And so are Ski and Tyler"

"OK, I'll let you go, but you have to check in with the MASH doctor at Baldy daily. Maybe twice a day. Agreed? And make sure your two compadres do the same. I'm going to call the doc at Baldy."

I nodded and said, "Thanks."

"I'll call your CO and good luck. Try to stay out of my office."

Back in the company area, I knocked on Top's door. He saw me and said, "Come in Mac."

"Good morning, Top. I've got a question and a request. Did the flight surgeon call? And I'd like to extend."

Top said, "Yes and OK. The doc called and cleared you to fly. Check with your platoon leader. The CO told me you'd be in here for the extension. Are you sure?"

"Yes Top, absolutely."

"Here's the form. It's signed by the CO. You have thirty days remaining here, then back to the world for thirty days, and then back here for six months. Sign and you're done. By the way, Wilder is off today, so you check with him and you could probably fly tomorrow. Ski and Tyler have been cleared also."

"Thanks Top."

I walked out and straight to the platoon leader's hooch. A short discussion ensued, and I discovered I was being sent to Hong Kong for five days of R & R. He told me I was "going native" and needed to clear my head. "You leave tomorrow." Shit, my head was spinning.

This last week and a few days was the longest I'd gone without flying since arriving in hell. *Shit, I hope I remember how to start the damn thing. I won't put this in the manual.*

I checked in with Ski and Tyler, and they were as ready as I was. So was Clearwater, my wing. He said, "I can't wait to get back in the air with you." Vandercamp, my co-pilot was also ready.

Ski and Tyler told me they had orders to go to Thailand for R & R for five days.

I said, "Shit I'm being sent to Hong Kong for five days. OK guys we meet back here in five days to kick some serious ass."

I reported in to CL tower the next day and was flown to Hong Kong.

Chapter 72.

SOPHIE

After a very dull oration on sex safety to prevent venereal diseases, we were bused to our Hotels. I checked in and put my small bag of civilian clothes in my room and then went straight to the bar.

Thirty GIs were bellied up to the bar. The haircuts gave them away. They were almost as loud as the Birds.

I was invited to join them, and then everything got blurry in thirty minutes. One of the more inebriated guys said in a very loud voice that he challenged everyone to Rickshaw races. I was thinking that a Firebird can't walk away from a challenge.

The next thing I realized I was sitting in a Rickshaw with four others in a line in the middle of the street. From what I could hear with all the yelling, we would start on the count of three and race one block. The winner would get five dollars in Hong Kong money, which was a lot. We then raced back to the Hotel and had a new winner. Someone said he needed a beer, so after telling the rickshaw drivers to rest, we all went in to the bar and got two travelers (beers to drink during the races). One beer for the first race, and one for the return race to the hotel.

The streets were terrible. Just as bad as CL. One of the drivers/runners fell in one of the deep ruts and the rickshaw ran over him. When we arrived at the Hotel/finish line several of us ran back to see if he was alive. He was, but it sounded like swearing in a language we didn't understand. I gave him five dollars, and he stopped whatever he was yelling and smiled at me and nodded his head and began recovering what remained of his rickshaw. After this strenuous racing, we went back to the bar and began discussing women and how you deal with the mamasan (lady who runs the brothel or night club and is in charge of the women). Only one guy in the group had done this before, as this was his second tour in VN. We followed him over to a far corner where the mamasan sat with about fifteen Asian girls who looked like they were about fourteen. All ten of us picked a girl as the old timer was negotiating. We paid her very little money. Mine was named Linda. *Yeah right.*

As we rode up to my floor in the elevator, I was feeling guilty because of Steph. However, between the booze and Linda getting undressed, I was rationalizing that Steph would understand.

Linda's first question was, "What do you like? I do everything, and I do it good." Her accent was pretty thick, but I got the message.

I understood her broken English, so we got in bed and did everything for most of the night. In the morning, after only three hours of sleep, I remembered what the old timer had told us after we had chosen our girls. "They will try to talk you into spending your entire R & R with them. That insures them four more nights of charging you for sex, and then they'll serve as your tour guides and encourage you to spend money on them. Don't do it. It's cheaper to get another girl." When she woke up, I braced myself for the tongue lashing I was about to receive. I gently said, "Goodbye and thank you for last night."

She looked at me with her hands on her naked hips and said, "You no want me anymore?"

I looked at her and just shook my head *no.*

She said in her very thick accent, "You are the mean son of the bitch that I have ever seen."

Then, she dressed and slammed the door as she stormed out of the room.

I think that went well?

Then, I went downstairs to the restaurant and ate with several of the guys from last night. We started tossing out ideas for what to do that day. One guy suggested that the four of us take the ferry boat out to Hong Kong Island and ride the tram to the top for lunch. A brochure said this was a "don't-miss sight."

We had a tough decision to make when we bought our ferry tickets. The top deck was five cents and the bottom was three cents. We laughed and bought the three cent ticket and said we'd save the two cents for booze.

The laugh was on us. The lower deck was for animals: goats, sheep, pigs and chickens. It smelled like VN, and there was no clean place to walk or stand. Fortunately, it was a short ride. After we got off, we tried scraping our shoes on a weeded area by the sidewalk.

We found the tram entrance. The slope up the mountain must have been 60 degrees. The ride took less than five minutes, and what a view! We could see into China and at least 100 ships in the harbor.

After that, we walked into a very fancy-looking restaurant and saw four beautiful Caucasian ladies sitting at a rather large table. One of them walked up to us and invited us to join them. *Something like this doesn't happen very often. Like never.*

We sat down and tried our best to be nice and no war talk. Their names were Sophie, Martha, Sarah, and Susan. I originally thought they were models, but they said they were students at the University of Hong Kong and on a break before the fall semester began. All four were from England and in their third year of a Dental program.

They told us they had two apartments next to each other and near the school. Telling us about their apartments couldn't help but tickle our expectations. We ate and talked for an hour, and then we went to a movie, followed by a dinner of western barbecue, all of which we guys felt obligated to pay for.

Into the evening, we just slowly paired up. My date was Sophie.

We stopped at a very nice bar. It made our hotel bar looked like the Baldy Hilton. After a couple of drinks, they suggested we go to their places for a nightcap. We guys looked at each other and raised our eyebrows. What was going on? We never spoke of VN, but our haircuts made our GI status obvious. I think the girls felt sorry for us.

After the drinks, Sophie invited me to her bedroom and began a very seductive undressing. My god, she was hot. I started to help, and then she began to undress me.

We jumped in bed, and let nature take its course. She was very inventive and radiated mischievous high fun. Her sense of play was infectious, and her life force took over. To my surprise, I discovered I could feel alive again. I don't know how long this went on. I just know I didn't want it to end. She acted like she had known me forever, and in that moment I felt I could live forever. A part of me knew I could die any day after I returned to VN. But right then I didn't have to think about that.

We finally went to sleep or passed out. I don't really remember which.

The next morning, after a very sexy shower and sex, she checked on her roomies; one was in the next bedroom and then she called the two next door. They decided we would have breakfast in thirty minutes and then spend the day together being tourists.

We were taken to a museum, a shopping district so we could buy new shirts, and then Ocean Park which was part zoo.

An incredible lunch followed. Then, it was off to a bay tour on a Chinese Junk which stopped at some ancient Chinese Pagodas. These were intricate and beautiful.

I told Sophie, "They are almost as pretty as you.'"

She blushed and asked me for my address in VN.

I was startled but gave it to her. She asked me what I did in VN. I told her I flew helicopters, and she threw her arms around me and was crying.

She said, "We don't see any exciting men here, just students and professors. No one is adventurous or faces danger. You really impress me. I'm going to miss you when we have to go back to our lives. You just wait until tonight. I'm going to do things with you I've only read about. I want to feel alive, Kevin. We started last night. Let's not sleep at all tonight."

"OK, wow, you're amazing," I said. "You're beautiful and smart. You knew everything about the museum and the Pagodas." I didn't know what to say about being in bed with her. She'd already said it, and if I said it, it would sound gross.

And then it hit me what I was doing.

Shit Kev, what's going on? You just lost the love of your life. Are you doing this because you want to feel alive again? Steph had said, "You have to grab every moment because you can die anytime in this god-forsaken shithole." You don't know if you should feel guilty or lucky right now. You're probably feeling both.

Sophie startled me out of my thoughts. "Do you want to have a drink before dinner? I spoke to my friends, and we decided to eat separately tonight. They all said they were having a great time. The four of you are living like there's no tomorrow, and we find that so exciting. I understand, as much as someone can from the sidelines. You risk your life daily. I know it sounds sick, but I admire that. You are passionate about what you do there and also here with me."

We were looking into each other's eyes, and hers were glowing with pleasure and admiration. I was smitten.

"I'm going to take you to the most fabulous restaurant tonight," she said, smiling with pleasure at the idea. "We'll order Peking Duck. It's incredible. One half of the duck is cut into about 26 pieces, and it literally melts in your mouth. They stuff it with spices and seasoning and seal it and slow roast it on a rotisserie all day. I guarantee it will turn you on almost as much as me tonight."

I gave her a good laugh and said, "I really don't want to leave in two days. I could live here with you forever." *Kev, you're an asshole.*

Back home, I'd hunted ducks. My brothers and I had tried every conceivable way to cook them. Pressure cooker, crock pot, baked, broiled, or roasted: they always tasted like "flying liver." We tried stuffing them with everything: oranges, apples, onions and spices. We finally said, "Fuck it," and gave them to the neighbors. They loved us for it. We probably should have asked them for their recipe.

I was wondering how I was going to fake it tonight when I took my first bite of that duck.

Sophie said, "Kev, let's write to each other and learn more about each other. I really like you, and yet I've only known you one night and two days. I guess it's the same with you. I hope it's not just loneliness. You for your home and me for mine. I have no one at home. How about you?"

"I only write lies home to my parents and brothers."

Later, at the restaurant, I was bracing myself for my "duck ordeal." *I've landed a burning helicopter. I can do this.*

"Here comes the duck," Sophie said, her excitement overflowing.

The waiter put half of a very large duck in front of us on a platter and proceeded to cut it into pieces. We were served mashed potatoes, carrots, and bok choy. The bok choy tasted awful. The duck was truly to die for.

I'd never tasted anything so good. Sophie was watching me as I took my first bite. I smiled and said, "Incredible. Thank you for introducing me to most fantastic meal I've ever eaten. You are really a gem."

She was glowing.

"Sophie, I hope this isn't just a weekend. I don't know how someone can have these kinds of feelings after only two days, but damn you're incredible."

I'm sorry, Steph. I'm clinging to life. I promise I will never forget you.

"Well Mac, so are you. Let's try to build on this relationship. I know you have time left in VN, and I have another year here. Do you think there's any chance for us, Mac.?"

"I don't know Sophie. I've extended for six months."

"Let's talk about it tonight. I really want to get to know you better. I think we might have something together. It's strange. We just picked each other out based on, I don't know what. You and I could have been with any of our three friends. It's really wild when you think about it."

"Let's go in the bar," I suggested, "and have a night cap and continue this very deep and serious talk."

"We've started with an instant attachment," Sophie pointed out, after we had settled in the bar. "My girlfriends and I have never done this before. I haven't been with a man in over two years. I'd given up on men when you walked into the restaurant and told us about your ferry boat ride and trying to clean your shoes afterwards. Not many guys would tell that story about themselves; too macho. Now tell me the truth about your mission in VN."

"I fly a helicopter gunship. I shoot North Vietnamese army troops during the day and half the night. My job is to protect Americans. In other words, I kill people without any remorse. I'm 22, and I'm protecting kids younger than me. The average age of a GI in VN is 19. Most of those kids have never felt love or seen much of the world. Their parents raise them to 18, and then the military drafts them. Thousands have already been killed, and for what? We aren't fighting this war to win. VN will probably end up like Korea. We fought there for nearly three years and then stopped and gave back all the land we conquered and split the country in half. We lost 46,000 kids there, and it was for nothing.

"I got bored at college after two years and had the urge to fly. I spent a year in flight school, and I've spent nearly another year in VN. After my six-month extension, I'll owe Uncle Sam a year and a half to pay them back for my training. Then, I'll go back to college, and it won't be my old major, math. I don't know right now what it will be.

"I've lost so many friends that I don't make friends anymore. Someone I know is killed, and they just replace him, and I continue flying. I've been shot down four times, chased through the jungle by enemy troops for 24 hours, wounded so many times I've lost count. I don't know how many kids have been killed flying with me. I have to put it all out of my mind. I'm the pilot, and the crew is my responsibility. I will carry their deaths for the rest of my life. I'm telling you this because I might not be a good choice for you. I have two more weeks and then home for thirty days and then return to hell. Remaining alive is not a sure thing."

Sophie looked stunned. I guess she wasn't expecting so much reality from me, a guy she'd met in a bar the day before. But she pulled herself together.

"God, Kev," she said, "my god, thank you so much for all your honesty. I really admire that. Let's go to bed and talk more."

"OK."

In the kitchen alcove of her apartment, she poured two glasses of wine and then said, "Follow me."

I did, and we turned from talking to touching. The slow kissing on the bed was a different universe. We sipped wine and kissed, and then sipped wine and kissed again. When the glasses were empty, we slowly undressed each other and continued the touch to include every part of our bodies.

We tried to last all night, but fatigue won out. We woke in each other's arms. Then, we talked about a possible future together and agreed to write.

After we eight had breakfast together, we did a fantastic day of sight-seeing. We guys ate our first sushi. After a hesitant first bite, it was like the Peking Duck. We laughed when someone said, "How are we going to eat C-rations after this?" Then, we explained what C-rations were, and all four girls scrunched up their faces in disgust.

Sophie and I caught ourselves looking into each other's eyes. Damn, I got the butterflies in my stomach.

All four girls got up to use the restroom. If guys did that, we'd be ruined.

I suggested we buy them dinner that night as it was our last night in heaven. All agreed, but we'd let them choose the restaurant.

When they returned, we told them our plan. They said *yes* with happy smiles. We decided to go to a movie, and then went to their rooms so we could "get ready for tonight." It was only 2:30. I knew what they wanted to do, and I was all for it.

Two glasses of wine and into Sophie's bedroom. We sat on the bed not knowing what to say, when she put down her glass and said, "Fuck it. Let's get into a more comfortable position to talk."

"My dentist never spoke to me like that back home."

She said, "This is my tough side. Not everyone is happy about females entering the dental profession, so we've had to toughen up to tolerate all the crap."

"You're spectacular and continue to surprise me," I told her. "Wow, how did I get so lucky 10,000 miles from home? With your determination and brains, you'll get anything you want. I'm amazed you might want me."

"I really like you, Kev. You're fun, funny, honest, caring, very lovable, and incredible in bed. I don't want this relationship to end."

"Life isn't any good unless you have someone to share it with," I said. "Someone to help you plan a future, have a family, enjoys each other's company, and try every day to keep the love alive."

I thought, *Love? It does feel like love, but it's happening so quickly, like with Steph. Should I pass up this chance? I lost one love, but I can't stop living my life.*

As we made love, we talked about our backgrounds. She was the youngest with two older brothers. She told me she was definitely the black sheep of the family because her parents and brothers disapproved of her going into a male profession. They also disapproved of her leaving the country for her schooling. Being three years in Hong Kong and going home only once had increased the rift between them. She felt very distant from her family. She said, 'My three friends were all I had, until I met you."

I filled her in on my family background, and then we decided to shower for dinner.

The restaurant was beautifully elegant and old, like a museum, and the food was out of this world. We tried to keep the conversation going, but everyone knew it was the last night, and then we'd all say goodbye in the morning.

Sophie and I didn't go to sleep that last night. It was sex, but it was more. We now knew some of each other's hopes and disappointments. We wanted to make each other feel that life could be good, that our touch could mean something really like love. We knew this was all happening too fast. But it felt real for both of us.

We showered at 6:00, so we would have time for an unhurried goodbye before the bus arrived. It was painful. Sophie was crying as were two of her girlfriends. My stomach was doing calisthenics. Our final kiss was soft and slow, which made letting go gut wrenching.

Chapter 73.

THE SUMMER OF '69

It was now August 1969. I had been in VN for almost a whole year.

I slept all the way to CL. Smitty was there with the jeep and asked, "How was the R & R."

"Incredible Smitty. It made coming back here painful."

I checked in with the CO, and he said, "Baldy tomorrow morning. We're very short of pilots. A firebird ship went down with all killed, as did a slick. Another slick went down, but the crew was rescued."

No drinking tonight, so I wrote a letter to Sophie. I told her how amazed I was at our serendipitous meeting. I told her I thought I could love her, and I wanted a chance to let our connection become more than just a fling; it really had felt so much deeper than that. I left the letter at our mailbox, which was in the bar, hoping I'd get a letter from her soon. Not sure if that was a reasonable hope.

We loaded our equipment and ourselves the next morning to hat up and get outta here; returning to the Hilton. *Oh joy.*

I asked Tyler and Ski, "How was R & R?"

They smiled, looked at each other and in unison said, "We have no brains, Mac. Those girls fucked our brains out."

I chuckled and told them, "Great, you two deserved it."

After we were in the air, I said, "I want to fly up the beach and show all of you what a slick pilot taught me when I was an FNG." I turned toward the beach and started flying very low right at the tide line on the beach. Out in front of me were at least fifty local villagers squatting to take a dump. The idea was that when they dropped their load, the tide would take it away. As I was approaching, you could see the look of fear as each one fell down in the deposit left by the guy next to him. They were falling like dominoes. This low-level PR from the USA continued for a 100 meters.

My crew was laughing so loud I could hear them without the IC. 9-9 called and said he was laughing so hard he was either going to wet his pants or crash.

"Well guys, you see how war turns you into a twisted fuck."

We rat raced all the way to Baldy. Our copilots were getting very good at staying in position. Vic, Bob Clearwater's copilot, and Gary, mine, made only one mistake each in forty-five minutes of playing /teaching.

The tired sorry-looking groups of Birds were very happy to see us. They were standing next to their ships, which they had moved out of the revetments so we could park ours, looking at their watches to let us know we were late. *Hell, it was only five minutes. Fussy fucks.*

The tired crews departed with all of them giving us the bird. It was a gesture of endearment. They really were a great bunch of guys.

Now we waited for the red phone to ring. We turned to reading our novels. We got tired of that and went outside to check our ships to help pass time. That took up a few hours. Then back to the Hilton.

It was night, 2100, before the red phone did finally ring and interrupt our boredom.

"Mac, LZ Center is being overrun. They're at the wire."

I called back Ski and said, "Throw in a few Flechettes. The NVA are out in the open."

A few minutes later, when we were up and flying, I called Center for a sit rep. The RTO said, "The bad guys are in the wire. Hundreds are running towards us from the north, the flattest ground to our wire."

I said, "Get your heads down and stay in your trenches. Our flare ship will be there a minute ahead of me. We'll come in shooting. See you in four minutes."

"Please make it three."

The flare ship had lit up the area, and as I rolled in, I could see literally hundreds of NVA running towards the wire. *Shit, they have to be on something.* The Flechettes stopped that charge. There were bodies all over the ground.

Gary was already doing great shooting at the wire. I went in to join him, when something opened up on me. *Oh fuck, they have a 51.*

I said, "51" and turned and fired three pair of rockets. A hell of a large secondary explosion blasted fifty feet in the air, and the 51 was dead. I had to turn sharply to avoid flying through the flames and debris.

"9-7 breaking right." The door gunners and mini guns were doing a great job. 9-9 fired a few rockets into the crowd near the wire. He was receiving considerable fire.

I put rockets on muzzle flashes, people, and near the trees 400 meters from the wire where the NVA were coming out. The flare ship put two more flares over the trees and lit up all of the open ground. It was turning into a turkey shoot. The NVA were totally disoriented and confused and running in all directions.

"Again Gary, as I've said before, 'Confusion is terrifying to an untrained person.'"

Now, I saw only a few errant muzzle flashes and heard a few pops as the rounds passed through my rotor wash.

Center had repositioned two of their 50s, so the enemy was taking fire from three of those monsters while retreating. Center called and asked us to pull back for a couple of minutes so they could drop mortars on those shits. They were far enough away that there was no danger of the mortars blowing up their own concertina wire.

I said, "Great and put some in those trees and walk them in 200 meters."

"Roger."

We circled south of Center while they dumped thirty to forty mortar shells all over those suicidal troops. I know they had to be on drugs to run across 400 meters (quarter of a mile) of open ground. The theory must have been to send out more troops than Center could shoot. It might have succeeded if we hadn't shown up or if that 51 gunner had got on target a little quicker; meaning, if he'd had me in his sights.

"Two more passes Center, then we're going to refuel and rearm in case those NVA want to continue this party later tonight. I don't see any movement down there now."

Baldy called and said, "We are being attacked by a large wave of troops."

"We're on our way. Be there in four minutes. Where are they attacking?"

"On the south side on the other side of the runway. We've put mortars on them and have two 50s working."

"We'll approach from the west, shoot and break over Baldy. Have your guys stop all firing when we come in on our gun run. We're two minutes out. Tell your guys on the 50s to get their heads down." *Shit I have only 10 rockets remaining.* "9-9, how many rockets do you have?"

He said, "Four and not much mini gun ammo."

I said, "Let's shoot single rockets. Is everyone ready?" I received numerous clicks over the radio.

"Baldy, stop all firing." He rogered, and I hoped everyone down there was onboard.

This looked exactly like Center. Start shooting at the wire and work your way away from Baldy and into the trees. The crew rained down hell on those bonsai shits. I turned the nose slightly, but not enough to affect the crew's shooting, and fired a single rocket into two different groups. That caused the charge to slow, and they turned their guns on me. My crew was shooting at every muzzle flash while I broke. Wing followed suit. I think I felt some hits, but no warning lights. The cannon was working just fine.

I had only eight remaining rockets, so I called Baldy. "Continue shooting, and we'll hold out to the west and see if they copy Center and try another charge."

The 50s were chewing up the few stragglers remaining that were trying to run back into the trees, lightly forested but no jungle. It was well lit as the arty was shooting their own flares with parachutes.

Shit, here they came again, stretched out in an even longer line. It looked to be 200 meters long. I put my rockets on single shot and told Baldy to cease fire, and I rolled in. I was shooting along the charging line which was looking very disordered. Some were running fast, but their speed varied down to a few standing motionless. As I broke, a sick thought flashed through my head: If we let a few get through the wire, they might burn down the Hilton. Now that WOULD help the war effort.

Suddenly, I was knocked back to reality by a mortar explosion fifty meters in front of me. I laid the ship over sixty degrees on the right side to get out of the area before another shell exploded. At the same time, I got on the radio to Baldy HQ and told them some son of a bitch was still shooting mortars, too close for comfort. "Find that jerk and inform him that it's the gunships' turn to shoot! I will be circling until you get that cowboy under control."

Actually, we were going to have to land soon. We were all short of ammo, and I had just gotten a yellow warning light for low fuel.

"9-9," I radioed, "Dump everything. My bird is thirsty."

"So's mine," was all he said.

Baldy, the Firebirds are out of everything, fuel and ammo. If you can get a few guys down to the Hilton and help us rearm and refuel, we can get back in the air pretty quick."

"Roger wilco 9-7. Sorry about the independent mortar operator."

"Great shootin' you guys," I said. "I'd go hunting with you any time. Gary, land this bird before we run out of gas. As you know, if we do run dry, it's the copilot's fault."

He said, "I know, Mac. God I love this job. Never had responsibility anywhere close to this back in the world."

With all the help, we were fueled and rearmed in fifteen minutes. I called Baldy on the red phone and asked how things were at Center and at our own perimeter.

"Fine everywhere, Mac. Get some sleep."

I said, "What's that?" That got a laugh out of the RTO.

The phone rang at 0600. They needed the guns to escort resupply ships into Center.

We scrambled out of Baldy, and I called Center. They said, "Heavy machine-gun fire coming out of the forest to the north. Same direction as last night. We've got arty and mortars on 'em. Every time a slick tries to land, they open up and the slick has to break away."

"OK, we're on it. Coming in from the east. How far in the trees are they located?"

"We estimate 200 meters."

"Turn off your arty and mortars. I'm beginning my run."

I punched several pair into the woods to see if I could piss any-one off. It worked. Up came some off-target tracers from two loca-tions, so I gave each a pair of rockets of good will from my office, and this started a fire at one location. I added, "Gary, you see how quick you have to make decisions when you're in this seat?"

He just nodded.

I called the slicks and said, "Are the first two ready?" (Center had two helo landing pads.)

As they did high overheads, I shot into the area again and spread out my rockets in case the bad guys were trying to retreat or relocate.

A few sporadic rounds got fired at the slicks, but I tried to stop that nonsense with my rockets. The slicks landed from the south, discharged their loads, and took off the way they had come in. That made for a long shot for the enemy, as they were on the other side of the small mountain called LZ Center. They tried, but their muzzle blasts made great targets for the gunships. Two additional flights of two slicks brought in more supplies: ammo, water, and food.

Back at Baldy, it was SOS (same old shit), or Double S, Double D (same shit, different day).

Basically, we just waited for the red phone so we could do our thing.

Ski said, "Come here Mac and see what those shits did to our new ship. Two holes in the tail boom with no internal damage, just through and through, and a hole in the belly that hit something hard because it would have come through the floor back in my area, but it didn't. I'll pull open an access panel and see what stopped that AK-47 bullet." Later, Ski told me it had struck a main beam support-ing the floor in the back.

The red phone rang, and everyone was out the door as I picked it up. The RTO spoke quickly, because he knew we got in the air fast. "No scramble Mac; sniffer mission in an hour." I stuck my head out the door and gave a slashing motion with my hand across my neck. The guys immediately stopped all activity to ready the ships for flight and began the process of putting the ships back to bed.

I received the info for the mission. Most of the guys lay down and read for an hour. I ran to the MASH unit to have my hands and hamstring checked. Fortunately, all were clean and no sign of infection.

A Huey landed by the gunships as I was leaving the MASH unit. I walked over to see Rattler 2-4, Tommy Bell, one of the pilots who had pulled out some downed pilots on a messy mission while I flew cover for him.

We shook hands and made some small talk as a truck drove up and stopped by Tommy's ship and began transferring the sniffing equipment.

"We're checking the area north of LZ Center where I spent last night and this morning," I said. "A lot of bad guys out there in bonsai charges to the wire. Turn your crew loose and tell them to shoot at any and everything. Stay alert. After last night, I'm going to be very trigger happy. If you see something off to the side, tell me because the sniffer won't pick it up. A few small fires when we left the area this morning. Most everything burnt last night."

"Thanks Mac. Here comes some yo-yo to give us our coordinates."

Fifteen minutes later, we were ready to take off for Center.

"Rock and roll guys." We bounced into the air.

We reached our starting point and a minute into the run drew some fire. The slick broke away, and I shot rockets; routine. Then we resumed the mission. On the next pass, I shot rockets into the area the slick would be flying over as it was right beside our last pass. No problem.

When we started a return pass, damned if they didn't shoot at us again. So more rockets, cannon and door gunners. I called 2-4 and said, "Why don't we try this new technique? I'll shoot, and then you fly by?"

"Sounds great and to add some excitement, my door gunners are going to randomly shoot even if there's no targets."

"I like that, mine are doing the same. I'm coming up to our last stopping point. Is everyone ready?"

9-9 and 2-4 said, "Ready."

"Here are the first rockets." I fired them at the same time I was talking. When they exploded, enemy tracers immediately came out of the trees, so the gunners in the sniffer ship started shooting, as did all my crew to include my rockets. We broke off the flight path and the slick circled away from the guns as I rolled in on that hot spot and walked rockets past that spot and out ahead of what would be our flight path. Shots were fired at me 100 meters off to the side of our intended flight path, so we targeted those guys.

Suddenly, my ship's nose turned twenty degrees right. "Shit, I said, "some lucky bastard just shot out my tail rotor." That tail rotor counteracts the main rotor's torque. As long as I had speed, the wind passing along the sides of the ship would keep it from spinning. The trick would be the landing. You have to add or reduce power and up and down on the collective to put friction on the runway to slow that forward speed. I broke off the mission and turned towards Baldy. I advised them of my situation and told them the sniffer ship and my wingman would wait for me to land first in case I lost control. I didn't want to bounce or crash into any other ships.

As I began flaring to slow my speed, the ship began to spin so my only choice was to close the throttle to stop the spinning and do a hovering autorotation. I was about twelve feet off the ground when I pulled my collective pitch up as far as it would go. This put a maximum amount of pitch (angle) in the blades, 25 degrees, so they would seize the most air possible and slow the descent. It wasn't my best landing, but I didn't break my new ship, and we all climbed out and walked away unharmed. There is a lot of truth in the saying: any landing you walk away from is a good landing. *YES.*

If I'd tried a running landing, the friction of the skids on the ground would have prevented the spin. But I could have caught a skid and flipped the ship over, and the blades and the ship would have been torn apart. With that could have come a fire, an explosion, or even the blades coming through the windshield.

Baldy had already called CL, and another lead gunship and Snake Doctor were on their way. A Chinook would be a half hour behind them. If Snake Doctor couldn't revive the ship, the Chinook could haul it to CL.

Fifty minutes later, the two Hueys landed. Out came Martin. He looked at my tail rotor and shook his head.

Martin said, "This brand new ship has to be taken back to CL by a Chinook." Lots of emphasis on the words, brand new ship.

"Hell Martin, it was a one in a million shot."

We called it "the golden BB," when a single bullet brings down a ship, as had just happened to me. There were three additional holes: two in the tail boom and one in the belly.

"Mac, you have no respect for Government property: you, for one, and your ships, for another."

"Do you want to grab some lunch? The food is better than CL."

"Sure thing, and we can avoid the sandblasting that everyone around that shit hook is about to receive."

"Wow," Martin said when he saw the cheeseburgers cooking on the large griddle. "They're going to be great. Look at all the grease and fat bubbling as they cook."

We heard the Chinook outside hooking up my ship.

"Oh Mac, I almost forgot," Martin said, "The CO asked me to give you this letter."

I took it. "Thanks." Then, I saw the return address. It said Rheem and Los Angeles. This was from Steph's parents. *I think I'm going to be sick.*

"Martin, I have to leave."

"The CO told me who it was from. He asked me to watch you when you got it. Damn Mac, I'm truly very sorry. Are you OK?"

I nodded and walked outside. I didn't want to open the envelope. Then I said, "What the hell. I know they're hurting too." I found a secluded spot and opened it.

"Dear Kevin: We feel as if we've known you forever. Steph was so detailed with her letter writing. You opened her eyes to see something other than books and opened her heart to love. Both were new and exciting. She felt so fortunate to have fallen in love in the most unlikely place on earth. You made her laugh. You taught her toughness. You caused her to cry every time you two were apart. She was so worried when you flew because you took chances, though calculated she said, but they were still chances.

"She told me things that I haven't told her father. She really opened up to me and that was a first. I felt closer to her than any time previous. She shared her most intimate thoughts and your most intimate moments. They made me feel young again, especially when she said things that reminded me of when her father and I couldn't keep our hands off each other.

"I spit out a mouth full of good wine when she told me the pussy brain story. I cried when she told me about the battle with the machine gun and you and Derek kept returning to check on her and the caring bath afterwards. She told me she had no remorse as she was helping Americans. I spit out wine again when she told me she had dick brain.

"She said you could go from a tender caring and loving person to a stone-cold killer. She had no problem with any of that. She felt as you do when you told her you were protecting American troops. She told me about the enemy she killed as a door gunner and sharks of all things, while in the pilot's seat. She said sex is the only thing more thrilling than flying and shooting. And you created all of those thrills.

"She learned from Derek about your missions and successes. She said you almost choked when she called Derek her godfather. The look on your face was priceless.

"Derek said you were the most competent soldier he has ever known or worked with, and that's quite a complement from a General about a Warrant Officer. He admires you and told us you brought Stephanie out of the shell she never knew she was in; hiding from herself. Even though her life ended much too early, she was able to live an exciting part of life and fall in love. She really felt loved by you.

"I'm going to stop now. I'm crying like a baby. I know you are crying as well. She told me you're a sensitive human being, so I know you are hurting as much as we are.

"I will write again soon. God I miss her.

"Love from the entire Rheem family."

Hell, I was going to have to return to the Hilton with these red teary eyes. Thank god for sun glasses.

And thank god for work. I did my next two missions with an intense focus, forcing every other thought out of my brain. There was a ROK insertion we had to do immediately. That took hours. Then something new for me. HQ wanted some areas of vegetation that had been killed by Agent Orange to be burned. The idea was to remove every trace of cover the enemy might use. We flew out with WP rockets and started a bunch of fires.

When we finished that, the fucking red phone rang once again and told me there were a couple hundred NVA coming across rice paddies north of Cacti heading south. Cacti is only eight to nine clicks west of Baldy, and they were two to three clicks north. "You are to contact GB Outlook 6."

"We'll be there in a few minutes."

Wow, the Green Berets were in trouble. Those guys were moving into combat. Previously, they had just been training locals to fight and inform on the enemy. Working especially with the Montagnards on the Laotian border. They hate the NVA.

"Outlook 6, this is Firebird 9-7 with a team of gunships two minutes out to your west; give me a sit rep."

"We're at the bottom of the hill Cacti sits on, about a half click from the wire on the north side. We are a team of eight and have two wounded. We can't get them up to Cacti without being overrun. The terrain is too steep to carry the wounded with any speed. The enemy is at least a company and are out in the open one click north."

"Not to worry. Give us thirty seconds, and we'll come in shooting. Keep your heads down and preferably behind a tree or a rock. We'll start shooting close and work north. Have you ever worked with guns before?"

"Hell yes. I hear you, and now I see you, and here's a pre-thank you."

"9-7 rolling in." *Shit, it looks like ants all over that open ground.* I punched my first pair 400 meters from the friendlies, then raised the nose slightly and fired two more, then two more. I turned slightly and shot at two groups: one north and one west, both completely in the open. Then, I received some enemy fire. Gary and the door gunners were all over those ants. I punched two pair at each group and broke, for my wingman to continue with his crew.

Clearwater, 9-9 called, as he was rolling in with all the crew shooting, "Taking fire." Tyler was helping by also shooting at 9-9's targets. The fire looked heavy, so I broke early and started shooting at a group behind a dike who were shooting at 9-9 on full auto. The dike was only two feet tall and offered no protection. Then, I switched my attention to the other group and said, "Break right, 9-9, and I'll get those bastards shooting at you."

"9-9 breaking right."

I fired, and they were history. Then, I got a fast-talking transmission from 9-9 that his crew chief and copilot had both been wounded on that last pass. "I'm headed to Baldy."

I said, "OK, We're going to dump our entire ordinance, and then we're behind you." I called Outlook 6 and asked, "How are you doing with those wounded?"

"We're at Cacti now. Wounded are doing OK. Great shootin' 9-7. We're watching you. Hell, I wouldn't want to be on the ground with those little shits."

I continued shooting everywhere, all across the open areas and to the north where they came from. I got a call from Cacti when I broke, and they asked me if I was finished.

"Yes, we've depleted our entire ordinance and are returning to Baldy to rearm and check on our wing-ship's crew."

"Roger 9-7 and thanks."

Baldy called and said that 9-9 had called CL with their report, and another crew chief and copilot were on the way.

I thanked them, and called 9-9. "How's everything?"

"We're OK, the wounds are not life threatening. I'm just now landing and an ambulance and medics are swarming all over my ship here at the Hilton. Our ship is OK. We're going to rearm and refuel at the revetments and wait for the replacements. Hell, the crew are comparing wounds."

I said, "Roger that. I'm landing at POL. See ya in a few."

We rearmed and then had to wait for the replacements. Nothing positive to do until the new guys got there. *This place is crazy. Someone is killed, someone is wounded; neither rhyme nor reason. Fuck, what a mess.*

I heard a Huey coming our way and hoped it was for us. I had called HQ earlier and asked how Cacti was doing. They said all was quiet out there. The two wounded were stable and could be evacuated out any time.

Fuck, I'm going to bed. I walked into the Hilton, and it didn't seem as shitty as usual. I fell asleep and didn't feel the least bit guilty.

I woke an hour later, and nothing was happening. 9-9 had briefed his new guys. Neil Bettencourt was going to be my copilot, and Vandercamp was promoted to wing copilot. All of this was out of necessity. The new crew chief was Joe Gibbs. His Pilot, Rivers 9-5, had gone home. Good for him.

Not a bad day. Everyone lived, our two birds and the two Green Berets. *We won today you sons of bitches.*

The next few days were relatively quiet. One daylight mission each day and no night missions. Then, a new gun crew flew up to relieve us. As we took off to my "rock and roll," I could taste that first cold beer back at the birdhouse.

We rat raced for thirty minutes, then moved west to fly down the beach. This place would make a great vacation spot if it weren't for two things: the war and the humidity.

After landing in CL, we followed all the military protocols for our beloved gunships, and then it was straight to our respective clubs to try to forget about the last week. It also helped wash the taste of dust and gunpowder out of our mouths.

I chugged the first beer and a shot of Crown Royal, then I hit the shower and scraped off six days of growth from my face. Clean clothes feel great and are taken for granted back in the world.

I wrote a letter of lies to send to my parents, took a nap, and wrote Sophie while I waited for lunch.

This place is just full of things to do. Yeah right. I'm thankful for booze.

Another nap after lunch and then I grabbed one of the nasty books off the shelves in the Birdhouse and proceeded to read and fantasize. This stimulated me to write Sophie again. This girl was really on my mind. She was so sensual, kind, and smart, and she seemed to really care for me.

At 1700, I walked to the mess hall with two other Birds and ate something I couldn't identify.

I was in a bad mood, so when I finished trying to eat, I thought, what the hell, and decided to ask the private who was scooping up the slop that he splattered on my tray a question. "What the hell's in that fucking pot?"

Without a moment's pause he said, "Water Buffalo shit, sir."

"That's great. I thought for a moment it might be something I couldn't eat!" Then, I just walked out. I was too tired to tell the kid that I was just fuckin' with him. I'm sure he'd heard all the complaints before.

I'm putting that in my manual. Don't bother complaining about the food to privates who have no choice about what they're serving.

Now it was time to drink myself into oblivion. Since things were slow in the AO, quite a few pilots had tomorrow off, so the place was busier than usual, which meant loud as hell. My head was throbbing a minute after I entered that den of perverts. *Well shit, look who's talking.* There were quite a few new faces. *Wow, as Marcus Aurelius said, "How quickly everything changes."*

I talked with both Birds and Rattlers. No tension tonight. Everyone was just glad to be alive.

Suddenly, someone rang the bell and the place was instantly quiet. The CO stepped forward and said, "Would Mr. McNally please come up here." I had no clue what was happening. I walked up trying to think of any reason I would be called up before this mob of future felons.

The CO said, "Mac, it gives me great pleasure to promote you to Chief Warrant Officer, W 2. Congratulations. Now go put $10 in the pot."

I walked over and put in my money and then walked back to the CO, so he could pin my new rank on the front of my collar. There was an instant roar and cheering as I heard them yelling, "Chief Mac," over and over. I grabbed a crown and chugged it. It didn't burn too much which meant I was half in the bag.

The revelry continued to include me. The CO walked up beside me and asked if there was room for one more at the famous 71st bar.

I said, "Of course sir." *I mean, after all, what else could you say to the boss?*

"Mac, I could order you to do this, but I want you to feel comfortable with it."

"Sir, you have piqued my interest."

"Would you consider flying a mission with me as your copilot?"

Without a pause I said, "Certainly, sir, my pleasure. You might consider flying out of CL so you are not subjected to the condemned Firebird Hilton. There is one slick pilot who slept in his ship when he had flare duty."

"I looked in there the other day when I flew to Baldy with Martin. It is a cesspool. The place was worse than the rumors. I've talked to Malko about getting new mattresses and pillows. My clerk said he would put them on a couple of slicks so they could mysteriously arrive. I haven't told anyone. I thought the guys could use the surprise."

"Thank you, sir. The only reason I sleep there is because I'm too tired to think about it. Sir, why don't you use some of that CO power you have worked so hard to attain and requisition a lead gunship? Then, we could do some training at Target Practice Island before we go on that mission into tiger country."

"Excellent idea, Mr. McNally. I'll get right on that. Meet me at my office at 0900. It's your day off, so I'll let you sleep in."

"Yes sir. Are you still thirsty?"

"I shouldn't, but what the hell? It's only 2030 (twenty thirty or 8:30 pm civilian time) and tomorrow isn't really a mission."

I paid our bill out of the pot, and we sipped our beer at a lonely table in a corner away from the crowd. "Sir, how difficult was it for you as a pilot to trade off flying time for desk time?"

"At first Mac, it was tougher than I thought it would be, but I knew I'd have to sacrifice one for the other. I love the military, so I made my choice."

The CO philosophized a bit about the cost of wars in terms of young lives lost and the price of freedom. I was content to listen. He wasn't happy about so many men dying with nothing significant being accomplished. He mentioned Korea. He was clearly referring also to VN, although he wouldn't come out and say that explicitly.

Suddenly, he caught himself and stopped.

"Well Mac, that's enough of that. I'd love to continue the drinking and the talking, but I have other duties. See ya' in the morning. Good night."

"Good night, sir."

Things were the usual back at the Birdhouse, a bunch of loud and rowdy drunks. Even though I was flying out to the Island with the CO the next day, technically tomorrow was a day off, so fuck it. I walked into the party room and yelled, "Shut up. I'm trying to sleep." Their answer was to increase the volume of the debauchery. So I said, "What are we drinking tonight?" I regretted it as soon as I opened my mouth, because I was given a purple motherfucker and was expected to chug it.

I obliged and, besides tasting like water buffalo piss, it burned all the way down. So in true Firebird tradition I said, "Gimmy another.

I want to wash out that foul taste from that first drink you handed me." Well, that drew a big laugh as the second drink was the same as the first. From there, it went downhill fast. We increased the volume on the tape recorder and started dancing. *War can really fuck you up, mentally as well as physically.* There are not many ways to unwind here. I met two new wing pilots, but I didn't bother trying to remember their names. I'd be going home in two weeks.

I thought I had had enough booze in me to sleep through the noise, so I went to bed. I didn't bother undressing. I lay there and thought of Steph and did eventually get to sleep.

Then, it was morning with the sun full in my face. It was 0700, so I had plenty of time to make myself presentable.

The CO and I took off for Target Practice Island at 0930. The CO did a three bounce TO. After the last bounce to get him in the air, he said, "Shit Mac, are all the TO like this?"

"Sir, the answer is 'sometimes yes, sometimes no,' meaning: wind in your face on a cool day is great, only one bounce. On a very hot day with high density air, you just slide along until you have some speed, and then you try slowly to pull the collective up, and then you get a few bounces. You have to have some speed when you're 1500 pounds over gross, as you are today. Nice TO, sir."

"1500 pounds overweight?" He said with incredulity in his voice.

"Yes sir, it's called the maximum firepower theory. If you shoot more and bigger ammo than they do, then you have a better chance of winning. We choose to carry more ammo; hence, the overloaded condition. Holds true for everything except those fucking 51 calibers. Then, you have to be fast and careful. We call them helicopter killers."

He had a good touch on the controls. I explained some of the weapon control switches. As we got near the Island, I said, "Set the controls so you have single rockets, so you can make twice the rocket runs."

He set the switches with a little help, and we rolled in. I watched as he fired at a dead truck. The first was short and the second was long. I said, "Sir, be gentle when you push the rocket button. Like you're holding a baby. Have you ever held one?"

We rolled in a half a dozen times, and he was getting the idea and settled down. I wondered what he'd do when the tracers were coming up at him. Some people couldn't ignore the danger and focus on shooting. I had him try the 40 mm cannon. He loved that. He could walk the rounds right into the target and was able to shift his fire to other areas as I created other situations for him to fire on. I said, "Over to your left in that truck, there are NVA shooting at us." He responded quite well. I then started calling out targets on the right, then the left, then straight out in front close in, then far out. I was jumping all over the board, and he calmly hit the targets.

I said, "We still have some rockets sitting in the pods."

"Let's get rid of them so this bird will be easier for me to land."

I was laughing when I replied, "You'd make a great Firebird; thinking ahead."

I called the target, and he walked in the rockets, requiring two or three additional shots before he hit it.

I said, "Let's get on that nose cannon as you will be firing that tomorrow. You have 450 rounds remaining so you can shoot quite a few on each gun run."

"Got it Mac. I'll kill every Bastard down there. Now I know how you feel. If I don't see 'em, point 'em out."

I liked this guy. He had what it took to do this dangerous and shitty job. We continued these cannon runs, and he was shooting the targets as fast as I could point them out. He was good. I asked him if he had ever flown in the guns.

He said, "Yes, a couple of times, but I didn't get the training you gave me today. I'll be much better prepared when we go out for real. Bring 'em on. Fuck those bastards. Just point your nose in the direction you want me to shoot."

"Damn sir, you talk like a Firebird. You're shooting like one, and I love your attitude. Actually sir, I won't always have my nose facing your targets. My nose will be facing my targets for the rockets. Your cannon swivels wherever you are looking. But you know that. Look for targets in the open, tracers and muzzle flashes. Then kill 'em." This continued for another hour. The CO was dripping wet, and I hadn't touched the controls. This will be good for him in case I get hit.

The CO flew us back to CL. As he was approaching the ground, the tower operator asked, "How'd it go out there?"

I thought this was a great chance to repeat what I'd said about

TOP. I said, "Tower, he got a dozen gophers, some dead palms, a naval vessel, and a hard on."

The tower operator and the CO were laughing almost to the point of not being understandable on the radio.

After we landed, I looked over and said, "You're excellent, sir, both flying and shooting. Now, sir, your day here is done. Ski and Tyler are coming down to help me rearm. As both a Major and a CO, you are exempt from rearming on training days. When the shit hits the fan, you'll be working for Tyler when we're on the ground, and I'll work for Ski."

"Thanks Mac, that was a great lesson. Enjoy your day off tomorrow. Maybe I can hunt you down for another run to TPI."

"Just call and we'll take Ski and Tyler along, so you can get a taste of those 60s behind your head. They're loud, and you'll feel like your head is going to blow up after they deafen you."

Prior to landing, I had asked the tower to call the 71st and ask Ski and Tyler to come down to the flight line. As we were rearming, I told them about tomorrow. "If the CO is busy, we'll just take a new Firebird out to TPI."

Ski asked, "How'd the CO do out there?"

"Pretty damn good; smooth, calm, and good with the weapons. The day after tomorrow, we'll really see how calm he is with tracers coming at him. What are you two doing after we rearm this Hog?"

Almost in unison they said, "Get drunk. Is there anything else to do in this hell hole?"

"Are you two drinking that swill in your club or do you want me to bring over some good shit? Do you like scotch?"

"Does it have alcohol in it?"

"Hell yes. You don't think I'd bring Kool Aid like you two pussies drank in high school?"

"Bring it over Mac, and we'll decide."

"I want to check my mail box first."

I walked over to the bar where our mail boxes were located and was surprised to see a letter from Sophie. I found a private spot on the beach and opened it.

"Dear Mac, I just received word that my mom and one of my brothers were killed in a car wreck on the autobahn. I don't know why they were in Germany. I'm in shock, Mac. I know everyone back home was against in my choice of profession, but it doesn't mean I don't love them. I'm flying out this afternoon for England. I will contact you later. Love, Sophie"

I felt a rush of different feelings. Sophie had written me and signed the letter "Love"; that made me feel a surge of that hope for the future I'd felt when we were together. But Sophie's mother and brother were killed; that was horrible. Sudden death was common here and we were supposed to just shrug it off, but out in the world—I was numb from war but I could still feel it—deaths like that were major tragedies. How was she going to get past it? I would write her. But would her Hong Kong address still work? And, really, what could I say? I'd write her... later, but for now... I had more immediate things to think about.

I went to the birdhouse to find that bottle of Scotch. I walked over to Ski and Tyler's hooch. I tried to put on a straight face, so they wouldn't guess I'd just received upsetting news.

"This will be a new experience for you," I told them. "You have to sip it and enjoy the flavor. It's potent, but you get the buzz without feeling so full and bloated and having to piss every ten minutes after the third beer."

"OK, Mac, we're game."

I handed the bottle to them and said, "Don't spill a drop or I'll shoot you."

"It's that good?" They opened it up, and I handed each a tin cup. I finagled these from Malko in supply. "Just pour in a half an inch and take a small sip. It might burn a little, so just hold it in your mouth and breathe in through your mouth and savor the flavor." I poured some in my cup and raised it up and said, "Here's to living another day." We touched cups and sipped.

Tyler replied, "It's stronger than what we're used to, but I'll bet I like it before the night is over."

Ski said, "No shit. Mac, where did you get this?"

"The last slick run to Danang picked up a few bottles for us. Keep this between the three of us. My hooch paid for this nectar of the gods."

We sipped for an hour and tried to talk about anything except the war. We ended up on the topic of what we'd do back in the world. Tyler talked about farming. Ski said he wanted to be an airline mechanic. I said I'd probably go back to college.

"Guys, we should wrap this up. The CO could call us at 0700 or 0800, and we'll be hurtin' big time if we finish this bottle."

"You're right," they agreed, "but we like this stuff."

"Take the bottle. Hide it in a safe spot, and we'll finish it next time."

We said, "Goodnight," and I returned to my hooch.

In spite of everything, I was asleep before my head touched the pillow. I woke up at 0800. *Shit, this is a gentleman's war.* I staggered into the mess hall and choked down something with ketchup. I didn't ask what it was. I thought it might piss off the cook. I didn't want him to spit in the spoon he used to sling the slop on my tray. BOHICA (Bend Over Here It Comes Again).

I cleaned up and stopped by HQ to see when the CO wanted to go blow up dead things. Top told me, "Come back at 1000 hours, and he'll be ready."

I had an hour. I could write to Sophie. But what? I just couldn't think. I told myself I should wait for her to send me her new address. A stupid excuse, but it gave me a way to put it off for another day.

At 0950, I went to find the CO. He had his personal jeep and drove us to the flight line. I could see Ski and Tyler had everything ready because they were sitting on the cargo deck hanging their feet outside. They jumped up as they saw us approach and walked toward the jeep.

They asked the CO if they could carry any of his gear. He said. "No thank you. I only have a helmet and a chicken board."

Ski and Tyler said the ship was ready, so I strapped it on and told the CO to do the same. I explained the "strap on" technique versus the "strap in" method, and he liked it.

I said, "It's your ship sir. Let's go to TPI."

He said, "Roger that."

I said "You're in the right seat today. That makes you the AC, and you use a real rocket sight, not a circle on your windshield. You will also shoot the cannon through the same sight."

He flew to the Island, and I made it a point to not touch the controls during the entire mission.

I said, "Pick a target sir and blow the shit out of it."

He called the target and made his gun run. He was short the first two and over compensated on the next two. Then he broke, and he looked at me, and I just nodded. We came in again, and he walked three rockets into the target with the third one a bull's eye.

He yelled, "All right."

"A couple more runs, sir, and let's switch to the cannon. That's your baby tomorrow, all 500 rounds."

We killed the dead palms, dead trees, a dead truck, and some big rocks as well. The CO was learning to deal with descending and watching the rotor and engine rpm. He was climbing out after a run and cautious not to overtorque the engine. He was monitoring the trim (keeping his nose on the targets).

Ski and Tyler were killing everything he killed. They were having fun, probably because no one was trying to kill them. This went on for more than an hour. I still hadn't touched the controls. He changed the armament system from cannon to rockets and to single rockets. This continued for another hour. Then we flew back to CL.

After he landed and hovered into the revetment I looked over and said, "Outstanding sir. I'm feeling good about tomorrow. I've an excellent pilot and gunner sitting next to me. Now sir, today your day is done. Remember, tomorrow, when on the ground, you work for Tyler, the gentleman behind me. I say gentleman only because it sounds nice. Actually, he's a murdering heathen, but I trust him with my life. He also is a friend, as is Ski, sitting behind you, sir."

Tyler said, "What's that 'murdering heathen' about?"

"Don't worry. I would never tell your mother."

The CO said, "Thanks men. See you at the briefing at 0600 in the mess hall."

"Well, Firebirds, let's rearm this beast. I'll call for fuel and then help."

"Make it a quick call," Ski said. "We want you to help with some of it."

"Hey guys, come on, I always help. Remember, even before I was a Bird."

We finished in twenty minutes, then checked all systems and pronounced the ship ready to rock and roll.

Ski and Tyler approached me and said, "How about a sip of the officer shit? That bottle of scotch is still hidden in our hooch."

"OK, but I'm beat, and tomorrow's CA is going to be very hot."

I really was worried about that CA. I hoped they'd prepped it with arty. Shit, the area was large enough to contain four companies of NVA, and that added up to 800 troops. There'd be 51s, mortars, RPGs and a lot of AK-47s.

When we arrived in the Company area, Ski said "I'll get that officer shit we enjoy so much."

No one spoke while we each took two small sips and called it a night. Everyone was thinking about tomorrow.

I slept poorly. Tomorrow's mission just didn't feel right. *Fuck it. I have seven days remaining before I go home for thirty days. I'll probably just sit around, thinking about Steph and wondering about Sophie. At least here I'm so busy flying, I don't have much time to think or wonder about anything.*

Chapter 74.

IT'S NOT ME MAC

We met in the mess hall at 0600 and received the briefing. There would be twenty slicks and my gun team. Our LZ was Cacti, and the base of the mountain that Cacti sits on, and north of that as far as we found the enemy. There would be two insertions of 140 grunts each time. Then, it would be the usual resupply for the rest of the day.

"Cacti have sent out several patrols, and they've reported extensive activity, so it's expected to be hot," the CO told us. "There will be an artillery barrage prior. The troops will be inserted as the smoke clears. Firebirds in first in case the arty missed anything."

We all received our freqs, coords and call sign Bad Boy 6. *That's interesting. I hope it's true.*

"OK Birds," I said, "strap on those gunships. We're going hunting. See you Rattlers at Baldy."

I called my wing, Clearwater (9-9), and said, "Those poor bastards in the 198th are going into the shit again. They just did this in that narrow valley a few days ago." *Damn, I'm glad I went to flight school.*

I looked over to the CO and said, "It's all yours, sir."

The CO landed and refueled at the turnaround, and then we went in the Hilton for a nap. I saw the new sheets and mattresses. I looked at the CO and mouthed a "thank you." The nap was short as twenty Hueys landing can create a lot of noise, not to mention a lot of dust. And here came the big trucks with the first group of grunts. We'd be back for the second insertion a few minutes after we took off as the LZ was only four and a half miles away.

One of the truck drivers said, "They are shelling the LZ. When they stop, you all TO. Good luck."

"That's encouraging," I commented to my people. "Between the arty and us no one near the LZ is going home to North Vietnam alive. Got that!"

Back came the click clicks.

We were off and now in battle mode. The slicks were on our tail, so we rolled in and started shooting. Back came an incredible amount of enemy fire. *Shit, where are those bastards hiding?* Even down in tunnels the concussion of exploding artillery shells can kill. They've found NVA dead in those tunnels with blood coming out of every orifice in their heads.

I began shooting out in front and just walked the rockets across the front end of the LZ and over to the other side, then I had to break. I was getting closer than I should to the ground. Some of the intensity lessened. I watched 9-9 do the same thing.

"9-9, let's make another run before our guys are dropped into that killing field." As we rolled in, I called the lead Rattler and said, "There's now only sporadic enemy fire." We were all on the same frequency, so he had been following our gun runs.

"OK, 9-7, here we come, and everyone shoot."

I started shooting just prior to the three Rattlers flaring to land and the grunts jumping out. I shot at the far end of the LZ. That was the only way for the flights to TO after disgorging their troops because there were eight additional flights coming in right on each other's tails.

The wing ship and I kept up our race-track pattern but shooting much less on each run as we had to cover all the flights. I called Baldy and asked them to send some extra people to our revetments to help us rearm. "We have to get back out with the second lift."

All the ships proceeded to Baldy after leaving the LZ. As the grunts were climbing into the Hueys, the door gunners were grabbing more ammo. A half-dozen guys were waiting to help the guns rearm. As they were loading rockets with guidance from the door gunners, the rest of us assisted with loading the mini guns and the cannon.

Our eyes were burning from sweat, and the sticky air smelled like shit. I was watching the slicks loading the grunts and saw that we were going to have to return with less than our full capacity of ammo. We had to get this second group of 140 into the fight ASAP to reinforce those kids in that LZ. I yelled, "Wrap it guys. We've got to get out of here."

The mini guns had about 8000 rounds and the cannon about 350. We did have a full complement of rockets.

One slick had to shut down with red warning lights right after taking off. His seven grunts each jumped into the back-up ship. *Shit, a slick just called. He's returning to Baldy because his exhaust is spewing smoke.*

The lead slick called out for everyone to close up the formation and fill in the gaps.

I called the lead Rattler and said, "Guns are rolling in." Tracers were flying both ways in the LZ which made it easy to locate muzzle flashes, and all four of us picked our targets at the jungle's border with the LZ. They must have reinforced the NVA as we were receiving more fire than on our last run.

A Huey blew up in the second flight of three. *Goddammit, a ship in the third flight can't take off.* Its engine had been damaged by enemy fire. The crew jumped out and ran to a ship in the next flight and jumped in after the troops jumped out. I take all of this personally. My job is to protect these ships and troops.

How the hell had we been so lucky in the first insertion? War is insane. All the slicks were shooting, and the guns were shooting, and we were making little headway.

Another call: the sixth flight just lost a crew chief and copilot. Other slicks were calling Baldy with wounded crew. This was becoming another SNAFU. My copilot (the CO) yelled, "Something just hit my shoulder."

"Can you still shoot?"

"Fuckin' A Mac."

"Guns, dump everything on this run. Sir, are you OK?"

He replied in a shaky voice, "Yes."

The grunts were calling for evac of wounded.

We were rearming and refueling as fast as possible.

The Major's shoulder didn't look serious, and he showed his true Firebird attitude. "Mac, I'm fine. Let's go kill that fucker who just shot me."

Baldy loaded three slicks to the ceiling with ammo. After

dumping it, they would become the Medivac ships. I noticed two holes in my windshield and two in the chin bubble. A radio was smoking, and I had two yellow lights.

Off we went, and my instrument panel was a priority on my list of problems to be aware of and check frequently.

I rolled in to protect the rattler going in for wounded. I shot at anything and everything on the ground and told everyone in the ship to do the same.

The NVA were more concerned about our rockets than the slick flaring to land, so I said, "Guns, keep shooting while they load that slick." Wing was firing before I broke off my run. I had to turn quicker than usual to cover him.

The slick called, "We're loaded and pulling pitch."

"OK Rattler, we've got you covered. Get out of there and stay low as long as you can."

There was a lot of traffic on the radios about slicks to haul out additional wounded after they dumped their cargo. The grunts were in desperate need of more ammo. We returned to Baldy for fuel and ammo as well.

We loaded some rockets in both gunships and took off after the slicks loaded and pulled pitch. Again, we didn't have enough time to rearm completely. I asked the slicks to slow down so we Birds could go in first and soften the area. They agreed and circled while we made a gun run on those fuckers.

They were still shooting at us, but it was minimal, which I appreciated.

"OK Rattlers, go in. Stay tight and don't stop shooting."

I was shooting before I called them. I shot at new muzzle flashes and at old ones I remembered from my last run 20 minutes before. They were shooting at me, but it was lackluster. I broke, and wing said, "the enemy wasn't shooting with any enthusiasm." I grinned at that comment.

I glanced at the CO, and he was fully engaged.

"OK Birds. Two more runs. We shoot everything 'till we're empty."

Just then, one of the three slicks called Mayday. He had just lost his engine and was auto rotating into a wet rice paddy. One of the other two ships said he was following to rescue the crew. He then said, "Firebirds, it's a 51. It's 200 meters from the LZ. They must have just set it up; it wasn't operating before."

"I see the smoke from the ship's engine. Land so you put the downed ship between you and that 51."

"Firebirds rolling in." I started shooting, as did my crew, when suddenly my chin bubble exploded in a million pieces.

I looked at the CO, and he was covered in blood and what looked like pieces of raw meat on his chicken board, right arm, and faceplate. The first thing out of my mouth was, "SHIT. Sir, can you hear me?"

He grabbed the controls and said, "It's not me, Mac. It's you."

I looked down at the floor and saw a piece of muscle hanging out my torn pant leg and attached to the lower half of my shin bone to my boot lying on the floor. I felt nothing and reached down and picked up the piece of leg and stood it upright on the floor. That was when I noticed the blood was coming out of the leg like it was being pumped. I knew that was from an artery. Strange that there was no pain.

I told Ski, "I needed a tourniquet." He laid down his gun and grabbed the back of my seat to pull him up to look over my shoulder and in a loud voice said, "FUCK." He pulled off his belt and handed it to me.

I wrapped it tightly on my thigh and was pulling as tight as possible to slow the blood flow when what turned out to be an AK-47 bullet struck the inside of my left elbow. I lightly put my right hand on the cyclic and gently keyed the transmit trigger switch. "Baldy, 9-7 is coming in. I've been hit."

Then, the CO cut in and said he was landing at the MASH unit.

Ski and Tyler released the back of my seat. This release is designed so you can pull a wounded or dead pilot away from the controls and/or offer aid. Tyler shoved an extra machine gun barrel under the belt and twisted until the blood flow was seriously reduced. They couldn't pull me out of my seat and into their area as the leg was barely attached.

I still didn't feel anything, but I knew it was bad. Thankfully, my body was in shock. I noticed my collective pitch lever and throttle were seriously damaged. I was feeling light headed as we were landing at Baldy. I noticed the overhead circuit breakers for the weapon systems had not been pulled. This a safety measure to ensure no rockets or the cannon could fire. I pulled all the breakers.

When we landed, the medics ran towards me with a stretcher. They looked in and saw my leg. I could see from their expressions that I was in deep shit. As they were trying to lift me out of my seat and lift the damaged lower leg over the cyclic, it struck the tip of the cyclic, and I felt intense pain.

I was placed on a table, and people were all over me with scissors cutting off my clothes down to my undershorts. The doc asked me if I felt pain.

I said, "Only when they were pulling me out of the ship."

I knew the doc from previous visits. He said, "Mac, I'm going to give you a shot of morphine so we can get ahead of the pain." I didn't even feel the shot. At least, it wasn't that syrup in the butt routine.

Shock does crazy things to your head as well as your body. I tried to sit up and stop the medic from cutting off my boots. I wanted to keep those boots because they had steel plates in the sole to prevent the grunts from stepping on punji sticks. I thought they would make great hunting boots.

The doc looked at me and in a very stern voice said, "Lie down or I'll put you out." *Another shot.*

Now the stretcher was picked up, and I was taken outside and placed in the medivac ship for a ride to the large hospital in Danang. When we landed, the stretcher and I were placed on a gurney as someone was pouring betadine on my leg while he was explaining what he was doing. All this time, they were running and pushing the gurney. Then they put me out.

I woke up after surgery and felt the worse pain I could ever have imagined. I lifted my head slightly and saw two feet under the sheet. That actually surprised me. I thought for sure that leg would not be there.

As I looked up a little higher, I saw Ski and Tyler at the foot of the bed and Firebirds on both sides along with the CO. I tried to smile. Even that made the leg hurt more.

One of the Birds said, "The doc said you got to keep the leg because you were on the operating table in surgery only nineteen minutes after you got hit. The nurses said we had to make this visit short. You're in recovery now, and they have to get you back to your isolation room.

I looked at the CO. "I'm glad I was flying with you sir. Because of you, I'm keeping my leg." I added, "Sorry, sir, for splattering it all over you."

"Don't even think about that, Mac. It all washes off. You just worry about getting better."

After we all said our goodbyes, the Birds and the CO departed.

Then the doctor came back in. He gave my chart a quick glance, and he then turned to look me in the eye. "Well Mac," he said. "It looks like you're going home."

AUTHOR'S NOTES

Mac's story is fiction, but it is based on my experiences and fellow pilots in Vietnam. 304,000 Vietnam veterans were seriously injured in combat but survived to have civilian lives in the decades following, like me, and (we may imagine) like Mac. I've managed to stay in touch with some of the people I met during the war. Others, most others, have gone on into their own futures. We've followed Mac on his journey as a soldier, but as he enters civilian life, we can let him go. He should be allowed to have his life after the war without us looking over his shoulder.

Mac's story reflects what life was like for an individual soldier in Vietnam. This novel was meant to entertain and to divert you but also to remind you how war is lived day by day. We civilians should remember that, whatever else we do.

2,709,918 American men served in uniform in Vietnam, and 58,148 were killed. Of those killed, 61% were younger than 21 years old. These facts, and all the other facts about the war, remain to be considered and debated by historians and others over the coming decades and centuries. We will let that "big picture" go, too. Except . . .

I can't resist adding one "big picture" note on "battle fatigue" and PTSD that I've been mulling over for the last forty years. The men and women who come home from war are forever changed — the trauma of the war continues in the minds of the participants, even those who escaped physical injury. This fact has been noted since the earliest times:

Source	Date	Damage
Homer's Iliad & Odyssey	8th Century BC	After lengthy battles, soldiers would appear blind and deaf
Shakespeare	15th century	A doctor cannot treat a mind diseased by the "memory of a rooted sorrow" (from Shakespeare's *Macbeth*)
Napoleonic Wars	17th century	Home sickness
American Civil War	19th century	Soldiers heart (later called battle fatigue)
World War I	1914-18	Shell shock
World War II	1939-45	Battle fatigue
Korean War	1950-53	Operational Exhaustion or Situational Disorder
Vietnam War	1955-1975	Post Traumatic Stress Disorder (named in the 1980's)
Desert storm, Desert Shield,	1990-present and current wars	

Complex post-traumatic stress disorder: acute and chronic (cptsd). Beginning in the 1990's, treatment paradigms for PTSD began to include an approach to treatment called "PTSD growth" or "growth after trauma." Sufferers from trauma, as in a soldier's PTSD, can free themselves from their destructive visceral reactivity. They will always remember the traumatic events, but with healing, they are no longer prisoners to the reactivity and can move on with their lives.

FINAL THOUGHTS

There are not many of us Vietnam veterans remaining, but we still exchange emails, even manage a few reunions. We honor our dead whenever we get together, whether they died in Vietnam or later. We are still a unit. We were called "Gods own Lunatics" not because we were lunatics but because it seemed to one newspaper reporter than only crazy men would risk what we had to risk. But we didn't feel we had any choice. It was our first helicopter war, and we were learning as went along. Our troops were depending on us. We did what we had to do.

As we Firebirds still say: *All gave some, some gave all.*

Kelly McHugh, January 20, 2021

GLOSSARY

A
ALPHA

AC	Aircraft Commander. Pilot In charge of the aircraft
Agent Orange	Vegetation killer sprayed on the jungle to kill everything and later burned to eliminate areas of concealment for the enemy
AK-47	Russian made automatic rifle. Used by the NVA. Very dependable
Ammo	The ordinance we fire from our helo: cannon, rockets and machine guns
AMMO	Acronym for Attention, Mission, Motivation and Objective
Ammo dump	Storage for all our fire power
AO	Area of operation. Our area of our responsibility
APC	All purpose capsule: aspirin
Arc light	B-52 air strike. The area bombed looked like the glow on hot metal from a welders torch.
Areca	Fruit from a palm that produces betel nut, a narcotic chewed by the Vietnamese. Causes lips, gums, and tongue to turn coal black. Keeps you in a buzz all day.
ARTY	Artillery or large cannons able to shoot up to twenty miles
ARVN	Army of the Republic of Vietnam (South

Vietnamese army)

At Ease	Military term to stand with your feet apart and your hands behind your back with the back of one hand in the palm of the other. A more relaxed pose from the rigid position of attention
Auto Rotate	Landing a helo without an engine. As you free fall you reduce all the pitch in the collective and the air passing through the rotor blades keeps the blades spinning at operational rpm. As you near the ground you pull the cyclic back and slow your forward speed and then pull up the collective pitch lever and it grabs the air and slows you to a landing.
AWOL	Absent without leave; usually a deserter
Avionics	Refers to our radios

B

BRAVO

Bazooka	A short-range tubular rocket launcher. Originally designed as an anti-tank weapon. It packs a lot of explosive power.
Baldy	Fire Support Base where the Firebirds would live so as to quickly support all the troops in the field and/or the other Fire Support bases in our AO
Barrage Artillery	Shooting enough rounds to saturate an area up to several thousand yards long and the width to be determined. These rounds fall only 30 meters apart.
Bee-hive Round	Artillery shell with pellets like a shotgun shell
Bees	Short for King Bees, the South Vietnamese Air Force
Betel Nut	Name of the narcotic from the Areca nut. Keeps the locals in a constant state of Buzz
BFD	Big Fucking Deal
Big Three	Food, water and ammo

Binocs/Binos	Short for binoculars
Birdhouse	Nickname for the Firebirds hooch in Chu Lai.
Blood Chit	Created by George Washington. A piece of paper signed by him to allow his spies to cross out of our front lines and into the British lines. Also allowed our spies to pass back across our lines. In VN, it was a piece of silk 12 by 12 inches you carried in your wallet stating you were an American and saying so in fifteen languages with an American flag. You were supposed to show this to a farmer and hope he was not a Vietcong. It says the U S will reward you, but how many VN farmers could read?
Body Bag	How most deceased American soldiers are removed from the battle field
BOHICA	Bend over; here it comes again.
Brass	Officers, Majors to Generals
Breaking	This word along with left or right is transmitted by a gun pilot to inform the other ship in the team that he is turning away from the target and to put rockets under and slightly behind him.
Brigade	1500 to 3500 troops
Bullet Magnet	Humorous term given to a pilot who has received many hits to his ship
Bush	Wild untamed jungle and usually enemy territory

C

CHARLIE	
Charlie	The enemy. "Charlie" began as "Victor Charlie" for Viet Cong and later shortened to Charlie.
CA	Combat assault. A number of Huey Slicks usually escorted in to a landing zone by Gunships to deposit ground troops to attack enemy forces
C & C	Command and Control. Name of the Huey flying high over a Combat Assault Landing Zone to help direct the mission on the ground

Caliber	Size of a bullet. For example, M-16 is 5.56 mm and a 50 caliber is 12.7mm
Call Sign	Name and a number given to the leaders in the field and pilots of a Huey
Chi Com	Nickname for weapons produced by Russia and China. Chinese Communists
Chinook	Name of the large tandem rotor Helicopter used by the Army. All Army helos are named after Indian tribes, except one: the Cobra.
Civvies	Term in the military for your civilian clothes you may wear when off duty
CL	Chu Lai. Small town 60 miles south of Danang and the home of the 71st Assault Helicopter Company
Claymore	Small, but powerful anti-personnel mine. Placed above ground and detonated by trip wire or electrically by a soldier
Click-Click	The sound in your ear phones from another Huey transmitting the sound by pulling twice on his transmit button. A quick non-verbal communication saying, "yes, I heard you"
Clicks	Nickname for a kilometer or .6 of a mile. Maps in VN were in Kilometers
C model Huey	Our Gunships. Produced by Bell Helicopter
CO	Commanding officer
Comm	Communications
Commo check	The Hueys check in to ensure their radios are operating prior to a mission.
Coords	Coordinates on a map
C-rations	Food in cans eaten by troops in the field. Not very good and no date on the can
Crew Chief	Person in charge of the Huey when on the ground. Also a door gunner when in the air
Crown	Crown Royal, a very nice Bourbon. How it got to VN I'll never know.

CS	The defining component of tear gas
CYA	Cover your ass.
Cyclic	The main control in the Huey. A shaft comes out of the floor up between your thighs. Used for control of all directions. Also contains radio transmit button, firing weapons and several additional functions.

D

DELTA

Daisy Cutter	A large 15,000 pound bomb used to clear landing areas in the jungle
Debrief	Debriefing after a mission. Talking over everything that was done, good and bad, and what could be done to improve the mission.
DEROS	Date estimated return from overseas (going home)
Dinks	Derogatory term used to describe the VN. They were small, hence dinky or small.
Dink Wheat	Rice
Division	10,000 to 18,000 soldiers
DMZ	Demilitarized Zone. Neutral territory separating two warring factions. A no man's land. One exists between North and South Korea.
DN	Da Nang. Large port city in VN
Dog Tags	Two small metal plates with name, blood type, religious preference, and serial number. Worn by all military personnel on a small beaded chain around the neck. This makes identification easier in case of death or to give the medical personnel the correct blood type, if wounded.
Door Gunners	The Door Gunner on the right side of the Huey and the Crew Chief, who serves as a Door Gunner when in the air, on the left side. They had a non-mounted Machine Gun used to cover all areas outside of the Huey when in combat.

Doughnut Dollies.	Women working through the Red Cross in Vietnam. They provided entertainment and a morale booster for troops in the field. A dangerous job and the only job other than nursing for women in VN; all in combat areas. Very brave and patriotic ladies
Dust off	The call sign for the helicopter ambulance corps, the medevac Hueys. They were used only to pick up wounded, and believe it or not they were unarmed. The bad guys knew they were unarmed and used the large Red Cross on the side door as a target.

E
ECHO

E & E	Escape and Evasion. This is what the helo pilots and crews did in VN when shot down.
EM	Enlisted man. Non-officer
Evac	Evacuation of personnel from a hostile area, especially wounded troops. Also picking up troops after a mission.
Eval	Evaluation of a pilot's skill as to whether he is promoted to copilot and eventually to pilot in command. Also, checking on anyone's performance of their work

F
FOXTROT

FAC	Forward Air Controller. Small propeller plane directing jets to a ground target using smoke rockets to mark the target.
Fast movers	The Jet Aircraft in VN.
FB	(1) Firebird Gunships in VN. Heavily armed. Main duty was to protect ground troops. (2) a member of a FB crew
F 4	The Phantom Jet with the large shark mouth painted on its nose. Best looking fighter plane

ever built. It looked mean.

50 or 51 caliber	Weapon is still used today. We called them Helicopter killers.
FIGMO	Fuck it got my orders. Orders to return to the world, (home)
Firebirds	The gunship platoon in the 71st Assault Helicopter Company
Fire Fight	When warring factions are in close combat; whether on the ground or in the air
Fire Fly	Helicopter mission at night. A slick shines a bright light on to a river and if any sampans are on the river the gunships destroy them. No one is allowed on the rivers at night as they were assumed to be carrying enemy troops, food and/or ammunitions for those troops.
FNG	Fucking new guy. A new pilot in their first 30 days in VN, where you learn how to fly in combat. Not like we flew in flight school.
F O	Fuck off
Free Fire Zone	An area where no one is allowed. The helo pilots were supposed to kill anyone in a free fire zone.
Freq	Frequency on our radios. Hueys had four radios
Frog	Cannon on the nose of the gunship
FSB	Fire-Support Base
FTA	Fuck the Army. Our answer to what we believed was a military mistake.
FUBAR	Fucked up beyond all recognition. Needs no explanation.

G

GOLF

Gatling gun	Multi barreled machine gun invented during the civil war; hand cranked at that time. The modern version is electric powered and fiercely destructive. The wing gunship had two electric Gatling

guns, also called miniguns. Historic note: Custer left his three Gatling guns behind at the Battle of Big Horn, because he thought they would be a burden.

GB	Green Berets. Also called Special Forces, tasked with: Unconventional warfare, foreign internal defense, special reconnaissance, direct action and counter-terrorism. "Snake eaters" is one nickname
GED	General Education Degree. Your senior year of High school completed in Basic training as a 17 year old to enter helo flight training of 11 months; thus an 18 year old pilot in combat.
GI	Government Issue. In other words, a soldier. The military owns you. When you join the military, you sign a blank check that includes your life.
Grunts	Term for Army ground troops in VN.
Gunship	Helo armed with rockets, machine guns, cannon and Gatling guns. Manned with a pilot, copilot, crew chief and door gunner. Gunships flew as a team of two.

H
HOTEL

Hamlet	Small VN village
Hot area	Lots of enemy. Helos and ground troops received heavy fire
Harold Robbins	Author of 25 Best Sellers. Lots of sex and action. Many were made into movies.
Hat Up	Let's get out of here; let's go. When you go outside in the military, you put on your cover (cap, or hat).
HE	High Explosive. Powerful munitions. Rockets or artillery shells
High Overhead	Method to land a slick on a fire support base

when enemy are present. Lay the Huey on its side and fall out of the sky like a rock. At the last moment, level the ship and pull back on the cyclic to slow any forward air speed until you are over the landing area and gently land.

HO	Nickname for Ho Chi Minh, Leader of North Vietnam during the VN war
Hog	Name of the lead gunship. Named this because it sits low on the ground and with the large rocket pods on the sides and the cannon on the nose; looks like a hog.
Hooch	Several meanings: Small buildings the GIs lived in at the 71st Helicopter Company. Six men to a building. Bottom 1/2 was wood and the top 1/2 was screen (the air conditioner). Also name given to the small buildings the rural Vietnamese lived in; some with corrugated tin roofs, (complements of Uncle Sam). Others with thatched roofs.
Hook	Short for Chinook; a large tandem rotor helo for carrying heavy loads
Hot Refueling	Refueling the Huey with the rotor blades turning so as to take off quickly if the enemy drops mortars on the ships.
Huey	Nickname for the UH-1 Iroquois Helicopter. Taken from the Baby Huey comics. Powerful and can do most anything.

I
INDIA

IC	Intercom. Radio for the four crewmen in the Huey to speak to one another
ID	Identification
IG	Inspector General. Group tasked to inspect all aspects of military bases to ensure they're maintained and in readiness

INOP	Inoperative
Intel	Intelligence gathering

J
JULIET

Jarhead	Nickname for a Marine due to their 'high and tight' haircut.
JP-4	High octane jet fuel used by the Hueys turbine engine.

K
KILO

Khe Sanh	Marine Fire Support Base just south of the DMZ
KIA	Killed in action
Kilo	Kilogram or 2.2 pounds
Kilometer	1000 meters or .62 miles
King Bees	VN Airforce flying old outdated post Korean War helos
Knot	1.15 nautical miles per hour

L
LIMA

Lifer	Career soldier
Lima Charlie	Loud and Clear
LT	Lieutenant, Lowest ranking officer
LRRP	Long Range Reconnaissance Patrol. Looks for enemy locations. Pronounced "lurp"
LZ	Landing zone. Area where Hueys deposit troops. Can be on a combat assault or inserting troops on any mission

M
MIKE

Magazine	Often incorrectly called a clip. The device holding the bullets, i.e. on an M-16 or AK-47 rifle.
MASH	Mobile Army Surgical Hospital. Located out in

	the field near the battle zone.
Mayday	This international distress signal is called out three successive times when an aircraft is in distress. From the French word m'aidez, "come help me"
Mercs	Mercenaries. Troops working for hire in war time. From countries other than the warring parties
Mess Hall	Military for kitchen and dining room. From the French word mes, meaning a portion of food
Mess Kit	Portable cup and plate for eating out in the field, if you're fortunate enough to have food other than C rations.
Meter	Metric measurement for distance; 39.37 inches
MIA	Missing in action. Unknown location of a soldier after a battle
Mic	Microphone. The metal arm on the Helo's crew's helmet that sits just in front of the lips and holds the microphone.
MP	Military police
MPC	Military payment certificate. Looks like Monopoly money and the same size. Used to pay troops in VN. Comes in denominations of 5, 10, 25 and 50 cents; 1, 5, 10 and 20 dollars.
Mortar	Short barrel tube for shooting rocket like projectiles at high angles, to drop them onto enemy close to your location.
MOS	Military Occupational Specialty. Your job description. Stated as an alpha numeric; 100B is a Helicopter Gunship Pilot.

N
NOVEMBER

Nape	Napalm; a highly flammable jellified gasoline delivered in bombs. It sticks to skin and causes 3rd degree burns.

NB	November Bravo. Means No Balls or coward.
NCO	Non Commissioned Officer. Sergeant up to first sergeant.
Nubee	A new guy
Number 1	VN way of saying you or the situation are the best.
Number 10	VN way of saying you or the situation are the worst.
NVA	North Vietnamese Army. America's enemy in VN.

0

OSCAR

O Club	Officers' club
O Dark Hundred	Really early in the AM
Off the Grid	Give no quarter (leave no survivors)
OJT	On the job training; where most of a soldier's training is realistically done.
OP	Operations. The people who do all the planning of missions.
OPHA	One pass haul ass. Use your entire ordinance on your first pass over the enemy

P

PAPA

PIC	Pilot in Command
PICS	Pictures
Peter Pilot	Derogatory name for a copilot
Plenum Chamber	An important filter to keep particles out of our spinning turbine blades.
Plexiglas	The very thin light acrylate glass used for a Helo's windshields
POL	Petroleum, Oil and Lubricants. Our gas stations in VN
Pop Smoke	Request by a helo to locate ground troops, by asking them to release a colored smoke grenade, for pick up or for the gunships to shoot in a given

	distance and direction to protect the troops.
POW	Prisoner of war. Soldier captured by the enemy
PR	Public Relations
PSP	Pierced Steel Planking. Interlocking large sheets of light-weight metal to build a quick runway. Holes are cut out in the sheets to reduce weight
Pucker Factor	The amount of force your anal sphincter exerts on the seat when you're in very hot action
Pull Pitch	Pull up the lever in your left hand to increase the angle of the blade striking the air and this creates lift.
P-38	Small manual can opener hooked on the dog-tag chain. Used to open C ration cans.
Punji Sticks	Bamboo shaved at an angle sharp as a knife. These are dipped in feces then buried in a hole with the sharp point upward and covered with twigs and leaves. The GI steps in the hole and his foot is penetrated by several of these sticks. It doesn't kill him, but he gets a terrible infection and is out of combat for a considerable period of time.
Purple Heart	This award was created by George Washington. You receive one for being killed or wounded in combat.
PX	Post Exchange. Army general store. Analogous to Walmart.

Q
QUEBEC

QT	Quang Tri. Northern most city in South VN. Near the DMZ
Quinine	Taken to prevent Malaria. Chloroquine was also used.

R
ROMEO

R & R	Rest and Recuperation. After you had been in Vietnam for over 8 months you could request a five day vacation to Australia, Thailand, Philippines or Hong Kong. It was really a big drunk, no sleep, and a lot of women. Married men would meet their wives in Hawaii.
Rat Race	Gunships flying around trees, hills and across rice paddies. This was done with Armed Forces VN radio blaring away. It was for training the wingman to stay in position to be able to shoot at anyone that shoots at the lead gunship.
RECON	Reconnaissance. Patrols out in the Jungle looking for the enemy. On the ground or in the air
REMF	Rear Echelon Mother Fucker. A high ranking officer that has not been in combat for a considerable amount of time. We would sometimes question their decisions as their knowledge for the mission appeared limited.
Revetment	Areas where we parked our Hueys. In VN they were constructed with 55 gallon drums filled with sand and set two wide in the shape of an L. A third barrel was centered on top of the two. This protected the ships from shrapnel from incoming rockets and mortars.
RHIP	Rank has its privileges
RLO	Real Live Officer. Derogatory term
RMI	Radio magnetic indicator. It shows the originating direction of a radio transmission.
Rockets	Solid fuel with a 17 pound warhead. Lead Gunship carried 38.
Roger	Means OK in military lingo
Roger wilco	Yes, I will comply.
ROK	Republic of South Korean soldiers. Fearsome

	soldiers. Great allies
Rotor Blades	Large blades on top of the Huey. Serve as a wing and propeller
Rotor wash	Wind created by the rotor blades
Rounds	Another name for bullets
RP	Rock pile. An LZ and FSB near the DMZ
RPG	Rocket Propelled Grenade. Fires from a shoulder held tube. Deadly against a helo as it was designed as an anti-tank weapon. Russian made
rpm	Revolutions per minutes. Refers to the turbine blades and/or the rotor blades speed.
Runway	Rectangle strips of land for aircraft to take off and land.

S

SIERRA	
Sampans	Small boats used on rivers by the VN to transport people or supplies to and from the market. Also transport illegal contraband after dark: weapons, ammunitions, troops and food. No boats were allowed on the water after dark.
Scramble	Taking off aircraft as quickly as possible
Scrambled Eggs	The raised gold designed on the bill of a Field Grade Officer, Major to General.
Shit hook	Term of endearment for the Chinook
Short Final	On approach to a runway at an airport you are close to landing
Short Timer	Very close to the end of your tour of duty in VN; less than 30 days
Shoulder Harness	4 point harness vs the three point in your car. There is a strap over each shoulder and the two across the waist. The four are then attached at your belt buckle area. A lever locks them in place when flying to hold you tight against the seat you so can't slide out if shot.

Side Arms	A pistol worn in a holster; either around the waist or as a shoulder holster
Sit Rep	Situation report. Pilots receive this from the ground troops to report their position and/or the enemy's position.
6 (six)	Number given the person in charge, whether in the air or on the ground. Also as part of a numeric: Bulldog 6, Firebird 9-6.
Slick	Name given to a Huey that hauls ass and/or trash: people and/or supplies. It has no rockets or Gatling guns hanging off the sides; hence, it has smooth or slick sides.
Sling Load	Supplies carried underneath a helo. Can be in a net or a sling; equipment, vehicles, artillery pieces or tanks of water
Smoke Grenade	Releases smoke to mark a position on the ground. No explosion or shrapnel
Smokey	A slick used to provide cover on a combat assault by flying low around the LZ while emitting a thick white smoke.
SNAFU	Situation Normal, All Fucked Up
SOP	Standard operating procedure. Things done the same way on every occasion.

T
TANGO

TAC Officer	Training, Advising and Counseling. Also a disciplinarian. Officer in charge of a group of flight-school students, and a returning pilot from VN.
Tail Rotor	Small spinning blade on the tail of the Huey to counteract the torque of the main rotor blades. Without a tail rotor, the helicopter would spin in the opposite direction of the main rotor blades. Actual name is anti-torque blade.
TET	Name of the VN New Year. Most important

	celebration in their culture.
TO	Take off and fly
TOP	The First Sergeant. The top enlisted soldier in a company
T & G	Touch and Goes. Practice landings and TO. Stay in the traffic pattern and essentially you're just flying in a circle.
TPI	Target practice island. Island a mile south of CL used to teach new members of the Firebirds to shoot cannons, rockets and machine guns.
Tracers	Bullet with a small depression in the base and packed with Phosphorus. This ignites when the bullet is fired and allows the shooter to see where his bullet is impacting. Usually every fifth bullet, meaning there are four bullets between each tracer. Used when firing a machine gun.
Triage	Deciding the degree of urgency of wounds to decide the order of treatment.
Translational Lift	Term used to describe the moment a helicopter is flying.
Trip Wires	Wire across a trail. When stepped on, it can detonate an explosive device.
TS	Tough Shit.
Turnaround	Area on an airport where air craft are able to turn in a direction needed and off the runway.
Twenty Four Hour Clock	Uses all 24 hours of the day. Before noon all times are preceded by a zero, such as 0600 for six am and all times after 12 noon just add 12, such as 3pm is 1500.

U

UNIFORM	
Un Ass Yourself	Depart an area. Get off your ass and move.
Uncle Ho	Nickname for Ho Chi minh
USO	United Services Organization, Private non-profit

organization (not Federal Government) to entertain troops.

V
VICTOR

Viet Cong	South VN individuals fighting for the North.
VN	Vietnamese people or the country.

W
WHISKEY

Warning Lights	Lights on the instrument panel informing you that something is wrong with a working part of the Huey: yellow is a warning and should be looked at when you land and red usually means land now or die.
WIA	Wounded in action
WILCO	Radio talk for "will comply"
WO	Warrant Officer. Rank of most of the army helo pilots
World	Name for the United States
WP	White Phosphorus. Also called Willy Pete or Wilson Picket. Burns at 5000 degrees. Rockets used to kill by concussion, shrapnel, burns or asphyxiation. Also used in artillery shells.

X
X RAY

XO	Executive Officer. Second in command after the Commanding Officer.

Y
YANKEE

Z
ZULU